W9-AEH-526

D A T E	D U E	
ILL-2016		

A Garland Series

Classics of Children's Literature 1621-1932

A collection of 117 titles
reprinted in photo-facsimile
in 73 volumes

Selected and arranged by
Alison Lurie
and
Justin G. Schiller

The Daisy Chain

Charlotte Yonge

*with a preface
for the Garland edition by*

Susan M. Kenney

Garland Publishing, Inc., New York & London

1977

Bibliographical note:

This facsimile has been
made from a copy in
The British Library
(12618.f.12)

Library of Congress Cataloging in Publication Data

Yonge, Charlotte Mary, 1823-1901.
  The daisy chain.

  (Classics of children's literature, 1621-1932)
  Reprint of the 1868 ed. published by Macmillan,
London.
  Bibliography: p.
  SUMMARY: Portrays a mid-Victorian family, their
confrontations with calamity, and their development of
Christian goodness.
  [1. Christian life--Fiction. 2. Family life--
Fiction] I. Title. II. Series.
PZ6.Y6Dai15   [Fic]   75-32169
ISBN 0-8240-2282-3

Printed in the United States of America

Preface

Charlotte Mary Yonge, whose life so nearly spans the Victorian Age and whose novels most often depict the bustling domestic affairs of those large intrepid families we have come to associate with that period, was born in 1823 at her family's modest country estate in Otterbourne, near Winchester, Hampshire, England. She was the only daughter of William and Fanny Bargus Yonge, both of whom came from neighboring families of the Devonshire landed gentry. This small but by all accounts happy family circle, completed in 1830 by the birth of a son, Julian, formed the center of Charlotte's existence, enlarged occasionally by childhood visits to cousins in Devonshire and Plymouth. Charlotte never married, whether out of timidity or principle it is hard to say; thus the chronicles of sprawling family life that are her major contribution to children's literature are entirely the work of a fertile and perhaps wishful imagination.

William Yonge believed in higher education for women, but not freedom, so Charlotte's education, like that of her heroine Ethel May, took place at home under the guidance of her mother and father. She progressed so rapidly with her combination of intelligence and dutiful perseverance that by the age of seven she was teaching Sunday School to the village children, an occupation she followed, incredibly, for the next seventy-one years. It is probable that she began writing, or at least making up stories, at a similarly early age, though none have survived. The education of the young, especially girls, and her writing were to be the sole activities of her remarkably uneventful adult life, directed both to "making goodness attractive" and to inculcating the Christian principles of charity, humility, and devotion to good works in her students and readers.

Aside from her parents, the most important influence in Charlotte's life was John Keble, with Newman the leader of the Oxford Movement. Keble in 1835 took the living of the nearby parish of Hursley, and in 1838 he presided at Charlotte's confirmation both as priest and family friend. His motto, "pro Ecclesia Dei," became the working principle of Charlotte's life, and it was at his suggestion that she determined to use her gift for storytelling as a way of teaching their religious principles to the poor and uneducated. Six months after her confirmation, her first work, a story in French heavily revised by Keble and William Yonge, was published in order to raise money for a village school. The proceeds of Charlotte's later works likewise went "for the Church of God," the only condition on which she felt she could justify writing fiction.

This early story was followed a few years later by her first novel, *Abbeychurch, or Self-control and Self-conceit*. Two more novels followed, published anonymously; in 1853 Charlotte achieved her first notable success with the appearance of *The Heir of Redclyffe*, still her most popular and widely read novel, the substantial profits of which bought an entire schooner for Bishop Selwyn's Melanesian mission. After the enthusiastic reception of *The Heir of Redclyffe*, Charlotte Yonge's novels of family life strenuously imbued with Christian principles and the struggle to be good, historical romances, schoolroom tales of popular history, and biographies appeared at the awesome rate of two or three a year, so that at the end of her life in 1901 she had nearly 160 titles to her credit.

The Daisy Chain, written just after *The Heir of Redclyffe*, appeared in book form in 1856, delayed two years by the death of William Yonge. Second only to *The Heir* in popularity, this long and detailed account of the May family depicts seven years in the life of Dr. May and his eleven children, from the death of the mother and crippling of the eldest daughter in an accident through a series of domestic calamities ranging in seriousness from schoolboy pranks to the loss at sea of a prospective son-in-law, ending with the death of the invalid daughter, Margaret. The plot of *The Daisy Chain* is at best episodic if one reads on solely to find out what happens next to whom, but the main action of the story is actually the development of Christian goodness in the older May children, symbolized by Ethel May's determination to build first a school and then a church in the squalid and heathenish settlement of Cocksmoor. The book is really about the difficulties and rewards of being good, as each of the May children and their father struggle against their own not very evil natures and the temptations of worldly circumstance to find "God's work in all we do and are." The novel ends with the establishment of the new church and with the dedication of Ethel May, the novel's main character, to a selfless spinsterhood spent caring for the needs of others. And it is plain, awkward, intellectual Ethel May who influenced a new generation of literary heroines; she is the prototype of such figures as Jo March in *Little Women*, who like Ethel are neither wholly good nor wholly beautiful, but human.

PREFACE

It hardly sounds like escapist reading, or even worth reading, yet there is something about *The Daisy Chain* that inspires even the most reluctant and cynical reader to continue with the affairs of the Mays. It is Charlotte Yonge's gift for delineating character that leads us on, that and its being, unlike many Victorian novels of greater genius, moral without being moralistic, tender without being mawkish, full of Christian devotion to good without being self-righteously homiletic. The understanding and drawing of those small details that make a character live is Charlotte Yonge's great strength as a novelist, and it is a small indication of her art that after relatively few pages one can without difficulty name and picture the eleven May children as individuals.

Charlotte Yonge wrote about what was familiar to her, and given her limited and sheltered existence, *The Daisy Chain*, like most of her other novels, is a plausible and perhaps even realistic portrait of a mid-Victorian family of the professional class, untroubled, like Charlotte Yonge herself, by either money worries or religious doubts, able to concentrate without distraction on the function and development of Christian ideals. Yet the goodness is attractive, and if this is the task Charlotte Yonge set for herself, one can only admire the energy and lack of sentimentality with which she went about her work.

Susan M. Kenney

SUSAN M. KENNEY is an Assistant Professor of English at Colby College in Waterville, Maine. Married and the mother of two children, she is currently completing a study of the novels of Virginia Woolf.

viii

CHARLOTTE MARY YONGE (1823-1901)

Bibliography of Her Books for Children:

Kings of England: A History for Young Children. London 1848.

The Little Duke or Richard the Fearless. London 1854.

Heartsease or the Brother's Wife. London 1854. Illustrated by Kate Greenaway 1879.

The History of Sir Thomas Thumb. Edinburgh 1855.

The Daisy Chain or Aspirations. London 1856.

The Instructive Picture-Book or Lessons from the Vegetable-World. Edinburgh 1857.

The Mice at Play. London [1860].

The Strayed Falcon. London [1860].

A Book of Golden Deeds of All Times and All Lands. London 1864.

A Book of Worthies. Gathered from the Old Histories, &c. London 1869.

A Storehouse of Stories. Edited by Charlotte Mary Yonge. London 1871.

ix

PREFACE

Little Lucy's Wonderful Globe. London 1871.

History of France. Part VIII, Historical Courses for Schools. London 1872.

Aunt Charlotte's Stories of English History. London 1873.

Aunt Charlotte's Stories of Bible History. London 1875.

Aunt Charlotte's Stories of Greek History. London 1876.

Aunt Charlotte's Stories of Roman History. London 1877.

Aunt Charlotte's Stories of German History. London 1877.

Aunt Charlotte's Evenings at Home with the Poets. London 1881.

Aunt Charlotte's Stories of American History. London 1883.

Shakespeare's Plays for Schools, Abridged and Annotated. London 1883.

Higher Reading-Book for Schools, Colleges and General Use. London 1885.

"Pixie Lawn," in *Please Tell Me a Tale. Short Original Stories for Children.* London 1885.

Teachings on the Catechism for the Little Ones. London 1886.

Just One Tale More. London 1886.

Aunt Charlotte's Stories of French History. London 1893.

The Story of Easter. London [1894].

PREFACE

Selected References:

Coleridge, Christabel. *Charlotte Mary Yonge: Her Life and Letters*. London 1903.

Mare, Margaret L. and A. C. Percival. *Victorian Best-Seller: The World of Charlotte M. Yonge*. London 1947.

DAISY CHAIN.

THE DAISY CHAIN:

OR,

ASPIRATIONS.

A FAMILY CHRONICLE.

BY

THE AUTHOR OF "THE HEIR OF REDCLYFFE,"

ETC.

> " To the highest room,
> Earth's lowliest flowers our Lord receives
> Close to His heart a place He gives,
> Where they shall ever bloom."

THE NINTH EDITION, WITH ILLUSTRATIONS.

London:

MACMILLAN AND CO.

1868.

LONDON:
R CLAY, SON, AND TAYLOR, PRINTERS,
BREAD STREET HILL.

PREFACE.

No one can be more sensible than is the Author that the present is an overgrown book of a nondescript class, neither the 'tale' for the young, nor the novel for their elders, but a mixture of both.

Begun as a series of conversational sketches, the story outran both the original intention and the limits of the periodical in which it was commenced; and, such as it has become, it is here presented to those who have already made acquaintance with the May family, and may be willing to see more of them. It would beg to be considered merely as what it calls itself, a Family Chronicle — a domestic record of home events, large and small, during those years of early life when the character is chiefly formed, and as an endeavour to trace the effects of those aspirations which are a part of every youthful nature. That the young should take one hint, to think whether their hopes and upward-breathings are truly upwards, and founded in lowliness, may be called the moral of the tale.

For those who may deem the story too long, and the characters too numerous, the Author can only beg their pardon for any tedium that they may have undergone before giving it up.

FEB. 22ND, 1856.

THE

DAISY CHAIN.

PART I.

THE DAISY CHAIN.

CHAPTER I.

'Si douce est la Marguerite.'—CHAUCER.

MISS WINTER, are you busy? Do you want this after-noon? Can you take a good long walk?'

'Ethel, my dear, how often have I told you of your impe-tuosity—you have forgotten.'

'Very well'—with an impatient twist—'I beg your pardon. Good morning, Miss Winter,' said a thin, lank, angular, sallow girl, just fifteen, trembling from head to foot with restrained eagerness, as she tried to curb her tone into the requisite civility.

'Good morning, Ethel, good morning, Flora,' said the prim, middle-aged, daily governess, taking off her bonnet, and arranging the stiff little rolls of curl at the long, narrow looking-glass, the border of which distorted the countenance.

'Good morning,' properly responded Flora, a pretty, fair girl, nearly two years older than her sister.

'Will you—' began to burst from Etheldred's lips again, but was stifled by Miss Winter's inquiry, 'Is your mamma pretty well to-day?'

'Oh! very well,' said both at once; 'she is coming to the read-ing.' And Flora added, 'Papa is going to drive her out to-day.'

'I am very glad. And the baby?'

'I do believe she does it on purpose!' whispered Ethel to herself, wriggling fearfully on the wide window-seat on which she had precipitated herself, and kicking at the bar of the table, by which manifestation she of course succeeded in deferring her hopes, by a reproof which caused her to draw herself into a rigid, melancholy attitude, a sort of penance of decorum, but a rapid motion of the eyelids, a tendency to crack the joints of the fingers, and an un-quietness at the ends of her shoes, betraying the restlessness of the digits therein contained.

It was such a room as is often to be found in old country town houses, the two large windows looking out on a broad old-fashioned street, through heavy framework, and panes of glass scratched with various names and initials. The walls were painted blue, the skirting almost a third of the height, and so wide at the top as to form a narrow shelf. The fire-place, constructed in the days when fires were made to give as little heat as possible, was ornamented with blue and white Dutch tiles bearing marvellous representations of Scripture history, and was protected by a very tall green guard; the chairs were much of the same date, solid and heavy, the seats in faded carpet-work, but there was a sprinkling of lesser ones and of stools; a piano; a globe; a large table in the middle of the room, with three desks on it; a small one, and a light cane chair by each window; and loaded book-cases. Flora began, 'If you don't want this afternoon to yourself—'

Ethel was on her feet, and open-mouthed. 'O, Miss Winter! if you would be so kind as to walk to Cocksmoor with us.'

'To Cocksmoor, my dear!' exclaimed the governess, in dismay.

'Yes, yes, but hear,' cried Ethel. 'It is not for nothing. Yesterday—'

'No, the day before,' interposed Flora.

'There was a poor man brought into the hospital. He had been terribly hurt in the quarry, and papa says he'll die. He was in great distress, for his wife has just got twins, and there were lots of children before. They want everything—food and clothes— and we want to walk and take it.'

'We had a collection of clothes ready, luckily,' said Flora; 'and we have a blanket, and some tea and some arrowroot, and a bit of bacon, and mamma says she does not think it too far for us to walk, if you will be so kind as to go with us.'

Miss Winter looked perplexed. 'How could you carry the blanket, my dear?'

'O, we have settled that,' said Ethel, 'we mean to make the donkey a sumpter-mule, so, if you are tired, you may ride home on her.'

'But, my dear, has your mamma considered? They are such a set of wild people at Cocksmoor; I don't think we could walk there alone.'

'It is Saturday,' said Ethel, 'we can get the boys.'

'If you would reflect a little! They would be no protection. Harry would be getting into scrapes, and you and Mary running wild.'

'I wish Richard was at home!' said Flora.

'I know!' cried Ethel. 'Mr. Ernescliffe will come. I am sure he can walk so far now. I'll ask him.'

Ethel had clapped after her the heavy door, with its shining brass lock, before Miss Winter well knew what she was about, and the governess seemed annoyed. 'Ethel does not consider,' said she. 'I don't think your mamma will be pleased.'

'Why not?' said Flora.

'My dear—a gentleman walking with you, especially if Margaret is going.'

'I don't think he is strong enough,' said Flora; 'but I can't think why there should be any harm. Papa took us all out walking with him yesterday—little Aubrey and all, and Mr. Ernescliffe went.'

'But, my dear—'

She was interrupted by the entrance of a fine, tall, blooming girl of eighteen, holding in her hand a pretty little maid of five. 'Good morning, Miss Winter. I suppose Flora has told you the request we have to make to you?'

'Yes, my dear Margaret; but did your mamma consider what a lawless place Cocksmoor is?'

'That was the doubt,' said Margaret, 'but papa said he would answer for it nothing would happen to us, and mamma said if you would be so kind.'

'It is unlucky,' began the governess, but stopped at the incursion of some new comers, nearly tumbling over each other, Ethel at the head of them. 'Oh! Harry!' as the gathers of her frock gave way in the rude grasp of a twelve-years-old boy. 'Miss Winter, 'tis all right—Mr. Ernescliffe says he is quite up to the walk, and will like it very much, and he will undertake to defend you from the quarrymen.'

'Is Miss Winter afraid of the quarrymen?' hallooed Harry. 'Shall I take a club?'

'I'll take my gun and shoot them,' valiantly exclaimed Tom; and while threats were passing among the boys, Margaret asked, in a low voice, 'Did you ask him to come with us?'

'Yes; he said he should like it of all things. Papa was there, and said it was not too far for him—besides, there's the donkey. Papa says it, so we must go, Miss Winter.'

Miss Winter glanced unutterable things at Margaret, and Ethel began to perceive she had done something wrong. Flora was going to speak, when Margaret, trying to appear unconscious of a certain deepening colour in her own cheeks, pressed a hand on her shoulder, and whispering, 'I'll see about it. Don't say any more, please,' glided out of the room.

'What's in the wind?' said Harry. 'Are many of your reefs out there, Ethel?'

'Harry can talk nothing but sailor's language,' said Flora,

'and I am sure he did not learn that of Mr. Ernescliffe. You never hear slang from him.'

'But aren't we going to Cocksmoor?' asked Mary, a blunt, downright girl of ten.

'We shall know soon,' said Ethel. 'I suppose I had better wait till after the reading to mend that horrid frock?'

'I think so, since we are so nearly collected,' said Miss Winter; and Ethel, seating herself on the corner of the window-seat, with one leg doubled under her, took up a Shakespeare, holding it close to her eyes, and her brother Norman, who, in age, came between her and Flora, kneeling on one knee on the window-seat, and supporting himself with one arm against the shutter, leant over her, reading it too, disregarding a tumultuous skirmish going on in that division of the family collectively termed 'the boys,' namely, Harry, Mary, and Tom; until Tom was suddenly pushed down, and tumbled over into Ethel's lap, thereby upsetting her and Norman together, and there was a general downfall, and a loud scream, 'The sphinx!'

'You've crushed it,' cried Harry, dealing out thumps indiscriminately.

'No, here 'tis,' said Mary, rushing among them, and bringing out a green sphinx caterpillar, on her finger—''tis not hurt.'

'*Pax! Pax!*' cried Norman, over all, with the voice of an authority, as he leapt up lightly and set Tom on his legs again. 'Harry! you had better do that again,' he added, warningly. 'Be off, out of this window, and let Ethel and me read in peace.'

'Here's the place,' said Ethel—'Crispin, Crispian's day. How I do like Henry V.'

'It is no use to try to keep those boys in order!' sighed Miss Winter.

'Saturnalia, as papa calls Saturday,' replied Flora.

'Is not your eldest brother coming home to-day?' said Miss Winter, in a low voice to Flora, who shook her head, and said, confidentially, 'He is not coming till he has passed that examination. He thinks it better not.'

Here entered, with a baby in her arms, a lady with a beautiful countenance of calm sweetness, looking almost too young to be the mother of the tall Margaret, who followed her. There was a general hush as she greeted Miss Winter, the girls crowding round to look at their little sister, not quite six weeks old.

'Now, Margaret, will you take her up to the nursery?' said the mother, while the impatient speech was repeated, 'Mamma, can we go to Cocksmoor?'

'You don't think it will be too far for you?' said the mother to Miss Winter, as Margaret departed.

'O no, not at all, thank you, that was not— But Margaret has explained.'

'Yes, poor Margaret,' said Mrs. May, smiling. 'She has settled it by choosing to stay at home with me. It is no matter for the others, and he is going on Monday, so that it will not happen again.'

'Margaret has behaved very well,' said Miss Winter.

'She has indeed,' said her mother, smiling. 'Well, Harry, how is the caterpillar?'

'They've just capsized it, mamma,' answered Harry, 'and Mary is making all taut.'

Mrs. May laughed, and proceeded to advise Ethel and Norman to put away Henry V., and find the places in their Bibles, 'or you will have the things mixed together in your heads,' said she.

In the meantime Margaret, with the little babe, to-morrow to be her god-child, lying gently in her arms, came out into the matted hall, and began to mount the broad shallow-stepped staircase, protected by low stout balusters, with a very thick, flat, and solid mahogany hand-rail, polished by the boys' constant riding up and down upon it. She was only on the first step, when the dining-room door opened, and there came out a young man, slight, and delicate-looking, with bright blue eyes, and thickly-curling light hair. 'Acting nurse?' he said, smiling. 'What an odd little face it is! I didn't think little white babies were so pretty! Well, I shall always consider myself as the real godfather—the other is all a sham.'

'I think so,' said Margaret, 'but I must not stand with her in a draught,' and on she went, while he called after her,—'So we are to have an expedition to-day.'

She did not gainsay it, but there was a little sigh of disappointment; and when she was out of hearing, she whispered, 'Oh! lucky baby, to have so many years to come before you are plagued with troublesome propriety!'

Then depositing her little charge with the nurse, and trying to cheer up a solemn-looking boy of three, who evidently considered his deposition from babyhood as a great injury, she tripped lightly down again, to take part in the Saturday's reading and catechising.

It was pleasant to see that large family in the hush and reverence of such teaching, the mother's gentle power preventing the outbreaks of recklessness to which even at such times the wild young spirits were liable. Margaret and Miss Winter especially rejoiced in it on this occasion, the first since the birth of the baby, that she had been able to preside. Under her, though seemingly without her taking any trouble, there was none of the smothered laughing at the little ones' mistakes, the fidgetting of the boys, or Harry's audacious impertinence to Miss Winter; and no less glad was Harry to have his mother there, and be guarded from himself.

The Catechism was repeated, and a comment on the Sunday Services read aloud. The Gospel was that on the taking the lowest place; and when they had finished, Ethel said, 'I like the verse which explains that:

> 'They who now sit lowest here,
> When their Master shall appear,
> He shall bid them higher rise,
> And be highest in the skies.''

'I did not think of that being the meaning of 'when He that bade thee cometh,'' said Norman, thoughtfully.

'It seemed to be only our worldly advantage that was meant before,' said Ethel.

'Well, it means that too,' said Flora.

'I suppose it does,' said Mrs. May; 'but the higher sense is the one chiefly to be dwelt on. It is a lesson how those least known and regarded here, and humblest in their own eyes, shall be the highest hereafter.'

And Margaret looked earnestly at her mother, but did not speak.

'May we go, mamma?' said Mary.

'Yes, you three—all of you, indeed, unless you wish to say any more.'

The 'boys' availed themselves of the permission. Norman tarried to put his books into a neat leather case, and Ethel stood thinking. 'It means altogether—it is a lesson against ambition,' said she.

'True,' said her mother, 'the love of eminence for its own sake.'

'And in so many different ways!' said Margaret.

'Aye, worldly greatness, riches, rank, beauty,' said Flora.

'All sorts of false flash and nonsense, and liking to be higher than one ought to be,' said Norman. 'I am sure there is nothing lower, or more mean and shabby, than getting places and praise a fellow does not deserve.'

'Oh, yes!' cried Ethel, 'but no one fit to speak to would do that!'

'Plenty of people do, I can tell you,' said Norman.

'Then I hope I shall never know who they are!' exclaimed Ethel. 'But I'll tell you what I was thinking of, mamma. Caring to be clever, and get on, only for the sake of beating people.'

'I think that might be better expressed.'

'I know,' said Ethel, bending her brow, with the fulness of her thought—'I mean caring to do a thing only because nobody else can do it—wanting to be first more than wanting to do one's best.'

'You are quite right, my dear Ethel,' said her mother; 'and I am glad you have found in the Gospel a practical lesson, that should be useful to you both. I had rather you did so than that you read it in Greek, though that is very nice, too,' she added, smiling, as she put her hand on a little Greek Testament, in which Ethel had been reading it, within her English Bible. 'Now, go and mend that deplorable frock, and if you don't dream over it, you won't waste too much of your holiday.'

'I'll get it done in no time!' cried Ethel, rushing headlong upstairs, twice tripping in it, before she reached the attic, where she slept, as well as Flora and Mary—a large room in the roof, the windows gay with bird-cages and flowers, a canary singing loud enough to deafen any one but girls to whom headaches were unknown, plenty of books and treasures, and a very fine view, from the dormer-window, of the town sloping downwards, and the river winding away, with some heathy hills in the distance. Poking and peering about with her short-sighted eyes, Ethel lighted on a work-basket in rare disorder, pulled off her frock, threw on a shawl, and sat down cross-legged on her bed, stitching vigorously, while meantime she spouted with great emphasis an ode of Horace, which Norman having learnt by heart, she had followed his example; it being her great desire to be even with him in all his studies, and though eleven months younger, she had never yet fallen behind him. On Saturday, he showed her what were his tasks for the week, and as soon as her rent was repaired, she swung herself downstairs in search of him for this purpose. She found him in the drawing-room, a pretty pleasant room—its only fault that it was rather too low. It had windows opening down to the lawn, and was full of pretty things, works, and knicknacks. Ethel found the state of affairs unfavourable to her. Norman was intent on a book on the sofa, and at the table sat Mr. Ernescliffe, hard at work with calculations and mathematical instruments. Ethel would not, for the world, that any one should guess at her classical studies—she scarcely liked to believe that even her father knew of them, and to mention them before Mr. Ernescliffe would have been dreadful. So she only shoved Norman, and asked him to come.

'Presently,' he said.

'What have you there?' said she, poking her head into the book. 'Oh! no wonder you can't leave off. I've been wanting you to read it all the week.'

She read over him a few minutes, then recoiled: 'I forgot

mamma told me not to read those stories in the morning. Only five minutes, Norman.'

'Wait a bit, I'll come.'

She fidgetted, till Mr. Ernescliffe asked Norman if there was a table of logarithms in the house.

'O yes,' she answered; 'don't you know, Norman? In a brown book on the upper shelf in the dining-room. Don't you remember papa's telling us the meaning of them, when we had the grand book-dusting?'

He was conscious of nothing but his book; however, she found the logarithms, and brought them to Mr. Ernescliffe, staying to look at his drawing, and asking what he was making out. He replied, smiling at the impossibility of her understanding, but she wrinkled her brown forehead, hooked her long nose, and spent the next hour in amateur navigation.

Market Stoneborough was a fine old town. The Minster, grand with the architecture of the time of Henry III., stood beside a broad river, and round it were the buildings of a Convent, made by a certain good Bishop Whichcote, the nucleus of a grammar school, which had survived the Reformation, and trained up many good scholars; among them, one of England's princely merchants, Nicholas Randall, whose effigy knelt in a niche in the chancel wall, scarlet-cloaked, white-ruffed, and black doubletted, a desk bearing an open Bible before him, and a twisted pillar of Derbyshire spar on each side. He was the founder of thirteen almshouses, and had endowed two scholarships at Oxford, the object of ambition of the Stoneborough boys, every eighteen months.

There were about sixty or seventy boarders, and the town boys slept at home, and spent their weekly holiday there on Saturday —the happiest day in the week to the May family, when only they had the company at dinner of Norman and Harry, otherwise known by their school names of June and July, given them because their elder brother had begun the series of months as May.

Some two hundred years back, a Dr. Thomas May had been head master, but ever since that time there had always been an M.D., not a D.D., in the family, owning a comfortable demesne of spacious garden, and field enough for two cows, still green and intact, among modern buildings and improvements.

The present Dr. May stood very high in his profession, and might soon have made a large fortune in London, had he not held fast to his home attachments. He was extremely skilful and clever, with a boyish character that seemed as if it could never grow older; ardent, sensitive, and heedless, with a quickness of sympathy and tenderness of heart that were increased, rather than blunted, by exercise in scenes of suffering.

At the end of the previous summer holidays, Dr. May had been called one morning to attend a gentleman who had been taken very ill, at the Swan Inn.

He was received by a little boy of ten years old, in much grief, explaining that his brother had come two days ago from London, to bring him to school here; he had seemed unwell ever since they met, and last night had become much worse. And extremely ill the Doctor found him; a youth of two or three-and-twenty, suffering under a severe attack of fever, oppressed, and scarcely conscious, so as quite to justify his little brother's apprehensions. He advised the boy to write to his family, but was answered by a look that went to his heart—'Alan' was all he had in the world—father and mother were dead, and their relations lived in Scotland, and were hardly known to them.

'Where have you been living, then?'

'Alan sent me to school at Miss Lawler's, when my mother died, and there I have been ever since, while he has been these three years and a half on the African station.'

'What, is he in the navy?'

'Yes,' said the boy, proudly, 'Lieutenant Ernescliffe. He got his promotion last week. My father was in the battle of Trafalgar; and Alan has been three years in the West Indies, and then he was in the Mediterranean, and now on the coast of Africa, in the Atalantis. You must have heard about him, for it was in the newspaper, how, when he was mate, he had the command of the Santa Isabel, the slaver they captured.'

The boy would have gone on for ever, if Dr. May had not recalled him to his brother's present condition, and proceeded to take every measure for the welfare and comfort of the forlorn pair.

He learnt from other sources that the Ernescliffes were well connected. The father had been a distinguished officer, but had been ill able to provide for his sons; indeed, he died without ever having seen little Hector, who was born during his absence on a voyage—his last, and Alan's first. Alan, the elder by thirteen years, had been like a father to the little boy, showing judgment and self-denial that marked him of a high cast of character. He had distinguished himself in encounters with slave ships, and in command of a prize that he had had to conduct to Sierra Leone, he had shown great coolness and seamanship, in several perilous conjunctures, such as a sudden storm, and an encounter with another slaver, when his Portuguese prisoners became mutinous, and nothing but his steadiness and intrepidity had saved the lives of himself and his few English companions. He was, in fact, as Dr. May reported, pretty much of a hero. He had not, at the time, felt the effects of the climate, but, owing to sickness and death among the other officers, he had suffered much fatigue, and pressure of mind and body. Immediately on his return, had followed his examination, and though he had passed with great credit, and it had been at once followed by well-earned promotion, his nervous excitable frame had been over-tasked, and the consequence was a long and severe illness.

The Swan Inn was not forty yards from Dr. May's back gate, and, at every spare moment, he was doing the part of nurse as well as doctor, professionally obliged to Alan Ernescliffe for bringing him a curious exotic specimen of fever, and requiting him by the utmost care and attention, while, for their own sakes, he delighted in the two boys with all the enthusiasm of his warm heart. Before the first week was at an end, they had learnt to look on the Doctor as one of the kindest friends it had been their lot to meet with, and Alan knew that if he died, he should leave his little brother in the hands of one who would comfort him as a father.

No sooner was young Ernescliffe able to sit up, than Dr. May insisted on conveying him to his own house, as his recovery was likely to be tedious, in solitude at the Swan. It was not till he had been drawn in a chair along the sloping garden, and placed on the sofa to rest, that he discovered that the time the good Doctor had chosen for bringing a helpless convalescent to his house, was two days after an eleventh child had been added to his family.

Mrs. May was too sorry for the solitary youth, and too sympathizing with her husband, to make any objection, though she was not fond of strangers, and had some anxieties. She had the utmost dependence on Margaret's discretion, but there was a chance of awkward situations, which papa was not likely to see or guard against. However, all seemed to do very well, and no one ever came into her room without some degree of rapture about Mr. Ernescliffe. The Doctor reiterated praises of his excellence, his principle, his ability and talent, his amusing talk; the girls were always bringing reports of his perfections. Norman retracted his grumbling at having his evenings spoilt; and 'the boys' were bursting with the secret that he was teaching them to rig a little ship that was to astonish mamma on her first coming down-stairs, and to be named after the baby; while Blanche did all the coquetry with him, from which Margaret abstained. The universal desire was for mamma to see him, and when the time came, she owned that papa's swan had not turned out a goose.

There were now no grounds for prolonging his stay; but it was very hard to go, and he was glad to avail himself of the excuse of remaining for the christening, when he was to represent the absent godfather. After that, he must go; he had written to his Scottish cousins to offer a visit, and he had a promise that he should soon be afloat again. No place would ever seem to him so like home as Market Stoneborough. He was quite like one of themselves, and took a full share in the discussions on the baby's name, which, as all the old family appellations had been used up, was an open question. The Doctor protested against Alice and Edith, which he said were the universal names in the present day. The boys hissed every attempt of their sisters at a romantic name, and then Harry wanted it to be Atalantis! At last Dr. May announced that he should have her named Dowsabel if they did not agree, and Mrs. May advised all the parties concerned to write their choice on a slip of paper, and little Aubrey should draw two out of her bag, trusting that Atalantis Dowsabel would not come out, as Harry confidently predicted.

However, it was even worse, Aubrey's two lots were Gertrude and Margaret. Ethel and Mary made a vehement uproar to discover who could have written Margaret, and at last traced it home to Mr. Ernescliffe, who replied that Flora, without saying why, had desired him to set down his favourite name. He was much disconcerted, and did not materially mend the matter by saying it was the first name that came into his head.

CHAPTER II.

' Meadows trim with daisies pied.'—MILTON.

ETHEL'S navigation lesson was interrupted by the dinner-bell. That long table was a goodly sight. Few ever looked happier than Dr. and Mrs. May, as they sat opposite to each other, presenting a considerable contrast in appearance as in disposition. She was a little woman, with that smooth pleasant plumpness that seems to belong to perfect content and serenity, her complexion fair and youthful, her face and figure very pretty, and full of quiet grace and refinement, and her whole air and expression denoting a serene, unruffled, affectionate happiness, yet with much authority in her mildness—warm and open in her own family, but reserved beyond it, and shrinking from general society.

The Doctor, on the contrary, had a lank, bony figure, nearly six feet high, and looking more so from his slightness; a face sallow, thin, and strongly marked, an aquiline nose, highly developed forehead, and peculiar temples, over which the hair strayed in thin curling flakes. His eyes were light-coloured, and were seldom seen without his near-sighted spectacles, but the expressions of the mouth were everything—so varying, so bright, and so sweet were the smiles that showed beautiful white teeth—moreover, his hand was particularly well made, small and delicate; and it always turned out that no one ever recollected that Dr. May was plain, who had ever heard his kindly greeting.

The sons and daughters were divided in likeness to father and mother; Ethel was almost an exaggeration of the Doctor's peculiarities, especially at the formed, but unsoftened age of fifteen; Norman had his long nose, sallow complexion, and tall figure, but was much improved by his mother's fine blue eyes, and was a very pleasant-looking boy, though not handsome; little Tom was a thin, white, delicate edition of his father; and Blanche contrived to combine great likeness to him with a great deal of prettiness. Of those that, as nurse said, favoured their mamma, Margaret was tall and blooming, with the same calm eyes, but with the brilliance of her father's smile; Flora had greater regularity of feature, and was fast becoming a very pretty girl, while Mary and Harry could not boast of much beauty, but were stout sturdy pictures of health; Harry's locks in masses of small tight yellow curls, much given to tangling and matting, unfit to be seen all the week, till nurse put him to torture every Saturday, by combing them out so as, at least, to make him for once, like, she said, a gentleman, instead of a young lion.

Little Aubrey was said by his papa to be like nothing but the full moon. And there he shone on them, by his mamma's side, announcing in language few could understand, where he had been with papa.

'He has been a small doctor,' said his father, beginning to cut the boiled beef as fast as if his hands had been moved by machinery. 'He has been with me to see old Mrs. Robins, and she made so much of him, that if I take you again you'll be regularly spoilt, young master.'

'Poor old woman, it must have been a pleasure to her,' said Mrs. May—'it is so seldom she has any change.'

'Who is she?' asked Mr. Ernescliffe.

'The butcher's old mother,' said Margaret, who was next to him. 'She is one of papa's pet patients, because he thinks her desolate and ill-used.'

'Her sons bully her,' said the Doctor, too intent on carving to perceive certain deprecatory glances of caution cast at him by his wife, to remind him of the presence of man and maid—'and that smart daughter is worse still. She never comes to see the old lady but she throws her into an agitated state, fit to bring on another attack. A meek old soul, not fit to contend with them!'

'Why do they do it?' said Ethel.

'For the cause of all evil! That daughter marries a grazier, and wants to set up for gentility; she comes and squeezes presents out of her mother, and the whole family are distrusting each other, and squabbling over the spoil before the poor old creature is dead! It makes one sick! I gave that Mrs. Thorn a bit of my mind at last; I could not stand the sight any longer. Madam, said I, you'll have to answer for your mother's death, as sure as my name's Dick May—a harpy dressed up in feathers and lace.'

There was a great laugh, and an entreaty to know whether this was really his address—Ethel telling him she knew he had muttered it to himself quite audibly, for which she was rewarded by a pretended box on the ear. It certainly was vain to expect order at dinner on Saturday, for the Doctor was as bad as the boys, and Mrs. May took it with complete composure, hardly appearing sensible of the Babel which would sometimes almost deafen its promoter, papa; and yet her interference was all-powerful, as now when Harry and Mary were sparring over the salt, with one gentle 'Mary!' and one reproving glance, they were reduced to quiescence.

Meanwhile Dr. May, in a voice above the tumult, was telling 'Maggie,' as he always called his wife, some piece of news about Mr. Rivers, who had bought Abbotstoke Grange; and Alan Ernescliffe, in much lower tones, saying to Margaret how he delighted in the sight of these home scenes, and this free household mirth.

'It is the first time you have seen us in perfection,' said Margaret, 'with mamma at the head of the table—no, not quite perfection either, without Richard.'

'I am very glad to have seen it,' repeated Alan. 'What a blessing it must be to your brothers to have such a home!'

'Yes, indeed,' said Margaret, earnestly.

'I cannot fancy any advantage in life equal to it. Your father and mother so entirely one with you all.'

Margaret smiled, too much pleased to speak, and glanced at her mother's sweet face.

'You can't think how often I shall remember it, or how rejoiced I—' He broke off, for the noise subsided, and his speech was not intended for the public ear, so he dashed into the general conversation, and catching his own name, exclaimed, 'What's that base proposal, Ethel?'

'To put you on the donkey,' said Norman.

'They want to see a sailor riding,' interposed the Doctor.

'Dr. May!' cried the indignant voice of Hector Ernescliffe, as his honest Scottish face flushed like a turkey cock, 'I assure you that Alan rides like——'

'Like a horse marine,' said Norman.

Hector and Harry both looked furious, but 'June' was too great a man in their world, for them to attempt any revenge, and it was left for Mary to call out, 'Why, Norman, nonsense! Mr. Ernescliffe rode the new black kicking horse till he made it quite steady.'

'Made it steady! No, Mary, that is saying too much for it,' said Mr. Ernescliffe.

'It has no harm in it—capital horse—splendid,' said the Doctor; 'I shall take you out with it this afternoon, Maggie.'

'You have driven it several times?' said Alan.

'Yes, I drove him to Abbotstoke yesterday—never started, except at a fool of a woman with an umbrella, and at the train—and we'll take care not to meet that.'

'It is only to avoid the viaduct at half-past four,' said Mrs. May, 'and that is easily done.'

'So you are bound for Cocksmoor?' said the Doctor. 'I told the poor fellow you were going to see his wife, and he was so thankful, that it did one's heart good.'

'Is he better? I should like to tell his wife,' said Flora.

The Doctor screwed up his face. 'A bad business,' he said; 'he is a shade better to-day; he may get through yet; but he is not my patient. I only saw him because I happened to be there when he was brought in, and Ward was not in the way.'

'And what's his name?'

'I can't tell—don't think I ever heard.'

'We ought to know,' said Miss Winter; 'it would be awkward to go without.'

'To go roaming about Cocksmoor asking where the man in the hospital lives!' said Flora. 'We can't wait till Monday.'

'I've done,' said Norman; 'I'll run down to the hospital and find out. May I, mamma?'

'Without your pudding, old fellow?'

'I don't want pudding,' said Norman, slipping back his chair. 'May I, mamma?'

'To be sure you may;' and Norman, with a hand on the back of Ethel's chair, took a flying leap over his own, that set all the glasses ringing.

'Stop, stop! know what you are going after, sir,' cried his father. 'What will they know there of Cocksmoor, or the man whose wife has twins? You must ask for the accident in number five.'

'And oh! Norman, come back in time,' said Ethel.

'I'll be bound I'm back before Etheldred the Unready wants me,' he answered, bounding off with an elasticity that caused his mother to say the boy was made of Indian rubber, and then putting his head in by the window to say, 'By-the-bye, if there's any pudding owing to me, that little chorister fellow of ours, Bill Blake, has got a lot of voracious brothers that want anything that's going. Tom and Blanche might take it down to 'em; I'm off! Hooray!' and he scampered headlong up the garden, prolonging his voice into a tremendous shout as he got further off, leaving every one laughing, and his mother tenderly observing that he was going to run a quarter of a mile and back, and lose his only chance of pudding for the week—old Bishop Whichcote's rules contemplating no fare but daily mutton, to be bought at a shilling per sheep. A little private discussion ensued between Harry and Hector, on the merits of the cakes at Ballhatchet's gate, and old Nelly's pies, which led the Doctor to mourn over the loss of the tarts of the cranberries, that used to grow on Cocksmoor, before it was inhabited, and to be the delight of the scholars of Stoneborough, when he was one of them—and then to enchant the boys by relations of ancient exploits, especially his friend Spencer climbing up, and engraving a name on the top of the market-cross, now no more, swept away by the Town Council in a fit of improvement, which had for the last twenty years enraged the Doctor at every remembrance of it. Perhaps at this moment his wife could hardly sympathize, when she thought of her boys emulating such deeds.

'Papa,' said Ethel, 'will you lend me a pair of spectacles for the walk?'

'And make yourself one, Ethel,' said Flora.

'I don't care—I want to see the view.'

'It is very bad for you, Ethel,' further added her mother; 'you will make your sight much shorter if you accustom your eyes to them.'

'Well, mamma, I never do wear them about the house.'

'For a very good reason,' said Margaret; 'because you haven't got them.'

'No, I believe Harry stole them in the holidays.'

'Stole them!' said the Doctor; 'as if they weren't my property, unjustifiably appropriated by her!'

'They were that pair that you never could keep on, papa,' said Ethel—'no use at all to you. Come, do lend me some.'

'I'm sure I shan't let you wear them,' said Harry. 'I shan't go, if you choose to make yourself such an object.'

'Ah!' said the father, 'the boys thought it time to put a stop to it when it came to a caricature of the little Doctor in petticoats.'

'Yes, in Norman's Lexicon,' said Ethel, 'a capital likeness of you, papa; but I never could get him to tell me who drew it.'

Nor did Ethel know that that caricature had been the cause of the black eye that Harry had brought home last summer. Harry returned, to protest that he would not join the walk, if she chose to be seen in the spectacles, while she undauntedly continued her petition, though answered that she would attract the attacks of the quarrymen, who would take her for an attenuated owl.

'I wish you were obliged to go about without them yourself, papa!' cried Ethel, 'and then you would know how tiresome it is not to see twice the length of your own nose.'

'Not such a very short allowance, either,' said the Doctor, quaintly, and therewith the dinner concluded. There was apt to be a race between the two eldest girls, for the honour of bringing down the baby; but this time their father strode up three steps at once, turned at the top of the first flight, made his bow to them, and presently came down with his little daughter in his arms, nodded triumphantly at the sisters, and set her down on her mother's lap.

'There, Maggie, you are complete, you old hen-and-chicken daisy. Can't you take her portrait in the character, Margaret?'

'With her pink cap, and Blanche and Aubrey as they are now, on each side?' said Flora.

'Margaret ought to be in the picture herself,' said Ethel. 'Fetch the artist in Norman's Lexicon, Harry.'

'Since he has hit off one of us so well,' said the Doctor. 'Well! I'm off. I must see old Southern. You'll be ready by three? Good-bye, hen and chicken.'

'And I may have the spectacles?' said Ethel, running after him; 'you know I am an injured individual, for mamma won't let me carry baby about the house, because I am so blind.'

'You are welcome to embellish yourself, as far as I am concerned.'

A general dispersion ensued, and only Mrs. May, Margaret, and the baby, remained.

'O no!' sighed Margaret; 'you can't be the hen-and-chicken daisy properly, without all your chickens. It is the first christening we ever had without our all being there.'

'It was best not to press it, my dear,' said her mother. 'Your papa would have had his thoughts turned to the disappointment again, and it makes Richard himself so unhappy to see his vexation that I believe it is better not to renew it.'

'But to miss him for so long!' said Margaret. 'Perhaps it is best, for it is very miserable, when papa is sarcastic and sharp and he cannot understand it, and takes it as meaning so much more than it really does, and grows all the more frightened and diffident. I cannot think what he would do without you to encourage him.'

'Or you, you good sister,' said her mother, smiling. 'If we could only teach him not to mind being laughed at, and to have some confidence in himself, he and papa would get on together.'

'It is very hard,' cried Margaret, almost indignantly, 'that papa won't believe it, when he does his best!'

'I don't think papa can bear to bring himself to believe that it is his best.'

'He is too clever himself to see how other people can be slow,' said Margaret; 'and yet'—the tears came into her eyes—'I cannot bear to think of his telling Richard it was no use to think of being a clergyman, and he had better turn carpenter at once, just because he failed in his examination.'

'My dear, I wish you would forget that,' said Mrs. May. 'You know papa sometimes says more than he means, and he was excessively vexed and disappointed. I know he was pleased with Ritchie's resolve not to come home again till he had passed, and it is best that it should not be broken.'

'The whole vacation, studying so hard, and this Christening!' said Margaret; 'it is treating him as if he had done wrong. I do believe Mr. Ernescliffe thinks he has—for papa always turns away the conversation, if his name is mentioned! I wish you would explain it, mamma; I can't bear *that*.'

'If I can,' said Mrs. May, rather pleased that Margaret had not taken on herself this vindication of her favourite brother at her father's expense. 'But, after all, Margaret, I never feel quite sure that poor Ritchie does exert himself to the utmost; he is too desponding to make the most of himself.'

'And the more vexed papa is, the worse it grows!' said Margaret. 'It is provoking, though. How I do wish sometimes to give Ritchie a jog, when there is some stumbling-block that he sticks fast at. Don't you remember those sums, and those declensions? When he is so clear and sensible about practical matters too—anything but learning—I cannot think why—and it is very mortifying!'

'I dare say it is very good for us not to have our ambition gratified,' said her mother. 'There are so many troubles worse than these failures, that it only shows how happy we are that we should take them so much to heart.'

'They are a very real trouble!' said Margaret. 'Don't smile, mamma. Only remember how wretched his school days were, when papa could not see any difficulty in what to him was so hard, and how all papa's eagerness only stupified him the more.'

'It is a comfort not to have that over again! Yet,' said the mother, 'I often think there is more fear for Norman. I dread his talent and success being snares.'

'There is no self-sufficiency about him,' said Margaret.

'I hope not, and he is so transparent, that it would be laughed down at the first bud; but the universal good report, and certainty of success, and being so often put in comparison with Richard, is hardly safe. I was very glad he heard what Ethel said to-day.'

'Ethel spoke very deeply,' said Margaret; 'I was a good deal struck by it—she often comes out with such solid thoughts.'

'She is an excellent companion for Norman.'

'The desire of being first!' said Margaret, 'I suppose that is a form of caring for oneself! It set me thinking a good deal, mamma, how many forms of ambition there are. The craving for rank, or wealth, or beauty, are so clearly wrong, that one does not question about them; but I suppose, as Ethel said, the caring to be first in attainments is as bad.'

'Or in affection,' said Mrs. May.

'In affection—oh! mamma, there is always some one person with whom one is first,' said Margaret, eagerly; and then, her colour deepening, as she saw her mother looking at her, she said hastily, 'Ritchie—I never considered it—but I know—it is my great pleasure—oh, mamma!'

'Well, my dear, I do not say but that you are the first with Richard, and that you well deserve to be so; but is the seeking to be the first even in that way safe? Is it not self-seeking again?'

'Well, perhaps, it is. I know it is what makes jealousy.'

'The only plan is not to think about ourselves at all,' said Mrs. May. 'Affection is round us like sunshine, and there is no use in measuring and comparing. We must give it out freely ourselves, hoping for nothing again.'

'O, mamma, you don't mean that!'

'Perhaps I should have said, bargaining for nothing again. It will come of itself, if we don't exact it; but rivalry is the sure means of driving it away, because that is trying to get oneself worshipped.'

'I suppose, then, you have never thought of it,' said Margaret, smiling.

'Why, it would have been rather absurd,' said Mrs. May, laughing, 'to begin to torment myself, whether you were all fond of me!

you all have just as much affection for me, from beginning to end, as is natural, and what's the use of thinking about it ? No, no, Margaret, don't go and protest that you love me, more than is natural,' as Margaret looked inclined to say something very eager, 'that would be in the style of Regan and Goneril. It will be natural by-and-by that you should, some of you, love some one else better, and if I cared for being first, what should I do then ?'

'O, mamma! — But,' said Margaret, suddenly, ' you are always sure of papa.'

'In one way, yes,' said Mrs. May; 'but how do I know how long—' Calm as she was, she could not finish that sentence. 'No, Margaret, depend upon it, the only security is, not to think about ourselves at all, and not to fix our mind on any affection on earth. The least share of the Love above, is the fulness of all blessing, and if we seek that first, all these things will be added unto us, and are,' she whispered, more to herself than to Margaret

CHAPTER III.

Wee modest crimson-tipped flower,
Thou'st met me in an evil hour,
For I maun crush amang the stoure
        Thy slender stem.
To spare thee now is past my power,
        Thou bonnie gem.—BURNS.

'Is this all the walking party ?' exclaimed Mr. Ernescliffe, as Miss Winter, Flora, and Norman gathered in the hall.

'Harry won't go because of Ethel's spectacles,' answered Flora; 'and Mary and he are inseparable, so they are gone with Hector to have a shipwreck in the field.'

'And your other sisters ?'

'Margaret has ratted—she is going to drive out with mamma,' said Norman; 'as to Etheldred the Unready, I'll run up and hurry her.'

In a moment he was at her door. 'Oh! Norman, come in. Is it time ?'

'I should think so! You're keeping every one waiting.'

'Oh dear! go on; only just tell me the past participle of *offero*, and I'll catch you up.'

'*Oblatus.*'

'O, yes, how stupid. The *a* long or short ? Then that's right. I had such a line in my head, I was forced to write it down. Is not it a capital subject this time ?'

'The devotion of Decius ? Capital. Let me see ?' said Nor-

man, taking up a paper scribbled in pencil, with Latin verses.
'O, you have taken up quite a different line from mine. I began
with Mount Vesuvius spouting lava like anything.'

'But Mount Vesuvius didn't *spout* till it overthrew Pompeii.'

'Murder!' cried Norman, 'I forgot! It's lucky you put me in
mind. I must make a fresh beginning. There go my six best
lines! However, it was an uncanny place, fit for hobgoblins, and
shades, and funny customers, which will do as well for my purpose.
Ha! that's grand about its being so much better than the *vana
gloria triumphalis*—only take care of the scanning there—'

'If it was but English. Something like this:—

> For what is equal to the fame
> Of forgetting self in the aim ?

That's not right, but—'

'Ethel, Norman, what are you about?' cried Flora. 'Do you
mean to go to Cocksmoor to-day?'

'Oh yes!' cried Ethel, flying into vehement activity; 'only
I've lost my blue-edged handkerchief—Flora, have you seen it?'

'No; but here is your red scarf.'

'Thank you, there is a good Flora. And oh! I finished a frock
all but two stitches. Where is it gone? Go on, all of you, I'll
overtake you—

> Purer than breath of earthly fame,
> Is losing self in a glorious aim.

Is that better, Norman?'

'You'll drive us out of patience,' said Flora, tying the handkerchief round Ethel's throat, and pulling out the fingers of her
gloves, which of course were inside out; 'are you ready?'

'Oh, my frock! my frock! There 'tis—three stitches—go on,
and I'll come,' said Ethel, seizing a needle, and sewing vehemently at a little pink frock. 'Go on, Miss Winter goes slowly
up the hill, and I'll overtake you.'

'Come, Norman, then; it is the only way to make her come
at all.'

'I shall wait for her,' said Norman. 'Go on, Flora, we shall
catch you up in no time;' and, as Flora went, he continued,
'Never mind your aims and fames and trumpery English rhymes.
Your verses will be much the best, Ethel; I only went on a little
about Mount Vesuvius and the landscape, as Alan described it the
other day, and Decius taking a last look, knowing he was to die.
I made him beg his horse's pardon, and say how they will both
be remembered, and their self-devotion would inspire Romans
to all posterity, and shout with a noble voice!' said Norman, repeating some of his lines, correcting them as he proceeded.

'Oh! yes; but oh! dear, I've done. Come along,' said Ethel, crumpling her work into a bundle, and snatching up her gloves—then, as they ran down-stairs, and emerged into the street, 'it is a famous subject.'

'Yes, you have made a capital beginning. If you won't break down somewhere, as you always do, with some frightful false quantity, that you would get an imposition for, if you were a boy. I wish you were. I should like to see old Hoxton's face, if you were to show him up some of these verses.'

'I'll tell you what, Norman, if I was you, I would not make Decius flatter himself with the fame he was to get—it is too like the stuff every one talks in stupid books. I want him to say—Rome—my country—the eagles—must win, if they do—never mind what becomes of me.'

'But why should he not like to get the credit of it, as he did? Fame and glory—they are the spirit of life, the reward of such a death.'

'O no, no,' said Ethel. 'Fame is coarse and vulgar—blinder than ever they draw Love or Fortune—she is only a personified newspaper, trumpeting out all that is extraordinary, without minding whether it is good or bad. She misses the delicate and lovely—I wished they would give us a theme to write about her. I should like to abuse her well.'

'It would make a very good theme, in a new line,' said Norman; 'but I don't give into it, altogether. It is the hope and the thought of fame, that has made men great, from first to last. It is in every one that is not good for nothing, and always will be! The moving spirit of man's greatness!'

'I'm not sure,' said Ethel; 'I think looking for fame is like wanting a reward at once. I had rather people forgot themselves. Do you think Arnold von Winkelried thought about fame, when he threw himself on the spears?'

'He got it,' said Norman.

'Yes; he got it for the good of other people, not to please himself. Fame does those that admire it good, not those that win it.'

'But!' said Norman, and both were silent for some short interval, as they left the last buildings of the town, and began to mount a steep hill. Presently Norman slackened his pace, and driving his stick vehemently against a stone, exclaimed, 'It is no use talking, Ethel, it is all a fight and à race. One is always to try to be foremost. That's the spirit of the thing—that's what the great, from first to last, have struggled, and fought, and lived, and died for.'

'I know it is a battle, I know it is a race. The Bible says so,' replied Ethel; 'but is not there the difference, that here all may win—not only one? One may do one's best, not care whether one is first or last. That's what our reading to-day said.'

'That was against trumpery vanity—false elevation—not what one has earned for oneself, but getting into other people's places that one never deserved. That every one despises!'

'Of course! That they do. I say, Norman, didn't you mean Harvey Anderson?'

Instead of answering, Norman exclaimed, 'It is pretension that is hateful—true excelling is what one's life is for. No, no, I'll never be beat, Ethel—I never have been beat by any one, except by you, when you take pains,' he added, looking exultingly at his sister, 'and I never will be.'

'O Norman!'

'I mean, of course, while I have senses. I would not be like Richard for all the world.'

'O no, no, poor Richard!'

'He is an excellent fellow in everything else,' said Norman; 'I could sometimes wish I was more like him—but how he can be so amazingly slow, I can't imagine. That examination paper he broke down in—I could have done it as easily as possible.'

'I did it all but one question,' said Ethel, 'but so did he, you know, and we can't tell whether we should have it done well enough.'

'I know I must do something respectable when first I go to Oxford, if I don't wish to be known as the man whose brother was plucked,' said Norman.

'Yes,' said Ethel; 'if papa will but let you try for the Randall scholarship next year, but he says it is not good to go to Oxford so young.'

'And I believe I had better not be there with Richard,' added Norman. 'I don't like coming into contrast with him, and I don't think he can like it, poor fellow, and it isn't his fault. I had rather stay another year here, get one of the open scholarships, and leave the Stoneborough ones for those who can do no better.'

In justice to Norman, we must observe that this was by no means said as a boast. He would scarcely have thus spoken to any one but Etheldred, to whom, as well as to himself, it seemed mere matter-of-fact. The others had in the meantime halted at the top of the hill, and were looking back at the town—the great old Minster, raising its twin towers and long roof, close to the river, where rich green meadows spread over the valley, and the town rising irregularly on the slope above, plentifully interspersed with trees and gardens, and one green space on the banks of the river, speckled over with a flock of little black dots in rapid motion.

'Here you are!' exclaimed Flora. 'I told them it was of no use to wait when you and Norman had begun a dissertation.'

'Now, Mr. Ernescliffe, I should like you to say,' cried Ethel, 'which do you think is the best, the name of it, or the thing?' Her eloquence always broke down with any auditor but her brother, or, perhaps, Margaret.

'Ethel!' said Norman, 'how is any one to understand you? The argument is this: Ethel wants people to do great deeds, and be utterly careless of the fame of them; I say, that love of glory is a mighty spring.'

'A mighty one!' said Alan; 'but I think, as far as I understand the question, that Ethel has the best of it.'

'I don't mean that people should not serve the cause first of all,' said Norman, 'but let them have their right place and due honour.'

'They had better make up their minds to do without it,' said Alan. 'Remember—

'The world knows nothing of its greatest men.''

'Then it is a great shame,' said Norman.

'But do you think it right,' said Ethel, 'to care for distinction? It is a great thing to earn it, but I don't think one should care for the outer glory.'

'I believe it is a great temptation,' said Alan. 'The being over elated or over depressed by success or failure in the eyes of the world, independently of the exertion we have used—'

'You call it a temptation?' said Ethel.

'Decidedly so.'

'But one can't live or get on without it,' said Norman.

There they were cut short. There was a plantation to be crossed, with a gate that would not open, and that seemed an effectual barrier against both Miss Winter and the donkey, until by persuasive eloquence and great gallantry, Mr. Ernescliffe performed the wonderful feat of getting the former over the tall fence, while Norman conducted the donkey a long way round, undertaking to meet them at the other side of the plantation.

The talk became desultory, as they proceeded for at least a mile along a cart-track, through soft tufted grass and heath, and young fir trees. It ended in a broad open moor, stony and full of damp boggy hollows, forlorn and desolate under the autumn sky. Here they met Norman again, and walked on along a very rough and dirty road, the ground growing more decidedly into hills and valleys as they advanced, till they found themselves before a small, but very steep hillock, one side of which was cut away into a slate quarry. Round this stood a colony of roughly-built huts, of mud, turf, or large blocks of the slate. Many workmen were engaged in splitting up the slates, or loading wagons with them, rude wild-looking men, at the sight of whom the ladies shrank up to their protectors, but who seemed too busy even to spare time for staring at them.

They were directed to John Taylor's house, a low mud cottage, very wretched looking, and apparently so smoky, that Mr. Ernescliffe and Norman were glad to remain outside and survey the quarry, while the ladies entered.

Inside they found more cleanliness and neatness than they had expected, but there was a sad appearance of poverty, insufficient furniture, and the cups and broken tea-pot on the table, holding nothing but toast and water, as a substitute for their proper contents. The poor woman was sitting by the fire with one twin on her lap, and the other on a chair by her side, and a larger child was in the corner by the fire, looking heavy and ill, while others of different ages lounged about listlessly. She was not untidy, but very pale, and she spoke in a meek, subdued way, as if the ills of life were so heavy on her that she had no spirit even to complain. She thanked them for their gifts but languidly, and did not visibly brighten when told that her husband was better.

Flora asked when the babes would be christened.

'I can't hardly tell, Miss—'tis so far to go.'

'I suppose none of the children can go to school. I don't know their faces there,' said Flora, looking at a nice tall, smooth-haired girl, of thirteen or fourteen.

'No, Miss—'tis so far. I am sorry they should not, for they always was used to it where we lived before, and my oldest girl, she can work very nicely. I wish I could get a little place for her.'

'You would hardly know what to do without her,' said Miss Winter.

'No, ma'am; but she wants better food than I can give her, and it is a bad wild place for a girl to grow up. It is not like what I was used to, ma'am; I was always used to keep to my school and to my church—but it is a bad place to live in here.'

No one could deny it, and the party left the cottage gravely. Alan and Norman joined them, having heard a grievous history of the lawlessness of the people, from a foreman with whom they had met. There seemed to be no visible means of improvement. The parish church was Stoneborough, and the living was very poor, the tithes having been appropriated to the old Monastery, and since its dissolution having fallen into possession of a body that never did anything for the town. The incumbent, Mr.

Ramsden, had small means, and was not a high stamp of clergy-man, seldom exerting himself, and leaving most of his parish work to the two under masters of the school, Mr. Wilmot and Mr. Harrison, who did all they had time and strength for, and more too, within the town itself. There was no hope for Cocksmoor!

'There would be a worthy ambition!' said Etheldred, as they turned their steps homeward. 'Let us propose that aim to our-selves, to build a church on Cocksmoor!'

'How many years do you give us to do it in?' said Norman.

'Few or many, I don't care. I'll never leave off thinking about it till it is done.'

'It need not be long,' said Flora, 'if one could get up a sub-scription.'

'A penny subscription?' said Norman. 'I'd rather have it my own doing.'

'You agree then,' said Ethel, 'do you, Mr. Ernescliffe?'

'I may safely do so,' he answered, smiling.

Miss Winter looked at Etheldred reprovingly, and she shrank into herself, drew apart, and indulged in a reverie. She had heard in books, of girls writing poetry, romance, history—gaining fifties and hundreds. Could not some of the myriads of fancies floating in her mind thus be made available? She would com-pose, publish, earn money—some day call papa, show him her hoard, beg him to take it, and, never owning whence it came, raise the building. Spire and chancel—pinnacle and buttress rose before her eyes—and she and Norman were standing in the porch, with an orderly, religious population, blessing the unknown benefactor, who had caused the news of salvation to be heard among them.

They were almost at home, when the sight of a crowd in the main street checked them. Norman and Mr. Ernescliffe went forward to discover the cause, and spoke to some one on the out-skirts—then Mr. Ernescliffe hurried back to the ladies. 'There's been an accident,' he said, hastily—'you had better go down the lane, and in by the garden.'

He was gone in an instant, and they obeyed in silence. Whence came Ethel's certainty that the accident concerned themselves? In an agony of apprehension, though without one outward sign of it, she walked home. They were in the garden—all was ap-parently as usual, but no one was in sight. Ethel had been first, but she held back, and let Miss Winter go forward into the house. The front door was open—servants were standing about in confusion, and one of the maids, looking dreadfully frightened, gave a cry, 'Oh! Miss—Miss—have you heard?'

'No—what? What has happened? Not Mrs. May—' exclaimed Miss Winter.

'Oh! ma'am! it's all of them. The carriage is overturned, and—'

'Who's hurt? Mamma! papa! Oh! tell me!' cried Flora.

'There's nurse,' and Ethel flew up to her. 'What is it? Oh! nurse!'

'My poor, poor children,' said old nurse, passionately kissing Ethel. Harry and Mary were on the stairs behind her, clinging together.

A stranger looked into the house, followed by Adams, the stableman. 'They are going to bring Miss May in,' some one said.

Ethel could bear it no longer. As if she could escape, she fled up-stairs, into her room, and, falling on her knees, hid her face on her bed.

There were heavy steps in the house, then a sound of hasty feet coming up to her. Norman dashed into the room, and threw himself on a chair. He was ghastly pale, and shuddered all over.

'Oh! Norman, Norman, speak. What is it?'

He groaned, but could not speak; he rested his head against her, and gasped. She was terribly frightened. 'I'll call—' and she would have gone, but he held her. 'No—no—they can't!' He was prevented from saying more, by chattering teeth and deadly faintness. She tried to support him, but could only guide him as he sank, till he lay at full length on the floor, where she put a pillow under his head, and gave him some water. 'Is it —oh! tell me. Are they much hurt? Oh, try to say.'

'They say Margaret is alive,' said Norman, in gasps; 'but— And papa—he stood up—sat—walked—was better—'

'Is he hurt—much hurt?'

'His arm—' and the tremor and fainting stopped him again.

'Mamma?' whispered Ethel; but Norman only pressed his face into the pillow.

She was so bewildered as to be more alive to the present distress of his condition, than to the vague horrors down-stairs. Some minutes passed in silence, Norman lying still, excepting a nervous trembling that agitated his whole frame. Again was heard the strange tread, doors opening and shutting, and suppressed voices, and he turned his face upwards, and listened, with his hand pressed to his forehead, as if to keep himself still enough to listen.

'Oh! what is the matter? What is it?' cried Ethel, startled and recalled to the sense of what was passing. 'Oh! Norman!' then springing up, with a sudden thought, 'Mr. Ward! Oh! is he there?'

P. 27.

NORMAN AND ETHEL.

'Yes,' said Norman, in a low, hopeless tone, 'he was at the place. He said it—'

'What?'

'Again Norman's face was out of sight.

'Mamma?' Ethel's understanding perceived, but her mind refused to grasp the extent of the calamity. There was no answer, save a convulsive squeezing of her hand.

Fresh sounds below recalled her to speech and action. 'Where is she? What are they doing for her? What—'

'There's nothing to be done. She—when they lifted her up, she was—'

'Dead?'

'Dead.'

The boy lay with his face hidden, the girl sat by him on the floor, too much crushed for even the sensations belonging to grief, neither moving nor looking. After an interval Norman spoke again, 'The carriage turned right over—her head struck on the kerb stone—'

'Did you see?' said Ethel, presently.

'I saw them lift her up.' He spoke at intervals, as he could get breath, and bear to utter the words. 'And papa—he was stunned—but soon he sat up, said he would go to her—he looked at her—felt her pulse, and then—sank down over her!'

'And did you say, I can't remember—was he hurt?'

The shuddering came again, 'His arm—all twisted—broken,' and his voice sank into a faint whisper; Ethel was obliged to sprinkle him again with water. 'But he won't die?' said she, in a tone calm from its bewilderment.

'Oh! no, no, no—'

'And Margaret?'

'They were bringing her home. I'll go and see. O! what's the meaning of this?' exclaimed he, scolding himself, as sitting up, he was forced to rest his head on his shaking hand.

'You are still faint, dear Norman; you had better lie still, and I'll go and see.'

'Faint—stuff—how horridly stupid!' but he was obliged to lay his head down again; and Ethel, scarcely less trembling, crept carefully towards the stairs, but a dread of what she might meet came over her, and she turned towards the nursery.

The younger ones sat there in a frightened huddle. Mary was on a low chair by the infant's cot, Blanche in her lap, Tom and Harry leaning against her, and Aubrey almost asleep. Mary held up her finger as Ethel entered, and whispered, 'Hush! don't wake baby for anything!'

The first true pang of grief shot through Ethel like a dart, stabbing and taking away her breath, 'Where are they?' she said; 'how is papa? who is with him?'

'Mr. Ward and Alan Ernescliffe,' said Harry.   'Nurse came up just now, and said they were setting his arm.'

'Where is he?'

'On the bed in his dressing-room,' said Harry.

'Has he come to himself—is he better?'

They did not seem to know, and Ethel asked where to find Flora. 'With Margaret,' she was told, and she was thinking whether she could venture to seek her, when she herself came fast up the stairs. Ethel and Harry both darted out. 'Don't stop me,' said Flora—'they want some handkerchiefs.'

'What, is not she in her own room?'

'No,' said Harry, 'in mamma's;' and then his face quivered all over, and he turned away. Ethel ran after her sister, and pulling out drawers without knowing what she sought, begged to hear how papa and Margaret were.

'We can't judge of Margaret—she has moved, and made a little moaning—there are no limbs broken, but we are afraid for her head. Oh! if papa could but—'

'And papa?'

'Mr. Ward is with him now—his arm is terribly hurt.'

'But oh! Flora—one moment—is he sensible?'

'Hardly; he does not take any notice—but don't keep me.'

'Can I do anything?' following her to the head of the stairs.

'No; I don't see what you can do. Miss Winter and I are with Margaret; there's nothing to do for her.'

It was a relief. Etheldred shrank from what she might have to behold, and Flora hastened down, too busy and too useful to have time to think. Harry had gone back to his refuge in the nursery, and Ethel returned to Norman. There they remained for a long time, both unwilling to speak or stir, or even to observe to each other on the noises that came in to them, as their door was left ajar, though in those sounds they were so absorbed, that they did not notice the cold of a frosty October evening, or the darkness that closed in on them.

They heard the poor babe crying, one of the children going down to call nurse, and nurse coming up; then Harry, at the door of the room where the boys slept, calling Norman in a low voice. Norman, now nearly recovered, went and brought him into his sister's room, and his tidings were, that their father's arm had been broken in two places, and the elbow frightfully injured, having been crushed and twisted by the wheel. He was also a good deal bruised, and though Mr. Ward trusted there was no positive harm to the head, he was in an unconscious state, from which the severe pain of the operation had only roused him, so far as to evince a few signs of suffering. Margaret was still insensible.

The piteous sound of the baby's wailing almost broke their hearts. Norman walked about the room in the dark, and said he should go down, he could not bear it; but he could not make up his mind to go; and after about a quarter of an hour, to their great relief, it ceased.

Next Mary opened the door, saying, 'Norman, here's Mr. Wilmot come to ask if he can do anything—Miss Winter sent word that you had better go to him.'

'How is baby?' asked Harry.

'Nurse has fed her, and is putting her to bed; she is quiet now,' said Mary; 'will you go down, Norman?'

'Where is he?'

'In the drawing-room.'

Norman paused to ask what he was to say. 'Nothing,' said Mary, 'nobody can do anything. Make haste. Don't you want a candle?'

'No, thank you, I had rather be in the dark. Come up as soon as you have seen him,' said Etheldred.

Norman went slowly down, with failing knees, hardly able to conquer the shudder that came over him, as he passed those rooms. There were voices in the drawing-room, and he found a sort of council there, Alan Ernescliffe, the surgeon, and Mr. Wilmot. They turned as he came in, and Mr. Wilmot held out his hand, with a look of affection and kindness that went to his heart, making room for him on the sofa, while going on with what he was saying. 'Then you think it would be better for me not to sit up with him.'

'I should decidedly say so,' replied Mr. Ward. 'He has recognised Mr. Ernescliffe, and any change might excite him, and lead him to ask questions. The moment of his full consciousness is especially to be dreaded.'

'But you do not call him insensible?'

'No, but he seems stunned—stupified by the shock, and by pain. He spoke to Miss Flora when she brought him some tea.'

'And admirably she managed,' said Alan Ernescliffe. 'I was much afraid of some answer that would rouse him, but she kept her self-possession beautifully, and seemed to compose him in a moment.'

'She is valuable indeed—so much judgment and activity,' said Mr. Ward. 'I don't know what we should have done without her. But we ought to have Mr. Richard—has no one sent to him?'

Alan Ernescliffe and Norman looked at each other.

'Is he at Oxford, or at his tutor's ?' asked Mr. Wilmot.

'At Oxford; he was to be there to-day, was he not, Norman?'

'What o'clock is it ? Is the post gone—seven—no ; it is all safe,' said Mr. Ward.

Poor Norman! he knew he was the one who ought to write, but his icy trembling hand seemed to shake more helplessly than ever, and a piteous glance fell upon Mr. Wilmot.

'The best plan would be,' said Mr. Wilmot, 'for me to go to him at once, and bring him home. If I go by the mail-train, I shall get to him sooner than a letter could.'

'And it will be better for him,' said Mr. Ward. 'He will feel it dreadfully, poor boy. But we shall all do better when we have him. You can get back to-morrow evening.'

'Sunday,' said Mr. Wilmot, 'I believe there is a train at four.'

'Oh! thank you, sir,' said Norman.

'Since that is settled, perhaps I had better go up to the Doctor,' said Alan ; 'I don't like leaving Flora alone with him,' and he was gone.

'How fortunate that that youth is here,' said Mr. Wilmot; 'he seems to be quite taking Richard's place.'

'And to feel it as much,' said Mr. Ward. 'He has been invaluable with his sailor's resources and handiness.'

'Well, what shall I tell poor Richard ?' asked Mr. Wilmot.

'Tell him there is no reason his father should not do very well, if we can keep him from agitation—but there's the point. He is of so excitable a constitution, that his faculties being so far confused, is the best thing, perhaps, that could be. Mr. Ernescliffe manages him very well—used to illness on that African coast, and the Doctor is very fond of him. As to Miss May, one can't tell what to say about her yet—there's no fracture, at least —it must be a work of time to judge.'

Flora at that moment half-opened the door, and called Mr. Ward, stopping for a moment to say it was nothing of any consequence. Mr. Wilmot and Norman were left together. Norman put his hands over his face and groaned—his master looked at him with kind anxiety, but did not feel as if it were yet time to speak of consolation.

'God bless and support you, and turn this to your good, my dear boy,' said he, affectionately, as he pressed his hand; 'I hope to bring your brother to-morrow.'

'Thank you, sir,' was all Norman could say; and as Mr. Wilmot went out by the front door, he slowly went up again, and lingering on the landing-place, was met by Mr. Ward, who told him to his relief—for the mere thinking of it renewed the faint sensation—that he had better not go to his father's room.

There was nothing to be done but to return to Ethel and Harry, and tell them all; with some humiliation at being helpless, where Flora was doing so much, and to leave their father to be watched by a stranger. If he had been wanted, Norman might have made the effort, but being told that he would be worse than useless, there was nothing for him but to give way.

They sat together in Ethel's room till somewhere between eight and nine o'clock, when good old nurse, having put her younger ones to bed, came in search of them. 'Dear, dear! poor darlings,' said she, as she found them sitting in the dark; she felt their cold hands, and made them all come into the nursery, where Mary was already, and, fondling them, one by one, as they passively obeyed her, she set them down on their little old stools round the fire, took away the high fender, and gave them each a cup of tea. Harry and Mary ate enough to satisfy her from a weary craving feeling, and for want of employment; Norman sat with his elbow on his knee, and a very aching head resting on his hand, glad of drink, but unable to eat; Ethel could be persuaded to do neither, till she found old nurse would let her have no peace.

The nurse sent them all to bed, taking the two girls to their own room, undressing them, and never leaving them until Mary was in a fair way of crying herself to sleep—for saying her prayers had brought the tears; while Ethel lay so wide awake that it was of no use to wait for her, and then she went to the boys, tucked them each in, as when they were little children, and saying, 'Bless your dear hearts!' bestowed on each of them a kiss which came gratefully to Norman's burning brow, and which even Harry's boyish manliness could not resist.

Flora was in Margaret's room, too useful to be spared.

So ended that dreadful Saturday.

CHAPTER IV.

'They may not mar the deep repose
  Of that immortal flower;
Though only broken hearts are found
  To watch her cradle by,
No blight is on her slumbers found,
  No touch of harmful eye.'—LYRA INNOCENTIUM.

SUCH a strange sad Sunday! No going to church, but all the poor children moving in awe and oppression about the house, speaking under their breath, as they gathered in the drawing-room. Into the study they might not go; and when Blanche would have asked why, Tom pressed her hand and shuddered.

Etheldred was allowed to come and look at Margaret, and even to sit in the room for a little while, to take the place of Miss Winter; but she was not sensible of sufficient usefulness to relieve the burden of fear and bewilderment in the presence of that still, pale form; and, what was almost worse, the sight of the familiar objects, the chair by the fire, the sofa, the books, the work-basket, the letter-case, the dressing things, all these were too oppressive. She sat crouched up, with her face hidden in her hands, and the instant she was released, hastened back to Norman. She was to tell him that he might go into the room, but he did not move, and Mary alone went in and out with messages.

Dr. May was not to be visited, for he was in the same half-conscious state, apparently sensible only of bodily suffering, though he answered when addressed, and no one was trusted to speak to him but Flora and Alan Ernescliffe.

The rest wore through the day as best they might. Harry slept a good deal, Ethel read to herself, and tried to get Norman to look at passages which she liked, Mary kept the little ones from being troublesome, and at last took them to peep behind the school-room blinds for Richard's coming.

There was a simultaneous shout when, at four o'clock, they caught sight of him, and though, at Ethel's exclamation of wonder, Mary and Tom hung their heads at having forgotten themselves, the association of gladness in seeing Richard was refreshing; the sense of being desolate and forsaken was relieved, and they knew that now they had one to rely on and to comfort them.

Harry hastened to open the front-door, and Richard, with his small trim figure, and fresh, fair young face, flushed, though not otherwise agitated, was among them, almost devoured by the younger ones, and dealing out quiet caresses to them, as he caught from the words and looks of the others, that at least his father and sister were no worse. Mr. Wilmot had come with him, but only stayed to hear the tidings.

'Can I see papa?' were Richard's first audible words—all the rest had been almost dumb show.

Ethel thought not, but took him to Margaret's room, where he stood for many minutes without speaking; then whispered to Flora that he must go to the others, she should call him if—and went down, followed by Ethel.

Tom and Blanche had fallen into teasing tricks, a sort of melancholy play to relieve the tedium. They grew cross. Norman was roused to reprove sharply, and Blanche was beginning to cry; but Richard's entrance set all at peace—he sat down among them, and, with soft voice, and arm round Blanche, as she leaned against him, made her good in a moment; and she listened while he talked over with Norman and Ethel all they could bear to speak of.

Late in the day, Flora came into her father's room, and stood gazing at him, as he lay with eyes closed, breathing heavily, and his brows contracted by pain. She watched him with piteous looks, as if imploring him to return to his children. Poor girl, to-day's quiet, after the last evening's bustle, was hard to bear. She had then been distracted from thought by the necessity of exertion, but it now repaid itself, and she knew not how to submit to do nothing but wait and watch.

'No change?' inquired Alan Ernescliffe; looking kindly in her face.

'No,' replied she, in a low, mournful tone. 'She only once said, 'Thank you.''

A voice which she did not expect, asked inquiringly, 'Margaret?' and her heart beat as if it would take away her breath, as she saw her father's eyes intently fixed on her. 'Did you speak of her?' he repeated.

'Yes, dear papa,' said Flora, not losing presence of mind, though in extreme fear of what the next question might be. 'She is quiet and comfortable, so don't be uneasy, pray.'

'Let me hear,' he said; and his whole voice and air showed him to be entirely roused. 'There is injury? What is it—'

He continued his inquiries till Flora was obliged fully to explain her sister's condition; and then he dismayed her by saying he would get up and go to see her. Much distressed, she begged him not to think of it, and appealed to Alan, who added his entreaties that he would at least wait for Mr. Ward; but the Doctor would not relinquish his purpose, and sent her to give notice that he was coming.

Mr. Ernescliffe followed her out of the room, and tried to console her, as she looked at him in despair.

'You see he is quite himself—quite collected,' he said; 'you heard how clear and coherent his questions were.'

'Can't it be helped? Do try to stop him till I can send to Mr. Ward.'

'I will try, but I think he is in a state to judge for himself. I do, upon my word; and I believe trying to prevent him would be more likely to do him harm than letting him satisfy himself. I really think you need not be alarmed.'

PART I.   D

'But you know,' said Flora, coming nearer, and almost gasping as she whispered and signed towards the door, 'she is there—it is mamma's room, that will tell all.'

'I believe he knows,' said Alan. 'It was *that* which made him faint after the accident, for he had his perceptions fully at first. I have suspected all day that he was more himself than he seemed, but I think he could not bear to awaken his mind to understand it, and that he was afraid to hear about her—your sister, so that our mention of her was a great relief, and did him good. I am convinced he knows the rest. Only go on, be calm, as you have been, and we shall do very well.'

Flora went to prepare. Ethel eagerly undertook to send to Mr. Ward, and hastened from the room, as if in a sort of terror, shrinking perhaps from what might lead to an outburst of grief. She longed to *have* seen her father, but was frightened at the chance of meeting him. When she had sent her message, and told her brothers what was passing, she went and lingered on the stairs and in the passage for tidings. After what seemed a long time, Flora came out, and hastened to the nursery, giving her intelligence on the way.

'Better than could be hoped; he walked alone into the room, and was quite calm and composed. Oh! if this will not hurt him; if the seeing baby was but over!'

'Does he want her?'

'Yes; he would have come up here himself, but I would not let him—Nurse, do you hear? Papa wants baby—let me have her.'

'Bless me, Miss Flora, you can't hold her while you are all of a tremble! And he has been to Miss Margaret?'

'Yes, nurse; and he was only rather stiff and lame.'

'Did Margaret seem to know him?' said Ethel.

'She just answered in that dreamy way when he spoke to her. He says he thinks it is as Mr. Ward believes, and that she will soon come to herself. He is quite able to consider—'

'And he knows all?'

'I am sure he does. He desired to see baby, and he wants you, nurse. Only mind you command yourself—don't say a word you can help—do nothing to agitate him.'

Nurse promised, but the tears came so fast, and sobs with them as she approached her master's room, that Flora saw no composure could be expected from her; and taking the infant from her, carried it in, leaving the door open for her to follow when wanted. Ethel stood by listening. There was silence at first, then some sounds from the baby, and her father's voice soothing it, in his wonted caressing phrases and tones, so familiar, that they seemed to break the spell, drive away her vague terrors, and restore her father. Her heart bounded, and a sudden impulse carried her to the bedside, at once forgetting all dread of seeing him, and chance of doing him harm. He lay, holding the babe close to him, and his face was not altered, so that there was nothing in the sight to impress her with the need of caution, and, to the consternation of the anxious Flora, she exclaimed, abruptly and vehemently, 'Papa! should not she be christened?'

Dr. May looked up at Ethel, then at the infant; 'Yes,' he said, 'at once.' Then added, feebly and languidly, 'Some one must see to it.'

There was a pause, while Flora looked reproachfully at her sister, and Ethel became conscious of her imprudence; but in a few moments Dr. May spoke again, first to the baby, and then asking—'Is Richard here?'

'Yes, papa.'

'Send him up presently. Where's nurse?'

Ethel retreated, much alarmed at her rash measure, and when she related it, she saw that Richard and Mr. Ernescliffe both thought it had been a great hazard.

'Papa wants you,' was a welcome sound to the ears of Richard, and brought a pink glow into his face. He was never one who readily showed his feelings, and there was no danger of his failing in self-command, though grievously downcast, not only at the loss of the tender mother, who had always stood between him and his father's impatience, but by the dread that he was too dull and insignificant to afford any help or comfort in his father's dire affliction.

Yet there was something in the gentle sad look that met him, and the low tone of the 'How d'ye do, Ritchie?' that drove off all thought of not being loved; and when Dr. May further added, 'You'll see about it all—I am glad you are come,' he knew he was of use, and was encouraged and cheered. That his father had full confidence and reliance in him, and that his presence was a satisfaction and relief, he could no longer doubt; and this was a drop of balm beyond all his hopes; for loving and admiring his father intensely, and with depressed spirits and a low estimate of himself, he had begun to fancy himself incapable of being anything but a vexation and burthen.

He sat with his father nearly all the evening, and was to remain with him at night. The rest were comforted by the assurance that Dr. May was still calm, and did not seem to have been injured by what had passed. Indeed, it seemed as if the violence and suddenness of the shock, together with his state of suffering, had deadened his sensations; for there was far less agitation about him than could have been thought possible in a man of such strong, warm affections and sensitive temperament.

Ethel and Norman went up arm-in-arm at bed-time.

'I am going to ask if I may wish papa good-night,' said Ethel. 'Shall I say anything about your coming?'

Norman hesitated, but his cheeks blanched; he shuddered, shook his head without speaking, ran up after Harry, and waved her back when she would have followed.

Richard told her that she might come in; and, as she slowly advanced, she thought she had never seen anything so ineffably mournful as the affectionate look on her father's face. She held his hand, and ventured—for it was with difficulty she spoke—to hope he was not in pain.

'Better than it was, thank you, my dear,' he said, in a soft, weak tone; then, as she bent down to kiss his brow, 'You must take care of the little ones.'

'Yes, papa,' she could hardly answer, and a large drop gathered slowly in each eye, long in coming, as if the heart ached too much for them to flow freely.

'Are they all well?'

'Yes, papa.'

'And good?' He held her hand, as if lengthening the interview. 'Yes, very good all day.'

A long deep sigh. Ethel's two tears stood on her cheeks.

'My love to them all. I hope I shall see them to-morrow. God bless you, my dear, good night.'

Ethel went up-stairs, saddened and yet soothed. The calm silent sorrow, too deep for outward tokens, was so unlike her father's usually demonstrative habits, as to impress her all the more, yet those two tears were followed by no more; there was much strangeness and confusion in her mind in the newness of grief.

She found poor Flora, spent with exertion, under the reaction of all she had undergone, lying on her bed, sobbing as if her heart would break, calling in gasps of irrepressible agony on mamma! mamma! yet with her face pressed down on the pillow that she might not be heard. Ethel, terrified and distressed, timidly implored her to be comforted, but it seemed as if she were not even heard; she would have fetched some one, but whom? Alas! alas! it brought back the sense that no mother would ever soothe them—Margaret, papa, both so ill, nurse engaged with Margaret! Ethel stood helpless and despairing, and Flora sobbed on, so that Mary awakened to burst out in a loud frightened fit of crying; but in a few moments a step was at the door, a knock, and Richard asked, 'Is anything the matter?'

He was in the room in a moment, caressing and saying affectionate things with gentleness and fondling care, like his mother, and which recalled the days when he had been proud to be left for a little while the small nurse and guardian of the lesser ones. Mary was hushed in a moment, and Flora's exhausted weeping was gradually soothed, when she was able to recollect that she was keeping him from her father; with kind good nights, he left Ethel to read to her till she could sleep. Long did Ethel read, after both her sisters were slumbering soundly; she went on in a sort of dreamy grief, almost devoid of pain, as if all this was too terrible to be true; and she had imagined herself into a story, which would give place at dawn to her ordinary life.

At last she went to bed, and slept till wakened by the return of Flora, who had crept down in her dressing-gown to see how matters were going. Margaret was in the same state, papa was asleep, after a restless, distressing night, with much pain and some fever; and whenever Richard had begun to hope, from his tranquillity, that he was falling asleep, he was undeceived by hearing an almost unconsciously uttered sigh of 'Maggie, my Maggie!' and then the head turned wearily on the pillow, as if worn out with the misery from which there was no escape. Towards morning, the pain had lessened, and, as he slept, he seemed much less feverish than they could have ventured to expect.

Norman looked wan and wretched, and could taste no breakfast; indeed Harry reported that he had been starting and talking in his sleep half the night, and had proceeded to groaning and crying out till, when it could be borne no longer, Harry waked him, and finished his night's rest in peace.

The children were kept in the drawing-room that morning, and there were strange steps in the house; but only Richard and Mr. Ernescliffe knew the reason. Happily there had been witnesses enough of the overturn to spare any reference to Dr. May—the violent start of the horses had been seen, and Adams and Mr. Ernescliffe agreed, under their breath, that the new black one was not fit to drive, while the whole town was so used to Dr. May's headlong driving, that every one was recollecting their own predictions of accidents. There needed little to account for the disaster—the only wonder was, that it had not happened sooner.

'I say,' announced Harry, soon after they were released again, 'I've been in to papa. His door was open, and he heard me, and called me. He says he should like any of us to come in and see him. Hadn't you better go, Norman?'

Norman started up and walked hastily out of the room, but his hand shook so, that he could hardly open the door; and Ethel, seeing how it was with him, followed him quickly, as he dashed, at full speed, up the stairs. At the top, however, he was forced to cling to the rail, gasping for breath, while the moisture started on his forehead.

'Dear Norman,' she said, 'there's nothing to mind. He looks just as usual. You would not know there was anything the matter.' But he rested his head on his hand, and looked as if he could not stir. 'I see it won't do,' said Ethel—'don't try—you will be better by-and-by, and he has not asked for you in particular.'

'I won't be beat by such stuff,' said Norman, stepping hastily forwards, and opening the door suddenly. He got through the greeting pretty well, there was no need for him to speak, he only gave his hand and looked away, unable to bring himself to turn his eyes on his father, and afraid of letting his own face be seen. Almost at the same moment, nurse came to say something about Margaret, and he seized the opportunity of withdrawing his hand and hurrying away, in good time, for he was pale as death, and was obliged to sit down on the head of the stairs, and lean his head against Etheldred.

'What does make me so ridiculous?' he exclaimed, faintly, but very indignantly.

The first cure was the being forced to clear out of Mr. Ward's way, which he could not effect without being seen; and Ethel, though she knew that he would be annoyed, was not sorry to be obliged to remain, and tell what was the matter with him. 'Oh,' said Mr. Ward, turning and proceeding to the dining-room, 'I'll set that to rights in a minute, if you will ask for a tumbler of hot water, Miss Ethel.'

And armed with the cordial he had prepared, Ethel hunted up her brother, and persuaded him, after scolding her a little, to swallow it, and take a turn in the garden; after which he made a more successful attempt at visiting his father.

There was another room whither both Norman and Etheldred wished to go, though they dared not hint at their desire. At last, Richard came to them, as they were wandering in the garden, and, with his usual stillness of manner, shaded with additional seriousness, said, 'Would you like to come into the study?'

Etheldred put one hand into his, Norman took the other, and soon they stood in that calm presence. Fair, cold, white, and intensely still—that face brought home to them the full certainty that the warm, brightening look would never beam on them, the soft blue eyes never guide, check, and watch them, the smile never

approve or welcome them. To see her unconscious of their presence
was too strange and sad, and all were silent, till, as they left the
room, Ethel looked out at Blanche and Aubrey in the garden.
'They will never remember her! Oh! why should it be?'

Richard would fain have moralized and comforted, but she felt
as if she knew it all before, and heard with languid attention.
She had rather read than talk, and he sat down to write letters.

There were no near relations to be sent for. Dr. May was an
only son, and his wife's sister, Mrs. Arnott, was in New Zealand;
her brother had long been dead, and his widow, who lived in
Edinburgh, was scarcely known to the May family. Of friends
there were many, fast bound by affection and gratitude, and notes,
inquiries, condolences, and offers of services came in thickly, and
gave much occupation to Flora, Richard, and Alan Ernescliffe,
in turn. No one from without could do anything for them—
they had all the help they wanted in Miss Winter and in Alan,
who was invaluable in sharing with Richard the care of the
Doctor, as well as in giving him the benefit of his few additional
years' experience, and relieving him of some of his tasks. He
was indeed like one of themselves, and a most valuable help and
comforter. Mr. Wilmot gave them all the time he could, and
on this day saw the Doctor, who seemed to find some solace in
his visit, though saying very little.

On this day the baby was to be baptized. The usual Stoneborough fashion was to collect all the christenings for the month
into one Sunday, except those for such persons as thought themselves too refined to see their children christened before the
congregation, and who preferred an empty church and a week-
day. The little one had waited till she was nearly six weeks old
for 'a Christening Sunday,' and since that had been missed, she
could not be kept unbaptized for another month; so, late in the
day, she was carried to Church.

Richard had extremely gratified old nurse, by asking her to
represent poor Margaret, Mrs. Hoxton stood for the other godmother, and Alan Ernescliffe was desired to consider himself
absolutely her sponsor, not merely a proxy. The younger children
alone were to go with them: it was too far off, and the way lay too
much through the town for it to be thought proper for the others
to go. Ethel wished it very much, and thought it nonsense to
care whether people looked at her; and in spite of Miss Winter's
seeming shocked at her proposing it, had a great mind to persist.
She would even have appealed to her papa, if Flora had not
stopped her, exclaiming, 'Really, Ethel, I think there never was
a person so entirely without consideration as you are.'

Much abashed, Ethel humbly promised that if she might go into papa's room she would not say one word about the christening unless he should begin, and, to her great satisfaction, he presently asked her to read the service to him. Flora came to the door-way of Margaret's room, and listened; when she had finished, all were silent.

'How shall we, how can we virtuously bring up our motherless little sister?' was the thought with each of the girls. The answers were, in one mind, 'I trust we shall do well by her, dear little thing. I see, on an emergency, that I know how to act. I never thought I was capable of being of so much use, thanks to dear, dear mamma's training. I shall manage, I am sure, and so they will all depend on me, and look up to me. How nice it was to hear dear papa say what he did about the comfort of my being able to look after Margaret.'

In the other, 'Poor darling, it is saddest of all for her, because she knows nothing, and will never remember her mamma. But if Margaret is but better, she will take care of her, and oh! how we ought to try—and I, such a naughty wild thing—if I should hurt the dear little ones by carelessness, or by my bad example! Oh! what shall I do, for want of some one to keep me in order? If I should vex papa by any of my wrong ways!'

They heard the return of the others, and the sisters both sprang up, 'May we bring her to you?' said Flora.

'Yes, do, my dears.'

The sisters all came in together with the little one, and Flora put her down within the arm her father stretched out for her. He gazed into the baby face, which, in its expressionless placidity, almost recalled her mother's tranquil sweetness.

'Gertrude Margaret,' said Flora, and with a look that had more of tenderness than grief, he murmured, 'My Daisy blossom, my little Maggie.'

'Might we?' said Ethel, when Flora took her again, 'might we take her to her godmother to see if she would notice her?'

He looked as if he wished it; but said 'No, I think not, better not rouse her,' and sighed heavily; then, as they stood round his bed, unwilling to go, he added, 'Girls, we must learn carefulness and thoughtfulness. We have no one to take thought for us now.'

Flora pressed the babe in her arms, Ethel's two reluctant tears stood on her cheeks, Mary exclaimed, 'I'll try not to be naughty;' and Blanche climbed up to kiss him, saying, 'I will be always good, papa.'

'Daisy—papa's daisy—your vows are made,' whispered Ethel,

gaining sole possession of the babe for a minute. 'You have promised to be good and holy. We have the keeping of you, mamma's precious flower, her pearl of truth! Oh, may God guard you to be an unstained jewel, till you come back to her again—and a blooming flower, till you are gathered into the wreath that never fades—my own sweet poor little motherless Daisy!'

CHAPTER V.

Through lawless camp, through ocean wild,
    Her prophet eye pursues her child;
Scans mournfully her poet's strain,
    Fears for her merchant, loss alike and gain.'—LYRA INNOCENTIUM.

DR. MAY took the management of himself into his own hands, and paid so little attention to Mr. Ward's recommendations, that his sons and daughters were in continual dread of his choosing to do something that might cause injurious agitation.

However, he did not attempt to go farther than Margaret's bedside, where he sat hour after hour, his eyes fixed upon her, as she continued in a state bordering on insensibility. He took little notice of anything else, and hardly spoke. There were heavy sighs now and then, but Richard and Flora, one or other of whom were always watching him, could hardly tell whether to ascribe them to the oppression of sorrow, or of suffering. Their great fear was of his insisting on seeing his wife's face, and it was a great relief that he never alluded to her, except once, to desire Richard to bring him her ring. Richard silently obeyed, and, without a word, he placed it on his little finger. Richard used to read the Psalms to him in the morning, before he was up, and Flora would bring little Daisy and lay her by his side.

To the last moment, they dreaded his choosing to attend the funeral, and Flora had decided on remaining at home, though trembling at the thought of what there might be to go through. They tried to let him hear nothing about it, but he seemed to know everything; and when Flora came into Margaret's room, without her bonnet, he raised his head, and said, 'I thought you were all going.'

'The others are—but may I not stay with you and her, papa?'

'I had rather be alone, my dear. I will take care of her. I should wish you all to be there.'

They decided that his wishes ought to be followed, and that the patients must be entrusted to old nurse. Richard told Flora, who looked very pale, that she would be glad of it afterwards, and she had his arm to lean upon.

The grave was in the cloister attached to the Minster, a smooth green square of turf, marked here and there with small flat lozenges of stone, and bearing the date and initials of those who lay there, and many of them recording former generations of Mays, to whom their descent from the head-master had given a right of burial there. Dr. Hoxton, Mr. Wilmot, and the surgeon, were the only friends whom Richard had asked to be with them, but the Minster was nearly full, for there was a very strong attachment and respect for Dr. and Mrs. May throughout the neighbourhood, and every one's feelings were strongly excited.

'In the midst of life, we are in death—' There was a universal sound, as of a sort of sob, that Etheldred never disconnected from those words.—Yet hardly one tear was shed by the young things who stood as close as they could round the grave. Harry and Mary did indeed lock their hands together tightly, and the shoulders of the former shook as he stood, bowing down his head, but the others were still and quiet, in part from awe and bewilderment, but partly, too, from a sense that it was against her whole nature that there should be clamorous mourning for her. The calm still day seemed to tell them the same, the sun beaming softly on the grey arches and fresh grass, the sky clear and blue, and the trees that showed over the walls bright with autumn colouring, all suitable to the serenity of a life unclouded to its last moment. Some of them felt as if it were better to be there, than in their saddened desolate home.

But home they must go, and, before going up-stairs, as Flora and Etheldred stood a moment or two with Norman, Ethel said, in a tone of resolution and of some cheerfulness, 'Well, we have to begin afresh.'

'Yes,' said Flora, 'it is a great responsibility. I do trust we may be enabled to do as we ought.'

'And now Margaret is getting better, she will be our stay,' said Ethel.

'I must go to her,' and Flora went up-stairs.

'I wish I could be as useful as Flora,' said Ethel, 'but I mean to try, and if I can but keep out of mischief, it will be something.'

'There is an object for all one does, in trying to be a comfort to papa.'

'That's no use,' said Norman, listlessly. 'We never can.'

'O but, Norman, he won't be always as he is now—I am sure he cares for us enough to be pleased, if we do right and get on.'

'We used to be so happy!' said Norman.

Ethel hesitated a little, and presently answered, 'I don't think it can be right to lament for our own sakes so much, is it?'

'I don't want to do so,' said Norman, in the same dejected way.

'I suppose we ought not to feel it either.' Norman only shook his head. 'We ought to think of her gain. You can't? Well, I am glad, for no more can I. I can't think of her liking for papa and baby and all of us to be left to ourselves. But that's not right of me, and of course it all comes right where she is; so I always put that out of my head, and think what is to come next in doing, and pleasing papa, and learning.'

'That's grown horrid,' said Norman. 'There's no pleasure in getting on, nor in anything.'

'Don't you care for papa and all of us being glad, Norman?'

As Norman could not just then say that he did, he would not answer.

'I wish—' said Ethel, disappointed, but cheering up the next minute. 'I do believe it is having nothing to do. You will be better when you get back to school on Monday.'

'That is worst of all!'

'You don't like going among the boys again? But that must be done some time or other. Or shall I get Richard to speak to Dr. Hoxton to let you have another week's leave?'

'No, no, don't be foolish. It can't be helped.'

'I am very sorry, but I think you will be better for it.'

She almost began to fancy herself unfeeling, when she found him so much more depressed than she was herself, and unable to feel it a relief to know that the time of rest and want of occupation was over. She thought it light-minded, though she could not help it, to look forward to the daily studies where she might lose her sad thoughts, and be as if everything were as usual. But suppose she should be to blame, where would now be the gentle discipline? Poor Ethel's feelings were not such as to deserve the imputation of levity, when this thought came over her; but her buoyant mind, always seeking for consolation, recurred to Margaret's improvement, and she fixed her hopes on her.

Margaret was more alive to surrounding objects, and, when roused, she knew them all, answered clearly when addressed, had even, more than once, spoken of her own accord, and shown solicitude at the sight of her father's bandaged, helpless arm, but he soon soothed this away. He was more than ever watchful over her, and could scarcely be persuaded to leave her for one moment, in his anxiety to be at hand to answer, when first she should speak of her mother, a moment apprehended by all the rest, almost as much for his sake as for hers.

So clear had her perceptions been, and so much more awake did she appear, on this evening, that he expected the enquiry to

:ome every moment, and lingered in her room; till she asked the hour, and begged him to go to bed.

As he bent over her, she looked up in his face, and said, softly, 'Dear papa.'

There was that in her tone which showed she perceived the truth, and he knelt by her side kissing her, but not daring to relax his restraint of feeling.

'Dear papa,' she said again, 'I hope I shall soon be better, and be some comfort to you.'

'My best—my own—my comfort,' he murmured, all he could say without giving way.

'Baby—is she well?'

'Yes, thank Heaven, she has not suffered at all.'

'I heard her this morning, I must see her to-morrow. But don't stay, dear, dear papa, it is late, and I am sure you are not at all well. Your arm—is it very much hurt?'

'It is nothing you need think about, my dear. I am much better than I could have imagined possible.'

'And you have been nursing me all the time! Papa, you must let me take care of you now. Do pray go to bed at once, and get up late. Nurse will take good care of me. Good night, dear papa.'

When Dr. May had left her, and tried to tell Richard how it had been, the tears cut him short, and had their free course: but there was much of thankfulness, for it might be looked on as the restoration of his daughter; the worst was over, and the next day he was able to think of other things, had more attention to spare for the rest, and when the surgeon came, took some professional interest in the condition of his own arm, inquired after his patients, and even talked of visiting them.

In the meantime, Margaret sent for her eldest brother, begging him to tell her the whole, and it was heard as calmly and firmly as it was told. Her bodily state lulled her mind; and besides it was not new; she had observed much while her faculties were still too much benumbed for her to understand all, or to express her feelings. Her thoughts seemed chiefly occupied with her father. She made Richard explain to her the injury he had suffered, and begged to know whether his constant attendance on her could do him harm. She was much rejoiced when her brother assured her that nothing could be better for him, and she began to say, with a smile, that very likely her being hurt had been fortunate. She asked who had taken care of him before Richard's arrival, and was pleased to hear that it was Mr. Ernescliffe. A visit from the little Gertrude Margaret was happily accomplished, and on the whole, the day was most satisfactory—she herself declaring that she could not see that there was anything the matter with her, except that she felt lazy, and did not seem able to move.

Thus the next Sunday morning dawned with more cheerfulness. Dr. May came down-stairs for the first time, in order to go to church with his whole flock, except the two Margarets. He looked very wan and shattered, but they clustered gladly round him, when he once more stood among them, little Blanche securing his hand, and nodding triumphantly to Mr. Ernescliffe, as much as to say, 'Now I have him, I don't want you.'

Norman alone was missing; but he was in his place at church among the boys. Again in returning, he slipped out of the party, and was at home the first, and when this recurred in the afternoon, Ethel began to understand his motive. The High-street led past the spot where the accident had taken place, though neither she nor any of the others knew exactly where it was, except Norman, on whose mind the scene was branded indelibly; she guessed that it was to avoid it that he went along what was called Randall's Alley, his usual short cut to school.

That Sunday brought back to the children that there was no one to hear their hymns; but Richard was a great comfort, watching over the little ones more like a sister than a brother. Ethel was ashamed of herself when she saw him taking thought for them, tying Blanche's bonnet, putting Aubrey's gloves on, teaching them to put away their Sunday toys, as if he meant them to be as neat and precise as himself.

Dr. May did not encounter the family dinner, nor attempt a second going to church; but Blanche was very glorious, as she led him down to drink tea, and, before going up again, he had a conversation with Alan Ernescliffe, who felt himself obliged to leave Stoneborough early on the morrow.

'I can endure better to go now,' said he, 'and I shall hear of you often; Hector will let me know, and Richard has promised to write.'

'Aye, you must let us often have a line. I should guess you were a letter writing man.'

'I have hitherto had too few friends who cared to hear of me to write much, but the pleasure of knowing that any interest is taken in me here—'

'Well,' said the Doctor, 'mind that a letter will always be welcome, and when you are coming southwards, here are your old quarters. We cannot lose sight of you any way, especially—' and his voice quivered, 'after the help you gave my poor boys and girls in their distress.'

'It would be the utmost satisfaction to think I had been of the smallest use,' said Alan, hiding much under these common-place words.

'More than I know,' said Dr. May; 'too much to speak of— Well, we shall see you again, though it is a changed place, and you must come and see your god-daughter—poor child—may she only be brought up as her sisters were! They will do their best, poor things, and so must I, but it is sad work!'

Both were too much overcome for words, but the Doctor was the first to continue, as he took off his dimmed spectacles. He seemed to wish to excuse himself for giving way; saying, with a look that would fain have been a smile, 'The world has run so light and easy with me hitherto, that you see I don't know how to bear with trouble. All thinking and managing fell to my Maggie's share, and I had as little care on my hands as one of my own boys—poor fellows. I don't know how it is to turn out, but of all the men on earth to be left with eleven children, I should choose myself as the worst.'

Alan tried to say somewhat of 'Confidence—affection—daughters,' and broke down, but it did as well as if it had been connected.

'Yes, yes,' said the Doctor, 'they are good children, every one of them. There's much to be thankful for, if one could only pluck up heart to feel it.'

'And you are convinced that Marga—that Miss May is re-covering?'

'She has made a great advance to-day. The head is right, at least,' but the Doctor looked anxious, and spoke low, as he said, 'I am not satisfied about her yet. That want of power over the limbs is more than the mere shock and debility, as it seems to me, though Ward thinks otherwise, and I trust he is right; but I cannot tell yet as to the spine. If this should not soon mend, I shall have Fleet to see her. He was a fellow-student of mine, very clever, and I have more faith in him than in any one else in that line.'

'By all means— Yes—' said Alan, excessively shocked. 'But you will let me know how she goes on—Richard will be so kind.'

'We will not fail,' said Dr. May, more and more touched at the sight of the young sailor struggling in vain to restrain his emotion; 'you shall hear. I'll write myself, as soon as I can use my hand, but I hope she may be all right long before that is likely to be.'

'Your kindness—' Alan attempted to say, but began again. 'Feeling as I must—' then interrupting himself. 'I beg your pardon, 'tis no fit time, nor fit— But you will let me hear.'

'That I will,' said Dr. May; and as Alan hastily left the room, he continued, half aloud, to himself, ' Poor boy ! poor fellow ! I see. No wonder ! Heaven grant I have not been the breaking of their two young hearts, as well as my own ! Maggie looked doubtful —as much as she ever did when my mind was set on a thing, when I spoke of bringing him here. But after all, she liked him as much as the rest of us did—she could not wish it otherwise—he is one of a thousand, and worthy of our Margaret. That he is ! and Maggie thinks so. If he gets on in his profession, why then we shall see—' but the sigh of anguish of mind, here showed that the wound had but been forgotten for one moment.

'Pshaw ! What am I running on to ? I'm all astray for want of her ! My poor girl—'

Mr. Ernescliffe set out before sun-rise. The boys were up to wish him good-bye, and so were Etheldred and Mary, and some one else, for while the shaking of hands was going on in the hall, there was a call ' Mr. Ernthcliffe,' and over the balusters peeped a little rough curly head, a face glowing with carnation deepened by sleep, and a round, plump, bare arm and shoulder ; and down at Alan's feet there fell a construction of white and pink paper, while a voice lisped out ' Mr. Ernthcliffe, there's a white rothe for you.'

An indignant ' Miss Blanche !' was heard behind, and there was no certainty that any thanks reached the poor little heroine, who was evidently borne off summarily to the nursery, while Ethel gave way to a paroxysm of suppressed laughter, joined in, more or less, by all the rest ; and thus Alan, promising faithfully to preserve the precious token, left Dr. May's door, not in so much outward sorrow as he had expected.

Even their father laughed at the romance of the white 'rothe,' and declared Blanche was a dangerous young lady ; but the story was less successful with Miss Winter, who gravely said it was no wonder, since Blanche's elder sister had been setting her the example of forwardness in coming down in this way after Mr. Ernescliffe. Ethel was very angry, and was only prevented from vindicating herself by remembering there was no peace-maker now, and that she had resolved only to think of Miss Winter's late kindness, and bear with her tiresome ways.

Etheldred thought herself too sorrowful to be liable to her usual faults, which would seem so much worse now ; but she found herself more irritable than usual, and doubly heedless, because her mind was pre-occupied. She hated herself, and suffered more from sorrow than even at the first moment, for now she felt what it was to have no one to tame her, no eye over her ; she found herself going *à tort et à travers* all the morning, and with no one to set her right. Since it was so the first day, what would follow ?

Mary was on the contrary so far subdued, as to be exemplary in goodness and diligence, and Blanche was always steady. Flora was too busy to think of the school-room, for the whole house was on her hands, besides the charge of Margaret, while Dr. May went to the hospital, and to sundry patients, and they thought he seemed the better for the occupation, as well as gratified and affected by the sympathy he everywhere met with, from high and low.

The boys were at school, unseen except when, at the dinner play-hour, Norman ran home to ask after his father and sister, but the most trying time was at eight in the evening, when they came home. That was wont to be the merriest part of the whole day, the whole family collected, papa at leisure and ready for talk or for play, mamma smiling over her work-basket, the sisters full of chatter, the brothers full of fun, all the tidings of the day discussed, and nothing unwelcome but bed-time. How different now! The Doctor was with Margaret; and though Richard tried to say something cheerful, as his brothers entered, there was no response, and they sat down on the opposite sides of the fire, forlorn and silent, till Richard, who was printing some letters on card-board to supply the gaps in Aubrey's ivory Alphabet, called Harry to help him; but Ethel, as she sat at work, could only look at Norman, and wish she could devise anything likely to gratify him.

After a time Flora came down, and laying some sheets of closely written note paper before her sister, said, ' Here is dear mamma's unfinished letter to aunt Flora. Papa says we elder ones are to read it. It is a description of us all, and very much indeed we ought to learn from it. I shall keep a copy of it.'

Flora took up her work, and began to consult with Richard, while Ethel moved to Norman's side, and kneeling so as to lean against his shoulder, as he sat on a low cushion, they read their mother's last letter, by the fire-light, with indescribable feelings, as they went through the subjects that had lately occupied them, related by her who would never be among them again. After much of this kind, for her letters to Mrs. Arnott were almost journals, came,

' You say it is long since you had a portrait gallery of the chicken daisies, and if I do not write in these leisure days, you will hardly get it after I am in the midst of business again. The new Daisy is like Margaret at the same age—may she continue like her! Pretty creature, she can hardly be more charming than at present. Aubrey, the moon-faced, is far from reconciled to his deposition from babyhood; he is a sober, solemn gentleman, backward in talking, and with such a will of his own as will want much watching; very different from Blanche, who is Flora over again, perhaps prettier, and more fairy-like, unless this is only one's admiration for the buds of the present season. None of them has ever been so winning as this little maid, who even attracts Dr. Hoxton himself, and obtains sugar-plums and kisses. 'Rather she than I,' says Harry, but notice is notice to the white Mayflower, and there is my anxiety—I am afraid it is not wholesome to be too engaging ever to get a rebuff. I hope having a younger sister, and outgrowing baby charms may be salutary. Flora soon left off thinking about her beauty, and the fit of vanity does less harm at five than fifteen. My poor Tom has not such a happy life as Blanche, he is often in trouble at lessons, and bullied by Harry at play, in spite of his champion, Mary; and yet I cannot interfere, for it is good for him to have all this preparatory teazing before he goes into school. He has good abilities, but not much perseverance or energy, and I must take the teaching of him into my own hands till his school-days begin, in hopes of instilling them. The girlishness and timidity will be knocked out of him by the boys, I suppose; Harry is too kind and generous to do more than teaze him moderately, and Norman will see that it does not go too far. It is a common saying that Tom and Mary made a mistake, that he is the girl and she the boy, for she is a rough, merry creature, the noisiest in the house, always skirmishing with Harry in defence of Tom, and yet devoted to him, and wanting to do everything he does. Those two, Harry and Mary, are exactly alike, except for Harry's curly mane of lion-coloured wig. The 'yellow haired laddie' is papa's name for Harry, which he does not mind from him, though furious if the girls attempt to call him so. Harry is the thorough boy of the family, all spirits, recklessness, and mischief, but so true, and kind, and noble-hearted, that one loves him the better after every freely confessed scrape. I cannot tell you how grateful I am to my boy for his perfect confidence, the thing that chiefly lessens my anxiety for him in his half-school, half-home life, which does not seem to me to work quite well with him. There are two sons of Mrs. Anderson's at the school, who are more his friends than I like, and he is too easily led by the desire not to be out-done, and to show that he fears nothing. Lately, our sailor-guest has inspired him with a vehement wish to go to sea; I wish it was not necessary that the decision should be made so early in life, for this fault is just what would make us most fear to send him into the world very young, though in some ways it might not do amiss for him.

'So much for the younger bairns, whom you never beheld, dear Flora. The three whom you left, when people used to waste pity on me for their being all babies together, now look as if any pair of them were twins, for Norman is the tallest, almost outgrowing his strength, and Ethel's sharp face, so like her papa's, makes her look older than Flora. Norman and Ethel do indeed take after their papa, more than any of the others, and are much alike. There is the same brilliant cleverness, the same strong feeling, not easy of demonstration, though impetuous in action; but poor Ethel's old foibles, her harum-scarum nature, quick temper, uncouth manners, and heedlessness of all but one absorbing object, have kept her back, and caused her much discomfort; yet I sometimes think these manifest defects have occasioned a discipline that is the best thing for the character in the end. They are faults that show themselves, and which one can tell how to deal with, and I have full confidence that she has the principle within her that will conquer them.'

'If—' mournfully sighed Ethel; but her brother pointed on further.

'My great hope is her entire indifference to praise—not approval, but praise. If she has not come up to her own standard, she works on, not always with good temper, but perseveringly, and entirely unheeding of commendation, till she has satisfied herself, only thinking it stupid not to see the faults. It is this independence of praise that I want to see in her brother and sister. They justly earn it, and are rightly pleased with it; but I cannot feel sure whether they do not depend on it too much. Norman lives, like all school-boys, a life of emulation, and has never met with anything but success. I do believe Dr. Hoxton and Mr. Wilmot are as proud of him as we are; and he has never shown any tendency to conceit, but I am afraid he has the love of being foremost, and pride in his superiority, caring for what he is compared with others, rather than what he is himself.'

PART I.　　　　　　　E

'I know,' said Norman; 'I have done so, but that's over.
I see what it is worth. I'd give all the *quam optimès* I ever
got in my life to be the help Richard is to papa.'

'You would if you were his age.'

'Not I, I'm not the sort. I'm not like her. But are we to
go on about the elders?'

'Oh! yes, don't let us miss a word. There can't be anything
but praise of them.'

'Your sweet goddaughter. I almost feel as if I had spoken in disparagement
of her, but I meant no such thing, dear girl. It would be hard to find a fault in
her, since the childish love of admiration was subdued. She is so solid and steady,
as to be very valuable with the younger ones, and is fast growing so lovely, that
I wish you could behold her. I do not see any vanity, but there lies my dread,
not of beauty-vanity, but that she will find temptation in the being everywhere
liked and sought after. As to Margaret, my precious companion and friend, you
have heard enough of her to know her, and, as to telling you what she is like, I
could as soon set about describing her papa. When I thought of not being spared
to them this time, it was happiness indeed to think of her at their head, fit to be
his companion, with so much of his own talent as to be more up to conversation
with him than he could ever have found his stupid old Maggie. It was rather a
trial of her discretion to have Mr. Ernescliffe here while I was up-stairs, and very
well she seems to have come out of it. Poor Richard's last disappointment is still
our chief trouble. He has been working hard with a tutor all through the vacation, and has not even come home to see his new sister, on his way to Oxford. He
had made a resolution that he would not come to us till he had passed, and his
father thought it best that it should be kept. I hope he will succeed next time,
but his nervousness renders it still more doubtful. With him it is the very reverse
of Norman. He suffers too much for want of commendation, and I cannot wonder
at it, when I see how much each failure vexes his father, and Richard little knows
how precious is our perfect confidence in him, how much more valuable than any
honours he could earn. You would be amused to see how little he is altered from
the pretty little fair fellow, that you used to say was so like my old portrait, even
the wavy rings of light glossy hair sit on his forehead, just as you liked to twist
them; and his small trim figure is a fine contrast to Norman's long legs and arms,
which—'

There the letter broke off, the playful affection of the last
words making it almost more painful to think that the fond
hand would never finish the sentence.

CHAPTER VI.

'A drooping daisy changed into a cup,
In which her bright-eyed beauty is shut up.'—WORDSWORTH.

'So there you are up for the day—really you look very comfortable,' said Ethel, coming into the room where Margaret lay
on her bed, half raised by pillows, supported by a wooden frame.

'Yes, is not it a charming contrivance of Richard's? It quite
gives me the use of my hands,' said Margaret.

'I think he is doing something else for you,' said Ethel; 'I heard him carpentering at six o'clock this morning, but I suppose it is to be a secret.'

'And don't you admire her night-cap?' said Flora.

'Is it anything different?' said Ethel, peering closer. 'O, I see—so she has a fine day night-cap. Is that your taste, Flora?'

'Partly,' said Margaret, 'and partly my own. I put in all these little white puffs, and I hope you think they do me credit. Wasn't it grand of me?'

'She only despises you for them,' said Flora.

'I'm very glad you could,' said Ethel, gravely; 'but do you know? it is rather like that horrid old lady in some book, who had a paralytic stroke, and the first thing she did that showed she had come to her senses was to write, 'Rose-coloured curtains for the doctors.' '

'Well, it was for the Doctor,' said Margaret, 'and it had its effect. He told me I looked much better when he found me trying it on.'

'And did you really have the looking-glass and try it on?' cried Ethel.

'Yes, really,' said Flora. 'Don't you think one may as well be fit to be seen if one is ill? It is no use to depress one's friends by being more forlorn and disconsolate than one can help.'

'No—not disconsolate,' said Ethel; 'but the white puffiness —and the hemming—and the glass!'

'Poor Ethel can't get over it,' said Margaret. 'But, Ethel, do you think there is nothing disconsolate in untidiness?'

'You could be tidy without the little puffs! Your first bit of work too! Don't think I'm tiresome. If they were an amusement to you, I am sure I am very glad of them, but I can't see the sense of them.'

'Poor little things!' said Margaret, laughing. 'It is only my foible for making a thing look nice. And, Ethel,' she added, drawing her down close over her, 'I did not think the trouble wasted, if seeing me look fresher cheered up dear papa a moment.'

'I spoke to papa about nurse's proposal,' said Margaret, presently, to Flora, 'and he quite agrees to it. Indeed, it is impossible that Anne should attend properly to all the children while nurse is so much engaged with me.'

'I think so,' said Flora; 'and it does not answer to bring Aubrey into the school-room. It only makes Mary and Blanche idle, and Miss Winter does not like it.'

'Then the question is, who shall it be? Nurse has no one in view, and only protests against 'one of the girls out of the school here.' '

'That's a great pity,' said Flora. 'Don't you think we could make her take to Jane White, she is so very nice?'

'I thought of her, but it will never answer if we displease nurse. Besides, I remember at the time Anne came, dear mamma thought there was danger of a girl's having too many acquaintances, especially taking the children out walking. We cannot always be sure of sending her out with Anne.'

'Do you remember—' said Ethel, there stopping.

'Well,' said both sisters.

'Don't you recollect, Flora, that girl whose father was in the hospital—that girl at Cocksmoor?'

'I do,' said Flora. 'She was a very nice girl; I wonder whether nurse would approve of her?'

'How old?' said Margaret.

'Fourteen, and tall. Such a clean cottage!'

The girls went on, and Margaret began to like the idea very much, and consider whether the girl could be brought for inspection, before nurse was prejudiced by hearing of her Cocksmoor extraction. At that moment Richard knocked at the door, and entered with Tom, helping him to bring a small short-legged table, such as could stand on the bed at the right height for Margaret's meals or employments.

There were great exclamations of satisfaction and gratitude; 'it was the very thing wanted, only how could he have contrived it?'

'Don't you recognise it?' said he.

'O, I see; it is the old drawing-desk that no one used. And you have put legs to it—how famous! You are the best contriver, Richard!'

'Then see, you can raise it up for reading or writing; here's a corner for your ink to stand flat; and there it is down for your dinner.'

'Charming; you have made it go so easily, when it used to be so stiff. There—give me my work-basket, please, Ethel; I mean to make some more white puffs.'

'What's the matter, now, Ethel?' said Flora; 'you look as if you did not approve of the table.'

'I was only thinking it was as if she was settling herself to lie in bed for a very long time,' said Ethel.

'I hope not,' said Richard; 'but I don't see why she should not be as comfortable as she can while she is there.'

'I am sure I hope you will never be ill, Ethel,' said Flora. 'You would be horrid to nurse!'

'She will know how to be grateful when she is,' said Margaret.

'I say, Richard,' exclaimed Ethel, 'this is hospital-meeting day, so you wont be wanted to drive papa.'

'No, I am at your service; do you want a walk?'

So it was determined that Richard and Ethel should walk together to Cocksmoor.

No two people could be much more unlike than Richard and Etheldred May; but they were very fond of each other. Richard was sometimes seriously annoyed by Ethel's heedlessness, and did not always understand her sublimities, but he had a great deal of admiration for one who partook so much of his father's nature; and Ethel had a due respect for her eldest brother, gratitude and strong affection for many kindnesses, a reverence for his sterling goodness, and his exemption from her own besetting failings, only a little damped by compassionate wonder at his deficiency in talent, and by her vexation at not being always comprehended.

They went by the road, for the plantation gate was far too serious an undertaking for any one not in the highest spirits for enterprise. On the way there was a good deal of that desultory talk, very sociable and interesting, that is apt to prevail between two people, who would never have chosen each other for companions, if they were not of the same family, but who are nevertheless very affectionate and companionable. Ethel was anxious to hear what her brother thought of papa's spirits, and whether he talked in their drives.

'Sometimes,' said Richard. 'It is just as it happens. Now and then he goes on just like himself, and then at other times he will not speak for three or four miles.'

'And he sighs!' said Ethel. 'Those sighs are so very sad, and long, and deep! They seem to have whole volumes in them, as if there was such a weight on him.'

'Some people say he is not as much altered as they expected,' said Richard.

'Oh! do they? Well! I can't fancy any one feeling it more. He can't leave off his old self, of course, but—' Ethel stopped short.

'Margaret is a great comfort to him,' said Richard.

'That she is. She thinks of him all day long, and I don't think either of them is ever so happy as in the evening, when he sits with her. They talk about mamma then—'

It was just what Richard could not do, and he made some observation to change the subject, but Ethel returned to it, so far as to beg to know how the arm was going on, for she did not like to say anything about it to papa.

'It will be a long business, I am afraid,' said Richard. 'Indeed, he said the other day, he thought he should never have the free use of the elbow.'

'And do you think it is very painful? I saw the other day

when Aubrey was sitting on his knee and fidgetting, he shrank whenever he even came towards it, and yet it seemed as if he could not bear to put him down.'

'Yes, it is excessively tender, and sometimes gets very bad at night.'

'Ah!' said Ethel, 'there's a line—here—round his eyes, that there never used to be, and when it deepens, I am sure he is in pain, or has been kept awake.'

'You are very odd, Ethel; how do you see things in people's faces, when you miss so much at just the same distance?'

'I look after what I care about,' said Ethel. 'One sees more with one's mind than one's eyes. The best sight is inside.'

'But do you always see the truth?' said Richard, gravely.

'Quite enough. I see what is less common than the ordinary world,' said Ethel.

Richard shook his head, not quite satisfied, but not sure enough that he entered into her meaning to question it.

'I wonder you don't wear spectacles,' was the result of his meditation, and it made her laugh by being so inapposite to her own reflections; but the laugh ended in a melancholy look. 'Dear mamma did not like me to use them,' she said, in a low voice.

Thus they talked till they arrived at Cocksmoor, where poor Mrs. Taylor, inspirited by better reports of her husband and the hopes for her daughter, was like another woman. · Richard was very careful not to raise false expectations, saying it all depended on Miss May and nurse, and what they thought of her strength and steadiness, but these cautions did not seem capable of damping the hopes of the smooth-haired Lucy, who stood smiling and curtseying. The twins were grown and improved, and Ethel supposed they would be brought to church on the next Christening Sunday, but their mother looked helpless and hopeless about getting them so far, and how was she to get gossips? Ethel began to grow very indignant, but she was always shy of finding fault with poor people to their faces when she would not have done so to persons in her own station, and so she was silent, while Richard hoped they would be able to manage, and said it would be better not to wait another month for still worse weather and shorter days.

As they were coming out of the house, a big, rough-looking, uncivilized boy came up before them, and called out, 'I say— ben't you the young Doctor up at Stoneborough?'

'I am Dr. May's son,' said Richard; while Ethel, startled, clung to his arm, in dread of some rudeness.

'Granny's bad,' said the boy; proceeding without further explanation to lead the way to another hovel, though Richard tried to explain that the knowledge of medicine was not in his case hereditary. A poor old woman sat groaning over the fire, and two children crouched, half-clothed, on the bare floor.

Richard's gentle voice and kind manner drew forth some wonderful descriptions—'her head was all of a goggle, her legs all of a fur, she felt as if some one was cutting right through her.'

'Well,' said Richard, kindly, 'I am no doctor myself, but I'll ask my father about you, and perhaps he can give you an order for the hospital.'

'No, no, thank ye, sir; I can't go to the hospital, I can't leave these poor children; they've no father nor mother, sir, and no one to do for them but me.'

'What do you all live on, then?' said Richard, looking round the desolate hut.

'On Sam's wages, sir; that's that boy. He is a good boy to me, sir, and his little sisters; he brings it, all he gets, home to me, reg'lar, but 'tis but six shillings a week, and they makes 'em take half of it out in goods and beer, which is a bad thing for a boy like him, sir.'

'How old are you, Sam?'

Sam scratched his head, and answered nothing. His grandmother knew he was the age of her black bonnet, and as he looked about fifteen, Ethel honoured him and the bonnet accordingly, while Richard said he must be very glad to be able to maintain them all, at his age, and, promising to try to bring his father that way, since prescribing at second hand for such curious symptoms was more than could be expected, he took his leave.

'A wretched place,' said Richard, looking round. 'I don't know what help there is for the people. There's no one to do anything for them, and it is of no use to tell them to come to church when it is so far off, and there is so little room for them.'

'It is miserable,' said Ethel; and all her thoughts during her last walk thither began to rush over her again, not effaced, but rather burnt in, by all that had subsequently happened. She had said it should be her aim and effort to make Cocksmoor a christian place. Such a resolve must not pass away lightly; she knew it must be acted on, but how? What would her present means —one sovereign—effect? Her fancies, rich and rare, had nearly been forgotten of late, but she might make them of use in time— in time, and here were hives of children growing up in heathenism. Suddenly an idea struck her—Richard, when at home, was a very diligent teacher in the Sunday-school at Stoneborough, though it was a thankless task, and he was the only gentleman so engaged, except the two clergymen—the other male teachers being a formal, grave, little baker, and one or two monitors

'Richard,' said Ethel, 'I'll tell you what. Suppose we were to set up a Sunday-school at Cocksmoor. We could get a room, and walk there every Sunday afternoon, and go to church in the evening instead.'

He was so confounded by the suddenness of the project, that he did not answer, till she had time for several exclamations and 'Well, Richards!'

'I cannot tell,' he said. 'Going to church in the evening would interfere with tea-time—put out all the house—make the evening uncomfortable.'

'The evenings are horrid now, especially Sundays,' said Ethel.

'But missing two more would make them worse for the others.'

'Papa is always with Margaret,' said Ethel. 'We are of no use to him. Besides, those poor children—are not they of more importance?'

'And, then, what is to become of Stoneborough school?'

'I hate it,' exclaimed Ethel; then seeing Richard shocked, and finding she had spoken more vehemently than she intended —'It is not as bad for you among the boys, but while that committee goes on, it is not the least use to try to teach the girls right. Oh! the fusses about the books, and one's way of teaching! And fancy how Mrs. Ledwich used us. You know I went again last Sunday, for the first time, and there I found that class of Margaret's, that she had just managed to get into some degree of nice order, taken so much pains with, taught so well. She had been telling me what to hear them—there it is given away to Fanny Anderson, who is no more fit to teach than that stick, and all Margaret's work will be undone. No notice to us—not even the civility to wait and see when she gets better.'

'If we left them now for Cocksmoor, would it not look as if we were affronted?'

Ethel was slightly taken aback, but only said, 'Papa would be very angry if he knew it.'

'I am glad you did not tell him,' said Richard.

'I thought it would only tease him,' said Ethel, 'and that he might call it a petty female squabble; and when Margaret is well, it will come right, if Fanny Anderson has not spoilt the girls in the meantime. It is all Mrs. Ledwich's doing. How I did hate it when every one came up and shook hands with me, and asked after Margaret and papa, only just out of curiosity!'

'Hush, hush, Ethel, what's the use of thinking such things?'

A silence,—then she exclaimed, 'But, indeed, Richard, you don't fancy that I want to teach at Cocksmoor, because it is disagreeable at Stoneborough?'

'No, indeed.'

The rendering of full justice conveyed in his tone, so opened Ethel's heart, that she went on eagerly:—'The history of it is this. Last time we walked here, *that* day, I said, and I meant it, that I would never put it out of my head; I would go on doing and striving, and trying, till this place was properly cared for, and has a church and a clergyman. I believe it was a vow, Richard, I do believe it was,—and if one makes one, one must keep it. There it is. So, I can't give money, I have but one pound in the world, but I have time, and I would make that useful, if you would help me.'

'I don't see how,' was the answer, and there was a fragment of a smile on Richard's face, as if it struck him as a wild scheme, that Ethel should undertake, single handed, to evangelize Cocksmoor.

It was such a damper as to be most mortifying to an enthusiastic girl, and she drew into herself in a moment.

They walked home in silence, and when Richard warned her that she was not keeping her dress out of the dirt, it sounded like a sarcasm on her projects, and, with a slightly pettish manner, she raised the unfortunate skirt, its crape trimmings greatly bespattered with ruddy mud. Then recollecting how mamma would have shaken her head at that very thing, she regretted the temper she had betrayed, and in a '*larmoyante*' voice, sighed, 'I wish I could pick my way better. Some people have the gift; you have hardly a splash, and I am up to the ancles in mud.'

'It is only taking care,' said Richard; 'besides, your frock is so long and full. Can't you tuck it up, and pin it?'

'My pins always come out,' said Ethel, disconsolately, crumpling the black folds into one hand, while she hunted for a pin with the other.

'No wonder, if you stick them in that way,' said Richard. 'Oh! you'll tear that crape. Here, let me help you. Don't you see, make it go in and out that way; give it something to pull against.'

Ethel laughed. 'That's the third thing you have taught me —to thread a needle, tie a bow, and stick in a pin. I never could learn those things of anyone else; they show, but don't explain the theory.'

They met Dr. May at the entrance of the town, very tired, and saying he had been a long tramp, all over the place, and Mrs. Hoxton had been boring him with her fancies. As he took Richard's arm he gave the long heavy sigh that always fell so painfully on Ethel's ear.

'Dear, dear, dear papa!' thought she, 'my work must also be to do all I can to comfort him.'

Her reflections were broken off. Dr. May exclaimed, 'Ethel, don't make such a figure of yourself. Those muddy ancles and petticoats are not fit to be seen—there, now you are sweeping the pavement. Have you no medium? One would think you had never worn a gown in your life before!'

Poor Ethel stept on before with mud-encrusted heels, and her father speaking sharply in the weariness and soreness of his heart; her draggle-tailed petticoats weighing down at once her missionary projects at Cocksmoor, and her tender visions of comforting her widowed father; her heart was full to over-flowing, and where was the mother to hear her troubles?

She opened the hall-door, and would have rushed up-stairs, but nurse happened to be crossing the hall. 'Miss Ethel, Miss Ethel, you arn't going up with them boots on! I do declare you are just like one of the boys. And your frock!'

Ethel sat submissively down on the lowest step, and pulled off her boots. As she did so, her father and brother came in—the former desiring Richard to come with him to the study, and write a note for him. She hoped that thus she might have Margaret to herself, and hurried into her room. Margaret was alone, maids and children at tea, and Flora dressing. The room was in twilight, with the red gleam of the fire playing cheer-fully over it.

'Well, Ethel, have you had a pleasant walk?'

'Yes—no. Oh, Margaret!' and throwing herself across the bottom of the bed, she burst into tears.

'Ethel, dear, what is the matter? Papa——'

'No—no; only I draggled my frock, and Richard threw cold water. And I am good for nothing! Oh! if mamma was but here!'

'Darling Ethel, dear Ethel, I wish I could comfort you. Come a little nearer to me, I can't reach you! Dear Ethel, what has gone wrong?'

'Everything!' said Ethel. 'No—I am too dirty to come on your white bed; I forgot, you wont like it,' added she, in an injured tone.

'You are wet—you are cold—you are tired,' said Margaret. 'Stay here and dress, don't go up in the cold. There, sit by the fire, pull off your frock and stockings, and we will send for the others. Let me see you look comfortable—there. Now tell me who threw cold water.'

'It was figurative cold water,' said Ethel, smiling for a moment. 'I was only silly enough to tell Richard my plan, and it's horrid to talk to a person who only thinks one high-flying and nonsensical—and then came the dirt.'

'But what was the scheme, Ethel?'

'Cocksmoor,' said Ethel, proceeding to unfold it.

'I wish we could,' said Margaret. 'It would be an excellent thing. But how did Richard vex you?'

'I don't know,' said Ethel, 'only he thought it would not do. Perhaps he said right; but it was coldly, and he smiled.'

'He is too sober-minded for our flights,' said Margaret. 'I know the feeling of it, Ethel, dear; but you know if he did see that some of your plans might not answer, it is no reason you should not try to do something at once. You have not told me about the girl.'

Ethel proceeded to tell the history. 'There!' said Margaret, cheerfully, 'there are two ways of helping Cocksmoor already. Could you not make some clothes for the two grand-children? I could help you a little; and then, if they were well-clothed, you might get them to come to the Sunday-school. And as to the twins, I wonder what the hire of a cart would be to bring the christening party? It is just what Richard could manage.'

'Yes,' said Ethel; 'but those are only little isolated individual things.'

'But one must make a beginning.'

'Then, Margaret, you think it was a real vow? You don't think it silly of me?' said Ethel, wistfully.

'Ethel, dear, I don't think dear mamma would say we ought to make vows, except what the Church decrees for us. I don't think she would like the notion of your considering yourself pledged; but I do think that, after all you have said and felt about Cocksmoor, and being led there on that day, it does seem as if we might be intended to make it our especial charge.'

'O Margaret, I am glad you say so. You always understand.'

'But you know we are so young, that now we have not her to judge for us, we must only do little things that we are quite sure of, or we shall get wrong.'

'That's not the way great things were done.'

'I don't know, Ethel; I think great things can't be good unless they stand on a sure foundation of little ones.'

'Well, I believe Richard was right, and it would not do to begin on Sunday, but he was so tame; and then my frock, and the horrid deficiency in those little neatnesses.'

'Perhaps that is good for you in one way; you might get very high-flying if you had not the discipline of those little tiresome things; correcting them will help you, and keep your high things from being all romance. I know dear mamma used to say so; that the trying to conquer them was a help to you. O, here's Mary! Mary, will you get Ethel's dressing things? She has come home wet-footed and cold, and has been warming herself by my fire.'

Mary was happy to help, and Ethel was dressed and cheered by the time Dr. May came in, for a hurried visit and report of his doings; Flora followed on her way from her room. Then all went to tea, leaving Margaret to have a visit from the little ones under charge of nurse. Afterwards her father came for two hours' stay with her, that precious time when she knew that sad as the talk often was, it was truly a comfort to him. It ended when ten o'clock struck, and he went down—Margaret hearing the bell, the sounds of the assembling servants, the shutting of the door, the stillness of prayer-time, the opening again, the feet moving off in different directions, then brothers and sisters coming in to kiss her and bid her good-night, nurse and Flora arranging her for the night, Flora coming to sleep in her little bed in the corner of the room, and, lastly, her father's tender good-night, and melancholy look at her, and all was quiet, except the low voices and movements as Richard attended him in his own room.

Margaret could think: 'Dear, dear Ethel, how noble and high she is! But I am afraid! It is what people call a difficult, dangerous age, and the grander she is, the greater danger of not managing her rightly. If those high purposes should run only into romance like mine, or grow out into eccentricities and un-feminineness, what a grievous pity it would be! And I, so little older, so much less clever, with just sympathy enough not to be a wise restraint—I am the person who has the responsibility, and oh, what shall I do? Mamma trusted to me to be a mother to them; papa looks to me, and I so unfit, besides this help-lessness. But God sent it, and put me in my place. He made me lie here, and will raise me up if it is good; so I trust He will help me with my sisters.

'Grant me to have a right judgment in all things, and ever-more to rejoice in Thy holy comfort.'

CHAPTER VII.

'Something between a hindrance and a help.'—WORDSWORTH.

ETHELDRED awoke long before time for getting up, and lay pon-dering over her visions. Margaret had sympathized, and therefore they did not seem entirely aërial. To earn money by writing was her favourite plan, and she called her various romances in turn before her memory, to judge which might be brought down to sober pen and ink. She considered till it became not too unreasonably early to get up. It was dark, but there was a little light close to the window; she had no writing-paper, but she would interline her old exercise-book. Down she ran, and crouching in the school-room window-seat, she wrote on in a trance of eager composition, till Norman called her, as he went to school, to help him to find a book.

This done, she went up to visit Margaret, to tell her the story, and consult her. But this was not so easy. She found Margaret with little Daisy lying by her, and Tom sitting by the fire over his Latin.

'O, Ethel, good morning, dear! you are come just in time.'

'To take baby?' said Ethel, as the child was fretting a little.

'Yes, thank you; she has been very good, but she was tired of lying here, and I can't move her about,' said Margaret.

'O, Margaret, I have such a plan,' said Ethel, as she walked about with little Gertrude; but Tom interrupted.

'Margaret, will you see if I can say my lesson?' and the thumbed Latin grammar came across her just as Dr. May's door opened, and he came in, exclaiming, 'Latin grammar! Margaret, this is really too much for you. Good morning, my dears. Ha! Tommy, take your book away, my boy. You must not inflict that on sister now. There's your regular master, Richard, in my room, if it is fit for his ears yet. What, the little one here, too?'

'How is your arm, papa?' said Margaret. 'Did it keep you awake?'

'Not long—it set me dreaming, though; and a very romantic dream it was—worthy of Ethel herself.'

'What was it, papa?'

'O, it was an odd thing, joining on strangely enough with one I had three or four-and-twenty years ago, when I was a young man, hearing lectures at Edinburgh, and courting'—he stopped, and felt Margaret's pulse, asked her a few questions, and talked to the baby. Ethel longed to hear his dream, but thought he would not like to go on; however, he did presently.

'The old dream was the night after a pic-nic on Arthur's Seat with the Mackenzies; Mamma and Aunt Flora were there. 'Twas a regular boy's dream, a tournament, or something of that nature, where I was victor, the queen—you know who she was —giving me her token—a Daisy Chain.'

'That is why you like to call us your Daisy Chain,' said Ethel.

'Did you write it in verse?' said Margaret. 'I think I once saw some verses like it in her desk.'

'I was in love, and three-and-twenty,' said the Doctor, looking drolly guilty in the midst of his sadness. 'Aye, those fixed it in my memory, perhaps my fancy made it more distinct than it really was. An evening or two ago, I met with them, and that stirred it up, I suppose. Last night came the tournament again, but it was the mêlée, a sense of being crushed down, suffocated by the throng of armed knights and horses—pain and wounds—and I looked in vain through the opposing overwhelming host for my — my Maggie. Well, I got the worst of it, my sword arm was broken —I fell, was stifled—crushed—in misery—all I could do was to grasp my token—my Daisy Chain,' and he pressed Margaret's hand as he said so. 'And, behold, the tumult and despair were passed. I lay on the grass in the cloisters, and the Daisy Chain hung from the sky, and was drawing me upwards. There—it is a queer dream for a sober old country Doctor. I don't know why I told you, don't tell any one again.'

And he walked away, muttering, 'For he told me his dreams, talked of eating and drinking,' leaving Margaret with her eyes full of tears, and Ethel vehemently caressing the baby.

'How beautiful,' said Ethel.

'It has been a comfort to him, I am sure,' said Margaret.

'You don't think it ominous,' said Ethel, with a slight tremulous voice.

'More soothing than anything else. It is what we all feel, is it not? that this little daisy bud is the link between us and heaven?'

'But about him. He was victor at first—vanquished the next time.'

'I think—if it is to have an interpretation, though I am not sure we ought to take it so seriously, it would only mean that in younger days, people care for victory and distinction in this world, like Norman, or as papa most likely did then; but, as they grow older, they care less, and others pass them, and they know it does not signify, for in our race all may win.'

'But he has a great name. How many people come from a distance to consult him! he is looked upon, too, in other ways! he can do anything with the corporation.'

Margaret smiled. 'All this does not sound grand—it is not as if he had set up in London.'

'Oh dear, I am so glad he did not.'

'Shall I tell you what mamma told me he said about it, when uncle Mackenzie said he ought? He answered, that he thought

health and happy home attachments were a better provision for
us to set out in life with than thousands.'

'I am sure he was right,' said Ethel, earnestly. 'Then you
don't think the dream meant being beaten, only that our best
things are not gained by successes in this world?'

'Don't go and let it dwell on your mind as a vision,' said
Margaret. 'I think dear mamma would call that silly.'

An interruption occurred, and Ethel had to go down to breakfast with a mind floating between romance, sorrow, and high
aspirations, very unlike the actual world she had to live in. First,
there was a sick man walking into the study, and her father,
laying down his letters, saying, 'I must despatch him before
prayers, I suppose. I've a great mind to say I never will see
any one who wont keep to my days.'

'I can't imagine why they don't,' said Flora, as he went.
'He is always saying so, but never acting on it. If he would
once turn one away, the rest would mind.'

Richard went on in silence, cutting bread and butter.

'There's another ring,' said Mary.

'Yes, he is caught now, they'll go on in a stream. I shall not
keep Margaret waiting for her breakfast, I shall take it up.'

The morning was tiresome; though Dr. May had two regular
days for seeing poor people at his house, he was too good-natured
to keep strictly to them, and this day, as Flora had predicted, there
was a procession of them not soon got rid of, even by his rapid
queries and the talismanic figures made by his left hand on scraps
of paper, with which he sent them off to the infirmary. Ethel
tried to read; the children lingered about; it was a trial of temper
to all but Tom, who obtained Richard's attention to his lessons.
He liked to say them to his brother, and this was an incentive to
learn them quickly, that none might remain for Miss Winter when
Richard went out with his father. If mamma had been there, she
would have had prayers; but now no one had authority enough,
though they did at last even finish breakfast. Just as the gig came
to the door, Dr. May dismissed his last patient, rang the bell in
haste, and as soon as prayers were over, declared he had an appointment, and had no time to eat. There was a general outcry,
that it was bad enough when he was well, and now he must not
take liberties; Flora made him drink some tea; and Richard
placed morsels in his way, while he read his letters. He ran up for
a final look at Margaret, almost upset the staid Miss Winter as
he ran down again, called Richard to take the reins, and was off.

It was French day, always a trial to Ethel. M. Ballompré,
the master, knew what was good and bad French, but could not

render a reason, and Ethel, being versed in the principles of grammar, from her Latin studies, chose to know the why and wherefore of his corrections—she did not like to see her pages defaced, and have no security against future errors; while he thought her a troublesome pupil, and was put out by her questions. They wrangled, Miss Winter was displeased, and Ethel felt injured.

Mary's inability to catch the pronunciation, and her hopeless dull look when she found that *cœur* must not be pronounced *cour*, nor *cur*, but something between, to which her rosy English lips could never come—all this did not tease M. Ballompré, for he was used to it.

His mark for Ethel's lesson was '*de l'humeur.*'

'I am sorry,' said Miss Winter, when he was gone. 'I thought you had outgrown that habit of disputing over every phrase.'

'I can't tell how a language is to be learnt without knowing the reasons of one's mistakes,' said Ethel.

'That is what you always say, my dear. It is of no use to renew it all, but I wish you would control yourself. Now, Mary, call Blanche, and you and Ethel take your arithmetic.'

So Flora went to read to Margaret, while Blanche went lightly and playfully through her easy lessons, and Mary floundered piteously over the difficulties of Compound Long Division. Ethel's mind was in too irritated and tumultuous a state for her to derive her usual solace from Cube Root. Her sum was wrong, and she wanted to work it right; but Miss Winter, who had little liking for the higher branches of arithmetic, said she had spent time enough over it, and summoned her to an examination such as the governess was very fond of and often practised. Ethel thought it useless, and was teased by it; and though her answers were chiefly correct, they were given in an irritated tone. It was of this kind:—

> What is the date of the invention of paper?
> What is the latitude and longitude of Otaheite?
> What are the component parts of brass?
> Whence is cochineal imported?

When this was over, Ethel had to fetch her mending-basket, and Mary her book of selections; the piece for to-day's lesson was the quarrel of Brutus and Cassius; and Mary's dull droning tone was a trial to her ears; she presently exclaimed, 'O Mary, don't murder it!'

'Murder what?' said Mary, opening wide her light blue eyes.

'That use of exaggerated language——' began Miss Winter.

'I've heard papa say it,' said Ethel, only wanting to silence

Miss Winter. In a cooler moment she would not have used the argument.

'All that a gentleman may say, may not be a precedent for a young lady; but you are interrupting Mary.'

'Only let me show her. I can't bear to hear her; listen, Mary.

' " What shall one of us
That struck the foremost " '—

'That is declaiming,' said Miss Winter. 'It is not what we wish for in a lady. You are neglecting your work and interfering.'

Ethel made a fretful contortion, and obeyed. So it went on all the morning; Ethel's eagerness checked by Miss Winter's dry manner, producing pettishness, till Ethel, in a state between self-reproach and a sense of injustice, went up to prepare for dinner, and to visit Margaret on the way.

She found her sister picking a merino frock to pieces. 'See here,' she said, eagerly, 'I thought you would like to make up this old frock for one of the Cocksmoor children; but what is the matter?' as Ethel did not show the lively interest that she expected.

'O, nothing; only Miss Winter is so tiresome.'

'What was it?'

'Everything—it was all horrid. I was cross, I know; but sho and M. Ballompré made me so;' and Ethel was in the midst of the narration of her grievances, when Norman came in. The school was half-a-mile off, but he had not once failed to come home, in the interval allowed for play after dinner, to inquire for his sister.

'Well, Norman, you are out of breath, sit down and rest. What is doing at school?—are you *dux* of your class?'

'Yes,' said the boy, wearily.

'What mark for the verses?' said Ethel.

'*Quam benè.*'

'Not *optime!*'

'No, they were *tame*,' Dr. Hoxton said.

'What is Harry doing?' said Margaret.

'He is fourth in his form. I left him at football.'

'Dinner!' said Flora, at the door. 'What will you have, Margaret?'

'I'll fetch it,' said Norman, who considered it his privilege to wait on Margaret at dinner. When he had brought the tray, he stood leaning against the bed-post, musing. Suddenly, there was a considerable clatter of fire-irons, and his violent start surprised Margaret.

PART I.   F

'Ethel has been poking the fire,' she said, as if no more was
needed to account for their insecurity. Norman put them up
again, but a ringing sound betrayed that it was not with a firm
touch; and when, a minute after, he came to take her plate, she
saw that he was trying with effort to steady his hand.

'Norman, dear, are you sure you are well?'

'Yes, very well,' said he, as if vexed that she had taken any
notice.

'You had better not come racing home. I'm not worth inquiries now, I am so much better,' said she, smiling.

He made no reply, but this was not consenting silence.

'I don't like you to lose your football,' she proceeded.

'I could not—' and he stopped short.

'It would be much better for you,' said she, looking up in his
face with anxious affectionate eyes; but he shunned her glance,
and walked away with her plate.

Flora had been in such close attendance upon Margaret, that
she needed some cheerful walks; and though she had some doubts
how affairs at home would go on without her, she was overruled,
and sent on a long expedition with Miss Winter and Mary, while
Ethel remained with Margaret.

The only delay before setting out was, that nurse came in,
saying—'If you please, Miss Margaret, there is a girl come to
see about the place.'

The sisters looked at each other and smiled; while Margaret
asked whence she came, and who she was.

'Her name is Taylor, and she comes from Cocksmoor; but
she is a nice, tidy, strong-looking girl, and she says she has been
used to children.'

Nurse had fallen into the trap most comfortably, and seemed
bent upon taking this girl as a choice of her own. She wished
to know if Miss Margaret would like to see her.

'If you please, nurse; but if you think she will do, that is
enough.'

'Yes, Miss; but you should look to them things yourself. If
you please, I'll bring her up.' So nurse departed.

'Charming!' cried Ethel; 'that's your capital management,
Flora. Nurse thinks she has done it all herself.'

'She is your charge, though,' said Flora, 'coming from your
own beloved Cocksmoor.'

Lucy Taylor came in, looking very nice, and very shy, curtseying low, in extreme awe of the pale lady in bed. Margaret was
much pleased with her, and there was no more to be done but to
settle that she should come on Saturday, and to let nurse take her

into the town to invest her with the universal blackness of the household, where the two Margarets were the only white things.

This arranged, and the walking party set forth, Ethel sat down by her sister's bed, and began to assist in unpicking the merino, telling Margaret how much obliged she was to her for thinking of it, and how grieved at having been so ungrateful in the morning. She was very happy over her contrivances, cutting out under her sister's superintendence. She had forgotten the morning's annoyance, till Margaret said—'I have been thinking of what you said about Miss Winter, and really I don't know what is to be done.'

'O Margaret, I did not mean to worry you,' said Ethel, sorry to see her look uneasy.

'I like you to tell me everything,' dear Ethel; 'but I don't see clearly the best course. We must go on with Miss Winter.'

'Of course,' said Ethel, shocked at her murmurs having even suggested the possibility of a change, and having, as well as all the others, a great respect and affection for her governess.

'We could not get on without her, even if I were well,' continued Margaret; 'and dear mamma had such perfect trust in her, and we all know and love her so well—it would make us put up with a great deal.'

'It is all my own fault,' said Ethel, only anxious to make amends to Miss Winter. 'I wish you would not say anything about it.'

'Yes, it does seem wrong even to think of it,' said Margaret, 'when she has been so very kind. It is a blessing to have any one to whom Mary and Blanche may so entirely be trusted. But for you—'

'It is my own fault,' repeated Ethel.

'I don't think it is quite all your own fault,' said Margaret, 'and that is the difficulty. I know dear mamma thought Miss Winter an excellent governess for the little ones, but hardly up to you; and she saw that you worried and fidgetted each other, so, you know, she used to keep the teaching of you a good deal in her own hands.'

'I did not know that was the reason,' said Ethel, overpowered by the recollection of the happy morning's work she had often done in that very room, when her mother had not been equal to the bustle of the whole school-room. That watchful, protecting, guarding, mother's love, a shadow of Providence, had been round them so constantly on every side, that they had been hardly conscious of it till it was lost to them.

'Was it not like her?' said Margaret; 'but now, my poor

Ethel, I don't think it would be right by you or by Miss Winter, to take you out of the school-room. I think it would grieve her.'

' I would not do that for the world.'

' Especially after all her kind nursing of me; and even, with more reason, it would not be becoming in us to make changes. Besides, King Etheldred,' said Margaret, smiling, ' we all know you are a little bit of a sloven, and, as nurse says, some one must be always after you; and do you know?—even if I were well, I had rather it was Miss Winter than me.'

' O no, you would not be formal and precise—you would not make me cross.'

' Perhaps you might make me so,' said Margaret, ' or I should let you alone, and leave you a slattern. We should both hate it so! No, don't make me your mistress, Ethel dear—let me be your sister and play-fellow still, as well as I can.'

' You are, you are. I don't care half so much when I have got you.'

' And will you try to bear with her, and remember it is right in the main, though it is troublesome?'

' That I will. I won't plague you again. I know it is bad for you, you look tired.'

' Pray don't leave off telling me,' said Margaret—'it is just what I wish on my own account, and I know it is comfortable to have a good grumble.'

' If it does not hurt you, but I am sure you are not easy now —are you?'

' Only my back,' said Margaret. 'I have been sitting up longer than usual, and it is tired. Will you call nurse to lay me flat again?'

The nursery was deserted—all were out, and Ethel came back in trepidation at the notion of having to do it herself, though she knew it was only to put one arm to support her sister, while, with the other, she removed the pillows; but Ethel was conscious of her own awkwardness and want of observation, nor had Margaret entire trust in her. Still she was too much fatigued to wait, so Ethel was obliged to do her best. She was careful and frightened, and therefore slow and unsteady. She trusted that all was right, and Margaret tried to believe so, though still uneasy.

Ethel began to read to her, and Dr. May came home. She looked up smiling, and asked where he had been, but it was vain to try to keep him from reading her face. He saw in an instant that something was amiss, and drew from her a confession that her back was aching a little. He knew she might have said a great deal—she was not in a comfortable position—she must be moved. She shook her head—she had rather wait—there was a dread of being again lifted by Ethel, that she could not entirely hide. Ethel was distressed, Dr. May was angry, and, no wonder, when he saw Margaret suffer, felt his own inability to help, missed her who had been wont to take all care from his hands, and was vexed to see a tall strong girl of fifteen, with the full use of both arms, and plenty of sense, incapable of giving any assistance, and only doing harm by trying.

'It is of no use,' said he. 'Ethel will give no attention to anything but her books! I've a great mind to put an end to all the Latin and Greek! She cares for nothing else.'

Ethel could little brook injustice, and much as she was grieving, she exclaimed, 'Papa, papa, I do care—now don't I, Margaret? I did my best.'

'Don't talk nonsense. Your best, indeed! If you had taken the most moderate care—'

'I believe Ethel took rather too much care,' said Margaret, much more harassed by the scolding than by the pain. 'It will be all right presently. Never mind, dear papa.'

But he was not only grieved for the present, but anxious for the future; and, though he knew it was bad for Margaret to manifest his displeasure, he could not restrain it, and continued to blame Ethel with enough of injustice to set her on vindication, whereupon he silenced her, by telling her she was making it worse by self-justification when Margaret ought to be quiet. Margaret tried to talk of other things, but was in too much discomfort to exert herself enough to divert his attention.

At last Flora returned, and saw in an instant what was wanted. Margaret was settled in the right posture, but the pain would not immediately depart, and Dr. May soon found out that she had a head-ache, of which he knew he was at least as guilty as Etheldred could be.

Nothing could be done but keep her quiet, and Ethel went away to be miserable; Flora tried to comfort her by saying it was unfortunate, but no doubt there was a knack, and every one could not manage those things; Margaret was easier now, and as to papa's anger, he did not always mean all he said.

But consolation came at bed-time; Margaret received her with open arms when she went to wish her good-night. 'My poor Ethel,' she said, holding her close, 'I am sorry I have made such a fuss.'

'Oh, you did not, it was too bad of me—I am grieved; are you quite comfortable now?'

'Yes, quite, only a little head-ache, which I shall sleep off. It

has been so nice and quiet. Papa took up George Herbert, and
has been reading me choice bits. I don't think I have enjoyed
anything so much since I have been ill.'

'I am glad of that, but I have been unhappy all the evening.
I wish I knew what to do. I am out of heart about everything!'

'Only try to mind and heed, and you will learn. It will be
a step if you will only put your shoes side by side when you take
them off.'

Ethel smiled and sighed, and Margaret whispered, 'Don't grieve
about me, but put your clever head to rule your hands, and you
will do for home and Cocksmoor too. Good-night, dearest.'

'I've vexed papa,' sighed Ethel—and just then he came into
the room.

'Papa,' said Margaret, 'here's poor Ethel, not half recovered
from her troubles.'

He was now at ease about Margaret, and knew he had been
harsh to another of his motherless girls.

'Ah! we must send her to the infant-school to learn "this is
my right hand, and this is my left,"' said he, in his half-gay,
half-sad manner.

'I was very stupid,' said Ethel.

'Poor child!' said her papa; 'she is worse off than I am.   If
I have but one hand left, she has two left-hands.'

'I do mean to try, papa.'

'Yes, you must, Ethel. I believe I was hasty with you, my
poor girl. I was vexed, and we have no one to smooth us down.
I am sorry, my dear, but you must bear with me, for I never learnt
her ways with you when I might. We will try to have more
patience with each other.'

What could Ethel do but hang round his neck and cry, till he
said, but tenderly, that they had given Margaret quite disturbance
enough to-day, and sent her to bed, vowing to watch each little
action, lest she should again give pain to such a father and sister.

CHAPTER VIII.

' 'Tis not enough that Greek or Roman page
    At stated hours his freakish thoughts engage,
    Even in his pastimes he requires a friend
    To warn and teach him safely to unbend,
    O'er all his pleasures gently to preside,
    Watch his emotions, and control their tide.'—COWPER.

THE misfortunes of that day disheartened and disconcerted Etheldred. To do mischief where she most wished to do good, to grieve

where she longed to comfort, seemed to be her fate; it was vain
to attempt anything for any one's good, while all her warm feelings and high aspirations were thwarted by the awkward ungainly
hands, and heedless eyes that Nature had given her. Nor did the
following day, Saturday, do much for her comfort, by giving her
the company of her brothers. That it was Norman's sixteenth
birth-day seemed only to make it worse. Their father had apparently forgotten it, and Norman stopped Blanche, when she was
going to put him in mind of it; stopped her by such a look as
the child never forgot, though there was no anger in it. In
reply to Ethel's inquiry what he was going to do that morning,
he gave a yawn and stretch, and said, dejectedly, that he had
got some Euripides to look over, and some verses to finish.

'I am sorry; this is the first time you ever have not managed
so as to make a real holiday of your Saturday!'

'I could not help it, and there's nothing to do,' said Norman,
wearily.

'I promised to go and read to Margaret, while Flora does her
music,' said Ethel; 'I shall come after that and do my Latin
and Greek with you.'

Margaret would not keep her long, saying she liked her to be
with Norman, but she found him with his head sunk on his open
book, fast asleep. At dinner-time, Harry and Tom, rushing in,
awoke him with a violent start.

'Halloo! Norman, that was a jump!' said Harry, as his
brother stretched and pinched himself. 'You'll jump out of your
skin some of these days, if you don't take care!'

'It's enough to startle any one to be waked up with such a
noise,' said Ethel.

'Then he ought to sleep at proper times,' said Harry, 'and
not be waking me up with tumbling about, and hallooing out,
and talking in his sleep half the night.'

'Talking in his sleep; why, just now, you said he did not
sleep,' said Ethel.

'Harry knows nothing about it,' said Norman.

'Don't I? well, I only know, if you slept in school, and were
a junior, you would get a proper good licking for going on as you
do at night.'

'And I think you might chance to get a proper good licking
for not holding your tongue,' said Norman, which hint reduced
Harry to silence.

Dr. May was not come home; he had gone with Richard far
into the country, and was to return to tea. He was thought to
be desirous of avoiding the family dinners that used to be so

delightful. Harry was impatient to depart, and when Mary and Tom ran after him, he ordered them back.

'Where can he be going?' said Mary, as she looked wistfully after him.

'I know,' said Tom.

'Where? Do tell me.'

'Only don't tell papa. I went down with him to the playground this morning, and there they settled it. The Andersons, and Axworthy, and he, are going to hire a gun, and shoot peewits on Cocksmoor.'

'But they ought not; should they?' said Mary. 'Papa would be very angry.'

'Anderson said there was no harm in it, but Harry told me not to tell. Indeed, Anderson would have boxed my ears for hearing, when I could not help it.'

'But Harry would not let him?'

'Aye. Harry is quite a match for Harvey Anderson, though he is so much younger; and he said he would not have me bullied.'

'That's a good Harry! But I wish he would not go out shooting!' said Mary.

'Mind, you don't tell.'

'And where's Hector Ernescliffe? Would not he go?'

'No. I like Hector. He did not choose to go, though Anderson teazed him, and said he was a poor Scot, and his brother didn't allow him tin enough to buy powder and shot. If Harry would have stayed at home, he would have come up here, and we might have had some fun in the garden.'

'I wish he would. We never have any fun now,' said Mary; 'but oh! there he is:' as she spied Hector peeping over the gate which led, from the field, into the garden. It was the first time that he had been to Dr. May's since his brother's departure, and he was rather shy, but the joyful welcome of Mary and Tom took off all reluctance, and they claimed him for a good game at play in the wood house. Mary ran up-stairs to beg to be excused the formal walk, and, luckily for her, Miss Winter was in Margaret's room. Margaret asked if it was very wet and dirty and hearing 'not very,' gave gracious permission, and off went Mary and Blanche to construct some curious specimens of pottery, under the superintendence of Hector and Tom. There was a certain ditch where yellow mud was attainable, whereof the happy children concocted marbles and vases, which underwent a preparatory baking in the boys' pockets, that they might not crack in the nursery fire. Margaret only stipulated that her sisters should be well fenced in brown holland, and when Miss Winter looked grave, said, 'Poor things, a little thorough play will do them a great deal of good.'

Miss Winter could not see the good of groping in the dirt; and Margaret perceived that it would be one of her difficulties to know how to follow out her mother's views for the children, without vexing the good governess by not deferring to her.

In the meantime, Norman had disconsolately returned to his Euripides, and Ethel, who wanted to stay with him and look out his words, was ordered out by Miss Winter, because she had spent all yesterday in-doors. Miss Winter was going to stay with Margaret, and Ethel and Flora coaxed Norman to come with them, 'just one mile on the turnpike road and back again; he would be much fresher for his Greek afterwards.'

He came, but he did not enliven his sisters. The three plodded on, taking a diligent constitutional walk, exchanging very few words, and those chiefly between the girls. Flora gathered some hoary clematis, and red berries, and sought in the hedge-sides for some crimson 'fairy baths' to carry home; and, at the sight of the amusement Margaret derived from the placing the beauteous little Pezizas in a saucer of damp green moss, so as to hide the brown sticks on which they grew, Ethel took shame to herself for want of perception of little attentions. When she told Norman so, he answered, 'There's no one who does see what is the right thing. How horrid the room looks! Everything is no how!' added he, looking round at the ornaments and things on the tables, which had lost their air of comfort and good taste. It was not disorder, and Ethel could not see what he meant. 'What's wrong?' said she.

'O never mind—you can't do it. Don't try—you'll only make it worse. It will never be the same as long as we live.'

'I wish you would not be so unhappy!' said Ethel.

'Never mind,' again said Norman, but he put his arm round her.

'Have you done your Euripides? Can I help you? Will you construe it with me, or shall I look out your words?'

'Thank you, I don't mind that. It is the verses! I want some sense!' said Norman, running his fingers through his hair till it stood on end. ''Tis such a horrid subject, Coral Islands! As if there was anything to be said about them.'

'Dear me, Norman, I could say ten thousand things, only I must not tell you what mine are, as yours are not done.'

'No, don't,' said Norman, decidedly.

'Did you read the description of them in the Quarterly? I am sure you might get some ideas there. Shall I find it for you? It is an old number.'

'Well, do; thank you—'

He rested listlessly on the sofa while his sister rummaged in a chiffonnière. At last she found the article, and eagerly read him the description of the strange forms of the coral animals, and the beauties of their flower-like feelers and branching fabrics. It would once have delighted him, but his first comment was, 'Nasty little brutes!' However, the next minute he thanked her, took the book, and said he could hammer something out of it, though it was too bad to give such an unclassical subject. At dusk he left off, saying he should get it done at night, his senses would come then, and he should be glad to sit up.

'Only three weeks to the holidays,' said Ethel, trying to be cheerful; but his assent was depressing, and she began to fear that Christmas would only make them more sad.

Mary did not keep Tom's secret so inviolably, but that, while they were dressing for tea, she revealed to Ethel where Harry was gone. He was not yet returned, though his father and Richard were come in, and the sisters were at once in some anxiety on his account, and doubt whether they ought to let papa know of his disobedience.

Flora and Ethel, who were the first in the drawing-room, had a consultation.

'I should have told mamma directly,' said Flora.

'He never did so,' sighed Ethel; 'things never went wrong then.'

'O yes, they did; don't you remember how naughty Harry was about climbing the wall, and making faces at Mrs. Richardson's servants?'

'And how ill I behaved the first day of last Christmas holidays?'

'She knew, but I don't think she told papa.'

'Not that we knew of, but I believe she did tell him everything; and I think, Flora, he ought to know everything, especially now. I never could bear the way the Mackenzies used to have of thinking their parents must be like enemies, and keeping secrets from them.'

'They were always threatening each other, "I'll tell mamma,"' said Flora, 'and calling us tell-tales, because we told our own dear mamma everything. But it is not like that now—I neither like to worry papa, nor to bring Harry into disgrace—besides, Tom and Mary meant it for a secret.'

'Papa would not be angry with him if we told him it was a secret,' said Ethel; 'I wish Harry would come in. There's the door—oh! it is only you.'

'Whom did you expect?' said Richard, entering.

The sisters looked at each other, and Ethel, after an interval, explained their doubts about Harry.

'He is come in,' said Richard; 'I saw him running up to his own room, very muddy.'

'O, I'm glad! But do you think papa ought to hear it? I don't know what's to be done. 'Tis the children's secret,' said Flora.

'It will never do to have him going out with those boys continually,' said Ethel—'Harvey Anderson close by all the holidays!'

'I'll try what I can do with him,' said Richard. 'Papa had better not hear it now, at any rate. He is very tired and sad this evening, and his arm is painful again; so we must not worry him with histories of naughtiness among the children.'

'No,' said Ethel, decidedly; 'I am glad you were there, Ritchie. I never should have thought of one time being better than another.'

'Just like Ethel,' said Flora, smiling.

'Why should not you learn?' said Richard, gently.

'I can't,' said Ethel, in a desponding way.

'Why not? You are much sharper than most people; and, if you tried, you would know those things as much better than I do, as you know how to learn history.'

'It is quite a different sort of cleverness,' said Flora. 'Recollect Sir Isaac Newton, or Archimedes.'

'Then you must have both sorts,' said Ethel; 'for you can do things nicely, and yet you learn very fast.'

'Take care, Ethel, you are singeing your frock! Well, I really don't think you can help those things!' said Flora. 'Your short sight is the reason of it, and it is of no use to try to mend it.'

'Don't tell her so,' said Richard. 'It can't be all short sight —it is the not thinking. I do believe that if Ethel would think, no one would do things so well. Don't you remember the beautiful perspective drawing she made of this room, for me to take to Oxford? That was very difficult, and wanted a great deal of neatness and accuracy, so why should she not be neat and accurate in other things? And I know you can read faces Ethel— why don't you look there before you speak?'

'Ah! before instead of after, when I only see I have said something *mal-à-propos*,' said Ethel.

'I must go and see about the children,' said Flora; 'if the tea comes while I am gone, will you make it Ritchie?'

'Flora despairs of me,' said Ethel.

'I don't,' said Richard. 'Have you forgotten how to put in a pin yet?'

'No, I hope not.'

'Well, then, see if you can't learn to make tea; and, by-the-by, Ethel, which is the next Christening Sunday?'

'The one after next, surely. The first of December is Monday —yes, to-morrow week is the next.'

'Then I have thought of something; it would cost eighteen-pence to hire Joliffe's spring-cart, and we might have Mrs. Taylor and the twins brought to church in it. Should you like to walk to Cocksmoor and settle it?'

'O yes, very much indeed. What a capital thought. Margaret said you would know how to manage.'

'Then we will go the first fine day papa does not want me.'

'I wonder if I could finish my purple frocks. But here's the tea. Now, Richard, don't tell me to make it. I shall do something wrong, and Flora will never forgive you.'

Richard would not let her off. He stood over her, counted her shovelsfull of tea, and watched the water into the tea-pot— he superintended her warming the cups, and putting a drop into each saucer. 'Ah!' said Ethel, with a concluding sigh, 'it makes one hotter than double equations!'

It was all right, as Flora allowed, with a slightly superior smile. She thought Richard would never succeed in making a notable or elegant woman of Ethel, and it was best that the two sisters should take different lines. Flora knew that, though clever and with more accomplishments, she could not surpass Ethel in intellectual attainments, but she was certainly far more valuable in the house, and had been proved to have just the qualities in which her sister was most deficient. She did not relish hearing that Ethel wanted nothing but attention to be more than her equal, and she thought Richard mistaken. Flora's remembrance of their time of distress was less unmixedly wretched than it was with the others, for she knew she had done wonders.

The next day Norman told Ethel that he had got on very well with the verses, and finished them off late at night. He showed them to her before taking them to school on Monday morning, and Ethel thought they were the best he had ever written. There was too much spirit and poetical beauty, for a mere school-boy task, and she begged for the foul copy, to show it to her father. 'I have not got it,' said Norman. 'The foul copy was not like these; but when I was writing them out quite late, it was all, I don't know how. Flora's music was in my ears, and the room seemed to get larger, and like an ocean cave; and when the candle flickered, 'twas like the green glowing light of the sun through the waves.'

'As it says here,' said Ethel.

'And the words all came to me of themselves in beautiful flowing Latin, just right, as if it was anybody but myself doing it, and they ran off my pen in red and blue and gold, and all sorts of colours; and fine branching zig-zagging stars, like what the book described, only stranger, came dancing and radiating round my pen and the candle. I could hardly believe the verses would scan by daylight, but I can't find a mistake. Do you try them again.'

Ethel scanned. 'I see nothing wrong,' she said, 'but it seems a shame to begin scanning Undine's verses, they are too pretty. I wish I could copy them. It must have been half a dream.'

'I believe it was; they don't seem like my own.'

'Did you dream afterwards?'

He shivered. 'They had got into my head too much; my ears sang like the roaring of the sea, and I thought my feet were frozen on to an iceberg: then came darkness, and sea monsters, and drowning—it was too horrid!' and his face expressed all, and more than all, he said. 'But 'tis a quarter to seven—we must go,' said he, with a long yawn, and rubbing his eyes. 'You are sure they are right, Ethel? Harry, come along.'

Ethel thought those verses ought to make a sensation, but all that came of them was a *Quam optimè*, and when she asked Norman if no special notice had been taken of them, he said, in his languid way, 'No; only Dr. Hoxton said they were better than usual.'

Ethel did not even have the satisfaction of hearing that Mr. Wilmot, happening to meet Dr. May, said to him, 'Your boy has more of a poet in him than any that has come in my way. He really sometimes makes very striking verses.'

Richard watched for an opportunity of speaking to Harry, which did not at once occur, as the boy spent very little of his time at home, and, as if by tacit consent, he and Norman came in later every evening. At last, on Thursday, in the additional two hours' leisure allowed to the boys, when the studious prepared their tasks, and the idle had some special diversion, Richard encountered him running up to his own room to fetch a newly-invented instrument for projecting stones.

'I'll walk back to school with you,' said Richard.

'I mean to run,' returned Harry.

'Is there so much hurry?' said Richard. 'I am sorry for it, for I wanted to speak to you, Harry; I have something to show you.'

His manner conveyed that it related to their mother, and the sobering effect was instantaneous. 'Very well,' said he, forgetting his haste. 'I'll come into your room.'

The awe-struck, shy, yet sorrowful look on his rosy face, showed preparation enough, and Richard's only preface was to say, 'It is a bit of a letter that *she* was in course of writing to aunt Flora, a description of us all. The letter itself is gone, but here is a copy of it. I thought you would like to read what relates to yourself.'

Richard laid before him the sheet of note-paper on which this portion of the letter was written, and left him alone with it, while he set out on the promised walk with Ethel.

They found the old woman, Granny Hall, looking like another creature, smoke-dried, and withered indeed, but all briskness and animation.

'Well! be it you, sir, and the young lady?'

'Yes; here we are come to see you again,' said Richard. I hope you are not disappointed that I've brought my sister this time instead of the Doctor.'

'No, no, sir; I've done with the Doctor for this while,' said the old woman, to Ethel's great amusement. 'He have done me a power of good, and thank him for it heartily; but the young lady is right welcome here—but 'tis a dirty walk for her.'

'Never mind that,' said Ethel, a little shyly; 'I came—where are your grandchildren?'

'O, somewhere out among the blocks. They gets out with the other children; I can't be always after them.'

'I wanted to know if these would fit them,' said Ethel, beginning to undo her basket.

'Well, 'pon my word! If ever I see! Here!' stepping out to the door, 'Polly—Jenny! come in, I say, this moment! Come in, ye bad girls, or I'll give you the stick; I'll break every bone of you, that I will!' all which threats were bawled out in such a good-natured, triumphant voice, and with such a delighted air, that Richard and Ethel could not help laughing.

After a few moments, Polly and Jenny made their appearance, extremely rough and ragged, but compelled by their grandmother to duck down, by way of courtesies, and, with finger in mouth, they stood, too shy to show their delight, as the garments were unfolded; Granny talking so fast that Ethel would never have brought in the stipulation, that the frocks should be worn to school and church, if Richard, in his mild, but steady way, had not brought the old woman to listen to it. She was full of asseverations that they should go; she took them to church sometimes herself, when it was fine weather and they had clothes, and they could say their catechiz as well as anybody already; yes, they should come, that they should, and next Sunday. Ethel promised to be there to introduce them to the chief lady, the president of the committee, Mrs. Ledwich, and, with a profusion of thanks, they took leave.

They found John Taylor, just come out of the hospital, looking weak and ill, as he smoked his pipe over the fire, his wife bustling about at a great rate, and one of the infants crying. It seemed to be a great relief that they were not come to complain of Lucy, and there were many looks of surprise on hearing what their business really was. Mrs. Taylor thanked, and appeared not to know whether she was glad or sorry; and her husband, pipe in hand, gazed at the young gentleman as if he did not comprehend the species, since he could not be old enough to be a clergyman.

Richard hoped they would find sponsors by that time; and there Mrs. Taylor gave little hope; it was a bad lot—there was no one she liked to ask to stand, she said, in a dismal voice; but there her husband put in, ' I'll find some one, if that's all; my missus always thinks nobody can't do nothing.'

' To be sure,' said the lamentable Mrs. Taylor, ' all the elder ones was took to church, and I'm loth the little ones shouldn't; but you see, sir, we are poor people, and it's a long way, and they was set down in the gentleman's register book.'

' But you know that is not the same, Mrs. Taylor. Surely Lucy could have told you that, when she went to school.'

' No, sir, 'tis not the same—I knows that; but this is a bad place to live in—'

'Always the old song, Missus!' exclaimed her husband. ' Thank you kindly, sir—you have been a good friend to us, and so was Dr. May, when I was up to the hospital, through the thick of his own troubles. I believe you are in the right of it, sir, and thank you. The children shall be ready, and little Jack, too, and I'll find gossips, and let 'em be christened on Sunday.'

' I believe you will be glad of it,' said Richard; and he went on to speak of the elder children coming to school, on Sunday, thus causing another whining from the wife about distance and bad weather, and no one else going that way. He said the little Halls were coming, but Mrs. Taylor began saying she disliked their company for the children—granny let them get about so much, and they said bad words. The father again interfered. Perhaps Mr. Wilmot, who acted as chaplain at the hospital, had been talking to him, for he declared at once that they should come; and Richard suggested that he might see them home when he came from church; then, turning to the boy and girl, told them they would meet their sister Lucy, and asked them if they would not like that.

On the whole, the beginning was not inauspicious, though there might be a doubt whether old Mrs. Hall would keep all her promises. Ethel was so much diverted and pleased as to be convinced she would; Richard was a little doubtful as to her power over the wild girls. There could not be any doubt that John Taylor was in earnest, and had been worked upon just at the right moment; but there was danger that the impression would not last. 'And his wife is such a horrible whining dawdle!' said Ethel—'there will be no good to be done if it depends on her.'

Richard made no answer, and Ethel presently felt remorseful for her harsh speech about a poor ignorant woman, overwhelmed with poverty, children, and weak health.

'I have been thinking a great deal about what you said last time we took this walk,' said Richard, after a considerable interval.

'O have you!' cried Ethel, eagerly; and the black peaty pond she was looking at seemed to sparkle with sunlight.

'Do you really mean it?' said Richard, deliberately.

'Yes, to be sure,' she said, with some indignation.

'Because I think I see a way to make a beginning; but you must make up your mind to a great deal of trouble, and dirty walks, and you must really learn not to draggle your frock.'

'Well, well; but tell me.'

'This is what I was thinking. I don't think I can go back to Oxford after Christmas. It is not fit to leave you while papa is so disabled.'

'O no, he could not get on at all. I heard him tell Mr. Wilmot the other day that you were his right-hand.'

Ethel was glad she had repeated this, for there was a deepening colour and smiling glow of pleasure on her brother's face, such as she had seldom seen on his delicate, but somewhat impassive features.

'He is very kind!' he said, warmly. 'No, I am sure I cannot be spared till he is better able to use his arm, and I don't see any chance of that just yet. Then, if I stay at home, Friday is always at my own disposal, while papa is at the hospital meeting.'

'Yes, yes; and we could go to Cocksmoor, and set up a school. How delightful!'

'I don't think you would find it quite as delightful as you fancy,' said Richard; 'the children will be very wild and ignorant, and you don't like that at the National School.'

'O, but they are in such need; besides, there will be no Mrs. Ledwich over me. It is just right—I shan't mind anything. You are a capital Ritchie, for having thought of it!'

'I don't think—if I am ever to be what I wish, that is, if I can get through at Oxford—I don't think it can be wrong to begin this, if Mr. Ramsden does not object.'

'O Mr. Ramsden never objects to anything.'

'And if Mr. Wilmot will come and set us off. You know we cannot begin without that, or without my father's fully liking it.'

'Oh! there can be no doubt of that.'

'This one thing, Ethel, I must stipulate. Don't you go and tell it all out at once to him. I cannot have him worried about our concerns.'

'But how?—no one can question that this is right. I am sure he won't object.'

'Stop, Ethel; don't you see, it can't be done for nothing? If we undertake it, we must go on with it, and when I am away, it will fall on you and Flora. Well, then, it ought to be considered whether you are old enough and steady enough; and if it can be managed for you to go continually all this way, in this wild place. There will be expense, too.'

Ethel looked wild with impatience, but could not gainsay these scruples, otherwise than by declaring they ought not to weigh against the good of Cocksmoor.

'It will worry him to have to consider all this,' said Richard; 'and it must not be pressed upon him.'

'No,' said Ethel, sorrowfully; 'but you don't mean to give it up.'

'You are always in extremes, Ethel. All I want is, to find a good time for proposing it.'

She fidgetted, and gave a long sigh.

'Mind,' said Richard, stopping short, 'I'll have nothing to do with it, except on condition you are patient, and hold your tongue about it.'

'I think I can, if I may talk to Margaret.'

'O yes, to Margaret, of course. We could not settle anything without her help.'

'And I know what she will say,' said Ethel. 'O I am so glad;' and she jumped over three puddles in succession.

'And, Ethel, you must learn to keep your frock out of the dirt.'

'I'll do anything, if you'll help me at Cocksmoor.'

CHAPTER IX.

'For the structure that we raise,
    Time is with materials filled;
Our to-days and yesterdays,
    Are the blocks with which we build.

'Truly shape and fashion these,
    Leave no yawning gaps between;
Think not, because no man sees,
    Such things will remain unseen.'—LONGFELLOW.

WHEN Ethel came home, burning with the tidings of the newly-excited hopes for Cocksmoor, they were at once stopped by Margaret eagerly saying, 'Is Richard come in?—pray call him;' then, on his entrance, 'O, Richard, would you be so kind as to take this to the bank. I don't like to send it by any one else—it is so much;' and she took from under her pillows a velvet bag, so heavy that it weighed down her slender white hand.

'What, he has given you the care of his money?' said Ethel.

'Yes; I saw him turning something out of his waistcoat-pocket into the drawer of the looking-glass, and sighing in that very sad way. He said his fees had come to such an accumulation, that he must see about sending them to the Bank; and then he told me of the delight of throwing his first fee into dear mamma's lap, when they were just married, and his old uncle had given up to him, and how he had brought them to her ever since; he said she had spoiled him, by taking all trouble off his hands. He looked at it, as if it was so sorrowful to him to have to dispose of it, that I begged him not to plague himself any more, but let me see about it, as dear mamma used to do; so he said I was spoiling him too, but he brought me the drawer, and emptied it out here: when he was gone, I packed it up, and I have been waiting to ask Richard to take it all to the Bank, out of his sight.'

'You counted it?' said Richard.

'Yes—there's fifty—I kept seventeen towards the week's expenses. Just see that it is right,' said Margaret, showing her neat packets.

'Oh, Ritchie,' said Ethel, 'what can expense signify, when all that has been kicking about loose in an open drawer? What would not one of those rolls do?'

'I think I had better take them out of your way,' said Richard, quietly. 'Am I to bring back the book to you, Margaret?'

'Yes, do,' said Margaret; 'pray do not teaze him with it.' And as her brother left the room, she continued, 'I wish he was better. I think he is more oppressed now than even at first. The pain of his arm, going on so long, seems to me to have pulled him down; it does not let him sleep, and, by the end of the day, he gets worn and fagged, by seeing so many people, and exerting himself to talk and think; and often, when there is something that must be asked, I don't know how to begin, for it seems as if a little more would be too much for him.'

'Yes, Richard is right,' said Ethel, mournfully; 'it will not do to press him about our concerns; but do you think him worse to-day?'

'He did not sleep last night, and he is always worse when he does not drive out into the country; the fresh air, and being alone with Richard, are a rest for him. To-day is especially trying; he does not think poor old Mr. Southern will get through the evening, and he is so sorry for the daughter.'

'Is he there now?'

'Yes; he thought of something that might be an alleviation, and he would go, though he was tired. I am afraid the poor daughter will detain him, and he is not fit to go through such things now.'

'No, I hope he will soon come; perhaps Richard will meet him. But, O Margaret, what do you think Richard and I have been talking of?' and, without perception of fit times and seasons, Ethel would have told her story, but Margaret, too anxious to attend to her, said, 'Hark! was not that his step?' and Dr. May came in, looking mournful and fatigued.

'Well,' said he, 'I was just too late. He died as I got there, and I could not leave the daughter till old Mrs. Bowers came.'

'Poor thing,' said Margaret. 'He was a good old man.'

'Yes,' said Dr. May, sitting wearily down, and speaking in a worn-out voice. 'One can't lightly part with a man one has seen at church every Sunday of one's life, and exchanged so many friendly words with over his counter. 'Tis a strong bond of neighbourliness in a small place like this, and, as one grows old, changes come heavier — 'the clouds return again after the rain.' Thank you, my dear,' as Ethel fetched his slippers, and placed a stool for his feet, feeling somewhat ashamed of thinking it an achievement to have, unbidden, performed a small act of attention which would have come naturally from any of the others.

'Papa, you will give me the treat of drinking tea with me?' said Margaret, who saw the quiet of her room would suit him better than the bustle of the children downstairs. 'Thank you,' as he gave a smile of assent.

That Margaret could not be made to listen this evening was plain, and all that Ethel could do, was to search for some books on schools. In seeking for them, she displayed such confusion in the chiffonnière, that Flora exclaimed, ' Oh, Ethel, how could you leave it so ?'

' I was in a hurry, looking for something for Norman. I'll set it to rights,' said Ethel, gulping down her dislike to being reproved by Flora, with the thought that mamma would have said the same.

' My dear !' cried Flora, presently, jumping up, ' what are you doing ? piling up those heavy books on the top of the little ones ; how do you think they will ever stand ? let me do it.'

' No, no, Flora ;' and Richard, in a low voice, gave Ethel some advice, which she received, seated on the floor, in a mood between temper and despair.

' He is going to teach her to do it on the principles of gravitation,' said Flora.

Richard did not do it himself, but, by his means, Ethel, without being in the least irritated, gave the chiffonnière a thorough dusting and setting-to-rights, sorting magazines, burning old catalogues, and finding her own long-lost ' Undine,' at which she was so delighted, that she would have forgotten all ; in proceeding to read it, curled up on the floor amongst the heaps of pamphlets, if another gentle hint from Richard had not made her finish her task so well, as to make Flora declare it was a pleasure to look in, and Harry pronounce it to be all neat and ship-shape

There was no speaking to Margaret the next morning—it was French day—and Ethel had made strong resolutions to behave better ; and whether there were fewer idioms, or that she was trying to understand, instead of carping at the master's explanations, they came to no battle ; Flora led the conversation, and she sustained her part with credit, and gained an excellent mark.

Flora said afterwards to Margaret, ' I managed nicely for her. I would not let M. Ballompré blunder upon any of the subjects Ethel feels too deeply to talk of in good French, and really Ethel has a great talent for languages. How fast she gets on with Italian !'

' That she does,' said Margaret. ' Suppose you send her up, Flora—you must want to go and draw or practice, and she may do her arithmetic here, or read to me.'

It was the second time Margaret had made this proposal, and it did not please Flora, who had learnt to think herself necessary to her sister, and liked to be the one to do everything for her. She was within six weeks of seventeen, and surely she need not be sent down again to the school-room, when she had been so good a manager of the whole family. She was fond of study and of accomplishments, but she thought she might be emancipated from Miss Winter ; and it was not pleasant to her that a sister, only eighteen months older, and almost dependant on her, should have authority to dispose of her time.

'I practise in the evening,' she said, 'and I could draw here, if I wished, but I have some music to copy.'

Margaret was concerned at the dissatisfaction, though not understanding the whole of it; 'You know, dear Flora,' she said, 'I need not take up all your time now.'

'Don't regret that,' said Flora. 'I like nothing so well as waiting on you, and I can attend to my own affairs very well here.'

'I'll tell you why I proposed it,' said Margaret. 'I think it would be a relief to Ethel to escape from Miss Winter's beloved Friday questions.'

'Great nonsense they are,' said Flora. 'Why don't you tell Miss Winter they are of no use?'

'Mamma never interfered with them,' said Margaret. 'She only kept Ethel in her own hands, and if you would be so kind as to change sometimes and sit in the school-room, we could spare Ethel, without hurting Miss Winter's feelings.'

'Well, I'll call Ethel, if you like, but I shall go and practise in the drawing-room. The old school-room piano is fit for nothing but Mary to hammer upon.'

Flora went away, evidently annoyed, and Margaret's conjectures on the cause of it were cut short by Ethel running in with a slate in one hand, and two books in the other, the rest having all tumbled down on the stairs.

'O, Margaret, I am so glad to come to you. Miss Winter has set Mary to read 'To be, or not to be,' and it would have driven me distracted to have stayed there. I have got a most beautiful sum in Compound Proportion, about a lion, a wolf, and a bear eating up a carcase, and as soon as they have done it, you shall hear me say my ancient geography, and then we will do a nice bit of Tasso; and if we have any time after that, I have got such a thing to tell you—only I must not tell you now, or I shall go on talking and not finish my lessons.'

It was not till all were done, that Ethel felt free to exclaim, 'Now for what I have been longing to tell you—Richard is going to—' But the fates were unpropitious. Aubrey trotted in, expecting to be amused; next came Norman, and Ethel gave up in despair; and, after having affronted Flora in the morning, Margaret was afraid of renewing the offence, by attempting to secure Ethel as her companion for the afternoon; so not till after the walk, could Margaret contrive to claim the promised communication, telling Ethel to come and settle herself cosily by her.

'I should have been very glad of you last evening,' said she, 'for papa went to sleep, and my book was out of reach.'

'O, I am sorry; how I pity you, poor Margaret!'

'I suppose I have grown lazy,' said Margaret, 'for I don't mind those things now. I am never sorry for a quiet time to recollect and consider.'

'It must be like the waiting in the dark between the slides of a magic lantern,' said Ethel; 'I never like to be quiet. I get so unhappy.'

'I am glad of resting and recollecting,' said Margaret. 'It has all been so like a dream, that merry morning, and then, slowly waking to find myself here in dear mamma's place, and papa watching over me. Sometimes I think I have not half understood what it really is, and that I don't realize, that if I was up and about, I should find the house without her.'

'Yes; that is the aching part!' said Ethel. 'I am happy, sitting on her bed here with you. You are a little of her, besides being my own dear Peg-top! You are very lucky to miss the meal-times and the evenings.'

'That is the reason I don't feel it wrong to like to have papa sitting with me all the evening,' said Margaret, 'though it may make it worse for you to have him away. I don't think it selfish in me to keep him. He wants quiet so much, or to talk a little when it suits him; we are too many now, when he is tired.'

'O, it is best,' said Ethel. 'Nothing that you do is selfish— don't talk of it, dear Margaret. It will be something like old times when you come down again.'

'But all this time you are not telling me what I want so much to hear,' said Margaret, 'about Cocksmoor. I am so glad Richard has taken it up.'

'That he has. We are to go every Friday, and hire a room, and teach the children. Once a week will do a great deal, if we can but make them wish to learn. It is a much better plan than mine; for if they care about it, they can come to school here on Sunday.'

'It is excellent,' said Margaret, 'and if he is at home till Easter, it will give it a start, and put you in the way of it, and get you through the short days and dark evenings, when you could not so well walk home without him.'

'Yes, and then we can all teach; Flora, and Mary, and you, when you are well again. Richard says it will be disagreeable, but I don't think so—they are such unsophisticated people. That Granny Hall is such a funny old woman; and the whole place wants nothing but a little care, to do very well.'

'You must prepare for disappointments, dear Ethel.'

'I know; I know nothing is done without drawbacks; but I am so glad to make some beginning.'

'So am I. Do you know, mamma and I were one day talking over those kind of things, and she said she had always regretted that she had so many duties at home, that she could not attend as much to the poor as she would like; but she hoped now we girls were growing up, we should be able to do more.'

'Did she?' was all Ethel said, but she was deeply gratified.

'I've been wanting to tell you. I knew you would like to hear it. It seems to set us to work so happily.'

'I only wish we could begin,' said Ethel, 'but Richard is so slow! Of course we can't act without papa's consent and Mr. Wilmot's help, and he says papa must not be worried about it, and he must watch for his own time to speak about it.'

'Yes,' said Margaret.

'I know—I would not have it otherwise; but what is tiresome is this. Richard is very good, but he is so dreadfully hard to stir up, and what's worse, so very much afraid of papa, that while he is thinking about opportunities, they will all go by, and then it will be Easter, and nothing done!'

'He is not so much afraid of papa as he was,' said Margaret. 'He has felt himself useful and a comfort, and papa is gentler; and that has cheered him out of the desponding way that kept him back from proposing anything.'

'Perhaps,' said Ethel; 'but I wish it was you. Can't you? you always know how to manage.'

'No; it is Richard's affair, and he must do as he thinks fit. Don't sigh, dear Ethel—perhaps he may soon speak, and, if not, you can be preparing in a quiet way all the time. Don't you remember how dear mamma used to tell us that things, hastily begun, never turn out well?'

'But this is not hasty. I've been thinking about it these six weeks,' said Ethel. 'If one does nothing but think, it is all no better than a vision. I want to be doing.'

'Well, you can be doing—laying a sound foundation,' said Margaret. 'The more you consider, and the wiser you make yourself, the better it will be when you do set to work.'

'You mean by curing myself of my slovenly ways, and impatient temper?'

'I don't know that I was exactly thinking of that,' said Margaret, 'but that ought to be the way. If we are not just the thing in our niche at home, I don't think we can do much real good elsewhere.'

'It would be hollow, show-goodness,' said Ethel. 'Yes, that is true; and it comes across me now and then what a horrid wretch I am, to be wanting to undertake so much, when I leave so much undone. But, do you know, Margaret, there's no one such a help in those ways as Richard. Though he is so precise, he is never tiresome. He makes me see things, and do them neatly, without plaguing me, and putting me in a rage. I'm not ready to bite off my own fingers, or kick all the rattle-traps over and leave them, as I am when Miss Winter scolds me, or nurse, or even Flora sometimes; but it is as if I was gratifying him, and his funny little old bachelor tidyisms divert me; besides, he teaches me the theory, and never lays hold of my poor fingers, and, when they won't bend the wrong way, calls them frogs.'

'He is a capital master for you,' said Margaret, much amused and pleased, for Richard was her especial darling, and she triumphed in any eulogy from those who ordinarily were too apt to regard his dulness with superior compassion.

'If he would only read our books, and enter into poetry and delight in it; but it is all nonsense to him,' said Ethel. 'I can't think how people can be so different: but oh! here he comes. Ritchie, you should not come upon us before we are aware.'

'What? I should have heard no good of myself?'

'Great good,' said Margaret; 'she was telling me you would make a neat-handed woman of her in time.'

'I don't see why she should not be as neat as other people,' said Richard, gravely. 'Has she been telling you our plan?'

And it was again happily discussed; Ethel satisfied by finding him fully set upon the design, and Margaret giving cordial sympathy and counsel. When Ethel was called away, Margaret said, 'I am so glad you have taken it up; not only for the sake of Cocksmoor, but of Ethel. It is good for her not to spend her high soul in dreams.'

'I am afraid she does not know what she undertakes,' said Richard.

'She does not; but you will keep her from being turned back. It is just the thing to prevent her energies from running to waste, and her being so much with you, and working under you, is exactly what one would have chosen.'

'By contraries!' said Richard, smiling. 'That is what I was afraid of. I don't half understand or follow her; and when I think a thing nonsense, I see you all calling it very fine, and I don't know what to make of it—'

'You are making yourself out more dull than you are,' said Margaret, affectionately.

'1 know I am stupid, and seem tame and cold,' said Richard, 'and you are the only one that does not care about it. That is what makes me wish Norman was the eldest. If I were as clever as he, I could do so much with Ethel, and be so much more to papa.'

'No you would not. You would have other things in your head. You would not be the dear, dear old Ritchie that you are. You would not be a calm, cautious, steady balance to the quick-silver heads some of us have got. No, no; Norman's a very fine fellow—a very dear fellow; but he would not do half so well for our eldest—he is too easily up, and down again.'

'And I am getting into my old way of repining,' said Richard. 'I don't mind so much, since my father has at least one son to be proud of, and I can be of some use to him now.'

'Of the greatest, and to all of us. I am so glad you can stay after Christmas, and papa was pleased at your offering, and said he could not spare you at all, though he would have tried, if it had been any real advantage to you.'

'Well, I hope he will approve. I must speak to him as soon as I can find him with his mind tolerably disengaged.'

The scene that ensued that evening in the magic lantern before Margaret's bed, did not promise much for the freedom of her father's mind. Harry entered with a resolute manner. 'Margaret, I wanted to speak to you,' said he, spreading himself out, with an elbow on each arm of the chair. 'I want you to speak to papa about my going to sea. It is high time to see about it —I shall be thirteen on the fifth of May.'

'And you mean it seriously, Harry?'

'Yes, of course I do, really and truly; and if it is to come to pass, it is time to take measures. Don't you see, Margaret?'

'It is time, as you say,' answered Margaret, reflectingly; and sadly surveying the bright boy, rosy-cheeked, round-faced, and blue-eyed, with the childish gladsomeness of countenance, that made it strange that his lot in life should be already in the balance.

'I know what you will all tell me, that it is a hard life; but I must get my own living some way or other, and I should like that way the best,' said he, earnestly.

'Should you like to be always far from home?'

'I should come home sometimes, and bring such presents to Mary, and baby, and all of you; and I don't know what else to be, Margaret. I should hate to be a doctor—I can't abide sick people; and I couldn't write sermons, so I can't be a clergyman; and I won't be a lawyer, I vow, for Harvey Anderson is to be a lawyer—so there's nothing left but soldiers and sailors, and I mean to be a sailor!'

'Well, Harry, you may do your duty, and try to do right, if you are a sailor, and that is the point.'

'Aye, I was sure you would not set your face against it, now you know Alan Ernescliffe.'

'If you were to be like him—' Margaret found herself blushing, and broke off.

'Then you will ask papa about it?'

'You had better do so yourself. Boys had better settle such serious affairs with their fathers, without setting their sisters to interfere. What's the matter, Harry—you are not afraid to speak to papa?'

'Only for one thing,' said Harry. 'Margaret, I went out to shoot pee-wits last Saturday with two fellows, and I can't speak to papa while that's on my mind.'

'Then you had better tell him at once.'

'I knew you would say so; but it would be like a girl, and it would be telling of the two fellows.'

'Not at all; papa would not care about them.'

'You see,' said Harry, twisting a little, 'I knew I ought not; but they said I was afraid of a gun, and that I had no money. Now I see that was chaff, but I didn't then; and Norman wasn't there.'

'I am so glad you have told me all this, Harry dear, for I knew you had been less at home of late, and I was almost afraid you were not going on quite well.'

'That's what it is,' said Harry. 'I can't stand things at all, and I can't go moping about as Norman does. I can't live without fun, and now Norman isn't there, half the time it turns to something I am sorry for afterwards.'

'But, Harry, if you let yourself be drawn into mischief here for want of Norman, what would you do at sea?'

'I should be an officer!'

'I am afraid,' said Margaret, smiling, 'that would not make much difference inside, though it might outside. You must get the self-control, and leave off being afraid to be said to be afraid.'

Harry fidgetted. 'I should start fresh, and be out of the way of the Andersons,' he said. 'That Anderson junior is a horrid fellow—he spites Norman, and he bullied me, till I was big enough to show him that it would not do—and though I am so much younger, he is afraid of me. He makes up to me, and tries to get me into all the mischief that is going.'

'And you know that, and let him lead you? Oh, Harry!'

'I don't let him lead me,' said Harry, indignantly, 'but I won't have them say I *can't* do things.'

Margaret laughed, and Harry presently perceived what she meant, but instead of answering, he began to boast, 'There never was a May in disgrace yet, and there never shall be.'

'That is a thing to be very thankful for,' said Margaret; 'but you know there may be much harm without public disgrace. I never heard of one of the Andersons being in disgrace yet.'

'No—shabby fellows, that just manage to keep fair with old Hoxton, and make a show,' said Harry. 'They look at transla- tions, and copy old stock verses. O, it was such fun the other day. What do you think? Norman must have been dreaming, for he had taken to school, by mistake, Richard's old Gradus that Ethel uses, and there were ever so many rough copies of hers sticking in it.'

'Poor Ethel! What consternation she would be in! I hope no one found it out.'

'Why, Anderson junior was gaping about in despair for sense for his verses—he comes on that, and slyly copies a whole set of her old ones, done when she—Norman, I mean—was in the fifth form. His subject was a river, and hers Babylon; but altering a line or two, it did just as well. He never guessed I saw him, and thought he had done it famously. He showed them up, and would have got some noted good mark, but that, by great good luck, Ethel had made two of her pentameters too short, which he hadn't the wit to find out, thinking all Norman did must be right. So he has shown up a girl's verses—isn't that rare?' cried Harry, dancing on his chair with triumph.

'I hope no one knows they were hers?'

'Bless you, no!' said Harry, who regarded Ethel's attainments as something contraband. 'D'ye think I could tell? No, that's the only pity, that he can't hear it; but, after all, I don't care for anything he does, now I know he has shown up a girl's verses.'

'Are these verses of poor Ethel's safe at home?'

'Yes, I took care of that. Mind you don't tell any one, Margaret; I never told even Norman.'

'But all your school-fellows arn't like these? You have Hector Ernescliffe.'

'He's a nice fellow enough, but he is little, and down in the school. 'Twould be making a fourth form of myself to be after him. The fact is, Margaret, they are a low, ungentlemanly lot just now, about sixth and upper fifth form,' said Harry, lowering his voice into an anxious, confidential tone; 'and since Norman has been less amongst them, they've got worse; and you see, now home is different, and he isn't like what he was, I'm thrown on them, and I want to get out of it. I didn't know that was it before, but Richard showed me what set me on thinking of it, and I see she knew all about it.'

'That she did! There is a great deal in what you say, Harry, but you know she thought nothing would be of real use but changing within. If you don't get a root of strength in yourself, your ship will be no better to you than school—there will be idle midshipmen as well as idle school-boys.'

'Yes, I know,' said Harry; 'but do you think papa will consent? She would not have minded.'

'I can't tell. I should think he would; but if any scheme is to come to good, it must begin by your telling him of the going out shooting.'

Harry sighed. 'I'd have done it long ago if she was here,' he said. 'I never did anything so bad before without telling, and I don't like it at all. It seems to come between him and me when I wish him good night.'

'Then, Harry, pray do tell him. You'll have no comfort if you don't.'

'I know I shan't; but then he'll be so angry! And, do you know, Margaret, 'twas worse than I told you, for a covey of partridges got up, and unluckily I had got the gun, and I fired and killed one, and that was regular poaching, you know! And when we heard some one coming, how we did cut! Ax—the other fellow, I mean, got it, and cooked it in his bed-room, and ate it for supper; and he laughs about it, but I have felt so horrid all the week! Suppose a keeper had got a summons!'

'I can only say again, the only peace will be in telling.'

'Yes; but he will be so angry. When that lot of fellows a year or two ago, did something like it, and shot some of the Abbotstoke rabbits, don't you remember how much he said about its being disgraceful, and ordering us never to have anything to do with their gunnery? And he will think it so very bad to have gone out on a lark just now! O, I wish I hadn't done it.'

'So do I, indeed, Harry! but I am sure, even if he should be angry at first, he will be pleased with your confessing.'

Harry looked very reluctant and disconsolate, and his sister did not wonder—for Dr. May's way of hearing of a fault was never to be calculated on. 'Come, Harry,' said she, 'if he is ever so angry, though I don't think he will be, do you think that will be half as bad as this load at your heart? Besides, if you are not bold enough to speak to him, do you think you can ever be brave enough for a sailor?'

'I will,' said Harry, and the words were hardly spoken, before his father's hand was on the door. He was taken by surprise at the moment of trial coming so speedily, and had half a mind to retreat by the other door; he was stayed by the reflection that Margaret would think him a coward, unfit for a sailor, and he made up his mind to endure whatever might betide.

'Harry here? This is company I did not expect.'

'Harry has something to say to you, papa.'

'Eh! my boy, what is it?' said he, kindly.

'Papa, I have killed a partridge. Two fellows got me to hire a gun, and go out shooting with them last Saturday,' said Harry, speaking firmly and boldly now he had once begun. 'We meant only to go after pee-wits, but a partridge got up, and I killed it.'

Then came a pause. Harry stopped, and Dr. May waited, half expecting to hear that the boy was only brought to confession, by finding himself in a scrape. Margaret spoke. 'And he could not be happy till he had told you.'

'Is it so? Is that the whole?' said the Doctor, looking at his son with a keen glance, between affection and inquiry, as if only waiting to be sure the confession was free, before he gave his free forgiveness.

'Yes, papa,' said Harry, his voice and lip losing their firmness, as the sweetness of expression gained the day on his father's face. 'Only that I know—'twas very wrong—especially now—and I am very sorry—and I beg your pardon.'

The latter words came between sighs, fast becoming sobs, in spite of Harry's attempts to control them, as his father held out his arm, and drew him close to him. 'That's mamma's own bravo boy,' he said in his ear—in a voice which strong feeling had reduced to such a whisper, that even Margaret could not hear—she only saw how Harry, sobbing aloud, clung tighter and tighter to him, till he said, 'Take care of my arm!' and Harry sprung back at least a yard, with such a look of dismay, that the Doctor laughed. 'No harm done!' said he. 'I was only a little in dread of such a young lion. Come back, Harry,' and he took his hand. 'It was a bad piece of work, and it will never do for you to let yourself be drawn into every bit of mischief that is on foot; I believe I ought to give you a good lecture on it, but I can't do it, after such a straightforward confession. You must have gone through enough in the last week, not to be likely to do it again.'

'Yes, papa—thank you.'

'I suppose I must not ask you any questions about it, for fear of betraying the fellows,' said Dr. May, half smiling.

'Thank you, papa,' said Harry, infinitely relieved and grateful, and quite content for some space to lean in silence against the chair, with that encircling arm round him, while some talk passed between his father and Margaret.

What a world of thought passed through the boy's young soul in that space! First, there was a thrill of intense, burning love to his father, scarcely less fondness to his sweet motherly sister; a clinging feeling to every chair and table of that room, which seemed still full of his mother's presence; a numbering over of all the others with ardent attachment, and a flinging from him with horror the notion of asking to be far away from that dearest father, that loving home, that arm that was round him. Anything rather than be without them in the dreary world! But then came the remembrance of cherished visions, the shame of relinquishing a settled purpose, the thought of weary morrows, with the tempters among his playmates, and his home blank and melancholy; and the roaming spirit of enterprise stirred again, and reproached him with being a baby, for fancying he could stay at home for ever. He would come back again with such honours as Alan Ernescliffe had brought, and oh! if his father so prized them in a stranger, what would it be in his own son? Come home to such a greeting as would make up for the parting! Harry's heart throbbed again for the boundless sea, the tall ship, and the wondrous foreign climes, where he had so often lived in fancy. Should he, could he speak; was this the moment? and he stood gazing at the fire, oppressed with the weighty reality of deciding his destiny. At last Dr. May looked in his face, 'Well, what now, boy? You have your head full of something—what's coming next?'

Out it came, 'Papa, will you let me be a sailor?'

'Oh!' said Dr. May, 'that is come on again, is it? I thought that you had forgotten all that.'

'No, papa,' said Harry, with the manly coolness that the sense of his determination gave him—'it was not a mere fancy, and I have never had it out of my head. I mean it quite in earnest—I had rather be a sailor. I don't wish to get away from Latin and Greek, I don't mind them; but I think I could be a better sailor than anything. I know it is not all play, but I am willing to rough it; and I am getting so old, it is time to see about it, so will you consent to it, papa?'

'Well! there's some sense in your way of putting it,' said Dr. May. 'You have it strong in your head, then, and you know 'tis not all fair weather work!'

'That I do; Alan told me histories, and I've read all about it; but one must rough it anywhere, and if I am ever so far away, I'll try not to forget what's right. I'll do my duty, and not care for danger.'

'Well said, my man; but remember, 'tis easier talking by one's own fireside, than doing when the trial comes.'

'And will you let me, papa?'

'I'll think about it. I can't make up my mind as 'quick as directly,' you know, Harry,' said his father, smiling kindly, 'but I won't treat it as a boy's fancy, for you've spoken in a manly way, and deserve to be attended to. Now run down, and tell the girls to put away their work, for I shall come down in a minute to read prayers.'

Harry went, and his father sighed and mused! 'That's a fine fellow! So this is what comes of bringing sick sailors home—one's own boys must be catching the infection. Little monkey, he talks as wisely as if he were forty! He is really set on it, do you think, Margaret? I'm afraid so!'

'I think so,' said Margaret; 'I don't think he ever has it out of his mind!'

'And when the roving spirit once lays hold of a lad, he must have his way—he is good for nothing else,' said Dr. May.

'I suppose a man may keep from evil in that profession, as well as in any other,' said Margaret.

'Aha! you are bit too, are you?' said the Doctor; ''tis the husbandman and viper, is it?' Then his smile turned into a heavy sigh, as he saw he had brought colour to Margaret's pale cheek, but she answered calmly, 'Dear mamma did not think it would be a bad thing for him.'

'I know,' said the Doctor, pausing; 'but it never came to this with her.'

'I wish he had chosen something else, but'—and Margaret thought it right to lay before her father some part of what he had said of the temptations of the school at Stoneborough. The Doctor listened and considered; at last he rose, and said, 'Well, I'll set Ritchie to write to Ernescliffe, and hear what he says. What must be, must be. 'Tis only asking me to give up the boy, that's all;' and as he left the room, his daughter again heard his sigh and half-uttered words, 'O Maggie, Maggie.'

CHAPTER X.

'A tale
Would rouse adventurous courage in a boy,
And make him long to be a mariner,
That he might rove the main.'—SOUTHEY.

ETHELDRED had the satisfaction of seeing the Taylors at school on Sunday, but no Halls made their appearance, and, on inquiry,

she was told, ' Please, ma'am, they said they would not come;'
so Ethel condemned Granny Hall as ' a horrid, vile, false, hypo-
critical old creature! It was no use having anything more to
do with her.'

' Very well,' said Richard; ' then I need not speak to my father.'

' Ritchie now! you know I meant no such thing!'

' You know, it is just what will happen continually.'

' Of course there will be failures, but this is so abominable,
when they had those nice frocks, and those two beautiful eighteen-
penny shawls! There are three shillings out of my pound thrown
away!'

' Perhaps there was some reason to prevent them. We will
go and see.'

' We shall only hear some more palavering. I want to have no
more to say to—' but here Ethel caught herself up, and began
to perceive what a happiness it was that she had not the power
of acting on her own impulses.

The twins and their little brother of two years old were christened in the afternoon, and Flora invited the parents to drink tea
in the kitchen, and visit Lucy, while Ethel and Mary each
carried a baby up-stairs to exhibit to Margaret.

Richard, in the meantime, had a conversation with John Taylor, and learnt a good deal about the district, and the number of
the people. At tea, he began to rehearse his information, and
the Doctor listened with interest, which put Ethel in happy
agitation, believing that the moment was come, and Richard
seemed to be only waiting for the conclusion of a long tirade
against those who ought to do something for the place, when
behold! Blanche was climbing on her father's knee, begging for
one of his Sunday stories.

Etheldred was cruelly disappointed, and could not at first rejoice to see her father able again to occupy himself with his little
girl. The narration, in his low tones, roused her from her mood
of vexation. It was the story of David, which he told in language scriptural and poetical, so pretty and tender in its simplicity, that she could not choose but attend. Ever and anon there
was a glance towards Harry, as if he were secretly likening his
own ' yellow haired laddie' to the ' shepherd boy, ruddy, and of
a fair countenance.'

' So Tom and Blanche,' he concluded, ' can you tell me how we
may be like the shepherd-boy, David?'

' There arn't giants now,' said Tom.

' Wrong is a giant,' said his little sister.

' Right, my white May-flower, and what then?'

'We are to fight,' said Tom.

'Yes, and mind, the giant with all his armour may be some great thing we have to do : but what did David begin with when he was younger?'

'The lion and the bear.'

'Aye, and minding his sheep. Perhaps little things, now you are little children, may be like the lion and the bear—so kill them off—get rid of them—cure yourself of whining or dawdling, or whatever it be, and mind your sheep well,' said he, smiling sweetly in answer to the children's earnest looks as they caught his meaning, 'and if you do, you will not find it near so hard to deal with your great giant struggle when it comes.'

Ah! thought Ethel, it suits me as well as the children. I have a great giant on Cocksmoor, and here I am, not allowed to attack him, because, perhaps, I am not minding my sheep, and letting my lion and my bear run loose about the house.

She was less impatient this week, partly from the sense of being on probation, and partly because she, in common with all the rest, was much engrossed with Harry's fate. He came home every day at dinner-time with Norman to ask if Alan Ernescliffe's letter had come; and at length Mary and Tom met them open-mouthed with the news that Margaret had it in her room.

Thither they hastened. Margaret held it out with a smile of congratulation, 'Here it is, Harry; papa said you were to have it, and consider it well, and let him know, when you had taken time. You must do it soberly. It is once for all.'

Harry's impetuosity was checked, and he took the letter quietly. His sister put her hand on his shoulder, 'Would you mind my kissing you, dear Harry?' and as he threw his arms round her neck, she whispered, 'Pray that you may choose right.'

He went quietly away, and Norman begged to know what had been Alan Ernescliffe's advice.

'I can scarcely say he gave any direct advice,' said Margaret; 'he would not have thought that called for. He said, no doubt there were hardships and temptations, more or less, according to circumstances; but, weighing one thing with another, he thought it gave as fair a chance of happiness as other professions, and the discipline and regularity had been very good for himself, as well as for many others he had known. He said, when a man is willing to go wrong there is much to help him, but when he is resolved on doing right, he need not be prevented.'

'That is what you may say of anything,' said Norman.

'Just so; and it answered papa's question, whether it was exposing Harry to more temptation than he must meet with anywhere. That was the reason it was such a comfort to have any one to write to, who understands it so well.'

'Yes, and knows Harry's nature.'

'He said he had been fortunate in his captains, and had led, on the whole, a happy life at sea; and he thought if it was so with him, Harry was likely to enjoy it more, being of a hardy adventurous nature, and a sailor from choice, not from circumstances.'

'Then he advised for it? I did not think he would; you know he will not let Hector be a sailor.'

'He told me he thought only a strong natural bent that way made it desirable, and that he believed Hector only wished it from imitation of him. He said too, long ago, that he thought Harry cut out for a sailor.'

'A spirited fellow!' said Norman, with a look of saddened pride and approval, not at all like one so near the same age. 'He is up to anything, afraid of nothing, he can lick any boy in the school already. It will be worse than ever without him!'

'Yes, you will miss your constant follower. He has been your shadow ever since he could walk. But there's the clock, I must not keep you any longer; good-bye, Norman.'

Harry gave his brother the letter as soon as they were outside the house, and while he read it, took his arm and guided him. 'Well,' said Norman as he finished.

'It is all right,' said Harry; and the two brothers said no more; there was something rising up in their throats at the thought that they had very few more walks to take together to Bishop Whichcote's school; Norman's heart was very full at the prospect of another vacancy in his home, and Harry's was swelling between the ardour of enterprise and the thought of bidding good-bye to each familiar object, and, above all, to the brother who had been his model and admiration from babyhood.

'Jane!' at length he broke out, 'I wish you were going too. I should not mind it half so much if you were.'

'Nonsense, Harry! you want to be July after June all your life, do you? You'll be much more of a man without me.'

That evening Dr. May called Harry into his study to ask him if his mind was made up; he put the subject fairly before him, and told him not to be deterred from choosing what he thought would be for the best by any scruples about changing his mind. 'We shall not think a bit the worse of you; better now, than too late.'

There was that in his face and tone that caused Harry to say, in a stifled voice, 'I did not think you would care so much, papa; I won't go, if you do.'

Dr. May put his hand on his shoulder, and was silent. Harry

felt a strange mixture of hope and fear, joy and grief, disappointment and relief. ' You must not give it up on that account, my
dear,' he said, at length ; ' I should not let you see this if it did
not happen at a time when I can't command myself as I ought.
If you were an only son, it might be your duty to stay ; being one
of many, 'tis nonsense to make a rout about parting with you.
If it is better for you, it is better for all of us ; and we shall do
very well when you are once fairly gone. Don't let *that* influence
you for a moment.'

Harry paused, not that he doubted, but he was collecting his
energies—' Then, papa, I choose the Navy.'

' Then it is done, Harry. You have chosen in a dutiful, unselfish spirit, and I trust it will prosper with you ; for I am sure
your father's blessing—aye, and your mother's too, go with you!
Now then,' after a pause, ' go and call Richard. I want him to
write to Ernescliffe about that naval school. You must take your
leave of the Whichcote foundation on Friday. I shall go and give
Dr. Hoxton notice to-morrow, and get Tom's name down instead.'

And when the name of Thomas May was set down, Dr. Hoxton
expressed his trust that it would pass through the school as free
from the slightest blemish as those of Richard, Norman, and
Harry May.

Now that Harry's destiny was fixed, Ethel began to think of
Cocksmoor again, and she accomplished another walk there with
Richard, Flora, and Mary, to question Granny Hall about the
children's failure.

The old woman's reply was a tissue of contradictions : the girls
were idle hussies, all *contrary:* they plagued the very life out of her,
and she represented herself as using the most frightful threats if
they would not go to school. Breaking every bone in their skin
was the least injury she promised them ; till Mary, beginning to
think her a cruel old woman, took hold of her brother's coat-
tails for protection.

' But I am afraid, Mrs. Hall,' said Richard, in that tone which
might be either ironical or simple, ' if you served them so, they
would never be able to get to school at all, poor things.'

' Bless you, sir, d'ye think I'd ever lay a finger near them ? it's
only the way one must talk to children, you see,' said she, patronizing his inexperience.

' Perhaps they have found that out,' said Richard.

Granny looked much entertained, and laughed triumphantly
and shrewdly, ' aye, aye, that they have, the lasses—they be sharp
enough for anything, *that* they be. Why, when I tell little Jenny
that there's the black man coming after her, what does she do

but she ups and says, 'Granny, I know 'tis only the wind in the chimney.''

'Then I don't think it seems to answer,' said Richard. 'Just suppose you were to try for once, really punishing them when they won't obey you; perhaps they would do it next time.'

'Why, sir, you see, I don't like to take the stick to them; they've got no mother, you see, sir.'

Mary thought her a kind grandmother, and came out from behind her brother.

'I think it would be kinder to do it for once. What do you think they will do as they grow older, if you don't keep them in order when they are little?'

This was foresight beyond Granny Hall, who began to expatiate on the troubles she had undergone in their service, and the excellence of Sam. There was certainly a charm in her manners, for Ethel forgot her charge of ingratitude, the other sisters were perfectly taken with her, nor could they any of them help giving credence to her asseverations that Jenny and Polly should come to school next Sunday.

They soon formed another acquaintance; a sharp-faced woman stood in their path, with a little girl in her hand, and arrested them with a low curtsey, and not a very pleasant voice, addressing herself to Flora, who was quite as tall as Richard, and appeared the person of most consequence.

'If you please, Miss, I wanted to speak to you. I have got a little girl here, and I want to send her to school, only I have no shoes for her.'

'Why surely, if she can run about here on the heath, she can go to school,' said Flora.

'Oh! but there is all the other children to point at her. The poor thing would be daunted, you see, Miss; if I could but get some friend to give her a pair of shoes, I'd send her in a minute. I want her to get some learning; as I am always saying, I'd never keep her away, if I had but got the clothes to send her in. I never lets her be running on the common, like them Halls, as it's a shame to see them in nice frocks, as Mrs. Hall got by going hypercriting about.'

'What is your name?' said Richard, cutting her short.

'Watts, if you please, sir; we heard there was good work up here, sir, and so we came; but I'd never have set foot in it, if I had known what a dark heathenish place it is, with never a gospel minister to come near it,' and a great deal more to the same purpose.

Mary whispered to Flora something about having out-grown

her boots, but Flora silenced her by a squeeze of the hand, and the two friends of Cocksmoor felt a good deal puzzled.

At last Flora said,—'You will soon get her clothed if she comes regularly to school on Sundays, for she will be admitted into the club; I will recommend her if she has a good character and comes regularly. Good morning, Mrs. Watts. Now we must go, or it will be dark before we get home.' And they walked hastily away.

'Horrid woman!' was Ethel's exclamation.

'But, Flora,' said innocent Mary, 'why would you not let me give the little girl my boots?'

'Perhaps I may, if she is good and comes to school,' said Flora.

'I think Margaret ought to settle what you do with your boots,' said Richard, not much to Flora's satisfaction.

'It is all the same,' she said. 'If I approve, Margaret will not object.'

'How well you helped us out,' Flora, said Ethel; 'I did not know in the least what to say.'

'It will be the best way of testing her sincerity,' said Flora, 'and at least it will do the child good; but I congratulate you on the promising aspect of Cocksmoor.'

'We did not expect to find a perfect place,' said Ethel; 'if it were, it would be of no use to go to it.'

Ethel could answer with dignity, but her heart sank at the aspect of what she had undertaken. She knew there would be evil; but she had expected it in a more striking and less disagreeable form.

That walk certainly made her less impatient, though it did did not relax her determination, nor the guard over her lion and bear, which her own good feeling, aided by Margaret's counsel, showed her were the greatest hindrances to her doing anything good and great.

Though she was obliged to set to work so many principles and reflections to induce herself to wipe a pen, or to sit straight on her chair, that it was like winding up a steam-engine to thread a needle; yet the work *was* being done—she was struggling with her faults, humbled by them, watching them, and overcoming them.

Flora, meanwhile, was sitting calmly down in the contemplation of the unexpected services she had rendered, confident that her character for energy and excellence was established, believing it herself, and looking back on her childish vanity and love of domineering as long past and conquered. She thought her grown-up character had begun, and was too secure to examine it closely.

CHAPTER XI.

'One thing is wanting in the beamy cup
Of my young life! one thing to be poured in;
Aye, and one thing is wanting to fill up
The measure of proud joy, and make it sin.'—F. W. F.

HOPES that Dr. May would ever have his mind free, seemed as fallacious as mamma's old promise to Margaret, to make doll's clothes for her whenever there should be no live dolls to be worked for in the nursery.

Richard and Ethel themselves had their thoughts otherwise engrossed. The last week before the holidays was an important one. There was an examination, by which the standing of the boys in the school was determined; and this time it was of more than ordinary importance, as the Randall scholarship of £100 a year for three years would be open in the summer to the competition of the first six boys. Richard had never come within six of the top, but had been passed at every examination by younger boys, till his father could bear it no longer; and now Norman was too young to be likely to have much chance of being of the number. There were eight decidedly his seniors; and Harvey Anderson, a small, quick-witted boy, half-a-year older, who had entered the school at the same time, and had always been one step below him, had, in the last three months, gained fast upon him.

Harry, however, meant Norman to be one of the six, and declared all the fellows thought he would be, except Anderson's party. Mr. Wilmot, in a call on Ethel and Flora, told them that he thought their brother had a fair chance, but he feared he was over-working himself, and should tell the Doctor so, whenever he could catch him; but this was difficult, as there was a great deal of illness just then, and he was less at home than usual.

All this excited the home party, but Norman only seemed annoyed by talk about it, and though always with a book in his hand, was so dreamy and listless, that Flora declared there was no fear of his doing too much—she thought he would fail for want of trying.

'I mean to try,' said Norman; 'say no more about it, pray.'

The great day was the 20th of December, and Ethel ran out as the boys went to school, to judge of Norman's looks, which were not promising. 'No wonder,' said Harry, 'since he had stayed up doing Euripides and Cicero the whole length of a candle that had been new at bed-time. But never mind, Ethel, if he only beats Anderson, I don't care for anything else.'

'O, it will be unbearable if he does not! Do try, Norman dear.'

'Never you mind.'

'He'll light up at the last moment,' said Ethel, consolingly, to Harry; but she was very uneasy herself, for she had set her heart on his surpassing Harvey Anderson. No more was heard all day. Tom went at dinner-time to see if he could pick up any news; but he was shy, or was too late, and gained no intelligence. Dr. May and Richard talked of going to hear the speeches and *vivâ voce* examination in the afternoon—objects of great interest to all Stoneborough men—but just as they came home from a long day's work, Dr. May was summoned to the next town, by an electric telegraph, and, as it was to a bad case, he did not expect to be at home till the mail-train came in at one o'clock at night. Richard begged to go with him, and he consented, unwillingly, to please Margaret, who could not bear to think of his 'fending for himself' in the dark on the railroad.

Very long did the evening seem to the listening sisters. Eight, and no tidings; nine, the boys not come; Tom obliged to go to bed by sheer sleepiness, and Ethel unable to sit still, and causing Flora demurely to wonder at her fidgetting so much, it would be so much better to fix her attention to some employment; while Margaret owned that Flora was right, but watched, and started at each sound, almost as anxiously as Ethel.

It was ten, when there was a sharp pull at the bell, and down flew the sisters; but old James was beforehand, and Harry was exclaiming, 'Dux! James, he is Dux! Hurrah! Flossy, Ethel, Mary! There stands the Dux of Stoneborough! Where's papa?'

'Sent for to Whitford. But oh! Norman, Dux! Is he really?'

'To be sure, but I must tell Margaret;' and up he rushed, shouted the news to her, but could not stay for congratulation; broke Tom's slumber by roaring it in his ear, and dashed into the nursery, where nurse for once forgave him for waking the baby. Norman, meanwhile, followed his eager sisters into the drawing-room, putting up his hand as if the light dazzled him, and looking, by no means, as if he had just achieved triumphant success.

Ethel paused in her exultation: 'But is it, is it true, Norman?'

'Yes,' he said, wearily, making his way to his dark corner.

'But what was it for? How is it?'

'I don't know,' he answered.

'What's the matter?' said Flora. 'Are you tired, Norman dear; does your head ache?'

'Yes;' and the pain was evidently severe.

'Won't you come to Margaret?' said Ethel, knowing what was the greater suffering; but he did not move, and they forbore to torment him with questions. The next moment Harry came down in an ecstacy, bringing in, from the hall, Norman's beautiful prize books, and showing off their Latin inscription.

'Ah!' said he, looking at his brother, ' he is regularly done for. He ought to turn in at once. That Everard is a famous fellow for an examiner. He said he never had seen such a copy of verses sent up by a schoolboy, and could hardly believe June was barely sixteen. Old Hoxton says he is the youngest Dux they have had these fifty years that he has known the school, and Mr. Wilmot said 'twas the most creditable examination he had ever known, and that I might tell papa so. What did possess that ridiculous old landlubber at Whitford, to go and get on the sick-list on this, of all the nights of the year? June, how can you go on sitting there, when you know you ought to be in your berth?'

'I wish he was,' said Flora; ' but let him have some tea first.'

'And tell us more, Harry,' said Ethel. 'Oh! it is famous. I knew he would come right at last. It is too delightful, if papa was but here!'

'Isn't it? You should have seen how Anderson grinned—he is only fourth—down below Forder, and Cheviot, and Ashe.'

'Well, I did not think Norman would have been before Forder and Cheviot. That is grand.'

'It was the verses that did it,' said Harry; 'they had an hour to do Themistocles on the hearth of Admetus, and there he beat them all to shivers. 'Twas all done smack, smooth, without a scratch, in Alcaics, and Cheviot heard Wilmot saying, 'twas no mere task, but had poetry, and all that sort of thing in it. But I don't know whether that would have done, if he had not come out so strong in the recitation; they put him on in Priam's speech to Achilles, and he said it—Oh! 'twas too bad papa did not hear him! Every one held their breath and listened.'

'How you do go on!' muttered Norman; but no one heeded, and Harry continued: 'He construed a chorus in Sophocles without a blunder; but what did the business was this, I believe. They asked all manner of out-of-the-way questions—history and geography, what no one expected, and the fellows who read nothing they can help, were thoroughly posed. Forder had not a word to say, and the others were worse, for Cheviot thought Queen Elizabeth's Earl of Leicester was Simon de Montfort; and didn't know when that battle was, beginning with an E.—was it Evesham, or Edgehill?'

'O Harry, you are as bad yourself?'

'But any one would know Leicester, because of Kenilworth,' said Harry; 'and I'm not sixth form. If papa had but been there! Every one was asking for him, and wishing it. For Dr

Hoxton called me—they shook hands with me, and wished me joy of it, and told me to tell my father how well Norman had done.'

'I suppose you looked so happy, they could not help it,' said Flora, smiling at that honest beaming face of joy.

'Aye,' said Norman, looking up; 'they had something to say to him on his own score, which he has forgotten.'

'I should think not,' said Harry. 'Why, what d'ye think they said? That I had gone on as well as all the Mays, and they trusted I should still, and be a credit to my profession.'

'Oh! Harry! why didn't you tell us? Oh! that is grand!' and, as the two elder girls made this exclamation, Mary proceeded to a rapturous embrace. 'Get along, Mary, you are throttling one. Mr. Everard inquired for my father and Margaret, and said he'd call to-morrow, and Hoxton and Wilmot kept on wishing he was there.'

'I wish he had been!' said Ethel; 'he would have taken such delight in it; but, even if he could have gone, he doubted whether it would not have made Norman get on worse from anxiety.'

'Well, Cheviot wanted me to send up for him at dinner-time,' said Harry; 'for, as soon as we sat down in the hall, June turned off giddy, and could not stay, and looked so horrid, we thought it was all over with him, and he would not be able to go up at all.'

'And Cheviot thought you ought to send for papa!'

'Yes, I knew he would not be in, and so we left him lying down on the bench in the cloister till dinner was over.'

'What a place for catching cold!' said Flora.

'So Cheviot said, but I couldn't help it, and when we went to call him afterwards, he was all right. Wasn't it fun, when the names were called over, and May senior, at the head! I don't think it will be better when I am a post-captain myself! But Margaret has not heard half yet.'

After telling it once in her room, once in the nursery, in whispers like gusts of wind, and once in the pantry, Harry employed himself in writing—'Norman is Dux!' in immense letters, on pieces of paper, which he disposed all over the house, to meet the eyes of his father and Richard on their return.

Ethel's joy was sadly damped by Norman's manner. He hardly spoke—only just came in to wish Margaret good-night, and shrank from her affectionate sayings, departing abruptly to his own room.

'Poor fellow! he is sadly overdone,' said she, as he went.

'Oh!' sighed Ethel, nearly ready to cry, ''tis not like what I used to fancy it would be when he came to the head of the school!'

'It will be different to-morrow,' said Margaret, trying to console herself as well as Ethel. 'Think how he has been on the strain this whole day, and long before, doing so much more than older boys. ' No wonder he is tired and worn out.'

Ethel did not understand what mental fatigue was, for her active, vigorous spirit had never been tasked beyond its powers.

'I hope he will be like himself to-morrow!' said she, disconsolately. 'I never saw him rough and hasty before. It was even with you, Margaret.'

'No, no, Ethel, you arn't going to blame your own Norman for unkindness on this of all days in the year. You know how it was; you love him better; just as I do, for not being able to bear to stay in this room, where—'

'Yes,' said Ethel, mournfully; 'it was a great shame of me! How could I? Dear Norman! how he does grieve—what love his must have been! But yet, Margaret,' she said, impatiently, and the hot tears breaking out, 'I cannot—cannot bear it! To have him not caring one bit for all of us! I want him to triumph! I can't without him!'

'What, Ethel, you, who said you didn't care for mere distinction and praise? Don't you think dear mamma would say it was safer for him not to be delighted and triumphant?'

'It is very tiresome,' said Ethel, nearly convinced, but in a slightly petulant voice.

'And does not one love those two dear boys to-night!' said Margaret. 'Norman, not able to rejoice in his victory without her, and Harry in such an ecstacy with Norman's honours. I don't think I ever was so fond of my two brothers.'

Ethel smiled, and drew up her head, and said no boys were like them anywhere, and papa would be delighted, and so went to bed happier in her exultation, and in hoping that the holidays would make Norman himself again.

Nothing could be better news for Dr. May, who had never lost a grain of the ancient school-party-loyalty that is part of the nature of the English gentleman. He was a thorough Stoneborough boy, had followed the politics of the Whichcote foundation year by year all his life, and perhaps, in his heart, regarded no honour as more to be prized than that of Dux and Randall scholar. Harry was in his room the next morning as soon as ever he was stirring, a welcome guest—teased a little at first, by his pretending to take it all as a sailor's prank to hoax him and Richard, and then free to pour out to delighted ears the whole history of the examination, and of every one's congratulations.

Norman himself was asleep when Harry went to give this narration. He came down late, and his father rose to meet him as he entered. 'My boy,' he said, 'I had not expected this of you. Well done, Norman!' and the whole tone and gesture had a heartfelt approval and joy in them, that Ethel knew her brother was deeply thrilled by, for his colour deepened, and his lips quivered into something like a smile, though he did not lift his eyes.

Then came Richard's warm greeting and congratulation, he, too, showing himself as delighted as if the honours were his own; and then Dr. May again, in lively tones, like old times, laughing at Norman for sleeping late, and still not looking well awake, asking him if he was quite sure it was not all a dream.

'Well,' said Norman, 'I should think it was, if it were not that you all believe it.'

'Harry had better go to sleep next,' said Dr. May, 'and see what dreaming will make him. If it makes Dux of Norman, who knows but it may make Drakes of him? Ha! Ethel—

> 'O, give us for our Kings such Queens,
> And for our Ducks such Drakes.''

There had not been such a merry breakfast for months. There was the old confusion of voices; the boys, Richard, and the Doctor had much to talk over of the school doings of this week, and there was nearly as much laughing as in days past. Ethel wondered whether any one but herself observed that the voice most seldom heard was Norman's.

The promised call was made by Dr. Hoxton, and Mr. Everard, an old friend, and after their departure Dr. May came to Margaret's room with fresh accounts, corroborating what Harry had said of the clear knowledge and brilliant talent that Norman had displayed, to a degree that surprised his masters, almost as much as the examiners. The copy of verses Dr. May brought with him, and construed them to Margaret, commenting all the way on their ease, and the fulness of thought, certainly remarkable in a boy of sixteen.

They were then resigned to Ethel's keeping, and she could not help imparting her admiration to their author, with some apology for vexing him again.

'I don't want to be cross,' said Norman, whom these words roused to a sense that he had been churlish last night; 'but I cannot help it. I wish people would not make such a fuss about it.'

'I don't think you can be well, Norman.'

'Nonsense. There's nothing the matter with me.'

'But I don't understand your not caring at all, and not being the least pleased.'

'It only makes it worse,' said Norman; 'I only feel as if I wanted to be out of the way. My only comfortable time yesterday was on that bench in the cool quiet cloister. I don't think I could have got through without that, when they left me in peace, till Cheviot and Harry came to rout me up, and I knew it was all coming.'

'Ah! you have overworked yourself, but it was for something. You have given papa such pleasure and comfort, as you can't help being glad of. That is very different from us foolish young ones and our trumpeting.'

'What comfort can it be? I've not been the smallest use all this time. When he was ill, I left him to Ernescliffe, and lay on the floor like an ass; and if he were to ask me to touch his arm, I should be as bad again. A fine thing for me to have talked all that arrogant stuff about Richard! I hate the thought of it; and, as if to make arrows and barbs of it, here's Richard making as much of this as if it was a double first class! He afraid to be compared with me, indeed!'

'Norman, indeed this is going too far. We can't be as useful as the elder ones; and when you know how papa was vexed about Richard, you must be glad to have pleased him.'

'If I were he, it would only make me miss her more. I believe he only makes much of me that he may not disappoint me.'

'I don't think so. He is really glad, and the more because she would have been so pleased. He said it would have been a happy day for her, and there was more of the glad look than the sorry one. It was the glistening look that comes when he is watching baby, or hearing Margaret say pretty things to her. You *see* it is the first bright morning we have had.'

'Yes,' said Norman; 'perhaps it was, but I don't know. I thought half of it was din.'

'Oh, Norman!'

'And another thing, Ethel, I don't feel as if I had fairly earned it. Forder or Cheviot ought to have had it. They are both more really good scholars than I am, and have always been above me. There was nothing I really knew better, except those historical questions that no one reckoned on; and not living at home with their sisters and books, they had no such chance, and it is very hard on them, and I don't like it.'

'Well, but you really and truly beat them in everything.'

'Aye, by chance. There were lots of places in construing, where I should have broken down if I had happened to be set on in them; it was only a wonder I did not in that chorus, for I had only looked at it twice; but Everard asked me nothing but what I knew; and now and then I get into a funny state, when nothing is too hard for me, and that was how it was yesterday evening.

Generally, I feel as dull as a post,' said Norman, yawning and stretching; 'I could not make a nonsense hexameter this minute, if I was to die for it.'

'A sort of Berserkar fury!' said Ethel, 'like that night you did the coral-worm verses. It's very odd. Are you sure you are well, dear Norman?'

To which he answered, with displeasure, that he was as well as possible, ordered her not to go and make any more fuss, and left her hastily. She was unhappy, and far from satisfied; she had never known his temper so much affected, and was much puzzled; but she was too much afraid of vexing him, to impart her perplexity even to Margaret. However, the next day, Sunday, as she was reading to Margaret after church, her father came in, and the first thing he said was, 'I want to know what you think of Norman.'

'How do you mean?' said Margaret; 'in health or spirits?'

'Both,' said Dr. May. 'Poor boy! he has never held up his head since October, and, at his age, that is hardly natural. He goes moping about, has lost flesh and appetite, and looks altogether out of order, shooting up like a May-pole, too.'

'Mind and body,' said Margaret, while Ethel gazed intently at her father, wondering whether she ought to speak, for Margaret did not know half what she did; nothing about the bad nights, nor what he called the 'funny state.'

'Yes, both. I fancied it was only his rapid growth, and the excitement of this examination, and that it would go off, but I think there's more amiss. He was lounging about doing nothing, when the girls were going to school after dinner, and I asked him to walk down with me to the Almshouses. He did not seem very willing, but he went, and presently, as I had hold of his arm, I felt him shivering, and saw him turn as pale as a sheet. As soon as I noticed it, he flushed crimson, and would not hear of turning back, stoutly protesting he was quite well, but I saw his hand was quivering even when I got into church. Why, Ethel, you have turned as red as he did.'

'Then he has done it!' exclaimed Ethel, in a smothered voice.

'What do you mean? Speak, Ethel.'

'He has gone past it—the place,' whispered she.

The Doctor made a sound of sorrowful assent, as if much struck; then said, 'you don't mean he has never been there since?'

'Yes,' said Ethel, 'he has always gone round Randall's alley or the garden; he has said nothing, but has contrived to avoid it.'

'Well,' said Dr. May, after a pause, 'I hoped none of us knew the exact spot.'

'We don't; he never told us, but he was there.'

'Was he?' exclaimed her father; 'I had no notion of that. How came he there?'

'He went on with Mr. Ernescliffe, and saw it all,' said Ethel, as her father drew out her words, apparently with his eye; 'and then came up to my room so faint that he was obliged to lie on the floor ever so long.'

'Faint—how long did it last?' said her father, examining her without apparent emotion, as if it had been an indifferent patient.

'I don't know, things seemed so long that evening. Till after dark at least, and it came on in the morning—no, the Monday. I believe it was your arm—for talking of going to see you always brought it on, till Mr. Ward gave him a dose of brandy-and-water, and that stopped it.'

'I wish I had known this before. Derangement of the nervous system, no doubt—a susceptible boy like that—I wonder what sort of nights he has been having.'

'Terrible ones,' said Ethel; 'I don't think he ever sleeps quietly till morning; he has dreams, and he groans and talks in his sleep: Harry can tell you all that.'

'Bless me!' cried Dr. May, in some anger, 'what have you all been thinking about to keep this to yourselves all this time?'

'He could not bear to have it mentioned,' said Ethel, timidly; 'and I didn't know that it signified so much; does it?'

'It signifies so much, that I had rather have given a thousand pounds than have let him go on all this time, to be overworked at school, and wound up to that examination!'

'Oh dear! I am sorry!' said Ethel, in great dismay. 'If you had but been at home when Cheviot wanted Harry to have sent for you—because he did not think him fit for it!' And Ethel was much relieved by pouring out all she knew, though her alarm was by no means lessened by the effect it produced on her father, especially when he heard of the 'funny state.'

'A fine state of things,' he said; 'I wonder it has not brought on a tremendous illness by this time. A boy of that sensitive temperament meeting with such a shock—never looked after—the quietest and most knocked down of all, and therefore the most neglected—his whole system disordered—and then driven to school to be harassed and overworked; if we had wanted to occasion brain fever we could not have gone a better way to set about it. I should not wonder if health and nerves were damaged for life!'

'Oh! papa, papa!' cried Ethel, in extreme distress, 'what shall I do! I wish I had told you, but—'

'I'm not blaming you, Ethel, you knew no better, but it has been grievous neglect. It is plain enough there is no one to see after you,' said the Doctor, with a low groan.

'We may be taking it in time,' said Margaret's soft voice—'it is very well it has gone on no longer.'

'Three months is long enough,' said Dr. May.

'I suppose,' continued Margaret, 'it will be better not to let dear Norman know we are uneasy about him.'

'No, no, certainly not. Don't say a word of this to him. I shall find Harry, and ask about these disturbed nights, and then watch him, trusting it may not have gone too far; but there must be dreadful excitability of brain!'

He went away, leaving Margaret to comfort Ethel as well as she could, by showing her that he had not said the mischief was done, putting her in mind that he was wont to speak strongly; and trying to make her thankful that her brother would now have such care as might avert all evil results.

'But, oh,' said Ethel, 'his success has been dearly purchased!'

CHAPTER XII.

'It hath do me mochil woe.'
'Yea hath it? Use,' quod he, 'this medicine;
Every daie this Maie or that thou dine,
Go lokin in upon the freshe daisie,
And though thou be for woe in poinct to die,
That shall full gretly lessen thee of thy pine'—CHAUCER.

THAT night Norman started from, what was not so much sleep as a trance of oppression and suffering, and beheld his father's face watching him attentively.

'Papa! What's the matter?' said he, starting up. 'Is any one ill?'

'No; no one; lie down again,' said Dr. May, possessing himself of a hand, with a burning spot in the palm, and a throbbing pulse.

'But what made you come here? Have I disturbed any one? Have I been talking?'

'Only mumbling a little, but you looked very uncomfortable.'

'But I'm not ill—what are you feeling my pulse for?' said Norman, uneasily.

'To see whether that restless sleep has quickened it.'

Norman scarcely let his father count for a moment, before he asked, 'What o'clock is it?'

'A little after twelve.'

'What does make you stay up so late, papa?'

'I often do when my arm seems likely to keep me awake. Richard has done all I want.'

'Pray don't stay here in the cold,' said Norman, with feverish impatience, as he turned upwards the cool side of his pillow. 'Good night.'

'No hurry,' said his father, still watching him.

'There's nothing the matter,' repeated the boy.

'Do you often have such unquiet nights ?'

'Oh, it does not signify. Good night,' and he tried to look settled and comfortable.

'Norman,' said his father, in a voice betraying much grief, 'it will not do to go on in this way. If your mother was here, you would not close yourself against her.'

Norman interrupted him in a voice strangled with sobs: 'It is no good saying it—I thought it would only make it worse for you; but that's it. I cannot bear the being without her.'

Dr. May was glad to see that a gush of tears followed this exclamation, as Norman hid his face under the coverings.

'My poor boy,' said he, hardly able to speak, 'only One can comfort you truly; but you must not turn from me; you must let me do what I can for you, though it is not the same.'

'I thought it would grieve you more,' said Norman, turning his face towards him again.

'What, to find my children feeling with me, and knowing what they have lost ? Surely not, Norman.'

'And it is of no use,' added Norman, hiding his face again, 'no one can comfort—'

'There you are wrong,' said Dr. May; with deep feeling; 'there is much of comfort in everything, in everybody, in kindness, in all around, if one can only open one's mind to it. But I did not come to keep you awake with such talk; I saw you were not quite well, so I came up to see about you; and now, Norman, you will not refuse to own that something is the matter.'

'I did not know it,' said Norman; 'I really believe I am well, if I could get rid of these horrible nights. I either lie awake, tumbling and tossing, or I get all sorts of unbearable dreams.'

'Aye, when I asked master Harry about you, all the answer I could get was, that he was quite used to it, and did not mind it at all. As if I asked for his sake! How fast that boy sleeps— he is fit for a midshipman's berth !'

'But do you think there is anything amiss with me ?'

'I shall know more about that to-morrow morning. Come to my room as soon as you are up, unless I come to you. Now, I have something to read before I go to bed, and I may as well try if it will put you to sleep.'

Norman's last sight that night was of the outline of his father's profile, and he was scarcely awake the next morning before Dr. May was there again.

Unwilling as he had been to give way, it was a relief to relinquish the struggle to think himself well, and to venture to lounge and dawdle, rest his heavy head, and stretch his inert limbs without fear of remark.   His father found him after breakfast lying on the sofa in the drawing-room with a Greek play by his side, telling Ethel what words to look out.

'At it again!' exclaimed Dr. May. 'Carry it away, Ethel. I will have no Latin or Greek touched these holidays.'

'You know,' said Norman, 'if I don't sap, I shall have no chance of keeping up.'

'You'll keep no where, if you don't rest.'

'It is only Euripides, and I can't do anything else,' said Norman, languidly.

'Very likely—I don't care. You have to get well first of all, and the Greek will take care of itself. Go up to Margaret. I put you in her keeping while I am gone to Whitford. After that, I dare say Richard will be very glad to have a holiday, and let you drive me to Abbotstoke.'

Norman rose, and wearily walked up-stairs, while his sister lingered to excuse herself. 'Papa, I did not think Euripides would hurt him—he knows it all so well; and he said he could not read anything else.'

'Just so, Ethel. Poor fellow, he has not spirits or energy for anything; his mind was forced into those classicalities when it wanted rest, and now it has not spring enough to turn back again.'

'Do you think him so very ill?'

'Not exactly; but there's low fever hanging about him, and we must look after him well, and I hope we may get him right. I have told Margaret about him; I can't stop any longer now.'

Norman found the baby in his sister's room, and this was just what suited him.   The Daisy showed a marked preference for her brothers; and to find her so merry and good with him, pleased and flattered him far more than his victory at school. He carried her about, danced her, whistled to her, and made her admire her pretty blue eyes in the glass most successfully, till nurse carried her off.   But perhaps he had been sent up rather too soon; for as he sat in the great chair by the fire, he was teased by the constant coming and going, all the petty cares of a large household transacted by Margaret—orders to butcher and cook—Harry racing in to ask to take Tom to the river— Tom, who was to go when his lesson was done, coming perpetually to try to repeat the same unhappy bit of *As in Præsenti*, each time in a worse whine.

'How can you bear it, Margaret?' said Norman, as she finally dismissed Tom, and laid down her account-book, taking up some delicate fancy-work. 'Mercy, here's another,' as enter a message about lamp-oil, in the midst of which Mary burst in to beg Margaret to get Miss Winter to let her go to the river with Harry and Tom.

'No, indeed, Mary, I could not think of such a thing. You had better go back to your lessons, and don't be silly,' as she looked much disposed to cry.

'No one but a Tom-boy would dream of it,' added Norman; and Mary departed disconsolate, while Margaret gave a sigh of weariness, and said, as she returned to her work, 'There, I believe I have done. I hope I was not cross with poor Mary, but it was rather too much to ask.'

'I can't think how you can help being cross to every one,' said Norman, as he took away the books she had done with.

'I am afraid I am,' said Margaret, sadly. 'It does get trying at times.'

'I should think so! This eternal worrying must be more than any one can bear; always lying there, too.'

'It is only now and then that it grows tiresome,' said Margaret. 'I am too happy to be of some use, and it is too bad to repine, but sometimes a feeling comes of its being always the same, as if a little change would be *such* a treat.'

'Arn't you very tired of lying in bed?'

'Yes, very, sometimes. I fancy—but it is only fancy—that I could move better if I was up and dressed. It has seemed more so lately, since I have been stronger.'

'When do you think they will let you get up?'

'There's the question. I believe papa thinks I might be lifted to the sofa now—and oh! how I long for it—but then Mr. Ward does not approve of my sitting up, even as I am doing now, and wants to keep me flat. Papa thinks that of no use, and likely to hurt my general health, and I believe the end of it will be that he will ask Sir Matthew Fleet's opinion.'

'Is that the man he calls Mat?'

'Yes, you know they went through the University together, and were at Edinburgh and Paris, but they have never met since he set up in London, and grew so famous. I believe it would be a great treat to papa to have him, and it would be a good thing for papa too; I don't think his arm is going on right—he does not trust to Mr. Ward's treatment, and I am sure some one else ought to see it.'

'Did you know, Margaret, that he sits up quite late, because he cannot sleep for it?'

'Yes, I hear him moving about, but don't tell him so; I would not have him guess for the world, that it kept me awake.'

'And does it?'

'Why, if I think he is awake and in pain, I cannot settle myself to sleep, but that is no matter; having no exercise, of course I don't sleep so much. But I am very anxious about him—he looks so thin, and gets so fagged—and no wonder.'

'Ah! Mr. Everard told me he was quite shocked to see him, and would hardly have known him,' and Norman groaned from the bottom of his heart.

'Well, I shall hope much from Sir Matthew's taking him in hand,' said Margaret, cheerfully; 'he will mind him, though he will not Mr. Ward.'

'I wish the holidays were over!' said Norman, with a yawn, as expressive as a sigh.

'That's not civil, on the third day,' said Margaret, smiling, 'when I am so glad to have you to look after me, so as to set Flora at liberty.'

'What, can I do you any good?' said Norman, with a shade of his former alacrity.

'To be sure you can, a great deal. Better not come near me otherwise, for I make every one into a slave. I want my morning reading now, that book on Advent, there.'

'Shall I read it to you?'

'Thank you, that's nice, and I shall get on with baby's frock.'

Norman read, but, ere long, took to yawning; Margaret begged for the book, which he willingly resigned, saying, however, that he liked it, only he was stupid. She read on aloud, till she heard a succession of heavy breathings, and saw him fast asleep, and so he continued till waked by his father's coming home.

Richard and Ethel were glad of a walk, for Margaret had found them a pleasant errand. Their Cocksmoor children could not go home to dinner between service and afternoon school, and Margaret had desired the cook to serve them up some broth in the back kitchen, to which the brother and sister were now to invite them. Mary was allowed to take her boots to Rebekah Watts, since Margaret held that goodness had better be profitable, at least at the outset; and Harry and Tom joined the party.

Norman, meantime, was driving his father—a holiday preferment highly valued in the days when Dr. May used only to assume the reins, when his spirited horses showed too much consciousness that they had a young hand over them, or when the old hack took a fit of laziness. Now, Norman needed Richard's assurance that the bay was steady, so far was he from being troubled with his ancient desire, that the steed would rear right up on his hind legs.

He could neither talk nor listen till he was clear out of the town, and found himself master of the animal, and even then the words were few, and chiefly spoken by Dr. May, until after going along about three miles of the turnpike road, he desired Norman to turn down a cross-country lane.

'Where does this lead?'

'It comes out at Abbotstoke, but I have to go to an outlying farm.'

'Papa,' said Norman, after a few minutes, 'I wish you would let me do my Greek.'

'Is that what you have been pondering all this time? What, may not the *bonus Homerus* slumber sometimes?'

'It is not Homer, it is Euripides. I do assure you, papa, it is no trouble, and I get much worse without it.'

'Well, stop here, the road grows so bad that we will walk, and let the boy lead the horse to meet us at Woodcote.'

Norman followed his father down a steep narrow lane, little better than a stony water-course, and began to repeat, 'If you would but let me do my work! I've got nothing else to do, and now they have put me up, I should not like not to keep my place.'

'Very likely, but—hollo—how swelled this is!' said Dr. May, as they came to the bottom of the valley, where a stream rushed along, coloured with a turbid creamy yellow, making little whirl-pools where it crossed the road, and brawling loudly just above where it roared and foamed between two steep banks of rock, crossed by a foot-bridge of planks, guarded by a handrail of rough poles. The Doctor had traversed it, and gone a few paces beyond, when, looking back, he saw Norman very pale, with one foot on the plank, and one hand grasping the rail. He came back, and held out his hand, which Norman gladly caught at, but no sooner was the other side attained, than the boy, though he gasped with relief, exclaimed, 'This is too bad! Wait one moment, please, and let me go back.'

He tried, but the first touch of the shaking rail, and glance at the chasm, disconcerted him, and his father, seeing his white cheeks and rigid lips, said, 'Stop, Norman, don't try it. You are not fit,' he added, as the boy came to him reluctantly.

'I can't bear to be such a wretch!' said he. 'I never used to be. I will not—let me conquer it;' and he was turning back, but the Doctor took his arm, saying, decidedly, 'No, I won't have it done. You are only making it worse, by putting a force on yourself.'

But the further Norman was from the bridge, the more displeased he was with himself, and more anxious to dare it again. 'There's no bearing it,' he muttered; 'let me only run back. I'll overtake you. I must do it if no one looks on.'

'No such thing,' said the Doctor, holding him fast. 'If you do, you'll have it all over again at night.'

'That's better than to know I am worse than Tom.'

'I tell you, Norman, it is no such thing. You will recover your tone if you will only do as you are told, but your nerves have had a severe shock, and when you force yourself in this way, you only increase the mischief.'

'Nerves,' muttered Norman, disdainfully; 'I thought they were only fit for fine ladies.'

Dr. May smiled. 'Well, will it content you if I promise that as soon as I see fit, I'll bring you here, and let you march over that bridge as often as you like?'

'I suppose I must be contented, but I don't like to feel like a fool.'

'You need not, while the moral determination is sound.'

'But my Greek, papa.'

'At it again—I declare, Norman, you are the worst patient I ever had!'

Norman made no answer, and Dr. May presently said, 'Well, let me hear what you have to say about it. I assure you it is not that I don't want you to get on, but that I see you are in great need of rest.'

'Thank you, papa. I know you mean it for my good, but I don't think you do know how horrid it is. I have got nothing on earth to do or care for—the school work comes quite easy to me, and I'm sure thinking is worse; and then,' Norman spoke vehemently, 'now they have put me up, it will never do to be beaten, and all the four others ought to be able to do it. I did not want or expect to be Dux, but now I am, you could not bear me not to keep my place, and to miss the Randall scholarship, as I certainly shall, if I do not work these whole holidays.'

'Norman, I know it,' said his father, kindly. 'I am very sorry for you, and I know I am asking of you what I could not have done at your age—indeed, I don't believe I could have done it for you a few months ago. It is my fault that you have been let alone, to have an overstrain and pressure on your mind, when you were not fit for it, and I cannot see any remedy but complete freedom from work. At the same time, if you fret and harass yourself about being surpassed, that is, as you say, much worse for you than Latin and Greek. Perhaps I may be wrong, and study might not do you the harm I think it would; at any rate, it is better than tormenting yourself about next half year, so I will not positively forbid it, but I think you had much better let it alone. I don't want to make it a matter of duty. I only tell you this, that you may set your mind at rest as far as I am concerned. If you do lose your place, I will consider it as my own doing, and not be disappointed. I had rather see you a healthy, vigórous, useful man, than a poor puling nervous wretch of a scholar, if you were to get all the prizes in the University.'

Norman made a little murmuring sound of assent, and both were silent for some moments, then he said: 'Then you will not be displeased, papa, if I do read, as long as I feel it does me no harm.'

'I told you I don't mean to make it a matter of obedience. Do as you please—I had rather you read than vexed yourself.'

'I am glad of it. Thank you, papa,' said Norman, in a much-cheered voice.

They had, in the meantime, been mounting a rising ground, clothed with stunted wood, and came out on a wide heath, brown with dead bracken; a hollow, traced by the tops of leafless trees, marked the course of the stream that traversed it, and the inequalities of ground becoming more rugged in outlines and greyer in colouring as they receded, till they were closed by a dark fir wood, beyond which rose in extreme distance, the grand mass of Welsh mountain heads, purpled against the evening sky, except where the crowning peaks bore a veil of snow. Behind, the sky was pure gold, gradually shading into pale green, and then into clear light wintry blue, while the sun setting behind two of the loftiest, seemed to confound their outlines, and blend them in one flood of soft hazy brightness. Dr. May looked at his son, and saw his face clear up, his brow expand, and his lips unclose with admiration.

'Yes,' said the Doctor, 'it is very fine, is it not? I used to bring mamma here now and then for a treat, because it put her in mind of her Scottish hills. Well, yours are the golden hills of heaven, now, my Maggie!' he added, hardly knowing that he spoke aloud. Norman's throat swelled, as he looked up in his face, then cast down his eyes hastily to hide the tears that had gathered on his eyelashes.

'I'll leave you here,' said Dr. May; 'I have to go to a farm-house close by, in the hollow behind us, there's a girl recovering from a fever. I'll not be ten minutes, so wait here.'

When he came back, Norman was still where he had left him, gazing earnestly, and the tears standing on his cheeks. He did not move till his father laid his hand on his shoulder—they walked away together without a word, and scarcely spoke all the way home.

Dr. May went to Margaret, and talked to her of Norman's fine character, and intense affection for his mother, the determined temper, and quietly borne grief, for which the Doctor seemed to have worked himself into a perfect enthusiasm of admiration; but lamenting that he could not tell what to do with him—study or no study hurt him alike—and he dreaded to see health and spirits shattered for ever. They tried to devise change of scene, but it did not seem possible just at present; and Margaret, besides her fears for Norman, was much grieved to see this added to her father's troubles.

At night Dr. May again went up to see whether Norman, whom he had moved into Margaret's former room, were again suffering from fever. He found him asleep in a restless attitude, as if he had just dropped off, and waking almost at the instant of his entrance, he exclaimed,—'Is it you? I thought it was mamma. She said it was all ambition.'

Then starting, and looking round the room, and at his father, he collected himself, and said, with a slight smile,—'I didn't know I had been asleep. I was awake just now, thinking about it. Papa, I'll give it up. I'll try to put next half out of my head, and not mind if they do pass me.'

'That's right, my boy,' said the Doctor.

'At least if Cheviot and Forder do, for they ought. I only hope Anderson won't. I can stand anything but that. But that is nonsense too.'

'You are quite right, Norman,' said the Doctor; 'and it is a great relief to me that you see the thing so sensibly.'

'No, I don't see it sensibly at all, papa. I hate it all the time, and I don't know whether I can keep from thinking of it, when I have nothing to do; but I see it is wrong. I thought all ambition and nonsense was gone out of me, when I cared so little for the examination; but now I see, though I did not want to be made first, I can't bear not to be first; and that's the old story, just as *she* used to tell me to guard against ambition. So I'll take my chance; and if I should get put down, why 'twas not fair that I should be put up, and it is what I ought to be, and serves me right into the bargain—'

'Well, that's the best sort of sense, your mother's sense,' said the Doctor, more affected than he liked to show. 'No wonder she came to you in your dream, Norman, my boy, if you had come to such a resolution. I was half in hopes you had some such notion when I came upon you on Far-view Down.'

' I think that sky did it,' said Norman, in a low voice; ' it made me think of her in a different way—and what you said too.'

' What did I say ?   I don't remember.'

But Norman could not repeat the words, and only murmured ' golden hills'—It was enough.

' I see,' said the Doctor, ' you had dwelt on the blank here, not taken home what it is to her.'

' Aye'—almost sobbed Norman, ' I never could before—that made me,' after a long silence, ' and then I know how foolish I was, and how she would say it was wrong to make this fuss, when you did not like it, about my place, and that it was not for the sake of my duty, but of ambition; I knew that, but till I went to bed to-night, I could not tell whether I could make up my mind, so I would say nothing.'

CHAPTER XIII.

' The days are sad, it is the Holy tide,
    When flowers have ceased to blow and birds to sing.'—F. TENNYSON.

IT had been a hard struggle to give up all thoughts of study, and Norman was not at first rewarded for it, but rather exemplified the truth of his own assertion, that he was worse without it; for when this sole occupation for his mind was taken away, he drooped still more. He would willingly have shown his father that he was not discontented, but he was too entirely unnerved to be either cheerful or capable of entering with interest into any occupation.   If he had been positively ill, the task would have been easier; but the low intermittent fever that hung about him did not confine him to bed, only kept him lounging, listless and forlorn, through the weary day, not always able to go out with his father, and on Christmas-day unfit even for Church.

All this made the want of his mother, and the vacancy in his home, still more evident, and nothing was capable of relieving his sadness, but his father's kindness, which was a continual surprise to him.   Dr. May was a parent who could not fail to be loved and honoured; but, as a busy man, trusting all at home to his wife, he had only appeared to his children either as a merry playfellow, or as a stern paternal authority, not often in the intermediate light of guiding friend, or gentle guardian; and it affected Norman exceedingly to find himself, a tall school-boy, watched and soothed with motherly tenderness and affection; with complete comprehension of his feelings, and delicate care of them. His father's solicitude and sympathy were round him day and night; and this, in the midst of so much toil, pain, grief, and anxiety of his own, that Norman might well feel overwhelmed with the swelling, inexpressible feelings of grateful affection.

How could his father know exactly what he would like—say the very things he was thinking—see that his depression was not wilful repining—find exactly what best soothed him! He wondered, but he could not have said so to any one, only his eye brightened; and, as his sisters remarked, he never seemed half so uncomfortable when papa was in the room. Indeed, the certainty that his father felt the sorrow as acutely as himself, was one reason of his opening to him. He could not feel that his brothers and sisters did so, for, outwardly, their habits were unaltered, their spirits not lowered, their relish for things around much the same as before, and this had given Norman a sense of isolation. With his father it was different. Norman knew he could never appreciate what the bereavement was to him—he saw its traces in almost every word and look, and yet perceived that something sustained and consoled him, though not in the way of forgetfulness. Now and then Norman caught at what gave this comfort, and it might be hoped he would do so increasingly; though, on this Christmas-day, Margaret felt very sad about him, as she watched him sitting over the fire, cowering with chilliness and headache, while every one was gone to Church, and saw that the reading of the service with her had been more of a trouble than a solace.

She tried to think it bodily ailment, and strove hard not to pine for her mother, to comfort them both, and say the fond words of refreshing, cheering pity, that would have made all light to bear. Margaret's home Christmas was so spent in caring for brother, father, and children, that she had hardly time to dwell on the sad change that had befallen herself.

Christmas was a season that none of them knew well how to meet: Blanche was overheard saying to Mary, that she wished it would not come, and Mary, shaking her head, and answering that she was afraid that was naughty, but it was very tiresome to have no fun. Margaret did her best up-stairs, and Richard down-stairs, by the help of prints and hymns, to make the children think of the true joy of Christmas; and in the evening their father gathered them round, and told them the stories of the Shepherds and of the Wise Men, till Mary and Blanche agreed, as they went up to bed, that it had been a very happy evening.

The next day Harry discomfited the school-room by bursting in with the news, that ' Louisa and Fanny Anderson were bearing down on the front door.' Ethel and Flora were obliged to appear in the drawing-room, where they were greeted by two girls, rather older than themselves. A whole shower of inquiries for Dr. May, for Margaret, and for the dear little baby, were first poured out; then came hopes that Norman was well, as they had not seen him at Church yesterday.

'Thank you; he was kept at home by a bad headache, but it is better to-day.'

'We came to congratulate you on his success—we could not help it—it must have been such a pleasure to you.'

'That it was!' exclaimed Ethel, pleased at participation in her rejoicing. 'We were so surprised.'

Flora gave a glance of warning, but Ethel's short-sighted eyes were beyond the range of correspondence, and Miss Anderson continued. 'It must have been a delightful surprise. We could hardly believe it when Harvey came in and told us. Every one thought Forder was sure, but they all were put out by the questions of general information—those were all Mr. Everard's doing.'

'Mr. Everard was very much struck with Norman's knowledge and scholarship too,' said Flora.

'So every one says. It was all Mr. Everard's doing, Miss Harrison told mamma; but, for my part, I am very glad for the sake of Stoneborough; I like a town boy to be at the head.'

'Norman was sorry for Forder and Cheviot—' began Ethel. Flora tried to stop her, but Louisa Anderson caught at what she said, and looked eagerly for more. 'He felt,' said she, only thinking of exalting her generous brother, 'as if it was hardly right, when they are so much his seniors, and he could scarcely enjoy it.'

'Ah! that is just what people say,' replied Louisa. 'But it must be very gratifying to you; and it makes him certain of the Randall scholarship, too, I suppose. It is a great thing for him! He must have worked very hard.'

'Yes, that he has,' said Flora; 'he is so fond of study, and that goes half-way.'

'So is dear Harvey. How earnest he is over his books! Mamma sometimes says, "Now, Harvey dear, you'll be quite stupified—you'll be ill; I really shall get Dr. May to forbid you." I suppose Norman is very busy too; it is quite the fashion for boys not to be idle now.'

'Poor Norman can't help it,' said Ethel, piteously. 'Papa will not hear of his doing any Latin or Greek these whole holidays.'

'He thinks he will come to it better again for entire rest,' said Flora, launching another look at her sister, which again fell short

A great deal of polite inquiry whether they were uneasy about him followed, mixed with a little boasting of dear Harvey's diligence.

'By-the-bye, Ethel, it is you that are the great patroness of the wild Cocksmoor children—are not you?'

Ethel coloured, and mumbled, and Flora answered for her. 'Richard and Ethel have been there once or twice. You know our under nursery-maid is a Cocksmoor girl.'

'Well, mamma said she could not think how Miss May could take one from thence. The whole place is full of thieves, and do you know, Bessie Boulder has lost her gold pencil-case.'

'Has she?' said Flora.

'And she had it on Sunday when she was teaching her class.'

'Oh!' cried Ethel, vehemently; 'surely she does not suspect any of those poor children!'

'I only know such a thing never happened at school before,' said Fanny, 'and I shall never take anything valuable there again.'

'But is she sure she lost it at school?'

'O yes, quite certain. She will not accuse any one, but it is not comfortable. And how those children do behave at church!'

'Poor things! they have been sadly neglected,' said Flora.

'They are quite spoiling the rest, and they are such figures! Why don't you, at least, make them cut their hair? You know it is the rule of the school.'

'I know, but half the girls in the first class wear it long.'

'O yes, but those are the superior people, that one would not be strict with, and they dress it so nicely too. Now these are like little savages.'

'Richard thinks it might drive them away to insist at first,' said Ethel; 'we will try to bring it about in time.'

'Well, Mrs. Ledwich is nearly resolved to insist, so you had better be warned, Ethel. She cannot suffer such untidiness and rags to spoil the appearance of the school, and, I assure you, it is quite unpleasant to the teachers.'

'I wish they would give them all to me!' said Ethel. 'But I do hope Mrs. Ledwich will have patience with them, for they are only to be gained gently.'

The visitors took their leave, and the two sisters began exclaiming—Ethel at their dislike of her *protégés*, and Flora at what they had said of Norman. 'And you, Ethel, how could you go and tell them we were surprised, and Norman thought it was hard on the other boys? They'll have it all over the town that he got it unjustly, and knows it, as they say already it was partiality of Mr. Everard's.'

'O no, no, they never can be so bad!'. cried Ethel; 'they must have understood better that it was his noble humility and generosity.'

'They understand anything noble! No indeed! They think

every one like their own beautiful brother! I knew what they came for all the time; they wanted to know whether Norman was able to work these holidays, and you told them the very thing they wanted to hear. How they will rejoice with that Harvey, and make sure of the Randall!'

'O no, no!' cried Ethel; 'Norman must get that!'

'I don't think he will,' said Flora, 'losing all this time, while they are working. It cannot be helped, of course, but it is a great pity.'

'I almost wish he had not been put up at all, if it is to end in this way,' said Ethel. 'It is very provoking, and to have them triumphing as they will! There's no bearing it!'

'Norman, certainly, is not at all well, poor fellow,' said Flora, 'and I suppose he wants rest, but I wish papa would let him do what he can. It would be much better for him than moping about as he is always doing now; and the disappointment of losing his place will be grievous, though now he fancies he does not care for it.'

'I wonder when he will ever care for anything again. All I read and tell him only seems to tease him, though he tries to thank me.'

'There is a strange apathy about him,' said Flora, 'but I believe it is chiefly for want of exertion. I should like to rouse him if papa would let me; I know I could, by telling him how these Andersons are reckoning on his getting down. If he does, I shall be ready to run away, that I may never meet any one here again.'

Ethel was very unhappy till she was able to pour all this trouble out to Margaret, and worked herself almost into crying about Norman's being passed by 'that Harvey,' and his sisters exulting, and papa being vexed, and Norman losing time and not caring.

'There you are wrong,' said Margaret; 'Norman did care very much, and it was not till he had seen clearly that it was a matter of duty to do as papa thought right, and not agitate his mind about his chances of keeping up, that he could bear to give up his work;' and she told Ethel a little of what had passed.

Ethel was much struck. 'But oh! Margaret, it is very hard, just to have him put up for the sake of being put down, and pleasing the Andersons!'

'Dear Ethel, why should you mind so much about the Andersons? May they not care about their brother as we do for ours?'

'Such a brother to care about!' said Ethel.

'But I suppose they may like him the best,' said Margaret, smiling.

'I suppose they do,' said Ethel, grudgingly; 'but still I cannot bear to see Norman doing nothing, and know Harvey Anderson will beat him.'

'Surely you had rather he did nothing than made himself ill.'

'To be sure, but I wish it wasn't so.'

'Yes; but, Ethel, whose doing is his getting into this state?'

Ethel looked grave. 'It was wrong of me,' said she, 'but then papa is not sure that Greek would hurt him.'

'Not sure, but he thinks it not wise to run the risk. But, Ethel dear, why are you so bent on his being Dux at all costs?'

'It would be horrid if he was not.'

'Don't you remember you used to say that outward praise or honour was not to be cared for as long as one did one's duty, and that it might be a temptation?'

'Yes, I know I did,' said Ethel, faltering, 'but that was for one's self.'

'It is harder, I think, to feel so about those we care for,' said Margaret; 'but after all, this is just what will show whether our pride in Norman is the right true loving pride, or whether it is only the family vanity of triumphing over the Andersons.'

Ethel hung her head. 'There's some of that,' she said, 'but it is not all. No—I don't want to triumph over them, nobody would do that.'

'Not outwardly perhaps, but in their hearts.'

'I can't tell,' said Ethel, 'but it is the being triumphed over that I cannot bear.'

'Perhaps this is all a lesson in humility for us,' said Margaret. 'It is teaching us, "Whosoever exalteth himself shall be abased, and he that humbleth himself shall be exalted."'

Ethel was silent for some little space, then suddenly exclaimed, 'And you think he will really be put down?'

Margaret seemed to have been talking with little effect, but she kept her patience, and answered, 'I cannot guess, Ethel, but I'll tell you one thing—I think there's much more chance if he comes to his work fresh and vigorous after a rest, than if he went on dulling himself with it all this time.'

With which Ethel was so far appeased that she promised to think as little as she could of the Andersons; and a walk with Richard to Cocksmoor turned the current of her thoughts. They had caught some more Sunday-school children by the help of Margaret's broth, but it was up-hill work; the servants did not like such guests in the kitchen, and they were still less welcome at school.

'What do you think I heard, Ethel?' said Flora, the next Sunday, as they joined each other in the walk from School to

Church; 'I heard Miss Graves say to Miss Boulder, "I declare I must remonstrate. I undertook to instruct a national, not a ragged school;" and then Miss Boulder shook out her fine watered silk and said, "It positively is improper to place ladies in contact with such squalid objects." '

'Ladies!' cried Ethel. 'A stationer's daughter and a banker's clerk's! Why do they come to teach at school at all?'

'Because our example makes it genteel,' said Flora.

'I hope you did something more in hopes of making it genteel.'

'I caught one of your ragged regiment with her frock gaping behind, and pinned it up. Such rags as there were under it! O Ethel!'

'Which was it?'

'That merry Irish-looking child. I don't know her name.'

'Oh! it is a real charming Irish name, Una M'Carthy. I am so glad you did it, Flora. I hope they were ashamed.'

'I doubt whether it will do good. We are sure of our station and can do anything—they are struggling to be ladies.'

'But we ought not to talk of them any more, Flora; here we are a most at the Churchyard.'

The Tuesday of this week was appointed for the visit of the London surgeon, Sir Matthew Fleet, and the expectation caused Dr. May to talk much to Margaret of old times, and the days of his courtship, when it had been his favourite project that his friend and fellow-student should marry Flora Mackenzie, and there had been a promising degree of liking, but 'Mat' had been obliged to be prudent, and had ended by never marrying at all. This the Doctor, as well as his daughters, believed was for the sake of Aunt Flora, and thus the girls were a good deal excited about his coming, almost as much on his own account as because they considered him as the arbiter of Margaret's fate. He only came in time for a seven o'clock dinner, and Margaret did not see him that night, but heard enough from her sisters, when they came up to tell the history of their guest, and of the first set dinner when Flora had acted as lady of the house. The dinner, it appeared, had gone off very well. Flora had managed admirably, and the only mishap was some awkward carving of Ethel's which had caused the dish to be changed with Norman. As to the guest, Flora said he was very good-looking and agreeable. Ethel abruptly pronounced, 'I am very glad Aunt Flora married Uncle Arnott instead.'

'I can't think why,' said Flora. 'I never saw a person of pleasanter manners.'

'Did they talk of old times?' said Margaret.

'No,' said Ethel; 'that was the thing.'

'You would not have them talk of those matters in the middle of dinner,' said Flora.

'No,' again said Ethel; 'but papa has a way—don't you know, Margaret, how one can tell in a moment if it is company talk.'

'What was the conversation about?' said Margaret.

'They talked over some of their old fellow-students,' said Flora.

'Yes,' said Ethel; 'and then when papa told him that beautiful history of Dr. Spencer going to take care of those poor emigrants in the fever, what do you think he said? " Yes, Spencer was always doing extravagant things." Fancy that to papa, who can hardly speak of it without having to wipe his spectacles, and who so longs to hear of Dr. Spencer.'

'And what did he say?'

'Nothing; so Flora and Sir Matthew got to pictures and all that sort of thing, and it was all company talk after that.'

'Most entertaining in its kind,' said Flora: 'but—oh, Norman!' as he entered—'why they are not out of the dining-room yet!'

'No; they are talking of some new invention, and most likely will not come for an hour.'

'Are you going to bed?'

'Papa followed me out of the dining-room to tell me to do so after tea.'

'Then sit down there, and I'll go and make some, and let it come up with Margaret's. Come, Ethel. Good night, Norman. Is your head aching to-night?'

'Not much, now I have got out of the dining-room.'

'It would have been wiser not to have gone in,' said Flora, leaving the room.

'It was not the dinner, but the man,' said Norman. 'It is incomprehensible to me how my father could take to him. I'd as soon have Harvey Anderson for a friend!'

'You are like me,' said Ethel, 'in being glad he is not our uncle.'

'He presume to think of falling in love with Aunt Flora!' cried Norman, indignantly.

'Why, what is the matter with him?' asked Margaret. 'I can't find much ground for Ethel's dislike, and Flora is pleased.'

'She did not hear the worst, nor you either, Ethel,' said Norman. 'I could not stand the cold hard way he spoke of hospital patients. I am sure he thinks poor people nothing but a study, and rich ones nothing but a profit. And his half sneers! But what I hated most was his way of avoiding discussions. When he saw he had said what would not go down with papa, he did not honestly stand up to the point, and argue it out, but seemed to have no mind of his own, and to be only talking to please papa—but not knowing how to do it. He understand my father indeed!'

Norman's indignation had quite revived him, and Margaret was much entertained with the conflicting opinions. The next was Richard's, when he came in late to wish her good night, after he had been attending on Sir Matthew's examination of his father's arm. He did nothing but admire the surgeon's delicacy of touch and understanding of the case, his view agreeing much better with Dr. May's own than with Mr. Ward's. Dr. May had never been entirely satisfied with the present mode of treatment, and Richard was much struck by hearing him say, in answer to Sir Matthew, that he knew his recovery might have been more speedy and less painful if he had been able to attend to it at first, or to afford time for being longer laid up. A change of treatment was now to be made, likely soon to relieve the pain, to be less tedious and troublesome, and to bring about a complete cure in three or four months at latest. In hearing such tidings, there could be little thought of the person who brought them, and Margaret did not, till the last moment, learn that Richard thought Sir Matthew very clever and sensible, and certain to understand her case. Her last visitor was her father: 'Asleep, Margaret? I thought I had better go to Norman first in case he should be awake.'

'Was he?'

'Yes, but his pulse is better to-night. He was lying awake to hear what Fleet thought of me. I suppose Richard told you.'

'Yes, dear papa, what a comfort it is!'

'Those fellows in London do keep up to the mark! But I would not be there for something. I never saw a man so altered. However, if he can only do for you as well—but it is of no use talking about it. I may trust you to keep yourself calm, my dear?'

'I am trying—indeed I am, dear papa. If you could help being anxious for me—though I know it is worse for you, for I only have to lie still, and you have to settle for me. But I have been thinking how well off I am, able to enjoy so much, and be employed all day long. It is nothing to compare with that poor girl you told me of, and you need not be unhappy for me. I have some verses to say over to myself to-night:

> " O Lord my God, do Thou Thy holy will,
> I will lie still,
> I will not stir, lest I forsake Thine arm
> And break the charm
> That lulls me, clinging to my Father's breast
> In perfect rest."

Is not that comfortable?'

'My child—my dear child—I will say no more, lest I should

break your sweet peace with my impatience. I will strive for the same temper, my Margaret. Bless you, dearest, good-night.'

After a night spent in waking intervals of such thoughts, Margaret found the ordinary morning, and the talk she could not escape, somewhat oppressive. Her brothers and sisters disturbed her by their open expressions of hope and anxiety; she dreaded to have the balance of tranquillity overset; and then blamed herself for selfishness in not being as ready to attend to them as usual. Ethel and Norman came up after breakfast, their aversion by no means decreased by further acquaintance. Ethel was highly indignant at the tone in which he had exclaimed, 'What, May, have you one as young as this?' on discovering the existence of the baby; and when Norman observed that was not so atrocious either, she proceeded, 'You did not hear the contemptuous compassionate tone when he asked papa what he meant to do with all these boys.'

'I'm glad he has not to settle,' said Norman.

'Papa said Harry was to be a sailor, and he said it was a good way to save expenses of education—a good thing.'

'No doubt,' said Norman, 'he thinks papa only wants to get rid of us, or if not, that it is an amiable weakness.'

'But I can't see anything so shocking in this,' said Margaret.

'It is not the words,' said Norman, 'the look and tone convey it; but there are different opinions. Flora is quite smitten with him, he talks so politely to her.'

'And Blanche!' said Ethel. 'The little affected pussy-cat made a set at him, bridled and talked in her mincing voice, with all her airs, and made him take a great deal of notice of her.'

Nurse here came to prepare for the surgeon's visit.

It was over, and Margaret awaited the judgment. Sir Matthew had spoken hopefully to her, but she feared to fasten hopes on what might have no meaning, and could rely on nothing, till she had seen her father, who never kept back his genuine opinion, and would least of all from her. She found her spirits too much agitated to talk to her sisters, and quietly begged them to let her be quite alone till the consultation was over, and she lay trying to prepare herself to submit thankfully, whether she might be bidden to resign herself to helplessness, or to let her mind open once more to visions of joyous usefulness. Every step she hoped would prove to be her father's approach, and the longest hour of her life was that before he entered her room. His face said that the tidings were good, and yet she could not ask.

'Well, Margaret, I am glad we had him down. He thinks you may get about again, though it may be a long time first.'

'Does he—oh papa!' and the colour spread over her face, as she squeezed his hand very fast.

'He has known the use of the limbs return almost suddenly after even a year or two,' and Dr. May gave her the grounds of the opinion, and an account of other like cases, which he said had convinced him, 'though, my poor child,' he said, 'I feared the harm I had done you was irremediable, but thanks—' He turned away his face, and the clasp of their hands spoke the rest.

Presently he told Margaret that she was no longer to be kept prostrate, but she was to do exactly as was most comfortable to her, avoiding nothing but fatigue. She might be lifted to the sofa the next day, and if that agreed with her, she might be carried down-stairs.

This, in itself, after she had been confined to her bed for three months, was a release from captivity, and all the brothers and sisters rejoiced as if she was actually on her feet again. Richard betook himself to constructing a reading-frame for the sofa; Harry tormented Miss Winter by insisting on a holiday for the others, and gained the day by an appeal to his father; then declared he should go and tell Mr. Wilmot the good news; and Norman, quite enlivened, took up his hat, and said he would come too.

In all his joy, however, Dr. May could not cease bewailing the alteration in his old friend, and spent half the evening in telling Margaret how different he had once been, in terms little less measured than Ethel's: 'I never saw such a change. Mat Fleet was one of the most warm, open-hearted fellows in the world, up to anything. I can hardly believe he is the same—turned into a mere machine, with a moving spring of self-interest! I don't believe he cares a rush for any living thing! Except for your sake, Margaret, I wish I had never seen him again, and only remembered him as he was at Edinburgh, as I remember dear old Spencer. It is a grievous thing! Ruined entirely! No doubt that London life must be trying—the constant change and bewilderment of patients preventing much individual care and interest. It must be very hardening. No family ties either, nothing to look to but pushing his way. Yes! there's great excuse for poor Mat. I never knew fully till now the blessing it was that your dear mother was willing to take me so early, and that this place was open to me with all its home connexions and interests. I am glad I never had anything to do with London!'

And when he was alone with Norman, he could not help saying, 'Norman, my boy, I'm more glad than ever you yielded to me about your Greek these holidays, and for the reason you did. Take care the love of rising and pushing never gets hold of you; there's nothing that faster changes a man from his better self.'

Meanwhile, Sir Matthew Fleet had met another old college friend in London, and was answering his inquiries for the Dick May of ancient times.

'Poor May! I never saw a man so thrown away. With his talent and acuteness, he might be the most eminent man of his day, if he had only known how to use them. But he was always the same careless, soft-hearted fellow, never knowing how to do himself any good, and he is the same still, not a day older nor wiser. It was a fatal thing for him that there was that country practice ready for him to step into, and even of that he does not make as good a thing as he might. Of course he married early, and there he is, left a widower with a house full of children—screaming babies, and great tall sons growing up, and he without a notion what he shall do with them, as heedless as ever—saving nothing, of course. I always knew it was what he would come to, if he would persist in burying himself in that wretched little country town, but I hardly thought, after all he has gone through, to find him such a mere boy still. And yet he is one of the cleverest men I ever met—with such talent, and such thorough knowledge of his profession, that it does one good to hear him talk. Poor May! I am sorry for him, he might have been anything, but that early marriage and country practice were the ruin of him.'

CHAPTER XIV.

'To thee, dear maid, each kindly wile
    Was known, that elder sisters know,
To check the unseasonable smile
    With warning hand and serious brow.

'From dream to dream with her to rove,
    Like fairy nurse with hermit child;
Teach her to think, to pray, to love,
    Make grief less bitter, joy less wild.'
                LINES ON A MONUMENT AT LICHFIELD.

SIR MATTHEW FLEET'S visit seemed like a turning-point with the May family, rousing and giving them revived hopes. Norman began to shake off his extreme languor and depression, the Doctor was relieved from much of the wearing suffering from his hurt, and his despondency as to Margaret's ultimate recovery had been driven away. The experiment of taking her up succeeded so well, that on Sunday she was fully attired, 'fit to receive company.' As she lay on the sofa there seemed an advance toward recovery. Much sweet coquetry was expended in trying to look her best for her father; and her best was very well, for though the brilliant bloom of health was gone, her cheeks had not lost their

K 2

pretty rounded contour, and still had some rosiness, while her large bright blue eyes smiled and sparkled. A screen shut out the rest of the room, making a sort of little parlour round the fire, where sundry of the family were visiting her after coming home from church in the afternoon. Ethel was in a vehement state of indignation at what had that day happened at school. 'Did you ever hear anything like it! When the point was, to teach the poor things to be Christians, to turn them back, because their hair was not regulation length.'

'What's that? Who did?' said Dr. May, coming in from his own room, where he had heard a few words.

'Mrs. Ledwich. She sent back three of the Cocksmoor children this morning. It seems she warned them last Sunday without saying a word to us.'

'Sent them back from church,' said the Doctor.

'Not exactly from church,' said Margaret.

'It is the same in effect,' said Ethel, 'to turn them from school; for if they did try to go alone, the pew-openers would drive them out.'

'It is a wretched state of things!' said Dr. May, who never wanted much provocation to begin storming about parish affairs. 'When I am churchwarden again, I'll see what can be done about the seats; but it's no sort of use, while Ramsden goes on as he does.'

'Now my poor children are done for!' said Ethel. 'They will never come again. And it's horrid, papa; there are lots of town children who wear immense long plaits of hair, and Mrs. Ledwich never interferes with them. It is entirely to drive the poor Cocksmoor ones away—for nothing else, and all out of Fanny Anderson's chatter.'

'Ethel, my dear,' said Margaret, pleadingly.

'Didn't I tell you, Margaret, how, as soon as Flora knew what Mrs. Ledwich was going to do, she went and told her this was the children's only chance, and if we affronted them for a trifle, there would be no hope of getting them back. She said she was sorry, if we were interested for them, but rules must not be broken; and when Flora spoke of all who do wear long hair unmolested, she shuffled and said, for the sake of the teachers, as well as the other children, rags and dirt could not be allowed; and then she brought up the old story of Miss Boulder's pencil, though she has found it again, and ended by saying Fanny Anderson told her it was a serious annoyance to the teachers, and she was sure we should agree with her, that something was due to voluntary assistants and subscribers.'

'I am afraid there has been a regular set at them,' said Margaret, 'and perhaps they are troublesome, poor things.'

'As if school keeping were for luxury!' said Dr. May. 'It is the worst thing I have heard of Mrs. Ledwich yet! One's blood boils to think of those poor children being cast off because our fine young ladies are too grand to teach them! The clergyman leaving his work to a set of conceited women, and they turning their backs on ignorance, when it comes to their door. Voluntary subscribers, indeed! I've a great mind I'll be one no longer.'

'Oh! papa, that would not be fair—' began Ethel; but Margaret knew he would not act on this, squeezed her hand, and silenced her.

'One thing I've said, and I'll hold to it,' continued Dr. May; 'if they outvote Wilmot again in your Ladies' Committee, I'll have no more to do with them, as sure as my name's Dick May. It is a scandal the way things are done here!'

'Papa,' said Richard, who had all the time been standing silent, 'Ethel and I have been thinking, if you approved, whether we could not do something towards teaching the Cocksmoor children, and breaking them in for the Sunday school.'

What a bound Ethel's heart gave, and how full of congratulation and sympathy was the pressure of Margaret's hand!

'What did you think of doing?' said the Doctor.

Ethel burnt to reply, but her sister's hand admonished her to remember her compact. Richard answered, 'We thought of trying to get a room, and going perhaps once or twice a week to give them a little teaching. It would be little enough, but it might do something towards civilizing them, and making them wish for more.'

'How do you propose to get a room?'

'I have reconnoitred, and I think I know a cottage with a tolerable kitchen, which I dare say we might hire for an afternoon for sixpence.'

Ethel, unable to bear it any longer, threw herself forward, and sitting on the ground at her father's feet, exclaimed, 'O papa! papa! do say we may!'

'What's all this about?' said the Doctor, surprised.

'Oh! you don't know how I have thought of it day and night these two months!'

'What! Ethel, have a fancy for two whole months, and the whole house not hear of it!' said her father, with a rather provoking look of incredulity.

'Richard was afraid of bothering you, and wouldn't let me. But do speak, papa. May we?'

'I don't see any objection.'

She clasped her hands in ecstacy. 'Thank you! thank you, papa! Oh! Ritchie! Oh! Margaret!' cried she, in a breathless voice of transport.

'You have worked yourself up to a fine pass,' said the Doctor, patting the agitated girl fondly, as she leant against his knee. 'Remember, slow and steady.'

'I've got Richard to help me,' said Ethel.

'Sufficient guarantee,' said her father, smiling archly as he looked up to his son, whose fair face had coloured deep red. 'You will keep the Unready in order, Ritchie.'

'He does,' said Margaret; 'he has taken her education into his hands, and I really believe he has taught her to hold up her frock and stick in pins.'

'And to know her right hand from her left, eh, Ethel? Well, you deserve some credit, then. Suppose we ask Mr. Wilmot to tea, and talk it over.'

'O thank you, papa! When shall it be? To-morrow?'

'Yes, if you like. I have to go to the town-council meeting, and am not going into the country, so I shall be in early.'

'Thank you. O how very nice!'

'And what about cost? Do you expect to rob me?'

'If you would help us,' said Ethel, with an odd shy manner; 'wo meant to make what we have go as far as may be, but mine is only fifteen and sixpence.'

'Well, you must make interest with Margaret for the turn-out of my pocket to-morrow.'

'Thank you, we are very much obliged,' said the brother and sister, earnestly; 'that is more than we expected.'

'Ha! don't thank too soon. Suppose to-morrow should be a blank day.'

'Oh, it won't!' said Ethel. 'I shall tell Norman to make you go to paying people.'

'There's avarice!' said the Doctor. 'But look you here, Ethel, if you'll take my advice, you'll make your bargain for Tuesday. I have a note appointing me to call at Abbotstoke Grange on Mr. Rivers, at twelve o'clock, on Tuesday. What do you think of that, Ethel? An old banker, rich enough for his daughter to curl her hair in bank notes. If I were you, I'd make a bargain for him.'

'If he had nothing the matter with him, and I only got one guinea out of him!'

'Prudence! Well, it may be wiser.'

Ethel ran up to her room, hardly able to believe that the mighty proposal was made; and it had been so readily granted, that it seemed as if Richard's caution had been vain in making such a delay, that even Margaret had begun to fear that the street of by-and-by was leading to the house of never. Now, however, it was plain that he had been wise. Opportunity was everything; at another moment, their father might have been harassed and oppressed, and unable to give his mind to concerns, which now he could think of with interest, and Richard could not have caught a more favourable conjuncture.

Ethel was in a wild state of felicity all that evening and the next day, very unlike her brother, who, dismayed at the open step he had taken, shrank into himself, and in his shyness dreaded the discussion in the evening, and would almost have been relieved, if Mr. Wilmot had been unable to accept the invitation. So quiet and grave was he, that Ethel could not get him to talk over the matter at all with her, and she was obliged to bestow all her transports and grand projects on Flora or Margaret, when she could gain their ears, besides conning them over to herself, as an accompaniment to her lessons, by which means she tried Miss Winter's patience almost beyond measure. But she cared not—she saw a gathering school and rising church, which eclipsed all thought of present inattentions and gaucheries. She monopolized Margaret in the twilight, and rhapsodized to her heart's content, talking faster and faster, and looking more and more excited. Margaret began to feel a little overwhelmed, and while answering 'yes' at intervals, was considering whether Ethel had not been flying about in an absent inconsiderate mood all day, and whether it would seem unkind to damp her ardour, by giving her a hint that she was relaxing her guard over herself. Before Margaret had steeled herself, Ethel was talking of a story she had read, of a place something like Cocksmoor. Margaret was not ready with her recollection, and Ethel, saying it was in a magazine in the drawing-room chiffonnière, declared she would fetch it.

Margaret knew what it was to expect her visitors to return 'in one moment,' and with a 'now-or-never' feeling she began, 'Ethel, dear, wait;' but Ethel was too impetuous to attend. 'I'll be back in a twinkling,' she called out, and down she flew, in her speed whisking away, without seeing it, the basket with Margaret's knitting and all her notes and papers, which lay scattered on the floor far out of reach, vexing Margaret at first, and then making her grieve at her own impatient feeling.

Ethel was soon in the drawing-room, but the right number of the magazine was not quickly forthcoming, and in searching she became embarked in another story. Just then, Aubrey, whose stout legs were apt to carry him into every part of the house where he was neither expected nor wanted, marched in at the open door, trying by dint of vehement gestures to make her understand, in his imperfect speech, something that he wanted. Very particularly troublesome she thought him, more especially as she could not make him out, otherwise than that he wanted her to do something with the newspaper and the fire. She made a boat for him with an old newspaper, a very hasty and frail performance, and told him to sail it on the carpet, and be Mr. Ernescliffe going away; and she thought him thus safely disposed of. Returning to her book and her search, with her face to the cupboard, and her book held up to catch the light, she was soon lost in her story, and thought of nothing more till suddenly roused by her father's voice in the hall, loud and peremptory with alarm, 'Aubrey! put that down!' She looked, and beheld Aubrey brandishing a great flaming paper—he dropped it at the exclamation—it fell burning on the carpet. Aubrey's white pinafore! Ethel was springing up, but in her cramped, twisted position, she could not do so quickly, and even as he called, her father strode by her, snatched at Aubrey's merino frock, which he crushed over the scarcely lighted pinafore, and trampled out the flaming paper with his foot. It was a moment of dreadful fright, but the next assured them that no harm was done.

'Ethel!' cried the Doctor, 'are you mad? What were you thinking of?'

Aubrey, here recollecting himself enough to be frightened at his father's voice and manner, burst into loud cries; the Doctor pressed him closer on his breast, caressed and soothed him. Ethel stood by, pale and transfixed with horror. Her father was more angry with her than she had ever seen him, and with reason, as she knew, as she smelt the singeing, and saw a large burnt hole in Aubrey's pinafore, while the front of his frock was scorched and brown. Dr. May's words were not needed, 'What could make you let him?'

'I didn't see—' she faltered.

'Didn't see! Didn't look, didn't think, didn't care! That's it, Ethel. 'Tis very hard one can't trust you in a room with the child any more than the baby herself. His frock perfect tinder. He would have been burnt to a cinder, if I had not come in.'

Aubrey roared afresh, and Dr. May, kissing and comforting him, gathered him up in his left arm, and carried him away, looking back at the door to say, 'There's no bearing it! I'll put a stop to all schools and Greek, if it is to lead to this, and make you good for nothing.'

Ethel was too much terrified to know where she was, or anything, but that she had let her little brother run into fearful peril, and grievously angered her father; she was afraid to follow him, and stood still, annihilated, and in despair, till roused by his return; then, with a stifled sob, she exclaimed, 'Oh, papa!' and could get no further for a gush of tears.

But the anger of the shock of terror was over, and Dr. May

was sorry for her tears, though still he could not but manifest some displeasure. 'Yes, Ethel,' he said, 'it was a frightful thing,' and he could not but shudder again. 'One moment later! It is an escape to be for ever thankful for—poor little fellow—but Ethel, Ethel, do let it be a warning to you.'

'O, I hope—I'll try—' sobbed Ethel.

'You have said you would try before.'

'I know I have,' said Ethel, choked. 'If I could but—'

'Poor child,' said Dr. May, sadly; then looking earnestly at her, 'Ethel, my dear, I am afraid of its being with you as—as it has been with me;' he spoke very low, and drew her close to him. 'I grew up, thinking my inbred heedlessness a sort of grace, so to say, rather manly—the reverse of finikin. I was spoilt as a boy, and my Maggie carried on the spoiling, by never letting me feel its effects. By the time I had sense enough to regret this as a fault, I had grown too old for changing of ingrain, long-nurtured habits—perhaps I never wished it really. You have seen,' and his voice was nearly inaudible, 'what my carelessness has come to —let that suffice at least, as a lesson that may spare you—what your father must feel as long as he lives.'

He pressed his hand tightly on her shoulder, and left her, without letting her see his face. Shocked and bewildered, she hurried up-stairs to Margaret. She threw herself on her knees, felt her arms round her, and heard her kind soothing, and then, in broken words, told how dreadful it had been, and how kind papa had been, and what he had said, which was now the uppermost thought. 'Oh! Margaret, Margaret, how very terrible it is! And does papa really think *so* ?'

'I believe he does,' whispered Margaret.

'How can he, can he bear it!' said Ethel, clasping her hands. 'O it is enough to kill one—I can't think why it did not !'

'He bears it,' said Margaret, 'because he is so very good, that help and comfort do come to him. Dear papa! He bears up because it is right, and for our sakes, and he has a sort of rest in that perfect love they had for each other. He knows how she would wish him to cheer up and look to the end, and support and comfort are given to him, I know they are; but oh, Ethel! it does make one tremble and shrink, to think what he has been going through this autumn, especially when I hear him moving about late at night, and now and then comes a heavy groan— whenever any especial care has been on his mind.'

Ethel was in great distress. 'To have grieved him again !' said she, 'and just as he seemed better and brighter! Everything

I do turns out wrong, and always will; I can't do anything well by any chance.'

'Yes you can, when you mind what you are about.'

'But I never can—I'm like him, every one says so, and he says the heedlessness is ingrain, and can't be got rid of.'

'Ethel, I don't really think he could have told you so.'

'I'm sure he said ingrain.'

'Well, I suppose it is part of his nature, and that you have inherited it, but—' Margaret paused—and Ethel exclaimed,

'He said his was long-nurtured; yes, Margaret, you guessed right, and he said he could not change it, and no more can I.'

'Surely, Ethel, you have not had so many years. You are fifteen instead of forty-six, and it is more a woman's work than a man's to be careful. You need not begin to despair. You were growing much better; Richard said so, and so did Miss Winter.'

'What's the use of it, if in one moment it is as bad as ever? And to-day, of all days in the year, just when papa had been so very, very kind, and given me more than I asked.'

'Do you know, Ethel, I was thinking whether dear mamma would not say that was the reason. You were so happy, that perhaps you were thrown off your guard.'

'I should not wonder if that was it,' said Ethel, thoughtfully. 'You know it was a sort of probation that Richard put me on. I was to learn to be steady before he spoke to papa, and now it seemed to be all settled and right, and perhaps I forgot I was to be careful still.'

'I think it was something of the kind. I was a little afraid before, and I wish I had tried to caution you, but I did not like to seem unkind.'

'I wish you had,' said Ethel. 'Dear little Aubrey! Oh! if papa had not been there! And I cannot think how, as it was, he could contrive to put the fire out, with his one hand, and not hurt himself. Margaret, it was terrible! How could I mind so little! Did you see how his frock was singed?'

'Yes, papa showed it to me. How can we be thankful enough! One thing I hope, that Aubrey was well frightened, poor little boy.'

'I know! I see now!' cried Ethel; 'he must have wanted me to make the fire blaze up, as Richard did one evening when we came in and found it low; I remember Aubrey clapping his hands and shouting at the flame; but my head was in that unhappy story, and I never had sense to put the things together, and reflect that he would try to do it himself. I only wanted to get him out of my way, dear little fellow. Oh, dear! how bad it was of me!

All from being uplifted, and my head turned, as it used to be when we were happier. Oh! I wish Mr. Wilmot was not coming!'

Ethel sat for a long time with her head hidden in Margaret's pillows, and her hand clasped by her good elder sister. At last she looked up and said, 'O Margaret, I am so unhappy. I see the whole meaning of it now. Do you not? When papa gave his consent at last, I was pleased and set up, and proud of my plans. I never recollected what a silly, foolish girl I am, and how unfit. I thought Mr. Wilmot would think great things of it— it was all wrong and self-satisfied. I never prayed at all that it might turn out well, and so now it won't.'

'Dearest Ethel, I don't see that. Perhaps it will do all the better for your being humbled about it now. If you were wild and high-flying, it would never go right.'

'Its hope is in Richard,' said Ethel.

'So it is,' said Margaret.

'I wish Mr. Wilmot was not coming to-night,' said Ethel again. 'It would serve me right, if papa were to say nothing about it.'

Ethel lingered with her sister till Harry and Mary came up with Margaret's tea, and summoned her, and she crept down-stairs, and entered the room so quietly, that she was hardly perceived behind her boisterous brother. She knew her eyes were in no presentable state, and cast them down, and shrank back as Mr. Wilmot shook her hand and greeted her kindly.

Mr. Wilmot had been wont to come to tea whenever he had anything to say to Dr. or Mrs. May, which was about once in ten or twelve days. He was Mary's godfather, and their most intimate friend in the town; and he had often been with them, both as friend and clergyman, through their trouble—no later than Christmas-day, he had come to bring the feast of that day to Margaret in her sick room. Indeed, it had been chiefly for the sake of the Mays that he had resolved to spend the holidays at Stoneborough, taking the care of Abbotstoke, while his brother, the vicar, went to visit their father. This was, however, the first time he had come in his old familiar way to spend an even-ing, and there was something in the resumption of former habits that painfully marked the change.

Ethel, on coming in, found Flora making tea, her father lean-ing back in his great chair in silence, Richard diligently cutting bread, and Blanche sitting on Mr. Wilmot's knee, chattering fast and confidentially. Flora made Harry dispense the cups, and called every one to their places; Ethel timidly glanced at her father's face as he rose and came into the light. She thought the lines and hollows were more marked than ever, and that he looked fatigued and mournful, and she felt cut to the heart; but he began to exert himself, and to make conversation, not, however, about Cocksmoor, but asking Mr. Wilmot what his brother thought of his new squire, Mr. Rivers.

'He likes him very much,' said Mr. Wilmot. 'He is a very pleasing person, particularly kind-hearted and gentle, and likely to do a great deal for the parish. They have been giving away beef and blankets at a great rate this Christmas.'

'What family is there?' asked Flora.

'One daughter, about Ethel's age, is there with her governess. He has been twice married, and the first wife left a son, who is in the Dragoons, I believe. This girl's mother was Lord Cosham's daughter.'

So the talk lingered on, without much interest or life. It was rather keeping from saying nothing than conversation, and no one was without the sensation that she was missing, round whom all had been free and joyous—not that she had been wont to speak much herself, but nothing would go on smoothly or easily without her. So long did this last, that Ethel began to think her father meant to punish her by not beginning the subject that night; and though she owned that she deserved it, she could not help being very much disappointed.

At length, however, her father began :—' We wanted you to talk over a scheme that these young ones have been concocting. You see, I am obliged to keep Richard at home this next term— it won't do to have no one in the house to carry poor Margaret. We can't do without him any way; so he and Ethel have a scheme of seeing what can be done for that wretched place, Cocksmoor.'

'Indeed!' said Mr. Wilmot, brightening and looking interested. 'It is sadly destitute. It would be a great thing if anything could be done for it. You have brought some children to school already, I think. I saw some rough-looking boys, who said they came from Cocksmoor.'

This embarked the Doctor in the history of the ladies being too fine to teach the poor Cocksmoor girls, which he told with kindling vehemence and indignation, growing more animated every moment, as he stormed over the wonted subject of the bad system of management—ladies' committee—negligent incumbent —insufficient clergy—misappropriated tithes—while Mr. Wilmot, who had mourned over it, within himself, a hundred times already, and was doing a curate's work on sufferance, with no pay, and little but mistrust from Mr. Ramsden, and absurd false reports among the more foolish part of the town, sat listening patiently, glad to hear the Doctor in his old strain, though it was a hopeless matter for discussion, and Ethel dreaded that the lamentation would go on till bedtime, and Cocksmoor be quite forgotten.

After a time they came safely back to the project, and Richard was called on to explain. Ethel left it all to him; and he, with rising colour, and quiet, unhesitating, though diffident manner, detailed designs that showed themselves to have been well matured. Mr. Wilmot heard, cordially approved, and, as all agreed that no time was to be lost while the holidays lasted, he undertook to speak to Mr. Ramsden on the subject the next morning, and if his consent to their schemes could be gained, to come in the afternoon to walk with Richard and Ethel to Cocksmoor, and set their affairs in order. All the time Ethel said not a word, except when referred to by her brother; but when Mr. Wilmot took leave, he shook her hand warmly, as if he was much pleased with her. 'Ah!' she thought, 'if he knew how ill I have behaved! It is all show and hollowness with me.'

She did not know that Mr. Wilmot thought her silence one of the best signs for the plan, nor how much more doubtful he would have thought her perseverance, if he had seen her wild and vehement. As it was, he was very much pleased, and when the Doctor came out with him into the hall, he could not help expressing his satisfaction in Richard's well-judged, and sensibly-described project.

'Aye, aye!' said the Doctor, 'there's much more in the boy than I used to think. He's a capital fellow, and more like his mother than any of them.'

'He is,' said Mr. Wilmot; 'there was a just, well-weighed sense and soberness in his plans that put me in mind of her every moment.'

Dr. May gave his hand a squeeze, full of feeling, and went up to tell Margaret. She, on the first opportunity, told Richard, and made him happier than he had been for months, not so much in Mr. Wilmot's words, as in his father's assent to, and pleasure in them.

CHAPTER XV.

'Pitch thy behaviour low, thy projects high,
    So shalt thou humble and magnanimous be;
Sink not in spirit; who aimeth at the sky
    Shoots higher much than he that means a tree.
    A grain of glory mixed with humbleness,
    Cures both a fever and lethargicness.'—HERBERT.

'NORMAN, do you feel up to a long day's work?' said Dr. May, on the following morning. 'I have to set off after breakfast to see old Mrs. Gould, and to be at Abbotstoke Grange by twelve; then

I thought of going to Fordholm, and getting Miss Cleveland to give us some luncheon—there are some poor people on the way to look at; and that girl on Far-view Hill; and there's another place to call at in coming home. You'll have a good deal of sitting in the carriage, holding Whitefoot, so if you think you shall be cold or tired, don't scruple to say so, and I'll take Adams to drive me.'

'No, thank you,' said Norman, briskly. 'This frost is famous.'

'It will turn to rain, I expect—it is too white,' said the Doctor, looking out at the window. 'How will you get to Cocksmoor, good people?'

'Ethel won't believe it rains unless it is very bad,' said Richard.

Norman set out with his father, and prosperously performed the expedition, arriving at Abbotstoke Grange at the appointed hour.

'Ha!' said the Doctor, as the iron gates of ornamental scroll work were swung back, 'there's a considerable change in this place since I was here last. Well kept up, indeed! Not a dead leaf left under the old walnuts, and the grass looks as smooth as if they had a dozen gardeners rolling it every day.'

'And the drive,' said Norman, 'more like a garden walk than a road! But oh! what a splendid cedar!'

'Isn't it! I remember that as long as I remember anything. All this fine rolling of turf, and trimming up of the place, does not make much difference to you, old fellow, does it? You don't look altered since I saw you last, when old Jervis was letting the place go to rack and ruin. So they have a new entrance—very handsome conservatory—flowers—the banker does things in style. There,' as Norman helped him off with his plaid, 'wrap yourself up well, don't get cold. The sun is gone in, and I should not wonder if the rain were coming after all. I'll not be longer than I can help.'

Dr. May disappeared from his son's sight through the conservatory, where, through the plate-glass, the exotics looked so fresh and perfumy, that Norman almost fancied that the scent reached him. 'How much poor Margaret would enjoy one of those camellias,' thought he, 'and these people have bushels of them for mere show. If I were papa, I should be tempted to be like Beauty's father, and carry off one. How she would admire it!'

Norman had plenty of time to meditate on the camellias, and then to turn and speculate on the age of the cedar, whether it could have been planted by the monks of Stoneborough Abbey, to whom the Grange had belonged, brought from Lebanon by a pilgrim, perhaps; and then he tried to guess at the longevity of cedars, and thought of asking Margaret, the botanist of the family. Then he yawned, moved the horse a little about, opined that Mr. Rivers must be very prosy, or have some abstruse complaint, considered the sky, and augured rain, buttoned another button of his rough coat, and thought of Miss Cleveland's dinner. Then he thought there was a very sharp wind, and drove about till he found a sheltered place on the lee side of the great cedar, looked up at it, and thought it would be a fine subject for verses, if Mr. Wilmot knew of it, and then proceeded to consider what he should make of them.

In the midst he was suddenly roused by the deep-toned note of a dog, and beheld a large black Newfoundland dog leaping about the horse in great indignation. 'Rollo! Rollo!' called a clear young voice, and he saw two ladies returning from a walk. Rollo, at the first call, galloped back to his mistress, and was evidently receiving an admonition, and promising good behaviour. The two ladies entered the house, while he lay down on the step, with his lion-like paw hanging down, watching Norman with a brilliant pair of hazel eyes. Norman, after a little more wondering when Mr. Rivers would have done with his father, betook himself to civil demonstrations to the creature, who received them with dignity, and presently, after acknowledging with his tail, various whispers of 'Good old fellow,' and 'Here, old Rollo!' having apparently satisfied himself that the young gentleman was respectable, he rose, and vouchsafed to stand up with his fore-paws in the gig, listening amiably to Norman's delicate flatteries. Norman even began to hope to allure him into jumping on the seat; but a great bell rang, and Rollo immediately turned round, and dashed off, at full speed, to some back region of the house. 'So, old fellow, you know what the dinner-bell means,' thought Norman. 'I hope Mr. Rivers is hungry too. Miss Cleveland will have eaten up her whole luncheon, if this old bore won't let my father go soon! I hope he is desperately ill—'tis his only excuse! Heigh ho! I must jump out to warm my feet soon! There, there's a drop of rain! Well, there's no end to it! I wonder what Ethel is doing about Cocksmoor. It is setting in for a wet afternoon!' and Norman disconsolately put up his umbrella.

At last Dr. May and another gentleman were seen in the conservatory, and Norman gladly proceeded to clear the seat; but Dr. May called out, 'Jump out, Norman, Mr. Rivers is so kind as to ask us to stay to luncheon.'

With boyish shrinking from strangers, Norman privately wished Mr. Rivers at Jericho, as he gave the reins to a servant, and entered the conservatory, where a kindly hand was held out to him by a gentleman of about fifty, with a bald smooth forehead, soft blue eyes, and gentle pleasant face. 'Is this your eldest son?' said he, turning to Dr. May,—and the manner of both was as if they were already well acquainted. 'No, this is my second. The eldest is not quite such a long-legged fellow,' said Dr. May. And then followed the question addressed to Norman himself, where he was at school.

'At Stoneborough,' said Norman, a little amused at the thought how angry Ethel and Harry would be that the paragraph of the county paper, where 'N. W. May' was recorded as prizeman and foremost in the examination, had not penetrated even to Abbotstoke Grange, or rather to its owner's memory.

However, his father could not help adding, 'He is the head of the school—a thing we Stoneborough men think much of.'

This, and Mr. Rivers's civil answer, made Norman so hot, that he did not notice much in passing through a hall full of beautiful vases, stuffed birds, busts, &c. tastefully arranged, and he did not look up till they were entering a handsome dining-room, where a small square table was laid out for luncheon near a noble fire.

The two ladies were there, and Mr. Rivers introduced them as his daughter and Mrs. Larpent. It was the most luxurious meal that Norman had ever seen, the plate, the porcelain, and all the appointments of the table so elegant, and the viands, all partaking of the Christmas character, and of a *recherché* delicate description quite new to him. He had to serve as his father's right hand, and was so anxious to put everything as Dr. May liked it, and without attracting notice, that he hardly saw or listened till Dr. May began to admire a fine Claude, on the opposite wall, and embarked in a picture discussion. The Doctor had much taste for art, and had made the most of his opportunities of seeing paintings during his time of study at Paris, and in a brief tour to Italy. Since that time, few good pictures had come in his way, and these were a great pleasure to him, while Mr. Rivers, a regular connoisseur, was delighted to meet with one who could so well appreciate them. Norman perceived how his father was enjoying the conversation, and was much interested both by the sight of the first fine paintings he had ever seen, and by the talk about their merits; but the living things in the room had more of his attention and observation, especially the young lady who sat at the head of the table; a girl about his own age; she was on a very small scale, and seemed to him like a fairy, in the airy lightness and grace of her movements, and the blithe gladsomeness of her gestures and countenance. Form and features, though perfectly healthful and brisk, had the peculiar finish and delicacy of a miniature painting, and were enhanced by the sunny glance of her dark soft smiling eyes. Her hair was in black silky braids, and her dress, with its gaiety of well-assorted colour, was positively refreshing to his eye, so long accustomed to the deep mourning of his sisters. A little Italian greyhound, perfectly white, was at her side, making infinite variations of the line of beauty and grace, with its elegant outline, and S-like tail, as it raised its slender nose in hopes of a fragment of bread which she from time to time dispensed to it.

Luncheon over, Mr. Rivers asked Dr. May to step into his library, and Norman guessed that they had been talking all this time, and had never come to the medical opinion. However, a good meal and a large fire made a great difference in his toleration, and, it was so new a scene, that he had no objection to a prolonged waiting, especially when Mrs. Larpent said, in a very pleasant tone, 'Will you come into the drawing-room with us?'

He felt somewhat as if he was walking in enchanted ground as he followed her into the large room, the windows opening into the conservatory, the whole air fragrant with flowers, the furniture and ornaments so exquisite of their kind, and all such a fit scene for the beautiful little damsel, who, with her slender dog by her side, tripped on demurely, and rather shyly, but with a certain skipping lightness in her step. A very tall overgrown school-boy did Norman feel himself for one bashful moment, when he found himself alone with the two ladies; but he was ready to be set at ease by Mrs. Larpent's good-natured manner, when she said something of Rollo's discourtesy. He smiled, and answered that he had made great friends with the fine old dog, and spoke of his running off to the dinner, at which little Miss Rivers laughed, and looked delighted, and began to tell of Rollo's perfections and intelligence. Norman ventured to inquire the name of the little Italian, and was told it was Nipen, because it had once stolen a cake, much like the wind-spirit in ' Feats on the Fiord.' Its beauty and tricks were duly displayed, and a most beautiful Australian parrot was exhibited. Mrs. Larpent taking full interest in the talk, in so lively and gentle a manner, and she and her pretty pupil evidently on such sister-like terms, that Norman could hardly believe her to be the governess, when he thought of Miss Winter.

Miss Rivers took up some brown leaves which she was cutting out with scissors, and shaping.—'Our holiday work,' said Mrs. Larpent, in answer to the inquiring look of Norman's eyes. 'Meta has been making a drawing for her papa, and is framing it in leather work. Have you ever seen any?'

PART I.   L

'Never!' and Norman looked eagerly, asking questions, and watching while Miss Rivers cut out her ivy leaf and marked its veins, and showed how she copied it from nature. He thanked her, saying, 'I wanted to learn all about it, for I thought it would be such nice work for my eldest sister.'

A glance of earnest interest from little Meta's bright eyes at her governess, and Mrs. Larpent, in a kind, soft tone that quite gained his heart, asked, 'Is she the invalid?'

'Yes,' said Norman. 'New fancy work is a great gain to her.'

Mrs. Larpent's sympathetic questions, and Meta's softening eyes, gradually drew from him a great deal about Margaret's helpless state, and her patience, and capabilities, and how everyone came to her with all their cares; and Norman, as he spoke, mentally contrasted the life, untouched by trouble and care, led by the fair girl before him, with that atmosphere of constant petty anxieties round her namesake's couch, at years so nearly the same.

'How very good she must be,' said little Meta, quickly and softly; and a tear was sparkling on her eyelashes.

'She is indeed,' said Norman, earnestly. 'I don't know what papa would do but for her.'

Mrs. Larpent asked kind questions whether his father's arm was very painful, and the hopes of its cure; and he felt as if she was a great friend already. Thence they came to books. Norman had not read for months past, but it happened that Meta was just now reading 'Woodstock,' with which he was of course familiar; and both grew eager in discussing that and several others. Of one, Meta spoke in such terms of delight, that Norman thought it had been very stupid of him to let it lie on the table for the last fortnight without looking into it.

He was almost sorry to see his father and Mr. Rivers come in, and hear the carriage ordered, but they were not off yet, though the rain was now only Scotch mist. Mr. Rivers had his most choice little pictures still to display, his beautiful early Italian masters, finished like illuminations, and over these there was much lingering and admiring. Meta had whispered something to her governess, who smiled, and advanced to Norman. 'Meta wishes to know if your sister would like to have a few flowers?' said she.

No sooner said than done; the door into the conservatory was opened, and Meta, cutting sprays of beautiful geranium, delicious heliotrope, fragrant calycanthus, deep blue tree violet, and exquisite hothouse ferns; perfect wonders to Norman, who, at each addition to the bouquet, exclaimed by turns, 'Oh! thank you,' and 'how she will like it!'

Her father reached a magnolia blossom from on high, and the

quick warm grateful emotion trembled in Dr. May's features and voice, as he said, 'It is very kind in you; you have given my poor girl a great treat. Thank you with all my heart.'

Margaret Rivers cast down her eyes, half smiled, and shrank back, thinking she had never felt anything like the left-handed grasp, so full of warmth and thankfulness. It gave her confidence to venture on the one question on which she was bent. Her father was in the hall, showing Norman his Greek nymph; and lifting her eyes to Dr. May's face, then casting them down, she coloured deeper than ever, as she said, in a stammering whisper, 'O please—if you would tell me—do you think—is papa very ill?'

Dr. May answered in his softest, most re-assuring tones: 'You need not be alarmed about him, I assure you. You must keep him from too much business,' he added, smiling; 'make him ride with you, and not let him tire himself, and I am sure you can be his best doctor.'

'But do you think,' said Meta, earnestly looking up, 'do you think he will be quite well again?'

'You must not expect doctors to be absolute oracles,' said he. 'I will tell you what I told him—I hardly think his will ever be sound health again, but I see no reason why he should not have many years of comfort, and there is no cause for you to disquiet yourself on his account—you have only to be careful of him.'

Meta tried to say 'thank you,' but not succeeding, looked imploringly at her governess, who spoke for her. 'Thank you, it is a great relief to have an opinion, for we were not at all satisfied about Mr. Rivers.'

A few words more, and Meta was skipping about like a sprite, finding a basket for the flowers—she had another shake of the hand, another grateful smile, and 'thank you,' from the Doctor; and then, as the carriage disappeared, Mrs. Larpent exclaimed, 'What a very nice, intelligent boy that was.'

'Particularly gentlemanlike,' said Mr. Rivers. 'Very clever— the head of the school, as his father tells me—and so modest and unassuming—though I see his father is very proud of him.'

'O, I am sure they are so fond of each other,' said Meta; 'didn't you see his attentive ways to his father at luncheon. And, papa, I am sure you must like Dr. May, Mr. Wilmot's doctor, as much as I said you would.'

'He is the most superior man I have met with for a long time,' said Mr. Rivers. 'It is a great acquisition to find a man of such taste and acquirements in this country neighbourhood, when there is not another who can tell a Claude from a Poussin. I declare, when once we began talking, there was no leaving off—

I have not met a person of so much conversation since I left town. I thought you would like to see him, Meta.'

'I hope I shall know the Miss Mays some time or other.'

'That is the prettiest little fairy I ever did see!' was Dr. May's remark, as Norman drove from the door.

'How good-natured they are!' said Norman; 'I just said something about Margaret, and she gave me all these flowers. How Margaret will be delighted! I wish the girls could see it all!'

'So you got on well with the ladies, did you?'

'They were very kind to me. It was very pleasant!' said Norman, with a tone of enjoyment that did his father's heart good.

'I was glad you should come in. Such a curiosity shop is a sight, and those pictures were some of them well worth seeing. That was a splendid Titian.'

'That cast of the Pallas of the Parthenon—how beautiful it was —I knew it from the picture in Smith's dictionary. Mr. Rivers said he would show me all his antiques if you would bring me again.'

'I saw he liked your interest in them. He is a good, kind-hearted dilettante sort of old man; he has got all the talk of the literary, cultivated society in London, and must find it dullish work here.'

'You liked him, didn't you?'

'He is very pleasant—I found he knew my old friend, Benson, whom I had not seen since we were at Cambridge together, and we got on that and other matters—London people have an art of conversation not learnt here, and I don't know how the time slipped away, but you must have been tolerably tired of waiting.'

'Not to signify,' said Norman. 'I only began to think he must be very ill; I hope there is not much the matter with him.'

'I can't say. I am afraid there is organic disease, but I think it may be kept quiet a good while yet, and he may have a pleasant life for some time to come, arranging his prints, and petting his pretty daughter. He has plenty to fall back upon.'

'Do you go there again?'

'Yes, next week. I am glad of it. I shall like to have another look at that little Madonna of his—it is the sort of picture that does one good to carry away in one's eye. Whay! Stop. There's an old woman in here. It is too late for Fordholm, but these cases won't wait.'

He went into the cottage, and soon returned, saying, 'Fine new blankets, and a great kettle of soup, and such praises of the ladies at the Grange!' And, at the next house, it was the same story. 'Well, 'tis no mockery now, to tell the poor creatures they want nourishing food. Slices of meat and bottles of port wine rain down on Abbotstoke.'

A far more talkative journey than usual ensued: the discussion of the paintings and antiques was almost equally delightful to the father and son, and lasted till, about a mile from Stoneborough, they descried three figures in the twilight.

'Ha! How are you, Wilmot? So you braved the rain, Ethel. Jump in,' called the Doctor, as Norman drew up.

'I shall crowd you—I shall hurt your arm, papa; thank you.'

'No, you won't—jump in—there's room for three threadpapers in one gig. Why, Wilmot, your brother has a very jewel of a squire! How did you fare?'

'Very well on the whole,' was Mr. Wilmot's answer, while Ethel scrambled in, and tried to make herself small, an art in which she was not very successful; and Norman gave an exclamation of horrified warning, as she was about to step into the flower-basket; then she nearly tumbled out again in dismay, and was relieved to find herself safely wedged in, without having done any harm, while her father called out to Mr. Wilmot, as they started, 'I say! You are coming back to tea with us.'

That cheerful tone, and the kindness to herself, were a refreshment and revival to Ethel, who was still sobered and shocked by her yesterday's adventure, and by the sense of her father's sorrowful displeasure. Expecting further to be scolded for getting in so awkwardly, she did not venture to volunteer anything, and even when he kindly said, 'I hope you were prosperous in your expedition,' she only made answer, in a very grave voice, 'Yes, papa, we have taken a very nice tidy room.'

'What do you pay for it?'

'Fourpence for each time.'

'Well, here's for you,' said Dr. May. 'It is only two guineas to-day; that banker at the Grange beguiled us of our time, but you had better close the bargain for him, Ethel—he will be a revenue for you, for this winter at least.'

'O thank you, papa,' was all Ethel could say; overpowered by his kindness, and more repressed by what she felt so unmerited, than she would have been by coldness, she said few words, and preferred listening to Norman, who began to describe their adventures at the Grange.

All her eagerness revived, however, as she sprung out of the carriage, full of tidings for Margaret; and it was almost a race between her and Norman to get up-stairs, and unfold their separate budgets.

Margaret's lamp had just been lighted, when they made their entrance, Norman holding the flowers on high.

'Oh! how beautiful, how delicious! For me? Where did you get them?'

'From Abbotstoke Grange; Miss Rivers sent them to you.'

'How very kind! What a lovely geranium, and oh, that fern! I never saw anything so choice. How came she to think of me?'

'They asked me in because it rained, and she was making the prettiest things, leather leaves and flowers for picture frames. I thought it was work that would just suit you, and learnt how to do it. That made them ask about you, and it ended by her sending you this nosegay.'

'How very kind everybody is! Well, Ethel, are you come home too?'

'Papa picked me up—O Margaret, we have found such a nice room, a clean sanded kitchen—'

'You never saw such a conservatory—'

'And it is to be let to us for fourpence a time—'

'The house is full of beautiful things, pictures and statues. Only think of a real Titian, and a cast of the Apollo!'

'Twenty children to begin with, and Richard is going to make some forms.'

'Mr. Rivers is going to show me all his casts.'

'O, is he? But only think how lucky we·were to find such a nice woman; Mr. Wilmot was so pleased with her.'

Norman found one story at a time was enough, and relinquished the field, contenting himself with silently helping Margaret to arrange the flowers, holding the basket for her, and pleased with her gestures of admiration. Ethel went on with her history. 'The first place we thought of would not do at all; the woman said she would not take half-a-crown a week to have a lot of children stabbling about, as she called it; so we went to another house, and there was a very nice woman indeed, Mrs. Green, with one little boy, whom she wanted to send to school, only it is too far. She says she always goes to church at Fordholm because it is nearer, and she is quite willing to let us have the room. So we settled it, and next Friday we are to begin. Papa has given us two guineas, and that will pay for, let me see, a hundred and twenty-six times, and Mr. Wilmot is going to give us some books, and Ritchie will print some alphabets. We told a great many of the people, and they are so glad. Old Granny Hall said, 'Well, I never!' and told the girls they must be as good as gold now the gentlefolks was coming to teach them. Mr. Wilmot is coming with us every Friday as long as the holidays last.'

Ethel departed on her father's coming in to ask Margaret if she would like to have a visit from Mr. Wilmot. She enjoyed this very much, and he sat there nearly an hour, talking of many matters, especially the Cocksmoor scheme, on which she was glad to hear his opinion at first hand.

'I am very glad you think well of it,' she said. 'It is most desirable that something should be done for those poor people, and Richard would never act rashly; but I have longed for advice whether it was right to promote Ethel's undertaking. I suppose Richard told you how bent on it she was, long before papa was told of it.'

'He said it was her great wish, and had been so for a long time past.'

Margaret, in words more adequate to express the possession the project had gained of Ethel's ardent mind, explained the whole history of it. 'I do believe she looks on it as a sort of call,' said she, 'and I have felt as if I ought not to hinder her, and yet I did not know whether it was right, at her age, to let her undertake so much.'

'I understand,' said Mr. Wilmot; 'but from what I have seen of Ethel, I should think you had decided rightly. There seems to me to be such a spirit of energy in her, that if she does not act, she will either speculate and theorize, or pine and prey on herself. I do believe that hard homely work, such as this school-keeping, is the best outlet for what might otherwise run to extravagance—more especially as you say the hope of it has already been an incentive to improvement in home duties.'

'That I am sure it has,' said Margaret.

'Moreover,' said Mr. Wilmot, 'I think you were quite right in thinking that to interfere with such a design was unsafe. I do believe that a great deal of harm is done by prudent friends, who dread to let young people do anything out of the common way, and so force their aspirations to ferment and turn sour, for want of being put to use.'

'Still, girls are told they ought to wait patiently, and not to be eager for self-imposed duties.'

'I am not saying that it is not the appointed discipline for the girls themselves,' said Mr. Wilmot. 'If they would submit, and do their best, it would doubtless prove the most beneficial thing for them; but it is a trial in which they often fail, and I had rather not be in the place of such friends.'

'It is a great puzzle!' said Margaret, sighing.

'Ah! I daresay you are often perplexed,' said her friend, kindly.

'Indeed I am. There are so many little details that I cannot be always teasing papa with, and yet which I do believe form the character more than the great events, and I never know whether I act for the best. And there are so many of us, so many duties, I cannot half attend to any. Lately, I have been giving up almost everything to keep this room quiet for Norman in the morning, because he was so much harassed and hurt by bustle and confusion, and I found to-day that things have gone wrong in consequence.'

'You must do the best you can, and try to trust that while you work in the right spirit, your failures will be compensated,' said Mr. Wilmot. 'It is a hard trial.'

'I like your understanding it,' said Margaret, smiling sadly. 'I don't know whether it is silly, but I don't like to be pitied for the wrong thing. My being so helpless is what everyone laments over; but, after all, that is made up to me by the petting and kindness I get from all of them: but it is the being mistress of the house, and having to settle for everyone, without knowing whether I do right or wrong—that is my trouble.'

'I am not sure, however, that it is right to call it a trouble, though it is a trial.'

'I see what you mean,' said Margaret. 'I ought to be thankful. I know it is an honour, and I am quite sure I should be grieved if they did not all come to me and consult me as they do. I had better not have complained; and yet I am glad I did, for I like you to understand my difficulties.'

'And, indeed, I wish to enter into them, and do or say anything in my power to help you. But I don't know anything that can be of so much comfort as the knowledge that He who laid the burden on you will help you to bear it.'

'Yes,' said Margaret, pausing; and then, with a sweet look, though a heavy sigh, she said, 'It is very odd how things turn out! I always had a childish fancy that I would be useful and important; but I little thought how it would be! However, as long as Richard is in the house, I always feel secure about the others, and I shall soon be down-stairs myself. Don't you think dear papa in better spirits?'

'I thought so to-day—' and here the Doctor returned, talking of Abbotstoke Grange, where he had certainly been much pleased. 'It was a lucky chance,' he said, 'that they brought Norman in. It was exactly what I wanted to rouse and interest him; and he took it all in so well, that I am sure they were pleased with him. I thought he looked a very lanky specimen of too much leg and arm when I called him in; but he has such good manners, and is so ready and understanding, that they could not help liking him.

It was fortunate I had him instead of Richard—Ritchie is a very good fellow, certainly; but he had rather look at a steam-engine, any day, than at Raffaelle himself.'

Norman had his turn by-and-by. He came up after tea, reporting that papa was fast asleep in his chair, and the others would go on about Cocksmoor till midnight, if they were let alone; and made up for his previous yielding to Ethel, by giving, with much animation, and some excitement, a glowing description of the Grange, so graphic, that Margaret said she could almost fancy she had been there.

'O Margaret, I wonder if you ever will! I would give something for you to see the beautiful conservatory. It is a real bower for a maiden of romance, with its rich green fragrance in the midst of winter. It is like a picture in a dream. One could imagine it a fairy land, where no care, or grief, or weariness could come; all choice beauty and sweetness waiting on the creature within. I can hardly believe that it is a real place, and that I have seen it.'

'Though you have brought these pretty tokens that your fairy is as good as she is fair,' said Margaret, smiling.

CHAPTER XVI.

EVANS. Peace your tattlings. What is fair, William?
WILLIAM. PULCHER.
QUICKLY. Poulcats! there are fairer things than poulcats sure!
EVANS. I pray you have your remembrance, child, accusativo HING HANG HOG.
QUICKLY. HANG HOG is Latin for bacon, I warrant you.—SHAKESPEARE.

In a large family it must often happen, that since every member of it cannot ride the same hobby, nor at the same time, their several steeds must sometimes run counter to each other; and so Ethel found it, one morning when Miss Winter, having a bad cold, had given her an unwonted holiday.

Mr. Wilmot had sent a large parcel of books for her to choose from for Cocksmoor, but this she could not well do without consultation. The multitude bewildered her, she was afraid of taking too many or too few, and the being brought to these practical details made her sensible that though her schemes were very grand and full for future doings, they passed very lightly over the intermediate ground. The '*Paulò post futurum*' was a period much more developed in her imagination than the future, that the present was flowing into.

Where was her coadjutor, Richard? Writing notes for papa,

and not to be disturbed. She had better have waited tranquilly, but this would not suit her impatience, and she ran up to Margaret's room. There she found a great display of ivy leaves, which Norman, who had been turning half the shops in the town upside down in search of materials, was instructing her to imitate in leather work—a regular mania with him, and apparently the same with Margaret.

In came Ethel. 'Oh! Margaret, will you look at these "First Truths?" Do you think they would be easy enough? Shall I take some of the "Parables" and "Miracles" at once, or content myself with the book about "Jane Sparks?"'

'There's some very easy reading in "Jane Sparks," isn't there? I would not make the little books from the New Testament too common.'

'Take care, that leaf has five points,' said Norman.

'Shall I bring you up "Jane Sparks" to see? Because then you can judge,' said Ethel.

'There, Norman, is that right?—what a beauty! I should like to look over them by-and-by, dear Ethel, very much.'

Ethel gazed and went away, more put out than was usual with her. 'When Margaret has a new kind of fancy work,' she thought, 'she cares for nothing else! as if my poor children did not signify more than trumpery leather leaves!' She next met Flora.

'O Flora, see here, what a famous parcel of books Mr. Wilmot has sent us to choose from.'

'All those!' said Flora, turning them over as they lay heaped on the drawing-room sofa; 'what a confusion!'

'See, such a parcel of reading books. I want to know what you think of setting them up with "Jane Sparks," as it is week-day teaching.'

'You will be very tired of hearing those spelt over for ever; they have some nicer books at the national school.'

'What is the name of them? Do you see any of them here?'

'No, I don't think I do, but I can't wait to look now. I must write some letters. You had better put them together a little. If you were to sort them, you would know what is there. Now, what a mess they are in.'

Ethel could not deny it, and began to deal them out in piles, looking somewhat more fitting, but still felt neglected and aggrieved, at no one being at leisure but Harry, who was not likely to be of any use to her.

Presently she heard the study door open, and hoped; but though it was Richard who entered the room, he was followed by Tom, and each held various books that boded little good to her. Miss Winter had, much to her own satisfaction, been relieved from the charge of Tom, whose lessons Richard had taken upon himself; and thus Ethel had heard so little about them for a long time past, that even in her vexation and desire to have them over, she listened with interest, desirous to judge what sort of place Tom might be likely to take in school.

She did not perceive that this made Richard nervous and uneasy. He had a great dislike to spectators of Latin lessons; he never had forgotten an unlucky occasion, some years back, when his father was examining him in the Georgics, and he, dull by nature, and duller by confusion and timidity, had gone on rendering word for word—*enim* for, *seges* a crop, *lini* of mud, *urit* burns, *campum* the field, *avenœ* a crop of pipe, *urit* burns it, when Norman and Ethel had first warned him of the beauty of his translation by an explosion of laughing, when his father had shut the book with a bounce, shaken his head in utter despair, and told him to give up all thoughts of doing anything—and when Margaret had cried with vexation. Since that time, he had never been happy when any one was in earshot of a lesson; but to-day he had no escape—Harry lay on the rug reading, and Ethel sat forlorn over her books on the sofa. Tom, however, was bright enough, declined his Greek nouns irreproachably, and construed his Latin so well, that Ethel could not help putting in a word or two of commendation, and auguring the third form. 'Do let him off the parsing, Ritchie,' said she, coaxingly—' he has said it so well, and I want you so much.'

'I am afraid I must not,' said Richard; who, to her surprise, did not look pleased or satisfied with the prosperous translation; 'but come, Tom, you shan't have many words, if you really know them.'

Tom twisted and looked rather cross, but when asked to parse the word *viribus*, answered readily and correctly.

'Very well, only two more—*affuit ?*'

'Third person singular, præter perfect tense of the verb *affo, affis, affui, affere*,' gabbled off Tom with such confidence, that though Ethel gave an indignant jump, Richard was almost startled into letting it pass, and disbelieving himself. He remonstrated in a somewhat hesitating voice. 'Did you find that in the dictionary?' said he, 'I thought *affui* came from *adsum*.'

'O to be sure, stupid fool of a word, so it does!' said Tom, hastily. 'I had forgot—*adsum, ades, affui, adesse.*'

Richard said no more, but proposed the word *oppositus.*

'Adjective.'

Ethel was surprised, for she remembered that it was, in this passage, part of a passive verb, which Tom had construed correctly, 'it was objected,' and she had thought this very creditable to him, whereas he now evidently took it for *opposite;* however, on Richard's reading the line, he corrected himself and called it a participle, but did not commit himself further, till asked for its derivation.

'From *oppositor.*'

'Hallo!' cried Harry, who hitherto had been abstracted in his book, but now turned, raised himself on his elbow, and, at the blunder, shook his thick yellow locks, and showed his teeth like a young lion.

'No, now, Tom, pay attention,' said Richard, resignedly. 'If you found out its meaning, you must have seen its derivation.'

'*Oppositus,*' said Tom, twisting his fingers, and gazing first at Ethel, then at Harry, in hopes of being prompted, then at the ceiling and floor, the while he drawled out the word with a whine, 'why, *oppositus* from *op-posor.*'

'A poser! aint it?' said Harry.

'Don't Harry, you distract him,' said Richard. 'Come, Tom, say at once whether you know it or not—it is of no use to invent.'

'From *op*—' and a mumble.

'What? I don't hear—*op*—'

Tom again looked for help to Harry, who made a mischievous movement of his lips, as if prompting, and, deceived by it, he said boldly, 'From *op-possum.*'

'That's right! let us hear him decline it!' cried Harry, in an ecstasy, '*Oppossum, opottis, opposse,* or *oh-pottery!*'

'Harry,' said Richard, in a gentle reasonable voice, 'I wish you would be so kind as not to stay, if you cannot help distracting him.'

And Harry, who really had a tolerable share of forbearance and consideration, actually obeyed, contenting himself with tossing his book into the air and catching it again, while he paused at the door to give his last unsolicited assistance. 'Decline *oppossum*, you say, I'll tell you how: *O-possum re-poses* up a gum-tree. *O-pot-you-I* will, says the *O-posse* of Yankees, come out to *ketch* him. Opossum poses them and declines in *O-pot-esse* by any manner of means of *o-potting-di-do-dum*, was quite *oppositum-oppositu*, in fact, quite *contrairy.*'

Richard, with the gravity of a victim, heard this sally of school-boy wit, which threw Ethel back on the sofa in fits of laughing, and declaring that the Opossum declined, not that he was declined; but, in the midst of the disturbance thus created, Tom stepped up to her and whispered 'Do tell me Ethel.'

'Indeed I shan't,' said she. 'Why don't you say fairly if you don't know?'

He was obliged to confess his ignorance, and Richard made him conjugate the whole verb *opponor* from beginning to end, in which he wanted a good deal of help.

Ethel could not help saying, 'How did you find out the meaning of that word, Tom, if you didn't look out the verb?'

'I—don't know,' drawled Tom, in the voice, half sullen, half piteous, which he always assumed when out of sorts.

'It is very odd,' she said, decidedly; but Richard took no notice, and proceeded to the other lessons, which went off tolerably well, except the arithmetic, where there was some great misunderstanding, into which Ethel did not enter for some time. When she did attend, she perceived that Tom had brought a right answer, without understanding the working of the sum, and that Richard was putting him through it. She began to be worked into a state of dismay and indignation at Tom's behaviour, and Richard's calm indifference, which made her almost forget 'Jane Sparks,' and long to be alone with Richard; but all the world kept coming into the room, and going out, and she could not say what was in her mind till after dinner, when, seeing Richard go up into Margaret's room, she ran after him, and entering it, surprised Margaret, by not beginning on her books, but saying at once, 'Ritchie, I wanted to speak to you about Tom. I am sure he shuffled about those lessons.'

'I am afraid he does,' said Richard, much concerned.

'What, do you mean that it is often so?'

'Much too often,' said Richard; 'but I have never been able to detect him; he is very sharp, and has some underhand way of preparing his lessons that I cannot make out.'

'Did you know it, Margaret?' said Ethel, astonished not to see her sister look shocked as well as sorry.

'Yes,' said Margaret, 'Ritchie and I have often talked it over, and tried to think what was to be done.'

'Dear me! why don't you tell papa? It is such a terrible thing!'

'So it is,' said Margaret, 'but we have nothing positive or tangible to accuse Tom of; we don't know what he does, and have never caught him out.'

'I am sure he must have found out the meaning of that *oppositum* in some wrong way—if he had looked it out, he would only have found opposite. Nothing but *opponor* could have shown him the rendering which he made.'

'That's like what I have said almost every day,' said Richard, 'but there we are—I can't get any further.'

'Perhaps he guesses by the context,' said Margaret.

'It would be impossible to do so always,' said both the Latin scholars at once.

'Well, I can't think how you can take it so quietly,' said Ethel. 'I would have told papa the first moment, and put a stop to it. I have a great mind to do so, if you won't.'

'Ethel, Ethel, that would never do!' exclaimed Margaret, 'pray don't. Papa would be so dreadfully grieved and angry with poor Tom.'

'Well, so he deserves,' said Ethel.

'You don't know what it is to see papa angry,' said Richard.

'Dear me, Richard!' cried Ethel, who thought she knew pretty well what his sharp words were. 'I'm sure papa never was angry with me, without making me love him more, and, at least, *want* to be better.'

'You are a girl,' said Richard.

'You are higher spirited, and shake off things faster,' said Margaret.

'Why, what do you think he would do to Tom?'

'I think he would be so very angry, that Tom, who, you know, is timid and meek, would be dreadfully frightened,' said Richard.

'That's just what he ought to be, frightened out of these tricks.'

'I am afraid it would frighten him into them still more,' said Richard, 'and perhaps give him such a dread of my father as would prevent him from ever being open with him.'

'Besides, it would make papa so very unhappy,' added Margaret. 'Of course, if poor dear Tom had been found out in any positive deceit, we ought to mention it at once, and let him be punished; but while it is all vague suspicion, and of what papa has such a horror of, it would only grieve him, and make him constantly anxious, without, perhaps, doing Tom any good.'

'I think all that is expediency,' said Ethel, in her bluff, abrupt way.

'Besides,' said Richard, 'we have nothing positive to accuse him of, and if we had, it would be of no use. He will be at school in three weeks, and there he would be sure to shirk, even if he left it off here. Every one does, and thinks nothing of it.'

'Richard!' cried both sisters, shocked. 'You never did?'

'No, we didn't, but most others do, and not bad fellows either. It is not the way of boys to think much of those things.'

'It is mean—it is dishonourable—it is deceitful!' cried Ethel.

'I know it is very wrong, but you'll never get the general run of boys to think so,' said Richard.

'Then Tom ought not to go to school at all till he is well armed against it,' said Ethel.

'That can't be helped,' said Richard. 'He will get clear of it in time, when he knows better.'

'I will talk to him,' said Margaret, 'and, indeed, I think it would be better than worrying papa.'

'Well,' said Ethel, 'of course I shan't tell, because it is not my business, but I think papa ought to know everything about us, and I don't like your keeping anything back. It is being almost as bad as Tom himself.'

With which words, as Flora entered, Ethel marched out of the room in displeasure, and went down, resolved to settle 'Jane Sparks' by herself.

'Ethel is out of sorts to-day,' said Flora. 'What's the matter?'

'We have had a discussion,' said Margaret. 'She has been terribly shocked by finding out what we have often thought about poor little Tom, and she thinks we ought to tell papa. Her principle is quite right, but I doubt—'

'I know exactly how Ethel would do it!' cried Flora; 'blurt out all on a sudden, "Papa, Tom cheats at his lessons!" then there would be a tremendous uproar; papa would scold Tom till he almost frightened him out of his wits, and then find out it was only suspicion.'

'And never have any comfort again,' said Margaret. 'He would always dread that Tom was deceiving him, and then think it was all for want of— O no, it will never do to speak of it, unless we find out some positive piece of misbehaviour.'

'Certainly,' said Flora.

'And it would do Tom no good to make him afraid of papa,' said Richard.

'Ethel's rule is right in principle,' said Margaret, thoughtfully, 'that papa ought to know all without reserve, and yet it will hardly do in practice. One must use discretion, and not tease him about every little thing. He takes them so much to heart, that he would be almost distracted; and, with so much business abroad, I think at home he should have nothing but rest, and, as far as we can, freedom from care and worry. Anything wrong about the children brings on *the* grief so much, that I cannot bear to mention it.'

Richard and Flora agreed with her, admiring the spirit which made her, in her weakness and helplessness, bear the whole burthen of family cares alone, and devote herself entirely to spare her father. He was, indeed, her first object, and she would have sacrificed anything to give him ease of mind; but, perhaps, she regarded him more as a charge of her own, than as, in very truth, the head of the family. She had the government in her

hands, and had never been used to see him exercise it much in
detail (she did not know how much her mother had referred
to him in private), and had succeeded to her authority at a time
when his health and spirits were in such a state as to make it
doubly needful to spare him.   It was no wonder that she sometimes carried her consideration beyond what was strictly right,
and forgot that he was the real authority, more especially as his
impulsive nature sometimes carried him away, and his sound
judgment was not certain to come into play at the first moment,
so that it required some moral courage to excite displeasure so
easy of manifestation; and of such courage there was, perhaps,
a deficiency in her character. Nor had she yet detected her own
satisfaction in being the first with every one in the family.

Ethel was put out, as Flora had discovered; and when she was
down-stairs she found it out, and accused herself of having been
cross to Margaret, and unkind to Tom—of wishing to be a tell-
tale.   But still, though displeased with herself, she was dissatis-
fied with Margaret; it might be right, but it did not agree with
her notions.   She wanted to see everyone uncompromising, as
girls of fifteen generally do; she had an intense disgust and
loathing of underhand ways; could not bear to think of Tom's
carrying them on, and going to a place of temptation with them
uncorrected; and she looked up to her father with the reverence
and enthusiasm of one like-minded.

She was vexed on another score.   Norman came home from
Abbotstoke Grange without having seen Miss Rivers, but with a
fresh basket of choice flowers, rapturous descriptions of Mr. Rivers's
prints, and a present of an engraving, in shading, such as to give
the effect of a cast, of a very fine head of Alexander.   Nothing
was to be thought of but a frame for this—olive, bay, laurel—
everything appropriate to the conqueror.   Margaret and Norman
were engrossed in the subject; and to Ethel, who had no toleration for fancy-work, who expected everything to be either useful
or intellectual, this seemed very frivolous. She heard her father
say how glad he was to see Norman interested and occupied, and
certainly, though it was only in leather leaves, it was better than
drooping and attending to nothing.   She knew, too, that Margaret did it for his sake; but, said Ethel to herself, ' It was very
odd that people should find amusement in such things. Margaret
always had a turn for them, but it was very strange in Norman.'

Then came the pang of finding out that this was aggravated
by the neglect of herself; she called it all selfishness, and felt
that she had had an uncomfortable, unsatisfactory day, with
everything going wrong.

CHAPTER XVII.

'Gently supported by the ready aid
Of loving hands, whose little work of toil
Her grateful prodigality repaid
With all the benediction of her smile,
She turned her failing feet
To the softly cushioned seat,
Dispensing kindly greetings all the time.'—R. M. MILNES.

THREE great events signalized the month of January. The first was, the opening of the school at Cocksmoor, whither a cart transported half-a-dozen forms, various books, and three dozen plumbuns, Margaret's contribution, in order that the school might begin with éclat. There walked Mr. Wilmot, Richard, and Flora, with Mary, in a jumping capering state of delight, and Ethel, not knowing whether she rejoiced. She kept apart from the rest, and hardly spoke, for this long probation had impressed her with a sense of responsibility, and she knew that it was a great work to which she had set her hand—a work in which she must persevere, and in which she could not succeed in her own strength.

She took hold of Flora's hand, and squeezed it hard, in a fit of shyness, when they came upon the hamlet, and saw the children watching for them; and when they reached the house, she would fain have shrunk into nothing; there was a swelling of heart that seemed to overwhelm and stifle her, and the effect of which was to keep her standing unhelpful, when the others were busy bringing in the benches and settling the room.

It was a tidy room, but it seemed very small when they ranged the benches, and opened the door to the seven-and-twenty children, and the four or five women who stood waiting. Ethel felt some dismay when they all came pushing in, without order or civility, and would have been utterly at a loss what to do with her scholars now she had got them, if Richard and Flora had not marshalled them to the benches.

Rough heads, torn garments, staring vacant eyes, and mouths gaping in shy rudeness—it was a sight to disenchant her of visions of pleasure in the work she had set herself. It was well that she had not to take the initiative.

Mr. Wilmot said a few simple words to the mothers about the wish to teach their children what was right, and to do the best at present practicable; and then told the children that he hoped they would take pains to be good, and mind what they were taught. Then he desired all to kneel down; he said the Collect, 'Prevent us, O Lord, in all our doings—' and then the Lord's Prayer.

PART I.   M

Ethel felt as if she could bear it better, and was more up to the work after this. Next, the children were desired to stand round the room, and Mr. Wilmot tried who could say the Catechism—the two biggest, a boy and a girl, had not an idea of it, and the boy looked foolish, and grinned at being asked what was his name. One child was tolerably perfect, and about half-a-dozen had some dim notions. Three were entirely ignorant of the Lord's Prayer, and many of the others did not by any means pronounce the words of it. Jane and Fanny Taylor, Rebekah Watts, and Mrs. Green's little boy, were the only ones who, by their own account, used morning and evening prayers, though, on further examination, it appeared that Polly and Jenny Hall, and some others, were accustomed to repeat the old rhyme about ' Matthew, Mark, Luke, and John,' and Una M'Carthy and her little brother Fergus said something that nobody could make out, but which Mr. Wilmot thought had once been an ' Ave Maria.'

Some few of the children could read, and several more knew their letters. The least ignorant were selected to form a first-class, and Mr. Wilmot promised a Prayer-book to the first who should be able to repeat the Catechism without a mistake, and a Bible to the first who could read a chapter in it.

Then followed a setting of tasks, varying from a verse of a Psalm, or the first answer in the Catechism, down to the distinction between A, B, and C; all to be ready by next Tuesday, when, weather permitting, a second lesson was to be given. Afterwards, a piece of advice of Margaret's was followed, and Flora read aloud to the assembly the story of ' Margaret Fletcher.' To some this seemed to give great satisfaction, especially to Una, but Ethel was surprised to see that many, and those not only little ones, talked and yawned. They had no power of attention even to a story, and the stillness was irksome to such wild colts. It was plain that it was time to leave off, and there was no capacity there which did not find the conclusion agreeable, when the basket was opened, and Ethel and Mary distributed the buns, with instructions to say ' thank you.'

The next Tuesday, *some* of the lessons were learnt, Una's perfectly; the big ignorant boy came no more; and some of the children had learnt to behave better, while others behaved worse; Ethel began to know what she was about; Richard's gentleness was eminently successful with the little girls, impressing good manners on them in a marvellous way ; and Mary's importance and happiness with alphabet scholars, some bigger than herself, were edifying. Cocksmoor was fairly launched.

The next memorable day was that of Margaret's being first carried down-stairs. She had been willing to put it off as long as she could, dreading to witness the change below-stairs, and feeling, too, that in entering on the family room, without power of leaving it, she was losing all quiet and solitude, as well as giving up that monopoly of her father in his evenings, which had been her great privilege.

However, she tried to talk herself into liking it; and was rewarded by the happy commotion it caused, though Dr. May was in a state of excitement and nervousness at the prospect of seeing her on the stairs, and his attempts to conceal it only made it worse, till Margaret knew she should be nervous herself, and wished him out of sight and out of the house till it was over, for without him she had full confidence in the coolness and steadiness of Richard, and by him it was safely and quietly accomplished. She was landed on the sofa, Richard and Flora settling her, and the others crowding round and exclaiming, while the newness of the scene and the change gave her a sense of confusion, and she shut her eyes to recover her thoughts, but opened them the next instant at her father's exclamation that she was overcome, smiled to reassure him, and declared herself not tired, and to be very glad to be among them again. But the bustle was oppressive, and her cheerful manner was an effort; she longed to see them all gone, and Flora found it out, sent the children for their walk, and carried off Ethel and the brothers.

Dr. May was called out of the room at the same time, and she was left alone. She gazed round her, at the room where, four months before, she had seen her mother with the babe in her arms, the children clustered round her, her father exulting in his hen-and-chicken daisies, herself full of bright undefined hope, radiant with health and activity, and her one trouble such that she now knew the force of her mother's words, that it only proved her happiness. It was not till that moment that Margaret realized the change: she found her eyes filling with tears, as she looked round, and saw the familiar furniture and ornaments.

They were instantly checked as she heard her father returning, but not so that he did not perceive them, and exclaim that it had been too much for her. 'O no—it was only the first time,' said Margaret, losing the sense of the painful vacancy in her absorbing desire not to distress her father, and thinking only of him as she watched him standing for some minutes leaning on the mantel-shelf, with his hand shading his forehead.

She began to speak as soon as she thought he was ready to have his mind turned away:—'How nicely Ritchie managed! He carried me so comfortably and easily. It is enough to spoil me to be so deftly waited on.'

'I am glad of it,' said Dr. May; 'I am sure the change is better for you;' but he came and looked at her still with great solicitude.

'Ritchie can take excellent care of me,' she continued, most anxious to divert his thoughts. 'You see it will do very well indeed for you to take Harry to school.'

'I should like to do so. I should like to see his master, and to take Norman with me,' said the Doctor. 'It would be just the thing for him now—we would show him the dockyard, and all those matters; and such a thorough holiday would set him up again.'

'He is very much better.'

'Much better—he is recovering spirits and tone very fast. That leaf-work of yours came at a lucky time. I like to see him looking out for a curious fern in the hedge-rows—the pursuit has quite brightened him up.'

'And he does it so thoroughly,' said Margaret. 'Ethel fancies it is rather frivolous of him, I believe; but it amuses me to see how men give dignity to what women make trifling. He *will* know everything about the leaves, hunts up my botany books, and has taught me a hundred times more of the construction and wonders of them than I ever learnt.'

'Aye,' said the Doctor, 'he has been talking a good deal to me about vegetable chemistry. He would make a good scientific botanist, if he were to be nothing else. I should be glad if he sticks to it as a pursuit—'tis pretty work; and I should like to have gone further with it, if I had ever had time for it.'

'I dare say he will,' said Margaret. 'It will be very pleasant if he can go with you. How he would enjoy the British Museum, if there was time for him to see it! Have you said anything to him yet?'

'No; I waited to see how you were, as it all depends on that.'

'I think it depends still more on something else; whether Norman is as fit to take care of you as Richard is.'

'That's another point. There's nothing but what he could manage now; but I don't like saying anything to him. I know he would undertake anything I wished, without a word; and then, perhaps, dwell on it in fancy, and force himself, till it would turn to a perfect misery, and upset his nerves again. I'm sorry for it. I meant him to have followed my trade, but he'll never do for that. However, he has wits enough to make himself what he pleases, and I dare say he will keep at the head of the school after all.'

'How very good he has been in refraining from restlessness!'

'It's beautiful!' said Dr. May, with strong emotion. 'Poor boy! I trust he'll not be disappointed, and I don't think he will; but I've promised him I won't be annoyed if he should lose his place—so we must take especial care not to show any anxiety. However, for this matter, Margaret, I wish you would sound him, and see whether it would be more pleasure or pain. Only mind you don't let him think that I shall be vexed, if he feels that he can't make up his mind; I would not have him fancy that for more than I can tell.'

This consultation revived the spirits of both; and the others returning, found Margaret quite disposed for companionship. If to her the evening was sad and strange, like a visit in a dream to some old familiar haunt, finding all unnatural, to the rest it was delightful. The room was no longer dreary, now that there was a centre for care and attentions, and the party was no longer broken up—the sense of comfort, cheerfulness, and home-gathering had returned, and the pleasant evening household gossip went round the table almost as it used to do. Dr. May resumed his old habit of skimming a club-book, and imparting the cream to the listeners; and Flora gave them some music, a great treat to Margaret, who had long only heard its distant sounds.

Margaret found an opportunity of talking to Norman, and judged favourably. He was much pleased at the prospect of the journey, and of seeing a ship, so as to have a clearer notion of the scene where Harry's life was to be spent, and though the charge of the arm was a drawback, he did not treat it as insurmountable.

A few days' attendance in his father's room gave him confidence in taking Richard's place, and, accordingly, the third important measure was decided on, namely, that he and his father should accompany Harry to the naval school, and be absent three nights. Some relations would be glad to receive them in London, and Alan Ernescliffe, who was studying steam navigation at Woolwich, volunteered to meet them, and go with them to Portsmouth.

It was a wonderful event; Norman and Harry had never been beyond Whitford in their lives, and none of the young ones could recollect their papa's ever going from home for more than one night. Dr. May laughed at Margaret for her anxiety and excitement on the subject, and was more amused at overhearing Richard's precise directions to Norman over the packing up.

'Aye, Ritchie,' said the Doctor, as he saw his portmanteau locked, and the key given to Norman, 'you may well look grave upon it. You won't see it look so tidy when it comes back again, and I believe you are thinking it will be lucky if you see it at all.'

There was a very affectionate leave-taking of Harry, who, growing rather soft-hearted, thought it needful to be disdainful, scolded Mary and Blanche for 'lugging off his figure-head,' and

assured them they made as much work about it as if he was
going to sea at once. Then, to put an end to any more embraces,
he marched off to the station with Tom, and nearly caused the
others to be too late, by the search for him that ensued.

In due time, Dr. May and Norman returned, looking the better
for the journey. There was, first, to tell of Harry's school and
its master, and Alan Ernescliffe's introduction of him to a nice-
looking boy of his own age; then they were eloquent on the
wonders of the dockyard, the Victory, the block machinery.
And London—while Dr. May went to transact some business,
Norman had been with Alan at the British Museum, and though
he had intended to see half London besides, there was no tearing
him away from the Elgin marbles; and nothing would serve him,
but bringing Dr. May the next morning to visit the Ninevite
bulls. Norman further said, that whereas papa could never go
out of his house without meeting people who had something to
say to him, it was the same elsewhere. Six acquaintances he
had met unexpectedly in London, and two at Portsmouth.

So the conversation went on all the evening, to the great
delight of all. It was more about things than people, though
Flora inquired after Mr. Ernescliffe, and was told he had met
them at the station, had been everywhere with them, and had
dined at the Mackenzies each day. 'How was he looking?'
Ethel asked; and was told pretty much the same as when he
went away; and, on a further query from Flora, it appeared that
an old naval friend of his father's had hopes of a ship, and had
promised to have him with him, and thereupon warm hopes were
expressed that Harry might have a berth in the same.

'And when is he coming here again, papa?' said Ethel.

'Eh! oh! I can't tell. I say, isn't it high time to ring?'

When they went up at night, every one felt that half the say
had not been said, and there were fresh beginnings on the stairs.
Norman triumphantly gave the key to Richard, and then called to
Ethel: 'I say, won't you come into my room while I unpack?'

'O yes, I should like it very much.'

Ethel sat on the bed, rolled up in a cloak, while Norman
undid his bag, announcing at the same time: 'Well, Ethel,
papa says I may get to my Euripides to-morrow, if I please,
and only work an hour at a time!'

'O, I am so glad. Then he thinks you quite well?'

'Yes, I am quite well. I hope I've done with nonsense.'

'And how did you get on with his arm?'

'Very well—he was so patient, and told me how to manage.
You heard that Sir Matthew said it had got much better in
these few weeks. O here it is! There's a present for you.'

THE DAISY CHAIN.

'O, thank you. From you, or from papa?'

'This is mine. Papa has a present for every one in his bag. He said, at last, that a man with eleven children hadn't need go to London very often.'

'And you got this beautiful Lyra Innocentium for me. How very kind of you, Norman. It is just what I wished for. Such lovely binding—and those embossed edges to the leaves. Oh! they make a pattern as they open! I never saw anything like it.'

'I saw such a one on Miss Rivers's table, and asked Ernescliffe where to get one like it. See here's what my father gave me.'

'Bishop Ken's Manual. That is in readiness for the Confirmation.'

'Look. I begged him to put my name, though he said it was a pity to do it with his left hand; I didn't like to wait, so I asked him at least to write N. W. May, and the date.'

'And he has added Prov. xxiii. 24, 25. Let me look it out.' She did so, and instead of reading it aloud, looked at Norman full of congratulation.

'How it ought to make one—' and there Norman broke off from the fulness of his heart.

'I'm glad he put both verses,' said Ethel, presently. 'How pleased with you he must be!'

A silence while brother and sister both gazed intently at the crooked characters, till at last Ethel, with a long breath, resumed her ordinary tone, and said, 'How well he has come to write with his left hand now.'

'Yes. Did you know that he wrote himself to tell Ernescliffe Sir Matthew's opinion of Margaret?'

'No: did he?'

'Do you know, Ethel,' said Norman, as he knelt on the floor, and tumbled miscellaneous articles out of his bag, 'it is my belief that Ernescliffe is in love with her, and that papa thinks so.'

'Dear me!' cried Ethel, starting up. 'That is famous. We should always have Margaret at home when he goes to sea!'

'But mind, Ethel, for your life you must not say one word to any living creature.'

'O no, I promise you I won't, Norman, if you'll only tell me how you found it out.'

'What first put it in my head was the first evening, while I was undoing the portmanteau; my father leant on the mantelshelf, and sighed and muttered, 'Poor Ernescliffe! I wish it may end well.' I thought he forgot that I was there, so I would not seem to notice, but I soon saw it was *that* he meant.'

'How?' cried Ethel, eagerly.

'O, I don't know—by Alan's way.'

'Tell me—I want to know what people do when they are in love.'

'Nothing particular,' said Norman, smiling.

'Did you hear him inquire for her? How did he look?'

'I can't tell. That was when he met us at the station before I thought of it, and I had to see to the luggage. But I'll tell you one thing, Ethel; when papa was talking of her to Mrs. Mackenzie, at the other end of the room, all his attention went away in an instant from what he was saying. And once, when Harry said something to me about her, he started, and looked round so earnestly.'

'O yes—that's like people in books. And did he colour?'

'No; I don't recollect that he did,' said Norman; 'but I observed he never asked directly after her if he could help it, but always was trying to lead, in some round-about way, to hearing what she was doing.'

Did he call her Margaret?'

'I watched; but to me he always said, "Your sister," and if he had to speak of her to papa, he said, "Miss May." And then you should have seen his attention to papa. I could hardly get a chance of doing anything for papa.'

'O I am sure of it!' cried Ethel, clasping her hands. 'But, poor man, how unhappy he must have been at having to go away when she was so ill!'

'Aye, the last time he saw her was when he carried her up-stairs.'

'O dear! I hope he will soon come here again!'

'I don't suppose he will. Papa did not ask him.'

'Dear me, Norman! Why not? Isn't papa very fond of him? Why shouldn't he come?'

'Don't you see, Ethel, that would be of no use while poor Margaret is no better. If he gained her affections, it would only make her unhappy.'

'O, but she is much better. She can raise herself up now without help, and sat up ever so long this morning, without leaning back on her cushions. She is getting well—you know Sir Matthew said she would.'

'Yes; but I suppose papa thinks they had better say nothing till she is quite well.'

'And when she is! How famous it will be!'

'Then there's another thing; he is very poor, you know.'

'I am sure papa doesn't care about people being rich.'

'I suppose Alan thinks he ought not to marry, unless he could make his wife comfortable.'

'Look here—it would be all very easy: she should stay with us, and be comfortable here, and he go to sea, and get lots of prize money.'

'And that's what you call domestic felicity!' said Norman, laughing.

'He might have her when he was at home,' said Ethel.

'No, no; that would never do,' said Norman. 'Do you think Ernescliffe is a man that would marry a wife for her father to maintain her?'

Why, papa would like it very much. He is not a mercenary father in a book.'

'Hey! what's that?' said a voice Ethel little expected. 'Contraband talk at contraband times? What's this!'

'Did you hear, papa?' said Ethel, looking down.

'Only your last words, as I came up to ask Norman what he had done with my pocket-book. Mind, I ask no impertinent questions; but, if you have no objection, I should like to know what gained me the honour of that compliment.'

'Norman?' said Ethel, interrogatively, and blushing in emulation of her brother, who was crimson.

'I'll find it,' said he, rushing off with a sort of nod and sign, that conveyed to Ethel that there was no help for it.

So, with much confusion, she whispered into her papa's ear that Norman had been telling her something he guessed about Mr. Ernescliffe.

Her father at first smiled, a pleased amused smile. 'Ah! ha! so Master June has his eyes and ears open, has he? A fine bit of gossip to regale you with on his return!'

'He told me to say not one word,' said Ethel.

'Right—mind you don't,' said Dr. May, and Ethel was surprised to see how sorrowful his face became. At the same moment Norman returned, still very red, and said, 'I've put out the pocket-book, papa. I think I should tell you I repeated what, perhaps, you did not mean me to hear—you talked to yourself something of pitying Ernescliffe.'

The Doctor smiled again at the boy's high-minded openness, which must have cost an effort of self-humiliation. 'I can't say *little* pitchers have long ears, to a May-pole like you, Norman,' said he; 'I think I ought rather to apologize for having inadvertently tumbled in among your secrets; I assure you I did not come to spy you.'

'O, no, no, no, *no!*' repeated Ethel, vehemently. 'Then you didn't mind our talking about it?'

'Of course not, as long as it goes no further. It is the use of sisters to tell them one's private sentiments. Is not it, Norman?'

'And do you really think *it* is *so*, papa?' Ethel could not help whispering.

'I'm afraid it is!' said Dr. May, sighing; then, as he caught her earnest eyes, 'The more I see of Alan, the finer fellow I think him, and the more sorry I am for him. It seems presumptuous, almost wrong, to think of the matter at all while my poor Margaret is in this state; and, if she were well, there are other difficulties which would, perhaps, prevent his speaking, or lead to long years of waiting and wearing out hope.'

'Money?' said Ethel.

'Aye! Though I so far deserve your compliment, Miss, that I should be foolish enough, if she were but well, to give my consent to-morrow, because I could not help it; yet one can't live forty-six years in this world without seeing it is wrong to marry without a reasonable dependence—and there won't be much among eleven of you. It makes my heart ache to think of it, come what may, as far as I can see, and without *her* to judge. The only comfort is, that poor Margaret herself knows nothing of it, and is at peace so far. It will be ordered for them, any how. Good night, my dear.'

Ethel sought her room, with graver, deeper thoughts of life than she had carried up-stairs.

CHAPTER XVIII.

'Saw ye never in the meadows,
    Where your little feet did pass,
Down below, the sweet white daisies
    Growing in the long green grass?

'Saw you never lilac blossoms,
    Or acacia white and red,
Waving brightly in the sunshine,
    On the tall trees over head?'

HYMNS FOR CHILDREN, C. F. A.

'My dear child, what a storm you have had! how wet you must be!' exclaimed Mrs. Larpent, as Meta Rivers came bounding up the broad staircase at Abbotstoke Grange.

'Oh, no; I am quite dry; feel.'

'Are you sure?' said Mrs. Larpent, drawing her darling into a luxurious bed-room, lighted up by a glowing fire, and full of pretty things. 'Here, come and take off your wet things, my dear, and Bellairs shall bring you some tea.'

'I'm dry; I'm warm,' said Meta, tossing off her plumy hat, as she established herself, with her feet on the fender. 'But where do you think I have been? You have so much to hear; but first—three guesses where we were in the rain?'

'In the Stoneborough Cloisters, that you wanted to see? My dear, you did not keep your papa in the cold there?'

'No, no; we never got there at all; guess again.'

'At Mr. Edward Wilmot's?'

'No!'

'Could it have been at Dr. May's? Really, then, you must tell me.'

'There! you deserve a good long story; beginning at the beginning,' said Meta, clapping her hands, 'wasn't it curious? as we were coming up the last hill, we met some girls in deep mourning with a lady, who looked like their governess. I wondered whether they could be Dr. May's daughters, and so it turned out they were. Presently there began to fall little square lumps, neither hail, nor snow, nor rain; it grew very cold, and rain came on. It would have been great fun, if I had not been afraid papa would catch cold, and he said he would canter on to the inn. But, luckily, there was Dr. May walking up the street, and he begged us to come into his house. I was so glad! We were tolerably wet, and Dr. May said something about hoping the girls were at home; well, when he opened the drawing-room door, there was the poor daughter lying on the sofa.'

'Poor girl! tell me of her.'

'O! you must go and see her; you won't look at her without losing your heart. Papa liked her so much—see if he does not talk of her all the evening. She looks the picture of goodness and sweetness. Only think of her having some of the Maidenhair and Cape Jessamine still in water, that we sent her so long ago. She shall have some flowers every three days. Well, Dr. May said, 'There is one, at least, that is sure to be at home.' She felt my habit, and said I must go and change it, and she called to a little thing of six, telling her to show me the way to Flora. She smiled, and said she wished she could go herself, but Flora would take care of me. Little Blanche came and took hold of my hand, chattering away, up we went, up two staircases, and at the top of the last stood a girl about seventeen, so pretty! such deep blue eyes, and such a complexion! "That's Flora," little Blanche said; "Flora, this is Miss Rivers, and she's wet, and Margaret says you are to take care of her."'

'So that was your introduction?'

'Yes; we got acquainted in a minute. She took me into her room—such a room! I believe Bellairs would be angry if she had such an one; all up in the roof, no fire, no carpet, except little strips by the beds; there were three beds. Flora used to sleep there till Miss May was ill, and now she dresses there. Yet I am sure they are as much ladies as I am.'

'You are an only daughter, my dear, and a petted one,' said

Mrs. Larpent, smiling. 'There are too many of them to make much of, as we do of our Meta.'

'I suppose so; but I did not know gentlewomen lived in such a way,' said Meta. 'There were nice things about, a beautiful inlaid work-box of Flora's, and a rose-wood desk, and plenty of books, and a Greek book and dictionary were spread open. I asked Flora if they were hers, and she laughed and said no; and that Ethel would be much discomposed that I had seen them. Ethel keeps up with her brother Norman—only fancy! and he at the head of the school. How clever she must be!'

'But, my dear, were you standing in your wet things all this time?'

'No; I was trying on their frocks, but they trailed on the ground upon me, so she asked if I would come and sit by the nursery fire till my habit was dry; and there was the dear little good-humoured baby, so fair and pretty. She is not a bit shy, will go to anybody, but, they say, she likes no one so well as her brother Norman.'

'So you had a regular treat of baby nursing?'

'That I had; I could not part with her, the darling. Flora thought we might take her down, and I liked playing with her in the drawing-room and talking to Miss May, till the fly came to take us home. I wanted to have seen Ethel; but, only think, papa has asked Dr. May to bring Flora some day; how I hope he will!'

Little Meta having told her story, and received plenty of sympathy, proceeded to dress, and while her maid braided her hair, a musing fit fell upon her. 'I have seen something of life to-day,' thought she. 'I had thought of the great difference between us and the poor, but I did not know ladies lived in such different ways. I should be very miserable without Bellairs, or without a fire in my room. I don't know what I should do if I had to live in that cold, shabby den, and do my own hair, yet they think nothing of it, and they are cultivated and lady-like! Is it all fancy and being brought up to it? I wonder if it is right? Yet dear papa likes me to have these things, and can afford them. I never knew I was luxurious before, and yet I think I must be! One thing I do wish, and that is, that I was of as much use as those girls. I ought to be. I am a motherless girl like them, and I ought to be everything to papa, just as Miss May is, even lying on the sofa there, and only two years older than I am. I don't think I am of any use at all; he is fond of me, of course, dear papa; and if I died, I don't know what would become of him, but that's only because I am his daughter—he has only George besides to care for. But, really and truly, he would get on as well without me. I never do anything for him, but now and then playing to him in the evening, and that not always, I am afraid, when I want to be about anything else. He is always petting me, and giving me all I want, but I never do anything but my lessons, and going to the school and the poor people, and that is all pleasure. I have so much that I never miss what I give away. I wonder whether it is all right. Leonora and Agatha have not so much money to do as they please with — they are not so idolized. George said, when he was angry, that papa idolizes me; but they have all these comforts and luxuries, and never think of anything but doing what they like. They never made me consider as these Mays do. I should like to know them more. I do so much want a friend of my own age. It is the only want I have. I have tried to make a friend of Leonora, but I cannot; she never cares for what I do. If she saw these Mays she would look down on them. Dear Mrs. Larpent is better than any one, but then she is so much older. Flora May shall be my friend. I'll make her call me Meta as soon as she comes. When will it be? The day after to-morrow?'

But little Meta watched in vain. Dr. May always came with either Richard or the groom to drive him, and if Meta met him and hoped he would bring Flora next time, he only answered that Flora would like it very much, and he hoped soon to do so.

The truth was, it was no such every-day matter as Meta imagined. The larger carriage had been broken, and the only vehicle held only the doctor—his charioteer—and in a very minute appendage behind, a small son of the gardener, to open gates and hold the horse.

The proposal had been one of those general invitations to be fulfilled at any time, and therefore easily set aside; and Dr. May, though continually thinking he should like to take his girls to Abbotstoke, never saw the definite time for so doing; and Flora herself, though charmed with Miss Rivers, and delighted with the prospect of visiting her, only viewed it as a distant prospect.

There was plenty of immediate interest to occupy them at home, to say nothing of the increasing employment that Cocksmoor gave to thoughts, legs, and needles. There was the commencement of the half-year, when Tom's school-boy life was to begin, and when it would be proved whether Norman were able to retain his elevation.

Margaret had much anxiety respecting the little boy about to be sent into a scene of temptation. Her great confidence was in Richard, who told her that boys did many more wrong things than were known at home, and yet turned out very well, and that Tom would be sure to right himself in the end. Richard had been blameless in his whole school course; but though never partaking of the other boys' evil practices, he could not form an independent estimate of character, and his tone had been a little hurt, by sharing the school public opinion of morality. He thought Stoneborough and its temptations inevitable, and only wished to make the best of it. Margaret was afraid to harass her father by laying the case before him. All her brothers had gone safely through the school, and it never occurred to her that it was possible that, if her father knew the bias of Tom's disposition, he might choose, for the present, at least, some other mode of education.

She talked earnestly to Tom, and he listened impatiently. There is an age when boys rebel against female rule, and are not yet softened by the chivalry of manhood, and Tom was at this time of life. He did not like to be lectured by a sister, secretly disputed her right, and, proud of becoming a schoolboy, had not the generous deference for her weakness felt by his elder brothers; he was all the time peeling a stick, as if to show that he was not attending, and he raised up his shoulder pettishly whenever she came to a mention of the religious duty of sincerity. She did not long continue her advice; and, much disappointed and concerned, tried to console herself with hoping that he might have heeded more than he seemed to do.

He was placed tolerably high in the school, and Norman, who had the first choice of fags, took him instead of Hector Ernescliffe, who had just passed beyond the part of the school liable to be fagged. He said he liked school, looked bright when he came home in the evening, and the sisters hoped all was right.

Every one was just now anxiously watching Norman, especially his father, who strove in vain to keep back all manifestation of his earnest desire to see him retain his post. Resolutely did the Doctor refrain from asking any questions when the boys came in, but he could not keep his eyes from studying the face, to see whether it bore marks of mental fatigue, and from following him about the room, to discover whether he found it necessary, as he had done last autumn, to spend the evening in study. It was no small pleasure to see him come in with his hand full of horse-chesnuts and hazel-buds, and proceed to fetch the miscroscope and botany books, throwing himself eagerly into the study of the wonders of their infant forms, searching deeply into them with Margaret, and talking them over with his father, who was very glad to promote the pursuit—one in which he had always taken great interest.

Another night Dr. May was for a moment disturbed by seeing the school-books put out; but Norman had only some notes to compare, and while he did so, he was remarking on Flora's music, and joining in the conversation so freely, as to prove it was no labour to him. In truth, he was evidently quite recovered, entirely himself again, except that he was less boyish. He had been very lively and full of merry nonsense; but his ardour for play had gone off with his high spirits, and there was a manliness of manner, and tone of mind, that made him appear above his real age.

At the end of a fortnight he volunteered to tell his father that all was right. 'I am not afraid of not keeping my place,' he said; 'you were quite right, papa. I am more up to my work than I was ever before, and it comes to me quite fresh and pleasant. I don't promise to get the Randall scholarship, if Forder and Cheviot stay on, but I can keep quite up to the mark in school-work.'

'That's right,' said Dr. May, much rejoiced. 'Are you sure you do it with ease, and without its haunting you at night?'

'Oh, yes; quite sure. I can't think what has made Dr. Hoxton set us on in such easy things this time. It is very lucky for me, for one gets so much less time to oneself as dux.'

'What! with keeping order?'

'Aye,' said Norman. 'I fancy they think they may take liberties because I am new and young. I must have my eye in all corners of the hall at once, and do my own work by snatches, as I can.'

'Can you make them attend to you?'

'Why yes, pretty well, when it comes to the point—"will you, or will you not." Cheviot is a great help, too, and has all the weight of being the eldest fellow amongst us.'

'But still you find it harder work than learning? You had rather have to master the dead language than the live tongues?'

'A pretty deal,' said Norman; then added, 'one knows what to be at with the dead, better than with the living; they don't make parties against one. I don't wonder at it. It was very hard on some of those great fellows to have me set before them; but I do not think it is fair to visit it by putting up the little boys to all sorts of mischief.'

'Shameful!' said the Doctor, warmly; 'but never mind, Norman, keep your temper, and do your own duty, and you are man enough to put down such petty spite.'

'I hope I shall manage rightly,' said Norman; 'but I shall be glad if I can get the Randall and get away to Oxford; school is not what it used to be, and if you don't think me too young—'

'No, I don't; certainly not. Trouble has made a man of you, Norman, and you are fitter to be with men than boys. In the meantime, if you can be patient with these fellows, you'll be of great use where you are. If there had been any one like you at the head of the school in my time, it would have kept me out of no end of scrapes. How does Tom get on?—he is not likely to fall into this set, I trust.'

'I am not sure,' said Norman; 'he does pretty well on the whole. Some of them began by bullying him, and that made him cling to Cheviot and Ernescliffe, and the better party; but lately, I have thought Anderson junior rather making up to him, and I don't know whether they don't think that tempting him over to them, would be the surest way of vexing me. I have an eye over him, and I hope he may get settled into the steadier sort before next half.'

After a silence, Norman said,—'Papa, there's a thing I can't settle in my own mind. Suppose there had been wrong things done when older boys, and excellent ones, too, were at the head of the school, yet they never interfered, do you think I ought to let it go on?'

'Certainly not; or why is power given to you?'

'So I thought,' said Norman; 'I can't see it otherwise. I wish I could, for it will be horrid to set about it, and they'll think it a regular shame in me to meddle. O! I know what I came into the study for; I want you to be so kind as to lend me your pocket Greek Testament. I gave Harry my little one.'

'You are very welcome. What do you want it for?'

Norman coloured. 'I met with a sermon the other day that recommended reading a bit of it every day, and I thought I should like to try, now the Confirmation is coming. One can always have some quiet by getting away into the cloister.'

'Bless you, my boy! while you go on in this way, I have not much fear but that you'll know how to manage.'

Norman's rapid progress affected another of the household in an unexpected way.

'Margaret, my dear, I wish to speak to you,' said Miss Winter, reappearing when Margaret thought every one was gone out walking. She would have said, 'I am very sorry for it'—so ominous was the commencement—and her expectations were fulfilled when Miss Winter had solemnly seated herself, and taken out her netting. 'I wished to speak to you about dear Ethel,' said the governess; 'you know how unwilling I always am to make any complaint, but I cannot be satisfied with her present way of going on.'

'Indeed,' said Margaret. 'I am much grieved to hear this. I thought she had been taking great pains to improve.'

'So she was at one time. I would not by any means wish to

deny it, and it is not of her learning that I speak, but of a hurried, careless way of doing everything, and an irritability at being interfered with.'

Margaret knew how Miss Winter often tried Ethel's temper, and was inclined to take her sister's part. 'Ethel's time is so fully occupied,' she said.

'That is the very thing that I was going to observe, my dear. Her time is too much occupied; and my conviction is, that it is hurtful to a girl of her age.'

This was a new idea to Margaret, who was silent, longing to prove Miss Winter wrong, and not have to see poor Ethel pained by having to relinquish any of her cherished pursuits.

'You see there is that Cocksmoor,' said Miss Winter. 'You do not know how far off it is, my dear; much too great a distance for a young girl to be walking continually in all weathers.'

'That's a question for papa,' thought Margaret.

'Besides,' continued Miss Winter, 'those children engross almost all her time and thoughts. She is working for them, preparing lessons, running after them continually. It takes off her whole mind from her proper occupations, unsettles her, and I do think it is beyond what befits a young lady of her age.'

Margaret was silent.

'In addition,' said Miss Winter, 'she is at every spare moment busy with Latin and Greek, and I cannot think that to keep pace with a boy of Norman's age and ability can be desirable for her.'

'It is a great deal,' said Margaret, 'but—'

'I am convinced that she does more than is right,' continued Miss Winter. 'She may not feel any ill effects at present, but you may depend upon it, it will tell on her by-and-by. Besides, she does not attend to anything properly. At one time she was improving in neatness and orderly habits. Now, you surely must have seen how much less tidy her hair and dress have been.'

'I have thought her hair looking rather rough,' said Margaret, disconsolately.

'No wonder,' said Miss Winter, 'for Flora and Mary tell me she hardly spends five minutes over it in the morning, and with a book before her the whole time. If I send her up to make it fit to be seen, I meet with looks of annoyance. She leaves her books in all parts of the school-room for Mary to put away, and her table drawer is one mass of confusion. Her lessons she does well enough, I own, though what I should call much too fast; but have you looked at her work lately?'

PART I.   N

'She does not work very well,' said Margaret, who was at that moment, though Miss Winter did not know it, re-gathering a poor child's frock that Ethel had galloped through with more haste than good speed.

'She works a great deal worse than little Blanche,' said Miss Winter, 'and though it may not be the fashion to say so in these days, I consider good needlework far more important than accomplishments. Well, then, Margaret, I should wish you only just to look at her writing.'

And Miss Winter opened a French exercise book, certainly containing anything but elegant specimens of penmanship. Ethel's best writing was an upright, disjointed, niggle, looking more like Greek than anything else, except where here and there it made insane efforts to become running-hand, and thereby lost its sole previous good quality of legibility, while the lines waved about the sheet in almost any direction but the horizontal. The necessity she believed herself under of doing what Harry called writing with the end of her nose, and her always holding her pen with her fingers almost in the ink, added considerably to the difficulty of the performance. This being her best, the worst may be supposed to be indescribable, when dashed off in a violent hurry, and considerably garnished with blots. Margaret thought she had seen the worst, and was sighing at being able to say nothing for it, when Miss Winter confounded her by turning a leaf, and showing it was possible to make a still wilder combination of scramble, niggle, scratch, and crookedness—and this was supposed to be an amended edition! Miss Winter explained that Ethel had, in an extremely short time, performed an exercise in which no fault could be detected except the writing, which was pronounced to be too atrocious to be shown up to M. Ballompré. On being desired to write it over again, she had obeyed with a very bad grace, and some murmurs about Cocksmoor, and produced the second specimen, which, in addition to other defects, had some elisions from arrant carelessness, depriving it of its predecessor's merits of being good French.

Miss Winter had been so provoked, that she believed this to be an effect of ill temper, and declared that she should certainly have kept Ethel at home to write it over again, if it had not so happened that Dr. May had proposed to walk part of the way with her and Richard, and the governess was unwilling to bring her into disgrace with him. Margaret was so grateful to her for this forbearance, that it disposed her to listen the more patiently to the same representations put in, what Miss Winter fancied, different forms. Margaret was much perplexed. She could not but see much truth in what Miss Winter said, and yet she could not bear to thwart Ethel, whom she admired with her whole heart; and that dry experience, and prejudiced preciseness, did not seem capable of entering into her sister's thirst for learning and action. When Miss Winter said Ethel would grow up odd, eccentric, and blue, Margaret was ready to answer that she would be superior to every one: and when the governess urged her to insist on Cocksmoor being given up, she felt impatient of that utter want of sympathy for the good work.

All that evening Margaret longed for a quiet time to reflect, but it never came till she was in bed; and when she had made up her mind how to speak to Ethel, it was five times harder to secure her alone. Even when Margaret had her in the room by herself, she looked wild and eager, and said she could not stay, she had some Thucydides to do.

'Won't you stay with me a little while, quietly?' said Margaret; 'we hardly ever have one of our talks.'

'I didn't mean to vex you, dear Margaret, I like nothing so well, only we are never alone, and I've no time.'

'Pray do spare me a minute, Ethel, for I have something that I must say to you, and I am afraid you won't like it—so do listen kindly.'

'Oh!' said Ethel, 'Miss Winter has been talking to you. I know she said she would tell you that she wants me to give up Cocksmoor. You aren't dreaming of it, Margaret!'

'Indeed, dear Ethel, I should be very sorry, but one thing I am sure of, that there is something amiss in your way of going on.'

'Did she show you that horrid exercise?'

'Yes.'

'Well, I know it was baddish writing, but just listen, Margaret. We promised six of the children to print them each a verse of a hymn on a card to learn. Ritchie did three, and then could not go on, for the book, that the others were in, was lost till last evening, and then he was writing for papa. So I thought I would do them before we went to Cocksmoor, and that I should squeeze time out of the morning; but I got a bit of Sophocles that was so horridly hard, it ate up all my time, and I don't understand it properly now; I must get Norman to tell me. And that ran in my head, and made me make a mistake in my sum, and have to begin it again. Then, just as I thought I had saved time over the exercise, comes Miss Winter and tells me I must do it over again, and scolds me, besides, about the ink on my fingers. She would send me up at once to get it off, and I could not find nurse and her bottle of stuff for it, so that wasted ever so much more time, and I was so vexed that, really and truly, my hand shook, and I could not write any better.'

'No, I thought it looked as if you had been in one of your agonies.'

'And she thought I did it on purpose, and that made me angry, and so we got into a dispute, and away went all the little moment I might have had, and I was forced to go to Cocksmoor as a promise breaker!'

'Don't you think you had better have taken pains at first?'

'Well, so I did with the sense, but I hadn't time to look at the writing much.'

'You would have made better speed if you had.'

'Oh! yes, I know I was wrong, but it is a great plague altogether. Really, Margaret, I shan't get Thucydides done.'

'You must wait a little longer, please, Ethel, for I want to say to you that I am afraid you are doing too much, and that prevents you from doing things well, as you were trying to do last autumn.'

'You are not thinking of my not going to Cocksmoor!' cried Ethel, vehemently.

'I want you to consider what is to be done, dear Ethel. You thought, last autumn, a great deal of curing your careless habits, now you seem not to have time to attend. You can do a great deal very fast, I know, but isn't it a pity to be always in a hurry?'

'It isn't Cocksmoor that is the reason,' said Ethel.

'No: you did pretty well when you began, but you know that was in the holidays, when you had no Latin and Greek to do.'

'O but, Margaret, they won't take so much time when I have once got over the difficulties, and see my way, but just now they have put Norman into such a frightfully difficult play, that I can hardly get on at all with it, and there's a new kind of Greek verses, too, and I don't make out from the book how to manage them. Norman showed me on Saturday, but mine won't be right. When I've got over that, I shan't be so hurried.'

'But Norman will go on to something harder, I suppose.'

'I dare say I shall be able to do it.'

'Perhaps you might, but I want you to consider if you are not working beyond what can be good for anybody. You see Norman is much cleverer than most boys, and you are a year younger; and besides doing all his work at the head of the school, his whole business of the day, you have Cocksmoor to attend to, and your own lessons, besides reading all the books that come into the house. Now isn't that more than is reason-able to expect any head and hands to do properly?'

'But if I can do it?'

'But can you, dear Ethel? Aren't you always racing from one thing to another, doing them by halves, feeling hunted, and then growing vexed?'

'I know I have been cross lately,' said Ethel, 'but it's the being so bothered.'

'And why are you bothered? Isn't it that you undertake too much?'

'What would you have me do?' said Ethel, in an injured, unconvinced voice. 'Not give up my children?'

'No,' said Margaret; 'but don't think me very unkind if I say, suppose you left off trying to keep up with Norman.'

'Oh! Margaret! Margaret!' and her eyes filled with tears. 'We have hardly missed doing the same every day since the first Latin grammar was put into his hands!'

'I know it would be very hard,' said Margaret, but Ethel continued, in a piteous tone, a little sentimental: 'From *hic hæc hoc* up to Alcaics and *beta* Thukididou we have gone on together, and I can't bear to give it up. I'm sure I can—'

'Stop, Ethel, I really doubt whether you can. Do you know that Norman was telling papa the other day, that it was very odd Dr. Hoxton gave them such easy lessons.'

Ethel looked very much mortified.

'You see,' said Margaret, kindly, 'we all know that men have more power than women, and I suppose the time has come for Norman to pass beyond you. He would not be cleverer than any one, if he could not do more than a girl at home.'

'He has so much more time for it,' said Ethel.

'That's the very thing. Now consider, Ethel. His work, after he goes to Oxford, will be doing his very utmost—and you know what an utmost that is. If you could keep up with him at all, you must give your whole time and thoughts to it, and when you had done so—if you could get all the honours in the University—what would it come to? You can't take a first-class.'

'I don't want one,' said Ethel; 'I only can't bear not to do as Norman does, and I like Greek so much.'

'And for that would you give up being a useful, steady daughter and sister at home? The sort of woman that dear mamma wished to make you, and a comfort to papa.'

Ethel was silent, and large tears were gathering.

'You own that that is the first thing?'

'Yes,' said Ethel, faintly.

'And that it is what you fail in most?'

'Yes.'

'Then, Ethel dearest, when you made up your mind to Cocksmoor, you knew those things could not be done without a sacrifice?'

'Yes, but I didn't think it would be this.'

Margaret was wise enough not to press her, and she sat down and sighed pitifully. Presently she said, 'Margaret, if you would only let me leave off that stupid old French, and horrid dull reading with Miss Winter, I should have plenty of time for everything; and what does one learn by hearing Mary read poetry, she can't understand?'

'You work, don't you? But indeed, Ethel, don't say that I can let you leave off anything. I don't feel as if I had that authority. If it be done at all, it must be by papa's consent, and if you wish me to ask him about it, I will, only I think it would vex Miss Winter; and I don't think dear mamma would have liked Greek and Cocksmoor to swallow up all the little common lady-like things.'

Ethel made two or three great gulps: 'Margaret, must I give up everything, and forget all my Latin and Greek?'

'I should think that would be a great pity,' said Margaret. 'If you were to give up the verse-making, and the trying to do as much as Norman, and fix some time in the day—half-an-hour, perhaps, for your Greek—I think it might do very well.'

'Thank you,' said Ethel, much relieved; 'I'm glad you don't want me to leave it all off. I hope Norman won't be vexed,' she added, looking a little melancholy.

But Norman had not by any means the sort of sentiment on the subject that she had: 'Of course, you know, Ethel,' said he, 'it must have come to this some time or other, and if you find those verses too hard, and that they take up too much of your time, you had better give them up.'

Ethel did not like anything to be said to be too hard for her, and was very near pleading she only wanted time, but some recollection came across her, and presently she said, 'I suppose it is a wrong sort of ambition to want to learn more, in one's own way, when one is told it is not good for one. I was just going to say I hated being a woman, and having these tiresome little trifles—my duty—instead of learning, which is yours, Norman.'

'I'm glad you did not,' said Norman, 'for it would have been very silly of you; and I assure you, Ethel, it is really time for you to stop, or you would get into a regular learned lady, and be good for nothing. I don't mean that knowing more than other people would make you so, but minding nothing else would.'

This argument from Norman himself, did much to reconcile Ethel's mind to the sacrifice she had made; and when she went to bed, she tried to work out the question in her own mind, whether her eagerness for classical learning was a wrong sort of ambition, to know what other girls did not, and whether it was right to crave for more knowledge than was thought advisable for her. She only bewildered herself, and went to sleep before she had settled anything, but that she knew she must make all give way to papa first, and, secondly, to Cocksmoor.

Meanwhile Margaret had told her father what had passed. He was only surprised to hear that Ethel had kept up so long with Norman, and thought that it was quite right that she should not undertake so much, agreeing more entirely than Margaret had expected with Miss Winter's view, that it would be hurtful to body as well as mind.

'It is perfectly ridiculous to think of her attempting it!' he said. 'I am glad you have put a stop to it.'

'I am glad I have,' said Margaret; 'and dear Ethel behaved so very well. If she had resisted, it would have puzzled me very much, I must have asked you to settle it. But it is very odd, papa, Ethel is the one of them all who treats me most as if I had real authority over her; she lets me scold her, asks my leave, never seems to recollect for a moment how little older I am, and how much cleverer she is. I am sure I never should have submitted so readily. And that always makes it more difficult to me to direct her; I don't like to take upon me with her, because it seems wrong to have her obeying me, as if she were a mere child.'

'She is a fine creature,' said Dr. May, emphatically. 'It just shows the fact, the higher the mind, the readier the submission. But you don't mean that you have any difficulty with the others?'

'O no, no. Flora never could need any interference, especially from me, and Mary is a thorough good girl. I only meant that Ethel lays herself out to be ruled in quite a remarkable way. I am sure, though she does love learning, her real love is for goodness, and for you, papa.'

Ethel would have thought her sacrifice well paid for, had she seen her father's look of mournful pleasure.

CHAPTER XIX.

'O ruthful scene! when from a nook obscure,
His little sister doth his peril see,
All playful as she sate, she grows demure,
She finds full soon her wonted spirits flee,
She meditates a prayer to set him free.'—SHENSTONE.

THE setting sun shone into the great west window of the school at Stoneborough, on its bare walls, the masters' desks, the forms polished with use, and the square, inky, hacked and hewed chests, carved with the names of many generations of boys.

About six or eight little boys were clearing away the books or papers that they, or those who owned them as fags, had left astray, and a good deal of talking and laughing was going on among them. 'Ha!' exclaimed one, 'here has Harrison left his book behind him that he was showing us the gladiators in!' and, standing by the third master's desk, he turned over a page or two of 'Smith's Antiquities,' exclaiming, 'It is full of pictures— here's an old man blowing the bellows—'

'Let me see!' cried Tom May, precipitating himself across the benches and over the desk, with so little caution, that there was an outcry; and, to his horror, he beheld the ink spilled over Mr. Harrison's book, while 'There, August! you've been and done it!' 'You'll catch it!' resounded on all sides.

'What good will staring with your mouth open do!' exclaimed Edward Anderson, the eldest present. 'Here! a bit of blotting paper this moment!'

Tom, dreadfully frightened, handed a sheet torn from an old paper-case that he had inherited from Harry, saying, despairingly, 'It won't take it out, will it?'

'No, little stupid head; but don't you see, I'm stopping it from running down the edges, or soaking in. He won't be the wiser till he opens it again at that place.'

'When he does, he will,' said the bewildered Tom.

'Let him. It won't tell tales.'

'He's coming!' cried another boy; 'he is close at the door.'

Anderson hastily shut the book over the blotting-paper, which he did not venture to retain in his hand, dragged Tom down from the desk, and was apparently entirely occupied with arranging his own box, when Mr. Harrison came in. Tom crouched behind the raised lid, quaking in every limb, conscious he ought to confess, but destitute of resolution to do so, and, in a perfect agony as the master went to his desk, took up the book, and carried it away, so unconscious, that Larkins, a great wag, only waited till his back was turned, to exclaim, 'Ha! old fellow, you don't know what you've got there!'

'Hollo! May junior, will you never leave off staring? you won't see a bit further for it,' said Edward Anderson, shaking him by the ear; 'come to your senses, and know your friends.'

'He'll open it!' gasped Tom.

'So he will; but I'd bet ninety to one, it is not at that page, or if he does, it won't tell tales, unless, indeed, he happened to see you standing there, crouching and shaking. That's the right way to bring him upon you.'

'But suppose he opens it, and knows who was in school?'

'What then? D'ye think we can't stand by each other, and keep our own counsel?'

'But the blotting-paper—suppose he knows that!'

There was a laugh all round at this, 'as if Harrison knew every one's blotting paper!'

'Yes; but Harry used to write his name all over his—see—and draw union-jacks on it.'

'If he did, the date is not there. Do you think the ink is going to say March 2nd? Why should not July have done it last half?'

'July would have told if he had,' said Larkins. 'That's no go.'

'Aye! That's the way—the Mays are all like girls—can't keep a secret—not one of them. There, I've done more for you than ever one of them would have done—own it—' and he strode up to Tom, and grasped his wrists, to force the confession from him.

'But—but he'll ask when he finds it out—'

'Let him. We know nothing about it. Don't be coming the good boy over me like your brothers. That won't do—I know whose eyes are not too short-sighted to read upside down.'

Tom shrank and looked abject, clinging to the hope that Mr. Harrison would not open the book for weeks, months, or years.

But the next morning, his heart died within him, when he beheld the unfortunate piece of blotting-paper, displayed by Mr. Harrison, with the inquiry whether any one knew to whom it belonged, and what made it worse was, that his sight would not reach far enough to assure him whether Harry's name was on it, and he dreaded that Norman or Hector Ernescliffe should recognise the nautical designs. However, both let it pass, and no one through the whole school attempted to identify it. One danger was past, but the next minute Mr. Harrison opened his 'Smith's Antiquities' at the page where stood the black witness. Tom gazed round in despair, he could not see his brother's face, but Edward Anderson, from the second form, returned him a glance of contemptuous encouragement.

'This book,' said Mr. Harrison, 'was left in school for a quarter of an hour yesterday. When I opened it again, it was in this condition. Do any of you know how it happened?' A silence, and he continued, 'Who was in school at the time? Anderson junior, can you tell me anything of it?'

'No, sir.'

'You know nothing of it?'

'No, sir.'

Cold chills crept over Tom, as Mr. Harrison looked round to refresh his memory. 'Larkins, do you know how this happened?'

'No, sir,' said Larkins, boldly, satisfying his conscience because he had not seen the manner of the overthrow.

'Ernescliffe, were you there?'

'No, sir.'

Tom's timid heart fluttered in dim hope that he had been overlooked, as Mr. Harrison paused, then said, 'Remember, it is con-
cealment that is the evil, not the damage to the book.   I shall
have a good opinion ever after of a boy honest enough to confess.
May junior, I saw you,' he added, hopefully and kindly. 'Don't
be afraid to speak out, if you did meet with a mischance.'

Tom coloured and turned pale. Anderson and Larkins grimaced
at him, to remind him that they had told untruths for his sake,
and that he must not betray him.   It was the justification he
wanted; he was relieved to fancy himself obliged to tell the
direct falsehood, for which a long course of petty acted deceits had
paved the way, for he was in deadly terror of the effects of truth.

'No, sir.'   He could hardly believe he had said the words, or
that they would be so readily accepted, for Mr. Harrison had only
the impression that he knew who the guilty person was, and would
not tell, and, therefore, put no more questions to him, but, after a
few more vain inquiries, was baffled, and gave up the investigation.

Tom thought he should have been very unhappy; he had
always heard that deceit was a heavy burthen, and would give
continual stings, but he was surprised to find himself very comfortable on the whole, and able to dismiss repentance as well as
terror.   His many underhand ways with Richard had taken away
the tenderness of his conscience, though his knowledge of what
was right was clear; and he was quite ready to accept the feeling
prevalent at Stoneborough, that truth was not made for school-
boys.

The axiom was prevalent, but not universal, and parties were
running high. Norman May, who, as head boy, had, in play-hours,
the responsibility, and almost the authority of a master, had taken
higher ground than was usual even with the well-disposed; and
felt it his duty to check abuses and malpractices that his prede-
cessors had allowed.   His friend, Cheviot, and the right-minded
set, maintained his authority with all their might; but Harvey
Anderson regarded his interference as vexatious, always took the
part of the offenders, and opposed him in every possible way,
thus gathering as his adherents not only the idle and mischievous,
but the weak and mediocre, and, among this set, there was a positive bitterness of feeling to May, and all whom they considered
as belonging to him.

In shielding Tom May and leading him to deceive, the younger

Anderson had gained a conquest—in him the Mays had fallen
from that pinnacle of truth which was a standing reproach to the
average Stoneborough code—and, from that time, he was under
the especial patronage of his friend.   He was taught the most
ingenious arts of saying a lesson without learning it, and of showing up other people's tasks; whispers and signs were directed
to him to help him out of difficulties, and he was sought out and
put forward whenever a forbidden pleasure was to be enjoyed by
stealth.   These were his stimulants under a heavy bondage; he
was teased and frightened, bullied and tormented, whenever it
was the fancy of Ned Anderson and his associates to make his
timidity their sport; he was scorned and ill-treated, and driven,
by bodily terror, into acts alarming to his conscience, dangerous
in their consequences, and painful in the perpetration; and yet,
among all his sufferings, the little coward dreaded nothing so much
as truth, though it would have set him free at once from this
wretched tyranny.

Excepting on holidays, and at hours when the town-boys were
allowed to go home, there were strict rules confining all except
the sixth form to their bounds, consisting of two large courts,
and an extensive field bordered by the river and the road.   On
the opposite side of the bridge was a turnpike gate, where the
keeper exposed stalls of various eatables, very popular among the
boys, chiefly because they were not allowed to deal there.
Ginger-beer could also be procured, and there were suspicions,
that the bottles so called, contained something contraband.

'August,' said Norman, as they were coming home from school
one evening, 'did I see you coming over the bridge?'

Tom would not answer.

'So you have been at Ballhatchet's gate? I can't think what
could take you there. If you want tarts, I am sure poor old
Betty's are just as good.   What made you go there?'

'Nothing,' said Tom.

'Well, mind you don't do it again, or I shall have to take you
in hand, which I shall be very sorry to do.   That man is a regular
bad character, and neither my father nor Dr. Hoxton would have
one of us have anything to do with him, as you know.'

Tom was in hopes it was over, but Norman went on.   'I am
afraid you are getting into a bad way.   Why won't you mind
what I have told you plenty of times before, that no good comes
of going after Ned Anderson, and Axworthy, and that set.
What were you doing with them to-day?' but receiving no
answer, he went on.   'You always sulk when I speak to you. I
suppose you think I have no right to row you, but I do it to save

you from worse. You can't *never* be found out.' This startled
Tom, but Norman had no suspicion. 'If you go on, you will
get into some awful scrape, and papa will be grieved. I would
not, for all the world, have him put out of heart about you.
Think of him, Tom, and try to keep straight.' Tom would say
nothing, only reflecting that his elder brother was harder upon
him than any one else would be, and Norman grew warmer. ' If
you let Anderson junior get hold of you, and teach you his tricks,
you'll never be good for anything. He seems good-natured now,
but he will turn against you, as he did with Harry. I know
how it is, and you had better take my word, and trust to me
and straightforwardness, when you get into a mess.'

'I'm in no scrape,' said Tom, so doggedly, that Norman lost
patience, and spoke with more displeasure. 'You will be, then,
if you go out of bounds, and run Anderson's errands, and shirk
work. You'd better take care. It is my place to keep order,
and I can't let you off for being my brother ; so remember, if I
catch you going to Ballhatchet's again, you may make sure of a
licking.'

So the warning closed—Tom more alarmed at the aspect of
right, which he fancied terrific, and Norman with some compunction at having lost temper and threatened, when he meant
to have gained him by kindness.

Norman recollected his threat with a qualm of dismay when,
at the end of the week, as he was returning from a walk with
Cheviot, Tom darted out of the gate-house. He was flying
across the bridge, with something under his arm, when Norman
laid a detaining hand on his collar, making a sign at the same
time to Cheviot to leave them.

'What are you doing here ?' said Norman, sternly, marching
Tom into the field. 'So you've been there again. What's that
under your jacket ?'

'Only—only what I was sent for,' and he tried to squeeze it
under the flap.

'What is it ? a bottle—'

'Only—only a bottle of ink.'

Norman seized it, and gave Tom a fierce angry shake, but the
indignation was mixed with sorrow. 'O Tom, Tom, these fellows
have brought you to a pretty pass. Who would have thought
of such a thing from us !'

Tom cowered, but felt only terror.

'Speak truth,' said Norman, ready to shake it out of him ; 'is
this for Anderson junior ?'

Under those eyes flashing with generous, sorrowful wrath, he dared not utter another falsehood, but Anderson's threats chained him, and he preferred his thraldom to throwing himself on the mercy of his brother who loved him. He would not speak.

'I am glad it is not for yourself,' said Norman; 'but do you remember what I said, in case I found you there again?'

'Oh! don't, don't!' cried the boy. 'I would never have gone if they had not made me.'

'Made you?' said Norman, disdainfully, 'how?'

'They would have thrashed me—they pinched my fingers in the box—they pulled my ears—Oh, don't—'

'Poor little fellow!' said Norman; 'but it is your own fault. If you won't keep with me, or Ernescliffe, of course they will bully you. But I must not let you off—I must keep my word!' Tom cried, sobbed, and implored in vain. 'I can't help it,' he said, 'and now, don't howl! I had rather no one knew it. It will soon be over. I never thought to have this to do to one of us.' Tom roared and struggled, till, releasing him, he said, 'There, that will do. Stop bellowing; I was obliged, and I can't have hurt you much—have I?' he added, more kindly, while Tom went on crying, and turning from him. 'It is nothing to care about, I am sure—look up;' and he pulled down his hands. 'Say you are sorry—speak the truth—keep with me, and no one shall hurt you again.'

Very different this from Tom's chosen associates; but he was still obdurate, sullen, and angry, and would not speak, nor open his heart to those kind words. After one more, 'I could not help it, Tom; you've no business to be sulky,' Norman took up the bottle, opened it, smelt, and tasted, and was about to throw it into the river, when Tom exclaimed, 'O don't, don't!—what will they do to me?—give it to me!'

'Did they give you the money to pay for it?'

'Yes, let me have it.'

'How much was it?'

'Fourpence.'

'I'll settle that,' and the bottle splashed in the river. 'Now, then, Tom, don't brood on it any more. Here's a chance for you of getting quit of their errands. If you will keep in my sight, I'll take care no one bullies you, and you may still leave off these disgraceful tricks, and do well.'

But Tom's evil spirit whispered that Norman had beaten him, that he should never have any diversion again, and that Anderson would punish him; and there was a sort of satisfaction in seeing that his perverse silence really distressed his brother.

'If you will go on in this way, I can't help it, but you'll be sorry some day,' said Norman; and he walked thoughtfully on, looking back to see whether Tom were following, as he did slowly, meditating on the way how he should avert his tyrant's displeasure.

Norman stood for a moment at the door, surveying the court, then walked up to a party of boys, and laid his hand on the shoulder of one, holding a silver fourpence to him. 'Anderson junior,' said he, 'there's your money. I am not going to let Stoneborough school be turned into a gin palace. I give you notice, it is not to be. Now, you are not to bully May junior for telling me. He did not—I found him out.'

Leaving Anderson to himself he looked for Tom; but not seeing him, he entered the cloister, for it was the hour when he was used to read there, but he could not fix his mind. He went to the bench where he had lain on the examination-day, and kneeling on it, looked out on the green grass where the graves were. 'Mother!—mother!' he murmured, 'have I been harsh to your poor little, tender, sickly boy? I couldn't help it. Oh! if you were but here! We are all going wrong! What shall I do? How should Tom be kept from this evil?—it is ruining him! Mean, false, cowardly, sullen—all that is worst—and your son—Oh! mother! and all I do only makes him shrink more from me. It will break my father's heart, and you will not be there to comfort him.'

Norman covered his face with his hands, and a fit of bitter grief came over him. But his sorrow was now not what it had been before his father's resignation had tempered it, and soon it turned to prayer, resolution, and hope.

He would try again to reason quietly with him, when the alarm of detection and irritation should have gone off, and he sought for the occasion; but, alas! Tom had learnt to look on all reproof as 'rowing,' and considered it as an additional injury from a brother, who, according to the Anderson view, should have connived at his offences, and turned a deafened ear and dogged countenance to all he said. The foolish boy sought after the Andersons still more, and Norman became more dispirited about him, greatly missing Harry, that constant companion and follower, who would have shared his perplexities, and removed half of them, in his own part of the school, by the influence of his high, courageous, and truthful spirit.

In the meantime, Richard was studying hard at home, with greater hopefulness and vigour than he had ever thrown into his work before. 'Suppose,' Ethel had once said to him, 'that when you are a clergyman, you could be curate of Cocksmoor, when there is a church there.'

'When!' said Richard, smiling at the presumption of the scheme, and yet it formed itself into a sort of definite hope. Perhaps they might persuade Mr. Ramsden to take him as a curate with a view to Cocksmoor; and this prospect, vague as it was, gave an object and hope to his studies. Every one thought the delay of his examination favourable to him, and he now read with a determination to succeed. Dr. May had offered to let him read with Mr. Harrison, but Richard thought he was getting on pretty well, with the help Norman gave him; for it appeared that ever since Norman's return from London, he had been assisting Richard, who was not above being taught by a younger brother; while, on the other hand, Norman, much struck by his humility, would not for the world have published that he was fit to act as his elder's tutor.

One evening, when the two boys came in from school, Tom gave a great start, and, pulling Mary by the sleeve, whispered, 'How came that book here?'

'It is Mr. Harrison's.'

'Yes, I know; but how came it here?'

'Richard borrowed it to look out something, and Ethel brought it down.'

A little re-assured, Tom took up an exciting story-book, and ensconced himself by the fire, but his agonies were great during the ensuing conversation.

'Norman,' Ethel was exclaiming in delight, 'do you know this book?'

'Smith? Yes, it is in the school library.'

'There's everything in it that one wants, I do believe. Here is such an account of ancient galleys—I never knew how they managed their banks of rowers before—Oh! and the Greek houses —look at the pictures, too.'

'Some of them are the same as Mr. Rivers' gems,' said Norman, standing behind her, and turning the leaves, in search of a favourite.

'Oh! what did I see? is that ink?' said Flora, from the opposite side of the table.

'Yes, didn't you hear?' said Ethel. Mr. Harrison told Ritchie when he borrowed it, that unluckily one day this spring he left it in school, and some of the boys must have upset an inkstand over it; but, though he asked them all round, each denied it. How I should hate for such things to happen! and it was a prize-book, too.'

While Ethel spoke she opened the marked page, to show the extent of the calamity, and as she did so Mary exclaimed, 'Dear me! how funny! why, how did Harry's blotting-paper get in there?'

Tom shrank into nothing, set his teeth, and pinched his fingers, ready to wish they were on Mary's throat, more especially as the words made some sensation. Richard and Margaret exchanged looks, and their father, who had been reading, sharply raised his eyes, and said, 'Harry's blotting-paper! How do you know that, Mary?'

'It is Harry's,' said she, all unconscious, 'because of that anchor up in one corner, and the union-jack in the other. Don't you see, Ethel?'

'Yes,' said Ethel, 'nobody drew that but Harry.'

'Aye, and there are his buttons,' said Mary, much amused and delighted with these relics of her beloved Harry. 'Don't you remember one day last holidays, papa desired Harry to write and ask Mr. Ernescliffe what clothes he ought to have for the naval school, and all the time he was writing the letter, he was drawing sailor's buttons on his blotting-paper. I wonder how ever it got into Mr. Harrison's book!'

Poor Mary's honest wits did not jump to a conclusion quite so fast as other people's, and she little knew what she was doing, when, as a great discovery, she exclaimed, 'I know! Harry gave his paper-case to Tom. That's the way it got to school!'

'Tom!' exclaimed his father, suddenly and angrily, 'where are you going?'

'To bed,' muttered the miserable Tom, twisting his hands. A dead silence of consternation fell on all the room. Mary gazed from one to the other, mystified at the effect of her words, frightened at her father's loud voice, and at Tom's trembling confusion. The stillness lasted for some moments, and was first broken by Flora, as if she had caught at a probability. 'Some one might have used the first blotting-paper that came to hand.'

'Come here, Tom,' said the Doctor, in a voice not loud, but trembling with anxiety; then laying his hand on his shoulder, 'Look in my face.' Tom hung his head, and his father put his hand under his chin, and raised the pale, terrified face.

'Don't be afraid to tell us the meaning of this. If any of your friends have done it, we will keep your secret. Look up, and speak out. How did your blotting-paper come there?'

Tom had been attempting his former system of silent sullenness, but there was anger at Mary, and fear of his father to agitate him, and in his impatient despair at thus being held and questioned, he burst out into a violent fit of crying.

'I can't have you roaring here to distress Margaret,' said Dr. May. 'Come into the study with me.'

But Tom, who seemed fairly out of himself, would not stir, and a screaming and kicking scene took place, before he was carried

into the study by his brothers, and there left with his father.
Mary, meantime, dreadfully alarmed, and perceiving that, in some
way, she was the cause, had thrown herself upon Margaret, sobbing
inconsolably, as she begged to know what was the matter, and why
papa was angry with Tom—had she made him so?

Margaret caressed and soothed her, to the best of her ability,
trying to persuade her that, if Tom had done wrong, it was better
for him it should be known, and assuring her that no one could
think her unkind, nor a tell-tale; then dismissing her to bed, and
Mary was not unwilling to go, for she could not bear to meet
Tom again, only begging in a whisper to Ethel, 'that, if dear
Tom had not done it, she would come and tell her.'

'I am afraid there is no hope of that!' sighed Ethel, as the
door closed on Mary.

'After all,' said Flora, 'he has not said anything. If he has
only done it, and not confessed, that is not so bad—it is only the
usual fashion of boys.'

'Has he been asked? Did he deny it?' said Ethel, looking in
Norman's face, as if she hardly ventured to put the question, and
she only received sorrowful signs as answers. At the same moment
Dr. May called him. No one spoke. Margaret rested her head on
the sofa, and looked very mournful, Richard stood by the fire
without moving limb or feature, Flora worked fast, and Ethel
leant back on an arm-chair, biting the end of a paper-knife.

The Doctor and Norman came back together. 'I have sent
him up to bed,' said Dr. May. 'I must take him to Harrison
to-morrow morning. It is a terrible business!'

'Has he confessed it?' said Margaret.

'I can hardly call such a thing a confession—I wormed it out
bit by bit—I could not tell whether he was telling truth or not,
till I called Norman in.'

'But he has not said anything more untrue—'

'Yes, he has though!' said Dr. May, indignantly. 'He said
Ned Anderson put the paper there, and had been taking up the
ink with it—'twas his doing—then when I came to cross-examine
him, I found that though Anderson did take up the ink, it was
Tom himself who knocked it down—I never heard anything like
it—I never could have believed it!'

'It must all be Ned Anderson's doing!' cried Flora. 'They
are enough to spoil anybody.'

'I am afraid they have done him a great deal of harm,' said
Norman.

'And what have you been about all the time?' exclaimed the
Doctor, too keenly grieved to be just. 'I should have thought

that with you at the head of the school, the child might have been kept out of mischief; but there have you been going your own way, and leaving him to be ruined by the very worst set of boys!'

Norman's colour rose with the extreme pain this unjust accusation caused him, and his voice, though low, was not without irritation. ' I *have* tried. I have not done as much as I ought, perhaps, but—'

'No, I think not, indeed!' interrupted his father. 'Sending a boy there, brought up as he had been, without the least tendency to deceit—'

Here no one could see Norman's burning cheeks, and brow bent downwards in the effort to keep back an indignant reply, without bursting out in exculpation; and Richard looked up, while the three sisters all at once began, ' O no, no, papa—' and left Margaret to finish—' Poor little Tom had not always been quite sincere.'

'Indeed! and why was I left to send him to school without knowing it? The place of all others to foster deceit.'

' It was my fault, papa,' said Margaret.

' And mine,' put in Richard; and she continued, ' Ethel told us we were very wrong, and I wish we had followed her advice. It was by far the best, but we were afraid of vexing you.'

' Every one seems to have been combined to hide what they ought not!' said Dr. May, though speaking to her much more softly than to Norman, to whom he turned angrily again. 'Pray, how came you not to identify this paper?'

' I did not know it,' said Norman, speaking with difficulty.

' He ought never to have been sent to school,' said the Doctor, ' that tendency was the very worst beginning.'

' It was a great pity; I was very wrong,' said Margaret, in great concern.

' I did not mean to blame you, my dear,' said her father, affectionately. ' I know you only meant to act for the best, but—' and he put his hand over his face, and then came the sighing groan, which pained Margaret ten thousand times more than reproaches, and which, in an instant, dispersed all the indignation burning within Norman, though the pain remained at his father's thinking him guilty of neglect, but he did not like, at that moment, to speak in self-justification.

After a short space, Dr. May desired to hear what were the deceptions to which Margaret had alluded, and made Norman tell what he knew of the affair of the blotted book. Ethel spoke hopefully when she had heard it. ' Well, do you know, I think he will do better now. You see, Edward made him conceal it, and he has been going on with it on his mind, and in that boy's power ever since; but now it is cleared up and confessed, he will begin afresh and do better. Don't you think so, Norman? don't you, papa?'

'I should have more hope, if I had seen anything like confession or repentance,' said Dr. May; 'but that provoked me more than all—I could only perceive that he was sorry to be found out, and afraid of punishment.'

'Perhaps, when he has recovered the first fright, he will come to his better self,' said Margaret; for she guessed, what indeed was the case, that the Doctor's anger on this first shock of the discovery of the fault he most abhorred, had been so great, that a fearful cowering spirit would be completely overwhelmed; and, as there had been no sorrow shown for the fault, there had been none of that softening and relenting that won so much love and confidence.

Every one felt that talking only made them more unhappy, they tried to return to their occupations, and so passed the time till night. Then, as Richard was carrying Margaret up-stairs, Norman lingered to say, 'Papa, I am very sorry you should think I neglected Tom. I dare say I might have done better for him, but, indeed, I have tried.'

'I am sure you have, Norman. I spoke hastily, my boy—you will not think more of it. When a thing like this comes on a man, he hardly knows what he says.'

'If Harry were here,' said Norman, anxious to turn from the real loss and grief, as well as to talk away that feeling of being apologized to, 'it would all do better. He would make a link with Tom; but I have so little, naturally, to do with the second form, that it is not easy to keep him in sight.'

'Yes, yes, I know that very well. It is no one's fault but my own; I should not have sent him there without knowing him better. But you see how it is, Norman—I have trusted to her, till I have grown neglectful, and it is well if it is not the ruin of him!'

'Perhaps he will take a turn, as Ethel says,' answered Norman, cheerfully. 'Good night, papa.'

'I have a blessing to be thankful for in you, at least,' murmured the Doctor to himself. 'What other young fellow of that age and spirit would have borne so patiently with my injustice? Not I—I am sure! A fine father I show myself to these poor children—neglect, helplessness, temper—O Maggie!'

Margaret had so bad a head-ache the next day, that she could not come down-stairs. The punishment was, they heard, a flogging at the time, and an imposition so long, that it was likely to occupy a large portion of the play-hours till the end of the half-year. His father said, and Norman silently agreed, 'a very good thing, it will keep him out of mischief;' but Margaret only wished she could learn it for him, and took upon herself all the blame from beginning to end. She said little to her father, for it distressed him to see her grieved; he desired her not to dwell on the subject, caressed her, called her his comfort and support, and did all he could to console her, but it was beyond his power; her sisters, by listening to her, only made her worse. 'Dear, dear papa,' she exclaimed, 'how kind he is! But he can never depend upon me again—I have been the ruin of my poor little Tom.'

'Well,' said Richard, quietly, 'I can't see why you should put yourself into such a state about it.'

This took Margaret by surprise. 'Have not I done very wrong, and perhaps hurt Tom for life?'

'I hope not,' said Richard. 'You and I made a mistake; but it does not follow that Tom would have kept out of this scrape, if we had told my father our notion.'

'It would not have been on my conscience,' said Margaret— 'he would not have sent him to school.'

'I don't know that,' said Richard. 'At any rate, we meant to do right, and only made a mistake. It was unfortunate; but I can't tell why you go and make yourself ill, by fancying it worse than it is. The boy has done very wrong, but people get cured of such things in time; and it is nonsense to fret as if he were not a mere child of eight years old. You did not teach him deceit.'

'No, but I concealed it—papa is disappointed, when he thought he could trust me.'

'Well! I suppose no one could expect never to make mistakes,' said Richard, in his sober tone.

'Self-sufficiency!' exclaimed Margaret; 'that has been the root of all! Do you know, Ritchie, I believe I was expecting that I could always judge rightly.'

'You generally do,' said Richard; 'no one else could do half what you do.'

'So you have said, papa, and all of you, till you have spoilt me. I have thought it myself, Ritchie.'

'It is true,' said Richard.

'But then,' said Margaret, 'I have grown to think much of it, and not like to be interfered with. I thought I could manage by myself; and when I said I would not worry papa, it was half because I liked the doing and settling all about the children myself. Oh! if it could have been visited in any way but by poor Tom's faults!'

'Well,' said Richard, 'if you felt so, it was a pity, though I never should have guessed it. But you see, you will never feel so again; and as Tom is only one, and there are nine to govern, it is all for the best.'

His deliberate common sense made her laugh a little, and she owned he might be right. 'It is a good lesson against my love of being first. But, indeed, it is difficult—papa can so little bear to be harassed.'

'He could not at first, but now he is strong and well, it is different.'

'He looks terribly thin and worn still,' sighed Margaret; 'so much older!'

'Aye, I think he will never get back his young looks; but except his weak arm, he is quite well.'

'And then his—his quick way of speaking may do harm.'

'Yes, that was what I feared for Tom,' said Richard, 'and there was the mistake. I see it now. My father always is right in the main, though he is apt to frighten one at first, and it is what ought to be, that he should rule his own house. But now, Margaret, it is silly to worry about it any more—let me fetch baby, and don't think of it.'

And Margaret allowed his reasonableness, and let herself be comforted. After all, Richard's solid soberness had more influence over her than anything else.

CHAPTER XX.

'Think how simple things and lowly,
　Have a part in Nature's plan,
How the great have small beginnings,
　And the child will be a man.
Little efforts work great actions,
　Lessons in our childhood taught
Mould the spirit of that temper
　Whereby blessed deeds are wrought.
Cherish, then, the gifts of childhood,
　Use them gently, guard them well,
For their future growth and greatness
　Who can measure, who can tell!'—MORAL SONGS.

THE first shock of Tom's misdemeanour passed away, though it still gave many an anxious thought to such of the family as felt responsible for him.

The girls were busily engaged in preparing an Easter feast for Cocksmoor. Mr. Wilmot was to examine the scholars, and buns and tea were provided, in addition to which Ethel designed to make a present to every one—a great task, considering that the

Cocksmoor funds were reserved for absolute necessaries, and were at a very low ebb. So that twenty-five gifts were to be composed out of nothing.

There was a grand turn out of drawers of rubbish, all over Margaret, raising such a cloud of dust as nearly choked her. What cannot rubbish and willing hands effect! Envelopes and wafer-boxes were ornamented with pictures, bags, needle-cases, and pincushions, beautiful balls, tippets, both of list and gay print, and even sun-bonnets and pinafores were contrived, to the supreme importance and delight of Mary and Blanche, who found it as good or better than play, and ranged their performances in rows, till the room looked like a bazaar. To provide for boys was more difficult; but Richard mended old toys, and repaired the frames of slates, and Norman's contribution of half-a-crown bought mugs, marbles, and penny knives, and there were even hopes that something would remain for bodkins, to serve as nozzles to the bellows, which were the pride of Blanche's heart.

Never were Easter gifts the source of more pleasure to the givers, especially when the nursery establishment met Dr. Hoxton near the pastry-cook's shop, and he bestowed on Blanche a packet of variegated sugar-plums, all of which she literally poured out at Ethel's feet, saying, 'I don't want them. Only let me have one for Aubrey, because he is so little. All the rest are for the poor children on Cocksmoor.'

After this, Margaret declared that Blanche must be allowed to buy the bodkin, and give her bellows to Jane Taylor, the only Cocksmoor child she knew, and to whom she always destined in turn every gift that she thought most successful.

So Blanche went with Flora to the toy-shop, and there fell in love with a little writing-box, that so eclipsed the bellows, that she tried to persuade Flora to buy it for Jane Taylor, to be kept till she could write, and was much disappointed to hear that it was out of the question. Just then a carriage stopped, and from it stepped the pretty little figure of Meta Rivers.

'Oh! how do you?' How delightful to meet you! I was wondering if we should! Little Blanche, too!' kissing her; 'and here's Mrs. Larpent. Mrs. Larpent—Miss Flora May. How is Miss May?'

This was all uttered in eager delight, and Flora, equally pleased, answered the inquiries. 'I hope you are not in a hurry, proceeded Meta, 'I want your advice. You know all about schools, don't you? I am come to get some Easter presents for our children, and I am sure you can help me.'

'Are the children little or big?' asked Flora.

'Oh! all sorts and sizes. I have some books for the great sensible ones, and some stockings and shoes for the tiresome stupid ones; but there are some dear little pets that I want nice things for. There—there's a doll that looks just fit for little curly-headed Annie Langley; don't you think so, Mrs. Larpent?'

The price of the doll was a shilling, and there were quickly added to it, boxes of toys, elaborate bead-work pincushions, polished blue and green boxes, the identical writing-case—even a small Noah's ark. Meta hardly asked the prices, which certainly were not extravagant, since she had nearly twenty articles for little more than a pound.

'Papa has given me a benefaction of £5 for my school-gifts,' said she; 'is not that charming? I wish you would come to the feast. Now, do!—it is on Easter Tuesday. Won't you come?'

'Thank you, I am afraid we can't. I should like it very much.'

'You never will come to me. You have no compassion.'

'We should enjoy coming very much. Perhaps in the summer, when Margaret is better.'

'Could not she spare any of you? Well, I shall talk to papa, and make him talk to Dr. May. Mrs. Larpent will tell you I always get my way. Don't I? Good-bye. See if I don't.'

She departed, and Flora returned to her own business; but Blanche's interest was gone. Dazzled by the more lavish gifts, she looked listlessly and disdainfully at bodkins, three for twopence. 'I wish I might have bought the writing box for Jane Taylor! Why does not papa give us money to get pretty things for the children?' said she, as soon as they came out.

'Because he is not so rich as Miss Rivers's papa.'—Flora was interrupted by meeting the Miss Andersons, who asked, 'Was not that carriage Mr. Rivers's, of Abbotstoke Grange?'

'Yes. We like Miss Rivers very much,' said Flora, resolved to show that she was acquainted.

'Oh! do you visit her? I knew he was a patient of Dr. May.' Flora thought there was no need to tell that the only call had been owing to the rain, and continued, 'She has been begging us to come to her school feast, but I do not think we can manage it.'

'Oh! indeed, the Grange is very beautiful, is it not?'

'Very,' said Flora. 'Good morning.'

Flora had a little uneasiness in her conscience, but it was satisfactory to have put down Louisa Anderson, who never could aspire to an intimacy with Miss Rivers. Her little sister looked up—'Why, Flora, have you seen the Grange?'

'No, but papa and Norman said so.'

And Blanche showed that the practical lesson on the pumps

of the world was not lost on her, by beginning to wish they were
as rich as Miss Rivers. Flora told her it was wrong to be discontented, but the answer was, 'I don't want it for myself, I
want to have pretty things to give away.'

And her mind could not be turned from the thought by any
attempt of her sister. Even when they met Dr. May coming
out of the hospital, Blanche renewed the subject. She poured
out the catalogue of Miss Rivers's purchases, making appealing
attempts at looking under his spectacles into his eyes, and he
perfectly understood the tenor of her song.

'I have had a sight, too, of little maidens preparing Easter
gifts,' said he.

'Have you, papa? What were they? Were they as nice as
Miss Rivers's?'

'I don't know, but I thought they were the best sort of gifts,
for I saw that plenty of kind thought and clever contrivance
went to them, aye, and some little self-denial too.'

'Papa, you look as if you meant *something;* but ours are
nothing but nasty old rubbish.'

'Perhaps some fairy, or something better, has brought a wand
to touch the rubbish, Blanche; for I think that the maidens
gave what would have been worthless kept, but became precious
as they gave it.'

'Do you mean the list of our flannel petticoats, papa, that
Mary has made into a tippet?'

'Perhaps I meant Mary's own time and pains, as well as the
tippet. Would she have done much good with them otherwise?'

'No, she would have played. Oh! then you like the presents
because they are our own making? I never thought of that.
Was that the reason you did not give us any of your sovereigns
to buy things with?'

'Perhaps I want my sovereigns for the eleven gaping mouths at
home, Blanche. But would not it be a pity to spoil your pleasure?
You would have lost all the chattering and laughing and buzzing
I have heard round Margaret of late, and I am quite sure Miss
Rivers can hardly be as happy in the gifts that cost her nothing,
as one little girl who gives her sugar-plums out of her own mouth!'

Blanche clasped her papa's hand tight, and bounded five or
six times. 'They are our presents, not yours,' said she. 'Yes,
I see. I like them better now.'

'Aye, aye,' said the Doctor. 'Seeing Miss Rivers's must not
take the shine out of yours, my little maids; for if you can't give
much, you have the pleasure of giving the best of all, your labour
of love.' Then thinking on, and speaking to Flora, 'The longer I

live, the more I see the blessing of being born in a state of life where you can't both both eat your cake and give it away.'

Flora never was at ease in a conversation with her father; she could not follow him, and did not like to show it. She answered aside from the mark, ' You would not have Blanche underrate Miss Rivers ?'

' No, indeed, she is as good and sweet a creature as ever came across me—most kind to Margaret, and loving to all the world. I like to see one whom care and grief have never set their grip upon. Most likely she would do like Ethel, if she had the oppor-tunity, but she has not.'

' So she has not the same merit ?' said Flora.

' We don't talk of merit. I meant that the power of sacrifice is a great advantage. The habit of small sacrifice that is made necessary in a large family is a discipline that only children are without; and so, with regard to wealth, I think people are to be pitied who can give extensively out of such abundance that they can hardly feel the want.'

' In effect, they can do much more,' said Flora.

' I am not sure of that. They *can*, of course, but it must be at the cost of personal labour and sacrifice. I have often thought of the words, " Silver and gold have I none, but such as I have give I thee." And *such as we have* it is that does the good; the gold, if we have it, but, at any rate, the personal influence; the very proof of sincerity, shown by the exertion and self-denial, tells far more than money lightly come by, lightly spent.'

' Do you mean that a person who maintained a whole school would do less good than one who taught one child ?'

' If the rich person take no pains, and leave the school to take care of itself—nay, if he only visit it now and then, and never let it inconvenience him, has he the least security that the scholars are obtaining any real good from it ? If the teacher of the one child is doing his utmost, he is working for himself at least.'

' Suppose we could build, say our church and school, on Cocks-moor at once, and give our superintendence besides ?'

' If things were ripe for it, the means would come. As it is, it is a fine field for Ethel and Richard. I believe it will be the making of them both. I am sure it is training Ethel, or making her train herself, as we could never have done without it. But here, come in and see old Mrs. Robins. A visit from you will cheer her up.'

Flora was glad of the interruption, the conversation was uncom-fortable to her. She almost fancied her papa was moralizing for their good, but that he carried it too far, for wealthy people assuredly had it in their power to do great things, and might work as hard themselves; besides, it was finer in them, there was so much *éclat* in their stooping to charity.   But her knowledge of his character would not allow her to think for a moment that he could say aught but from the bottom of his heart—no, it was one of his one-sided views that led him into paradox.   ' It was just like papa,' and so there was no need to attend to it.   It was one of his enthusiasms, he was so very fond of Ethel, probably be-cause of her likeness to himself.   Flora thought Ethel put almost too forward—they all helped at Cocksmoor, and Ethel was very queer and unformed, and could do nothing by herself.   The only thing Flora did keep in her mind was, that her papa had spoken to her, as if she were a woman compared with Ethel.

Little Blanche made her report of the conversation to Mary, ' that it was so nice; and now she did not care about Miss Rivers's fine presents at all, for papa said what one made one's self was better to give than what one bought.   And papa said, too, that it was a good thing not to be rich, for then one never felt the miss of what one gave away.'

Margaret, who overheard the exposition, thought it so much to Blanche's credit, that she could not help repeating it in the even-ing, after the little girl was gone to bed, when Mr. Wilmot had come in to arrange the programme for Cocksmoor.   So the little fit of discontent and its occasion, the meeting with Meta Rivers, were discussed.

'Yes,' said Mr. Wilmot, 'those Riverses are open-handed.   They really seem to have so much money, that they don't know what to do with it.   My brother is ready to complain that they spoil his parish.   It is all meant so well, and they are so kind-hearted and excellent, that it is a shame to find fault, and I tell Charles and his wife that their grumbling at such a squire proves them the most spoilt of all.'

' Indiscriminate liberality?' asked the Doctor.   ' I should guess the old gentleman to be rather soft !'

' That's one thing.   The parish is so small, and there are so few to shower all this bounty on, and they are so utterly unused to country people.   They seem to think by laying out money they can get a show set of peasants in rustic cottages, just as they have their fancy cows and poultry—all that offends the eye out of the way.'

' Making it a matter of taste,' said the Doctor.

' I'm sure I would,' said Norman, aside, to Ethel,   ' What's the use of getting one's self disgusted ?'

' One must not begin with showing dislike,' began Ethel, ' or—

' Aye—you like rags, don't you ? but hush.'

'That is just what I should expect of Mr. Rivers,' said Dr. May; 'he has cultivated his taste till it is getting to be a disease, but his daughter has no lack of wit.'

'Perhaps not. Charles and Mary are very fond of her, but she is entirely inexperienced, and that is a serious thing with so much money to throw about. She pays people for sending their children to school, and keeping their houses tidy; and there is so much given away, that it is enough to take away all independence and motive for exertion. The people speculate on it, and take it as a right; by-and-by there will be a reaction—she will find out she is imposed upon, take offence, and for the rest of her life will go about saying how ungrateful the poor are!'

'It is a pity good people won't have a little common sense,' said Dr. May. 'But there's something so bewitching in that little girl, that I can't give her up. I verily believe she will right herself.'

'I have scarcely seen her,' said Mr. Wilmot.

'She has won papa's heart by her kindness to me,' said Margaret, smiling. 'You see her beautiful flowers? She seems to me, made to lavish pleasures on others wherever she goes.'

'O yes, they are most kind-hearted,' said Mr. Wilmot. 'It is only the excess of a virtue that could be blamed in them, and they are most valuable to the place. She will learn experience in time—I only hope she will not be spoilt.'

Flora felt as if her father must be thinking his morning's argument confirmed, and she was annoyed. But she thought there was no reason why wealth should not be used sensibly, and if she were at the head of such an establishment as the Grange, her charity should be so well regulated as to be the subject of general approbation.

She wanted to find some one else on her side, and, as they went to bed, she said to Ethel, 'Don't you wish we had some of this superfluity of the Riverses for poor Cocksmoor?'

'I wish we had *anything* for Cocksmoor! Here's a great hole in my boot, and nurse says I must get a new pair, that is seven-and-sixpence gone! I shall never get the first pound made up towards building!'

'And pounds seem nothing to them,' said Flora.

'Yes, but if they don't manage right with them—I'll tell you, Flora, I got into a fit of wishing the other day; it does seem such a grievous pity to see those children running to waste for want of daily teaching, and Jenny Hall had forgotten everything. I was vexed, and thought it was all no use while we could not do more; but just then I began to look out the texts Ritchie had marked for me to print for them to learn, and the first was, "Be thou faithful over a few things, and I will make thee ruler over many things," and then I thought perhaps we were learning to be faithful with a few things. I am sure what they said to-night showed it was lucky we have not more in our hands. I should do wrong for ever with the little we have if it were not for Ritchie and Margaret. By the time we have really got the money together for the school, perhaps I shall have more sense.'

'Got the money! As if we ever could!'

'Oh, yes! we shall and will. It need not be more than £70, Ritchie says, and I have twelve shillings for certain, put out from the money for hire of the room, and the books and clothes, and, in spite of these horrid boots, I shall save something out of this quarter, half-a-crown at least. And I have another plan besides—'

But Flora had to go down to Margaret's room to bed. Flora was always ready to throw herself into the present, and liked to be the most useful person in all that went forward, so that no thoughts of greatness interfered with her enjoyment at Cocksmoor.

The house seemed wild that Easter Monday morning. Ethel, Mary, and Blanche, flew about in all directions, and in spite of much undoing of their own arrangements, finished their preparations so much too early, that at half-past eleven, Mary complained that she had nothing to do, and that dinner would never come.

Many were the lamentations at leaving Margaret behind, but she answered them by talking of the treat of having papa all to herself, for he had lent them the gig, and promised to stay at home all the afternoon with her.

The first division started on foot directly after dinner, the real council of education, as Norman called them, namely, Mr. Wilmot, Richard, Ethel, and Mary; Flora, the other member, waited to take care of Blanche and Aubrey, who were to come in the gig, with the cakes, tea-kettles, and prizes, driven by Norman. Tom and Hector Ernescliffe were invited to join the party, and many times did Mary wish for Harry.

Supremely happy were the young people as they reached the common, and heard the shout of tumultuous joy raised by their pupils, who were on the watch for them. All was now activity. Everybody trooped into Mrs. Green's house, while Richard and Ethel ran different ways to inspect the fires, where their kettles full of tea were to be boiled.

Then when the kitchen was so full that it seemed as if it could hold no more, some kind of order was produced, the children were seated on their benches, and, while the mothers stood behind to listen, Mr. Wilmot began to examine, as well as he could in so crowded an audience.

There *was* progress. Yes, there was. Only three were as

utterly rude and idealess as they used to be at Christmas. Glimmerings had dawned on most, and one—Una M'Carthy—was fit to come forward to claim Mr. Wilmot's promise of a Prayer-book. She could really read and say the Catechism, her Irish wit and love of learning had out-stripped all the rest, and she was the pride of Ethel's heart, fit, now, to present herself on equal terms with the Stoneborough set, as far as her sense was concerned—though, alas! neither present nor exhortation had succeeded in making her anything, in looks, but a picturesque tatterdemalion, her sandy elf locks streaming over a pair of eyes, so dancing and *gracieuses*, that it was impossible to scold her.

With beating heart, as if her own success in life depended for ever on the way her flock acquitted themselves, Ethel stood by Mr. Wilmot, trying to read answers coming out of the dull mouths of her children, and looking exultingly at Richard whenever some good reply was made, especially when Una answered an unexpected question. It was too delightful to hear how well she remembered all the history up to the flood, and how prettily it came out in her Irish accent! That made up for all the atrocious stupidity of others, who, after being told every time since they had begun, who gave their names, now chose to forget.

In the midst, while the assembly were listening with admiration to the reading of the scholar next in proficiency to Una, a boy, who could read words of five letters without spelling, there was a fresh squeezing at the door, and, the crowd opening as well as it could, in came Flora and Blanche, while Norman's head was seen for a moment in the doorway.

Flora's whisper to Ethel was her first discovery, that the closeness and heat of the room were nearly overpowering. Her excitement had made all be forgotten. 'Could not a window be opened?'

Mrs. Green interfered—it had been nailed up because her husband had the rheumatiz!

'Where's Aubrey?' asked Mary.

'With Norman. Norman said he would not let him go into the black-hole, so he has got him out of doors. Ethel! we must come out! You don't know what an atmosphere it is! Blanche, go out to Norman!'

'Flora, Flora! you don't consider,' said Ethel, in an agony.

'Yes, yes. It is not at all cold. Let them have their presents out of doors, and eat their buns.'

Richard and Mr. Wilmot agreed with Flora, and the party were turned out. Ethel did own, when she was in the open air, 'that it had been rather hot.'

Norman's face was a sight, as he stood holding Aubrey in his arms, to gratify the child's impatience. The stifling den, the uncouth aspect of the children, the head girl so very ragged a specimen, thoroughly revolted his somewhat fastidious disposition. This was Ethel's delight! to this she made so many sacrifices! this was all that her time and labour had effected! He did not wish to vex her, but it was more than he could stand.

However, Ethel was too much engrossed to look for sympathy. It was a fine spring day, and on the open space of the common the arrangements were quickly made. The children stood in a long line, and the baskets were unpacked. Flora and Ethel called the names, Mary and Blanche gave the presents, and assuredly the grins, courtesies, and pulls of the forelock they elicited, could not have been more hearty for any of Miss Rivers's treasures. The buns and the kettles of tea followed—it was perfect delight to entertainers and entertained, except when Mary's dignity was cruelly hurt by Norman's authoritatively taking a kettle out of her hands, telling her she would be the death of herself or somebody else, and reducing her to the mere rank of a bun distributor, which Blanche and Aubrey could do just as well; while he stalked along with a grave and resigned countenance, filling up the cups held out to him by timid-looking children. Mary next fell in with Granny Hall, who had gone into such an ecstasy over Blanche and Aubrey, that Blanche did not know which way to look; and Aubrey, in some fear that the old woman might intend to kiss him, returned the compliments by telling her she was 'ugly up in her face,' at which she laughed heartily, and uttered more vehement benedictions.

Finally, the three best children, boys and girls, were to be made fit to be seen, and recommended by Mr. Wilmot to the Sunday-school and penny-club at Stoneborough, and, this being proclaimed, and the children selected, the assembly dispersed. Mr. Wilmot rejoicing Ethel and Richard, by saying, 'Well, really, you have made a beginning. There is an improvement in tone among those children, that is more satisfactory than any progress they may have made.'

Ethel's eyes beamed, and she hurried to tell Flora. Richard coloured and gave his quiet smile, then turned to put things in order for their return.

'Will you drive home, Richard?' said Norman, coming up to him.

'Don't you wish it?' said Richard, who had many minor arrangements to make, and would have preferred walking home independently.

'No, thank you, I have a head-ache, and walking may take it

off,' said Norman, taking off his hat and passing his fingers through his hair.

'A head-ache again—I am sorry to hear it.'

'It is only that suffocating den of yours. My head ached from the moment I looked into it. How can you take Ethel into such a hole, Richard? It is enough to kill her to go on with it for ever.'

'It is not so every day,' said the elder brother, quietly. 'It is a warm day, and there was an unusual crowd.'

'I shall speak to my father,' exclaimed Norman, with somewhat of the supercilious tone that he had now and then been tempted to address to his brother. 'It is not fit that Ethel should give up everything, health and all, to such a set as these. They look as if they had been picked out of the gutter—dirt, squalor, everything disgusting, and summer coming on, too, and that horrid place with no window to open! It is utterly unbearable!'

Richard stooped to pick up a heavy basket, then smiled and said, 'You must get over such things as these if you mean to be a clergyman, Norman.'

'Whatever I am to be, it does not concern the girls being in such a place as this. I am surprised that you could suffer it.'

There was no answer—Richard was walking off with his basket, and putting it into the carriage. Norman was not pleased with himself, but thought it his duty to let his father know his opinion of Ethel's weekly resort. All he wished was to avoid Ethel herself, not liking to show her his sentiments, and he was glad to see her put into the gig with Aubrey and Mary.

They rushed into the drawing-room, full of glee, when they came home, all shouting their news together, and had not at first leisure to perceive that Margaret had some tidings for them in return. Mr. Rivers had been there, with a pressing invitation to his daughter's school-feast, and it had been arranged that Flora and Ethel should go and spend the day at the Grange, and their father come to dine, and fetch them home in the evening. Margaret had been much pleased with the manner in which the thing was done. When Dr. May, who seemed reluctant to accept the proposal that related to himself, was called out of the room, Mr. Rivers had, in a most kind manner, begged her to say whether she thought it would be painful to him, or whether it might do his spirits good. She decidedly gave her opinion in favour of the invitation, Mr. Rivers gained his point, and she had ever since been persuading her father to like the notion, and assuring him it need not be made a precedent for the renewal of invitations to dine out in the town. He thought the change would be pleasant for his girls, and had, therefore, consented.

'O, papa, papa! thank you!' cried Ethel, enraptured, as soon as he came into the room. 'How very kind of you! How I have wished to see the Grange, and all Norman talks about! Oh dear! I am so glad you are going there, too!'

'Why, what should you do with me?' said Dr. May, who felt and looked depressed at this taking up of the world again.

'Oh dear! I should not like it at all without you! It would be no fun at all by ourselves. I wish Flora would come home How pleased she will be! Papa! I do wish you would look as if you didn't mind it. I can't enjoy it if you don't like going.'

'I shall when I am there, my dear,' said the Doctor, affectionately, putting his arm around her as she stood by him. 'It will be a fine day's sport for you.'

'But can't you like it beforehand, papa?'

'Not just this minute, Ethel,' said he, with his bright sad smile. 'All I like just now, is my girl's not being able to do without me; but we'll do the best we can—So your flock acquitted themselves brilliantly? Who is your Senior Wrangler?'

Ethel threw herself eagerly into the history of the examination, and had almost forgotten the invitation till she heard the front door open. Then it was not she, but Margaret, who told Flora— Ethel could not, as she said, enjoy what seemed to sadden her father. Flora received it much more calmly. 'It will be very pleasant,' said she; 'it was very kind of papa to consent. You will have Richard and Norman, Margaret, to be with you in the evening.'

And as soon as they went up-stairs, Ethel began to write down the list of prizes in her school journal, while Flora took out the best evening frocks, to study whether the crape looked fresh enough.

The invitation was a convenient subject of conversation, for Norman had so much to tell his sisters of the curiosities they must look for at the Grange, that he was not obliged to mention Cocksmoor. He did not like to mortify Ethel by telling her his intense disgust, and he knew he was about to do what she would think a great injury by speaking to his father on the subject; but he thought it for her real welfare, and took the first opportunity of making to his father and Margaret a most formidable description of Ethel's black-hole. It quite alarmed Margaret, but the Doctor smiled, saying, 'Aye, aye, I know the face Norman puts on if he looks into a cottage.'

'Well,' said Norman, with some mortification, 'all I know is, that my head ached all the rest of the day.'

'Very likely; but your head is not Ethel's, and there were twice as many people as the place was intended to hold.'

'A stuffy hole, full of peat-smoke, and with a window that can't open at the best of times.'

' Peat-smoke is wholesome,' said Dr. May, looking provoking.

' You don't know what it is, papa, or you would never let Ethel spend her life there. It is poisonous!'

' I'll take care of Ethel,' said Dr. May, walking off and leaving Norman in a state of considerable annoyance at being thus treated. He broke out into fresh exclamations against the horrors of Cocksmoor, telling Margaret she had no idea what a den it was.

' But, Norman, it can't be so very bad, or Richard would not allow it.'

' Richard is deluded!' said Norman ; ' but if he chooses to run after dirty brats, why should he take Ethel there ?'

' My dear Norman, you know it is all Ethel's doing.'

' Yes ; I know she has gone crazy after them, and given up all her Greek for it. It is past endurance!' said Norman, who had worked himself up into great indignation.

' Well, but surely, Norman, it is better they should do what they can for those poor creatures, than for Ethel to learn Greek.'

' I don't know that. Let those who are fit for nothing else go and drone over A,B,C, with ragged children, if they like. It is just their vocation; but there is an order in everything, Margaret, and minds of a superior kind are intended for higher purposes, not to be wasted in this manner.'

' I don't know whether they are wasted!' said Margaret, not quite liking Norman's tone, though she had not much to say to his arguments.

' Not wasted ? Not in doing what any one can do ? I know what you'll say about the poor. I grant it, but high ability must be given for a purpose, not to be thrown away. It is common sense, that some one must be meant to do the dirty work.'

' I see what you mean, Norman, but I don't quite like that to be called by such a name. I think—' she hesitated. ' Don't you think you dislike such things more than—'

' Any one must abominate dirt and slovenliness. I know what you mean. My father thinks 'tis all nonsense in me, but his profession has made him insensible to such things, and he fancies every one else is the same! Now, Margaret, am I unreasonable?'

' I am sure I don't know, dear Norman,' said Margaret, hesitating, and feeling it her duty to say something, ' I dare say it was very disagreeable.'

' And you think, too, that I made a disturbance for nothing?'

' No, indeed I don't, nor does dear papa. I have no doubt he will see whether it is proper for Ethel. All I think he meant is, that perhaps your not being well last winter, has made you a little more sensitive in such things.'

Norman paused, and coloured. He remembered the pain it had given him to find himself incapable of being of use to his father, and that he had resolved to conquer the weakness of nerve of which he was ashamed; but he did not like to connect this with his fastidious feelings of refinement. He would not own to himself that they were over nice, and, at the bottom of all this justification, rankled Richard's saying, that he who cared for such things was unfit for a clergyman. Norman's secret thought was, it was all very well for those who could only aspire to parish work in wretched cottages—people who could distinguish themselves were more useful at the University, forming minds, and opening new discoveries in learning.

Was Norman quite proof against the consciousness of daily excelling all his competitors? His superiority had become even more manifest this Easter, when Cheviot and Forder, the two elder boys whom he had outstripped, left the school, avowedly, because it was not worth while for them to stay, since they had so little chance of the Randall scholarship. Norman had now only to walk over the course, no one even approaching him but Harvey Anderson.

Meta Rivers always said that fine weather came at her call, and so it did—glowing sunshine streaming over the shaven turf, and penetrating even the solid masses of the great cedar.

The carriage was sent for the Miss Mays, and, at two o'clock, they arrived. Flora, extremely anxious that Ethel should comport herself discreetly; and Ethel full of curiosity and eagerness, the only drawback, her fears that her papa was doing what he disliked. She was not in the least shy, and did not think about her manner enough to be troubled by the consciousness that it had a good deal of abruptness and eagerness, and that her short sight made her awkward. Meta met them with outstretched hands, and a face beaming with welcome. 'I told you I should get my way!' she said, triumphantly, and, after her warm greeting, she looked with some respect at the face of the Miss May who was so very clever. It certainly was not what she expected, not at all like either of the four sisters she had already seen—brown, sallow, and with that sharp long nose, and the eager eyes, and brow a little knit by the desire to see as far as she could. It was pleasanter to look at Flora.

Ethel left the talk chiefly to Flora—there was wonder and study enough for her in the grounds and garden, and when Mrs. Larpent tried to enter into conversation with her, she let it drop two or three times, while she was peering hard at a picture, and trying to make out its subject. However, when they all went out to walk to church, Ethel lighted up, and talked, admired, and asked questions in her quick, eager way, which interested Mrs. Larpent greatly. The governess asked after Norman, and no more was wanted to produce a volume of histories of his successes, till Flora turned as she walked before with Meta, saying, 'Why, Ethel, you are quite overwhelming Mrs. Larpent.'

But some civil answer convinced Ethel that what she said was interesting, and she would not be stopped in her account of their anxieties on the day of the examination. Flora was pleased that Meta, catching some words, begged to hear more, and Flora gave an account of the matter, soberer in terms, but quietly setting Norman at a much greater distance from all his competitors.

After church came the feast in the school. It was a large commodious building. Meta declared it was very tiresome that it was so good inside, it was so ugly, she should never rest till papa had built her a real beauty. They found Mr. and Mrs. Charles Wilmot in the school, with a very nice well-dressed set of boys and girls, and—but there is no need to describe the roast-beef and plum-pudding, 'the feast ate merrily,' and Ethel was brilliantly happy waiting on the children, and so was sunny-hearted Meta. Flora was too busy in determining what the Riverses might be thinking of her and her sister to give herself up to the enjoyment.

Ethel found a small boy looking ready to cry at an untouched slice of beef. She examined him whether he could cut it, and at last discovered that, as had been the case with one or two of her own brothers at the same age, meat was repugnant to him. In her vehement manner, she flew off to fetch him some pudding, and hurrying up, as she thought, to Mr. Charles Wilmot, who had been giving it out, she thrust her plate between him and the dish, and had begun her explanation, when she perceived it was a stranger, and she stood, utterly discomfited, not saying, 'I beg your pardon,' but only blushing, awkward and confused, as he spoke to her, in a good-natured, hospitable manner, which showed her it must be Mr. Rivers. She obtained her pudding, and, turning hastily, retreated.

'Meta,' said Mr. Rivers, as his daughter came out of the school with him, for, open and airy as it was, the number and the dinner made him regard it as Norman had viewed the Cocksmoor room, 'was that one of the Miss Mays?'

'Yes, papa; Ethel, the third—the clever one.'

'I thought she must be one of them from her dress; but what a difference between her and the others!'

Mr. Rivers was a great admirer of beauty, and Meta, brought

up to be the same, was disappointed. but consoled herself by admiring Flora.   Ethel, after the awkwardness was over, thought
no more of the matter, but went on in full enjoyment of the
feast.   The eating finished, the making of presents commenced,
and choice ones they were.   The smiles of Meta and of the
children were a pretty sight, and Ethel thought she had never
seen anything so like a beneficent fairy.   Mr. and Mrs. Wilmot
said their words of counsel and encouragement, and by five
o'clock all was over.

'Oh! I am sorry!' said Meta, 'Easter won't come again for
a whole year, and it has been so delightful.   How that dear
little Annie smiled and nursed her doll!   I wish I could see her
show it to her mother!   Oh! how nice it is!   I am so glad papa
brought me to live in the country.   I don't think anything can
be so charming in all the world as seeing little children happy!'

Ethel could not think how the Wilmots could have found it
in their heart to regret the liberality of this sweet damsel, on
whom she began to look with Norman's enthusiastic admiration.

There was time for a walk round the grounds, Meta doing the
honours to Flora, and Ethel walking with Mrs. Larpent.   Both
pairs were very good friends, and the two sisters admired and
were charmed with the beauty of the gardens and conservatories
—Ethel laying up a rich store of intelligence for Margaret; but
still she was not entirely happy; her papa was more and more
on her mind.   He had looked dispirited at breakfast; he had
a long hard day's work before him; and she was increasingly
uneasy at the thought that it would be a painful effort to him
to join them in the evening.   Her mind was full of it when
she was conducted, with Flora, to the room where they were to
dress; and when Flora began to express her delight, her answer
was only that she hoped it was not very unpleasant to papa.

'It is not worth while to be unhappy about that, Ethel.   If
it is an effort, it will be good for him when he is once here.   I
know he will enjoy it.'

'Yes, I should think he would—I hope he will.   He must like
you to have such a friend as Miss Rivers.   How pretty she is!'

'Now, Ethel, it is high time to dress.   Pray make yourself
look nice—don't twist up your hair in that anyhow fashion.'

Ethel sighed, then began talking fast about some hints on
school-keeping which she had picked up for Cocksmoor.

Flora's glossy braids were in full order, while Ethel was still
struggling to get her plait smooth, and was extremely beholden
to her sister for taking it into her own hands, and doing the
best with it that its thinness and roughness permitted.   And

then Flora pinched and pulled and arranged Ethel's frock, in vain attempts to make it sit like her own—those sharp high bones resisted all attempts to disguise them. 'Never mind, Flora, it is quite tidy, I am sure, there—do let me be in peace. You are like old nurse.'

'So those are all the thanks I get?'

'Well, thank you very much, dear Flora. You are a famous person. How I wish Margaret could see that lovely mimosa!'

'And, Ethel, do take care. Pray don't poke and spy when you come into the room, and don't frown when you are trying to see. I hope you won't have anything to help at dinner. Take care how you manage.'

'I'll try,' said Ethel, meekly; though a good deal tormented, as Flora went on with half-a-dozen more injunctions, closed by Meta's coming to fetch them. Little Meta did not like to show them her own bed-room—she pitied them so much when she thought of the contrast. She would have liked to put Flora's arm through hers, but she thought it would look neglectful of Ethel, so she only showed the way down-stairs. Ethel forgot all her sister's orders; for there stood her father, and she looked most earnestly at his face. It was cheerful, and his voice sounded well-pleased as he greeted Meta; then resumed an animated talk with Mr. Rivers. Ethel drew as near him as she could; she had a sense of protection, and could open to full enjoyment when she saw him bright. At the first pause in the conversation, the gentlemen turned to the young ladies. Mr. Rivers began talking to Flora, and Dr. May, after a few pleasant words to Meta, went back to Ethel. He wanted her to see his favourite pictures—he led her up to them, made her put on his spectacles to see them better, and showed her their special merits. Mr. Rivers and the others joined them; Ethel said little, except a remark or two in answer to her papa, but she was very happy—she felt that he liked to have her with him; and Meta, too, was struck by the soundness of her few sayings, and the participation there seemed to be in all things between father and daughter.

At dinner Ethel went on pretty well. She was next to her father, and was very glad to find the dinner so grand, that no side-dish fell to her lot to be carved. There was a great deal of pleasant talk, such as the girls could understand, though they did not join much in it, except that now and then Dr. May turned to Ethel as a reference for names and dates. To make up for silence at dinner, there was a most confidential chatter in the drawing-room. Flora and Meta on one side, hand in hand, calling each other by their Christian names, Mrs. Larpent and Ethel on the other. Flora dreaded only that Ethel was talking too much, and revealing too much in how different style they lived. Then came the gentlemen, Dr. May begging Mr. Rivers to show Ethel one of his prints, when Ethel stooped more than ever, as if her eyelashes were feelers, but she was in transports of delight, and her embarrassment entirely at an end in her admiration, as she exclaimed and discussed with her papa, and by her hearty appreciation made Mr. Rivers for the time forget her plainness. Music followed: Flora played nicely, Meta like a well-taught girl; Ethel went on musing over the engravings. The carriage was announced, and so ended the day in Norman's fairy land. Ethel went home, leaning hard against her papa, talking to him of Raffaelle's Madonnas; and looking out at the stars, and thinking how the heavenly beauty of those faces, that in the prints she had been turning over, seemed to be connected with the glories of the darkblue sky and glowing stars. 'As one star differeth from another star in glory,' murmured she; 'that was the lesson to-day, papa;' and when she felt him press her hand, she knew he was thinking of that last time she had heard the lesson, when he had not been with her, and her thoughts went with his, though not another word was spoken.

Flora hardly knew when they ceased to talk. She had musings equally engrossing of her own. She saw she was likely to be very intimate with Meta Rivers, and she was roaming away into schemes for not letting the intercourse drop, and hopes of being admitted to many a pleasure, as yet little within her reach—parties, balls, London itself, and, above all, the satisfaction of being admired. The certainty that Mr. Rivers thought her pretty and agreeable, had gratified her all the evening, and if he, with his refined taste, thought so, what would others think? Her only fear was, that Ethel's awkwardness might make an unfavourable impression, but, at least, she said to herself, it was anything but vulgar awkwardness.

Their reflections were interrupted by the fly stopping. It was at a little shop in the outskirts of the town, and Dr. May explained that he wanted to inquire for a patient. He went in for a moment, then came back to desire that they would go home, for he should be detained some little time. No one need sit up for him—he would let himself in.

It seemed a comment on Ethel's thoughts, bringing them back to the present hour. That daily work of homely mercy, hoping for nothing again, was surely the true way of doing service.

CHAPTER XXI.

WATCHMAN. How, if he will not stand?
DOGBERRY. Why, then, take no note of him, but let him go.
MUCH ADO ABOUT NOTHING.

DR. MAY promised Margaret that he would see whether the black hole of Cocksmoor was all that Norman depicted it, and, accordingly, he came home that way on Tuesday evening, the next week, much to the astonishment of Richard, who was in the act of so mending the window that it might let in air when open, and keep it out when shut, neither of which purposes had it ever yet answered.

Dr. May walked in, met his daughter's look of delight and surprise, spoke cheerfully to Mrs. Green, a hospital acquaintance of his, like half the rest of the country, and made her smile and courtesy by asking if she was not surprised at such doings in her house; then looked at the children, and patted the head that looked most fit to pat, inquired who was the best scholar, and offered a penny to whoever could spell copper tea-kettle, which being done by three merry mortals, and having made him extremely popular, he offered Ethel a lift, and carried her off between him and Adams, on whom he now depended for driving him, since Richard was going to Oxford at once.

It was possible to spare him now. Dr. May's arm was as well as he expected it ever would be; he had discarded the sling, and could use his hand again, but the arm was still stiff and weak—he could not stretch it out, nor use it for anything requiring strength; it soon grew tired with writing, and his daughters feared that it ached more than he chose to confess, when they saw it resting in the breast of his waistcoat. Driving he never would have attempted again, even if he could, and he had quite given up carving—he could better bear to sit at the side, than at the bottom of the dinner-table.

Means of carrying Margaret safely had been arranged by Richard, and there was no necessity for longer delaying his going to Oxford, but he was so unwillingly spared by all, as to put him quite into good spirits. Ethel was much concerned to lose him from Cocksmoor, and dreaded hindrances to her going thither without his escort; but she had much trust in having her father on her side, and meant to get authority from him for the propriety of going alone with Mary.

She did not know how Norman had jeopardized her projects, but the danger blew over. Dr. May told Margaret that the place was clean and wholesome, and though more smoky than might be preferred, there was nothing to do any one in health any harm, especially when the walk there and back was over the fresh moor. He lectured Ethel herself on opening the window, now that she could; and advised Norman to go and spend an hour in the school, that he might learn how pleasant peat-smoke was—a speech Norman did not like at all. The real touchstone of temper is ridicule on a point where we do not choose to own ourselves fastidious, and if it had been from any one but his father, Norman would not have so entirely kept down his irritation.

Richard passed his examination successfully, and Dr. May wrote himself to express his satisfaction. Nothing went wrong just now except little Tom, who seemed to be justifying Richard's fears of the consequence of exciting his father's anger. At home, he shrank and hesitated at the simplest question if put by his father suddenly; and the appearance of cowardice and prevarication displeasing Dr. May further, rendered his tone louder, and frightened Tom the more, giving his manner an air of sullen reserve that was most unpleasant. At school, it was much the same—he kept aloof from Norman, and threw himself more into the opposite faction, by whom he was shielded from all punishment, except what they chose themselves to inflict on him.

Norman's post as head of the school was rendered more difficult by the departure of his friend Cheviot, who had always upheld his authority; Harvey Anderson did not openly transgress, for he had a character to maintain, but it was well known throughout the school that there was a wide difference between the boys, and that Anderson thought it absurd, superfluous, and troublesome in May not to wink at abuses which appeared to be licensed by long standing. When Edward Anderson, Axworthy, and their set, broke through rules, it was with the understanding that the second boy in the school would support them, if he durst.

The summer, and the cricket season, brought the battle of Ballhatchet's house to issue. The cricket ground was the field close to it, and for the last two or three years there had been a frequent custom of despatching juniors to his house for tarts and ginger-beer bottles. Norman knew of instances last year in which this had led to serious mischief, and had made up his mind that, at whatever loss of popularity, it was his duty to put a stop to the practice.

He was an ardent cricketer himself, and though the game did not, in anticipation, seem to him to have all the charms of last year, he entered into it with full zest when once engaged. But his eye was on all parts of the field, and especially on the corner by the bridge, and the boys knew him well enough to attempt nothing unlawful within the range of that glance. However the constant vigilance was a strain too great to be always kept up, and he had reason to believe he was eluded more than once.

At last came a capture, something like that of Tom, one which he could not have well avoided making. The victim was George Larkins, the son of a clergyman in the neighbourhood, a wild, merry varlet, who got into mischief rather for the sake of the fun than from any bad disposition.

His look of consternation was exaggerated into a most comical caricature, in order to hide how much of it was real.

'So you are at that trick, Larkins.'

'There! that bet is lost!' exclaimed Larkins. 'I laid Hill half-a-crown that you would not see me when you were mooning over your verses!'

'Well, I have seen you. And now ?—'

'Come, you would not thrash a fellow when you have just lost him half-a-crown! Single misfortunes never come alone, they say; so there's my money and my credit gone, to say nothing of Ballhatchet's ginger-beer!'

The boy made such absurd faces, that Norman could hardly help laughing, though he wished to make it a serious affair. 'You know, Larkins, I have given out that such things are not to be. It is a melancholy fact.'

'Aye! so you must make an example of me!' said Larkins, pretending to look resigned. 'Better call all the fellows together, hadn't you, and make it more effective? It would be grateful to one's feelings, you know—and Juno,' added he, with a ridiculous confidential air, 'if you'll only lay it on soft, I'll take care it makes noise enough. Great cry, little wool, you know.'

'Come with me,' said Norman. 'I'll take care you are example enough. What did you give for those articles ?'

'Fifteen-pence half-penny. Rascally dear, isn't it ? but the old rogue makes one pay double for the risk! You are making his fortune, you have raised his prices fourfold.'

'I'll take care of that.'

'Why, where are you taking me ? Back to him ?'

'I am going to gratify your wish to be an example.'

'A gibbet! a gibbet!' cried Larkins. 'I'm to be turned off on the spot where the crime took place—a warning to all beholders. Only let me send home for old Neptune's chain, if you please, sir— if you hang me in the combined watch-chains of the school, I fear they would give way, and defeat the purposes of justice.'

They were by this time at the bridge. 'Come in,' said Norman, to his follower, as he crossed the entrance of the little shop, the

first time he had ever been there.   A little cringing shrivelled
old man stood up in astonishment.

'Mr. May! can I have the pleasure, sir?'

'Mr. Ballhatchet, you know that it is contrary to the rules
that there should be any traffic with the school without special
permission.'

'Yes, sir—just nothing, sir—only when the young gentlemen
come here, sir—I'm an old man, sir, and I don't like not to oblige
a young gentleman, sir,' pleaded the old man, in a great fright.

'Very likely,' said Norman, 'but I am come to give you fair
notice.   I am not going to allow the boys here to be continually
smuggling spirits into the school.'

'Spirits! bless you, sir, I never thought of no such a thing!
'Tis nothing in life but ginger-beer—very cooling drink, sir, of
my wife's making; she had the receipt from her grandmother up
in Leicestershire.   Won't you taste a bottle, sir?' and he hastily
made a cork bounce, and poured it out.

That, of course, was genuine, but Norman was 'up to him,'
in schoolboy phrase.

'Give me yours, Larkins.'

No pop ensued.   Larkins, enjoying the detection, put his
hands on his knees, and looked wickedly up in the old man's
face to see what was coming.

'Bless me! it is a little flat.   I wonder how that happened?
I'll be most happy to change it, sir.   Wife! what's the meaning
of Mr. Larkins' ginger-pop being so flat?'

'It is very curious ginger-beer indeed, Mr. Ballhatchet,' said
Norman; 'and since it is liable to have such strange properties,
I cannot allow it to be used any more at the school.'

'Very well, sir—as you please, sir.   You are the first gentleman
as has objected, sir.'

'And once for all, I give you warning,' added Norman, 'that
if I have reason to believe you have been obliging the young
gentlemen, the magistrates and the trustees of the road shall
certainly hear of it.'

'You would not hurt a poor man, sir, as is drove to it—you
as has such a name for goodness?'

'I have given you warning,' said Norman.   'The next time
I find any of your bottles in the school-fields, your licence goes.
Now, there are your goods.   Give Mr. Larkins back the fifteen-
pence.   I wonder you are not ashamed of such a charge!'

Having extracted the money, Norman turned to leave the shop.
Larkins, triumphant, 'Ha! there's Harrison!' as the tutor rode
by, and they touched their caps.   'How he stared! My eyes!

June, you'll be had up for dealing with old Ball!' and he went into an ecstasy of laughing. 'You've settled him, I believe. Well, is justice satisfied?'

'It would be of no use thrashing you,' said Norman, laughing, as he leant against the parapet of the bridge, and pinched the boy's ear. 'There's nothing to be got out of you but chaff.'

Larkins was charmed with the compliment.

'But I'll tell you what, Larkins, I can't think how a fellow like you can go and give in to these sneaking, underhand tricks that make you ashamed to look one in the face.'

'It is only for the fun of it.'

'Well, I wish you would find your fun some other way. Come, Larkins, recollect yourself a little—you have a home not so far off. How do you think your father and mother would fancy seeing you reading the book you had yesterday, or coming out of Ballhatchet's with a bottle of spirits, called by a false name?'

Larkins pinched his fingers; home was a string that could touch him, but it seemed beneath him to own it. At that moment a carriage approached, the boy's whole face lighted up, and he jumped forward. 'Our own!' he cried. 'There she is!'

She was, of course, his mother; and Norman, though turning hastily away that his presence might prove no restraint, saw the boy fly over the door of the open carriage, and could have sobbed at the thought of what that meeting was.

'Who was that with you?' asked Mrs. Larkins, when she had obtained leave to have her boy with her, while she did her shopping.

'That was May senior, our Dux.'

'Was it? I am very glad you should be with him, my dear George. He is very kind to you, I hope?'

'He is a jolly good fellow,' said Larkins, sincerely; though by no means troubling himself as to the appropriateness of the eulogy, nor thinking it necessary to explain to his mother the terms of the conversation.

It was not fruitless; Larkins did avoid mischief when it was not extremely inviting, was more amenable to May senior, and having been put in mind by him of his home, he was not ashamed to bring the thought to the aid of his eyes, when, on Sunday, during a long sermon of Mr. Ramsden's, he knew that Axworthy was making the grimace which irresistibly incited him to make a still finer one.

And Ballhatchet was so much convinced of 'that there young May' being in earnest, that he assured his persuasive customers that it was as much as his licence was worth to supply them.

Evil and insubordination were more easily kept under than

Norman had expected, when ho first made up his mind to the
struggle. Firmness had so far carried the day, and the power
of manful assertion of the right had been proved, contrary to
Cheviot's parting auguries that he would only make himself disliked, and do no good.

The whole of the school was extremely excited this summer
by a proceeding of Mr. Tomkins, the brewer, who suddenly
closed up the foot-way called Randall's-alley, declaring that there
was no right of passage through a certain field at the back of
his brewery. Not only the school, but the town was indignant,
and the Mays especially so. It had been the Doctor's way to
school forty years ago, and there were recollections connected
with it that made him regard it with personal affection. Norman,
too, could not bear to lose it; he had not entirely conquered his
reluctance to pass that spot in the High-street, and the loss of the
alley would be a positive deprivation to him. Almost every native
of Stoneborough felt strongly the encroachment of the brewer,
and the boys, of course, carried the sentiment to exaggeration.

The propensity to public speaking perhaps added to the
excitement, for Norman May and Harvey Anderson, for once in
unison, each made a vehement harangue in the school-court—
Anderson's a fine specimen of the village Hampden style, about
Britons never suffering indignities, and free-born Englishmen
swelling at injuries.

'That they do, my hearty,' interjected Larkins, pointing to
an inflamed eye that had not returned to its right dimensions.
However, Anderson went on, unmoved by the under titter, and
demonstrated, to the full satisfaction of all the audience, that
nothing could be more illegal and unfounded than the brewer's
claims.

Then came a great outburst from Norman, with all his father's
headlong vehemence; the way was the right of the town, the
walk had been trodden by their forefathers for generations past
—it had been made by the good old generous-hearted man who
loved his town and townspeople, and would have heard with
shame and anger of a stranger, a new inhabitant, a grasping
radical, caring, as radicals always did, for no rights, but for their
own chance of unjust gains, coming here to Stoneborough to cut
them off from their own path. He talk of liberalism, and the
rights of the poor! He who cut off Randall's poor old creatures
in the almshouses from their short way! And then came some
stories of his oppression as a poor-law guardian, which greatly
aggravated the wrath of the speaker and audience, though otherwise they did not exactly bear on the subject. 'What would

old Nicholas Randall say to these nineteenth-century doings?' finished Norman.

'Down with them!' cried a voice from the throng, probably Larkins's; but there was no desire to investigate, it was the universal sentiment. 'Down with it! Hoorah, we'll have our foot-path open again! Down with the fences! Britons never shall be slaves!' as Larkins finally ejaculated.

'That's the way to bring it to bear!' said Harvey Anderson. 'See if he dares to bring an action against us. Hoorah!'

'Yes, that's the way to settle it,' said Norman. 'Let's have it down. It is an oppressive, arbitrary, shameful proceeding, and we'll show him we won't submit to it!'

Carried along by the general feeling, the whole troop of boys dashed shouting up to the barricade at the entrance of the field, and levelled it with the ground. A handkerchief was fastened to the top of one of the stakes, and waved over the brewhouse wall, and some of the boys were for picking up stones and dirt, and launching them over, in hopes of spoiling the beer; but Norman put a stop to this, and brought them back to the school-yard, still in a noisy state of exultation.

It cooled a little by-and-by under the doubt how their exploit would be taken. At home, Norman found it already known; and his father, half glad, half vexed, enjoying the victory over Tomkins, yet a little uneasy on his son's behalf. 'What will Dr. Hoxton say to the *dux*?' said he. 'I didn't know he was to be *dux* in mischief as well as out of it.'

'You can't call it mischief, papa, to resent an unwarranted encroachment of our rights by such an old ruffian as that. One's blood is up to think of the things he has done!'

'He richly deserves it, no doubt,' said the Doctor, 'and yet I wish you had been out of the row. If there is any blame, you will be the first it will light on.'

'I am glad of it, that is but just. Anderson and I seem to have stirred it up—if it wanted stirring—for it was in every fellow there; indeed, I had no notion it was coming to this when I began.'

'Oratory,' said the Doctor, smiling. 'Ha, Norman! Think a little another time, my boy, before you take the law into your own hands, or, what is worse, into a lot of hands you can't control for good, though you may excite them to harm.'

Dr. Hoxton did not come into school at the usual hour, and, in the course of the morning, sent for May senior, to speak to him in his study.

He looked very broad, awful, and dignified, as he informed him that Mr. Tomkins had just been with him to complain of the damage that had been done, and he appeared extremely displeased that the *Dux* should have been no check on such proceedings.

'I am sorry, sir,' said Norman, 'but I believe it was the general feeling that he had no right to stop the alley, and, therefore, that it could not be wrong to break it down.'

'Whether he has a right or not, is not a question to be settled by you. So I find that you, whose proper office it is to keep order, have been inflaming the mischievous and aggressive spirit amongst the others. I am surprised at you; I thought you were more to be depended upon, May, in your position.'

Norman coloured a good deal, and simply answered, 'I am sorry, sir.'

'Take care, then, that nothing of the kind happens again,' said Dr. Hoxton, who was very fond of him, and did not find fault with him willingly.

That the first inflammatory discourse had been made by Anderson did not appear to be known—he only came in for the general reprimand given to the school.

It was reported the following evening, just as the town boys turned out to go to their homes, that 'old Tomkins had his fence up five times higher than before.'

'Have at him again, say I!' exclaimed Axworthy. 'What business has he coming stopping up ways that were made before he was born?'

'We shall catch it from the Doctor if we do,' said Edward Anderson. 'He looked in no end of a rage yesterday when he talked about the credit of the school.'

'Who cares for the credit of the school?' said the elder Anderson; 'we are out of the school now—we are townsmen—Stoneborough boys—citizens not bound to submit to injustice. No, no, the old rogue knew it would not stand if it was brought into court, so he brings down old Hoxton on us instead—a dirty trick he deserves to be punished for.'

And there was a general shout and yell in reply.

'Anderson,' said Norman, 'you had better not excite them again, they are ripe for mischief. It will go further than it did yesterday—don't you see?'

Anderson could not afford to get into a scrape without May to stand before him, and rather sulkily he assented.

'It is of no use to rave about old Tomkins,' proceeded Norman, in his style of popular oratory. 'If it is illegal, some one will go to law about it, and we shall have our alley again. We have shown him our mind once, and that is enough; if we let him alone now, he will see 'tis only because we are ordered, not for his sake. It would be just putting him in the right, and may be winning his cause for him, to use any more violence. There's law for you, Anderson. So now no more about it—let us all go home like rational fellows. August, where's August?'

Tom was not visible—he generally avoided going home with his brother; and Norman having seen the boys divide into two or three little parties, as their roads lay homewards, found he had an hour of light for an expedition of his own, along the bank of the river. He had taken up botany with much ardour, and sharing the study with Margaret was a great delight to both. There was a report that the rare yellow bog-bean grew in a meadow about a mile and a half up the river, and thither he was bound, extremely enjoying the summer evening walk, as the fresh dewy coolness sunk on all around, and the noises of the town were mellowed by distance, and the sun's last beams slanted on the green meadows, and the May-flies danced, and dragon-flies darted, and fish rose or leapt high in the air, or showed their spotted sides, and opened and shut their gills, as they rested in the clear water, and the evening breeze rustled in the tall reeds, and brought fragrance from the fresh-mown hay.

It was complete enjoyment to Norman after his day's study, and the rule and watch over the unruly crowd of boys, and he walked and wandered, and collected plants for Margaret till the sun was down, and the grasshoppers chirped clamorously, while the fern-owl purred, and the beetle hummed, and the skimming swallows had given place to the soft-winged bat, and the large white owl floating over the fields as it moused in the long grass.

The summer twilight was sobering every tint, when, as Norman crossed the cricket-field, he heard, in the distance, a loud shout. He looked up, and it seemed to him that he saw some black specks dancing in the forbidden field, and something like the waving of a flag, but it was not light enough to be certain, and he walked quickly home.

The front door was fastened, and, while he was waiting to be let in, Mr. Harrison walked by, and called out, 'You are late at home to-night—it is half-past nine.'

'I have been taking a walk, sir.'

A good-night was the answer, as he was admitted. Every one in the drawing-room looked up, and exclaimed, as he entered, 'Where's Tom?'

'What! he is not come home?'

'No! Was he not with you?'

'I missed him after school. I was persuaded he was come home. I have been to look for the yellow bog-bean. There, Margaret. Had not I better go and look for him?'

'Yes, do,' said Dr. May. 'The boy is never off one's mind'

A sort of instinctive dread directed Norman's steps down the open portion of Randall's Alley, and, voices growing louder as he came nearer, confirmed his suspicions. The fence at this end was down, and, on entering the field, a gleam of light met his eye on the ground—a cloud of smoke, black figures were flitting round it, pushing brands into red places, and feeding the bonfire.

'What have you been doing?' exclaimed Norman. 'You have got yourself into a tremendous scrape!'

A peal of laughter, and shout of 'Randall and Stoneborough for ever!' was the reply.

'August! May junior! Tom! answer me! Is he here?' asked Noman, not solicitous to identify any one.

But gruff voices broke in upon them. 'There they are, nothing like 'em for mischief.'

'Come, young gentlemen,' said a policeman, 'be off, if you please. We don't want to have none of you at the station to-night.'

A general hurry-skurry ensued. Norman alone, strong in innocence, walked quietly away, and, as he came forth from the darkness of the Alley, beheld something scouring away before him, in the direction of home. It popped in at the front door before him, but was not in the drawing-room. He strode up stairs, called, but was not answered, and found, under the bed-clothes, a quivering mass, consisting of Tom, with all his clothes on, fully persuaded that it was the policeman who was pursuing him.

CHAPTER XXII.

Oh Life, without thy chequered scene,
Of right and wrong, of weal and woe,
Success and failure, could a ground
For magnanimity be found?'—WORDSWORTH.

DOCTOR MAY was called for late the next day, Friday, and spent some time in one of the houses near the river. It was nearly eight o'clock when he came away, and he lingered, looking towards the school, in hopes of a walk home with his boys.

Presently he saw Norman come out from under the archway, his cap drawn over his face, and step, gesture, and manner, betraying that something was seriously wrong. He came up almost to his father without seeing him, until startled by his exclamation, 'Norman—why, Norman, what's the matter?'

Norman's lips quivered, and his face was pale—he seemed as if he could not speak.

'Where's Tom?' said the Doctor, much alarmed. 'Has he

got into disgrace about this business of Tomkins? That boy—'

'He has only got an imposition,' interrupted Norman. 'No, it is not that,—it is myself,—' and it was only with a gulp and struggle that he brought out the words, 'I am turned down in the school.'

The Doctor started back a step or two, aghast. 'What—how —speak, Norman. What have you done?'

'Nothing!' said Norman, recovering, in the desire to reassure his father, 'nothing!'

'That's right,' said the Doctor, breathing freely. 'What's the meaning of it . . . . a misunderstanding?'

'Yes,' said Norman, with bitterness. 'It is all Anderson's doing—a word from him would have set all straight—but he would not—I believe, from my heart, he held his tongue to get me down, that he might have the Randall!'

'We'll see you righted,' said the Doctor, eagerly. 'Come, tell me the whole story, Norman. Is it about this unlucky business?'

'Yes. The town-fellows were all up about it last evening, when we came out of school. Anderson senior himself began to put them up to having the fence down again. Yes, that he did—I remember his very words—that Tomkins could not bring it into Court, and so set old Hoxton at us. Well, I told them it would not do,—thought I had settled them—saw them off home—yes, Simpson, and Benson, and Grey, up the High Street, and the others their way. I only left Axworthy going into a shop when I set off on my walk. What could a fellow do more? How was I to know that that Axworthy would get them together again, and take them to this affair—pull up the stakes—saw them down—for they were hard to get down—shy all sorts of things over into the court—hoot at old Tomkins's man, when he told them to be off—and make a bonfire of the sticks at last?'

'And Harvey Anderson was there?'

'No—not he. He is too sharp. Born and bred attorney as he is—he talked them up to the mischief when my back was turned, and then sneaked quietly home, quite innocent, and out of the scrape.'

'But Doctor Hoxton can never entertain a suspicion that you had anything to do with it.'

'Yes, he does though. He thinks I incited them, and Tomkins and the policeman declare I was there in the midst of the row— and not one of these fellows will explain how I came at the last to look for Tom.'

'Not Tom himself?—'

PART I.

'He did try to speak, poor little fellow, but, after the other affair, his word goes for nothing, and so, it seems, does mine. I did think Hoxton would have trusted me!'

'And did not he?' exclaimed Dr. May.

'He did not in so many words accuse me of—of—but he told me he had serious charges brought against me—Mr. Harrison had seen me at Ballhatchet's, setting an example of disregard to rules—and, again, Mr. Harrison saw me coming in at a late hour last night. "I know he did," I said, and I explained where I had been, and they asked for proofs! I could hardly answer, from surprise, at their not seeming to believe me, but I said you could answer for my having come in with the flowers for my sister.'

'To be sure I will—I'll go this instant—' he was turning.

'It is of no use, papa, to-night; Dr. Hoxton has a dinner-party.'

'He is always having parties. I wish he would mind them less, and his business more. You disbelieved! but I'll see justice done you, Norman, the first thing to-morrow. Well—'

'Well, then, I said, old Ballhatchet could tell that I crossed the bridge at the very time they were doing this pretty piece of work, for he was sitting smoking in his porch when I went home, and, would you believe it? the old rascal would not remember who passed that evening! It is all his malice and revenge—nothing else!'

'Why—what have you been doing to him?'

Norman shortly explained the ginger-beer story, and adding, 'Cheviot told me I should get nothing but ill-will, and so I have—all those town-fellows turn against me now, and though they know as well as possible how it was, they won't say a word to right me, just out of spite, because I have stopped them from all the mischief I could!'

'Well, then—'

'They asked me whether—since I allowed that I had been there at last—I had dispersed the boys. I said no, I had no time. Then they desired to know who was there, and that I had not seen; it was all dark, and there had not been a moment, and if I guessed, it was no affair of mine to say. So they ordered me down, and had up Ned Anderson, and one or two more who were known to have been in the riot, and then they consulted a good while, and sent for me; Mr. Wilmot was for me, I am sure, but Harrison was against me. Dr. Hoxton sat there, and made me one of his addresses. He said he would not enter on the question whether I had been present at the repetition of the outrage, as he called it, but what was quite certain was, that I had abused my authority and influence in the school; I had been setting a bad example, and breaking the rules about Ballhatchet, and so far from repressing mischief, I had been the foremost in it, making inflammatory harangues, leading them to commit violence the first time, and the next, if not actually taking part in it personally, at any rate, not preventing it. In short, he said it was clear I had not weight enough for my post—it was some excuse I had been raised to it so young—but it was necessary to show that proficiency in studies did not compensate for disregard of discipline, and so he turned me down below the first six! So there's another May in disgrace!'

'It shall not last—it shall not last, my boy,' said Dr. May, pressing Norman's arm; 'I'll see you righted. Dr. Hoxton shall hear the whole story. I am not for fathers interfering in general, but if ever there was a case, this is! Why, it is almost actionable —injuring your whole prospects in life, and all because he will not take the trouble to make an investigation! It is a crying shame.'

'Every fellow in the school knows how it was,' said Norman; 'and plenty of them would be glad to tell, if they had only the opportunity; but he asked no one but those two or three worst fellows that were at the fire, and they would not tell, on purpose. The school will go to destruction now—they'll get their way, and all I have been striving for is utterly undone.'

'You setting a bad example! Dr. Hoxton little knows what you have been doing. It is a mockery, as I have always said, to see that old fellow sit wrapped up in his pomposity, eating his good dinners, and knowing no more what goes on among his boys than this umbrella! But he will listen to me—and we'll make those boys confess the whole—aye, and have up Ballhatchet himself, to say what your traffic with him was; and we will see what old Hoxton says to you then, Norman.'

Dr. May and his son felt keenly and spoke strongly. There was so much of sympathy and fellow-feeling between them, that there was no backwardness on Norman's part in telling his whole trouble, with more confidence than school-boys often show towards their fathers, and Dr. May entered into the mortification as if he were still at school. They did not go into the house, but walked long up and down the garden, working themselves up into, if possible, stronger indignation, and concerting the explanation for to-morrow, when Dr. May meant to go at once to the head master, and make him attend to the true version of the story, appealing to Harvey Anderson himself, Larkins, and many others, for witnesses. There could be hardly a doubt that Norman would be thus exculpated; but, if Dr. Hoxton would not see things in their true light, Dr. May was ready to take him away at once, rather than see him suffer injustice.

Still, though comforted by his father's entire reliance, Norman was suffering severely under the sense of indignity, and grieved that Dr. Hoxton, and the other masters, should have believed him guilty—that name of May could never again boast of being without reproach. To be in disgrace stung him to the quick, even though undeservedly, and he could not bear to go in, meet his sisters, and be pitied. · 'There's no need they should know of it,' said he, when the Minster clock pealing ten, obliged them to go in-doors, and his father agreed. They bade each other good-night, with the renewal of the promise that Dr. Hoxton should be forced to hear Norman's vindication the first thing to-morrow, Harvey Anderson be disappointed of what he meanly triumphed in, and Norman be again in his post at the head of the school, in more honour and confidence than ever, putting down evil, and making Stoneborough what it ought to be.

As Dr. May lay awake in the summer's morning, meditating on his address to Dr. Hoxton, he heard the unwelcome sound of a ring at the bell, and, in a few minutes, a note was brought to him.

'Tell Adams to get the gig ready—I'll let him know whether he is to go with me.'

And, in a few minutes, the Doctor opened Norman's door, and found him dressed, and standing by the window, reading. 'What, up already, Norman ? I came to tell you that our affairs must wait till the afternoon. It is very provoking, for Hoxton may be gone out; but Mr. Lake's son, at Groveswood, has an attack on the head, and I must go at once. It is a couple of dozen miles off or more. I have hardly ever been there, and it may keep me all day.'

'Shall you go in the gig ? Shall I drive you ?' said Norman, looking rather blank.

'That's what I thought of, if you like it. I thought you would sooner be out of the way.'

'Thank you—yes, papa. Shall I come and help you to finish dressing ?'

'Yes, do, thank you; it will hasten matters. Only, first order in some breakfast. What makes you up so early ? Have not you slept ?'

'Not much—it has been such a hot night.'

'And you have a head-ache. Well, we will find a cure for that before the day is over. I have settled what to say to old Hoxton.'

Before another quarter of an hour had passed, they were driving through the deep lanes, the long grass thickly laden with morning dew, which beaded the webs of the spiders, and rose in clouds of mist under the influence of the sun's rays. There was stillness in the air at first, then the morning sounds, the labourer going forth, the world wakening to life, the opening houses, the children coming out to school. In spite of the tumult of feeling, Norman could not but be soothed and refreshed by the new and fair morning scene, and both minds quitted the school politics, as Dr. May talked of past enjoyment of walks or drives home in early dawn, the more delicious after a sad watch in a sick room, and told of the fair sights he had seen at such unwonted hours.

They had far to go, and the heat of the day had come on before they entered the place of their destination. It was a woodland village, built on a nook in the side of the hill, sloping greenly to the river, and shut in by a white gate, which seemed to gather all in one, the little low old-fashioned church, its yard, shaded with trees, and enclosed by long white rails; the parsonage, covered with climbing plants and in the midst of a gay garden; and one or two cottages. The woods cast a cool shadow, and, in the meadows by the river, rose cocks of new-made hay; there was an air of abiding serenity about the whole place, save that there stood an old man by the gate, evidently watching for the physician's carriage; and where the sun fell on that parsonage-house was a bedroom window wide open, with the curtains drawn.

'Thank Heaven, you are come, sir,' said the old man—'he is fearfully bad.'

Norman knew young Lake, who had been a senior boy when he first went to school, was a Randall scholar, and had borne an excellent character, and highly distinguished himself at the University. And now, by all accounts, he seemed to be dying—in the height of honour and general esteem. Dr. May went into the house, the old man took the horse, and Norman lingered under the trees in the church-yard, watching the white curtains now and then puffed by the fitful summer breeze, as he lay on the turf in the shade, under the influence of the gentle sadness around, resting, mind and body, from the tossing tumultuous passionate sensations that had kept him restless and miserable through the hot night.

He waited long—one hour, two hours had passed away, but he was not impatient, and hardly knew how long the time had been before his father and Mr. Lake came out of the house together, and, after they parted, Dr. May summoned him. He of course asked first for the patient. 'Not quite so hopeless as at first,' and the reasons for having been kept so long were detailed, with many circumstances of the youth's illness, and the parents' resignation, by which Dr. May was still too deeply touched to have room in his mind for anything besides.

They were more than half-way home, and a silence had succeeded the conversation about the Lake family, when Norman spoke:

'Papa, I have been thinking about it, and I believe it would be better to let it alone, if you please.'

'Not apply to Dr. Hoxton!' exclaimed his father.

'Well, I think not. I have been considering it, and it does hardly seem to me the right thing. You see, if I had not you close at hand, this could never be explained, and it seems rather hard upon Anderson, who has no father, and the other fellows, who have theirs further off—'

'Right, Norman, that is what my father before me always said, and the way I have always acted myself; much better let a few trifles go on not just as one would wish, than be for ever interfering. But I really think this is a case for it, and I don't think you ought to let yourself be influenced by the fear of any party-spirit.'

'It is not only that, papa—I have been thinking a good deal to-day, and there are other reasons. Of course I should wish Dr. Hoxton to know that I spoke the truth about that walk, and I hope you will let him know, as I appealed to you. But, on cooler thoughts, I don't believe Dr. Hoxton could seriously suspect me of such a thing as that, and it was not on that ground that I am turned down, but that I did not keep up sufficient discipline, and allowed the outrage, as he calls it. Now, you know, that is, after a fashion, true. If I had not gone on like an ass the other day, and incited them to pull down the fences, they would not have done it afterwards, and perhaps, I ought to have kept on guard longer. It was my fault, and we can't deny it.'

Dr. May made a restless, reluctant movement. 'Well, well, I suppose it was—but it was just as much Harvey Anderson's— and is he to get the scholarship because he has added meanness to the rest?'

'He was not Dux,' said Norman, with a sigh. 'It was more shabby than I thought was even in him. But I don't know that the feeling about him is not one reason. There has always been a rivalry and bitterness between us two, and if I were to get the upper hand now, by means not in the usual course, such as the fellows would think ill of, it would be worse than ever, and I should always feel guilty and ashamed to look at him.'

'Over-refining, Norman,' muttered Dr. May.

'Besides, don't you remember, when his father died, how glad you and every one were to get him a nomination, and it was said that if he gained a scholarship, it would be such a relief to poor Mrs. Anderson? Now he has this chance, it does seem hard to deprive her of it. I should not like to know that I had done so.'

'Whew!' the Doctor gave a considering whistle.

'You could not make it straight, papa, without explaining about the dealing with Ballhatchet, and that would be unfair to them all, even the old rogue himself; for I promised to say nothing about former practices, as long as he did not renew them.'

'Well! I don't want to compromise you, Norman. You know your own ground best, but I don't like it at all. You don't know the humiliation of disgrace. Those who have thought highly of you, now thinking you changed—I don't know how to bear it for you.'

'I don't mind anything while you trust me,' said Norman, eagerly; 'not much, I mean, except Mr. Wilmot. You must judge, papa, and do as you please.'

'No, you must judge, Norman. Your confidence in me ought not to be a restraint. It has always been an understood thing that, what you say at home is, as if it had not been said, as regards my dealings with the masters.'

'I know, papa. Well, I'll tell you what brought me to this. I tumbled about all night in a rage, when I thought how they had served me, and of Hoxton's believing it all, and how he might only half give in to your representation, and then I gloried in Anderson's coming down from his height, and being seen in his true colours. So it went on till morning came, and I got up. You know you gave me my mother's little "Thomas à Kempis." I always read a bit every morning. To-day it was, "Of four things that bring much inward peace." And what do you think they were?'

"Be desirous, my son, to do the will of another rather than thine own.

"Choose always to have less rather than more.

"Seek always the lowest place, and to be inferior to every one.

"Wish always and pray that the will of God may be wholly fulfilled in thee."

'I liked them the more, because it was just like her last reading with us, and like that letter.—Well, then I wondered as I lay on the grass at Groveswood, whether she would have thought it best for me to be reinstated, and I found out that I should have been rather afraid of what you might say when she had talked it over with you.'

Dr. May smiled a little at the simplicity with which this last was said, but his smile ended in one of his heavy sighs. 'So you took her for your counsellor, my boy. That was the way to find out what was right.'

'Well, there was something in the place, and, in watching poor Lake's windows, that made me not able to dwell so much on getting on, and having prizes and scholarships. I thought that caring for those had been driven out of me, and you know I never felt as if it were my right when I was made Dux; but now I find it is all come back. It does not do for me to be first; I have been what she called elated, and been more peremptory than need with the lower boys, and gone on in my old way with Richard, and so I suppose this disgrace has come to punish me. I wish it were not disgrace, because of our name at school, and because it will vex Harry so much; but since it is come, considering all things, I suppose I ought not to struggle to justify myself at other people's expense.'

His eyes were so dazzled with tears, that he could hardly see to drive, nor did his father speak at first. 'I can't say anything against it, Norman, but I am sorry, and one thing more you should consider. If Dr. Hoxton should view this absurd business in the way he seems to do, it will stand in your way for ever in testimonials, if you try for anything else.'

'Do you think it will interfere with my having a Confirmation ticket?'

'Why no, I should not think—such a boyish escapade could be no reason for refusing you one.'

'Very well, then it had better rest. If there should be any difficulty about my being Confirmed, of course we will explain it.'

'I wish every one showed themselves as well prepared!' half-muttered the Doctor; then, after long musing, 'Well, Norman, I give up the scholarship. Poor Mrs. Anderson wants it more than we do, and if the boy is a shabby fellow, the more he wants a decent education. But what do you say to this? I make Hoxton do you full justice, and reinstate you in your proper place, and then I take you away at once—send you to a tutor—anything, till the end of the long vacation.'

'Thank you,' said Norman, pausing. 'I don't know, papa. I am very much obliged to you, but I think it would hardly do. You would be uncomfortable at seeing to quarrel with Dr. Hoxton, and it would be hardly creditable for me to go off in anger.'

'You are right, I believe,' said Dr. May. 'You judge wisely, though I should not have ventured to ask it of you. But what is to become of the discipline of the school? Is that all to go to the dogs?'

'I could not do anything with them if I were restored in this way; they would be more set against me. It is bad enough as it is, but, even for my own peace, I believe it is better to leave it alone. All my comfort in school is over, I know!' and he sighed deeply.

'It is a most untoward business!' said the Doctor. 'I am very sorry your school-days should be clouded—but it can't be helped and you will work yourself into a character again. You are full young, and can stay for the next Randall.'

Norman felt as if, while his father looked at him as he now did, the rest of the world were nothing to him; but, perhaps, the driving past the school brought him to a different mind, for he walked into the house slowly and dejectedly.

He told his own story to Ethel, in the garden, not without much difficulty, so indignant were her exclamations; and it was impossible to make her see that his father's interference would put him in an awkward position among the boys. She would argue vehemently that she could not bear Mr. Wilmot to think ill of him, that it was a great shame of Dr. Hoxton, and that it was dreadful to let such a boy as Harvey Anderson go unpunished. 'I really do think it is quite wrong of you to give up your chance of doing good, and leave him in his evil ways!' That was all the comfort she gave Norman, and she walked in to pour out a furious grumbling upon Margaret.

Dr. May had been telling the elder ones, and they were in conversation after he had left them—Margaret talking with animation, and Flora sitting over her drawing, uttering reluctant assents. 'Has he told you, poor fellow?' asked Margaret.

'Yes,' said Ethel. 'Was there ever such a shame?'

'That is just what I say,' observed Flora. 'I cannot see why the Andersons are to have a triumph over all of us.'

'I used to think Harvey the best of the two,' said Ethel. 'Now I think he is a great deal the worst. Taking advantage of such a mistake as this! How will he ever look Norman in the face?'

'Really,' said Margaret, 'I see no use in aggravating ourselves by talking of the Andersons.'

'I can't think how papa can consent,' proceeded Flora. 'I am sure, if I were in his place, I should not!'

'Papa is so much pleased with dear Norman's behaviour, that it quite makes up for all the disappointment,' said Margaret. 'Besides, he is very much obliged to him in one way; he would not have liked to have to battle the matter with Dr. Hoxton. He spoke of Norman's great good judgment.'

'Yes, Norman can persuade papa to anything,' said Flora.

'Yes, I wish papa had not yielded,' said Ethel. 'It would have been just as noble in dear Norman; and we should not have the apparent disgrace.'

'Perhaps it is best as it is, after all,' said Flora.

'Why, how do you mean?' said Ethel.

'I think it very likely things might have come out. Now, don't look furious, Ethel. Indeed I can't help it; but really I don't think it is explicable why Norman should wish to hush it up, unless there were something behind!'

'Flora!' cried Ethel; too much shocked to bring out another word.

'If you are unfortunate enough to have such suspicions,' said Margaret, quietly, 'I think it would be better to be silent.'

'As if you did not know Norman!' stammered Ethel.

'Well,' said Flora, 'I don't wish to think so. You know I did not hear Norman himself; and when papa gives his vehement accounts of things, it always puzzles us of the cooler-minded sort.'

'It is as great a shame as ever I heard!' cried Ethel, recovering her utterance. 'Who would you trust, if not your own father and brother?'

'Yes, yes,' said Flora, not by any means wishing to displease her sisters. 'If there is such a thing as an excess of generosity, it is sure to be among ourselves. I only know it does not suit me. It will make us all uncomfortable whenever we meet the Andersons, or Mr. Wilmot, or any one else; and as to such tenderness to Harvey Anderson, I think it is thrown away.'

'Thrown away on the object, perhaps,' said Margaret, 'but not in Norman.'

'To be sure,' broke out Ethel. 'Better be than seem! Oh, dear! I am sorry I was vexed with dear old June when he told me. I had rather have him now than if he had gained everything, and every one was praising him—that I had! Harvey Anderson is welcome to be Dux and Randall scholar for what I care, while Norman is—while he is, just what we thought of the last time we read that Gospel—you know, Margaret?'

'He is—that he is,' said Margaret; 'and, indeed, it is most beautiful to see how what has happened has brought him at once to what she wished, when, perhaps, otherwise it would have been a work of long time.'

Ethel was entirely consoled. Flora thought of the words *tête exaltée*, and considered herself alone to have sober sense enough to see things in a true light—not that she went the length of believing that Norman had any underhand motives, but she thought it very discreet in her to think a prudent father would not have been satisfied with such a desire to avoid investigation.

Dr. May would not trust himself to enter on the subject with Dr. Hoxton in conversation; he only wrote a note.

'June 16th.

'Dear Dr. Hoxton,

'My son has appealed to me to confirm his account of himself on Thursday evening last. I therefore distinctly state that he came in at half-past nine, with his hands full of plants from the river, and that he then went out again, by my desire, to look for his little brother.

'Yours, very truly,
'R. MAY.'

A long answer came in return, disclaiming all doubt of Norman's veracity, and explaining Dr. Hoxton's grounds for having degraded him. There had been misconduct in the school, he said, for some time past, and he did not consider that it was any very serious reproach to a boy of Norman's age, that he had not had weight enough to keep up his authority, and had been carried away by the general feeling. It had been necessary to make an example for the sake of principle, and though very sorry it should have fallen on one of such high promise and general good conduct, Dr. Hoxton trusted that it would not be any permanent injury to his prospects, as his talents had raised him to his former position in the school so much earlier than usual.

'The fact was,' said Dr. May, 'that old Hoxton did it in a passion, feeling he must punish somebody; and now, finding there's no uproar about it, he begins to be sorry. I won't answer this note. I'll stop after church to-morrow, and shake hands, and that will show we don't bear malice.'

What Mr. Wilmot might think, was felt by all to affect them more nearly. Ethel wanted to hear that he declared his complete conviction of Norman's innocence, and was disappointed to find that he did not once allude to the subject. She was only consoled by Margaret's conjecture that, perhaps, he thought the head-master had been hasty, and could not venture to say so— he saw into people's characters, and it was notorious that it was just what Dr. Hoxton did not.

Tom had spent the chief of that Saturday in reading a novel borrowed from Axworthy, keeping out of sight of every one. All Sunday he avoided Norman more scrupulously than ever, and again on Monday. That day was a severe trial to Norman; the taking the lower place, and the sense that, excel as much as ever he might in his studies, it would not avail to restore him to his former place, were more unpleasant, when it came to the point, than he had expected.

He saw the cold manner, so different from the readiness with which his tasks had always been met, certain as they were of being well done; he found himself among the common herd whom he had passed so triumphantly, and, for a little while, he had no heart to exert himself.

This was conquered by the strong will and self-rebuke for having merely craved for applause, but, in the play-ground, he found himself still alone—the other boys who had been raised by his fall, shrank from intercourse with one whom they had injured by their silence, and the Andersons, who were wont to say the Mays carried every tale home, and who still almost expected interference from Dr. May, hardly believed their victory secure, and the younger one, at least, talked spitefully, and triumphed in the result of May's meddling and troublesome over-strictness. 'Such prigs always come to a downfall,' was the sentiment.

Norman found himself left out of everything, and stood dispirited and weary on the bank of the river, wishing for Harry, wishing for Cheviot, wishing that he had been able to make a friend who would stand by him, thinking it could not be worse if he had let his father reinstate him—and a sensation of loneli-ness and injustice hung heavy at his heart.

His first interruption was a merry voice. 'I say, June, there's no end of river cray-fish under that bank,' and Larkins' droll face was looking up at him, from that favourite position, half-stooping, his hands on his knees, his expression of fun trying to conceal his real anxiety and sympathy.

Norman turned and smiled, and looked for the cray-fish, and, at the same time, became aware of Hector Ernescliffe, watching for an opportunity to say, 'I have a letter from Alan.' He knew they wanted, as far as little boys ventured to seek after one so much their elder, to show themselves his friends, and he was grateful; he roused himself to hear about Alan's news, and found it was important—his great friend, Captain Gordon, had got a ship, and hoped to be able to take him, and this might lead to Harry's going with him. Then Norman applied himself to the capture of cray-fish, and Larkins grew so full of fun and drollery, that the hours of recreation passed off less gloomily than they had begun.

If only his own brother would have been his adherent! But he saw almost nothing of Tom. Day after day he missed him, he was off before him in going and returning from school, and when he caught a sight of his face, it looked harassed, pale, and miserable, stealing anxious glances after him, yet shrinking from his eye. But, at the same time, Norman did not see him ming-ling with his former friends, and could not make out how he disposed of himself. To be thus continually shunned by his own brother, even when the general mass were returning to ordinary terms, became so painful, that Norman was always on the watch to seek for one more conversation with him.

He caught him at last in the evening, just as they were going home. 'Tom, why are you running away? Come with me,' said he, authoritatively; and Tom obeyed in trembling.

Norman led the way to the meads. 'Tom,' said he, 'do not let this go on. Why do you serve me in this way? You surely need not turn against me,' he said, with pleading melancholy in his voice.

It was not needed. Tom had flung himself upon the grass, and was in an agony of crying, even before he had finished the words.

'Tom, Tom! what is the matter? Have they been bullying you again? Look up, and tell me—what is it? You know I can stand by you still, if you'll only let me;' and Norman sat by him on the grass, and raised his face by a sort of force, but the kind words only brought more piteous sobs. It was a long time before they diminished enough to let him utter a word, but Norman went on patiently consoling and inquiring, sure, at least, that here had broken down the sullenness that had always repelled him.

At last came the words, 'Oh! I cannot bear it. It is all my doing!'

'What—how—you don't mean this happening to me? It is not your doing, August—what fancy is this?'

'O yes, it is,' said Tom, his voice cut short by gasps, the remains of the sobs. 'They would not hear me! I tried to tell them how you told them not, and sent them home. I tried to tell about Ballhatchet—but—but they wouldn't—they said if it had been Harry, they would have attended—but they would not believe me. Oh! if Harry was but here!'

'I wish he was,' said Norman, from the bottom of his heart; 'but you see, Tom, if this sets you on always telling truth, I shan't think any great harm done.'

A fresh burst, 'Oh! they are all so glad! They say such things! And the Mays were never in disgrace before. O Norman, Norman!'

'Never mind about that,—' began Norman.

'But you would mind,' broke in the boy, passionately, 'if you knew what Anderson junior and Axworthy say! They say it serves you right, and they were going to send me to old Ballhatchet's to get some of his stuff to drink confusion to the month of June, and all pragmatical meddlers; and when I said I could not go, they vowed if I did not, I should eat the corks for them! And Anderson junior called me names, and licked me. Look there.' He showed a dark blue-and-red stripe, raised on the palm of his hand. 'I could not write well for it these three days, and Hawes gave me double copies!'

'The cowardly fellows!' exclaimed Norman, indignantly. 'But you did not go?'

'No, Anderson senior stopped them. He said he would not have the Ballhatchet business begin again.'

'That is one comfort,' said Norman. 'I see he does not dare not to keep order. But if you'll only stay with me, August, I'll take care they don't hurt you.'

'Oh! June! June!' and he threw himself across his kind

brother. 'I am so very sorry! Oh! to see you put down—and hear them! And you to lose the scholarship! Oh, dear! oh, dear! and be in disgrace with them all!'

'But, Tom, do cheer up. It is nothing to be in such distress at. Papa knows all about it, and while he does, I don't care half so much.'

'O, I wish—I wish—'

'You see, Tom,' said Norman, 'after all, though it is very kind of you to be sorry for not being able to get me out of this scrape, the thing one wants you to be sorry about, is your own affair.'

'I wish I had never come to school! I wish Anderson would leave me alone! It is all his fault! A mean-spirited, skulking, bullying—'

'Hush, hush, Tom, he is bad enough, but now you know what he is, you can keep clear of him for the future. Now listen. You and I will make a fresh start, and try if we can't get the Mays to be looked on as they were when Harry was here. Let us mind the rules, and get into no more mischief.'

'You'll keep me from Ned Anderson and Axworthy?' whispered Tom.

'Yes, that I will. And you'll try and speak the truth, and be straightforward?'

'I will, I will,' said Tom, worn out in spirits by his long bondage, and glad to catch at the hope of relief and protection.

'Then let us come home,' and Tom put his hand into his brother's, as a few weeks back would have seemed most unworthy of schoolboy dignity.

Thenceforth Tom was devoted to Norman, and kept close to him, sure that the instant he was from under his wing, his former companions would fall on him to revenge his defection, but clinging to him also from real affection and gratitude. Indolence and timidity were the true root of what had for a time seemed like a positively bad disposition; beneath, there was a warm heart, and sense of right, which had been almost stifled for the time, in the desire, from moment to moment, to avoid present trouble or fear. Under Norman's care his better self had freer scope; he was guarded from immediate terror, and kept from the suggestions of the worse sort of boys, as much as was in his brother's power; and the looks they cast towards him, and the sly torments they attempted to inflict, by no means invited him back to them. The lessons, where he had a long inveterate habit of shuffling, came under Norman's eye at the same time. He always prepared them in his presence, instead of in the most secret manner possible, and with all Anderson's expeditious modes of avoiding the making them of any use. Norman sat by, and gave such help as was fair and just, showed him how to learn, and explained difficulties, and the ingenuity hitherto spent in eluding learning being now directed to gaining it, he began to make real progress, and find satisfaction in it. The comfort of being good dawned upon him once more, but still there was much to contend with; he had acquired such a habit of prevarication, that, if by any means taken by surprise, his impulse was to avoid giving a straightforward answer, and when he recollected his sincerity, the truth came with the air of falsehood. Moreover, he was an arrant coward, and provoked tricks by his manifest and unreasonable terrors. It was no slight exercise of patience that Norman underwent, but this was the interest he had made for himself; and the recovery of the boy's attachment, and his improvement, though slow, were a present recompence.

Ernescliffe, Larkins, and others of the boys, held fast to him, and after the first excitement was past, all the rest returned to their former tone. He was decidedly as much respected as ever, and, at the same time, regarded with more favour than when his strictness was resented. And as for the discipline of the school, that did not suffer. Anderson felt that, for his own credit, he must not allow the rules to be less observed than in May's reign, and he enforced them upon the reluctant and angry boys, with whom he had been previously making common cause. Dr. Hoxton boasted to the under-masters that the school had never been in such good order as under Anderson, little guessing that this was but reaping the fruits of a past victory, or that every boy in the whole school gave the highest place in their esteem to the deposed Dux.

To Anderson, Norman's cordial manner and ready support were the strangest part of all, only explained by thinking that he deemed it, as he tried to do himself, merely the fortune of war, and was sensible of no injury.

And, for Norman himself, when the first shock was over, and he was accustomed to the change, he found the cessation of vigilance a relief, and carried a lighter heart than any time since his mother's death. His sisters could not help observing that there was less sadness in the expression of his eyes, that he carried his head higher, walked with freedom and elasticity of step, tossed and flourished the Daisy till she shouted and crowed, while Margaret shrank at such freaks; and, though he was not much of a laugher himself, contributed much sport in the way of bright apposite sayings to the home circle.

It was a very unexpected mode of cure for depression of spirits, but there could be no question that it succeeded; and when a few Saturdays after, he drove Dr. May again to Groveswood to see young Mr. Lake, who was recovering, he brought Margaret home a whole pile of botanical curiosities, and drew his father into an animated battle over natural and Linnæan systems, which kept the whole party merry with the pros and cons every evening for a week.

CHAPTER XXIII.

Oh! the golden-hearted daisies,
  Witnessed there before my youth,
To the truth of things, with praises
  Of the beauty of the truth.'—E. B. BROWNING.'

'MARGARET, see here.'

The Doctor threw into her lap a letter, which made her cheeks light up.

Mr. Ernescliffe wrote that his father's friend, Captain Gordon, having been appointed to the frigate *Alcestis*, had chosen him as one of his lieutenants, and offered a nomination as naval cadet for his brother. He had replied that the navy was not Hector's destination; but, as Captain Gordon had no one else in view, had prevailed on him to pass on the proposal to Harry May.

Alan wrote in high terms of his captain, declaring that he esteemed the having sailed with him as one of the greatest advantages he had ever received; and adding, that, for his own part, Dr. May needed no promise from him, to be assured that he would watch over Harry like his own brother. It was believed that the *Alcestis* was destined for the South American station.

'A three years' business,' said Dr. May, with a sigh. 'But the thing is done, and this is as good as we can hope.'

'Far better!' said Margaret. 'What pleasure it must have given him! Dear Harry could not sail under more favourable circumstances.'

'No, I would trust to Ernescliffe as I would to Richard. It is kindly done, and I will thank him at once. Where does he date from?'

'From Portsmouth. He does not say whether he has seen Harry.'

'I suppose he waited for my answer. Suppose I enclose a note for him to give to Harry. There will be rapture enough, and it is a pity he should not have the benefit of it.'

The Doctor sat down to write, while Margaret worked and mused—perhaps on outfits and new shirts—perhaps on Harry's lion-locks beneath a blue cap and gold band—or, perchance, on the coral shoals of the Pacific.

It was one of the quiet afternoons, when all the rest were out, and which the Doctor and his daughter especially valued, when they were able to spend one together without interruption. Soon, however, a ring at the door brought an impatient exclamation from the Doctor; but his smile beamed out at the words, 'Miss Rivers.' They were great friends; in fact, on terms of some mutual sauciness; though Meta was, as yet, far less at home with his daughters, and came in, looking somewhat shy.

'Ah, your congeners are gone out!' was the Doctor's reception. 'You must put up with our sober selves.'

'Is Flora gone far?' asked Meta.

'To Cocksmoor,' said Margaret. 'I am very sorry she has missed you.'

'Shall I be in your way?' said Meta, timidly. 'Papa has several things to do, and said he would call for me here.'

'Good luck for Margaret,' said Dr. May.

'So they are gone to Cocksmoor!' said Meta. 'How I envy them!'

'You would not, if you saw the place,' said Dr. May. 'I believe Norman is very angry with me for letting them go near it.'

'Ah! but they are of real use there!'

'And Miss Meta is obliged to take to envying the black-hole of Cocksmoor, instead of being content with the eglantine bowers of Abbotstoke! I commiserate her!' said the Doctor.

'If I did any good instead of harm at Abbotstoke!'

'Harm!' exclaimed Margaret.

'They wont on very well without me,' said Meta; 'but ever since I have had the class, they have been getting naughtier and noisier every Sunday; and, last Sunday, the prettiest of all—the one I liked best, and had done everything for—she began to mimic me —held up her finger, as I did, and made them all laugh!'

'Well, that is very bad!' said Margaret; 'but I suppose she was a very little one.'

'No, a quick clever one, who knew much better, about nine years old. She used to be always at home in the week, dragging about a great baby; and we managed that her mother should afford to stay at home, and send her to school. It seemed such a pity her cleverness should be wasted.'

The Doctor smiled. 'Ah! depend upon it, the tyrant-baby was the best disciplinarian.'

Meta looked extremely puzzled.

'Papa means,' said Margaret, 'that if she was inclined to be conceited, the being teased at home might do her more good than being brought forward at school.'

PART I. B

'I have done everything wrong, it seems,' said Meta, with a shade of what the French call *dépit*. 'I thought it must be right and good—but it has only done mischief; and now papa says they are an ungrateful set, and that, if it vexes me, I had better have no more to do with them!'

'It does not vex you so much as that, I hope,' said Margaret.

'O, I could not bear that!' said Meta; 'but it is so different from what I thought!'

'Ah! you had an Arcadia of good little girls in straw hats, such as I see in Blanche's little books,' said the Doctor, 'all making the young lady an oracle, and doing wrong—if they do it at all —in the simplest way, just for an example to the others.'

'Dr. May! How can you know so well? But do you really think it is their fault, or mine?'

'Do you think me a conjuror?'

'Well, but what do you think?'

'What do Mr. and Mrs. Charles Wilmot think?'

'I know Mrs. Wilmot thinks I spoil my class. She spoke to me about making favourites, and sometimes has seemed surprised at things which I have done. Last Sunday, she told me she thought I had better have a steadier class, and I know whom she will give me—the great big, stupid ones, at the bottom of the first class! I do believe it is only out of good-nature that she does not tell me not to teach at all. I have a great mind I will not; I know I do nothing but harm.'

'What shall you say if I tell you I think so too?' asked the Doctor.

'O, Dr. May! you don't really? Now, does he, Miss May? I am sure I only want to do them good. I don't know what I can have done.'

Margaret made her perceive that the Doctor was smiling, and she changed her tone, and earnestly begged to be told what they thought of the case; for if she should show her concern at home, her father and governess would immediately beg her to cease from all connection with the school, and she did not feel at all convinced that Mrs. Wilmot liked to have her there. Feeling injured by the implied accusation of mismanagement, yet, with a sense of its truth, used to be petted, and new to rebuffs, yet with a sincere wish to act rightly, she was much perplexed by this, her first reverse, and had come partly with the view of consulting Flora, though she had fallen on other counsellors.

'Margaret, our adviser-general,' said the Doctor, 'what do you say? Put yourself in the place of Mrs. Charles Wilmot, and say, shall Miss Rivers teach or not?'

'I had rather you would, papa.'

'Not I—I never kept school.'

'Well, then, I being Mrs. Wilmot, should certainly be mortified if Miss Rivers deserted me, because the children were naughty. I think, I think I had rather she came and asked me what she had better do.'

'And you would answer "teach," for fear of vexing her,' said Meta.

'I should, and also for the sake of letting her learn to teach.'

'The point where only trial shows one's ignorance,' said Dr. May.

'But I don't want to do it for my own sake,' said Meta. 'I do everything for my own sake already.'

'For theirs, then,' said the Doctor. 'If teaching will not come by nature, you must serve an apprenticeship, if you mean to be of service in that line. Perhaps, it was the gift that the fairies omitted.'

'But will it do any good to them?'

'I can't tell; but I am sure it would do them harm for you to give it up, because it is disagreeable.'

'Well,' said Meta, with a sigh, 'I'll go and talk to Mrs. Wilmot. I could not bear to give up anything that seems right, just now, because of the Confirmation.'

Margaret eagerly inquired, and it appeared that the Bishop had given notice for a Confirmation in August, and that Mr. Wilmot was already beginning to prepare his candidates, whilst Mr. Ramsden, always tardy, never gave notice till the last moment possible. The hope was expressed that Harry might be able to profit by this opportunity; and Harry's prospects were explained to Meta; then the Doctor, recollecting something that he wished to say to Mr. Rivers, began to ask about the chance of his coming before the time of an engagement of his own.

'He said he should be here at about half-past four,' said Meta. 'He is gone to the station to inquire about the trains. Do you know what time the last comes in?'

'At nine forty-five,' said the Doctor.

'That is what we were afraid of. It is for Bellairs, my maid. Her mother is very ill, and she is afraid she is not properly nursed. It is about five miles from the Milbury Station, and we thought of letting her go with a day-ticket, to see about her. She could go in the morning, after I am up; but I don't know what is to be done, for she could not get back before I dress for dinner.'

Margaret felt perfectly aghast at the cool tone, especially after what had passed.

'It would be quite impossible,' said the Doctor. 'Even going

by the eight o'clock train, and returning by the last, she would
only have two hours to spare—short enough measure for a sick
mother.'

'Papa means to give her whatever she wants for any nurse she
may get.'

'Is there no one with her mother now?'

'A son's wife, who, they think, is not kind. Poor Bellairs was
so grateful for being allowed to go home. I wonder if I could
dress for once without her.'

'Do you know old Crabbe?' said the Doctor.

'The dear old man at Abbotstoke? O yes, of course.'

'There was a very sad case in his family. The mother was
dying of a lingering illness, when the son met with a bad accident. The only daughter was a lady's maid, and could not be
spared, though the brother was half crazy to see her, and there
was no one to tend them but a wretch of a woman, paid by the
parish. The poor fellow kept calling for his sister in his delirium, and, at last, I could not help writing to the mistress.'

'Did she let her come?' said Meta, her cheek glowing.

'As a great favour, she let her set out by the mail train, after
dressing her for a ball, with orders to return in time for her
toilette for an evening party the next day.'

'O, I remember,' said Margaret, 'her coming here at five in
the morning, and your taking her home.'

'And when we got to Abbotstoke, the brother was dead. That
parish nurse had not attended to my directions, and, I do believe,
was the cause of it. The mother had had a seizure, and was in
the most precarious state.'

'Surely, she stayed!'

'It was as much as her place was worth,' said the Doctor;
'and her wages were the chief maintenance of the family. So she
had to go back to dress her mistress, while the old woman lay
there, wailing after Betsy. She did give warning then, but,
before the month was out, the mother was dead.'

Meta did not speak, and Dr. May presently rose, saying, he
should try to meet Mr. Rivers in the town, and went out. Meta
sat thoughtful, and, at last, sighing, said, 'I wonder whether
Bellairs' mother is so very ill? I have a great mind to let Susan
try to do my hair, and let Bellairs stay a little longer. I never
thought of that.'

'I do not think you will be sorry,' said Margaret.

'Yes, I shall, for if my hair does not look nice, papa will not
be pleased, and there is Aunt Leonora coming. How odd it will
be to be without Bellairs! I will ask Mrs. Larpent.'

'Oh, yes!' said Margaret. 'You must not think we meant to advise; but papa has seen so many instances of distress, from servants not spared to their friends in illness, that he feels strongly on the subject.'

'And I really might have been as cruel as that woman!' said Meta. 'Well, I hope Mrs. Bellairs may be better, and able to spare her daughter. I don't know what will become of me without her.'

'I think it will have been a satisfaction in one way,' said Margaret.

'In what way?'

'Don't you remember what you began by complaining of, that you could not be of use? Now, I fancy this would give you the pleasure of undergoing a little personal inconvenience for the good of another.'

Meta looked half puzzled, half thoughtful, and Margaret, who was a little uneasy at the style of counsel she found herself giving, changed the conversation.

It was a memorable one to little Miss Rivers, opening out to her, as did almost all her meetings with that family, a new scope for thought and for duty. The code, to which she had been brought up, taught that servants were the machines of their employer's convenience. Good-nature occasioned much kindliness of manner and intercourse, and every luxury and indulgence was afforded freely; but where there was any want of accordance between the convenience of the two parties, there was no question. The master must be the first object, the servants' remedy was in their own hands.

Amiable as was Mr. Rivers, this, merely from indulgence and want of reflection, was his principle; and his daughter had only been acting on it, though she did not know it, till the feelings, that she had never thought of, were thus displayed before her. These were her first practical lessons that life was not meant to be passed in pleasing ourselves, and being good-natured at small cost.

It was an effort. Meta was very dependant, never having been encouraged to be otherwise, and Bellairs was like a necessary of life, in her estimation; but strength of principle came to aid her naturally kind-hearted feeling, and she was pleased by the idea of voluntarily undergoing a privation, so as to test her sincerity.

So when her father told her of the inconvenient times of the trains, and declared that Bellairs must give it up, she answered, by proposing to let her sleep a night or two there, gaily promised to manage very well, and satisfied him

Her maid's grateful looks and thanks recompensed her when she made the offer to her, and inspirited her to an energetic coaxing of Mrs. Larpent, who, being more fully aware than her father, of the needfulness of the lady's-maid, and also very anxious that her darling should appear to the best advantage before the expected aunt, Lady Leonora Langdale, was unwilling to grant more than one night at the utmost.

Meta carried the day, and her last assurance to Bellairs was, that she might stay as long as seemed necessary to make her mother comfortable.

Thereupon Meta found herself more helpful in some matters than she had expected, but at a loss in others. Susan, with all Mrs. Larpent's supervision, could not quite bring her dress to the air that was so peculiarly graceful and becoming; and she often caught her papa's eye looking at her, as if he saw something amiss, and could not discover what it was. Then came Aunt Leonora, always very kind to Meta, but the dread of the rest of the household, whom she was wont to lecture on the proper care of her niece. Miss Rivers was likely to have a considerable fortune, and Lady Leonora intended her to be a very fashionable and much-admired young lady, under her own immediate protection.

The two cousins, Leonora and Agatha, talked to her; the one of her balls, the other of her music—patronized her, and called her their good little cousin—while they criticised the stiff set of those unfortunate plaits made by Susan, and laughed, as if it was an unheard-of concession, at Bellairs' holiday.

Nevertheless, when 'Honoured Miss' received a note, begging for three days' longer grace, till a niece should come, in whom Bellairs could place full confidence, she took it on herself to return free consent. Lady Leonora found out what she had done, and reproved her, telling her it was only the way to make 'those people' presume, and Mrs. Larpent was also taken to task; but, decidedly, Meta did not regret what she had done, though she felt as if she had never before known how to appreciate comfort, when she once more beheld Bellairs stationed at her toilette table.

Meta was asked about her friends. She could not mention any one but Mrs. Charles Wilmot and the Miss Mays.

'Physician's daughters; oh!' said Lady Leonora.

And she proceeded to exhort Mr. Rivers to bring his daughter to London, or its neighbourhood, where she might have masters, and be in the way of forming intimacies suited to her connections.

Mr. Rivers dreaded London—never was well there, and did not like the trouble of moving—while Meta was so attached to the Grange, that she entreated him not to think of leaving it, and greatly dreaded her aunt's influence. Lady Leonora did, indeed, allow that the Grange was a very pretty place; her only complaint was, the want of suitable society for Meta; she could not bear the idea of her growing accustomed—for want of something better—to the Vicar's wife, and the pet Doctor's daughters.

Flora had been long desirous to effect a regular call at Abbotstoke, and it was just now that she succeeded. Mrs. Charles Wilmot's little girl was to have a birthday feast, at which Mary, Blanche, and Aubrey were to appear. Flora went in charge of them, and as soon as she had safely deposited them, and appointed Mary to keep Aubrey out of mischief, she walked up to the Grange, not a whit daunted by the report of the very fine ladies who were astonishing the natives of Abbotstoke.

She was admitted, and found herself in the drawing-room, with a quick, lively-looking lady, whom she perceived to be Lady Leonora, and who instantly began talking to her very civilly. Flora was never at a loss, and they got on extremely well; her ease and self-possession, without forwardness, telling much to her advantage. Meta came in, delighted to see her, but, of course, the visit resulted in no really intimate talk, though it was not without effect. Flora declared Lady Leonora Langdale to be a most charming person; and Lady Leonora, on her side, asked Meta who was that very elegant conversible girl. 'Flora May,' was the delighted answer, now that the aunt had committed herself by commendation. And she did not retract it; she pronounced Flora to be something quite out of the common way, and supposed that she had had unusual advantages.

Mr. Rivers took care to introduce to his sister-in-law, Dr. May, (who would fain have avoided it,) but ended by being in his turn pleased and entertained by her brilliant conversation, which she put forth for him, as her instinct showed her that she was talking to a man of high ability. A perfect gentleman she saw him to be, and making out some mutual connections far up in the family tree of the Mackenzies, she decided that the May family were an acquisition, and very good companions for her niece at present, while not yet come out.

So ended the visit, with this great triumph for Meta, who had a strong belief in Aunt Leonora's power and infallibility, and yet had not consulted her about Bellairs, nor about the school question.

She had missed one Sunday's school on account of her aunt's visit, but the resolution made beside Margaret's sofa had not been forgotten. She spent her Saturday afternoon in a call on Mrs. Wilmot, ending with a walk through the village; she confessed her ignorance, apologized for her blunders, and put herself

under the direction which once she had fancied too strict and
harsh to be followed.

And on Sunday, she was content to teach the stupid girls,
and abstain from making much of the smooth-faced engaging
set. She thought it very dull work, but she could feel that it
was something not done to please herself; and whereas her father
had feared she would be dull when her cousins were gone, he
found her more joyous than ever.

There certainly was a peculiar happiness about Margaret
Rivers; her vexations were but ripples, rendering the sunny
course of her life more sparkling, and each exertion in the way
of goodness was productive of so much present joy, that the
steps of her ladder seemed, indeed, to be of diamonds.

Her ladder—for she was, indeed, mounting upwards. She
was very earnest in her Confirmation preparation, most anxious
to do right and to contend with her failings; but the struggle
at present was easy; and the hopes, joys, and incentives, shone
out more and more upon her in this blithe stage of her life.

She knew there was a dark side, but hope and love were more
present to her than was fear. Happy those to whom such young
days are granted.

CHAPTER XXIV.

> ' It is the generous spirit, who, when brought
> Among the tasks of real life, hath wrought
> Upon the plan that pleased his childish thought,
> Whose high endeavours are an inward light,
> Making the path before them always bright.'—WORDSWORTH.

THE holidays had commenced about a week when Harry, now
duly appointed to H. M. S. *Alcestis*, was to come home on leave,
as he proudly expressed it.

A glad troop of brothers and sisters, with the Doctor himself,
walked up to the station to meet him, and who was happiest
when, from the window, was thrust out the rosy face, with the
gold band? Mary gave such a shriek and leap, that two passengers
and one guard turned round to look at her, to the extreme dis-
comfiture of Flora and Norman, evidenced by one by a grave
' Mary! Mary!' by the other, by walking off to the extreme end
of the platform, and trying to look as if he did not belong to
them, in which he was imitated by his shadow, Tom.

Sailor already, rather than school-boy, Harry cared not for
spectators; his bound from the carriage, and the hug between
him and Mary, would have been worthy of the return from the

voyage. The next greeting was for his father, and the sisters had had their share by the time the two brothers thought fit to return from their calm walk on the platform.

Grand was it to see that party return to the town—the naval cadet, with his arm linked in Mary's, and Aubrey clinging to his hand, and the others walking behind, admiring him as he turned his bright face every moment with some glad question or answer, 'How was Margaret?' Oh, so much better; she had been able to walk across the room, with Norman's arm round her—they hoped she would soon use crutches—and she sat up more. 'And the baby?' More charming than ever—four teeth—would soon walk—such a darling! Then came 'my dirk, the ship, our berth.' 'Papa, do ask Mr. Ernescliffe to come here. I know he could get leave.'

'Mr. Ernescliffe! You used to call him Alan!' said Mary.

'Yes, but that is all over now. You forget what we do on board. Captain Gordon himself calls me Mr. May!'

Some laughed, others were extremely impressed.

'Ha! There's Ned Anderson coming,' cried Mary. 'Now! Let him see you, Harry.'

'What matters Ned Anderson to me?' said Harry; and, with an odd mixture of shame-facedness and cordiality, he marched full up to his old school-fellow, and shook hands with him, as if able, in the plenitude of his officership, to afford plenty of good-humoured superiority. Tom had meantime subsided out of all view. But poor Harry's exultation had a fall.

'Well!' graciously inquired 'Mr. May,' 'and how is Harvey?'

'O, very well. We are expecting him home to-morrow.'

'Where has he been?'

'To Oxford, about the Randall.'

Harry gave a disturbed, wondering look round, on seeing Edward's air of malignant satisfaction. He saw nothing that re-assured him, except the quietness of Norman's own face, but even that altered as their eyes met. Before another word could be said, however, the Doctor's hand was on Harry's shoulder.

'You must not keep him now, Ned,' said he—'his sister has not seen him yet.'

And he moved his little procession onwards, still resting on Harry's shoulder, while a silence had fallen on all, and even the young sailor ventured no question. Only Tom's lips were quivering, and Ethel had squeezed Norman's hand. 'Poor Harry!' he muttered; 'this is worst of all! I wish we had written it to him.'

'So do I now, but we always trusted it would come right. Oh! if I were but a boy to flog that Edward!'

' Hush, Ethel, remember what we resolved.'

They were entering their own garden, where, beneath the shade of the tulip-tree, Margaret lay on her couch. Her arms were held out, and Harry threw himself upon her; but when he rose from her caress, Norman and Tom were gone.

' What is this ?' he now first ventured to ask.

' Come with me,' said Dr. May, leading the way to his study, where he related the whole history of the suspicion that Norman had incurred. He was glad that he had done so in private, for Harry's indignation and grief went beyond his expectations; and when at last it appeared that Harvey Anderson was actually Randall scholar, after opening his eyes with the utmost incredulity, and causing it to be a second time repeated, he gave a gulp or two, turned very red, and ended by laying his head on the table, and fairly sobbing and crying aloud, in spite of dirk, uniform, and manhood.

' Harry! why Harry, my boy ! We should have prepared you for this,' said the Doctor, affectionately. ' We have left off breaking our hearts about it. I don't want any comfort now, for having gold instead of glitter; though at first I was as bad as you.'

' O if I had but been there !' said Harry, combating unsuccessfully with his tears.

' Ah ! so we all said, Norman and all. Your word would have cleared him—that is, if you had not been in the thick of the mischief. Ha! July, should not you have been on the top of the wall ?'

' I would have stood by him, at least. Would not I have given Axworthy and Anderson two such black eyes as they could not have shown in school for a week ? They had better look out !' cried Harry, savagely.

' What ! An officer in Her Majesty's service ! Eh, Mr. May?'

' Don't, papa, don't. Oh ! I thought it would have been so happy, when I came home, to see Norman Randall scholar. Oh ! now I don't care for the ship, nor anything.'

Again Harry's face went down on the table.

' Come, come, Harry,' said Dr. May, pulling off the spectacles that had become very dewy, ' don't let us make fools of ourselves, or they will think we are crying for the scholarship.'

' I don't care for the scholarship, but to have June turned down —and disgrace—'

' What I care for, Harry, is having June what he is, and *that* I know better now.'

' He is ! he is—he is June himself, and no mistake !' cried Harry, with vehemence.

'The prime of the year, is not it?' said the Doctor, smiling, as he stroked down the blue sleeve, as if he thought that generous July did not fall far short of it.

'That he is!' exclaimed Harry. 'I have never met one fellow like him.'

'It will be a chance if you ever do,' said Dr. May. 'That is better than scholarships!'

'It should have been both,' said Harry.

'Norman thinks the disappointment has been very good for him,' said the Doctor. 'Perhaps it made him what he is now. All success is no discipline, you know.'

Harry looked as if he did not know.

'Perhaps you will understand better by-and-by, but this I can tell you, Harry, that the patient bearing of his vexation, has done more to renew Norman's spirits, than all his prosperity. See if it has not. I believe it is harder to every one of us, than to him. To Ethel, especially, it is a struggle to be in charity with the Andersons.'

'In charity!' repeated Harry. 'Papa! you don't want us to like a horrid, sneaking, mean-spirited pair like those, that have used Norman in that shameful way?'

'No, certainly not; I only want you to feel no more personal anger, than if it had been Cheviot, or some indifferent person, that had been injured.'

'I should have hated them all the same!' cried Harry.

'If it is *all the same,* and it is the treachery you hate, I ask no more,' said the Doctor.

'I can't help it, papa, I can't! If I were to meet those fellows, do you think I could shake hands with them? If I did not lick Ned all down Minster-street, he might think himself lucky.'

'Well, Harry, I won't argue any more. I have no right to preach forbearance. Your brother's example is better worth than my precept. Shall we go back to Margaret, or have you anything to say to me?'

Harry made no positive answer, but pressed close to his father, who put his arm round him, while the curly-head was laid on his shoulder. Presently, he said, with a great sigh, 'There's nothing like home.'

'Was that what you wanted to say?' asked Dr. May, smiling, as he held the boy more closely to him.

'No; but it will be a long time before I come back. They think we shall have orders for the Pacific.'

'You will come home our real lion,' said the Doctor 'How much you will have to tell!'

'Yes,' said Harry; 'but, oh! it is very different from coming home every night, not having any one to tell a thing to.'

'Do you want to say anything now?'

'I don't know. I told you in my letter about the half-sovereign.'

'Aye, never mind that.'

'And there was one night, I am afraid, I did not stand by a little fellow that they bullied about his prayers. Perhaps he would have gone on, if I had helped him!'

'Does he sail with you?'

'No, he was at school. If I had told him that he and I would stand by each other—but he looked so foolish, and began to cry! I am sorry now.'

'Weak spirits have much to bear,' said the Doctor, 'and you stronger ones, who don't mind being bullied, are meant, I suppose, to help them, as Norman has been doing by poor little Tommy.'

'It was thinking of Norman—that made me sorry. I knew there was something else, but you see I forget, when I don't see you and Margaret every day.'

'You have One always near, my boy.'

'I know, but I cannot always recollect. And there is such a row at night on board, I cannot think or attend as I ought,' murmured Harry.

'Yes, your life, sleeping at home in quiet, has not prepared you for that trial,' said the Doctor. 'But others have kept upright habits under the same, you know—and God helps those who are doing their best.'

Harry sighed.

'I mean to do my best,' he added; 'and if it was not for feeling bad, I should like it. I *do* like it'—and his eye sparkled, and his smile beamed, though the tear was undried.

'I know you do!' said Dr. May, smiling, 'and for feeling bad, my Harry, I fear you must do that by sea, or land, as long as you are in this world. God be thanked that you grieve over the feeling. But He is ready to aid, and knows the trial, and you will be brought nearer to Him, before you leave us.'

'Margaret wrote about the Confirmation. Am I old enough?'

'If you wish it, Harry, under these circumstances.'

'I suppose I do,' said Harry, uneasily twirling a button. 'But then, if I've got to forgive the Andersons—'

'We won't talk any more of that,' said the Doctor—'here is poor Mary, reconnoitring, to know why I am keeping you from her.'

Then began the scampering up and down the house, round and round the garden, visiting every pet or haunt, or contrivance;

Mary and Harry at the head, Blanche and Tom in full career after them, and Aubrey stumping and scrambling at his utmost speed, far behind.

Not a word passed between Norman and Harry on the school misadventure, but, after the outbreak of the latter, he treated it as a thing forgotten, and brought all his high spirits to enliven the family party. Richard, too, returned later on the same day, and though not received with the same uproarious joy as Harry, the elder section of the family were as happy in their way as what Blanche called the middle-aged. The Daisy was brought down, and the eleven were again all in the same room, though there were suppressed sighs from some, who reflected how long it might be before they could again assemble.

Tea went off happily in the garden, with much laughing and talking. 'Pity to leave such good company!' said the Doctor, unwillingly rising at last—'but I must go to the Union—I promised Ward to meet him there.'

'O let me walk with you!' cried Harry.

'And me!' cried other voices, and the Doctor proposed that they should wait for him in the meads, and extend the walk after the visit; Richard and Ethel both expressing their intention of adhering to Margaret—the latter observing how nice it would be to get rid of everybody, and have a talk.

'What have we been doing all this time?' said Dr. May, laughing.

'Chattering, not conversing,' said Ethel, saucily.

'Aye! the Cocksmoor board is going to sit,' said Dr. May.

'What is a board?' inquired Blanche, who had just come down prepared for her walk.

'Richard, Margaret, and Ethel, when they sit upon Cocksmoor,' said Dr. May.

'But Margaret never does sit on Cocksmoor, papa.'

'Only allegorically, Blanche,' said Norman.

'But I don't understand what is a board?' pursued Blanche.

'Mr. May in his ship,' was Norman's suggestion.

Poor Blanche stood in perplexity. 'What is it really?'

'Something wooden-headed,' continued the provoking papa.

'A board is all wooden, not only its head,' said Blanche.

'Exactly so, especially at Stoneborough!' said the Doctor.

'It is what papa is when he comes out of the council-room,' added Ethel.

'Or what every one is while the girls are rigging themselves,' sighed Harry. 'Ha! here's Polly—now we only want Flora.'

'And my stethoscope! Has any one seen my stethoscope?' exclaimed the Doctor, beginning to rush frantically into the study, dining-room, and his own room; but failing, quietly took up a book, and gave up the search, which was vigorously pursued by Richard, Flora, and Mary, until the missing article was detected, where Aubrey had left it in the nook on the stairs, after using it for a trumpet and a telescope.

'Ah! now my goods will have a chance!' said Dr. May, as he took it, and patted Richard's shoulder. 'I have my best right-hand, and Margaret will be saved endless sufferings.'

'Papa!'

'Aye! poor dear! don't I see what she undergoes, when nobody will remember that useful proverb, "A place for everything, and everything in its place?" I believe one use of her brains is to make an inventory of all the things left about the drawing-room; but, beyond it, it is past her power.'

'Yes,' said Flora, rather aggrieved; 'I do the best I can, but when nobody ever puts anything into its place, what can I do, single-handed? So no one ever goes anywhere without first turning the house up-side down, for their property; and Aubrey, and now even baby, are always carrying whatever they can lay hands on into the nursery. I can't bear it; and the worst of it is, that—' she added, finishing her lamentation, after the others were out at the door, 'Papa and Ethel have neither of them the least shame about it.'

'No, no, Flora, that is not fair!' exclaimed Margaret—but Flora was gone.

'I have shame,' sighed Ethel, walking across the room, disconsolately, to put a book into a shelf.

'And you don't leave things *trainants* as you used,' said Margaret. 'That is what I meant.'

'I wish I did not,' said Ethel; 'I was thinking whether I had better not make myself pay a forfeit. Suppose you keep a book for me, Margaret, and make a mark against me at everything I leave about; and if I pay a farthing for each, it will be so much away from Cocksmoor, so I must cure myself!'

'And what shall become of the forfeits?' asked Richard.

'Oh, they won't be enough to be worth having, I hope,' said Margaret.

'Give them to the Ladies' Committee,' said Ethel, making a face. 'Oh, Ritchie! they are worse than ever. We are so glad that Flora is going to join it, and see whether she can do any good.'

'We?' said Margaret, hesitating.

'Ah! I know you arn't, but papa said she might—and you know she has so much tact and management—'

'As Norman says,' observed Margaret, doubtfully. 'I cannot like the notion of Flora going and squabbling with Mrs. Ledwich and Louisa Anderson!'

'What do you think, Ritchie?' asked Ethel. 'Is it not too bad that they should have it all their own way, and spoil the whole female population? Why, the last thing they did was to leave off reading the Prayer-book prayers morning and evening! And it is much expected that next they will attack all learning by heart.'

'It is too bad,' said Richard, 'but Flora can hardly hinder them.'

'It will be one voice,' said Ethel; 'but oh! if I could only say half what I have in my mind, they must see the error. Why, these, these—what they call formal—these the ties—links on to the Church—on to what is good—if they don't learn them soundly—rammed down hard—you know what I mean—so that they can't remember the first—remember when they did not know them—they will never get to learn—know—understand when they can understand!'

'My dear Ethel, don't frown so horribly, or it will spoil your eloquence,' said Margaret.

'I don't understand either,' said Richard, gravely. 'Not understand when they can understand? What do you mean?'

'Why, Ritchie, don't you see? If they don't learn them—hard, firm, by rote when they can't—they won't understand when they can.'

'If they don't learn when they can't, they won't understand when they can?'—puzzled Richard—making Margaret laugh—but Ethel was too much in earnest for amusement.

'If they don't learn them by rote when they have strong memories. Yes, that's it!' she continued, 'they will not know them well enough to understand them when they are old enough!'

'Who won't learn or understand what?' said Richard.

'Oh! Ritchie, Ritchie! Why the children—the Psalms—the Gospels—the things. They ought to know them, love them, grow up to them, before they know the meaning, or they won't care. Memory, association, affection, all those come when one is younger than comprehension!'

'Younger than one's own comprehension?'

'Richard, you are grown more tiresome than ever. Are you laughing at me?'

'Indeed, I beg your pardon—I did not mean it,' said Richard. 'I am very sorry to be so stupid.'

'My dear Ritchie, it was only my blundering—never mind.'

'But what did you mean? I want to know, indeed, Ethel.'

'I mean that memory and association come before comprehension, so that one ought to know all good things—fa—with familiarity before one can understand, because understanding does not make one love. Oh! one does that before, and, when the first little gleam, little bit of a sparklet of the meaning does come, then it is so valuable and so delightful.'

'I never heard of a little bit of a sparklet before,' said Richard, 'but I think I do see what Ethel means; and it is like what I heard and liked in a University sermon some Sundays ago, saying that these lessons and holy words were to be impressed on us here from infancy on earth, that we might be always unravelling their meaning, and learn it fully at last—where we hope to be.'

'The very same thought!' exclaimed Margaret, delighted; 'but,' after a pause, ' I am afraid the Ladies' Committee might not enter into it in plain English, far less in Ethel's language.'

'Now, Margaret! You know I never meant myself. I never can get the right words for what I mean.'

'And you leave about your *faux commencements*, as M. Ballom-pré would call them, for us to stumble over,' said Margaret.

'But Flora would manage!' said Ethel. 'She has power over people, and can influence them. O Ritchie, don't persuade papa out of letting her go.'

'Does Mr. Wilmot wish it?' asked Richard.

'I have not heard him say, but he was very much vexed about the prayers,' said Ethel.

'Will he stay here for the holidays?'

'No, his father has not been well, and he is gone to take his duty. He walked with us to Cocksmoor before he went, and we did so wish for you.'

'How have you been getting on?'

'Pretty well, on the whole,' said Ethel; 'but, oh dear! oh dear, Richard, the M'Carthys are gone!'

'Gone, where?'

'Oh, to Wales. I knew nothing of it till they were off. Una and Fergus were missing, and Jane Taylor told me they were all gone. Oh, it is so horrid! Una had really come to be so good and so much in earnest. She behaved so well at school and church, that even Mrs. Ledwich liked her, and she used to read her Testament half the day, and bring her Sunday-school lessons to ask me about! Oh! I was so fond of her, and it really seemed to have done some good with her. And now it is all lost! Oh! I wish I knew what would become of my poor child!'

'The only hope is that it may not be all lost,' said Margaret.

'With such a woman for a mother!' said Ethel; 'and going to some heathenish place again! If I could only have seen her first, and begged her to go to Church and say her prayers. If I only knew where she is gone! but I don't. I did think Una would have come to wish me good-bye!'

'I am very sorry to lose her,' said Richard.

'Mr. Wilmot says it is bread cast on the waters,' said Margaret—'he was very kind in consoling Ethel, who came home quite in despair.'

'Yes, he said it was one of the trials,' said Ethel, 'and that it might be better for Una as well as for me. And I am trying to care for the rest still, but I cannot yet as I did for her. There are none of the eyes that look as if they were eating up one's words before they come, and that smile of comprehension! Oh! they all are such stupid little dolts, and so indifferent!'

'Why, Ethel!'

'Fancy last Friday—Mary and I found only eight there—'

'Do you remember what a broiling day Friday was?' interrupted Margaret. 'Miss Winter and Norman both told me I ought not to let them go, and I began to think so when they came home. Mary was the colour of a peony!'

'Oh! it would not have signified if the children had been good for anything, but all their mothers were out at work, and, of those that did come, hardly one had learnt their lessons—Willy Blake had lost his spelling-card—Anne Harris kicked Susan Pope, and would not say she was sorry. Mary Hall would not know M from N, do all our Mary would; and Jane Taylor, after all the pains I have taken with her, when I asked how the Israelites crossed the Red Sea, seemed never to have heard of them.'

Margaret could have said that Ethel had come in positively crying with vexation, but with no diminution of the spirit of perseverance. 'I am so glad you are come, Richard!' she continued. 'You will put a little new life into them. They all looked so pleased, when we told them Mr. Richard was coming.'

'I hope we shall get on,' said Richard:

'I want you to judge whether the Popes are civilized enough to be dressed for Sunday-school. Oh! and the money. Here is the account-book—'

'How neatly you have kept it, Ethel!'

'Ah! it was for you, you know. Receipts—see, ar'n't you surprized?'

'Four pounds, eighteen and eightpence! That is a great deal!'

'The three guineas were Mr. Rivers's fees, you know; then, Margaret gave us half-a-sovereign, and Mary a shilling, and there was one that we picked up, tumbling about the house, and papa said we might have, and the two-pence were little Blanche's savings. Oh, Ritchie!' as a bright coin appeared on the book.

'That is all I could save this term,' he said.

'Oh! it is famous. Now, I do think I may put another whole sovereign away into the purse for the church. See, here is what we have paid. Shoes—those did bring our money very low, and then I bought a piece of print which cost sixteen shillings, but it will make plenty of frocks. So, you see, the balance is actually two pounds nine! That is something. The nine shillings will go on till we get another fee; for I have two frocks ready made for the Popes, so the two pounds are a real nest-egg towards the Church.'

'The Church!' repeated Richard, half smiling.

'I looked in the paper the other day, and saw that a chapel had been built for nine hundred pounds,' said Ethel.

'And you have two!'

'Two in eight months, Ritchie, and more will come as we get older. I have a scheme in my head, but I won't tell you now.'

'Nine hundred! And a Church has to be endowed as well as built, you know, Ethel.'

'Oh! never mind that now. If we can begin and build, some good person will come and help. I'll run and fetch it, Ritchie. I drew out a sketch of what I want it to be.'

'What a girl that is!' said Richard, as Ethel dashed away.

'Is not she?' said Margaret. 'And she means all so heartily. Do you know she has spent nothing on her own pleasure—not a book, not a thing has she bought this year, except a present for Blanche's birthday, and some silk to net a purse for Harry.'

'I cannot help being sometimes persuaded that she will succeed,' said Richard.

'Faith, energy, self-denial, perseverance, they go a great way,' said Margaret. 'And yet when we look at poor dear Ethel, and her queer ungainly ways, and think of her building a Church!'

Neither Richard nor Margaret could help laughing, but they checked it at once, and the former said, 'That brave spirit is a reproof to us all.'

'Yes,' said Margaret; 'and so is the resolution to mend her little faults.'

Ethel came back, having, of course, mislaid her sketch, and, much vexed, wished to know if it ought to cause her first forfeit; but Margaret thought these should not begin till the date of the agreement, and the three resumed the Cocksmoor discussion.

It lasted till the return of the walking party, so late, that they had been star-gazing, and came in, in full dispute as to which

was Cygnus and which Aquila, while Blanche was talking very
grandly of Taurus Poniatouski, and Harry begging to be told
which constellations he should still see in the southern hemisphere. Dr. May was the first to rectify the globe for the
southern latitudes, and fingers were affectionately laid on Orion's
studded belt, as though he were a friend who would accompany
the sailor-boy. Voices grew loud and eager in enumerating the
stars common to both; and so came bed-time, and the globe stood
on the table in danger of being forgotten. Ethel diligently lifted
it up; and while Norman exclaimed at her tidiness, Margaret told
how a new leaf was to be turned, and of her voluntary forfeits.

'A very good plan,' cried the Doctor. 'We can't do better
than follow her example.'

'What you, papa? Oh! what fun!' exclaimed Harry.

'So you think I shall be ruined, Mr. Monkey. How do you
know I shall not be the most orderly of all? A penny for everything left about, confiscated for the benefit of Cocksmoor, eh?'

'And twopence for pocket-handkerchiefs, if you please,' said
Norman, with a gesture of disgust.

'Very well. From Blanche, upwards. Margaret shall have a
book, and set down marks against us—hold an audit every
Saturday night. What say you, Blanche?'

'O I hope Flora will leave something about!' cried Blanche,
dancing with glee.

CHAPTER XXV.

'O no, we never mention her,
We never breathe her name.'—Song.

A GREAT deal of merriment had come home with Harry, who
never was grave for ten minutes without a strong reaction, and
distracted the house with his noise and his antics, in proportion,
as it sometimes seemed, to the spaces of serious thought and reading spent in the study, where Dr. May did his best to supply Mr.
Ramsden's insufficient attention to his Confirmation candidates,
by giving an hour every day to Norman, Ethel, and Harry. He
could not lecture, but he read with them, and his own earnestness was very impressive.

The two eldest felt deeply, but Harry often kept it in doubt,
whether he were not as yet too young and wild for permanent
impressions, so rapid were his transitions, and so overpowering his
high spirits. Not that these were objected to; but there was a
feeling that there might as well be moderation in all things, and

that it would have been satisfactory if, under present circumstances, he had been somewhat more subdued and diligent

'There are your decimals not done yet, Harry.'

For Harry being somewhat deficient in arithmetic, had been recommended to work in that line during his visit at home—an operation usually deferred, as at present, to the evening.

'I am going to do my sums now, Flora,' said Harry, somewhat annoyed.

He really fetched his arithmetic, and his voice was soon heard asking how he was ever to put an end to a sum that *would* turn to nothing but everlasting threes.

'What have you been doing, young ladies?' asked Dr. May. 'Did you call on Miss Walkingham?'

'Flora and Blanche did,' said Ethel; 'I thought you did not want me to go, and I had not time. Besides, a London grand young lady—Oh!' and Ethel shook her head in disgust.

'That is not the way you treat Meta Rivers.'

'Oh! Meta is different. She has never been out!'

'I should have been glad for you to have seen Miss Walkingham,' said her father. 'Pretty manners are improving; besides, old Lady Walkingham begged me to send my daughters.'

'I should not have seen her,' said Ethel, 'for she was not well enough to let us in.'

'Was it not pushing?' said Flora. 'There were the Andersons leaving their card!'

'Those Andersons!' exclaimed the Doctor; 'I am sick of the very sound of the name. As sure as my name is Dick May, I'll include it in Margaret's book of fines.'

Flora looked dignified.

'They are always harping on that little trumpery girl's nonsense,' said Harry—'Aught, aught, eight, that is eight thousandths, eh, Norman! If it was about those two fellows, the boys—'

'You would harp only on what affects you?' said the Doctor.

'No, I don't; men never do. That is one hundred and twenty-fifth.'

'One man does it to an hundred and twenty-five women?' said Dr. May.

'It is rather a female defect, indeed,' said Margaret.

'Defect!' said Flora.

'Yes,' said Dr. May, 'since it is not only irksome to the hearers, but leads to the breaking of the ninth commandment.'

Many voices declared, in forms of varying severity, that it was impossible to speak worse of the Andersons than they deserved.

'Andersons again!' cried Dr. May; 'One, two, three, four, five, six forfeits!'

'Papa himself, for he said the name,' saucily put in Blanche.

'I think I should like the rule to be made in earnest,' said Ethel.

'What! in order to catch Flora's pence for Cocksmoor?' suggested Harry.

'No, but because it is malice. I mean, that is, if there is dislike, or a grudge in our hearts at them—talking for ever of nasty little miserable irritations makes it worse.'

'Then why do you do it?' asked Flora. 'I heard you only on Sunday declaiming about Fanny Anderson.'

'Ha!' cried out all at once. 'There goes Flora!'

She looked intensely serious and innocent.

'I know,' said Ethel. 'It is the very reason I want the rule to be made, just to stop us, for I am sure we must often say more than is right.'

'Especially when we come to the pass of declaring that the ninth commandment *cannot* be broken with regard to them,' observed the Doctor.

'Most likely they are saying much the same of us,' said Richard.

'Or worse,' rejoined Dr. May. 'The injured never hates as much as the injurer.'

'Now papa has said the severest thing of all!' whispered Ethel.

'Proving the inexpedience of personalities,' said Dr. May, 'and in good time enter the evening post.—Why! how now, Mr. May, are you gone mad?'

'Hallo! why ho, ha! hurrah!' and up went Harry's book of decimals to the ceiling, coming down upon a candle, which would have been overturned on Ethel's work, if it had not been dexterously caught by Richard.

'Harry!' indignantly cried Ethel and Flora, 'see what you have done;' and the Doctor's voice called to order, but Harry could not heed. 'Hear! hear! he has a fortune, an estate.'

'Who? Tell us—don't be so absurd. Who?'

'Why, Mr. Ernescliffe. Here is a letter from Hector. Only listen:

'"Did you know we had an old far-away English cousin, one Mr. Halliday? I hardly did, though Alan was named after him, and he belonged to my mother. He was a cross old fellow, and took no notice of us, but within the last year or two, his nephew, or son, or something, died, and now he is just dead, and the lawyer wrote to tell Alan he is heir-at-law. Mr. Ernescliffe of Maplewood! Does it not sound well? It is a beautiful great place in Shropshire, and Alan and I mean to run off to see it as soon as he can have any time on shore." '

Ethel could not help looking at Margaret, but was ashamed of her impertinence, and coloured violently, whereas her sister did not colour at all, and Norman, looking down, wondered whether Alan would make the voyage.

'Oh! of course he will; he must,' said Harry. 'He would never give up now.'

Norman further wondered whether Hector would remain on the Stoneborough foundation, and Mary hoped they should not lose him; but there was no great readiness to talk over the event, and there soon was a silence broken by Flora saying, 'He is no such nobody, as Louisa Anderson said, when we—'

Another shout, which caused Flora to take refuge in playing waltzes for the rest of the evening. Moreover, to the extreme satisfaction of Mary, she left her crochet-needle on the floor at night. While a tumultuous party were pursuing her with it to claim the penny, and Richard was conveying Margaret up-stairs, Ethel found an opportunity of asking her father if he were not very glad of Mr. Ernescliffe's good fortune.

'Yes, very. He is a good fellow, and will make a good use of it.'

'And now, papa, does it not make—you won't say *now* you are sorry he came here.'

She had no answer but a sigh, and a look that made her blush for having ventured so far. She was so much persuaded that great events must ensue, that, all the next day, she listened to every ring of the bell, and when one at last was followed by a light, though, to her ears, manly sounding tread, she looked up flushing with expectation.

Behold, she was disappointed. 'Miss Walkingham' was announced, and she rose surprised, for the lady in question had only come to Stoneborough for a couple of days with an infirm mother, who, having known Dr. May in old times, had made it her especial request that he would let her see his daughters. She was to proceed on her journey to-day, and the return of the visit had been by no means expected.

Flora went forward to receive her, wondering to see her so young-looking, and so unformed. She held out her hand, with a red wrist, and, as far as could be seen under her veil, coloured when presented to the recumbent Margaret. How she got into her chair, they hardly knew, for Flora was at that moment extremely annoyed by hearing an ill-bred peal of Mary's laughter in the garden, close to the window; but she thought it best to appear unconscious, since she had no power to stop it.

Margaret thought the stranger embarrassed, and kindly inquired for Lady Walkingham.

'Much the same, thank you,' mumbled a voice down in the throat.

A silence, until Margaret tried another question, equally briefly answered; and, after a short interval, the young lady contrived to make her exit, with the same amount of gaucherie as had marked her entrance.

Expressions of surprise at once began, and were so loud, that when Harry entered the room, his inquiry was, 'What's the row?'

'Miss Walkingham,' said Ethel, 'but you won't understand. She seemed half wild! Worse than me!'

'How did you like the pretty improving manners?' asked Harry.

'Manners! she had none,' said Flora. 'She, highly connected! used to the best society!'

'How do you know what the best society do?' asked Harry.

'The poor thing seemed very shy,' said Margaret.

'I don't know about shyness,' said Flora. 'She was stifling a laugh all the time, like a rude school-boy. And I thought papa said she was pretty!'

'Aye? Did you think her so?' asked Harry.

'A great broad red face—and so awkward!' cried Flora, indignantly.

'If one could have seen her face, I think she might have been nice-looking,' said Margaret. 'She had pretty golden curls, and merry blue eyes, rather like Harry's.'

'Umph!' said Flora—'beauty and manners seemed to me much on a par! This is one of papa's swans, indeed!'

'I can't believe it was Miss Walkingham at all!' said Ethel. 'It must have been some boy in disguise.'

'Dear me!' cried Margaret, starting with the painful timidity of helplessness. 'Do look whether anything is gone. Where's the silver inkstand?'

'You don't think she could put that into her pocket,' said Ethel, laughing, as she held it up.

'I don't know. Do, Harry, see if the umbrellas are safe in the hall. I wish you would, for now I come to remember, the Walkinghams went at nine this morning. Miss Winter said that she saw the old lady helped into the carriage, as she passed.' Margaret's eyes looked quite large and terrified. 'She must have been a spy—the whole gang will come at night! I wish Richard was here. Harry, it really is no laughing matter. You had better give notice to the police.'

The more Margaret was alarmed, the more Harry laughed. 'Never mind, Margaret, I'll take care of you! Here's my dirk. I'll stick all the robbers.'

'Harry! Harry! Oh! don't!' cried Margaret, raising herself up in an agony of nervous terror. 'Oh! where is papa? Will nobody ring the bell, and send James for the police?'

'Police, police! Thieves! Murder! Robbers! Fire! All hands ahoy!' shouted Harry, his hands making a trumpet over his mouth.

'Harry! how can you?' said Ethel, hastily; 'don't you see that Margaret is terribly frightened? Can't you say at once that it was you?'

'You!' and Margaret sank back, as there was a general outcry of laughter and wonder.

'Did you know it, Ethel?' asked Flora, severely.

'I only guessed it this moment,' said Ethel. 'How well you did it, Harry!'

'Well!' said Flora; 'I did think her dress very like Margaret's shot silk. I hope you did not do that any harm.'

'But how did you manage?' said Ethel. 'Where did your bonnet come from?'

'It was a new one of Adams' wife. Mary got it for me. Come in, Polly, they have found it out. Did you not hear her splitting with laughing outside the window? I would not let her come in for fear she should spoil all.'

'And I was just going to give her such a scolding for giggling in the garden,' said Flora, 'and to say we had been as bad as Miss Walkingham. You should not have been so awkward, Harry; you nearly betrayed yourself.'

'He had nobody to teach him but Mary,' said Ethel.

'Ah! you should have seen me at my ease in Minster Street. No one suspected me there.'

'In Minster Street. Oh! Harry! you don't really mean it.'

'I do. That was what I did it for. I was resolved to know what the nameless ones said of the Miss Mays.'

Hasty and eager inquiries broke out from Flora and Ethel.

'Oh, Dr. May was very clever, certainly, very clever. Had I seen the daughters? I said I was going to call there, and they said—'

'What, oh, what, Harry?'

'They said Flora was thought pretty, but—and as to Ethel, now, how do you think you came off, Unready?'

'Tell me. They could not say the same of me, at any rate.'

'Quite the reverse! They called Ethel very odd, poor girl.'

'I don't mind,' said Ethel. 'They may say what they please of me; besides that, I believe it is all Harry's own invention.'

'Nay, that is a libel on my invention!' exclaimed Harry. 'If I had drawn on that, could I not have told you something much droller?'

'And was that really all?' said Flora.

'They said—let me see—that all our noses were too long, and, that as to Flora's being a beauty! when their brothers called her —so droll of them—but Harvey called her a stuck-up duchess. In fact, it was the fashion to make a great deal of those Mays.'

'I hope they said something of the sailor brother,' said Ethel.

'No; I found if I stayed to hear much more, I should be knocking Ned down, so I thought it time to take leave before he suspected.'

All this had passed very quickly, with much laughter, and numerous interjections of amusement, and reprobation, or delight. So excited were the young people, that they did not perceive a step on the gravel, till Dr. May entered by the window, and stood among them. His first exclamation was of consternation. 'Margaret! my dear child, what is the matter?'

Only then did her brother and sisters perceive that Margaret was lying back on her cushions, very pale, and panting for breath. She tried to smile and say, 'it was nothing,' and 'she was silly,' but the words were faint, from the palpitation of her heart.

'It was Harry's trick,' said Flora, indignantly, as she flew for the scent-bottle, while her father bent over Margaret. 'Harry dressed himself up, and she was frightened.'

'O no—no—he did not mean it,' gasped Margaret.—'don't.'

'Harry! I did not think you could be so cowardly and un-feeling!' and Dr. May's look was even more reproachful than his words.

Harry was dismayed at his sister's condition, but the injustice of the wholesale reproach chased away contrition. 'I did nothing to frighten any one,' he said, moodily.

'Now, Harry, you know how you kept on,' said Flora, 'and when you saw she was frightened—'

'I can have no more of this,' said Dr. May, seeing that the discussion was injuring Margaret more and more. 'Go away to my study, sir, and wait till I come to you! All of you out of the room—Flora, fetch the sal volatile.'

'Let me tell you,' whispered Margaret. 'Don't be angry with Harry. It was—'

'Not now, not now, my dear. Lie quite still.'

She obeyed, took the sal volatile, and shut her eyes, while he sat leaning anxiously over, watching her. Presently, she opened them, and, looking up, said, rather faintly, and trying to smile, 'I don't think I can be better till you have heard the rights of it. He did not mean it.'

'Boys never do mean it,' was the Doctor's answer. 'I hoped better things of Harry.'

'He had no intention,' began Margaret, but she still was unfit to talk, and her father silenced her, by promising to go and hear the boy's own account.

In the hall, he was instantly beset by Ethel and Mary, the former exclaiming, 'Papa! you are quite mistaken. It was very foolish of Margaret to be so frightened! He did nothing at all to frighten any one.'

Ethel's mode of pleading was unfortunate; the 'very foolish of Margaret' were the very words to displease.

'Do not interfere!' said her father, sternly. 'You only encourage him in his wanton mischief, and no one takes any heed how he torments my poor Margaret.'

'Papa!' cried Harry, passionately bursting open the study door, 'tormenting Margaret was the last thing I would do.'

'That is not the way to speak, Harry. What have you been doing?'

With rapid agitated utterance, Harry made his confession. At another time the Doctor would have treated the matter as a joke carried too far, but which, while it called for censure, was very amusing; but now the explanation that the disguise had been assumed to impose on the Andersons, only added to his displeasure.

'You seem to think you have a licence to play off any impertinent freaks you please, without consideration for any one,' he said; 'but I tell you it is not so. As long as you are under my roof, you shall feel my authority, and you shall spend the rest of the day in your room. I hope quietness there will bring you to a better mind, but I am disappointed in you. A boy who can choose such a time, and such subjects, for insolent, unfeeling, practical jokes, cannot be in a fit state for Confirmation.'

'Oh! papa! papa!' cried the two girls, in tones of entreaty— while Harry, with a burning face and hasty step, dashed upstairs without a word.

'You have been as bad!' said Dr. May. 'I say nothing to you, Mary, you knew no better; but, to see you, Ethel, first encouraging him in his impertinence, and terrifying Margaret so that I dare say she may be a week getting over it, and now defending him, and calling her silly, is unbearable. I cannot trust one of you!'

'Only listen, papa!'

'I will have no altercation; I must go back to Margaret, since no one else has the slightest consideration for her.'

An hour had passed away, when Richard knocked at Ethel's door to tell her that tea was ready.

'I have a great mind not to go down,' said Ethel, as he looked in, and saw her seated with a book.

'What do you mean?'

'I cannot bear to go down while poor Harry is so unjustly used.'

'Hush, Ethel!'

'I cannot hush! Just because Margaret fancies robbers and murderers, and all sorts of nonsense, as she always did, is poor Harry to be accused of wantonly terrifying her, and shut up, and cut off from Confirmation? and just when he is going away, too! It is unkind, and unjust, and—'

'Ethel, you will be sorry—'

'Papa will be sorry,' continued Ethel, disregarding the caution. 'It is very unfair, and I *will* say so. It was all nonsense of Margaret's, but he will always make everything give way to her! And poor Harry, just going to sea. No, Ritchie, I cannot come down; I cannot behave as usual.'

'You will grieve Margaret much more,' said Richard.

'I can't help that—she should not have made such a fuss.'

Richard was somewhat in difficulties how to answer, but at that moment Harry's door, which was next, was slightly opened—and his voice said, 'Go down, Ethel. The Captain may punish any one he pleases, and it is mutiny in the rest of the crew to take his part.'

'Harry is in the right,' said Richard. 'It is our duty not to question our father's judgments. It would be wrong of you to stay up.'

'Wrong?' said Ethel.

'Of course. It would be against the articles of war,' said Harry, opening his door another inch. 'But, Ritchie, I say, do tell me whether it has hurt Margaret.'

'She is better now,' said Richard, 'but she has a head-ache, chiefly, I believe, from distress at having brought this on you. She is very sorry for her fright.'

'I had not the least intention of frightening the most fearsome little tender mouse on earth,' said Harry.

'No, indeed!' said Ethel.

'And at another time it would not have signified,' said Richard; but, you know, Margaret always was timid, and now, the not being able to move, and the being out of health, has made her nerves weak, so that she cannot help it.'

'The fault was in our never heeding her when we were so eager to hear Harry's story,' said Ethel. 'That was what made the palpitation so bad. But, now papa knows all, does he not understand about Harry?'

'He was obliged to go out as soon as Margaret was better,' said Richard, 'and was scarcely come in when I came up.'

'Go down, Ethel,' repeated Harry. 'Never mind me. Norman told me that sort of joke never answered, and I might have minded him.'

The voice was very much troubled, and it brought back that burning sensation of indignant tears to Ethel's eyes.

'O Harry! you did not deserve to be so punished for it.'

'That is what you are not to say,' returned Harry. 'I ought not to have played the trick, and—and just now too—but I always forget things—'

The door shut, and they fancied they heard sobs. Ethel groaned, but made no opposition to following her brother down to tea. Margaret lay, wan and exhausted, on the sofa—the Doctor looked very melancholy and rather stern, and the others were silent. Ethel had begun to hope for the warm reaction she had so often known after a hasty fit, but it did not really come; Harry was boy instead of girl—the fault and its consequence had been more serious—and the anxiety for the future was greater. Besides, he had not fully heard the story; Harry, in his incoherent narration, had not excused himself, and Margaret's panic had appeared more as if inspired by him, than, as it was, in fact, the work of her fancy.

Thus the evening passed gloomily away, and it was not till the others had said good night, that Dr. May began to talk over the affair with his eldest son, who then was able to lay before him the facts of the case, as gathered from his sisters. He listened with a manner as though it were a reproof, and then said, sadly, 'I am afraid I was in a passion.'

'It was very wrong in Harry,' said Richard, 'and particularly unlucky it should happen with the Andersons.'

'Very thoughtless,' said the Doctor, 'no more, even as regarded Margaret; but thoughtlessness should not have been treated as a crime.'

'I wish we could see him otherwise,' said Richard.

'He wants—' and there Dr. May stopped short, and, taking up his candle, slowly mounted the stairs, and looked into Harry's room. The boy was in bed, but started up on hearing his father's step, and exclaimed, 'Papa, I am very sorry! Is Margaret better?'

'Yes, she is; and I understand now, Harry, that her alarm was an accident. I beg your pardon for thinking for a moment that it was otherwise—'

'No,' interrupted Harry, 'of course I could never mean to frighten her; but I did not leave off the moment I saw she was afraid, because it was so very ridiculous, and I did not guess it would hurt her.'

'I see, my honest boy. I do not blame you, for you did not know how much harm a little terror does to a person in her helpless state. But, indeed, Harry, though you did not deserve such anger as mine was, it is a serious thing that you should be so much set on fun and frolic as to forget all considerations, especially at such a time as this. It takes away from much of my comfort in sending you into the world; and for higher things—how can I believe you really impressed and reverent, if the next minute—'

'I'm not fit! I'm not fit!' sobbed Harry, hiding his face.

'Indeed, I hardly know whether it is not so,' said the Doctor. 'You are under the usual age, and, though I know you wish to be a good boy, yet I don't feel sure that these wild sports do not carry away everything serious, and whether it is right to bring one so thoughtless to—'

'No, no,' and Harry cried bitterly, and his father was deeply grieved, but no more could then be said, and they parted for the night—Dr. May saying, as he went away, 'You understand, that it is not as punishment for your trick, if I do not take you to Mr. Ramsden for a ticket, but that I cannot be certain whether it is right to bring you to such solemn privileges, while you do not seem to me to retain steadily any grave or deep feelings. Perhaps your mother would have better helped you.'

And Dr. May went away to mourn over what he viewed as far greater sins than those of his son.

Anger had, indeed, given place to sorrow, and all were grave the next morning, as if each had something to be forgiven.

Margaret, especially, felt guilty of the fears which, perhaps, had not been sufficiently combated in her days of health, and now were beyond control, and had occasioned so much pain. Ethel grieved over the words she had yesterday spoken in haste of her father and sister; Mary knew herself to have been an accomplice in the joke; and Norman blamed himself for not having taken the trouble to perceive that Harry had not been talking rhodomontade when he had communicated 'his capital scheme' the previous morning.

The decision as to the Confirmation was a great grief to all.

Flora consoled herself by observing that, as he was so young, no
one need know it, nor miss him; and Ethel, with a trembling,
almost sobbing voice, enumerated all Harry's excellences, his
perfect truth, his kindness, his generosity, his flashes of intense
feeling—declared that nobody ought to be Confirmed if he were
not, and begged and entreated that Mr. Wilmot might be written
to, and consulted.   She would almost have done so herself, if
Richard had not shown her that it would be undutiful.

Harry himself was really subdued.   He made no question as to
the propriety of the decision, but rather felt his own unworthiness, and was completely humbled and downcast.   When a note
came from Mrs. Anderson, saying that she was convinced that it
could not have been Dr. May's wish that she should be exposed
to the indignity of a practical joke, and that a young lady of
the highest family should have been insulted, no one had spirits
to laugh at the terms; and when Dr. May said, ' What is to be
done ?' Harry turned crimson, and was evidently trying to utter
something.

' I see nothing for it but for him to ask their pardon,' said
Dr. May—and a sound was heard, not very articulate, but
expressing full assent.

' That is right,' said the Doctor.   ' I'll come with you.'

' O, thank you !' cried Harry, looking up.

They set off at once.   Mrs. Anderson was neither an unpleasing nor unkind person—her chief defect being a blind admiration
of her sons and daughters, which gave her, in speaking of them,
a tone of pretension that she would never have shown on her
own account.

Her displeasure was pacified in a moment by the sight of the
confused contrition of the culprit, coupled with his father's frank
and kindly tone of avowal, that it had been a foolish, improper
frolic, and that he had been much displeased with him for it.

' Say no more—pray say no more, Dr. May.   We all know
how to overlook a sailor's frolic, and, I am sure, Master Harry's
present behaviour—but you'll take a bit of luncheon,' and, as
something was said of going home to the early dinner, ' I am
sure you will wait one minute.   Master Harry must have a piece
of my cake, and allow me to drink to his success.'

Poor Mr. May! to be called Master Harry, and treated to
sweet cake!   But he saw his father thought he ought to endure,
and he even said, ' Thank you.'

The cake stuck in his throat, however, when Mrs. Anderson
and her daughters opened their full course of praise on their
dear Harvey and dearest Edward, telling all the flattering things

Dr. Hoxton had said of the order into which Harvey had brought the school, and insisting on Dr. May's reading the copy of the testimonial that he had carried to Oxford. 'I knew you would be kind enough to rejoice,' said Mrs. Anderson, 'and that you would have no—no feeling about Mr. Norman; for, of course, at his age, a little matter is nothing; and it must be better for the dear boy himself to be a little while under a friend like Harvey, than to have authority while so young.'

'I believe it has done him no harm,' was all that the Doctor could bring himself to say; and thinking that he and his son had endured quite enough, he took his leave as soon as Harry had convulsively bolted the last mouthful.

Not a word was spoken all the way home. Harry's own trouble had overpowered even this subject of resentment. On Sunday, the notice of the Confirmation was read. It was to take place on the following Thursday, and all those who had already given in their names, were to come to Mr. Ramsden to apply for their tickets. While this was read, large tear-drops were silently falling on poor Harry's book.

Ethel and Norman walked together in the twilight, in deep lamentation over their brother's deprivation, which seemed especially to humble them; 'for,' said Norman, 'I am sure no one can be more resolved on doing right than July, and he has got through school better than I did.'

'Yes,' said Ethel; 'if we don't get into his sort of scrape, it is only that we are older, not better. I am sure mine are worse, my letting Aubrey be nearly burnt—my neglects.'

'Papa must be doing right,' said Norman; 'but for July to be turned back when we are taken, makes me think of man judging only by outward appearance.'

'A few outrageous-looking acts of giddiness that are so much grieved over, may not be half so bad as the hundreds of wandering thoughts that one forgets, because no one else can see them!' said Ethel.

Meanwhile, Harry and Mary were sitting twisted together into a sort of bundle, on the same footstool, by Margaret's sofa. Harry had begged of her to hear him say the Catechism once more, and Mary had joined with him in the repetition. There was to be only one more Sunday at home.

'And that!' he said, and sighed.

Margaret knew what he meant, for the Feast was to be spread for those newly admitted to share it. She only said a caressing word of affection.

'I wonder when I shall have another chance,' said Harry. 'If we should get to Australia, or New Zealand—but then, perhaps, there would be no Confirmation going on, and I might be worse by that time.'

'O, you must not let that be!'

'Why, you see, if I can't be good here, with all this going on, what shall I do among those fellows, away from all?'

'You will have one friend!'

'Mr. Ernescliffe! You are always thinking of him, Margaret, but perhaps he may not go, and if he should, a lieutenant cannot do much for a midshipman. No, I thought, when I was reading with my father, that *somehow*, it might help me to do what *it* called putting away childish things—don't you know? I might be able to be stronger and steadier, *somehow*. And then, if—if—you know, if I did tumble overboard, or anything of that sort, there is *that* about the—what they will go to next Sunday, being necessary to salvation.'

Harry laid down his head and cried; Margaret could not speak for tears; and Mary was incoherently protesting against any notion of his falling overboard.

'It is *generally* necessary, Harry,' Margaret said, at last—'not in impossible cases.'

'Yes, if it had been impossible, but it was not; if I had not been a mad goose all this time, but when a bit of fun gets hold of me, I can't think. And if I am too bad for that, I am too bad for—for—and I shall never see mamma again! Margaret, it almost makes me af—afraid to sail.'

'Harry, don't, don't talk so!' sobbed Mary. 'O do come to papa, and let us beg and pray. Take hold of my hand, and Margaret will beg too; and when he sees how sorry you are, I am sure he will forgive, and let you be Confirmed.' She would have dragged him after her.

'No, Mary,' said Harry, resisting her. 'It is not that he does not forgive. You don't understand. It is what is right. And he cannot help it, or make it right for me, if I am such a horrid wretch that I can't keep grave thoughts in my head. I might do it again after that, just the same.'

'You have been grave enough of late!' said Mary.

'This was enough to make me so,' said Harry; 'but even at Church, since I came home, I have behaved ill! I kicked Tom, to make him look at old Levitt asleep, and then I went on, because he did not like it. I know I am too idle.'

On the Tuesday, Dr. May had said he would take Norman and Etheldred to Mr. Ramsden. Ethel was gravely putting on her walking-dress, when she heard her father's voice calling Harry and she started with a joyful hope.

There, indeed, when she came down stairs, stood Harry, his cap in his hand, and his face serious, but with a look on it that had as much subdued joy, as awe.

'Dear, dear Harry! you are going with us then?'

'Yes, papa wrote to ask what Mr. Wilmot thought, and he said—'

Harry broke off, as his father advanced, and gave her the letter itself to read. Mr. Wilmot answered, that he certainly should not refuse such a boy as Harry, on the proof of such entire penitence and deep feeling. Whether to bring him to the further privilege, might be another question; but, as far as the Confirmation was concerned, the opinion was decided.

Norman and Ethel were too happy for words, as they went arm in arm along the street, leaving their dear sailor to be leant on by his father.

Harry's sadness was gone, but he still was guarded and gentle, during the few days that followed; he seemed to have learnt thought, and in his gratitude for the privileges he had so nearly missed, to rate them more highly than he might otherwise have done. Indeed, the doubt for the Sunday gave him a sense of probation.

The Confirmation day came. Mr. Rivers had asked that his daughter might be with Miss May, and Ethel had therefore to be called for in the Abbotstoke carriage, quite contrary to her wishes, as she had set her heart on the walk to Church with her father and brothers. Flora would not come, for fear of crowding Mr. Rivers, who with Mrs. Larpent, accompanied his darling.

'O Margaret,' said Flora, after putting her sister into the carriage, 'I wish we had put Ethel into a veil! There is Meta all white from head to foot, with such a veil! and Ethel, in her little white cap, looks as if she might be Lucy Taylor, only not so pretty.'

'Mamma thought the best rule was to take the dress that needs least attention from ourselves, and will be least noticed,' said Margaret.

'There is Fanny Anderson gone by in the fly with a white veil on!' cried Mary, dashing in.

'Then I am glad Ethel has not one,' said Flora.

Margaret looked annoyed, but she had not found the means of checking Flora without giving offence; and she could only call Mary and Blanche to order, beg them to think of what the others were doing, and offer to read to them a little tale on Confirmation.

Flora sat and worked, and Margaret, stealing a glance at her understood, that, in her quiet way, she resented the implied reproof. 'Making the children think me worldly and frivolous!' she thought, 'as if Margaret did not know that I think and feel as much as any reasonable person!'

The party came home in due time, and, after one kiss to Margaret, given in silence, dispersed, for they could not yet talk of what had passed.

Only Ethel, as she met Richard on the stairs, said, 'Ritchie, do you know what the Bishop's text was? "No man having put his hand to the plough, and looking back, is fit for the kingdom of God."'

'Yes?' said Richard, interrogatively.

'I thought it might be a voice to me,' said Ethel; 'besides what it says to all, about our Christian course. It seems to tell me not to be out of heart about all those vexations at Cocksmoor. Is it not a sort of putting our hand to the plough?'

Dr. May gave his own history of the Confirmation to Margaret. 'It was a beautiful thing to watch,' he said, 'the faces of our own set. Those four were really like a poem. There was little Meta in her snowy whiteness, looking like innocence itself, hardly knowing of evil, or pain, or struggle, as that soft earnest voice made her vow to be ready for it all, almost as unscathed and unconscious of trial, as when they made it for her at her baptism—pretty little thing—may she long be as happy. And for our own Ethel, she looked as if she was promising on and on, straight into eternity. I heard her "I *do*," dear child, and it was in such a tone as if she meant to be ever *doing*.'

'And for the boys?'

'There was Norman grave and steadfast, as if he knew what he was about, and was manfully and calmly ready—he might have been a young knight, watching his armour.'

'And so he is!' said Margaret, softly. 'And poor Harry?'

The Doctor could hardly command voice to tell her. 'Poor Harry, he was last of all, he turned his back and looked into the corner of the seat, till all the voices had spoken, and then turned about in haste, and the two words came on the end of a sob.'

'You will not keep him away on Sunday?' said Margaret.

'Far be it from me. I know not who should come, if he should not.'

CHAPTER XXVI.

'What matter, whether through delight
Or led through vale of tears,
Or seen at once, or hid from sight,
The glorious way appears ?
If step by step the path we see,
That leads, my Saviour, up to thee !'

'I could not help it,' said Dr. May—'that little witch—'

'Meta Rivers? Oh! what, papa?'

'It seems that Wednesday is her birthday, and nothing will serve her but to eat her dinner in the old Roman camp.'

'And are we to go? O which of us?'

'Every one of anything like rational years. Blanche is especially invited.'

There were transports till it was recollected, that on Thursday morning school would recommence, and that on Friday Harry must join his ship.

However, the Roman camp had long been an object of their desires, and Margaret was glad that the last day should have a brilliancy, so she would not hear of any one remaining to keep her company, talked of the profit she should gain by a leisure day, and took ardent interest in every one's preparations and expectations, in Ethel's researches into county histories and classical dictionaries, Flora's sketching intentions, Norman's promises of *Campanula glomerata,* and a secret whispered into her ear by Mary and Harry.

'Meta's weather,' as they said, when the August sun rose fresh and joyous; and great was the unnecessary bustle, and happy confusion, from six o'clock till eleven, when Dr. May, who was going to visit patients some way further on the same road, carried off Harry and Mary, to set them down at the place.

The rest were called for by Mr. Rivers's carriage and break. Mrs. Charles Wilmot and her little girl were the only additions to the party, and Meta, putting Blanche into the carriage to keep company with her contemporary, went herself in the break. What a brilliant little fairy she was, in her pink summer robes, fluttering like a butterfly, and with the same apparent felicity in basking in joy, all gaiety, glee, and light-heartedness in making others happy! On they went, through honeysuckled lanes, catching glimpses of sunny fields of corn falling before the reaper, and happy knots of harvest folks dining beneath the shelter of their sheaves, with the sturdy old green umbrella sheltering them from the sun.

Snatches of song, peals of laughter, merry nonsense, passed from one to the other; Norman, roused into blitheness, found wit, the young ladies found laughter, and Richard's eyes and mouth looked very pretty, as they smiled their quiet diversion.

At last, his face drawn all into one silent laugh, he directed the eyes of the rest to a high green mound, rising immediately before them, where stood two little figures, one with a spy-glass, intently gazing the opposite way.

At the same time came the halt, and Norman, bounding out, sprang lightly and nimbly up the side of the mound, and, while the spy-glass was yet pointed full at Wales, had hold of a pair of stout legs, and with the words, 'Keep a good look-out!' had tumbled Mr. May headforemost down the grassy slope, with Mary rolling after.

Harry's first outcry was for his precious glass—his second was, not at his fall, but that they should have come from the east, when, by the compass, Stoneborough was north-north-west. And then the boys took to tumbling over one another, while Meta frolicked joyously, with Nipen after her, up and down the mounds, chased by Mary and Blanche, who were wild with glee.

By-and-by she joined Ethel, and Norman was summoned to help them to trace out the old lines of encampment, ditch, rampart, and gates—happy work on those slopes of fresh turf, embroidered with every minute blossom of the moor—thyme, birdsfoot, eye-bright, and dwarf purple thistle, buzzed and hummed over by busy, blacktailed, yellow-banded dumbledores, the breezy wind blowing softly in their faces, and the expanse of country-wooded hill, verdant pasture, amber harvest-field, winding river, smoke-canopied town, and brown moor, melting greyly away to the mountain-heads.

Now in sun, now in shade, the bright young antiquaries surveyed the old banks, and talked wisely of vallum and fossa, of legion and cohort, of Agricola and Suetonius, and discussed the delightful probability, that this might have been raised in the war with Caractacus, whence, argued Ethel, since Caractacus was certainly Arviragus, it must have been the very spot where Imogen met Posthumus again. Was not yonder the very high road to Milford Haven, and thus must not 'fair Fidele's grassy tomb' be in the immediate neighbourhood?

Then followed the suggestion that the mound in the middle was a good deal like an ancient tomb, where, as Blanche interposed with some of the lore lately caught from Ethel's studies, 'they used to bury their tears in wheelbarrows,' while Norman observed it was the more probable, as fair Fidele never was buried at all.

The idea of a search enchanted the young ladies. 'It was the right sort of vehicle, evidently,' said Norman, looking at Harry, who had been particularly earnest in recommending that it should be explored; and Meta declared that if they could but find the least trace, her papa would be delighted to go regularly to work, and reveal all the treasures.

Richard seemed a little afraid of the responsibility of treasure-trove, but he was overruled by a chorus of eager voices, and dis-possessed of the trowel, which he had brought to dig up some down-gentians for the garden. While Norman set to work as pioneer, some skipped about in wild ecstasy, and Ethel knelt down to peer into the hole.

Very soon there was a discovery—an eager outcry—some pottery! Roman vessels—a red thing that might have been a lamp, another that might have been a lachrymatory.

'Well,' said Ethel, 'you know, Norman, I always told you that the children's pots and pans in the clay ditch were very like Roman pottery.'

'Posthumus's pattypan!' said Norman, holding it up. 'No doubt this was the bottle filled with the old queen's tears when Cloten was killed.'

'You see it is very small,' added Harry; 'she could not squeeze out many.'

'Come now, I do believe you are laughing at it!' said Meta, taking the derided vessels into her hands. 'Now, they really are genuine, and very curious things, are not they, Flora?'

Flora and Ethel admired and speculated till there was a fresh and still more exciting discovery—a coin, actually a medal, with the head of an emperor upon it—not a doubt of his high nose being Roman. Meta was certain that she knew one exactly like him among her father's gems. Ethel was resolved that he should be Claudius, and began decyphering the defaced inscription THVRVS. She tried Claudius's whole torrent of names, and, at last, made it into a contraction of Tiberius, which highly satisfied her.

Then Meta, in her turn, read D. V. X., which, as Ethel said, was all she could wish—of course it was *dux et imperator*, and Harry muttered into Norman's ear, 'ducks and geese!' and then heaved a sigh, as he thought of the Dux no longer. 'V. V.,' continued Meta, 'what can that mean?'

'Five, five, of course,' said Flora.

'No, no! I have it, *Venus Victrix*,' said Ethel, 'the ancestral Venus! Ha! don't you see? there she is on the other side crowning Claudius.'

'Then there is an E.'

'Something about Æneas,' suggested Norman, gravely.

But Ethel was sure that could not be, because there was no diph-thong; and a fresh theory was just being started, when Blanche's head was thrust in to know what made them all so busy.

'Why, Ethel, what are you doing with Harry's old medal of the Duke of Wellington?'

Poor Meta and Ethel, what a downfall! Meta was sure that Norman had known it the whole time, and he owned to having guessed it from Harry's importunity for the search. Harry and Mary had certainly made good use of their time, and great was the mirth over the trap so cleverly set—the more when it was disclosed that Dr. May had been a full participator in the scheme, had suggested the addition of the pottery, had helped Harry to some liquid to efface part of the inscription, and had even come up with them to plant the snare in the most plausible corner for researches.

Meta, enchanted with the joke, flew off to try to take in her governess and Mrs. Wilmot, whom she found completing their leisurely promenade, and considering where they should spread the dinner.

The sight of those great baskets of good fare was appetizing, and the company soon collected on the shady turf, where Richard made himself extremely useful, and the feast was spread without any worse mishap than Nipen's running away with half a chicken, of which he was robbed, as Tom reported, by a surly-looking dog that watched in the outskirts of the camp, and caused Tom to return nearly as fast as the poor little white marauder.

Meta 'very immorally,' as Norman told her, comforted Nipen with a large share of her sandwiches. Harry armed himself with a stick, and Mary with a stone, and marched off to the attack, but saw no signs of the enemy, and had begun to believe him a figment of Tom's imagination, when Mary spied him under a bush, lying at the feet of a boy, with whom he was sharing the spoil.

Harry called out rather roughly, 'Hollo! what are you doing there?'

The boy jumped up, the dog growled, Mary shrank behind her brother, and begged him not to be cross to the poor boy, but to come away. Harry repeated his question.

'Please, sir, Toby brought it to me.'

'What, is Toby your dog?'

'Yes, sir.'

'Are you so hungry as to eat dog's meat?'

'I have not had nothing before to-day, sir.'

'Why, where do you live? hereabouts?'

'O no, sir; I lived with grandmother up in Cheshire, but she is dead now, and father is just come home from sea, and he wrote down I was to be sent to him at Portsmouth, to go to sea with him.'

'How do you live? do you beg your way?'

'No, sir; father sent up a pound in a letter, only Nanny Brooks said I owed some to her for my victuals, and I have not much of it left, and bread comes dear, so when Toby brought me this bit of meat, I was glad of it, sir, but I would not have taken it—'

The boy was desired to wait while the brother and sister, in breathless excitement, rushed back with their story.

Mrs. Wilmot was at first inclined to fear that the naval part of it had been inspired by Harry's uniform, but the examination of Jem Jennings put it beyond a doubt that he spoke nothing but the truth; and the choicest delight of the feast was the establishing him and Toby behind the barrow, and feeding them with such viands as they had probably never seen before.

The boy could not read writing, but he had his father's letter in his pocket, and Mary capered at the delightful coincidence, on finding that Jem Jennings was actually a quarter-master on board the Alcestis. It gave a sort of property in the boy, and she almost grudged Meta the having been first to say that she would pay for the rest of his journey, instead of doing it by subscription.

However, Mary had a consolation, she would offer to take charge of Toby, who, as Harry observed, would otherwise have been drowned—he could not be taken on board. To be sure, he was a particularly ugly animal, rough, grisly, short-legged, long-backed, and with an apology for a tail—but he had a redeeming pair of eyes, and he and Jem lived on terms of such close friendship, that he would have been miserable in leaving him to the mercy of Nanny Brooks.

So, after their meal, Jem and Toby were bidden to wait for Dr. May's coming, and fell asleep together on the green bank, while the rest either sketched, or wandered, or botanized. Flora acted the grown-up lady with Mrs. Wilmot, and Meta found herself sitting by Ethel, asking her a great many questions about Margaret, and her home, and what it could be like to be one of such a numerous family. Flora had always turned aside from personal matters, as uninteresting to her companion, and, in spite of Meta's admiration, and the mutual wish to be intimate, confidence did not spring up spontaneously, as it had done with the Doctor, and, in that single hour, with Margaret. Blunt as Ethel was, her heartiness of manner gave a sense of real progress in friendship. Their Confirmation vows seemed to make a link, and Meta's unfeigned enthusiasm for the Doctor was the sure road to Ethel's heart. She was soon telling how glad Margaret was that he had been drawn into taking pleasure in to-day's scheme, since, not only were his spirits tried by the approach of Harry's departure, but he had, within the last few days, been made very sad by reading and answering Aunt Flora's first letter on the news of last October's misfortune.

'My aunt in New Zealand,' explained Ethel.

'Have you an aunt in New Zealand?' cried Meta. 'I never heard of her!'

'Did not you? Oh! she does write such charming long letters!'

'Is she Dr. May's sister?'

'No; he was an only child. She is dear mamma's sister. I don't remember her, for she went out when I was a baby, but Richard and Margaret were so fond of her. They say she used to play with them, and tell them stories, and sing Scotch songs to them. Margaret says, the first sorrow of her life was Aunt Flora's going away.'

'Did she live with them?'

'Yes; after grandpapa died, she came to live with them, but then Mr. Arnott came about. I ought not to speak evil of him, for he is my godfather, but we do wish he had not carried off Aunt Flora! That letter of hers showed me what a comfort it would be to papa to have her here.'

'Perhaps she will come.'

'No; Uncle Arnott has too much to do. It was a pretty story altogether. He was an officer at Edinburgh, and fell in love with Aunt Flora, but my grandfather Mackenzie thought him too poor to marry her, and it was all broken off, and they tried to think no more of it. But grandpapa died, and she came to live here, and somehow Mr. Arnott turned up again, quartered at Whitford, and papa talked over my Uncle Mackenzie, and helped them— and Mr. Arnott thought the best way would be to go out to the colonies. They went when New Zealand was very new, and a very funny life they had! Once they had their house burnt in Heki's rebellion—and Aunt Flora saw a Maori walking about in her best Sunday bonnet—but, in general, everything has gone on very well, and he has a great farm, besides an office under government.'

'Oh! so he went out as a settler; I was in hopes it was as a missionary.'

'I fancy Aunt Flora has done a good deal that may be called missionary work,' said Ethel, 'teaching the Maori women and girls. They call her mother, and she has quite a doctor's shop for them, and tries hard to teach them to take proper care of their poor little children, when they are ill—and she cuts out clothes for the whole pah, that is, the village.'

'And are they Christians?'

'Oh! to be sure they are now! They meet in the pah for prayers every morning and evening—they used to have a hoe struck against a bit of metal for a signal, and when papa heard of it, he gave them a bell, and they were so delighted. Now there comes a Clergyman every fourth Sunday, and, on the others, Uncle Arnott reads part of the service to the English near, and the Maori teacher to his people.'

Meta asked ravenously for more details, and when she had pretty well exhausted Ethel's stock, she said, 'How nice it must be! Ethel, did you ever read the "Faithful Little Girl"?'

'Yes; it was one of Margaret's old Sunday books. I often recollected it before I was allowed to begin Cocksmoor.'

'I'm afraid I am very like Lucilla!' said Meta.

'What? In wishing to be a boy, that you might be a Missionary?' said Ethel. 'Not in being quite so cross at home?' she added, laughing.

'I am not cross, because I have no opportunity,' said Meta.

'No opportunity! Oh, Meta! if people wish to be cross, it is easy enough to find grounds for it. There is always the moon to cry for.'

'Really and truly,' said Meta, thoughtfully, 'I never do meet with any reasonable trial of temper, and I am often afraid it cannot be right or safe to live so entirely at ease, and without contradictions.'

'Well, but—' said Ethel, 'it is the state of life in which you are placed.'

'Yes; but are we meant never to have vexations?'

'I thought you had them,' said Ethel. 'Margaret told me about your maid. That would have worried some people, and made them horridly cross.'

'Oh! no rational person,' cried Meta. 'It was so nice to think of her being with the poor mother, and I was quite interested in managing for myself; besides, you know, it was just a proof how one learns to be selfish, that it had never occurred to me that I ought to spare her.'

'And your school children—you were in some trouble about them?'

'Oh! that is pleasure.'

'I thought you had a class you did not like.'

'I like them now—they are such steady plodding girls, so much in earnest, and one, that has been neglected, is so pleased and touched by kindness. I would not give them up for anything now—they are just fit for my capacity.'

'Do you mean that nothing ever goes wrong with you, or that you do not mind anything—which?'

'Nothing goes wrong enough with me to give me a handsome excuse for minding it.'

'Then it must be all your good temper.'

'I don't think so,' said Meta—'it is that nothing is ever disagreeable to me.'

'Stay,' said Ethel, 'if the ill-temper was in you, you would only be the crosser for being indulged—at least, so books say. And I am sure myself, that it is not whether things are disagreeable or not, but whether one's will is with them, that signifies.'

'I don't quite understand.'

'Why—I have seen the boys do for play, and done myself, what would have been a horrid hardship if one had been made to do it. I never liked any lessons as well as those I did without being obliged, and always, when there is a thing I hate very much in itself, I can get up an interest in it, by resolving that I will do it well, or fast, or something—if I *can* stick my will to it, it is like a lever, and it is done. Now, I think it must be the same with you, only your will is more easily set at it than mine.'

'What makes me uncomfortable is, that I feel as if I never followed anything but my will.'

Ethel screwed up her face, as if the eyes of her mind were nursuing some thought almost beyond her. 'If our will and our duty run the same,' she said, 'that can't be wrong. The better people are, the more they "love what He commands," you know. In Heaven they have no will but His.'

'Oh! but Ethel,' cried Meta, distressed, 'that is putting it too high. Won't you understand what I mean? We have learnt so much lately about self-denial, and crossing one's own inclinations, and enduring hardness. And here I live with two dear kind people, who only try to keep every little annoyance from my path. I can't wish for a thing without getting it—I am waited on all day long, and I feel like one of the women that are at ease—one of the careless daughters.'

'I think still papa would say it was your happy contented temper that made you find no vexation.'

'But that sort of temper is not goodness. I was born with it; I never did mind anything, not even being punished, they say, unless I knew papa was grieved, which always did make me unhappy enough. I laughed, and went to play most saucily, whatever they did to me. If I had striven for the temper, it would be worth having, but it is my nature. And Ethel,' she added, in a low voice, as the tears came into her eyes, 'don't you remember last Sunday? I felt myself so vain and petted a thing! as if I had no share in the Cup of suffering, and did not deserve to call myself a member—it seemed ungrateful.'

Ethel felt ashamed, as she heard of warmer feelings than her own had been, expressed in that lowered trembling voice, and she sought for the answer that would only come to her mind in sense, not at first in words. 'Discipline,' said she, 'would not that show the willingness to have the part? Taking the right times for refusing oneself some pleasant thing.'

'Would not that be only making up something for oneself?' said Meta.

'No, the Church orders it. It is in the Prayer-book,' said Ethel. 'I mean one can do little secret things—not read story-books on those days, or keep some tiresome sort of work for them. It is very trumpery, but it keeps the remembrance, and it is not so much as if one did not heed.'

'I'll think,' said Meta, sighing. 'If only I felt myself at work, not to please myself, but to be of use. Ha!' she cried, springing up, 'I do believe I see Dr. May coming!'

'Let us run and meet him,' said Ethel.

They did so, and he called out his wishes of many happy returns of blithe days to the little birthday queen, then added, 'You both look grave, though—have they deserted you?'

'No, papa, we have been having a talk,' said Ethel. 'May I tell him, Meta? I want to know what he says.'

Meta had not bargained for this, but she was very much in earnest, and there was nothing formidable in Dr. May, so she assented.

'Meta is longing to be at work—she thinks she is of no use,' said Ethel—'she says she never does anything but please herself.'

'Pleasing oneself is not the same as trying to please oneself,' said Dr. May, kindly.

'And she thinks it cannot be safe or right,' added Ethel, 'to live that happy bright life, as if people without care or trouble could not be living as Christians are meant to live. Is that it, Meta?'

'Yes, I think it is,' said Meta. 'I seem to be only put here to be made much of!'

'What did David say, Meta?' returned Dr. May.

> ' My Shepherd is the living Lord,
>   Nothing therefore I need:
> In pastures fair, near pleasant streams,
>   He setteth me to feed.'

Then you think,' said Meta, much touched, 'that I ought to look on this as "the pastures fair," and be thankful. I hope I was not unthankful.'

'O, no,' said Ethel. 'It was the wish to bear hardness, and be a good soldier, was it not?'

'Ah! my dear,' he said, 'the rugged path and dark valley will come in His own fit time. Depend upon it, the good Shepherd is giving you what is best for you in the green meadow, and if you lay hold on His rod and staff in your sunny days—' He stopped short, and turned to his daughter.

'Ethel, they sang that Psalm the first Sunday I brought your mamma home!'

Meta was much affected, and began to put together what the father and daughter had said. Perhaps the little modes of secret discipline, of which Ethel had spoken, might be the true means of clasping the staff—perhaps she had been impatient, and wanting in humility in craving for the strife, when her armour was scarce put on.

Dr. May spoke once again. 'Don't let any one long for external trial. The offering of a free heart is the thing. To offer praise is the great object of all creatures in heaven and earth. If the happier we are, the more we praise, then all is well.'

But the serious discussion was suddenly broken off.

Others had seen Dr. May's approach, and Harry and Mary rushed down in dismay at their story having, as they thought, been forestalled. However, they had it all to themselves, and the Doctor took up the subject as keenly as could have been hoped, but the poor boy being still fast asleep, after, probably, much fatigue, he would not then waken him to examine him, but came and sat down in the semicircle, formed by a terraced bank of soft turf, where Mrs. Larpent, Mrs. Wilmot, Richard, and Flora, had for some time taken up their abode. Meta brought him the choice little basket of fruit which she had saved for him, and all delighted in having him there, evidently enjoying the rest and sport very much, as he reposed on the fragrant slope, eating grapes, and making inquiries as to the antiquities lately discovered.

Norman gave an exceedingly droll account of the great Roman Emperor, Tiberius V. V., and Meta correcting it, there was a regular gay skirmish of words, which entertained every one extremely—above all, Meta's indignation when the charge was brought home to her of having declared the 'old Duke' exactly like in turns to Domitian and Tiberius—his features quite forbidding.

This lasted till the younger ones, who had been playing and rioting till they were tired, came up, and throwing themselves down on the grass, Blanche petitioned for something that every one could play at.

Meta proposed what she called the story play. One was to be

sent out of earshot, and the rest to agree upon a word, which was then to be guessed by each telling a story, and introducing the word into it, not too prominently. Meta volunteered to guess, and Harry whispered to Mary it would be no go, but, in the meantime, the word was found, and Blanche eagerly recalled Meta, and sat in the utmost expectation and delight. Meta turned first to Richard, but he coloured distressfully, and begged that Flora might tell his story for him—he should only spoil the game. Flora, with a little tinge of graceful reluctance, obeyed. 'No woman had been to the summit of Mont Blanc,' she said, 'till one young girl, named Marie, resolved to have this glory. The guides told her it was madness, but she persevered. She took the staff, and everything requisite, and, following a party, began the ascent. She bravely supported every fatigue, climbed each precipice, was undaunted by the giddy heights she attained, bravely crossed the fields of snow, supported the bitter cold, and finally, though suffering severely, arrived at the topmost peak, looked forth where woman had never looked before, felt her heart swell at the attainment of her utmost ambition, and the name of Marie was inscribed as that of the woman who alone has had the glory of standing on the summit of the Giant of the Alps.'

It was prettily enunciated, and had a pleasing effect. Meta stood conning the words—woman—giant—mountain—glory—and begged for another tale.

'Mine shall not be so stupid as Flora's,' said Harry. 'We have an old sailor on board the Alcestis—a giant he might be for his voice—but he sailed once in the Glory of the West, and there they had a monkey that was picked up in Africa, and one day this old fellow found his queer messmate, as he called him, spying through a glass, just like the captain. The captain had a glorious collection of old coins, and the like, dug up in some of the old Greek colonies, and whenever Master Monkey saw him overhauling them, he would get out a brass button, or a card or two, and turn 'em over, and chatter at them, and glory over them, quite knowing—' said Harry, imitating the gesture, 'and I dare say he saw V. V., and Tiberius Cæsar, as well as the best of them.'

'Thank you, Mr. Harry,' said Meta. 'I think we are at no loss for monkeys here. But I have not the word yet. Who comes next? Ethel—'

'I shall blunder, I forewarn you,' said Ethel, 'but this is mine. 'There was a young king, who had an old tutor, whom he despised because he was so strict, so he got rid of him, and took to idle sport. One day, when he was out hunting in a forest, a white hind came and ran before him, till she guided him to a castle, and there he found a lady, all dressed in white, with a beamy crown on her head, and so nobly beautiful, that he fell in love with her at once, and was only sorry to see another prince who was come to her palace too. She told them her name was Gloria, and that she had had many suitors, but the choice did not depend on herself—she could only be won by him who deserved her, and for three years they were to be on their probation, trying for her. So she dismissed them, only burning to gain her, and telling them to come back in three years' time. But they had not gone far before they saw another palace, much finer, all glittering with gold and silver, and their Lady Gloria came out to meet them, not in her white dress, but in one all gay and bright with fine colours, and her crown they now saw was of diamonds. She told them they had only seen her every-day dress and house, this was her best; and she showed them about the castle, and all the pictures of her former lovers. There was Alexander, who had been nearer retaining her than any one, only the fever prevented it; there was Pyrrhus, always seeking her, but slain by a tile—Julius Cæsar—Tamerlane —all the rest, and she hoped that one of these two would really prove worthy and gain her, by going in the same path as these great people.

'So our prince went home; his head full of being like Alexander and all the rest of them, and he sent for his good old tutor to reckon up his armies, and see whom he could conquer in order to win her. But the old tutor told him he was under a mistake; the second lady he had seen was a treacherous cousin of Gloria, who drew away her suitors by her deceits, and whose real name was Vana Gloria. If he wished to earn the true Gloria, he must set to work to do his subjects good, and to be virtuous. And he did; he taught them, and he did justice to them, and he bore it patiently and kindly when they did not understand. But by-and-by, the other king, who had no good tutor to help him, had got his armies together, and conquered ever so many people, and drawn off their men to be soldiers; and now he attacked the good prince, and was so strong that he gained the victory, though both prince and subjects fought manfully with heart and hand; but the battle was lost, and the faithful prince wounded and made prisoner, but bearing it most patiently, till he was dragged behind the other's triumphal car with all the rest, when the three years were up, to be presented to Vana Gloria. And so he was carried into the forest, bleeding and wounded, and his enemy drove the car over his body, and stretched out his arms to Vana Gloria, and found her a vain, ugly wretch, who grew frightful as soon as he grasped her. But the good dying prince saw the beautiful beamy face of his lady-love bending over him. "Oh!" he said, "vision of my life, hast thou come to lighten my dying eyes? Never—never, even in my best days, did I deem that I could be worthy of thee; the more I strove, the more I knew that Gloria is for none below—for me less than all."

'And then the lady came and lifted him up, and she said, "Gloria is given to all who do and suffer truly in a good cause, for faithfulness is glory, and that is thine."'

Ethel's language had become more flowing as she grew more eager in the tale, and they all listened with suspended interest. Norman asked where she got the story. 'Out of an old French book, the *Magazin des Enfans*,' was the answer.

'But why did you alter the end?' said Flora, 'why kill the poor man? He used to be prosperous, why not?'

'Because I thought,' said Ethel, 'that glory could not properly belong to any one here, and if he was once conscious of it, it would be all spoilt. Well, Meta, do you guess?'

'Oh! the word! I had forgotten all about it. I think I know what it must be, but I should so like another story. May I not have one?' said Meta, coaxingly. 'Mary, it is you.'

Mary fell back on her papa, and begged him to take hers. Papa told the best stories of all, she said, and Meta looked beseeching.

'My story will not be as long as Ethel's,' said the Doctor, yielding with a half-reluctant smile. 'My story is of a humming-bird, a little creature that loved its master with all its strength, and longed to do somewhat for him. It was not satisfied with its lot, because it seemed merely a vain and profitless creature. The nightingale sang praise, and the woods sounded with the glory of its strains; the fowl was valued for its flesh, the ostrich for its plume, but what could the little hummingbird do, save rejoice in the glory of the flood of sunbeams, and disport itself over the flowers, and glance in the sunny light, as its bright breastplate flashed from rich purple to dazzling flame-colour, and its wings supported it, fluttering so fast that the eye could hardly trace them, as it darted its slender beak into the deep-belled blossoms. So the little bird grieved, and could not rest, for thinking that it was useless in this world, that it sought merely its own gratification, and could do nothing that could conduce to the glory of its master. But, one night, a voice spoke to the little bird, "Why hast thou been placed here," it said, "but at the will of thy master? Was it not that he might delight himself in thy radiant plumage, and see thy joy in the sunshine? His gifts are thy buoyant wing, thy beauteous colours, the love of all around, the sweetness of the honey drop in the flowers, the shade of the palm leaf. Esteem them, then, as his; value thine own bliss, while it lasts, as the token of his care and love; and while thy heart praises him for them, and thy wings quiver and dance to the tune of that praise, then, indeed, thy gladness conduces to no vain-glory of thine own, in beauty, or in graceful flight, but thou art a creature serving as best thou canst to his glory.'"

'I know the word,' half whispered Meta, not without a trembling of the lip. 'I know why you told the story, Dr. May, but one is not as good as the hummingbirds.'

The elder ladies had begun to look at watches, and talk of time to go home; and Jem Jennings having been seen rearing himself up from behind the barrow, the Doctor proceeded to investigate his case, was perfectly satisfied of the boy's truth, and as ready as the young ones to befriend him. A letter should be written at once, desiring his father to look out for him on Friday, when he should go by the same train as Harry, who was delighted at the notion of protecting him so far, and begged to be allowed to drive him home to Stoneborough in the gig.

Consent was given; and Richard being added to give weight and discretion, the gig set out at once—the Doctor, much to Meta's delight, took his place in the break. Blanche, who, in the morning, had been inclined to despise it as something akin to a cart, now finding it a popular conveyance, was urgent to return in it; and Flora was made over to the carriage, not at all unwillingly, for, though it separated her from Meta, it made a senior of her.

Norman's fate conveyed him to the exalted seat beside the driver of the break, where he could only now and then catch the sounds of mirth from below. He had enjoyed the day exceedingly, with that sort of *abandon* more than ordinarily delicious to grave or saddened temperaments, when roused or drawn out for a time. Meta's winning grace and sweetness had a peculiar charm for him, and, perhaps, his having been originally introduced to her as ill, and in sorrow, had given her manner towards him a sort of kindness which was very gratifying.

And now he felt as if he was going back to a very dusky dusty world; the last and blithest day of his holidays was past, and he must return to the misapprehensions and injustice that had blighted his school career, be kept beneath boys with half his ability, and without generous feeling, and find all his attainments useless in restoring his position. Dr. Hoxton's dull scholarship would chill all pleasure in his studies—there would be no companiouship among the boys—even his supporters, Ernescliffe and Larkins, were gone, and Harry would leave him still under a cloud.

Norman felt it more as disgrace than he had done since the first, and wished he had consented to quit the school when the offer had been made—be made a man, instead of suffering these doubly irksome provocations, which rose before him in renewed force. 'And what would that little hummingbird think of me if she knew me disgraced,' thought he. 'But it is of no use to think of it. I must go through with it, and as I always *am* getting vain-glorious, I had better have no opportunity. I did not declare I renounced vain-pomp and glory last week, to begin coveting them now again.'

So Norman repressed the sigh as he looked at the school buildings, which never could give him the pleasures of memory they afforded to others.

The break had set out before the carriage, so that Meta had to come in and wait for her governess. Before the vehicle had disgorged half its contents, Harry had rushed out to meet them, 'Come in! come in, Norman! Only hear. Margaret shall tell you herself! Hurra!'

Is Mr. Ernescliffe come? crossed Ethel's mind, but Margaret was alone, flushed, and holding out her hands. 'Norman! where is he? Dear Norman, here is good news! Papa, Dr. Hoxton has been here, and he knows all about it—and oh! Norman, he is very sorry for the injustice, and you are Dux again!'

Norman really trembled so much that he could neither speak nor stand, but sat down on the window-seat, while a confusion of tongues asked more.

Dr. Hoxton and Mr. Larkins had come to call—heard no one was at home but Miss May—had, nevertheless, come in—and Margaret had heard that Mr. Larkins, who had before intended to remove his son from Stoneborough, had, in the course of the holidays, made discoveries from him, which he could not feel justified in concealing from Dr. Hoxton.

The whole of the transactions with Ballhatchet, and Norman's part in them, had been explained, as well as the true history of the affray in Randall's alley—how Norman had dispersed the boys, how they had again collected, and, with the full concurrence of Harvey Anderson, renewed the mischief, how the Andersons had refused to bear witness in his favour, and how Ballhatchet's ill-will had kept back the evidence which would have cleared him.

Little Larkins had told all, and his father had no scruple in repeating it, and causing the investigation to be set on foot. Nay, he deemed that Norman's influence had saved his son, and came, as anxious to thank him, as Dr. Hoxton, warm-hearted, though injudicious, was to repair his injustice. They were much surprised and struck by finding that Dr. May had been aware of the truth the whole time, and had patiently put up with the injustice, and the loss of the scholarship—a loss which Dr. Hoxton would have given anything to repair, so as to have sent up a scholar likely to do him so much credit; but it was now too late, and he had only been able to tell Margaret how dismayed he was at finding out that the boy to whom all the good order in his school was owing, had been so ill-used. Kind Dr. May's first feeling really seemed to be pity and sympathy for his old friend, the head master, in the shock of such a discovery. Harry was vociferously telling his version of the story to Ethel and Mary. Tom stood transfixed in attention. Meta, forgotten and bewildered, was standing near Norman, whose colour rapidly varied, and whose breath came short and quick as he listened. A quick half interrogation passed Meta's lips, heard by no one else.

'It is only that it is all right,' he answered, scarcely audibly; 'they have found out the truth.'

'What—who—you?' said Meta, as she heard words that implied the past suspicion.

'Yes,' said Norman, 'I was suspected, but never at home.'

'And is it over now?'

'Yes, yes,' he whispered huskily, 'all is right, and Harry will not leave me in disgrace.'

Meta did not speak, but she held out her hand in hearty congratulation; Norman, scarce knowing what he did, grasped and wrung it so tight, that it was positive pain, as he turned away his head to the window to struggle with those irrepressible tears. Meta's colour flushed into her cheek as she found it still held, almost unconsciously, perhaps, in his agitation; and she heard Margaret's words, that both gentlemen had said Norman had acted nobly, and that every revelation made in the course of their examination, had only more fully established his admirable conduct.

'O, Norman! Norman, I am so glad!' cried Mary's voice in the first pause; and, Margaret, asking where he was, he suddenly turned round, recollected himself, and found it was not the back of the chair that he had been squeezing, blushed intensely, but made no attempt at apology, for indeed he could not speak —he only leant down over Margaret, to receive her heartfelt embrace; and, as he stood up again, his father laid his hand on his shoulder, 'My boy, I am glad—' but the words were broken; and, as if neither could bear more, Norman hastily left the room, Ethel rushing after him.

'Quite overcome!' said the Doctor, 'and no wonder. He felt it cruelly, though he bore up gallantly. Well, July?'

'I'll go down to school with him to-morrow, and see him Dux again! I'll have three-times-three!' shouted Harry. 'Hip! hip! hurra!' and Tom and Mary joined in chorus.

'What is all this?' exclaimed Flora, opening the door—'is every one gone mad?'

Many were the voices that answered.

'Well! I am glad, and I hope the Andersons will make an apology. But where is poor Meta? Quite forgotten?'

'Meta would not wonder, if she knew all,' said the Doctor, turning, with a sweet smile that had in it something, nevertheless, of apology.

'Oh! I am so glad—so glad!' said Meta, her eyes full of tears, as she came forward.

And there was no helping it; the first kiss between Margaret May, and Margaret Rivers, was given in that overflowing sympathy of congratulation.

The Doctor gave her his arm to take her to the carriage, and, on the way his quick warm words filled up the sketch of Norman's behaviour; Meta's eyes responded better than her tongue, but, to her good-bye, she could not help adding, 'Now I *have* seen true glory.'

His answer was much such a gripe as her poor little fingers had already received; but though they felt hot and crushed, all the way home, the sensation seemed to cause such throbs of joy, that she would not have been without it.

CHAPTER XXVII.

' And full of hope, day followed day,
  While that stout ship at anchor lay
    Beside the shores of Wight.
  The May had then made all things green,
  And floating there, in pomp serene,
  That ship was goodly to be seen,
    His pride and his delight.

' Yet then when called ashore, he sought
  The tender peace of rural thought,
    In more than happy mood.
  To your abodes, bright daisy flowers,
  He then would steal at leisure hours,
  And loved you, glittering in your bowers,
    A starry multitude.'—WORDSWORTH.

HARRY's last home morning was brightened by going to the school to see full justice done to Norman, and enjoying the scene for him. It was, indeed, a painful ordeal to Norman himself, who could, at the moment, scarcely feel pleasure in his restoration, excepting for the sake of his father, Harry, and his sisters. To find the head-master making apologies to him, was positively painful and embarrassing, and his countenance would have been fitter for a culprit receiving a lecture. It was pleasanter when the two other masters shook hands with him, Mr. Harrison with a free confession that he had done him injustice, and Mr. Wilmot with a glad look of congratulation, that convinced Harry he had never believed Norman to blame.

Harry himself was somewhat of a hero; the masters all spoke to him, bade him good speed, and wished him a happy voyage; and all the boys were eager to admire his uniform, and wish themselves already men and officers like Mr. May. He had his long-desired three cheers for 'May Senior!' shouted with a thorough good-will by the united lungs of the Whichcote foundation, and a supplementary cheer arose for the good ship Alcestis, while hands were held out on every side; and the boy arrived at such a pitch of benevolence and good humour, as actually to volunteer a friendly shake of the hand to Edward Anderson, whom he encountered skulking apart.

'Never mind, Ned; we have often licked each other before now, and don't let us bear a grudge now I am going away. We are Stoneborough fellows both, you know, after all.'

Edward did not refuse the offered grasp; and though his words were only, 'Good-bye, I hope you will have plenty of fun!' Harry went away with a lighter heart.

The rest of the day Harry adhered closely to his father, though chiefly in silence. Dr. May had intended much advice and exhortation for his warm-hearted, wild-spirited son, but words would not come, not even when in the still evening twilight they walked down alone together to the cloister, and stood over the little stone-marked M.M. After standing there for some minutes, Harry knelt to collect some of the daisies in the grass.

'Are those to take with you?'

'Margaret is going to make a Cross of them for my Prayer-book.'

'Aye, they will keep it in your mind—say it all to you, Harry. She may be nearer to you everywhere, though you are far from us. Don't put yourself from her.'

That was all Dr. May contrived to say to his son, nor could Margaret do much more than kiss him, while tears flowed one by one over her cheeks, as she tried to whisper that he must remember and guard himself, and that he was sure of being thought of, at least, in every prayer; and then she fastened into his book the Cross, formed of flattened daisies, gummed upon a frame-work of paper. He begged her to place it at the Baptismal Service, for he said, 'I like that about fighting—and I always did like the Church being like a ship—don't you? I only found that prayer out the day poor little Daisy was christened.'

Margaret had, indeed, a thrill of melancholy pleasure in this task, when she saw how it was regarded. Oh! that her boy might not lose these impressions amid the stormy waves he was about to encounter.

That last evening of home good nights cost Harry many a choking sob ere he could fall asleep; but the morning of departure had more cheerfulness; the pleasure of patronizing Jem Jennings was as consoling to his spirits, as was to Mary the necessity of comforting Toby.

Toby's tastes were in some respects vulgar, as he preferred the stable and Will Adams to all Mary's attentions; but he attached himself vehemently to Dr. May, followed him everywhere, and went into raptures at the slightest notice from him. The Doctor said it was all homage to the master of the house. Margaret held that the dog was a physiognomist.

The world was somewhat flat after the loss of Harry—that element of riot and fun—Aubrey was always playing at 'poor Harry sailing away,' Mary looked staid and sober, and Norman was still graver, and more devoted to books, while Ethel gave herself up more completely to the thickening troubles of Cocksmoor.

Jealousies had arisen there; and these, with some rebukes for failures in sending children to be taught, had led to imputations on the character of Mrs. Green, in whose house the school was kept. Ethel was at first vehement in her defence; then, when stronger evidence was adduced of the woman's dishonesty, she was dreadfully shocked, and wanted to give up all connexion with her; and, in both moods, was equally displeased with Richard for pausing, and not going all lengths with her.

Mr. Wilmot was appealed to, and did his best to investigate; but the only result was, to discover that no one interrogated had any notion of truth, except John Taylor, and he knew nothing of the matter. The mass of falsehood, spite, violence, and dishonesty, that became evident, was perfectly appalling, and not a clue was to be found to the truth—scarcely a hope that minds so lost to honourable feeling were open to receive good impressions. It was a great distress to Ethel—it haunted her night and day—she lay awake pondering on the vain hopes for her poor children, and slept to dream of the angry faces and rude accusations. Margaret grew quite anxious about her, and her elders were seriously considering the propriety of her continuing her labours at Cocksmoor.

Mr. Wilmot would not be at Stoneborough after Christmas. His father's declining health made him be required at home, and since Richard was so often absent, it became matter of doubt whether the Miss Mays ought to be allowed to persevere, unassisted by older heads, in such a locality.

This doubt put Ethel into an agony. Though she had lately been declaring that it made her very unhappy to go—she could not bear the sight of Mrs. Green, and that she knew all her efforts were vain while the poor children had such homes; she now only implored to be allowed to go on; she said that the badness of the people only made it more needful to do their utmost for them—there were no end to the arguments that she poured forth upon her ever kind listener, Margaret.

'Yes, dear Ethel, yes, but pray be calm; I know papa and Mr. Wilmot would not put a stop to it, if they could possibly help it, but if it is not proper—'

'Proper! that is as bad as Miss Winter!'

'Ethel, you and I cannot judge of these things—you must leave them to our elders—'

'And men always are so fanciful about ladies—'

'Indeed, if you speak in that way, I shall think it is really hurting you.'

'I did not mean it, dear Margaret,' said Ethel, 'but if you knew what I feel for poor Cocksmoor, you would not wonder that I cannot bear it.'

'I do not wonder, dearest, but if this trial is sent you, perhaps it is to train you for better things.'

'Perhaps it is for my fault,' said Ethel. 'Oh! oh! if it be that I am too unworthy. And it is the only hope; no one will do anything to teach these poor creatures, if I give it up. What shall I do, Margaret?'

Margaret drew her down close to her, and whispered, 'Trust them, Ethel dear. The decision will be whatever is the will of God. If He thinks fit to give you the work, it will come; if not, He will give you some other, and provide for them.'

'If I have been too neglectful of home, too vain of persevering when no one but Richard would,' sighed Ethel.

'I cannot see that you have, dearest,' said Margaret, fondly, 'but your own heart must tell you that. And now, only try to be calm and patient. Getting into these fits of despair is the very thing to make people decide against you.'

'I will! I will! I will try to be patient,' sobbed Ethel; 'I know to be wayward and set on it would only hurt. I might only do more harm—I'll try. But oh! my poor children.'

Margaret gave a little space for the struggle with herself, then advised her resolutely to fix her attention on something else. It was a Saturday morning, and time was more free than usual, so Margaret was able to persuade her to continue a half-forgotten drawing, while listening to an interesting article in a review, which opened to her that there were too many Cocksmoors in the world.

The dinner hour sounded too soon, and, as she was crossing the hall, to put away her drawing materials, the front door gave the click peculiar to Dr. May's left-handed way of opening it. She paused, and saw him enter, flushed, and with a look that certified her that something had happened.

'Well, Ethel! he is come.'

'Oh papa! Mr. Ernes—'

He held up his finger, drew her into the study, and shut the door. The expression of mystery and amusement gave way to sadness and gravity as he sat down in his arm-chair, and sighed as if much fatigued. She was checked and alarmed, but she could not help asking, 'Is he here?'

'At the Swan. He came last night, and watched for me this morning, as I came out of the hospital. We have been walking over the meadows to Fordholm.'

No wonder Dr. May was hot and tired.

'But is he not coming?' asked Ethel.

'Yes, poor fellow; but hush, stop, say nothing to the others. I must not have her agitated till she has had her dinner in peace, and the house is quiet. You know she cannot run away to her room as you would.'

'Then he is really come for *that?*' cried Ethel, breathlessly; and, perceiving the affirmative, added, 'but why did he wait so long?'

'He wished to see his way through his affairs, and also wanted to hear of her from Harry. I am afraid poor July's colours were too bright.'

'And why did he come to the Swan instead of to us?'

'That was his fine, noble feeling. He thought it right to see me first, that if I thought the decision too trying for Margaret, in her present state, or if I disapproved of the long engagement, I might spare her all knowledge of his coming.'

'Oh papa! you won't!'

'I don't know but that I ought—but yet—the fact is, that I cannot. With that fine young fellow so generously, fondly attached, I cannot find it in my heart to send him away for four years without seeing her, and yet, poor things, it might be better for them both. O Ethel, if your mother were but here!'

He rested his forehead on his hands, and Ethel stood aghast at his unexpected reception of the addresses for which she had so long hoped. She did not venture to speak, and presently he roused himself as the dinner-bell rang. 'One comfort is,' he said, 'that Margaret has more composure than I. Do you go to Cocksmoor this afternoon?'

'I wished it.'

'Take them all with you. You may tell them why when you are out. I must have the house quiet. I shall get Margaret out into the shade, and prepare her, as best I can, before he comes at three o'clock.'

It was not flattering to be thus cleared out of the way, especially when full of excited curiosity, but any such sensation was quite overborne by sympathy in his great anxiety, and Ethel's only question was, 'Had not Flora better stay, to keep off company?'

'No, no,' said Dr. May, impatiently, 'the fewer the better;' and hastily passing her, he dashed up to his room, nearly running over the nursery procession, and, in a very few seconds, was seated at table, eating and speaking by snatches, and swallowing endless draughts of cold water.

'You are going to Cocksmoor!' said he, as they were finishing.

'It is the right day,' said Richard. 'Are you coming, Flora?'

'Not to-day, I have to call on Mrs. Hoxton.'

'Never mind Mrs. Hoxton,' said the Doctor—'you had better go to-day, a fine cool day for a walk.'

He did not look as if he had found it so.

'O yes, Flora, you must come,' said Ethel, 'we want you.'

'I have engagements at home,' replied Flora.

'And it really is a trying walk,' said Miss Winter.

'You must,' reiterated Ethel. 'Come to our room, and I will tell you why.'

'I do not mean to go to Cocksmoor till something positive is settled. I cannot have anything to do with that woman.'

'If you would only come up-stairs,' implored Ethel, at the door, 'I have something to tell you alone.'

'I shall come up in due time. I thought you had outgrown closetings and foolish secrets,' said Flora.

Her movements were quickened however by her father, who, finding her with Margaret in the drawing-room, ordered her up-stairs in a peremptory manner, which she resented, as treating her like a child, and therefore proceeded in no amiable mood to the room, where Ethel awaited her in wild tumultuous impatience.

'Well, Ethel, what is this grand secret?'

'O Flora! Mr. Ernescliffe is at the Swan! He has been speaking to papa about Margaret.'

'Proposing for her, do you mean?' said Flora.

'Yes, he is coming to see her this afternoon, and that is the reason that papa wants us to be all out of the way.'

'Did papa tell you this?'

'Yes,' said Ethel, beginning to perceive the secret of her displeasure, 'but only because I was the first person he met; and Norman guessed it long ago. Do put on your things! I'll tell you all I know when we are out. Papa is so anxious to have the coast clear.'

'I understand,' said Flora, 'but I shall not go with you. Do not be afraid of my interfering with any one. I shall sit here.'

'But papa said you were to go.'

'If he had done me the favour of speaking to me himself,' said Flora, 'I should have shown him that it is not right that Margaret should be left without any one at hand in case she should be overcome. He is of no use in such cases, only makes things worse. I should not feel justified in leaving Margaret with no one else; but he is in one of those hand-over-head moods, when it is not of the least use to say a word to him.'

'Flora! how can you? when he expressly ordered you.'

'All he meant was, do not be in the way, and I shall not show myself unless I am needed, when he would be glad enough of me. I am not bound to obey the very letter, like Blanche or Mary.'

Ethel looked horrified by the assertion of independence, but Richard called her from below, and with one more fruitless entreaty, she ran down stairs.

Richard had been hearing all from his father, and it was comfortable to talk the matter over with him, and hear explained the anxiety which frightened her, while she scarcely comprehended it; how Dr. May could not feel certain whether it was right or expedient to promote an engagement which must depend on health so uncertain as poor Margaret's, and how he dreaded the effect on the happiness of both.

Ethel's romance seemed to be turning to melancholy, and she walked on gravely and thoughtfully, though repeating that there could be no doubt of Margaret's perfect recovery by the time of the return from the voyage.

Her lessons were somewhat nervous and flurried, and even the sight of two very nice neat new scholars, of very different appearance from the rest, and of much superior attainments, only half interested her. Mary was enchanted at them as a pair of prodigies, actually able to read! and had made out their names, and their former abodes, and how they had been used to go to school, and had just come to live in the cottage deserted by the lamented Una.

Ethel thought it quite provoking in her brother to accede to Mary's entreaties that they should go and call on this promising importation. Even the children's information that they were taught now by 'Sister Cherry' failed to attract her; but Richard looked at his watch, and decided that it was too soon to go home, and she had to submit to her fate.

Very different was the aspect of the house from the wild Irish cabin appearance that it had had in the M'Carthy days. It was the remains of an old farm-house that had seen better days, some-what larger than the general run of the Cocksmoor dwellings. Respectable furniture had taken up its abode against the walls, the kitchen was well arranged, and, in spite of the wretched floor-ing and broken windows, had an air of comfort. A very tidy woman was bustling about, still trying to get rid of the relics of her former tenants, who might, she much feared, have left a legacy of typhus fever. The more interesting person was, however, a young woman of three or four-and-twenty, pale, and very lame, and with the air of a respectable servant, her manners particularly pleasing. It appeared that she was the daughter of a first wife, and, after the period of schooling, had been at service, but had been lamed by a fall down-stairs, and had been obliged to come home, just as scar-city of work had caused her father to leave his native parish, and seek employment at other quarries. She had hoped to obtain plain work, but all the family were dismayed and disappointed at the wild spot to which they had come, and anxiously availed them-selves of this introduction to beg that the elder boy and girl might be admitted into the town school, distant as it was. At another time, the thought of Charity Elwood would have engrossed Ethel's whole mind, now she could hardly attend, and kept looking eagerly at Richard as he talked endlessly with the good mother. When, at last, they did set off, he would not let her gallop home like a steam-engine, but made her take his arm, when he found that she could not otherwise moderate her steps. At the long hill, a figure appeared, and, as soon as Richard was certified of its identity, he let her fly, like a bolt from a cross-bow, and she stood by Dr. May's side.

A little ashamed, she blushed instead of speaking, and waited for Richard to come up and begin. Neither did he say anything, and they paused till, the silence disturbing her, she ventured a 'Well, papa!'

' Well, poor things. She was quite overcome when first I told her—said it would be hard on him, and begged me to tell him that he would be much happier if he thought no more of her.'

' Did Margaret ?' cried Ethel. ' Oh! could she mean it ?'

' She thought she meant it, poor dear, and repeated such things again and again; but when I asked whether I should send him away without seeing her, she cried more than ever, and said, ' You are tempting me! It would be selfishness.'

' O dear! she surely has seen him !'

' I told her that I would be the last person to wish to tempt her to selfishness, but that I did not think that either could be easy in settling such a matter through a third person.'

' It would have been very unkind,' said Ethel; ' I wonder she did not think so.'

' She did at last. I saw it could not be otherwise, and she said, poor darling, that when he had seen her, he would know the impossibility; but she was so agitated, that I did not know how it could be.'

' Has she ?'

' Aye, I told him not to stay too long, and left him under the tulip-tree with her. I found her much more composed—he was so gentle and considerate. Ah! he is the very man! Besides, he has convinced her now that affection brings him, not mere generosity, as she fancied.'

' O, then it is settled !' cried Ethel, joyously.

' I wish it were! She has owned that if—if she were in health —but that is all, and he is transported with having gained so much! Poor fellow. So far, I trust, it is better for them to know each other's minds, but how it is to be—'

' But, papa, you know Sir Matthew Fleet said she was sure to get well; and in three years' time—'

' Yes! yes, that is the best chance. But it is a dreary look-out for two young things. That is in wiser hands, however ! If only I saw what was right to do ! My miserable carelessness has undone you all !' he concluded, almost inaudibly.

It was, indeed, to him a time of great distress and perplexity, wishing to act the part of father and mother both towards his daughter, acutely feeling his want of calm decision, and torn to pieces at once by sympathy with the lovers, and by delicacy that held him back from seeming to bind the young man to an uncertain engagement, above all, tortured by self-reproach for the commencement of the attachment, and for the misfortune that had rendered its prosperity doubtful.

Ethel could find no words of comfort in the bewildered glimpse at his sorrow and agitation. Richard spoke with calmness and good sense, and his replies, though brief and commonplace, were not without effect in lessening the excitement and despondency which the poor Doctor's present mood had been aggravating.

At the door, Dr. May asked for Flora, and Ethel explained. If Flora had obtruded herself, he would have been irritated, but, as it was, he had no time to observe the disobedience, and saying that he hoped she was with Margaret, sent Ethel into the drawing-room.

Flora was not there, only Margaret lay on her sofa, and Ethel hesitated, shy, curious, and alarmed; but, as she approached, she was relieved to see the blue eyes more serene even than usual, while a glow of colour spread over her face, making her like the blooming Margaret of old times ; her expression was full of peace, but became somewhat amused at Ethel's timid, awkward pauses, as she held out her hands, and said, 'Come, dear Ethel.'

'O, Margaret, Margaret!'

And Ethel was drawn into her sister's bosom. Presently, she drew back, gazed at her sister, inquiringly, and said, in an odd, doubtful voice, 'Then you are glad?'

Margaret nearly laughed at the strange manner, but spoke with a sorrowful tone, 'Glad in one way, dearest, almost too glad, and grateful.'

'O, I am so glad!' again said Ethel; 'I thought it was making everybody unhappy.'

'I don't believe I could be that, now he has come, now I know;' and her voice trembled. 'There must be doubt and uncertainty,' she added, 'but I cannot dwell on them just yet. They will settle what is right, I know, and, happen what may, I have always *this* to remember.'

'Oh! that is right! Papa will be so relieved! He was afraid it had only been distress.'

'Poor papa! Yes, I did not command myself at first ; I was not sure whether it was right to see him at all.'

'Oh! Margaret, that was too bad!'

'It did not seem right to encourage any such—such,' the word was lost, 'to such a poor helpless thing as I am. I did not know what to do, and I am afraid I behaved like a silly child, and did not think of dear papa's feelings. But I will try to be good, and leave it all to them.'

'And you are going to be happy?' said Ethel, wistfully.

'For the present, at least. I cannot help it,' said Margaret. 'Oh! he is so kind, and so unselfish, and so beautifully gentle— and to think of his still caring—but there, dear Ethel, I am not going to cry—do call papa, or he will think me foolish again. I want him to be quite at ease about me before he comes'

'Then he is coming?'

'Yes, at tea-time—so run, dear Ethel, and tell Jane to get his room ready.'

This message quickened Ethel, and after giving it, and reporting consolingly to her father, she went up to Flora, who had been a voluntary prisoner up-stairs all this time, and was not peculiarly gratified at such tidings coming only through the medium of Ethel. She had before been sensible that, superior in discretion and effectiveness as she was acknowledged to be, she did not share so much of the confidence and sympathy as some of the others, and she felt mortified and injured, though in this case it was entirely her own fault. The sense of alienation grew upon her.

She dressed quickly, and hurried down, that she might see Margaret alone, but the room was already prepared for tea, and the children were fast assembling. Ethel came down a few minutes after, and found Blanche claiming Alan Ernescliffe as her lawful property, dancing round him, chattering, and looking injured if he addressed a word to any one else.

'How did lovers look?' was a speculation which had, more than once, occupied Ethel, and when she had satisfied herself that her father was at ease, she began to study it, as soon as a shamefaced consciousness would allow her, after Alan's warm shake of the hand.

Margaret looked much as usual, only with more glow and brightness—Mr. Ernescliffe, not far otherwise; he was as pale and slight as on his last visit, with the same soft blue eyes, capable, however, of a peculiar keen, steady glance when he was listening, and which now seemed to be attending to Margaret's every word or look, through all the delighted uproar which Aubrey, Blanche, and Mary kept up round him, or while taking his share in the general conversation, telling of Harry's popularity and good conduct on board the Alcestis, or listening to the history of Norman's school adventures, which he had heard, in part, from Harry, and how young Jennings was entered in the flag-ship, as a boy, though not yet to sail with his father.

After the storm of the day, the sky seemed quite clear, and Ethel could not see that being lovers made much difference—to be sure papa displeased Blanche, by calling her away to his side, when she would squeeze her chair in between Alan's and the sofa; and Alan took all the waiting on Margaret exclusively to himself. Otherwise, there was nothing remarkable, and he was very much the same Mr. Ernescliffe whom they had received a year ago.

In truth, the next ten days were very happy. The future was left to rest, and Alan spent his mornings in the drawing-room alone with Margaret, and looked ever more brightly placid, while with the rest, he was more than the former kind play-fellow, for he now took his place as the affectionate elder brother, entering warmly into all their schemes and pleasures, and winning for himself a full measure of affection from all; even his little god-daughter began to know him, and smile at his presence. Margaret and Ethel especially delighted in the look of enjoyment with which their father sat down to enter on the evening's conversation after the day's work; and Flora was well-pleased that Mrs. Hoxton should find Alan in the drawing-room, and ask afterwards about his estate; and that Meta Rivers, after being certified that this was *their* Mr. Ernescliffe, pronounced that her papa thought him particularly pleasing and gentlemanlike. There was something dignified in having a sister on the point of being engaged.

CHAPTER XXVIII.

'Sail forth into the sea, thou ship,
   Through breeze and cloud right onward steer;
The moistened eye, the trembling lip,
   Are not the signs of doubt or fear!'—LONGFELLOW.

TRANQUILLITY only lasted until Mr. Ernescliffe found it necessary to understand on what terms he was to stand. Every one was tender of conscience, anxious to do right, and desirous to yield to the opinion that nobody could, or would give. While Alan begged for a positive engagement, Margaret scrupled to exchange promises that she might never be able to fulfil, and both agreed to leave all to her father, who, in every way, ought to have the best ability to judge whether there was unreasonable presumption in such a betrothal; but this very ability only served to perplex the poor Doctor more and more. It is far easier for a man to decide when he sees only one bearing of a case, than when, like Dr. May, he not only sees them, but is rent by them in his inmost heart. Sympathizing in turn with each lover, bitterly accusing his own carelessness as the cause of all their troubles, his doubts contending with his hopes, his conviction clashing with Sir Matthew Fleet's opinion, his conscientious sincerity and delicacy conflicting with his affection and eagerness, he was perfectly incapable of coming to a decision, and suffered so cruelly, that Margaret was doubly distressed for his sake, and Alan felt himself guilty of having rendered everybody miserable.

Dr. May could not conceal his trouble, and rendered Ethel almost as unhappy as himself, after each conversation with her, though her hopes usually sprang up again, and she had a happy conviction that this was only the second volume of the novel. Flora was not often called into his councils; confidence never came spontaneously from Dr. May to her; there was something that did not draw it forth towards her, whether it resided in that half-sarcastic corner of her steady blue eye, or in the grave common sense of her gentle voice. Her view of the case was known to be that there was no need for so much perplexity—why should not Alan be the best judge of his own happiness? If Margaret were to be delicate for life, it would be better to have such a home to look to; and she soothed and comforted Margaret, and talked in a strain of unmixed hope and anticipation that often drew a smile from her sister, though she feared to trust to it.

Flora's tact and consideration in keeping the children away, when the lovers could best be alone, and letting them in, when the discussion was becoming useless and harassing, her cheerful smiles, her evening music that covered all sounds, her removal of all extra annoyances, were invaluable, and Margaret appreciated them, as, indeed, Flora took care that she should.

Margaret begged to know her eldest brother's judgment, but had great difficulty in dragging it out. Diffidently as it was proposed, it was clear and decided. He thought that his father had better send Sir Matthew Fleet a statement of Margaret's present condition, and abide by his answer as to whether her progress warranted the hope of her restoration.

Never was Richard more surprised than by the gratitude with which his suggestion was hailed, simple as it was, so that it seemed obvious that others should have already thought of it. After the tossings of uncertainty, it was a positive relief to refer the question to some external voice, and only Ethel and Norman expressed strong dislike to Sir Matthew becoming the arbiter of Margaret's fate, and were scarcely pacified by Dr. May's assurance, that he had not revealed the occasion of his inquiry. The letter was sent, and repose returned, but hearts beat high on the morning when the answer was expected.

Dr. May watched the moment when his daughter was alone, carried the letter to her, and kissing her, said, with an oppressed voice, 'I give you joy, my dear.'

She read with suspended breath and palpitating heart. Sir Matthew thought her improvement sure, though slow, and had barely a doubt, that, in a year, she would have regained her full strength and activity.

'You will show it to Alan,' said Dr. May, as Margaret lifted her eyes to his face inquiringly.

'Will not you?' she said.

'I cannot,' he answered. 'I wish I was more helpful to you,

my child,' he added, wistfully, ' but you will rest on him, and be happy together while he stays, will you not ?'

' Indeed I will, dear papa.'

Mr. Ernescliffe was with her as the Doctor quitted her. She held the letter to him, ' But,' she said, slowly, ' I see that papa does not believe it.'

' You promised to abide by it !' he exclaimed, between entreaty and authority.

' I do ; if you choose so to risk your hopes.'

' But,' cried he, as he glanced hastily over the letter, ' there can be no doubt ! These words are as certain as language can make them. Why will you not trust them ?'

' I see that papa does not.'

' Despondency and self-reproach make him morbidly anxious. Believe so, my Margaret ! You know he is no surgeon !'

' His education included that line,' said Margaret. ' I believe he has all but the manual dexterity. However, I would fain have faith in Sir Matthew,' she added, smiling, ' and perhaps I am only swayed by the habit of thinking that papa must know best.'

' He does in indifferent cases ; but it is an old axiom, that a medical man should not prescribe for his own family ; above all, in such a case, where it is but reasonable to believe an unprejudiced stranger, who alone is cool enough to be relied on. I absolutely depend on him !'

Margaret absolutely depended on the bright cheerful look of conviction. ' Yes,' she said, ' we will try to make papa take pleasure in the prospect. Perhaps I could do more if I made the attempt.'

' I am sure you could, if you would let me give you more support. If I were but going to remain with you !'

' Don't let us be discontented,' said Margaret, smiling, ' when so much more has been granted than I dare to hope. Be it as it may, let us be happy in what we have.'

' It makes you happy ?' said he, archly reading her face to draw out the avowal, but he only made her hide it, with a mute caress of the hand that held hers. She was glad enough to rest in the present, now that everything concurred to satisfy her conscience in so doing, and come what might, the days now spent together would be a possession of joy for ever.

Captain Gordon contrived to afford his lieutenant another fortnight's leave, perhaps because he was in dread of losing him altogether, for Alan had some doubts, and many longings to remain. Had it been possible to marry at once, he would have quitted the navy immediately ; and he would have given worlds

P. 304.

MARGARET AND ERNESCLIFFE.

to linger beside Margaret's couch, and claim her the first moment possible, believing his care more availing than all. He was, however, so pledged to Captain Gordon, that, without strong cause, he would not have been justified in withdrawing; besides, Harry was under his charge, and Dr. May and Margaret both thought, with the captain, that an active life would be a better occupation for him than watching her. He would never be able to settle down at his new home comfortably without her, and he would be more in the way of duty while pursuing his profession, so Margaret nerved herself against using her influence to detain him, and he thanked her for it.

Though hope and affection could not at once repair an injured spine, they had wonderful powers in inciting Margaret to new efforts. Alan was as tender and ready of hand as Richard, and more clever and enterprising; and her unfailing trust in him prevented all alarms and misgivings, so that wonders were effected, and her father beheld her standing with so little support, looking so healthful and so blithe, that his forebodings melted away, and he talked joyously of the future.

The great achievement was taking her round the garden. She could not bear the motion of wheels, but Alan adopted the hammock principle, and, with the aid of Richard and his crony, the carpenter, produced a machine in which no other power on earth could have prevailed on her to trust herself, but in which she was carried round the garden so successfully, that there was even a talk of next Sunday and of the Minster.

It was safely accomplished, and tired as she was, Margaret felt, as she whispered to Alan, that he had now crowned all the joy that he had brought to her.

Ethel used to watch them, and think how beautiful their countenances were, and talk them over with her father, who was quite happy about them now. She gave assistance, which Alan never once called unhandy, to all his contrivances, and often floundered in upon his conferences with Margaret, in a way that would have been very provoking, if she had not always blushed and looked so excessively discomfited, that they had only to laugh and reassure her.

Alan was struck by finding that the casual words spoken on the way from Cocksmoor had been so strenuously acted on, and he brought on himself a whole torrent of Ethel's confused narratives, which Richard and Flora would fain have checked; but Margaret let them continue, as she saw him a willing listener, and was grateful to him for comprehending the ardent girl.

He declared himself to have a share in the matter, reminding Ethel of her appeal to him to bind himself to the service of

Cocksmoor. He sent a sovereign at once, to aid in a case of the sudden death of a pig; and when securely established in his brotherly right, he begged Ethel to let him know what would help her most. She stood colouring, twisting her hands, and wondering what to say; whereupon he relieved her by a proposal to leave an order for ten pounds, to be yearly paid into her hands, as a fixed income for her school.

A thousand a year could hardly have been so much to Ethel. 'Thank you! Oh, this is charming! We could set up a regular school! Cherry Elwood is the very woman! Alan, you have made our fortune! Oh! Margaret! Margaret! I must go and tell Ritchie and Mary! This is the first real step to our Church and all!'

'May I do it?' said Alan, turning to Margaret, as Ethel frantically burst out of the room; 'perhaps I should have asked leave?'

'I was going to thank you,' said Margaret. 'It is the very kindest thing you could have done by dear Ethel! the greatest comfort to us. She will be at peace now, when anything hinders her from going to Cocksmoor.'

'I wonder,' said Alan, musing, 'whether we shall ever be able to help her more substantially. I cannot do anything hastily, for you know Maplewood is still in the hands of the executors, and I cannot tell what claims there may be upon me; but by-and-by, when I return, if I find no other pressing duty, might not a Church at Cocksmoor be a thankoffering for all I have found here?'

'Oh! Alan, what joy it would be!'

'It is a long way off,' he said, sadly; 'and, perhaps, her force of perseverance will have prevailed alone.'

'I suppose I must not tell her, even as a vision.'

'It is too uncertain; I do not know the wants of the Maplewood people, and I must provide for Hector. I would not let these vague dreams interfere with her resolute work; but, Margaret, what a vision it is! I can see you laying the first stone on that fine heathy brow.'

'Oh! your godchild should lay the first stone!'

'She shall, and you shall lead her. And there shall be Ethel's sharp face full of indescribable things as she marshals her children, and Richard shall be Curate, and read in his steady soft tone, and your father shall look sunny with his boys around him, and you—'

'Oh! Alan!' said Margaret, who had been listening with a smile, 'it is, indeed, a long way off!'

'I shall look to it as the haven where I would be,' said the sailor.

They often spoke together of this scheme, ever decking it in brighter colours. The topic seemed to suit them better than their own future, for there was no dwelling on that without an occasional misgiving, and the more glad the anticipation, the deeper the sigh that followed on Margaret's part, till Mr. Ernescliffe followed her lead, and they seldom spoke of these uncertainties, but outwardly smiled over the present, inwardly dwelt on the truly certain hopes. There were readings shared together, made more precious than all by the conversations that ensued.

The hour for parting came at last. Ethel never knew what passed in the drawing-room, whence everyone was carefully excluded. Dr. May wandered about, keeping guard over the door, and watching the clock, till, at the last moment, he knocked, and called, in a trembling voice, 'Ernescliffe! Alan! It is past the quarter! You must not stay!'

The other farewells were hurried; Alan seemed voiceless, only nodding in reply to Mary's vociferous messages to Harry, and huskily whispering to Ethel, 'Good luck to Cooksmoor!'

The next moment the door had shut on him, and Dr. May and Flora had gone to her sister, whom she found not tearful, but begging to be left alone.

When they saw her again, she was cheerful; she kept up her composure and animation without flagging, nor did she discontinue her new exertions, but seemed decidedly the happier for all that had passed.

Letters came every day for her, and presents to every one. Ethel had a gold chain and eye-glass, which, it was hoped, might cure her of frowning and stooping, though her various ways of dangling her new possession caused her to be so much teased by Flora and Norman, that, but for regard to Margaret's feelings, she would not have worn it for three days.

To Mary was sent a daguerreotype of Harry, her glory and delight. Say, who would, that it had pig's eyes, a savage frown, a pudding chin, there were his own tight rings of hair, his gold-banded cap, his bright buttons—how could she prize it enough? She exhibited it to the little ones ten times a day, she kissed it night and morning, and registered her vow always to sleep with it under her 'pilow,' in a letter of thanks, which Margaret defended and despatched, in spite of Miss Winter's horrors at its disregard of orthography.

It was nearly the last letter before the Alcestis was heard of at Spithead. Then she sailed; she sent in her letters to Plymouth, and her final greetings by a Falmouth cutter—poor Harry's wild scrawl in pencil, looking very sea-sick.

'Dear papa and all, good-bye. We are out of sight of land. Three years, and keep up a good heart. I shall soon be all right.

'Your H. MAY.'

It was inclosed in Mr. Ernescliffe's envelope, and with it came tidings that Harry's brave spirit was not failing, even under untoward circumstances, but he had struggled on deck, and tried to write, when all his contemporaries had given in; in fact, he was a fine fellow, every one liked him, and Captain Gordon, though chary of commendation, had held him up to the other youngsters as an example of knowing what a sailor was meant to be like.

Margaret smiled, and cried over the news when she imparted it—but all serenely—and though she was glad to be alone, and wrote journals for Alan, when she could not send letters, she exerted herself to be the same sister as usual to the rest of the household, and not to give way to her wandering musings.

From one subject her attention never strayed. Ethel had never found any lack of sympathy in her for her Cocksmoor pursuits; but the change now showed, that where once Margaret had been interested, merely as a kind sister, she now had a personal concern, and she threw herself into all that related to it as her own chief interest and pursuit—becoming the foremost in devising plans, and arranging the best means of using Mr. Ernescliffe's benefaction.

The Elwood family had grown in the good opinion of the Mays. Charity had hobbled to Church, leaning on her father's arm, and being invited to dinner in the kitchen, the acquaintance had been improved, and nurse herself had pronounced her such a tidy, good sort of body, that it was a pity she had met with such a misfortune. If Miss Ethel brought in nothing but the like of her, they should be welcome—poor thing, how tired she was !

Nurse's opinions were apt to be sagacious, especially when in the face of her prejudices, and this gave Margaret confidence. Cherry proved to have been carefully taught by a good clergyman and his wife, and to be of very different stamp from the persons to whom the girls were accustomed. They were charmed with her, and eagerly offered to supply her with books—respecting her the more when they found that Mr. Hazlewood had already lent her their chief favourites. Other and greater needs they had no power to fill up.

'It is so lone without the Church bells, you see, Miss,' said Mrs. Elwood. 'Our tower had a real fine peal, and my man was one of the ringers. I seems quite lost without them, and there was Cherry, went a'most every day with the children.'

'Every day!' cried Mary, looking at her with respect.

'It was so near,' said Cherry, 'I could get there easy, and I got used to it when I was at school.'

'Did it not take up a great deal of time?' said Ethel.

'Why, you see, Ma'am, it came morning and night, out of working times, and I can't be stirring much.'

'Then you miss it sadly,' said Ethel.

'Yes, Ma'am, it made the day go on well like, and settled a body's mind, when I fretted for what could not be helped. But I try not to fret after it now, and Mr. Hazlewood said, if I did my best wherever I was, the Lord would still join our prayers together.'

Mr. Hazlewood was recollected by Mr. Wilmot as an old College friend, and a correspondence with him fully confirmed the favourable estimate of the Elwoods, and was decisive in determining that the day-school, with Alan's ten pounds as a salary, and a penny a week from each child, should be offered to Cherry.

Mr. Hazlewood answered for her sound excellence, and aptitude for managing little children, though he did not promise genius, such as should fulfil the requirements of modern days. With these Cocksmoor could dispense at present; Cherry was humbly gratified, and her parents delighted with the honour and profit; there was a kitchen which afforded great facilities, and Richard and his carpenter managed the fitting to admiration; Margaret devised all manner of useful arrangements, settled matters with great earnestness, saw Cherry frequently, discussed plans, and learnt the history and character of each child, as thoroughly as Ethel herself. Mr. Ramsden himself came to the opening of the school, and said so much of the obligations of Cocksmoor to the young ladies, that Ethel would not have known which way to look, if Flora had not kindly borne the brunt of his compliments.

Every one was pleased, except Mrs. Green, who took upon herself to set about various malicious reports of Cherry Elwood; but nobody cared for them, except Mrs. Elwood, who flew into such passions, that Ethel was quite disappointed in her, though not in Cherry, who meekly tried to silence her mother, begged the young ladies not to be vexed, and showed a quiet dignity that soon made the shafts of slander fall inoffensively.

All went well; there was a school instead of a hubbub, clean faces instead of dirty, shining hair instead of wild elf-locks, orderly children instead of little savages. The order and obedience that Ethel could not gain in six months, seemed impressed in six days by Cherry; the neat work made her popular with the mothers, her firm gentleness won the hearts of the children, and the kitchen was filled not only with boys and girls from the quarry, but with some little ones from outlying cottages of Fordholm and Abbotstoke, and there was even a smart little farmer, who had been unbearable at home.

Margaret's unsuccessful Bath chair was lent to Cherry, and in it her scholars drew her to Stoneborough every Sunday, and slowly began to redeem their character with the ladies, who began to lose the habit of shrinking out of their way—the Stoneborough children did so instead; and Flora and Ethel were always bringing home stories of injustice to their scholars, fancied or real, and of triumphs in their having excelled any national school girl. The most stupid children at Cocksmoor always seemed to them wise in comparison with the Stoneborough girls, and the Sunday-school might have become to Ethel a school of rivalry, if Richard had not opened her eyes by a quiet observation, that the town girls seemed to fare as ill with her as the Cocksmoor girls did with the town ladies. Then she caught herself up, tried to be candid, and found that she was not always impartial in her judgments. Why would competition mingle even in the best attempts?

Cherry did not so bring forward her scholars, that Ethel could have many triumphs of this dangerous kind. Indeed, Ethel was often vexed with her; for though she taught needlework admirably, and enforced correct reading, and reverent repetition, her strong provincial dialect was a stumbling-block; she could not put questions without book, and nothing would teach her Ethel's rational system of arithmetic. That she was a capital dame, and made the children very good, was allowed; but now and then, when mortified by hearing what was done at Stoneborough, Fordholm, or Abbotstoke, Ethel would make vigorous efforts, which resulted only in her coming home fuming at Cherry's 'outrageous dulness.'

These railings always hurt Margaret, who had made Cherry almost into a friend, and generally liked to have a visit from her during the Sunday, when she always dined with the servants. Then school questions, Cocksmoor news, and the tempers of the children, were talked over, and Cherry was now and then drawn into home reminiscences, and descriptions of the ways of her former school. There was no fear of spoiling her—notice from her superiors was natural to her, and she had the lady-likeness of womanly goodness, so as never to go beyond her own place. She had had many trials too, and Margaret learnt the true history of them, as she won Cherry's confidence, and entered into them, feeling their likeness, yet dissimilarity, to her own.

Cherry had been a brisk happy girl in a good place, resting in one of the long engagements that often extend over half the life of a servant, enjoying the nod of her baker as he left his bread, and her walk from Church with him on alternate Sundays. But poor Cherry had been exposed to the perils of window cleaning; and, after a frightful fall, had wakened to find herself in a hospital, and her severe sufferings had left her a cripple for life.

And the baker had not been an Alan Ernescliffe! She did not complain of him—he had come to see her, and had been much grieved, but she had told him she could never be a useful wife; and before she had used her crutches, he was married to her pretty fellow-servant.

Cherry spoke very simply; she hoped it was better for Long, and believed Susan would make him a good wife. Ethel would have thought she did not feel, but Margaret knew better.

She stroked the thin slight fingers, and gently said, 'Poor Cherry!' and Cherry wiped away a tear, and said, 'Yes, Ma'am, thank you, it is best for him. I should not have wished him to grieve for what cannot be helped.'

'Resignation is the great comfort.'

'Yes, Ma'am. I have a great deal to be thankful for. I don't blame no one, but I do see how some, as are married, seem to get to think more of this world; and now and then I fancy I can see how it is best for me as it is.'

Margaret sighed, as she remembered certain thoughts before Alan's return.

'Then, Ma'am, there has been such goodness! I did vex at being a poor helpless thing, nothing but a burthen on father; and when we had to go from home, and Mr. and Mrs. Hazlewood and all, I can't tell you how bad it was, Ma'am.'

'Then you are comforted now?'

'Yes, Ma'am,' said Cherry, brightening. 'It seems as if He had given me something to do, and there are you and Mr. Richard, and Miss Ethel, to help. I should like, please God, to be of some good to those poor children.'

'I am sure you will, Cherry; I wish I could do as much.'

Cherry's tears had come again. 'Ah! Ma'am, you—' and she stopped short, and rose to depart. Margaret held out her hand to wish her good-bye. 'Please, Miss, I was thinking how Mr. Hazlewood said that God fits our place to us, and us to our place.'

'Thank you, Cherry, you are leaving me something to remember.'

And Margaret lay questioning with herself, whether the school-mistress had not been the most self-denying of the two; but withal gazing on the hoop of pearls which Alan had chosen as the ring of betrothal.

'The Pearl of great price,' murmured she to herself; 'if we hold that, the rest will soon matter but little! It remaineth that both they that have wives, be as they that have none, and they that weep as though they wept not, and they that rejoice as though they rejoiced not! If ever Alan and I have a home together upon earth, may all too confident joy be tempered by the fears that we have begun with! I hope this probation may make me less likely to be taken up with the cares and pleasures of his position, than I might have been last year. He is one who can best help the mind to go truly upward! But oh! that voyage!'

<hr>

CHAPTER XXIX.

'Heart affluence in household talk,
From social fountains never dry.'—TENNYSON.

'WHAT a bore!'

'What's the matter now?'

'Here has this old fellow asked me to dinner again!'

'A fine pass we are come to!' cried Dr. May, half amused, half irate. 'I should like to know what I should have said at your age, if the head-master had asked me to dinner.'

'Papa is not so very fond of dining at Dr. Hoxton's,' said Ethel.

'A whipper-snapper schoolboy, who might be thankful to dine anywhere!' continued Dr. May, while the girls burst out laughing, and Norman looked injured.

'It is very ungrateful of Norman,' said Flora; 'I cannot see what he finds to complain of.'

'You would know,' said Norman, 'if, instead of playing those perpetual tunes of yours, you had to sit it out in that perfumery drawing-room, without anything to listen to worth hearing. If I have looked over that Court Album once, I have a dozen times, and there is not another book in the place!'

'I am glad there is not,' said Flora. 'I am quite ashamed to see you for ever turning over those old pictures! You cannot guess how stupid you look. I wonder Mrs. Hoxton likes to have you,' she added, patting his shoulders between jest and earnest.

'I wish she would not, then! It is only to escort you.'

'Nonsense, Norman, you know better!' cried Ethel. 'You know it is for your own sake, and to make up for their injustice, that he invites you, or Flora either.'

'Hush, Ethel! he gives himself quite airs enough already,' said the Doctor.

'Papa!' said Ethel, in vexation, though he gave her a pinch to show it was all in good humour, while he went on, 'I am glad to hear they do leave him to himself in a corner. A very good thing too! Where else should a great gawky schoolboy be?'

'Safe at home, where I wish he would let me be,' muttered Norman, though he contrived to smile, and followed Flora out of the room, without subjecting himself to the imputation of offended dignity.

Ethel was displeased, and began her defence: 'Papa, I wish—' and there she checked herself.

'Eh! Miss Ethel bristles up!' said her father, who seemed in a somewhat mischievous mood of teasing.

'How could you, papa?' cried she.

'How could I what, Miss Etheldred?'

'Plague Norman,'—the words would come. 'Accuse him of airs.'

'I hate to see young fellows above taking an honour from their elders,' said Dr. May.

'Now, papa, papa, you know it is no such thing. Dr. Hoxton's parties are very dull—you know they are, and it is not fair on Norman. If he was set up and delighted at going so often, then you would call him conceited.'

'Conceit has a good many lurking-places,' said Dr. May. 'It is harder to go and be overlooked, than to stay at home.'

'Now, papa, you are not to call Norman conceited!' cried Ethel. 'You don't believe that he is any such thing.'

'Why, not exactly,' said Dr. May, smiling. 'The boy has missed it, marvellously; but, you see, he has everything that subtle imp would wish to feed upon, and it is no harm to give him a lick with the rough side of the tongue, as your canny Scots grandfather used to say.'

'Ah! if you knew, papa—' began Ethel.

'If I knew?'

'No, no, I must not tell.'

'What, a secret, is there?'

'I wish it was not; I should like to tell you very much, but then, you see, it is Norman's, and you are to be surprised.'

'Your surprise is likely to be very much like Blanche's birth-day presents, a stage aside.'

'No, I am going to keep it to myself.'

Two or three days after, as Ethel was going to the school-room after breakfast, Dr. May beckoned her back to the dining-room, and, with his merry look of significance, said, 'Well, ma'am, I have found out your mystery!'

'About Norman? Oh, papa! Did he tell you?'

'When I came home from the hospital last night, at an hour when all respectable characters, except doctors and police, should be in their warm beds, I beheld a light in Norman's window, so methought I would see what Gravity was doing out of his bed at midnight—'

'And you found him at his Greek—'

'So that was the meaning of his looking so lank and careworn, just as he did last year, and he the prince of the school! I could have found it in my heart to fling the books at his head!'

'But you consent, don't you, to his going up for the scholarship?'

'I consent to anything, as long as he keeps within due bounds, and does not work himself to death. I am glad of knowing it, for now I can put a moderate check upon it.'

'And did he tell you all about it?'

'He told me he felt as if he owed it to us to gain something for himself, since I had given up the Randall to gratify him—a pretty sort of gratification.'

'Yes, and he will be glad to get away from school. He says he knows it is bad for him—as it is uncomfortable to be singled out in the way Dr. Hoxton does now. You know,' pleaded Ethel, 'it is not ingratitude or elation, but it is, somehow, not *nice* to be treated as he is, set apart from the rest.'

'True; Dr. Hoxton never had taste or judgment. If Norman were not a *lusus naturæ*,' said Dr. May, hesitating for a word, 'his head would have been turned long ago. And he wants companions too—he has been forced out of boyhood too soon, poor fellow—and Harry gone too. He does not get anything like real relaxation, and he will be better among youths than boys. Stoneborough will never be what it was in my time!' added the Doctor, mournfully. 'I never thought to see the poor old place come to this; but there—when all the better class send their sons to the great public schools, and leave nothing but riff-raff here, one is forced, for a boy's own sake, to do the same.'

'Oh! I am so glad! Then you have consented to the rest of Norman's scheme, and will not keep poor little Tom at school here without him?'

'By what he tells me, it would be downright ruin to the boy. I little thought to have to take a son of mine away from Stoneborough; but Norman is the best judge, and he is the only person who seems to have made any impression on Tom, so I shall let it be. In fact,' he added, half smiling, 'I don't know what I could refuse old June.'

'That's right!' cried Ethel. 'That is so nice! Then, if Norman gets the scholarship, Tom is to go to Mr. Wilmot first, and then to Eton!'

'If Norman gains the scholarship, but that is an if,' said Dr. May, as though hoping for a loop-hole to escape offending the shade of Bishop Whichcote.

'Oh, papa, you cannot doubt of that!'

'I cannot tell, Ethel. He is *facile princeps* here in his own world, but we do not know how it may be when he is measured with public schoolmen, who have had more first-rate tutorship than poor old Hoxton's.'

'Ah! he says so, but I thought that was all his humility.'

'Better he should be prepared. If he had had all those advantages—but it may be as well after all. I always had a hankering to have sent him to Eton, but your dear mother used to say it was not fair on the others. And now, to see him striving in order to give the advantage of it to his little brother! I only hope Master Thomas is worthy of it—but it is a boy I can't understand.'

'Nor I,' said Ethel; 'he never seems to say anything he can help, and goes after Norman without talking to any one else.'

'I give him up to Norman's management!' said Dr. May. 'He says the boy is very clever, but I have not seen it; and, as to more serious matters.—However, I must take it on Norman's word, that he is wishing to learn truth. We made an utter mistake about him; I don't know who is to blame for it.'

'Have you told Margaret about Norman's plan?' asked Ethel.

'No; he desired me to say nothing. Indeed, I should not like Tom's leaving school to be talked of beforehand.'

'Norman said he did not want Flora to hear, because she is so much with the Hoxtons, and he said they would all watch him.'

'Aye, aye! and we must keep his secret. What a boy it is! But it is not safe to say conceited things. We shall have a fall yet, Ethel. Not seventeen, remember, and brought up at a mere grammar-school.'

'But we shall still have the spirit that made him try,' said Ethel, 'and that is the thing.'

'And, to tell you the truth,' said the Doctor, lingering, 'for my own part, I don't care a rush for it!' and he dashed off to his work, while Ethel stood laughing.

'Papa was so very kind,' said Norman, tremulously, when Ethel followed him to his room, to congratulate him on having gained his father's assent, of which he had been more in doubt than she.

'And you see he quite approves of the scheme for Tom, except for thinking it disrespect to Bishop Whichcote. He said he only hoped Tom was worthy of it.'

'Tom!' cried Norman. 'Take my word for it, Ethel, Tom will surprise you all. He will beat us all to nothing, I know!'

'If only he can be cured of—'

'He will,' said Norman, 'when once he has outgrown his frights, and that he may do at Mr. Wilmot's, apart from those fellows. When I go up for this scholarship, you must look after his lessons, and see if you are not surprised at his construing!'

'When you go. It will be in a month!'

'He has told no one, I hope.'

'No; but I hardly think he will bear not telling Margaret.'

'Well—I hate a thing being out of one's own keeping. I should not so much dislike Margaret's knowing, but I *won't* have Flora know—mind that, Ethel,' he said, with disproportionate vehemence.

'I only hope Flora will not be vexed. But, oh dear! how nice it will be when you have it, telling Meta Rivers, and all!'

'And this is a fine way of getting it, standing talking here. Not that I shall—You little know what public schools can do! But that is no reason against trying.'

'Good night, then. Only one thing more. You mean that, till further orders, Margaret should not know?'

'Of course,' said Norman, impatiently. 'She won't take any of Flora's silly affronts, and, what is more, she would not care half so much as before Alan Ernescliffe came.'

'Oh, Norman, Norman! I'm sure—'

'Why, it is what they always say. Everybody can't be first, and Ernescliffe has the biggest half of her, I can see.'

'I am sure I did not,' said Ethel, in a mortified voice.

'Why, of course, it always comes of people having lovers.'

'Then I am sure I won't!' exclaimed Ethel.

Norman went into a fit of laughing.

'You may laugh, Norman, but I will never let papa or any of you be second to any one!' she cried, vehemently.

A brotherly home-truth followed: 'Nobody asked you, sir,' she said!' was muttered by Norman, still laughing heartily.

'I know,' said Ethel, not in the least offended, 'I am very ugly, and very awkward, but I don't care. There never can be anybody in all the world that I shall like half as well as papa, and I am glad no one is ever likely to make me care less for him and Cocksmoor.'

'Stay till you are tried,' said Norman.

Ethel squeezed up her eyes, curled up her nose, showed her teeth in a horrible grimace, and made a sort of snarl: 'Yah! That's the face I shall make at them!' and then, with another good-night, ran to her own room.

Norman was, to a certain extent, right with regard to Margaret—her thoughts and interest had been chiefly engrossed by Alan Ernescliffe, and, so far drawn away from her own family, that when the Alcestis was absolutely gone beyond all reach of letters for the present, Margaret could not help feeling somewhat of a void, and as if the home concerns were not so entire an occupation for her mind as formerly.

She would fain have thrown herself into them again, but she became conscious that there was a difference. She was still the object of her father's intense tenderness and solicitude, indeed she could not be otherwise, but it came over her sometimes that she was less necessary to him than in the first year. He was not conscious of any change, and, indeed, it hardly amounted to a change, and yet Margaret, lying inactive and thoughtful, began to observe that the fullness of his confidence was passing to Ethel. Now and then it would appear that he fancied he had told Margaret little matters, when he had really told them to Ethel—and it was Ethel who would linger with him in the drawing-room after the others had gone up at night, or who would be late at the morning's reading, and disarm Miss Winter, by pleading that papa had been talking to her. The secret they shared together was, of course, the origin of much of this; but also Ethel was now more entirely the Doctor's own than Margaret could be after her engagement; and there was a likeness of mind between the father and daughter that could not but develop more in this year, that in all Ethel's life, when she had made the most rapid progress. Perhaps, too, the Doctor looked on Margaret rather as the authority and mistress of his house, while Ethel was more of a playfellow; and thus, without either having the least suspicion that the one sister was taking the place of the other, and without any actual neglect of Margaret, Ethel was his chief companion.

'How excited and anxious Norman looks!' said Margaret, one day, when he had rushed in at the dinner-hour, asking for his father, and, when he could not find him, shouting out for Ethel. 'I hope there is nothing amiss. He has looked thin and worn for some time, and yet his work at school is very easy to him.'

'I wish there may be nothing wrong there again,' said Flora. 'There! there's the front door banging! He is off! Ethel!'—stepping to the door, and calling in her sister, who came from the street door, her hair blowing about with the wind.—'What did Norman want?'

'Only to know whether papa had left a note for Dr. Hoxton,' said Ethel, looking very confused and very merry.

'That was not all,' said Flora. 'Now, don't be absurd, Ethel —I hate mysteries.'

'Last time I had a secret, you would not believe it,' said Ethel, laughing.

'Come!' exclaimed Flora, 'why cannot you tell us at once what is going on?'

'Because I was desired not,' said Ethel. 'You will hear it soon enough,' and she capered a little.

'Let her alone, Flora,' said Margaret. 'I see there is nothing wrong.'

'If she is desired to be silent, there is nothing to be said,' replied Flora, sitting down again, while Ethel ran away to guard her secret.

'Absurd!' muttered Flora. 'I cannot imagine why Ethel is always making mysteries!'

'She cannot help other people having confidence in her,' said Margaret, gently.

'She need not be so important, then,' said Flora—'always having private conferences with papa! I do not think it is at all fair on the rest.'

'Ethel is a very superior person,' said Margaret, with half a sigh.

Flora might toss her head, but she attempted no denial in words.

'And,' continued Margaret, 'if papa does find her his best companion and friend, we ought to be glad of it.'

'I do not call it just,' said Flora.

'I do not think it can be helped,' said Margaret; 'the best *must* be preferred.'

'As to that, Ethel is often very ridiculous and silly.'

'She is improving every day; and you know dear mamma always thought her the finest character amongst us.'

'Then you are ready to be left out, and have your third sister always put before you?'

'No, Flora, that is not the case. Neither she nor papa would ever be unfair; but, as she would say herself, what they can't help, they can't help; and, as she grows older, she must surpass me more and more.'

'And you like it?'

'I like it—when—when I think of papa, and of his dear, noble Ethel. I *do* like it, when I am not selfish.'

Margaret turned away her head, but presently looked up again.

'Only, Flora,' she said, 'pray do not say one word of this, on any account, to Ethel. She is so happy with papa, and I would not, for anything, have her think I feel neglected, or had any jealousy.'

'Ah,' thought Flora, 'you can give up sweetly, but you have Alan to fall back upon. Now I, who certainly have the best right, and a great deal more practical sense—'

Flora took Margaret's advice, and did not reproach Ethel, for a little reflection convinced her that she should make a silly figure in so doing, and she did not like altercations.

It was the same evening that Norman came in from school with his hands full of papers, and, with one voice, his father and Ethel exclaimed, 'You have them?'

'Yes;' and he gave a letter to his father, while Blanche, who had a very inquisitive pair of eyes, began to read from a paper he placed on the table.

'Norman Walter, son of Richard and Margaret May, High-street, Doctor of Medicine, December 21st, 18— Thomas Ramsden.'

'What is that for, Norman?' and, as he did not attend, she called Mary to share her speculations, and spell out the words.

'Ha!' cried Dr. May, 'this is capital! The old Doctor seems not to know how to say enough for you. Have you read it?'

'No, he only told me he had said something in my favour, and wished me all success.'

'Success!' cried Mary. 'Oh, Norman, you are not going to sea, too?'

'No, no!' interposed Blanche, knowingly—'he is going to be married. I heard nurse wish her brother success when he was going to marry the washerwoman with a red face.'

'No,' said Mary, 'people never are married till they are twenty.'

'But I tell you,' persisted Blanche, 'people always write like this, in a great book in Church, when they are married. I know, for we always go into Church with Lucy and nurse, when there is a wedding.'

'Well, Norman, I wish you success with the bride you are to court,' said Dr. May—much diverted with the young ladies' conjectures.

'But is it really?' said Mary, making her eyes as round as full moons.

'Is it really?' repeated Blanche—'Oh dear! is Norman going to be married? I wish it was to be Meta Rivers, for then I could always ride her dear little white pony.'

'Tell them,' whispered Norman, a good deal out of countenance, as he leant over Ethel, and quitted the room.

Ethel cried, 'Now then!' and looked at her father, while
Blanche and Mary reiterated inquiries—marriage, and going to
sea, being the only events that, in their imagination, the world
could furnish. Going to try for a Balliol scholarship! It was
a sad falling off, even if they understood what it meant. The
Doctor's explanations to Margaret had a tone of apology for
having kept her in ignorance, and Flora said few words, but felt
herself injured; she had nearly gone to Mrs. Hoxton that afternoon, and how strange it would have been if anything had been said
to her of her own brother's projects, when she was in ignorance.

Ethel slipped away to her brother, who was in his own room,
surrounded with books, flushed and anxious, and trying to glance
over each subject on which he felt himself weak.

'I shall fail! I know I shall!' was his exclamation. 'I wish I
had never thought of it!'

'What? did Dr. Hoxton think you not likely to succeed?'
cried Ethel, in consternation.

'Oh! he said I was certain, but what is that? We Stoneborough men only compare ourselves with each other. I shall
break down to a certainty, and my father will be disappointed.'

'You will do your best?'

'I don't know that. My best will all go away when it comes
to the point.'

'Surely not. It did not go away last time you were examined,
and why should it now?'

'I tell you, Ethel, you know nothing about it. I have not
got up half what I meant to have done. Here, do take this
book—try me whether I know this properly.'

So they went on; Ethel doing her best to help and encourage,
and Norman in an excited state of restless despair, which drove
away half his senses and recollection, and his ideas of the
superior powers of public school-boys magnifying every moment.
They were summoned down-stairs to prayers, but went up again
at once; and more than an hour subsequently, when their father
paid one of his domiciliary visits, there they still were, with their
Latin and Greek spread out, Norman trying to strengthen all
doubtful points, but in a desperate desultory manner, that only
confused him more and more, till he was obliged to lay his head
down on the table, shut his eyes, and run his fingers through his
hair, before he could recollect the simplest matter; his render-
ings alternated with groans, and cold as was the room, his cheeks
and brows were flushed and burning.

The Doctor checked all this, by saying, gravely and sternly, 'This is not right, Norman. Where are all your resolutions?'

'I shall never do it! I ought never to have thought of it! I shall never succeed!'

'What, if you do not?' said Dr. May, laying his hand on his shoulder.

'What?—why Tom's chance lost—you will all be mortified,' said Norman, hesitating in some confusion.

'I will take care of Tom,' said Dr. May.

'And he will have been foiled!' said Ethel.

'If he is?'

The boy and girl were both silent.

'Are you striving for mere victory's sake, Norman?' continued his father.

'I thought not,' murmured Norman.

'Successful or not, you will have done your utmost for us. You would not lose one jot of affection or esteem, and Tom shall not suffer. Is it worth this agony?'

'No, it is foolish,' said Norman, with trembling voice, almost as if he could have burst into tears. He was quite unnerved by the anxiety and toil with which he had overtasked himself, beyond his father's knowledge.

'Oh! papa!' pleaded Ethel, who could not bear to see him pained.

'It is foolish,' continued Dr. May, who felt it was the moment for bracing severity. 'It is rendering you unmanly. It is wrong.'

Again Ethel made an exclamation of entreaty.

'It is wrong, I know,' repeated Norman; 'but you don't know what it is to get into the spirit of the thing.'

'Do you think I do not?' said the Doctor; 'I can tell exactly what you feel now. If I had not been an idle dog, I should have gone through it all many more times.'

'What shall I do?' asked Norman, in a worn-out voice.

'Put all this out of your mind, sleep quietly, and don't open another book.'

Norman moved his head, as if sleep were beyond his power.

'I will read you something to calm your tone,' said Dr. May, and he took up a Prayer-Book. ' "Know ye not, that they which run in a race, run all, but one receiveth the prize? So run that ye may obtain. And every man that striveth for the mastery, is temperate in all things. Now they do it to obtain a corruptible crown, but we an incorruptible." And, Norman, that is not the struggle where the race is not to the swift, nor the battle to the strong; nor the contest where the conqueror only wins vanity and vexation of spirit.'

Norman had cast down his eyes, and hardly made answer, but the words had evidently taken effect. The Doctor only further bade him good night, with a whispered blessing; and, taking Ethel by the hand, drew her away.

When they met the next morning, the excitement had passed from Norman's manner, and he looked dejected and resigned. He had made up his mind to lose, and was not grateful for good wishes, he ought never to have thought, he said, of competing with men from public schools, and he knew his return of love of vain-glory deserved that he should fail. However, he was now calm enough not to be likely to do himself injustice by nervousness, and Margaret had hopes that Richard's steady, equable mind, would have a salutary influence. So, commending Tom's lessons to Ethel, and hearing, but not marking, countless messages to Richard, he set forth upon his *emprise*, while his anxiety seemed to remain as a legacy for those at home.

Poor Dr. May confessed that his practice by no means agreed with his precept, for he could think of nothing else, and was almost as bad as Norman, in his certainty that the boy would fail from mere nervousness. Margaret was the better companion for him now; attaching less intensity of interest to Norman's success, than did Ethel, she was the more able to compose him, and cheer his hopes.

CHAPTER XXX.

' Weary soul, and burdened sore,
    Labouring with thy secret load,
  Fear not all thy griefs to pour
    In this heart, love's true abode.'—LYRA INNOCENTIUM.

TEA had just been brought in on the eighth evening from Norman's departure, when there was a ring at the bell. There was a start, and look of expectation. ' Only a patient,' said the Doctor; but it surely was not for that reason that he rose with so much alacrity and opened the door, nor was ' Well, old fellow?' the greeting for his patients—so everybody sprang after him, and beheld something tall taking off a coat, while a voice said, ' I have got it.'

The mass of children rushed back to Margaret, screaming, ' He has got it!' and then Aubrey trotted out into the hall again to see what Norman had got.

' A happy face at least,' said Margaret, as he came to her. And that was not peculiar to Norman. The radiance had shone out upon every one in that moment, and it was one buzz of happy exclamation, query and answer—the only tone of regret when Mary spoke of Harry, and all at once took up the strain—how glad poor Harry would be. As to the examination, that had been much less difficult than Norman had expected; in fact, he said, it was lucky for him that the very subjects had been chosen in which he was most up—luck which, as the Doctor could not help observing, generally did attend Norman. And Norman had been so happy with Richard; the kind, wise, elder brother had done exactly what was best for him in soothing his anxiety, and had fully shared his feelings and exulted in his success. Margaret had a most triumphant letter, dwelling on the abilities of the candidates whom Norman had out-stripped, and the idea that every one had conceived of his talent. 'Indeed,' wrote Richard, 'I fancy the men had never believed that I could have a clever brother. I am glad they have seen what Norman can do.'

Margaret could not help reading this aloud, and it made Norman blush with the compunction that Richard's unselfish pride in him always excited. He had much to tell of his ecstasy with Oxford. Stoneborough Minster had been a training in appreciation of its hoary beauty, but the essentially prosaic Richard had never prepared him for the impression that the Reverend old University made on him, and he was already, heart and soul, one of her most loyal and loving sons, speaking of his College and of the whole University as one who had a right of property in them, and looking, all the time, not elated, but contented, as if he had found his sphere and was satisfied. He had seen Cheviot, too, and had been very happy in the renewed friendship; and had been claimed as a cousin by a Balliol man, a certain Norman Ogilvie, a name well known among the Mays. 'And how has Tom been getting on?' he asked, when he returned to home affairs.

'Oh! I don't know,' said Ethel. 'He will not have my help.'

'Not let you help him?' exclaimed Norman.

'No. He says he wants no girls,' said Ethel, laughing.

'Foolish fellow!' said Norman. 'I wonder what sort of work he has made.'

'Very funny, I should think,' said Ethel, 'judging by the verses I could see.'

The little pale, rough-haired Tom, in his perpetual coating of dust, softly crept into the room, as if he only wanted to elude observation; but Mary and Blanche were at once vociferating their news in his ears, though with little encouragement—he only shook them off abruptly, and would not answer when they required him to be glad.

Norman stretched out his arm, intercepting him as he was making for his hiding-place behind Dr. May's arm-chair

'Come, August, how have things gone on?'

'Oh! I don't know.'

'What's your place?'

'Thirteenth!' muttered Tom in his throat, and well he might, for two or three voices cried out that was too bad, and that it was all his own fault, for not accepting Ethel's help. He took little heed, but crept to his corner without another word, and Mary knew she should be thumped, if she should torment him there.

Norman left him alone, but the coldness of the little brother for whom he had worked, gave a greater chill to his pleasure than he could have supposed possible. He would rather have had some cordiality on Tom's part, than all the congratulations that met him the next day.

He could not rest contented while Tom continued to shrink from him, and he was the more uneasy when, on Saturday morning, no calls from Mary availed to find the little boy, and bring him to the usual reading and Catechism.

Margaret decided that they must begin without him, and poor Mary's verse was read, in consequence, with a most dolorous tone. As soon as the books were shut, she ran off, and a few words passed among the elder ones about the truant—Flora opining that the Andersons had led him away; Ethel suggesting that his gloom must arise from his not being well; and Margaret looking wistfully at Norman, and saying she feared they had judged much amiss last spring.

Norman heard in silence, and walked thoughtfully into the garden. Presently he caught Mary's voice in expostulation: 'How could you not come to read!'

'Girls' work!' growled another voice, out of sight.

'But Norman, and Richard, and Harry, always come to the reading. Everybody ought.'

Norman, who was going round the shrubs that concealed the speakers from him, here lost their voices, but, as he emerged in front of the old tool-house, he heard a little scream from Mary, and, at the same moment, she darted back, and fell over a heap of cabbage-stumps in front of the old tool-house. It was no small surprise to her to be raised by him, and tenderly asked whether she were hurt. She was not hurt, but she could not speak without crying, and when Norman begged to hear what was the matter, and where Tom was, she would only plead for him—that he did not intend to hurt her, and that she had been teasing him. What had he done to frighten her? Oh! he had *only* run at her with a hoe, because she was troublesome; she did not mind it, and Norman must not—and she clung to him as if to keep him back, while he pursued his researches in the tool-house, where, nearly concealed by a great bushel-basket, lurked Master Thomas, crouching down, with a volume of 'Gil Blas' in his hand.

'You here! Tom! What have you hidden yourself here for? What can make you so savage to Mary?'

'She should not bother me,' said Tom, sulkily.

Norman sent Mary away, pacifying her by promises that he would not revenge her quarrel upon Tom, and then, turning the basket upside down, and perching himself astride on it, he began: 'That is the kindest, most forgiving little sister I ever did see. What possesses you to treat her so ill?'

'I wasn't going to hurt her.'

'But why drive her away? Why don't you come to read?' No answer; and Norman, for a moment, felt as if Tom were really hopelessly ill-conditioned and sullen, but he persevered in restraining his desire to cuff the ill-humour out of him, and continued: 'Come! there's something wrong, and you will never be better till it is out. Tell me—don't be afraid. Those fellows have been at you again?'

He took Tom by the arm to draw him nearer, but a cry and start of pain were the result. 'So they have licked you? Eh? What have they been doing?'

'They said they would spiflicate me if I told!' sighed Tom.

'They shall never do anything to you—' and by-and-by a sobbing confession was drawn forth, muttered at intervals, as low as if Tom expected the strings of onions to hear and betray him to his foes. Looking on him as a deserter, these town-boys had taken advantage of his brother's absence, to heap on him every misery they could inflict. There had been a wager between Edward Anderson and Sam Axworthy as to what Tom could be made to do, and his personal timidity made him a miserable victim, not merely beaten and bruised, but forced to transgress every rule of right and wrong that had been enforced on his conscience. On Sunday, they had profited by the absence of their Dux to have a jollification at a little public-house, not far from the playing-fields; and here had Tom been dragged in, forced to partake with them, and frightened with threats that he had treated them all, and was liable to pay the whole bill, which, of course, he firmly believed, as well as that he should be at least half-murdered if he gave his father any suspicion that the whole had not been consumed by himself. Now, though poor Tom's conscience had lost many scruples during the last spring, the offence, into which he had been forced, was too heinous to a child brought up as he had been, to be palliated even in his own eyes. The profanation of Sunday, and the carousal in a public-house, had combined to fill him with a sense of shame and degradation, which was the real cause that he felt himself unworthy to come and read with his sisters. His grief and misery were extreme, and Norman's indignation was such as could find no utterance. He sat silent, quivering with anger, and clenching his fingers over the handle of the hoe.

'I knew it!' sighed Tom. 'None of you will ever speak to me again!'

'You! Why, August, man, I have better hopes of you than ever. You are more really sorry now than ever you were before.'

'I had never been at the Green Man before,' said poor Tom, feeling his future life stained.

'You never will again!'

'When you are gone—' and the poor victim's voice died away.

'Tom, you will not stay after me. It is settled that when I go to Balliol, you leave Stoneborough, and go to Mr. Wilmot as pupil. Those scamps shall never have you in their clutches again.'

It did not produce the ecstasy Norman had expected. The boy still sat on the ground, staring at his brother, as if the good news hardly penetrated the gloom; and, after a disappointing silence, recurred to the most immediate cause of distress: 'Eight shillings and tenpence-halfpenny! Norman, if you would only lend it to me, you shall have all my tin till I have made it up—sixpence a week, and half-a-crown on New Year's Day.'

'I am not going to pay Mr. Axworthy's reckoning,' said Norman, rather angrily. 'You will never be better till you have told my father the whole.'

'Do you think they will send in the bill to my father?' asked Tom, in alarm.

'No, indeed! that is the last thing they will do,' said Norman; 'but I would not have you come to him only for such a sneaking reason.'

'But the girls would hear it. Oh! if I thought Mary and Margaret would ever hear it—Norman, I can't—'

Norman assured him that there was not the slightest reason that these passages should ever come to the knowledge of his sisters. Tom was excessively afraid of his father, but he could not well be more wretched than he was already; and he was brought to assent when Norman showed him that he had never been happy since the affair of the blotting-paper, when his father's looks and tones had become objects of dread to his guilty conscience. Was not the only means of recovering a place in papa's esteem to treat him with confidence?

Tom answered not, and would only shudder when his brother took upon him to declare that free confession would gain pardon even for the doings at the Green Man.

Tom had grown stupified and passive, and his sole dependence was on Norman, so, at last, he made no opposition when his brother offered to conduct him to his father and speak for him. The danger now was that Dr. May should not be forthcoming, and the elder brother was as much relieved, as the younger was dismayed, to see, through the drawing-room window, that he was standing beside Margaret.

'Papa, can you come and speak to me?' said Norman, at the door.

'Coming! What now?' said the Doctor, entering the hall. 'What, Tom, my boy, what is it?' as he saw the poor child white, cold, almost sick with apprehension, with every pulse throbbing, and looking positively ill. He took the chilly, damp hand, which shook nervously, and would fain have withdrawn itself.

'Come, my dear, let us see what is amiss;' and before Tom knew what he was doing, he had seated him on his knee, in the arm-chair in the study, and was feeling his pulse. 'There, rest your head! Has it not been aching all day?'

'I do not think he is ill,' said Norman; 'but there is something he thinks I had better tell you.'

Tom would fain have been on his feet, yet the support of that shoulder was inexpressibly comfortable to his aching temples, and he could not but wait for the shock of being roughly shaken and put down. So, as his brother related what had occurred, he crouched and trembled more and more on his father's breast, till, to his surprise, he found the other arm passed round him in support, drawing him more tenderly close.

'My poor little fellow!' said Dr. May, trying to look into the drooping face; 'I grieve to have exposed you to such usage as this? I little thought it of Stoneborough fellows!'

'He is very sorry,' said Norman, much distressed by the condition of the culprit.

'I see it—I see it plainly,' said Dr. May. . 'Tommy, my boy, why should you tremble when you are with me?'

'He has been in great dread of your being displeased.'

'My boy, do you not know how I forgive you?'

Tom clung round his neck, as if to steady himself. 'Oh! papa! I thought you would never—'

'Nay, you need never have thought so, my boy! What have I done that you should fear me?'

Tom did not speak, but nestled up to him with more confidence; 'There! that's better! Poor child! what he must have suffered! He was not fit for the place! I had thought him looking ill. Little did I guess the cause.'

'He says his head has ached ever since Sunday,' said Norman; 'and I believe he has hardly eaten or slept properly since.'

'He shall never be under their power again! Thanks to you, Norman. Do you hear that, Tommy?'

The answer was hardly audible. The little boy was already almost asleep, worn out with all he had undergone. Norman began to clear the sofa, that they might lay him down, but his father would not hear of disturbing him, and, sending Norman away, sat still for more than an hour, until the child slowly awoke, and scarcely recalling what had happened, stood up between his father's knees, rubbing his eyes, and looking bewildered.

' You are better now, my boy?'

'I thought you would be very angry,' slowly murmured Tom, as the past returned on him.

'Never, while you are sorry for your faults, and own them freely.'

'I'm glad I did,' said the boy, still half asleep. 'I did not know you would be so kind.'

'Ah! Tom, I fear it was as much my fault as yours, that you did not know it. But, my dear, there is a pardon that can give you better peace than mine.'

'I think,' muttered Tom, looking down—'I think I could say my prayers again now, if—'

'If what, my dear?'

'If you would help me, as mamma used—'

There could be but one response to this speech.

Tom was still giddy and unwell, his whole frame affected by the troubles of the last week, and Dr. May arranged him on the sofa, and desired him to be quiet, offering to send Mary to be his companion. Tom was languidly pleased, but renewed his entreaty, that his confession might be a secret from his sisters. Dr. May promised, and Mary, quite satisfied at being taken into favour, asked no questions, but spent the rest of the morning in playing at draughts with him, and, in having inflicted on her the history of the Bloody Fire King's Ghost—a work of Tom's imagination, which he was wont to extemporize, to the extreme terror of much enduring Mary.

When Dr. May had called Mary, he next summoned Norman, who found him in the hall, putting on his hat, and looking very stern and determined.

'Norman!' said he, hastily, 'don't say a word—It must be done—Hoxton must hear of this.'

Norman's face expressed utter consternation.

'It is not your doing. It is no concern of yours,' said Dr. May, walking impetuously into the garden. 'I find my boy ill, broken down, shattered—it is the usage of this crew of fellows—what right have I to conceal it—leave other people's sons to be so served?'

'I believe they did so to Tom out of ill-will to me,' said Norman, 'and because they thought he had ratted.'

'Hush! don't argue against it,' said Dr. May, almost petulantly. 'I have stood a great deal to oblige you, but I cannot stand this. When it is a matter of corruption, base cruelty—no, Norman, it is not right—not another word!'

Norman's words had not been many, but he felt a conviction that in spite of the dismay and pain to himself, Dr. May ought to meet with submission to his judgment, and he acquiesced by silence.

'Don't you see,' continued the Doctor; 'if they act thus, when your back is turned, what is to happen next half? 'Tis not for Tom's sake, but how could we justify it to ourselves, to expose other boys to this usage?'

'Yes,' said Norman, not without a sigh. 'I suppose it must be.'

'That is right,' said Dr. May, as if much relieved. 'I knew you must see it in that light. I do not mean to abuse your confidence.'

'No, indeed,' answered Norman, warmly.

'But you see yourself, that where the welfare of so many is at stake, it would be wickedness — yes, wickedness to be silent. Could I see that little fellow prostrated, trembling in my arms, and think of those scamps inflicting the same on other helpless children—away from their homes!'

'I see, I see!' said Norman, carried along by the indignation and tenderness that agitated his father's voice in his vehemence —'it is the only thing to be done.'

'It would be sharing the guilt to hide it,' said Dr. May.

'Very well,' said Norman, still reluctantly. 'What do you wish me to do? You see, as Dux, I know nothing about it. It happened while I was away.'

'True, true,' said his father. 'You have learnt it as brother, not as senior boy. Yes, we had better have you out of the matter. It is I who complain of their usage of my son.'

'Thank you,' said Norman, with gratitude.

'You have not told me the names of these fellows. No, I had best not know them.'

'I think it might make a difference,' hesitated Norman.

'No, no, I will not hear them. It ought to make none. The fact is the same, be they who they may.'

The Doctor let himself out at the garden-gate, and strode off at a rapid pace, conscious, perhaps, in secret, that if he did not at once yield to the impulse of resentment, good-nature would overpower the sense of justice. His son returned to the house with a heavy sigh, yet honouring the generosity that had respected his scruples, when merely his own worldly loss was involved, but set them aside when the good of others was concerned. By-and-by Dr. May reappeared. The head-master had been thoroughly roused to anger, and had begged at once to examine May junior, for whom his father was now come.

Tom was quite unprepared for such formidable consequences of his confession, and began by piteous tears and sobs, and when these had, with some difficulty, been pacified, he proved to be really so unwell and exhausted, that his father could not take him to Minster-street, and was obliged to leave him to his brother's keeping, while he returned to the school.

Upon this, Dr. Hoxton came himself; and the sisters were extremely excited and alarmed by the intelligence that he was in the study with papa and Tom.

Then away went the gentlemen; and Mary was again called to comfort Tom, who, broken down into the mere longing for sympathy, sobbed out all his troubles to her, while her eyes expanded more and more in horror, and her soft heart giving way, she cried quite as pitifully, and a great deal more loudly; and so the other sisters learnt the whole, and Margaret was ready for her father, when he came in, in the evening, harassed and sorrowful. His anger was all gone now; and he was excessively grieved at finding that the ringleaders, Samuel Axworthy and Edward Anderson, could, in Dr. Hoxton's opinion, receive no sentence but expulsion, which was to be pronounced on them on Monday.

Sam Axworthy was the son of a low, uneducated man, and his best chance had been the going to this school; but he was of a surly, obstinate temper, and showed so little compunction, that even such superabundant kindness as Dr. May's could not find compassion for him; especially since it had appeared that Tom had been by no means the only victim, and that he had often been the promoter of the like mal-practices, which many boys were relieved to be forced to expose.

For Edward Anderson, however, or rather for his mother, Dr. May was very sorry, and had even interceded for his pardon; but Dr. Hoxton, though slow to be roused, was far less placable than the other Doctor, and would not hear of anything but the most rigorous justice.

'Poor Mrs. Anderson, with her pride in her children!' Flora spoke it with a shade of contemptuous pity, but it made her father groan.

'I shall never be able to look in her face again! I shall never see that boy without feeling that I have ruined him.'

'He needed nobody to do that for him,' said Flora.

'With every disadvantage!' continued Dr. May; 'unable even to remember his father! Why could I not be more patient and forbearing?'

'Oh! papa!' was the general cry—Norman's voice giving decision to the sisters' exclamation.

'Perhaps,' said Margaret, 'the shock may be the best thing for him.'

'Right, Margaret,' said her father. 'Sometimes such a thing is the first that shows what a course of evil really is.'

'They are an affectionate family, too,' said Margaret, 'and his mother's grief may have an effect on him.'

'If she does not treat him as an injured hero,' said Flora; 'besides, I see no reason for regret. These are but two, and the school is not to be sacrificed to them.'

'Yes,' said Norman; 'I believe that Ashe will be able to keep much better order without Axworthy. It is much better as it is, but Harry will be very sorry to hear it, and I wish this half was over.'

Poor Mrs. Anderson! her shower of notes rent the heart of the one Doctor, but were tossed carelessly aside by the other. On that Sunday, Norman held various conversations with his probable successor, Ashe, a gentle, well-disposed boy, hitherto in much dread of the post of authority, but owning, that, in Axworthy's absence the task would be comparatively easy, and that Anderson would probably originate far less mischief.

Edward Anderson himself fell in Norman's way in the street, and was shrinking aside, when a word, of not unfriendly greeting, caused him to quicken his steps, and say, hesitatingly, 'I say, how is August?'

'Better, thank you; he will be all right in a day or two.'

'I say, we would not have bullied him so, if he had not been in such a fright at nothing.'

'I dare say not.'

'I did not mean it all; but that sort of thing makes a fellow go on,' continued Edward, hanging down his head, very sorrowful and downcast.

'If it had only been fair bullying; but to take him to that place—to teach him falsehood—' said Norman.

Edward's eyes were full of tears; he almost owned the whole. He had not thought of such things, and then Axworthy—It was more evident from manner than words, that the boy did repent, and was greatly overcome both by his own disgrace, and his mother's distress, wishing earnestly to redeem his character, and declaring, from the bottom of his heart, that he would avoid his former offences. He was emboldened at last to say, with hesitation, 'Could not you speak to Doctor Hoxton for me?'

'My father has said all he could in your behalf.'

Edward's eye glanced towards Norman in wonder, as he recollected that the Mays must know that a word from him would have saved Norman from unjust punishment, and the loss of the scholarship, and he said, 'good night,' and turned aside to his own home, with a heavy sigh.

Norman took another turn, looked up at the sky, twisted his hands together in perplexity, mumbled something about hating to do a thing when it was all for no use, and then marched off towards Minster-street, with a pace like his father's the day before.

When he came forth again from Dr. Hoxton's study, he did not believe that his intercession had produced the least effect, and there was a sense of vexation at the position which he had assumed. He went home, and said nothing on the subject; but when, on Monday, the school was assembled, and the judgment announced, it was Axworthy alone whose friends had been advised to remove him.

Anderson received a severe punishment, as did all those who had shared in the revel at the Green Man. Even Tom, and another little boy, who had been likewise drawn in, were obliged to stay within narrow bounds, and to learn heavy impositions; and a stern reprimand and exhortation were given to the school collectively. Anderson, who had seen from the window that turn towards Minster-street, drew his own conclusions, and was not insensible to the generosity that had surpassed his hopes, though to his faltering attempt at thanks, Norman replied that he did not believe it was owing to him, and never exposed himself to Flora's wonder, by declaring at home what he had done.

So the last weeks of the half-year passed away with the boys in a subdued but hopeful manner, and the reformation, under Norman's auspices, progressed so well, that Ashe might fairly expect to reap the benefit of the discipline, established at so much cost.

Mr. Wilmot had looked on, and given his help, but he was preparing to leave Stoneborough, and there was great concern at the parting with such a friend. Ethel, especially, mourned the loss to Cocksmoor, and, for though hers had been the executive part, his had been the head, and he was almost equally grieved to go from the newly-begun work.

Margaret lamented the loss of her kind counsellor, and the ready hearer of her anxieties for the children. Writing could ill supply the place of their conversations, and she feared likewise that her father would feel the want of his companionship. The promise of visits, and the intercourse kept up by Tom's passing to and fro, was the best consolation.

Poor Margaret had begun to flag, both in strength and spirits, as winter approached, but there came a revival in the shape of 'Ship Letters!' Alan wrote cheerfully and graphically, with excellent accounts of Harry, who, on his side, sent very joyous and characteristic despatches, only wishing that he could present Mary with all the monkeys and parrots he had seen at Rio, as well as the little ruby-crested hummingbirds, that always reminded him of Miss Rivers.

With the Christmas holidays, Hector Ernescliffe came from Eton, as to a home, and was received by Margaret as a sort of especial charge. It was pretty to see how he turned to her as something peculiarly his own, and would sit on a footstool by her, letting himself be drawn into confidence, and dwelling on his brother's past doings, and on future schemes for Maplewood. For the rest, he restored to the house the atmosphere of boy, which had somewhat departed with Harry. Mary, who had begun to be tamed down, ran more wild than ever, to the utter despair of Miss Winter; and Tom, now that his connexion with the Whichcote foundation was over, and he was no more cowed by the sight of his tyrants, came out in a new light. He put on his boy-nature, rioted like the rest, acquired colour in his cheeks, divested his jacket of perpetual dust, had his hair cut, brushed up a crest on his head, and ran about no longer a little abject, but a merry lad.

Ethel said it was a change from Horrid-locks to Harfagre; Margaret said little, but, like her father, she blessed Norman in her heart for having given back the boy to his father's confidence, and saved him so far from the terrible course of deceit and corruption. She could not much take to heart the mad exploits of the so-called boys, even though she spent three hours in heart-beatings on Christmas Eve, when Hector, Mary, Tom, Blanche, and the dog Toby, were lost the whole day. However they did come back at six o'clock, having been deluded by an old myth of George Larkins, into starting for a common, three miles beyond

Cocksmoor, in search of mistletoe, with scarlet berries, and yellow holly, with leaves like a porcupine! Failing these wonders, they had been contenting themselves with scarlet holly, in the Drydale plantations, when a rough voice exclaimed, 'Who gave you leave to take that?' whereupon Tom had plunged into a thicket, and nearly 'scratched out both his eyes;' but Hector boldly standing his ground, with Blanche in his hand, the woodman discovered that here was the Miss Mary, of whom his little girls talked so much, thereupon cut down the choicest boughs, and promised to leave a full supply at Dr. May's. Margaret could have been angry at the taking the young ladies on so mad a scheme, but then Mary was so happy, and as to Hector, how scold him, when he had lifted Blanche over every ditch, and had carried her home one mile on his back, and another, Queen's-cushion fashion, between him and Mary?

Flora, meanwhile, went her own way. The desire of compensating for what had past with Norman, led to great civilities from Dr. and Mrs. Hoxton, which nobody was at liberty to receive except Flora. Pretty, graceful, and pleasing, she was a valuable companion to a gentle little, inane lady, with more time and money than she knew what to do with; and Mrs. Hoxton, who was of a superior grade to the Stoneborough ladies in general, was such a chaperon as Flora was glad to secure. Dr. May's old loyal feelings could not help regarding her notice of his daughter as a favour and kindness, and Margaret could find no tangible objections, nor any precedent from her mother's conduct, even had any one had the power to interfere with one so quiet, reasonable, and determined as Flora.

So the intimacy became closer and closer, and as the winter passed on, Flora gradually became established as the dear friend and assistant, without whom Mrs. Hoxton could give no party. Further, Flora took the grand step of setting up a copperplate and cards of 'Miss Flora May,' went out frequently on morning calls with Mrs. Hoxton and her bay horses, and when Dr. May refused his share of invitations to dinner with the neighbours in the country, Flora generally found that she could go under the Hoxtons' guardianship.

END OF PART I.

THE DAISY CHAIN.

PART II.

THE DAISY CHAIN.

CHAPTER I.

'Now have I then eke this condicion,
That above all the flouris in the mede;
Then love I most these flouris white and rede,
Soche that men callin daisies in our town.
To them have I so great affection,
As I said erst, when comin is the Maie,
That in my bed there dawith me no daie
That I am up and walking in the mede,
To see this floure agenst the sunne sprede.'—CHAUCER.

'THAT is better!' said Margaret, contemplating a butterfly of the penwiper class, whose constitution her dexterous needle had been rendering less ricketty than Blanche had left it.

Margaret still lay on the sofa, and her complexion had assumed the dead white of habitual ill-health. There was more languor of manner, and her countenance, when at rest, and not under the eye of her father, had a sadness of expression, as if any hopes that she might once have entertained, were fading away. The years of Alan Ernescliffe's absence that had elapsed had rather taken from her powers than added to them. Nevertheless, the habit of cheerfulness and sympathy had not deserted her, and it was with a somewhat amused glance that she turned towards Ethel, as she heard her answer by a sigh.

These years had dealt more kindly with Etheldred's outward appearance. They had rounded her angles, softened her features, and tinged her cheeks with a touch of red, that took off from the surrounding sallowness. She held herself better, had learnt to keep her hair in order, and the more womanly dress, plain though it was, improved her figure more than could have been hoped in the days of her lank, gawky girlhood. No one could call her pretty, but her countenance had something more than ever pleasing in the animated and thoughtful expression on those marked features. She was sitting near the window, with a book, a dictionary and pencil, as she replied to Margaret, with the sigh that made her sister smile.

'Poor Ethel! I condole with you.'

'And I wonder at you!' said Ethel, 'especially as Flora and Mrs. Hoxton say it is all for your sake;' then, nettled by Margaret's laugh, 'such a nice occupation for her, poor thing, as if you were Mrs. Hoxton, and had no resource but fancy-work.'

'You know I am base enough to be so amused,' said Margaret; 'but, seriously, Ethel dear, I cannot bear to see you so much hurt by it. I did not know you were really grieved.'

'Grieved! I am ashamed—sickened!' cried Ethel, vehemently. 'Poor Cocksmoor! As soon as anything is done there, Flora must needs go about implying that we have set some grand work in hand, and want only means—'

'Stop, Ethel; Flora does not boast.'

'No, she does not boast. I wish she did! That would be straightforward and simple; but she has too good taste for that —so she does worse—she tells a little, and makes that go a long way, as if she were keeping back a great deal! You don't know how furious it makes me!'

'Ethel!'

'So,' said Ethel, disregarding, 'she stirs up all Stoneborough to hear what the Miss Mays are doing at Cocksmoor. So the Ladies' Committee must needs have their finger in! Much they cared for the place when it was wild and neglected! But they go to inspect Cherry and her school—Mrs. Ledwich and all— and, back they come, shocked—no system, no order, the mistress untrained, the school too small, with no apparatus! They all run about in despair, as if we had ever asked them to help us. And so Mrs. Hoxton, who cares for poor children no more than for puppy-dogs, but who can't live without useless work, and has filled her house as full of it as it can hold, devises a bazaar—a field for her trumpery, and a show-off for all the young ladies; and Flora treats it like an inspiration! Off they trot, to the old Assembly Rooms. I trusted that the smallness of them would have knocked it on the head; but, still worse, Flora's talking of it makes Mr. Rivers think it our pet scheme; so, what does he do but offer his park, and so we are to have a regular fancy fair, and Cocksmoor school will be founded in vanity and frivolity! But, I believe you like it!'

'I am not sure of my own feeling,' said Margaret. 'It has been settled without our interposition, and I have never been able to talk it over calmly with you. Papa does not seem to disapprove.'

'No,' said Ethel. 'He *will* only laugh, and say it will spare him a great many of Mrs. Hoxton's nervous attacks. He thinks of it nearly as I do, at the bottom, but I cannot get him to stop it, nor even to say he does not wish Flora to sell.'

'I did not understand that you really had such strong objections,' said Margaret. 'I thought it was only as a piece of folly, and—'

'And interference with *my* Cocksmoor?' said Ethel. 'I had better own to what may be wrong personal feeling at first.'

'I can hardly call it wrong,' said Margaret, tenderly, 'considering what Cocksmoor is to you, and what the Ladies' Committee is.'

'Oh! Margaret, if the lawful authority—if a good clergyman would only come, how willingly would I work under him. But Mrs. Ledwich and—it is like having all the Spaniards and savages spoiling Robinson Crusoe's desert island!'

'It is not come to that yet,' said Margaret; 'but, about the Fancy Fair. We all know that the school is very much wanted.'

'Yes, but I hoped to wait in patience and perseverance, and do it at last.'

'All yourself?'

'Now Margaret! you know I was glad of Alan's help.'

'I should *think* so!' said Margaret. 'You need not make a favour of that!'

'Yes, but, don't you see, that came as almsgiving, in the way which brings a blessing. We want nothing to make us give money and work to Cocksmoor. We do all we can already; and I don't want to get a fine bag or a ridiculous pincushion in exchange!'

'Not you, but—'

'Well, for the rest. If they like to offer their money, well and good, the better for them; but why must they not give it to Cocksmoor—but for that unnatural butterfly of Blanche's, with black pins for horns, that they will go and sell at an extortionate rate.'

'The price will be given for Cocksmoor's sake!'

'Pooh! Margaret. Do you think it is for Cocksmoor's sake that Lady Leonora Langdale and her fine daughter come down from London? Would Mrs. Hoxton spend the time in making frocks for Cocksmoor children that she does in cutting out paper, and stuffing glass bottles with it? Let people be honest—alms, or pleasure, or vanity! let them say which they mean; but don't make charity the excuse for the others; and, above all, don't make my poor Cocksmoor the victim of it.'

'This is very severe,' said Margaret, pausing, almost confounded. 'Do you think no charity worth having but what is given on unmixed motives? Who, then, could give?'

'Margaret—we see much evil arise in the best-planned insti-
tutions; nay, in what are not human. Don't you think we
ought to do our utmost to have no flaw in the foundation?
Schools are not such perfect places that we can build them without fear, and, if the means are to be raised by a bargain for
amusement—if they are to come from frivolity instead of self-
denial, I am afraid of them. I do not mean that Cocksmoor has
not been the joy of my life, and of Mary's, but that was not
because we did it for pleasure.'

'No!' said Margaret, sighing, 'you found pleasure by the
way. But why did you not say all this to Flora.'

'It is of no use to talk to Flora,' said Ethel; 'she would say
it was high-flown and visionary. Oh! she wants it for the
bazaar's own sake, and that is one reason why I hate it.'

'Now, Ethel!'

'I do believe it was very unfortunate for Flora that the Hoxtons took to patronizing her, because Norman would not be
patronized. Ever since it began, her mind has been full of
visitings, and parties, and county families, and she has left off
the home usefulness she used to care about.'

'But you are old enough for that,' said Margaret. 'It would
be hard to keep Flora at home, now that you can take her place,
and do not care for going out. One of us must be the repre-
sentative Miss May, you know, and keep up the civilities; and
you may think yourself lucky it is not you.'

'If it was only that, I should not care, but I may as well tell
you, Margaret, for it is a weight to me. It is not the mere
pleasure in gaieties—Flora cares for them, in themselves, as little
as I do—nor is it neighbourliness, as a duty to others, for, you
may observe, she always gets off any engagement to the Wards,
or any of the town folk, to whom it would be a gratification to
have her—she either eludes them, or sends me. The thing is,
that she is always trying to be with the great people, the county
set, and I don't think that is the safe way of going on.'

Margaret mused sadly. 'You frighten me, Ethel! I cannot
say it is not so, and these are so like the latent faults that dear
mamma's letter spoke of—'

Ethel sat meditating, and, at last, said, 'I wish I had not told
you! I don't always believe it myself, and it is so unkind, and
you will make yourself unhappy too. I ought not to have
thought it of her! Think of her ever-ready kindness and help-
fulness; her pretty courteous ways to the very least; her
obligingness and tact!'

'Yes,' said Margaret, 'she is one of the kindest people there
is, and I am sure that she thought the gaining funds for Cocks-

moor was the best thing to be done, that you would be pleased, and a great deal of pleasant occupation provided for us all.'

'That is the bright side, the surface side,' said Ethel.

'And not an untrue one,' said Margaret; 'Meta will not be vain, and will work the more happily for Cocksmoor's sake. Mary and Blanche, poor Mrs. Boulder, and many good ladies who hitherto have not known how to help Cocksmoor, will do so now with a good will, and though it is not what we should have chosen, I think we had better take it in good part.'

'You think so?'

'Yes, indeed I do. If you go about with that dismal face and strong disapproval, it will really seem as if it was the having your dominion meddled with that you dislike. Besides, it is putting yourself forward to censure what is not absolutely wrong in itself, and that cannot be desirable.'

'No,' said Ethel, 'but I cannot help being sorry for Cocksmoor. I thought patience would prepare the way, and the means be granted in good time, without hastiness—only earnestness.'

'You have made a picture for yourself,' said Margaret, gently. 'Yes, we all make pictures for ourselves, and we are the foremost figures in them; but they are taken out of our hands, and we see others putting in rude touches, and spoiling our work, as it seems; but, by-and-by, we shall see that it is all guided.'

Ethel sighed. 'Then having protested to my utmost against this concern, you think I ought to be amiable about it.'

'And to let poor Mary enjoy it. She would be so happy, if you would not bewilder her by your gloomy looks, and keep her to the hemming of your endless glazed calico bonnet strings.'

'Poor old Mary! I thought that was by her own desire.'

'Only her dutiful allegiance to you; and, as making pincushions is nearly her greatest delight, it is cruel to make her think it, in some mysterious way, wrong and displeasing to you.'

Ethel laughed, and said, 'I did not think Mary was in such awe of me. I'll set her free, then. But, Margaret, do you really think I ought to give up my time to it?'

'Could you not just let them have a few drawings, or a little bit of your company work—just enough for you not to annoy every one, and seem to be testifying against them. You would not like to vex Meta.'

'It will go hard, if I do not tell Meta my mind. I cannot bear to see her deluded.'

'I don't think she is,' said Margaret; 'but she does not set her face against what others wish. As papa says of his dear little hummingbird, she takes the honey, and leaves the poison.'

'Yes; amid all that enjoyment, she is always choosing the

good, and leaving the evil; always sacrificing something, and then being happy in the sacrifice!'

'No one would guess it was a sacrifice, it is so joyously done—least of all Meta herself.'

'Her coming home from London was exactly a specimen of that sacrifice—and no sacrifice,' said Ethel.

'What was that?' said Norman, who had come up to the window unobserved, and had been listening to their few last sentences.

'Did not you hear of it? It was a sort of material turning away from vanity that made me respect the little rival Daisy, as much as I always admired her.'

'Tell me,' said Norman. 'When was it?'

'Last spring. You know Mr. Rivers is always ill in London; indeed, papa says it would be the death of him; but Lady Leonora Langdale thinks it dreadful that Meta should not go to all the gaieties; and, last year, when Mrs. Larpent was gone, she insisted on her coming to stay with her for the season. Now, Meta thought it wrong to leave her father alone, and wanted not to have gone at all, but, to my surprise, Margaret advised her to yield, and go for some short fixed time.'

'Yes,' said Margaret, 'as all her elders thought it right, I did not think we could advise her to refuse absolutely. Besides, it was a promise.'

'She declared she would only stay three weeks, and the Langdales were satisfied, thinking that, once in London, they should keep her. They little knew Meta, with her pretty ways of pretending that her resolution is only spoilt-child wilfulness. None of you quite trusted her, did you, Margaret? Even papa was almost afraid, though he wanted her very much to be at home; for poor Mr. Rivers was so low and forlorn without her, though he would not let her know, because Lady Leonora had persuaded him to think it was all for her good.'

'What did they do with her in London?' asked Norman.

'They did their utmost,' said Ethel. 'They made engagements for her, and took her to parties and concerts—those she did enjoy very much—and she had lessons in drawing and music, but whenever she wanted to see any exhibitions, or do anything, they always said there was time to spare. I believe it was very charming, and she would have been very glad to stay, but she never would promise, and she was always thinking of her positive duty at home. She seemed afterwards to think of her wishes to remain almost as if they had been a sin; but she said—dear little Meta—that nothing had ever helped her so much as that she used to say to herself, whenever she was going out, "I renounce the world." It came to a crisis at last, when Lady Leonora wanted her to be presented—the drawing-room was after the end of her three weeks—and she held out against it; though her aunt laughed at her, and treated her as if she was a silly, shy child. At last, what do you think Meta did? She went to her uncle, Lord Cosham, and appealed to him to say whether there was the least necessity for her to go to court.'

'Then she gained the day?' said Norman.

He was delighted with that spirited, yet coaxing way of hers, and admired her determination. He told papa so himself—for you must know, when he heard all Meta had to say, he called her a very good girl, and said he would take her home himself on the Saturday she had fixed, and spend Sunday at Abbotstoke. Oh! he was perfectly won by her sweet ways. Was not it lucky? for before this Lady Leonora had written to Mr. Rivers, and obtained from him a letter, which Meta had the next day, desiring her to stay for the drawing-room. But Meta knew well enough how it was, and was not to be conquered that way; so she said she must go home to entertain her uncle, and that if her papa really wished it, she would return on Monday.'

'Knowing well that Mr. Rivers would be only too glad to keep her.'

'Just so. How happy they both did look, when they came in here on their way from the station where he had met her! How she danced in, and how she sparkled with glee!' said Margaret, 'and poor Mr. Rivers was quite tremulous with the joy of having her back, hardly able to keep from fondling her every minute, and coming again into the room after they had taken leave, to tell me that his little girl had preferred her home, and her poor old father, to all the pleasures in London. Oh! I was so glad they came! That was a sight that did one good! And then, I fancy Mr. Rivers is a wee bit afraid of his brother-in-law, for he begged papa and Flora to come home and dine with them, but Flora was engaged to Mrs. Hoxton.'

'Ha! Flora!' said Norman, as if he rather enjoyed her losing something through her going to Mrs. Hoxton. 'I suppose she would have given the world to go!'

'I was so sorry,' said Ethel, 'but I had to go instead, and it was delightful. Papa made great friends with Lord Cosham, while Mr. Rivers went to sleep after dinner, and I had such a delightful wandering with Meta, listening to the nightingales, and hearing all about it. I never knew Meta so well before.'

'And there was no more question of her going back?' said Norman.

'No, indeed! She said, when her uncle asked in joke, on Monday morning, whether she had packed up to return with him, Mr. Rivers was quite nervously alarmed the first moment, lest she should intend it.'

'That little Meta,' said Margaret. 'Her wishes for substantial use have been pretty well realized!'

'Um!' said Ethel.

'What do you mean?' said Norman, sharply. 'I should call her present position the perfection of feminine usefulness.'

'So perhaps it is,' said Ethel; 'but though she does it beautifully, and is very valuable; to be the mistress of a great luxurious house, like that, does not seem to me the subject of aspirations like Meta's.'

'Think of the contrast with what she used to be,' said Margaret, gently, 'the pretty, gentle, playful toy that her father brought her up to be, living a life of mere accomplishments and self-indulgence; kind certainly, but never so as to endure any disagreeables, or make any exertion. But as soon as she entered into the true spirit of our calling, did she not begin to seek to live the sterner life, and train herself in duty? The quiet way she took always seemed to me the great beauty of it. She makes duties of her accomplishments by making them loving obedience to her father.'

'Not that they are not pleasant to her?' interposed Norman.

'Certainly,' said Margaret, 'but it gives them the zest, and confidence that they are right, which one could not have in such things merely for one's own amusement.'

'Yes,' said Ethel, 'she does more; she told me one day that one reason she liked sketching was, that looking into nature always made Psalms and Hymns sing in her ears, and so with her music and her beautiful copies from the old Italian devotional pictures. She says our papa taught her to look at them so as to see more than the mere art and beauty.'

'Think how diligently she measures out her day,' said Margaret; 'getting up early, to be sure of time for reading her serious books, and working hard at her tough studies.'

'And what I care for still more,' said Ethel, 'her being bent on learning plain needlework and doing it for her poor people. She is so useful amongst the cottagers at Abbotstoke!'

'And a famous little mistress of the house,' added Margaret. 'When the old housekeeper went away two years ago, she thought she ought to know something about the government of the house; so she asked me about it, and proposed to her father that the new one should come to her for orders, and that she should pay the wages and have the accounts in her hands. Mr. Rivers thought it was only a freak, but she has gone on steadily; and I assure you, she has had some difficulties, for she has come to me about them. Perhaps Ethel does not believe in them?'

'No, I was only thinking how I should hate ordering those fanciful dinners for Mr. Rivers. I know what you mean, and how she had difficulties about sending the maids to Church, and in dealing with the cook who did harm to the other servants, and yet sent up dinners that he liked, and how puzzled she was how to avoid annoying him. Oh! she has got into a peck of troubles by making herself manager.'

'And had she not been the Meta she is, she would either have fretted, or thrown it all up, instead of humming briskly through all. She never was afraid to speak to any one,' said Margaret, 'that is one thing; I believe every difficulty makes the spirit bound higher, till she springs over it, and finds it, as she says, only a pleasure.'

'She need not be afraid to speak,' said Ethel, 'for she always does it well and winningly. I have seen her give a reproof in so firm and kind a way, and so bright in the instant of forgiveness.'

'Yes,' said Margaret, 'she does those disagreeable things as well as Flora does in her way.'

'And yet,' said Ethel, 'doing things well does not seem to be a snare to her.'

'Because,' whispered Margaret, 'she fulfils more than almost any one—the—" Whatsoever ye do, do all to the glory of God."'

'Do you know,' said Norman, suddenly, 'the derivation of Margarita?'

'No further than those two pretty meanings, the pearl and the daisy,' said Ethel.

'It is from the Persian Mervarid, child of light,' said Norman; and, with a sudden flush of colour, he returned to the garden.

'A fit meaning for one who carries sunshine with her,' said Margaret. 'I feel in better tune, for a whole day, after her bright eyes have been smiling on me.'

'You want no one to put you in tune,' said Ethel, fondly— 'you, our own pearl of light.'

'No, call me only an old faded daisy,' said Margaret, sadly.

'Not a bit, only our moon, *la gran Margarita*,' said Ethel.

'I hear the real Daisy coming!' exclaimed Margaret, her face lighting up with pleasure as the two youngest children entered, and indeed, little Gertrude's golden hair, round open face, fresh red and white complexion, and innocent looks, had so much likeness to the flower, as to promote the use of the pet name, though protests were often made in favour of her proper appellation. Her temper was daisy-like too, serene and loving, and able to bear a great deal of spoiling, and resolve as they might, who was not her slave?

Miss Winter no longer ruled the school-room. Her sway had been brought to a happy conclusion by a proposal from a widowed sister to keep house with her; and Ethel had reason to rejoice that Margaret had kept her submissive under authority, which, if not always judicious, was both kind and conscientious.

Upon the change, Ethel had thought that the lessons could easily be managed by herself and Flora; while Flora was very anxious for a finishing governess, who might impart singing to herself, graces to Ethel, and accomplishments to Mary and Blanche.

Dr. May, however, took them both by surprise. He met with a family of orphans, the eldest of whom had been qualifying herself for a governess, and needed nothing but age and finish; and in ten minutes after the project had been conceived, he had begun to put it in execution, in spite of Flora's prudent demurs.

Miss Bracy was a gentle, pleasing young person, pretty to look at, with her soft olive complexion, and languid pensive eyes, obliging and intelligent; and the change from the dry, authoritative Miss Winter, was so delightful, that unedifying contrasts were continually being drawn. Blanche struck up a great friendship for her at once; Mary, always docile, ceased to be piteous at her lessons; and Ethel moralised on the satisfaction of having sympathy needed instead of repelled, and did her utmost to make Miss Bracy feel at home—and like a friend—in her new position.

For herself, Ethel had drawn up a beautiful time-table, with all her pursuits and duties most carefully balanced, after the pattern of that which Margaret Rivers had made by her advice, on the departure of Mrs. Larpent, who had been called away by the ill-health of her son. Meta had adhered to hers in an exemplary manner, but she was her own mistress in a manner that could hardly be the lot of one of a large family.

Margaret had become subject to languor and palpitations, and the headship of the household had fallen entirely upon Flora, who, on the other hand, was a person of multifarious occupations, and always had a great number of letters to write, or songs to copy and practise, which, together with her frequent visits to Mrs. Hoxton, made her glad to devolve, as much as she could, upon her younger sister; and, "O Ethel, you will not mind just doing this for me," was said often enough to be a tax upon her time.

Moreover, Ethel perceived that Aubrey's lessons were in an unsatisfactory state. Margaret could not always attend to them, and suffered from them when she did; and he was bandied about between his sisters and Miss Bracy in a manner that made him neither attentive nor obedient.

On her own principle, that to embrace a task heartily, renders it no longer irksome, she called on herself to sacrifice her studies and her regularity as far as was needful, to make her available for home requirements. She made herself responsible for Aubrey, and, after a few battles with his desultory habits, made him a very promising pupil, inspiring so much of herself into him, that he was, if anything, overfull of her classical tastes. In fact, he had such an appetite for books, and dealt so much in precocious wisdom, that his father was heard to say, 'Six years old! It is a comfort that he will soon forget the whole.'

Gertrude was also Ethel's pupil, but learning was not at all in her line; and the sight of 'Cobwebs to Catch Flies,' or of the venerated 'Little Charles,' were the most serious clouds, that made the Daisy pucker up her face, and infuse a whine into her voice.

However, to-day, as usual, she was half dragged, half coaxed, through her day's portion of the discipline of life, and then sent up for her sleep, while Aubrey's two hours were spent in more agreeable work, such as Margaret could not but enjoy hearing —so spirited was Ethel's mode of teaching—so eager was her scholar.

His play afterwards consisted in fighting o'er again the siege of Troy on the floor, with wooden bricks, shells, and the survivors of a Noah's ark, while Ethel read to Margaret until Gertrude's descent from the nursery, when the only means of preventing a dire confusion in Aubrey's camp was, for her elder sisters to become her playfellows, and so spare Aubrey's temper. Ethel good-humouredly gave her own time, till their little tyrant trotted out to make Norman carry her round the garden on his back.

So sped the morning till Flora came home, full of the intended bazaar, and Ethel would fain have taken refuge in puzzling out her Spanish, had she not remembered her recent promise to be gracious.

The matter had been much as she had described it. Flora had a way of hinting at anything she thought creditable, and thus the Stoneborough public had become aware of the exertions of the May family on behalf of Cocksmoor.

The plan of a Fancy Fair was started. Mrs. Hoxton became more interested than was her wont, and Flora was enchanted at the opening it gave for promoting the welfare of the forlorn district. She held a position which made her hope to direct the whole. As she had once declared, with truth, it only had depended on themselves, whether she and her sisters should sink to the level of the Andersons, and their set, or belong to the county society; and her tact had resulted in her being decidedly—as the little dress-maker's apprentice amused Ethel by saying—'One of our most distinguished patronesses'—a name that had stuck by her ever since.

Margaret looked on passively, inclined to admire Flora in everything, yet now and then puzzled; and her father in his simple-hearted way, felt only gratitude and exultation in the kindness that his daughter met with. As to the bazaar, if it had been started in his own family he might have weighed the objections; but, as it was not his daughter's own concern, he did not trouble himself about it, only regarding it as one of the many vagaries of the ladies of Stoneborough.

So the scheme had been further developed, till now Flora came in with much to tell. The number of stalls had been finally fixed. Mrs. Hoxton undertook one, with Flora as an aide-de-camp, and some nieces to assist; Lady Leonora was to *chaperon* Miss Rivers; and a third, to Flora's regret, had been allotted to Miss Cleveland, a good-natured, merry, elderly heiress, who would, Flora feared, bring on them the whole 'Stoneborough crew.' And then she began to reckon up the present resources—drawings, bags, and pincushions. 'That chip hat you plaited for Daisy, Margaret, you must let us have that. It will be lovely, trimmed with pink.'

'Do you wish for this?' said Ethel, heaving up a grim mass of knitting.

'Thank you,' said Flora; 'so ornamental, especially the original performance in the corner, which you would perpetrate, in spite of my best efforts.'

'I shall not be offended if you despise it. I only thought you might have no more scruple in robbing Granny Hall than in robbing Daisy.'

'Pray send it. Papa will buy it as your unique performance'

'No; you shall tell me what I am to do.'

'Does she mean it?' said Flora, turning to Margaret. 'Have you converted her? Well done! Then, Ethel, we will get some pretty *batiste*, and you and Mary shall make some of those nice sun-bonnets, which you really do to perfection.'

'Thank you. That is a more respectable task than I expected. People may have something worth buying,' said Ethel, who, like all the world, felt the influence of Flora's tact.

'I mean to study the useful,' said Flora. 'The Cleveland set will be sure to deal in frippery, and I have been looking over

Mrs. Hoxton's stores, where I see quite enough for mere decoration. There are two splendid vases in potichomanie, in an Etruscan pattern, which are coming for me to finish.'

'Mrs. Taylor, at Cocksmoor, could do that for you,' said Ethel. 'Her two phials, stuffed with chintz patterns and flour, are quite as original and tasteful.'

'Silly work,' said Flora, 'but it makes a fair show.'

'The essence of Vanity Fair,' said Ethel.

'It won't do to be satirical overmuch,' said Flora. 'You won't get on without humouring your neighbours' follies.'

'I don't want to get on.'

'But you want—or, at least, I want—Cocksmoor to get on.'

Ethel saw Margaret looking distressed, and, recalling her resolution, she said, 'Well, Flora, I don't mean to say any more about it. I see it can't be helped, and you all think you intend it for good; so there's an end of the matter, and I'll do anything for you in reason.'

'Poor old King Ethel!' said Flora, smiling in an elder-sisterly manner. 'You will see, my dear, your views are very pretty, but very impracticable, and it is a work-a-day world after all—even papa would tell you so. When Cocksmoor school is built, then you may thank me. I do not look for it before.'

CHAPTER II.

'Knowledge is second, not the first;
A higher hand must make her mild,
If all be not in vain, and guide
Her footsteps, moving side by side,
With wisdom; like the younger child,
For she is earthly of the mind,
But knowledge heavenly of the soul.'—IN MEMORIAM.

ETHELDRED had not answered her sister, but she did not feel at all secure that she should have anything to be thankful for, even if the school were built.

The invasion of Cocksmoor was not only interference with her own field of action, but it was dangerous to the improvement of her scholars. Since the departure of Mr. Wilmot, matters at Stoneborough National School had not improved, though the Miss Andersons talked a great deal about progress, science, and lectures.

The Ladies' Committee were constantly at war with the mistresses, and that one was a veteran who endured them, or whom they could endure beyond her first half-year. No mistress had stayed a year within the memory of any girl now at school. Perpetual change prevented any real education, and, as each lady held different opinions and proscribed all books not agreeing thereto, everything 'dogmatical' was excluded; and, as Ethel said, the children learnt nothing but facts about lions and steam-engines, while their doctrine varied with that of the visitor for the week. If the ten generals could only have given up to Miltiades, but alas! there was no Miltiades. Mr. Ramsden's health was failing, and his neglect told upon the parish in the dreadful evils reigning unchecked, and engulfing many a child whom more influential teaching might have saved. Mental arithmetic, and the rivers of Africa, had little power to strengthen the soul against temptation.

The scanty attendance at the National School attested the indifference with which it was regarded, and the borderers voluntarily patronized Cherry Elwood, and thus had, perhaps, first aroused the emulation that led Mrs. Ledwich on a visit of inspection, to what she chose to consider as an offshoot of the National School.

The next day, she called upon the Miss Mays. It was well that Ethel was not at home. Margaret received the lady's horrors at the sight of the mere crowded cottage kitchen, the stupid untrained mistress, without an idea of method, and that impertinent woman, her mother! Miss Flora and Miss Ethel must have had a great deal to undergo, and she would lose no time in convening the Ladies' Committee, and appointing a successor to 'that Elwood,' as soon as a fit room could be erected for her use. If Margaret had not known that Mrs. Ledwich sometimes threatened more than she could accomplish, she would have been in despair. She tried to say a good word for Cherry, but was talked down, and had reason to believe that Mrs. Elwood had mortally offended Mrs. Ledwich.

The sisters had heard the other side of the story at Cocksmoor. Mrs. Elwood would not let them enter the school, till they had heard how that there Mrs. Ledwich had come in, and treated them all as if it was her own place—how she had found fault with Cherry before all the children, and, as good as said, she was not fit to keep a school. She had even laid hands on one of the books, and said that she should take it home, and see whether it were a fit one for them to use; whereupon Mrs. Elwood had burst out in defence—it was Miss Ethel May's book, and should not be taken away—it was Miss Ethel as she looked to—and when it seemed that Mrs. Ledwich had said something disparaging of Miss Ethel, either as to youth, judgment, or doctrine, Mrs. Elwood had fired up into a declaration that 'Miss Ethel was a real lady—that she was! and that no real lady would ever come prying into other folk's work, and finding fault with what wasn't no business of theirs,' with more of a personal nature, which Flora could not help enjoying, even while she regretted it.

Cherry was only too meek, as her mother declared. She had said not a word, except in quiet reply, and being equally terrified by the attack and defence, had probably seemed more dull than was her wont. Her real feelings did not appear till the next Sunday, when, in her peaceful conference with Margaret, far from the sound of storms, she expressed that she well knew that she was a poor scholar, and that she hoped the young ladies would not let her stand in the children's light, when a better teacher could be found for them.

'I am sure!' cried Ethel, as she heard of this, 'it would be hard to find such a teacher in humility! Cherry bears it so much better than I, that it is a continual reproof!'

As to the dulness, against which Ethel used to rail, the attacks upon it had made her erect it into a positive merit; she was always comparing the truth, honesty, and respectful demeanour of Cherry's scholars, with the notorious faults of the National-school girls, as if these defects had been implanted either by Mrs. Ledwich, or by geography. It must be confessed that the violence of partisanship did not make her a pleasant companion.

However, the interest of the bazaar began somewhat to divert the current of the ladies' thoughts, and Ethel found herself walking day after day to Cocksmoor, unmolested by further reports of Mrs. Ledwich's proceedings. Richard was absent, preparing for Ordination, but Norman had just returned home for the Long Vacation, and, rather than lose the chance of a conversation with her, had joined her and Mary in a walk to Cocksmoor.

His talk was chiefly of Settlesham, old Mr. Wilmot's parish, where he had been making a visit to his former tutor, and talking over the removal to Eton of Tom, who had well responded to the care taken of him, and with his good principles confirmed, and his character strengthened, might be, with less danger, exposed to trial.

It had been a visit such as to leave a deep impression on Norman's mind. Sixty years ago, old Mr. Wilmot had been what he now was himself—an enthusiastic and distinguished Balliol man, and he had kept up a warm, clear-sighted interest in Oxford, throughout his long life. His anecdotes, his recollections, and comments on present opinions had been listened to with great eagerness, and Norman had felt it an infinite honour to give the venerable old man his arm, and to be shown by him his curious collection of books. His parish, carefully watched for so many years, had been a study not lost upon Norman, who detailed

particulars of the doings there, which made Ethel sigh to think
of the contrast with Stoneborough.—In such conversation they
came to the entrance of the hamlet, and Mary, with a scream of
joy, declared that she really believed that he was going to help
them! He did not turn away.

'Thank you!' said Ethel, in a low voice, from the bottom of
her heart.

She used him mercifully, and made the lessons shorter than
usual, but when they reached the open air again, he drew a long
breath; and when Mary eagerly tried for a compliment to their
scholars, asked if they could not be taught the use of eyelids.

'Did they stare?' said Ethel. 'That's one advantage of being
blind. No one can stare me out of countenance.'

'Why were you answering all your questions yourself?' asked
Mary.

'Because no one else would,' said Norman.

'You used such hard words,' replied Ethel.

'Indeed! I thought I was very simple.'

'O!' cried Mary, 'there were derive, and instruction, and
implicate, and—oh, so many.'

'Never mind,' said Ethel, seeing him disconcerted. 'It is
better for them to be drawn up, and you will soon learn their
language. If we only had Una M'Carthy here!'

'Then you don't like it?' said Mary, disappointed.

'It is time to learn not to be fastidious,' he answered. 'So,
if you will help me—'

'Norman, I am so glad!' said Ethel.

'Yes,' said Norman, 'I see now that these things that puff us
up, and seem the whole world to us now, all end in nothing but
such as this! Think of old Mr. Wilmot, once carrying all before
him, but deeming all his powers well bestowed in fifty years'
teaching of clowns!'

'Yes,' replied Ethel, very low. 'One soul is worth—' and she
paused from the fullness of thought.

'And these things, about which we are so elated, do not render
us so fit to teach—as you, Mary, or as Richard.'

'They do,' said Ethel. 'The ten talents were doubled.
Strength tells in power. The more learning, the fitter to teach
the simplest thing.'

'You remind me of old Mr. Wilmot, saying that the first thing
he learnt at his parish was, how little his people knew; the
second, how little he himself knew.'

So Norman persevered in the homely discipline that he had
chosen for himself, which brought out his deficiency in practical

work in a manner which lowered him in his own eyes, to a degree almost satisfactory to himself. He was not indeed without humility, but his nature was self-contemplative and self-conscious enough to perceive his superiority of talent, and it had been the struggle of his life to abase this perception, so that it was actually a relief not to be obliged to fight with his own complacency in his powers. He had learnt not to think too highly of himself—he had yet to learn to 'think soberly.' His aid was Ethel's chief pleasure through this somewhat trying summer, it might be her last peaceful one at Cocksmoor.

That bazaar! How wild it had driven the whole town, and even her own home!

Margaret herself, between good-nature and feminine love of pretty things, had become ardent in the cause. In her unvaried life, it was a great amusement to have so many bright, elegant things exhibited to her, and Ethel was often mortified to find her excited about some new device, or drawn off from 'rational employments,' to complete some trifle.

Mary and Blanche were far worse. From the time that consent had been given to the fancy-work being carried on in the school-room, all interest in study was over. Thenceforth, lessons were a necessary form, gone through without heart or diligence. These were reserved for pasteboard boxes, beplastered with rice and sealing-wax, for alum-baskets, dressed dolls, and every conceivable trumpery; and the governess was as eager as the scholars.

If Ethel remonstrated, she hurt Miss Bracy's feelings, and this was a very serious matter to both parties.

The governess was one of those morbidly sensitive people, who cannot be stopped when once they have begun arguing that they are injured. Two women together, each with the last-word instinct, have no power to cease; and, when the words are spent in explaining—not in scolding—conscience is not called in to silence them, and nothing but dinner, or a thunder-storm can check them. All Ethel's good sense was of no avail; she could not stop Miss Bracy, and, though she might resolve within herself, that real kindness would be to make one reasonable reply, and then quit the subject, yet, on each individual occasion, such a measure would have seemed mere impatience and cruelty. She found that if Miss Winter had been too dry, Miss Bracy went to the other extreme, and demanded a manifestation of sympathy and return to her passionate attachment that perplexed Ethel's undemonstrative nature. Poor good Miss Bracy, she little imagined how often she added to the worries of her dear Miss Ethel, all for want of self-command.

Finally, as the lessons were less and less attended to, and the needs of the stall became more urgent, Dr. May and Margaret concurred in a decision, that it was better to yield to the mania, and give up the studies till they could be pursued with a willing mind.

Ethel submitted, and only laughed with Norman at the display of treasures, which the girls went over daily, like the 'House that Jack built,' always starting from 'the box that Mary made.' Come when Dr. May would into the drawing-room, there was always a line of penwipers laid out on the floor, bags pendant to all the table-drawers, anti-macassars laid out everywhere.

Ethel hoped that the holidays would create a diversion, but Mary was too old to be made into a boy, and Blanche drew Hector over to the feminine party, setting him to gum, gild, and paste all the contrivances which, in their hands, were mere feeble gimcracks, but which now became fairly sound, or, at least, saleable.

The boys also constructed a beautiful little ship from a print of the Alcestis, so successfully, that the Doctor promised to buy it; and Ethel grudged the very sight of it to the bazaar.

Tom, who, in person, was growing like a little shadow or model of Norman, had, unlike him, a very dexterous pair of hands, and made himself extremely useful in all such works. On the other hand, the Cleveland stall seemed chiefly to rely for brilliance on the wit of Harvey Anderson, who was prospering at his College, and the pride of his family. A great talker, and extremely gallant, he was considered a far greater acquisition to a Stoneborough drawing-room, than was the silent, bashful Norman May, and rather looked down on his brother Edward, who, having gone steadily through the school, was in the attorney's office, and went on quietly and well, colouring up gratefully whenever one of the May family said a kind word to him.

CHAPTER III.

' Any silk, any thread,
  Any toys for your head,
Of the newest and finest wear-a ?
    Come to the pedlar,
    Money's a medlar,
  That doth utter all men's wear-a.'—WINTER'S TALE.

'THIS one day, and it will be over ! and we shall be rational again !' thought Ethel, as she awoke.

Flora was sleeping at the Grange, to be ready for action in the morning, and Ethel was to go early with Mary and Blanche, who were frantic to have a share in the selling. Norman and the boys were to walk at their own time, and the children to be brought later by Miss Bracy. The Doctor would be bound by no rules.

It was a pattern day, bright, clear, warm, and not oppressive, perfect for an out-of-doors *fête;* and Ethel had made up her mind to fulfil her promise to Margaret of enjoying herself. In the brilliant sunshine, and between two such happy sisters, it would have been surly, indeed, not to enter into the spirit of the day; and Ethel laughed gaily with them, and at their schemes and hopes; Blanche's heart being especially set on knowing the fate of a watch-guard of her own construction.

Hearing that the ladies were in the gardens, they repaired thither at once. The broad, smooth bowling-green lay before them; a marquee, almost converted into a bower, bounding it on either side, while, in the midst arose, gorgeous and delicious, a pyramid of flowers—contributions from all the hot-houses in the neighbourhood—to be sold for the benefit of the bazaar. Their freshness and fragrance gave a brightness to the whole scene, while shrinking from such light, as only the beauteous works of nature could bear, was the array accomplished by female fingers.

Under the wreathed canopies were the stalls, piled up with bright colours, most artistically arranged. Ethel, with her over-minute knowledge of every article, could hardly believe that yonder glowing Eastern pattern of scarlet, black and blue, was, in fact, a judicious mosaic of penwipers that she remembered, as shreds begged from the tailor, that the delicate lace-work consisted of Miss Bracy's perpetual anti-macassars, and that the potichomanie could look so dignified and Etruscan.

'Here you are!' cried Meta Rivers, springing to meet them. 'Good girls, to come early. Where's my little Daisy?'

'Coming in good time,' said Ethel. 'How pretty it all looks!'

'But where's Flora—where's my watch-guard?' anxiously asked Blanche.

'She was here just now,' said Meta, looking round. 'What a genius she is, Ethel! She worked wonders all yesterday, and let the Miss Hoxtons think it was all their own doing, and she was out before six this morning, putting finishing touches.'

'Is this your stall?' said Ethel.

'Yes, but it will not bear a comparison with hers. It has a lady's-maid-look by the side of hers. In fact, Bellairs and my aunt's maid did it chiefly, for papa was rather ailing yesterday, and I could not be out much.'

'How is he now?'

'Better; he will walk round by-and-by. I hope it will not be too much for him.'

'Oh! what beautiful *things!*' cried Mary, in ecstasy, at what she was forced to express by the vague substantive, for her imagination had never stretched to the marvels she beheld.

'Aye! we have been lazy, you see, and so Aunt Leonora brought down all these smart concerns. It is rather like Howell and James's, isn't it?'

In fact, Lady Leonora's marquee was filled with costly knick-knacks, which, as Meta justly said, had not half the grace and appropriate air that reigned where Flora had arranged, and where Margaret had worked, with the peculiar freshness and finish that distinguished everything to which she set her hand.

Miss Cleveland's counter was not ill set-out, but it wanted the air of ease and simplicity, which was even more noticeable than the perfect taste of Flora's wares. If there had been nothing facetious, the effect would have been better, but there was nothing to regret, and the whole was very bright and gay.

Blanche could hardly look; so anxious was she for Flora, to tell her the locality of her treasure.

'There she is,' said Meta, at last. 'George is fixing that branch of evergreen for her.'

'Flora! I did not know her,' cried each sister, amazed, while Mary added, 'Oh! how nice she looks.'

It was the first time of seeing her in the white muslin, and broad chip-hat—which all the younger saleswomen of the bazaar had agreed to wear. It was a most becoming dress, and she did, indeed, look strikingly elegant, and well dressed. It occurred to Ethel, for the first time, that Flora was decidedly the reigning beauty of the bazaar—no one but Meta Rivers could be compared to her, and that little lady was on so small a scale of perfect finish, that she seemed fit to act the fairy, where Flora was the enchanted princess.

Flora greeted her sisters eagerly, while Meta introduced her brother—a great contrast to herself, though not without a certain comeliness, tall and large, with ruddy complexion, deep lustreless black eyes, and a heavy straight bush of black moustache, veiling rather thick lips. Blanche reiterated inquiries for her watch-guard.

'I don't know,' said Flora. 'Somewhere among the rest.'

Blanche was in despair.

'You may look for it,' said Flora—who, however hurried, never failed in kindness—'if you will touch nothing.'

So Blanche ran from place to place in restless dismay, that caused Mr. George Rivers to ask what was the matter.

'The guards! the guards!' cried Blanche; whereupon he fell into a fit of laughter, which disconcerted her, because she could not understand him, and made Ethel take an aversion to him on the spot.

However, he was very good-natured; he took Blanche's reluctant hand, and conducted her all along the stall, even proceeding to lift her up where she could not command a view of the whole, thus exciting her extreme indignation. She shook herself out when he set her down, surveyed her crumpled muslin, and believed he took her for a *little* girl! She ought to have been flattered when the quest was successful, and he insisted on knowing which was *the* guard, and declared that he should buy it. She begged him to do no such thing, and he desired to know why—insisting that he would give five shillings—fifteen—twenty-five for that one! till she did not know whether he was in earnest, and she doing an injury to the bazaar!

Meantime, the hour had struck, and Flora had placed Mrs. Hoxton in a sheltered spot, where she could take as much, or as little trouble, as she pleased. Lady Leonora, and Miss Langdale, came from the house, and, with the two ladies'-maids in the background, took up their station with Miss Rivers. Miss Cleveland called her party to order, and sounds of carriages were heard approaching.

Mary and Blanche disbursed the first money spent in the 'Fancy Fair;' Mary, on a blotting-book for Harry, to be placed among the presents, to which she added on every birthday, while Blanche bought a sixpenny gift for every one, with more attention to the quantity than the quality. Then came a revival of her anxieties for the guards, and while Mary was simply desirous of the fun of being a shopwoman, and was made happy by Meta Rivers asking her help, Blanche was in despair, till she had sidled up to the neighbourhood of the 'guards,' and her piteous looks had caused good-natured Mrs. Hoxton to invite her to assist, when she placed herself close to the precious object.

A great fluttering of heart went to that manœuvre, but still felicity could not be complete. That great troublesome Mr. George Rivers, had actually threatened to buy nothing but that one watch-chain, and Blanche's eye followed him everywhere with fear, lest he should come that way. And there were many other gentlemen—what could they want but watch-guards, and of them—what—save this paragon?

Poor Blanche; what did she not undergo whenever any one

cast his eye over her range of goods? and this was not seldom, for there was an attraction in the pretty little eager girl, glowing and smiling. One old gentleman actually stopped, handled the guards themselves, and asked their price.

'Eighteen-pence,' said Blanche, colouring and faltering, as she held up one in preference.

'Eh! is not this the best?' said he, to the lady on his arm.

'Oh! please, take that instead?' exclaimed Blanche, in extremity.

'And why?' asked the gentleman, amused.

'I made this,' she answered.

'Is that the reason I must not have it?'

'No, don't tease her,' the lady said, kindly; and the other was taken.

'I wonder for what it is reserved!' the lady could not help saying, as she walked away.

'Let us watch her for a minute or two. What an embellishment children are! Ha! don't you see—the little maid is fluttering and reddening now! How pretty she looks! Ah! I see! here's the favoured! Don't you see that fine bronzed lad—Eton —one can see at a glance! It is a little drama. They are pretending to be strangers. He is turning over the goods with an air, she trying to look equally careless, but what a pretty carnation it is! Ha! ha! he has come to it—he has it! Now the acting is over, and they are having their laugh out! How joyously! What next! Oh! she begs off from keeping shop—she darts out to him, goes off in his hand—I declare that is the prettiest sight in the whole fair! I wonder who the little demoiselle can be?'

The great event of the day was over now with Blanche, and she greatly enjoyed wandering about with Hector and Tom. There was a post-office at Miss Cleveland's stall, where, on paying sixpence, a letter could be obtained to the address of the inquirer. Blanche had been very anxious to try, but Flora had pronounced it nonsense; however, Hector declared that Flora was not his master, tapped at the sliding panel, and charmed Blanche by what she thought a most witty parody of his name as Achilles Lionsrock, Esquire. When the answer came from within, 'Ship letter, sir, double postage,' they thought it almost uncanny; and Hector's shilling was requited by something so like a real ship letter, that they had some idea that the real post had somehow transported itself thither. The interior was decidedly oracular, consisting of this one line, 'I counsel you to persevere in your laudable undertaking.'

Hector said he wished he had any laudable undertaking, and Blanche tried to persuade Tom to try his fortune, but he pronounced that he did not care to hear Harvey Anderson's trash—he knew his writing, though disguised, and had detected his shining boots below the counter. There Mr. George Rivers came up, and began to tease Blanche about the guards, asking her to take his fifteen shillings—or five-and-twenty, and who had got that *one*, which alone he wanted; till the poor child, after standing perplexed for some moments, looked up with spirit, and said, 'You have no business to ask,' and, running away, took refuge in the back of Mrs. Hoxton's marquee, where she found Ethel packing up for Miss Hoxton's purchasers, and confiding to her that Mr. George Rivers was a horrid man, she ventured no more from her protection. She did, indeed, emerge, when told that papa was coming with Aubrey and Daisy, and Miss Bracy, and she had the pleasure of selling to them some of her wares, Dr. May bargaining with her to her infinite satisfaction; and little Gertrude's blue eyes opened to their full width, not understanding what could have befallen her sisters.

'And what is Ethel doing?' asked the Doctor.

'Packing up parcels, papa,' and Ethel's face was raised, looking very merry.

'Packing parcels! How long will they last tied up?' said Dr. May, laughing.

'Lasting is the concern of nothing in the fair, papa,' answered she, in the same tone.

For Ethel was noted as the worst packer in the house; but, having offered to wrap up a pincushion, sold by a hurried Miss Hoxton, she became involved in the office for the rest of the day—the same which Bellairs and her companion performed at the Langdale counter. Flora was too ready and dexterous to need any such aid, but the Miss Hoxtons were glad to be spared the trouble; and Blanche, whose fingers were far neater than Ethel's, made the task much easier, and was kept constant to it by her dread of the dark moustache, which was often visible near their tent, searching, she thought, for her.

Their humble employment was no sinecure; for this was the favourite stall with the purchasers of better style, since the articles were, in general, tasteful, and fairly worth the moderate price set on them. At Miss Cleveland's counter, there was much noisy laughter—many jocular cheats—tricks for gaining money, and refusals to give change; and it seemed to be very popular with the Stoneborough people, and to carry on a brisk trade. The only languor was in Lady Leonora's quarter—the articles were too costly, and hung on hand; nor were the ladies sufficiently well known, nor active enough, to gain custom, excepting Meta, who drove a gay traffic at her end of the stall, which somewhat redeemed the general languor.

Her eyes were, all the time, watching for her father, and, suddenly perceiving him, she left her trade in charge of the delighted and important Mary, and hastened to walk round with him, and show him the humours of the fair.

Mary, in her absence, had the supreme happiness of obtaining Norman as a customer. He wanted a picture for his rooms at Oxford, and water-coloured drawings were, as Tom had observed, suitable staple commodities for Miss Rivers. Mary tried to make him choose a brightly-coloured pheasant, with a pencil back-ground; and, then, a fine foaming sea-piece, by some unknown Lady Adelaide, that much dazzled her imagination; but nothing would serve him but a sketch of an old cedar-tree, with Stoneborough Minster in the distance, and the Welsh hills beyond, which Mary thought a remarkable piece of bad taste, since—could he not see all that any day of his life? and was it worth while to give fourteen shillings and sixpence for it? But he said it was all for the good of Cocksmoor, and Mary was only too glad to add to her hoard of coin; so she only marvelled at his extravagance, and offered to take care of it for him; but, to this, he would not consent. He made her pack it up for him, and had just put the whitey-brown parcel under his arm, when Mr. Rivers and his daughter came up, before he was aware. Mary proudly advertised Meta that she had sold something for her.

'Indeed! What was it?'

'Your great picture of Stoneborough!' said Mary.

'Is that gone? I am sorry you have parted with that, my dear; it was one of your best,' said Mr. Rivers, in his soft, sleepy, gentle tone.

'Oh! papa, I can do another. But, I wonder! I put that extortionate price on it, thinking no one would give it, and so that I should keep it for you. Who has it, Mary?'

'Norman, there. He would have it, though I told him it was very dear.'

Norman, pressed near them by the crowd, had been unable to escape, and stood blushing, hesitating, and doubting whether he ought to restore the prize, which he had watched so long, and obtained so eagerly.

'Oh! it is you?' said Mr. Rivers, politely. 'O, no, do not think of exchanging it. I am rejoiced that one should have it who can appreciate it. It was its falling into the hands of a stranger that I disliked. You think with me, that it is one of her best drawings.'

'Yes, I do,' said Norman, still rather hesitating.

'She did that with C——, when he was here last year. He taught her very well. Have you that other here, that you took with him, my dear? The view from the gate, I mean.'

'No, dear papa. You told me not to sell that.'

'Ah! I remember; that is right. But there are some very pretty copies from Prout here.'

While he was seeking them, Meta contrived to whisper—'If you could persuade him to go in-doors—-this confusion of people is so bad for him, and I must not come away. I was in hopes of Dr. May, but he is with the little ones.'

Norman signed comprehension, and Meta said, 'Those copies are not worth seeing, but, you know, papa, you have the originals in the library.'

Mr. Rivers looked pleased, but was certain that Norman could not prefer the sketches to this gay scene. However, it took very little persuasion to induce him to do what he wished, and he took Norman's arm, crossed the lawn, and arrived in his own study, where it was a great treat to him to catch any one who would admire his accumulation of prints, drawings, coins, &c.; and his young friend was both very well amused, and pleased to be setting Miss Rivers's mind at ease on her father's account. It was not till half-past four that Dr. May knocked at the door, and stood surprised at finding his son there. Mr. Rivers spoke warmly of the young Oxonian's kindness in leaving the fair for an old man, and praised Norman's taste in art. Norman rose to take leave, but still thought it incumbent on him to offer to give up the picture, if Mr. Rivers set an especial value on it. But Mr. Rivers went to the length of being very glad that it was in his possession, and added to it a very pretty drawing of the same size, by a noted master, which had been in the water-colour exhibition; and, while Norman walked away, well pleased, Mr. Rivers began to extol him to his father, as a very superior and sensible young man, of great promise, and began to wish George had the same turn.

Norman, on returning to the Fancy Fair, found the world in all the ardour of raffles. Lady Leonora's contributions were the chief prizes, which attracted every one, and, of course, the result was delightfully incongruous. Poor Ethel, who had been persuaded to venture a shilling to please Blanche, who had spent all her own, obtained the two jars in potichomanie, and was regarding them with a face worth painting. Harvey Anderson had a doll, George Rivers a wooden monkey that jumped over a stick; and, if Hector Ernescliffe was enchanted at winning a beautiful mother-of-pearl inlaid work-box, which he had vainly wished to buy for Margaret, Flora only gained a match-box of her own, well-known always to miss fire, but which had been decided to be good enough for the bazaar.

By fair means or foul, the commodities were cleared off; and, while the sunbeams faded from the trodden grass, the crowds disappeared, and the vague compliment—'a very good bazaar,' was exchanged between the lingering sellers and their friends.

Flora was again to sleep at the Grange, and return the next day, for a committee to be held over the gains, which were not yet fully ascertained. So Dr. May gathered his flock together, and packed them, boys and all, into the two conveyances, and Ethel bade Meta good-night, almost wondering to hear her merry voice say, 'It has been a delightful day—has it not? It was so kind of your brother to take care of papa.'

'Oh! it was delightful,' echoed Mary; 'and I took one pound fifteen and sixpence!'

'I hope it will do great good to Cocksmoor,' added Meta; 'but, if you want real help, you know, you must come to us.'

Ethel smiled, but hurried her departure, for she saw Blanche again tormented by Mr. George Rivers, to know what had become of the guard, telling her that, if she would not say, he should be furiously jealous.

Blanche hid her face on Ethel's arm when they were in the carriage, and almost cried with indignant 'shamefastness.' That long-desired day had not been one of unmixed happiness to her, poor child, and Ethel doubted whether it had been so to any one, except, indeed, to Mary, whose desires never soared so high but that they were easily fulfilled, and whose placid content was not easily wounded. All she was wishing now was, that Harry were at home to receive his paper-case.

The return to Margaret was real pleasure. The narration of all that had passed was an event to her. She was so charmed with her presents of every degree; things, unpleasant at the time, could, by drollery in the relating, be made mirthful fun ever after; Dr. May and the boys were so comical in their observations—Mary's wonder and simplicity came in so amusingly—and there was such merriment at Ethel's two precious jars, that she could hardly wish they had not come to her. On one head they were all agreed—in dislike of George Rivers, whom Mary pronounced to be a detestable man, and, when gently called to order by Margaret, defended it, by saying that Miss Bracy said it was better to detest than to hate, while Blanche coloured up to the ears, and hid herself behind the arm-chair; and Dr. May qualified the censure by saying, he believed there was no great harm in the youth, but that he was shallow-brained and extravagant, and, having been born in the days when Mr. Rivers had been working himself up in the world, had not had so good an education as his little half-sister.

'Well, what are you thinking of?' said her father, laying his hand on Ethel's arm, as she was wearily and pensively putting together the scattered purchases, before going up to bed.

'I was thinking, papa, that there is a great deal of trouble taken, in this world, for a very little pleasure.'

'The trouble is the pleasure, in most cases, most misanthropical Miss!'

'Yes, that is true; but if so, why cannot it be taken for some good?'

'They meant it to be good,' said Dr. May. 'Come, I cannot have you severe and ungrateful.'

'So I have been telling myself, papa, all along; but, now that the day has come, and I have seen what jealousies, and competitions, and vanities, and disappointments it has produced—not even poor little Blanche allowed any comfort—I am almost sick at heart, with thinking Cocksmoor was the excuse!'

'Spectators are more philosophical than actors, Ethel. Others have not been tying parcels all day.'

'I had rather do that than—but that is the "Fox and the Grapes,"' said Ethel, smiling. 'What I mean is, that the real gladness of life is not in these great occasions of pleasure, but in the little side delights, that come in the midst of one's work, don't they, papa? Why is it worth while to go and search for a day's pleasuring?'

'Ethel, my child! I don't like to hear you talk so,' said Dr. May, looking anxiously at her. 'It may be too true, but it is not youthful, nor hopeful. It is not as your mother or I felt in our young days, when a treat was a treat to us, and gladdened our hearts long before and after. I am afraid you have been too much saddened with loss and care—'

'O, no, papa!' said Ethel, rousing herself, though speaking huskily. 'You know I am your merry Ethel. You know I can be happy enough—only at home—'

And Ethel, though she had tried to be cheerful, leant against his arm, and shed a few tears.

'The fact is, she is tired out,' said Dr. May, soothingly, yet half laughing. 'She is not a beauty or a grace, and she is thoughtful and quiet, and so she moralizes, instead of enjoying, as the world goes by. I dare say a night's rest will make all the difference in the world.'

'Ah! but there is more to come. That Ladies' Committee at Cocksmoor!'

'They are not there yet, Ethel. Good-night, you tired little cynic.'

CHAPTER IV.

' Back then, complainer . . . . . .
Go, to the world return, nor fear to cast
Thy bread upon the waters, sure at last
In joy to find it after many days.'—CHRISTIAN YEAR.

THE next day Ethel had hoped for a return to reason, but, behold, the world was cross! The reaction of the long excitement was felt; Gertrude fretted, and was unwell; Aubrey was pettish at his lessons; and Mary and Blanche were weary, yawning and inattentive; every straw was a burthen, and Miss Bracy had feelings.

Ethel had been holding an interminable conversation with her in the school-room, interrupted at last by a summons to speak to a Cocksmoor woman at the back-door; and she was returning from the kitchen, when the Doctor called her into his study.

'Ethel! what is all this? Mary has found Miss Bracy in floods of tears in the school-room, because she says you told her she was ill-tempered.'

'I am sure you will be quite as much surprised,' said Ethel, somewhat exasperated, 'when you hear that you lacerated her feelings yesterday.'

'I? Why, what did I do?' exclaimed Dr. May.

'You showed your evident want of confidence in her.'

'I? What can I have done?'

'You met Aubrey and Gertrude in her charge, and you took them away at once to walk with you.'

'Well?'

'Well, that was it. She saw you had no confidence in her.'

'Ethel, what on earth can you mean? I saw the two children dragging on her, and I thought she would see nothing that was going on, and would be glad to be released; and I wanted them to go with me, and see Meta's gold pheasants.'

'That was the offence. She has been breaking her heart all this time, because she was sure, from your manner, that you were displeased to see them alone with her—eating *bon-bons*, I believe—and therefore took them away.'

'Daisy is the worse for her *bon-bons*, I believe, but the overdose of them rests on my shoulders. I do not know how to believe you, Ethel. Of course, you told her, nothing of the kind crossed my mind, poor thing.'

'I told her so, over and over again, as I have done forty times before, but her feelings are always being hurt!'

'Poor thing, poor thing! no doubt it is a trying situation, and she is sensitive. Surely you are all forbearing with her?'

'I hope we are,' said Ethel; 'but how can we tell what vexes her?'

'And what is this, of your telling her she was ill-tempered?' asked Dr. May, incredulously.

'Well, papa,' said Ethel, softened, yet wounded by his thinking it so impossible. 'I had often thought I ought to tell her that these sensitive feelings of hers were nothing but temper; and perhaps—indeed I know I do—I partake of the general fractiousness of the house to-day, and I did not bear it so patiently as usual. I did say that I thought it wrong to foster her fancies; for if she looked at them coolly, she would find they were only a form of pride and temper.'

'It did not come well from you, Ethel,' said the Doctor, looking vexed.

'No, I know it did not,' said Ethel, meekly; 'but oh! to have these janglings once a week, and to see no end to them!'

'Once a week?'

'It is really as often, or more often!' said Ethel. 'If any of us criticize anything the girls have done, if there is a change in any arrangement, if she thinks herself neglected—I can't tell you what little matters suffice; she will catch me, and argue with me, till—oh! till we are both half-dead, and yet cannot stop ourselves.'

'Why do you argue?'

'If I could only help it!'

'Bad management,' said the Doctor, in a low musing tone. 'You want a head!'—and he sighed.

'Oh! papa, I did not mean to distress you. I would not have told you, if I had remembered—but I am worried to-day, and off my guard—'

'Ethel, I thought you were the one on whom I could depend for hearing everything.'

'These were such nonsense!'

'What may seem nonsense to you, is not the same to her.

You must be forbearing, Ethel. Remember that dependance is prone to morbid sensitiveness, especially in those who have a humble estimate of themselves.'

'It seems to me that touchiness is more pride than humility,' said Ethel, whose temper, already not in the smoothest state, found it hard that, after having long borne patiently with these constant arguments, she should find Miss Bracy made the chief object of compassion.

Dr. May's chivalrous feeling caused him to take the part of the weak, and he answered, 'You know nothing about it. Among our own kin, we can afford to pass over slights, because we are sure the heart is right—we do not know what it is to be among strangers, uncertain of any claim to their esteem or kindness. Sad! sad!' he continued, as the picture wrought on him. 'Each trifle seems a token one way or the other! I am very sorry I grieved the poor thing yesterday. I must go and tell her so at once!'

He put Ethel aside, and knocked at the school-room door, while Ethel stood, mortified. 'He thinks I have been neglecting, or speaking harshly to her! For fifty times that I have borne with her maundering, I have, at last, once told her the truth: and for that I am accused of want of forbearance! Now he will go and make much of her, and pity her, till she will think herself an injured heroine, and be worse than ever; and he will do away with all the good of my advice, and want me to ask her pardon for it—but that I never will. It was only the truth, and I will stick to it.'

'Ethel!' cried Mary, running up to her, then slackening her pace, and whispering; 'You did not tell Miss Bracy she was ill-tempered.'

'No—not exactly. How could you tell papa I did?'

'She said so. She was crying, and I asked what was the matter, and she said, my sister Ethel said, she was ill-tempered.'

'She made a great exaggeration, then,' said Ethel.

'I am sure she was very cross all day!' said Mary.

'Well, that is no business of yours,' said Ethel, pettishly. 'What now? Mary! don't look out at the street window.'

'It is Flora—the Grange carriage—' whispered Mary, as the two sisters made a precipitate retreat into the drawing-room.

Meanwhile, Dr. May had been in the school-room. Miss Bracy had ceased her tears before he came—they had been her retort on Ethel, and she had not intended the world to know of them. Half-disconcerted, half-angry, she heard the Doctor approach. She was a gentle, tearful woman, one of those who are often called meek, under an erroneous idea, that meekness consisted in making herself exceedingly miserable under every kind of grievance; and she now had a sort of melancholy satisfaction in believing that the young ladies had fabricated an exaggerated complaint of her temper, and that she was going to become injured innocence. To think herself accused of a great wrong, excused her from perceiving herself guilty of a lesser one.

'Miss Bracy,' said Dr. May, entering with his frank, sweet look; 'I am concerned that I vexed you by taking the children to walk with me yesterday. I thought such little brats would be troublesome to any but their spoiling papa, but they would have been in safer hands with you. You would not have been as weak as I was, in regard to sugar-plums.'

Such amends as these confused Miss Bracy, who found it pleasanter to be lamentable with Ethel, than to receive a full apology, for her imagined offence, from the master of the house. Feeling both small and absurd, she murmured something of 'oh no;' and 'being sure,' and hoped he was going, so that she might sit down to pity herself, for those girls having made her appear so ridiculous.

No such thing! Dr. May put a chair for her, and sat down himself, saying with a smile, 'You see, you must trust us sometimes, and overlook it, if we are less considerate than we might be. We have rough, careless habits with each other, and forget that all are not used to them.'

Miss Bracy exclaimed, 'Oh! no, never, they were most kind.'

'We wish to be,' said Dr. May, 'but there are little neglects —or you think there are. I will not say there are none, for that would be answering too much for human nature, or that they are fanciful—for that would be as little comfort as to tell a patient that the pain is only nervous—'

Miss Bracy smiled, for she could remember instances when, after suffering much at the time, she had found the affront imaginary.

He was glad of that smile, and proceeded. 'You will let me speak to you, as to one of my own girls? To them I should say, use the only true cure. Don't brood over vexations, small or great, but think of them as trials that, borne bravely, become blessings.'

'Oh! but Dr. May!' she exclaimed, shocked; 'nothing in your house could call for such feelings.'

'I hope we are not very savage,' he said, smiling; 'but, indeed, I still say it is the safest rule. It would be the only one if you were really among unkind people; and, if you take so much to heart an unlucky neglect of mine, what would you do if the slight were a true one?'

'You are right; but my feelings were always over sensitive;' and this she said with a sort of complacency.

'Well, we must try to brace them,' said Dr. May, much as if prescribing for her. ' Will not you believe in our confidence and esteem, and harden yourself against any outward unintentional piece of incivility?'

She felt as if she could at that moment.

'Or at least, try to forgive and forget them. Talking them over only deepens the sense of them, and discussions do no good to any one. My daughters are anxious to be your best friends, as I hope you know.'

'Oh! they are most kind—'

'But, you see, I must say this—' added Dr. May, somewhat hesitating—' as they have no mother to—to spare all this—' and, then, growing clearer, he proceeded, ' I must beg you to be for-bearing with them, and not perplex yourself and them with argu-ing on what cannot be helped. They have not the experience that could enable them to finish such a discussion without unkind-ness; and it can only waste the spirits, and raise fresh subjects of regret. I must leave you—I hear myself called.'

Miss Bracy began to be sensible that she had somewhat abused Ethel's patience; and the unfortunate speech about the source of her sensitiveness, did not appear to her so direfully cruel as at first. She hoped every one would forget all about it, and resolved not to take umbrage so easily another time, or else be silent about it, but she was not a person of much resolution.

The Doctor found that Meta Rivers and her brother had brought Flora home, and were in the drawing-room, where Margaret was hearing another edition of the history of the fair, and a bye-play was going on, of teasing Blanche about the chain.

George Rivers was trying to persuade her to make one for him; and her refusal came out at last, in an almost passionate key, in the midst of the other conversation—'No! I say—no!'

'Another no, and that will be yes.'

'No! I won't! I don't like you well enough!'

Margaret gravely sent Blanche and the other children away, to take their walk, and the brother and sister, soon after, took leave, when Flora called Ethel to hasten to the Ladies' Committee, that they might arrange the disposal of the one hundred and fifty pounds, the amount of their gains.

'To see the fate of Cocksmoor,' said Ethel.

'Do you think I cannot manage the Stoneborough folk?' said

Flora, looking radiant with good humour, and conscious of power. 'Poor Ethel! I am doing you good against your will! Never mind, here is wherewith to build the school, and the management will be too happy to fall into our hands. Do you think every one is as ready as you are, to walk three miles, and back, continually?'

There was sense in this; there always was sense in what Flora said, but it jarred on Ethel; and it seemed almost unsympathizing in her to be so gay, when the rest were wearied or perturbed. Ethel would have been very glad of a short space to recollect herself, and recover her good temper; but it was late, and Flora hurried her to put on her bonnet, and come to the Committee. 'I'll take care of your interests,' she said, as they set out. 'You look as doleful as if you thought you should be robbed of Cocksmoor, but that is the last thing that will happen, you will see.'

'It would not be acting fairly to let them build for us, and then for us to put them out of the management,' said Ethel.

'My dear, they want importance, not action. They will leave the real power to us of themselves.'

'You like to build Cocksmoor with such instruments,' said Ethel, whose ruffled condition made her forget her resolution not to argue with Flora.

'Bricks are made of clay!' said Flora. 'There, that was said like Norman himself! On your plan, we might have gone cn for forty years, saving seven shillings a year, and spending six, whenever there was an illness in the place.'

'You, who used to dislike these people more than even I did!' said Ethel.

'That was when I was an infant, my dear, and did not know how to deal with them. I will take care—I will even save Cherry Elwood for you, if I can. Alan Ernescliffe's ten pounds is a noble weapon.'

'You always mean to manage everything, and then you have no time!' said Ethel, sensible all the time of her own ill-humour, and of her sister's patience and amiability, yet propelled to speak the unpleasant truths that in her better moods were held back.

Still Flora was good-tempered, though Ethel would almost have preferred her being provoked; 'I know,' she said, 'I have been using you ill, and leaving the world on your shoulders, but it was all in your service and Cocksmoor's; and now we shall begin to be reasonable and useful again.'

'I hope so,' said Ethel.

'Really, Ethel, to comfort you, I think I shall send you with Norman to dine at Abbotstoke Grange on Wednesday. Mr. Rivers begged us to come; he is so anxious to make it lively for his son.

'Thank you, I do not think Mr. George Rivers and I should be likely to get on together. What a bad style of wit! You heard what Mary said about him?' and Ethel repeated the doubt between hating and detesting.

'Young men never know how to talk to little girls,' was Flora's reply.

At this moment they came up with one of the Miss Andersons, and Flora began to exchange civilities, and talk over yesterday's events with great animation. Her notice always gave pleasure, brightened as it was by the peculiarly engaging address which she had inherited from her father, and which, therefore, was perfectly easy and natural. Fanny Anderson was flattered and gratified, rather by the manner than the words, and, on excellent terms, they entered the Committee-room, namely, the school-mistress's parlour.

There were nine ladies on the Committee—nine muses, as the Doctor called them, *because* they produced anything but harmony. Mrs. Ledwich was in the chair; Miss Rich was secretary, and had her pen and ink, and account-book ready. Flora came in, smiling and greeting; Ethel, grave, earnest, and annoyed, behind her, trying to be perfectly civil, but not at all enjoying the congratulations on the successful bazaar. The ladies all talked and discussed their yesterday's adventures, gathering in little knots, as they traced the fate of favourite achievements of their skill, while Ethel, lugubrious and impatient, beside Flora, the only one not engaged, was, therefore, conscious of the hubbub of clacking tongues.

At last, Mrs. Ledwich glanced at the mistress's watch, in its pasteboard tower, in Gothic architecture, and insisted on proceeding to business. So they all sat down round a circular table, with a very fine red, blue, and black oil-cloth, whose pattern was inseparably connected, in Ethel's mind, with absurdity, tedium, and annoyance.

The business was opened by the announcement of what they all knew before, that the proceeds of the Fancy Fair amounted to one hundred and forty-nine pounds, fifteen shillings and tenpence.

Then came a pause, and Mrs. Ledwich said that next they had to consider what was the best means of disposing of the sum gained in this most gratifying manner. Everyone except Flora, Ethel, and quiet Mrs. Ward, began to talk at once. There was a great deal about Elizabethan architecture, crossed by much more, in which normal, industrial, and common things, most often met Ethel's ear, with some stories, second-hand, from Harvey Anderson, of marvellous mistakes; and, on the opposite side of the table, there was Mrs. Ledwich, impressively saying something to the silent Mrs. Ward, marking her periods with emphatic beats with her pencil, and each seemed to close with "Mrs. Perkinson's niece," whom Ethel knew to be Cherry's intended supplanter. She looked piteously at Flora, who only smiled and made a sign with her hand to her to be patient. Ethel fretted inwardly at that serene sense of power; but she could not but admire how well Flora knew how to bide her time, when, having waited till Mrs. Ledwich had nearly wound up her discourse on Mrs. Elwood's impudence, and Mrs. Perkinson's niece, she leant towards Miss Boulder, who sat between, and whispered to her: 'Ask Mrs. Ledwich if we should not begin with some steps for getting the land.'

Miss Boulder, having acted as conductor, the president exclaimed, 'Just so, the land is the first consideration. We must at once take steps for obtaining it.' Thereupon Mrs. Ledwich, who 'always did things methodically,' moved, and Miss Anderson seconded, that the land requisite for the school must be obtained, and the nine ladies held up their hands, and resolved it.

Miss Rich duly recorded the great resolution, and Miss Boulder suggested that, perhaps, they might write to the National Society, or Government, or something; whereat Miss Rich began to flourish one of the very long goose-quills which stood in the inkstand before her, chiefly as insignia of office, for she always wrote with a small, stiff metal pen.

Flora here threw in a query, whether the National Society, or Government, or something, would give them a grant, unless they had the land to build upon?

The ladies all started off hereupon, and all sorts of instances of hardness of heart were mentioned; the most relevant of which was, that the Church Building Society would not give a grant to Mr. Holloway's proprietary Chapel at Whitford, when Mrs. Ledwich was suddenly struck with the notion that dear Mr. Holloway might be prevailed on to come to Stoneborough, to preach a sermon in the Minster, for the benefit of Cocksmoor, when they would all hold plates at the door. Flora gave Ethel a tranquillizing pat, and, as Mrs. Ledwich turned to her, asking whether she thought Dr. May, or Dr. Hoxton, would prevail on him to come, she said, with her winning look, 'I think that consideration had better wait till we have some more definite view. Had we not better turn to this land question?'

'Quite true!' they all agreed, but to whom did the land belong? —and what a chorus arose! Miss Anderson thought it belonged to Mr. Nicolson, because the wagons of slate had James Nicolson on them, and, if so, they had no chance, for he was an old miser— and six stories illustrative thereof ensued. Miss Rich was quite sure some Body held it, and Bodies were slow of movement. Mrs.

Ledwich remembered some question of enclosing, and thought all waste lands were under the Crown; she knew that the Stoneborough people once had a right to pasture their cattle, because Mr. Southron's cow had tumbled down a loam-pit, when her mother was a girl. No, that was on Far-view down, out the other way! Miss Harrison was positive that Sir Henry Walkinghame had some right there, and would not Dr. May apply to him? Mrs. Grey thought it ought to be part of the Drydale estate, and Miss Boulder was certain that Mr. Bramshaw knew all about it.

Flora's gentle voice carried conviction that she knew what she was saying, when, at last, they left a moment for her to speak—(Ethel would have done so long ago.) 'If I am not mistaken, the land is a copyhold of Sir Henry Walkinghame, held under the manor of Drydale, which belongs to M—— College, and is underlet to Mr. Nicolson.'

Everybody, being partially right, was delighted, and had known it all before; Miss Boulder agreed with Miss Anderson, that Miss May had stated it as lucidly as Mr. Bramshaw could. The next question was, to whom to apply? and, after as much as was expedient had been said in favour of each, it was decided that, as Sir Henry Walkinghame was abroad, no one knew exactly where, it would be best to go to the fountain-head, and write at once to the Principal of the College. But who was to write? Flora proposed Mr. Ramsden as the fittest person, but this was negatived. Every one declared that he would never take the trouble, and Miss Rich began to agitate her pens. By this time, however, Mrs. Ward, who was opposite to the Gothic clock-tower, began to look uneasy, and suggested, in a nervous manner, that it was half-past five, and she was afraid Mr. Ward would be kept waiting for his dinner. Mrs. Grey began to have like fears, that Mr. Grey would be come in from his ride, after banking hours. The other ladies began to think of tea, and the meeting decided on adjourning till that day next week, when the Committee would sit upon Miss Rich's letter.

'My dear Miss Flora!' began Miss Rich, adhering to her as they parted with the rest at the end of the street, 'how am I to write to a Principal? Am I to begin Reverend Sir, or my Lord, or is he Venerable, like an Archdeacon? What is his name, and what am I to say?'

'Why; it is not a correspondence much in my line,' said Flora, laughing.

'Ah! but you are so intimate with Dr. Hoxton, and your brothers at Oxford! You must know—'

I'll take advice,' said Flora, good-naturedly. 'Shall I come, and call before Friday, and tell you the result?'

'Oh! pray! It will be a real favour! Good morning—'

'There,' said Flora, as the sisters turned homewards; 'Cherry is not going to be turned out just yet!'

'How could you, Flora? Now they will have that man from Whitford, and you said not a word against it!'

'What was the use of adding to the hubbub? A little opposition would make them determined on having him. You will see, Ethel, we shall get the ground on our own terms, and then it will be time to settle about the mistress. If the harvest holidays were not over, we would try to send Cherry to a training-school, so as to leave them no excuse.'

'I hate all this management and contrivance. It would be more honest to speak our minds, and not pretend to agree with them.'

'My dear Ethel! have I spoken a word contrary to my opinion? It is not fit for me, a girl of twenty, to go disputing and dragooning as you would have me; but a little *scavoir faire*, a grain of common sense, thrown in among the babble, always works. Don't you remember how Mrs. Ward's sister told us that a whole crowd of tottering Chinese ladies would lean on her, because they felt her firm support, though it was out of sight?'

Ethel did not answer; she had self-control enough left, not to retort upon Flora's estimate of herself, but the irritation was strong; she felt as if her cherished views for Cocksmoor were insulted, as well as set aside, by the place being made the occasion of so much folly and vain prattle, the sanctity of her vision of self-devotion destroyed by such interference, and Flora's promises did not reassure her. She doubted Flora's power, and had still more repugnance to the means by which her sister tried to govern; they did not seem to her straightforward, and she could not endure Flora's complacency in their success. Had it not been for her real love for the place, and people, as well as the principle which prompted that love, she could have found it in her heart to throw up all concern with it, rather than become a fellow-worker with such a conclave.

Such were Ethel's feelings as the pair walked down the street; the one sister bright and smiling with the good-humour that had endured many shocks all that day, all good-nature and triumph, looking forward to success, great benefit to Cocksmoor, and plenty of management, with credit and praise to herself; the other, downcast and irritable, with annoyance at the interference with her schemes, at the prospects of her school, and at herself for being out of temper, prone to murmur or to reply tartly, and not able to recover from her mood, but only, as she neared the house, lapsing into her other trouble, and preparing to resist any misjudged, though kind attempt of her father, to make her unsay her rebuke to Miss Bracy. Pride and temper! Ah! Etheldred! where were they now?

Dr. May was at his study door, as his daughters entered the hall, and Ethel expected the order which she meant to question; but, instead of this, after a brief inquiry after the doings of the nine muses, which Flora answered, so as to make him laugh, he stopped Ethel, as she was going up-stairs, by saying, 'I do not know whether this letter is intended for Richard, or for me. At any rate, it concerns you most.'

The envelope was addressed to the Reverend Richard May, D.D., Market Stoneborough, and the letter began, 'Reverend Sir.' So far Ethel saw, and exclaimed, with amusement, then, with a longdrawn 'Ah!' and an interjection, 'My poor dear Una!' she became absorbed, the large tears—yes, Ethel's reluctant tears gathering slowly and dropping.

The letter was from a Clergyman far away in the north of England, who said he could not, though a stranger, resist the desire to send to Dr. May, an account of a poor girl, who seemed to have received great benefits from him, or from some of his family, especially as she had shown great eagerness on his proposing to write.

He said it was nearly a year since there had come into his parish a troop of railway men and their families. For the most part, they were completely wild and rude, unused to any pastoral care; but, even on the first Sunday, he had noticed a keen-looking, freckled, ragged, unmistakeably Irish girl, creeping into Church, with a prayer-book in her hand, and had afterwards found her hanging about the door of the school. 'I never saw a more engaging, though droll, wild expression, than that with which she looked up to me—' (Ethel's cry of delight was at that sentence—she knew that look so well, and had yearned after it so often!) 'I found her far better instructed than her appearance had led me to expect, and more truly impressed with the spirit of what she had learnt, than it has often been my lot to find children. She was perfect in the New Testament history—' ('Ah! that she was not, when she went away!') 'and was in the habit of constantly attending Church, and using morning and evening prayers—' ('Oh! how I longed, when she went away, to beg her to keep them up! Dear Una.') 'On my questions, as to how she had been taught, she always replied, 'Mr. Richard May,' or 'Miss Athel.' You must excuse me, if I have not correctly caught the name, from her Irish pronunciation—'

('I am afraid he thinks my name is Athaliah! But, oh! this dear girl! How I have wished to hear of her!') 'Everything was answered with 'Mr. Richard,' or 'Miss Athel;' and, if I inquired further, her face would light up with a beam of gratitude, and she would run on as long as I could listen, with instances of their kindness. It was the same with her mother, a wild, rude specimen of an Irishwoman, whom I never could bring to Church herself, but who ran on loudly with their praises, usually ending with, 'Heavens be their bed;' and saying that Una had been quite a different girl since the young ladies and gentleman found her out, and put them parables in her head.

'For my own part, I can testify that, in the seven months that she attended my school, I never had a serious fault to find with her, but far more often to admire the earnestness and devout spirit, as well as the kindness and generosity apparent in all her conduct. Bad living, and an unwholesome locality, have occasioned a typhus fever among the poor strangers in this place, and Una was one of the first victims. Her mother, almost from the first, gave her up, saying, she knew she was one marked for glory; and Una has been lying day after day, in a sort of half-delirious state, constantly repeating hymns and psalms, and generally, apparently very happy, except when one distress occurred again and again, whether delirious or sensible, namely, that she had never gone to wish Miss May good-bye, and thank her; and, that maybe, she and Mr. Richard thought her ungrateful, and she would sometimes beg, in her phraseology, to go on her bare knees to Stoneborough, only to see Miss Athel again.

'Her mother, I should say, told me the girl had been half-mad at not being allowed to go and take leave of Miss May; and she had been sorry herself, but her husband had come home suddenly from the search for work, and, having made his arrangements, removed them at once, early the next morning—too early to go to the young lady—though, she said, Una did—as they passed through Stoneborough—run down the street before she was aware, and she found her sobbing, fit to break her heart, before the house—' ('Oh! why, why was I not up, and at the window! Oh, my Una, to think of that!') 'When I spoke of writing to let Miss May hear how it was, the poor girl caught at the idea with the utmost delight. Her weakness was too great to allow her to utter many words distinctly, when I asked her what she would have me say, but these were as well as I could understand:—' The blessing of one, that they have brought peace unto. Tell them I pray, and will pray, that they may walk in the robe of glory—and tell Mr. Richard that I mind what he said to me, of taking hold on the sure hope. God crown all their crosses unto them, and fulfil all their desires unto everlasting life.' I feel that I am not rendering her words with all their fervour and beauty of Irish expression, but I would that I could fully retain and transmit them, for those who have so led her, must, indeed, be able to feel them precious. I never saw a more peaceful frame of penitence and joy. She died last night, sleeping herself away, without more apparent suffering, and will be committed to the earth on Sunday next, all her fellow-scholars attending; and, I hope, profiting by the example she has left.

'I have only to add my most earnest congratulations to those whose labour of love has borne such blessed fruit; and, hoping you will pardon the liberty, &c.'

Etheldred finished the letter through blinding tears, while rising sobs almost choked her. She ran away to her own room, bolted the door, and threw herself on her knees beside her bed —now confusedly giving thanks for such results—now weeping bitterly over her own unworthiness. Oh! what was she in the sight of Heaven, compared with what this poor girl had deemed her—with what this Clergyman thought her? She, the teacher, taught, trained, and guarded, from her infancy, by her wise mother, and by such a father! She, to have given way, all day, to pride, jealousy, anger, selfish love of her own will; when this poor girl had embraced, and held fast, the blessed hope, from the very crumbs they had brought her! Nothing could have so humbled the distrustful spirit that had been working in Ethel, which had been scotched into silence—not killed—when she endured the bazaar, and now had been indemnifying itself by repining at every stumbling-block. Her own scholar's blessing was the rebuke that went most home to her heart, for having doubted whether good could be worked in any way, save her own.

She was interrupted by Mary trying to open the door, and, admitting her, heard her wonder at the traces of her tears, and ask what there was about Una? Ethel gave her the letter, and Mary's tears showered very fast—they always came readily. 'Oh! Ethel! how glad Richard will be!'

'Yes; it is all Richard's doing. So much more good, and wise, and humble, as he is. No wonder his teaching—' and Ethel sat down and cried again.

Mary pondered. 'It makes me very glad,' she said; 'and yet I don't know why one cries. Ethel, do you think'—she came near, and whispered—'that Una has met dear mamma there?'

Ethel kissed her. It was almost the first time Mary had spoken of her mother; and she answered, 'Dear Mary, we cannot tell—we may think. It is all one Communion, you know.'

Mary was silent, and, next time she spoke, it was to hope that Ethel would tell the Cocksmoor children about Una.

Ethel was obliged to dress and go down-stairs to tea. Her father seemed to have been watching for her, with his study-door open, for he came to meet her, took her hand, and said, in a low voice, 'My dear child, I wish you joy. This will be a pleasant message, to bid poor Ritchie good speed for his Ordination, will it not?'

'That it will, papa—'

'Why, Ethel, have you been crying over it all this time?' said he, struck by the sadness of her voice.

'Many other things, papa. I am so unworthy—but it was not our doing—but the grace—'

'No; but thankful you may be, to have been the means of awakening the grace!'

Ethel's lips trembled. 'And, oh, papa! coming to-day, when I have been behaving so ill to you, and Miss Bracy, and Flora, and all.'

'Have you? I did not know you had behaved ill to me.'

'About Miss Bracy—I thought wrong things, if I did not say them. To her, I believe, I said what was true, though it was harsh of me to say it, and—'

'What? about pride and temper? It was true, and I hope it will do her good. Cure a piping turkey with a pepper-corn sometimes. I have spoken to her, and told her to pluck up a little spirit; not fancy affronts, and not to pester you with them. Poor child! you have been sadly victimized to-day and yesterday. No wonder you were bored past patience, with that absurd rabble of women!'

'It was all my own selfish, distrustful temper, wanting to have Cocksmoor taken care of in my own way, and angry at being interfered with. I see it now—and here this poor girl, that I thought thrown away—'

'Aye, Ethel, you will often see the like. The main object may fail or fall short, but the earnest painstaking will always be blessed some way or other, and where we thought it most wasted, some fresh green shoot will spring up, to show it is not we that give the increase. I suppose you will write to Richard with this?'

'That I shall.'

'Then you may send this with it. Tell him my arm is tired and stiff to-day, or I would have said more. He must answer the Clergyman's letter.'

Dr. May gave Ethel his sheet not folded. His written words were now so few as to be cherished amongst his children.

'DEAR RICHARD—May all your ministerial works be as blessed as this, your first labour of love. I give you hearty joy of this strengthening blessing.—Mine goes with it—'only be strong and of a good courage !'

'Your affectionate Father,   'R. MAY.

'P.S. Margaret does not gain ground this summer—you must soon come home and cheer her.'

CHAPTER V.

'As late, engaged by fancy's dream,
I lay beside a rapid stream,
I saw my first come gliding by,
Its airy form soon caught my eye;
Its texture frail, and colour various,
Like human hopes and life, precarious.
Sudden, my second caught my ear,
And filled my soul with instant fear;
I quickly rose, and home I ran,
My whole was hissing in the pan.'—RIDDLE.

FLORA revised the letter to the Principal, and the Ladies' Committee approved, after having proposed seven amendments, all of which Flora caused to topple over by their own weakness.

After interval sufficient to render the nine ladies very anxious, the Principal wrote from Scotland, where he was spending the Long Vacation, and informed them that their request should be laid before the next College meeting.

After the Committee had sat upon this letter, the two sisters walked home in much greater harmony than after the former meeting. Etheldred had recovered her candour, and was willing to own that it was not art, but good sense, that gave her sister so much ascendancy. She began to be hopeful, and to declare that Flora might yet do something even with the ladies. Flora was gratified by the approval that no one in the house could help valuing ; 'Positively,' said Flora, 'I believe I may in time. You see there are different ways of acting, as an authority, or as an equal.'

'The authority can move from without, the equal must from within,' said Ethel.

'Just so. We must circumvent their prejudices, instead of trying to beat them down.'

'If you only could have the proper Catechizing restored !'

'Wait ; you will see. Let me feel my ground.'

'Or if we could only abdicate into the hands of the rightful power !'

'The rightful power would not be much obliged to you.'

'That is the worst of it,' said Ethel. 'It is sad to hear the sick people say that Dr. May is more to them than any parson; it shows that they have so entirely lost the notion of what their Clergyman should be.'

'Dr. May is *the* man most looked up to in the town,' said Flora, 'and that gives weight to us in the Committee, but it is all in the using.'

'Yes,' said Ethel, hesitating.

'You see, we have the *prestige* of better birth, and better education, as well as of having the chief property in the town, and of being the largest subscribers, added to his personal character,' said Flora; 'so that everything conspires to render us leaders, and our age alone prevented us from assuming our post sooner.'

They were at home by this time, and, entering the hall, perceived that the whole party were in the lawn. The consolation of the children for the departure of Hector and Tom, was a bowl of soap-suds and some tobacco-pipes, and they had collected the house to admire and assist; even Margaret's couch being drawn close to the window.

Bubbles are one of the most fascinating of sports. There is the soft foamy mass, like driven snow or like whipped cream. Blanche bends down to blow "a honeycomb," holding the bowl of the pipe in the water; at her gurgling blasts there slowly heaves upwards the pile of larger, clearer bubbles, each reflecting the whole scene, and sparkling with rainbow tints, until Aubrey ruthlessly dashes all into fragments with his hand, and Mary pronounces it stiff enough, and presents a pipe to little Daisy, who, drawing the liquid into her mouth, throws it away with a grimace, and declares that she does not like bubbles! But Aubrey stands with swelled cheeks, gravely puffing at the sealing-waxed extremity. Out pours a confused assemblage of froth, but the glassy globe slowly expands, the little branching veins, flowing down on either side, bearing an enlarging miniature of the sky, the clouds, the tulip-tree. Aubrey pauses to exclaim! but where is it? Try again! A proud bubble, as Mary calls it, a peacock, in blended pink and green, is this transparent sphere, reflecting and embellishing house, wall, and shrubs! It is too beautiful! It is gone! Mary undertakes to give a lesson, and blows deliberately without the slightest result. Again! she waves her disengaged hand in silent exultation as the airy balls detach themselves, and float off on the summer breeze, with a tardy, graceful, uncertain motion. Daisy rushes after them, catches at them, and looks at her empty fingers with a puzzled 'All gone!' as plainly expressed by Toby, who snaps at them, and shakes his head with offended dignity at the shock of his meeting teeth, while the kitten frisks after them, striking at them with her paw, amazed at meeting vacancy.

Even the grave Norman is drawn in. He agrees with Mary that bubbles used to fly over the wall, and that one once went into Mrs. Richardson's garret window, when her housemaid tried to catch it with a pair of tongs, and then ran down-stairs screaming that there was a ghost in her room; but that was in Harry's time, the heroic age of the May nursery.

He accepts a pipe, and his greater height raises it into a favourable current of air—the glistening balloon sails off. It flies, it soars; no, it is coming down! The children shout at it, as if to drive it up, but it wilfully descends—they rush beneath, they try to waft it on high with their breath—there is a collision between Mary and Blanche—Aubrey perceives a taste of soapy water—the bubble is no more—it has vanished in his open mouth!

Papa himself has taken a pipe, and the little ones are mounted on chairs, to be on a level with their tall elders. A painted globe is swimming along, hesitating at first, but the dancing motion is tending upwards, the rainbow tints glisten in the sunlight—all rush to assist it; if breath of the lips can uphold it, it should rise, indeed! Up! above the wall! over Mrs. Richardson's elm, over the topmost branch—hurra! out of sight! Margaret adds her voice to the acclamations. Beat that if you can, Mary! That doubtful wind keeps yours suspended in a graceful minuet; its pace is accelerated—but earthwards! it has committed self-destruction by running foul of a rose-bush. A general blank!

'You here, Ethel?' said Norman, as the elders laughed at each other's baffled faces.

'I am more surprised to find you here,' she answered.

'Excitement!' said Norman, smiling; 'one cause is as good as another for it.'

'Very pretty sport,' said Dr. May. 'You should write a poem on it, Norman.'

'It is an exhausted subject,' said Norman; 'bubble and trouble are too obvious a rhyme.'

'Ha! there it goes! It will be over the house! That's right!' Every one joined in the outcry.

'Whose is it?'

'Blanche's—'

'Hurrah for Blanche! Well done, white Mayflower, there!' said the Doctor, 'that is what I meant. See the applause gained by a proud bubble that flies! Don't we all bow down to it, and waft it up with the whole force of our lungs, air as it is ; and when it fairly goes out of sight, is there any exhilaration or applause that surpasses ours ?'

'The whole world being bent on making painted bubbles fly over the house,' said Norman, far more thoughtfully than his father. 'It is a fair pattern of life and fame.'

'I was thinking,' continued Dr. May, 'what was the most unalloyed exultation, I remember.'

'Harry's, when you were made Dux,' whispered Ethel to her brother.

'Not mine,' said Norman, briefly.

'I believe,' said Dr. May, 'I never knew such glorification as when Aubrey Spencer climbed the poor old market-cross. We all felt ourselves made illustrious for ever in his person.'

'Nay, papa, when you got that gold medal must have been the grandest time,' said Blanche, who had been listening.

Dr. May laughed, and patted her. 'I, Blanche? Why, I was excessively amazed, that is all, not in Norman's way, but I had been doing next to nothing to the very last, then fell into an agony, and worked like a horse, thinking myself sure of failure, and that my mother and my uncle would break their hearts.'

'But when you heard that you had it ?' persisted Blanche.

'Why, then I found I must be a much cleverer fellow than I thought for !' said he, laughing ; 'but I was ashamed of myself, and of the authorities, for choosing such an idle dog, and vexed that other plodding lads missed it, who deserved it more than I.'

'Of course,' said Norman, in a low voice, 'that is what one always feels. I had rather blow soap-bubbles !'

'Where was Dr. Spencer ?' asked Ethel.

'Not competing. He had been ready a year before, and had gained it, or I should have had no chance. Poor Spencer ! what would I not give to see him, or hear of him ?'

'The last was—how long ago ?' said Ethel.

'Six years, when he was setting off, to return from Poonsheda-gore,' said Dr. May, sighing. 'I give him up ; his health was broken, and there was no one to look after him. He was the sort of man to have a nameless grave, and a name too blessed for fame.'

Ethel would have asked further of her father's dear old friend, but there were sounds, denoting an arrival, and Margaret beckoned to them, as Miss Rivers, and her brother, were ushered into the drawing-room ; and Blanche instantly fled away, with her basin, to hide herself in the school-room.

Meta skipped out, and soon was established on the grass, an attraction to all the live creatures, as it seemed ; for the kitten came, and was caressed, till her own graceful Nipen was ready to fight with the uncouth Toby, for the possession of a resting-place on the skirt of her habit, while Daisy nestled up to her, as claiming a privilege, and Aubrey kept guard over the dogs.

Meta inquired after a huge doll—Dr. Hoxton's gift to Daisy, at the bazaar.

'She is in Margaret's wardrobe,' was the answer, 'because Aubrey tied her hands behind her, and was going to offer her up on the nursery grate.'

'Oh! Aubrey, that was too cruel!'

'No,' returned Aubrey; 'she was Iphigenia, going to be sacrificed.'

'Mary unconsciously acted Diana,' said Ethel, 'and bore the victim away.'

'Pray, was Daisy a willing Clytemnestra?' asked Meta.

'Oh, yes, she liked it,' said Aubrey, while Meta looked discomfited.

'I never could get proper respect paid to dolls,' said Margaret; 'we deal too much in their natural enemies.'

'Yes,' said Ethel, 'my only doll was like a heraldic lion, couped in all her parts.'

'Harry and Tom once made a general execution,' said Flora; 'there was a doll hanging to every baluster—the number made up with rag.'

George Rivers burst out laughing—his first sign of life; and Meta looked as if she had heard of so many murders.

'I can't help feeling for a doll!' she said. 'They used to be like sisters to me.   I feel as if they were wasted on children, that see no character in them, and only call them Dolly.'

'I agree with you,' said Margaret. 'If there had been no live dolls, Richard and I should have reared our doll family as judiciously as tenderly. There are treasures of carpentry still extant, that he made for them.'

'Oh! I am so glad!' cried Meta, as if she had found another point of union. 'If I were to confess—there is a dear old Rose in the secret recesses of my wardrobe. I could as soon throw away my sister—'

'Ha!' cried her brother, laying hold of the child, 'here, little Daisy, will you give your doll to Meta?'

'My name is Gertrude Margaret May,' said the little round mouth.   The fat arm was drawn back, with all a baby's dignity, and the rosy face was hidden in Dr. May's breast, at the sound of George Rivers's broad laugh, and, 'Well done, little one!'

Dr. May put his arm round her, turned aside from him, and began talking to Meta about Mr. Rivers.

Flora and Norman made conversation for the brother; and he presently asked Norman to go out shooting with him; but, looked so amazed on hearing that Norman was no sportsman, that Flora tried to save the family credit, by mentioning Hector's love of a gun, which caused their guest to make a general tender of sporting privileges; 'Though,' added he, with a drawl, 'shooting is rather a nuisance, especially alone.'

Meta told Ethel, a little apart, that he was so tired of going out alone, that he had brought her here, in search of a companion.

'He comes in at eleven o'clock, poor fellow, quite tired with solitude,' said she, 'and comes to me to be entertained.'

'Indeed!' exclaimed Ethel. 'What can you do?'

'What I can,' said Meta, laughing. 'Whatever is not "a horrid nuisance" to him.'

'It would be a horrid nuisance to me,' said Ethel, bluntly, 'if my brothers wanted me to amuse them all the morning.'

'Your brothers, oh!' said Meta, as if that were very different; 'besides, you have so much more to do. I am only too glad and grateful, when George will come to me at all. You see, I have always been too young to be his companion, or find out what suited him, and now he is so very kind and good-natured to me.'

'But what becomes of your business?'

'I get time, one way or another. There is the evening, very often, when I have sung both him and papa to sleep. I had two hours, all to myself, yesterday night,' said Meta, with a look of congratulation, 'and I had a famous reading of "Thirlwall's Greece."'

'I should think that such evenings were as bad as the mornings.'

'Come, Ethel, don't make me naughty. Large families, like yours, may have merry, sociable evenings; but, I do assure you, ours are very pleasant. We are so pleased to have George at home; and we really hope that he is taking a fancy to the dear Grange. You can't think how delighted papa is, to have him content to stay quietly with us so long. I must call him, to go back now, though, or papa will be kept waiting.'

When Ethel had watched the tall, ponderous brother help the bright fairy sister to fly airily into her saddle, and her sparkling glance, and wave of the hand, as she cantered off, contrasting with his slow bend, and immobility of feature, she could not help saying that Meta's life certainly was not too charming, with her fanciful, valetudinarian father, and that stupid, idealess brother.

'He is very amiable and good-natured,' interposed Norman.

'Ha! Norman, you are quite won by his invitation to shoot! How he despised you for refusing—as much as you despised him.'

'Speak for yourself,' said Norman. 'You fancy no sensible man likes shooting, but you are all wrong. Some of our best men are capital sportsmen. Why, there is Ogilvie—you know what he is. When I bring him down here, you will see that there is no sort of sport that he is not keen after.'

'This poor fellow will never be keen after anything,' said Dr. May. 'I pity him! Existence seems hard work to him!'

'We shall have baby calling him "the detestable" next,' said Ethel. 'What a famous set down she gave him.'

'She is a thorough lady, and allows no liberties,' said Dr. May.

'Ah!' said Margaret, 'it is a proof of what I want to impress on you. We really must leave off calling her Daisy, when strangers are there.'

'It is so much nicer,' pleaded Mary.

'The very reason,' said Margaret, 'fondling names should be kept for our innermost selves, not spread abroad, and made common. I remember when I used to be called Peg-top—and Flora, Flossy—we were never allowed to use the names, when any visitor was near; and we were asked if we could not be as fond of each other by our proper names. I think it was felt that there was a want of reserve, in publishing our pet words to other people.'

'Quite true,' said Dr. May; 'baby-names never ought to go beyond home. It is the fashion to use them now; and, besides the folly, it seems, to me, an absolute injury to a girl, to let her grow up, with a nick-name attached to her.'

'Aye!' chimed in Norman; 'I hear men talking of Henny, and Loo, and the like; and you can't think how glad I have been, that my sisters could not be known by any absurd word!'

'It is a case, where self-respect would make others behave properly,' said Flora.

'True,' said Dr. May; 'but if girls won't keep up their own dignity, their friends' duty is to do it for them. The mischief is in the intimate friends, who blazon the words to every one.'

'And then they call one formal, for trying to protect the right name,' said Flora. 'It is, one-half of it, silliness, and, the other, affectation of intimacy.'

'Now I know,' said Mary, 'why you are so careful to call Meta Miss Rivers, to all the people here.'

'I should hope so!' cried Norman, indignantly.

'Why, yes, Mary,' said Margaret, 'I should hope lady-like feeling would prevent you from calling her Meta before—'

'The Andersons!' cried Ethel, laughing. 'Margaret was just going to say it. We only want Harry to exact the forfeit! Poor dear little hummingbird! It gives one an oppression on the chest, to think of her having that great do-nothing brother on her hands all day.'

'Thank you,' said Norman, 'I shall know where I am not to look when I want a sister.'

'Aye,' said Ethel, 'when you come yawning to me to find amusement for you, you will see what I shall do!'

'Stand over me with a stick while I print A B C for Cocksmoor, I suppose,' said Norman.

'Well! why not? People are much better doing something than nothing.'

'What, you won't even let me blow bubbles!' said Norman.

'That is too intellectual, as papa makes it,' said Ethel. 'By-the-by, Norman,' she added, as she had now walked with him a little apart, 'it always was a bubble of mine that you should try for the Newdigate Prize. Ha!' as the colour rushed into his cheeks, 'you really have begun!'

'I could not help it, when I heard the subject given out for next year. Our old friend, Decius Mus.'

'Have you finished?'

'By no means, but it brought a world of notions into my head, such as I could not but set down. Now, Ethel, do oblige me, do write another, as we used in old times.'

'I had better not,' said Ethel, standing thoughtful. 'If I throw myself into it, I shall hate everything else, and my wits will be woolgathering. I have neither time nor poetry enough.'

'You used to write English Verse.'

'I was cured of it.'

'How?'

'I wanted money for Cocksmoor, and after persuading papa, I got leave to send a ballad about a little girl, and a white rose, to that school magazine. I don't think papa liked it, but there were some verses that touched him, and one had seen worse. It was actually inserted, and I was in high feather, till, oh! Norman! imagine Richard getting hold of this unlucky thing, without a notion where it came from. Margaret put it before him, to see what he would say to it.'

'I am afraid it was not like a young lady's anonymous composition in a story.'

'By no means. Imagine Ritchie picking my poor metaphors to pieces, and weighing every sentimental line! And all in his dear old simplicity, because he wanted to understand it, seeing that Margaret liked it. He had not the least intention of hurting my feelings, but never was I so annihilated! I thought he was doing it on purpose, till I saw how distressed he was when he found it out; and, worse than all was, his saying at the end, that he supposed it was very fine, but he could not understand it.'

'Let me see it.'

'Some time or other; but let me see Decius.'

'Did you give up verses because Richard could not understand them?'

'No; because I had other fish to fry. And I have not given them up altogether. I do scrabble down things that tease me by running in my head, when I want to clear my brains, and know what I mean; but I can't do it without sitting up at night, and that stupifies me before breakfast. And as to making bubbles of them, Ritchie has cured me of that!'

'It is a pity!' said Norman.

'Nonsense, let me see Decius. I know he is splendid.'

'I wish you would have tried, for all my best ideas are stolen from you.'

Ethel prevailed by following her brother to his room, and perching herself on the window-sill, while he read his performance from many slips of paper. The visions of those boyish days had not been forgotten, the Vesuvius scenery was much as Ethel had once described it, but with far more force and beauty; there was Decius' impassioned address to the beauteous land he was about to leave, and the remembrances of his Roman hearth, his farm, his children, whom he quitted for the pale shadows of an uncertain Elysium. There was a great hiatus in the middle, and Norman had many more authorities to consult, but the summing up was nearly complete, and Ethel thought the last lines grand, as they spoke of the noble consul's name living for evermore, added to the examples that nerve ardent souls to devote life, and all that is precious, to the call of duty. Fame is not their object. She may crown their pale brows, but for the good of others, not their own, a beacon light to the world. Self is no object of theirs, and it is the casting self behind that wins—not always the visible earthly strife, but the combat between good and evil. They are the true victors, and whether chronicled, or forgotten, true glory rests on their heads, the sole true glory that man can attain, namely, the reflected beams that crown them as shadowy types of Him whom Decius knew not—the Prince who gave himself for His people, and thus rendered death, for Truth's sake, the highest boon to mortal man.

'Norman, you must finish it! When will it be given in?'

'Next spring, if at all, but keep the secret, Ethel. I cannot have my father's hopes raised.'

'I'll tell you of a motto,' said Ethel. 'Do you remember

Mrs. Hemans' mention of a saying of Sir Walter Scott—" Never let me hear that brave blood has been shed in vain. It sends a roaring voice down through all time?" '

'If—' said Norman, rather ashamed of the enthusiasm which, almost approaching to the so-called ' funny state,' of his younger days, had trembled in his voice, and kindled his eye, ' if you won't let me put " *nascitur ridiculus mus.*" '

'Too obvious,' said Ethel. 'Depend upon it every under-graduate has thought of it already.'

Ethel was always very happy over Norman's secrets, and went about smiling over Decius, and comparing *her* brother with such a one as poor Meta was afflicted with; wasting some super-fluous pity and contempt on the weary weight that was inflicted on the Grange.

'What do you think of me ?' said Margaret, one afternoon. ' I have had Mr. George Rivers here for two hours.'

'Alone! what could bring him here ?'

'I told him that every one was out, but he chose to sit down, and seemed to be waiting.'

'How could you get on ?'

'Oh! we asked a few questions, and brought out remarks, with great difficulty, at long intervals. He asked me if lying here was not a great nuisance, and, at last, he grew tired of twisting his moustache, and went away.'

' I thrush it was a call to take leave.'

' No, he thinks he shall sell out, for the army is a great nuisance.'

'You seem to have got into his confidence.'

'Yes, he said he wanted to settle down, but living with one's father was such a nuisance.'

'By-the-by !' cried Ethel, laughing, ' Margaret, it strikes me that this is a Dumbiedikes' courtship !'

'Of yourself ?' said Margaret, slyly.

'No, of Flora. You know, she has often met him at the Grange and other places, and she does contrive to amuse him, and make him almost animated. I should not think he found her a great nuisance.'

'Poor man ! I am sorry for him !' said Margaret.

'Oh! rejection will be very good for him, and give him some-thing to think of.'

'Flora will never let it come to that,' said Margaret. 'But not one word about it, Ethel !'

Margaret and Etheldred kept their eyes open, and sometimes imagined, sometimes laughed at themselves for their speculations, and so October began ; and Ethel laughed, as she questioned whether the Grange would feel the Hussar's return to his quarters, as much as home would the departure of their scholar for Balliol.

CHAPTER VI.

'So, Lady Flora, take my lay,
  And if you find a meaning there,
Oh! whisper to your glass, and say,
  What wonder if he thinks me fair.'—TENNYSON.

FLORA and Norman were dining with one of their county acquaintance, and Dr. May had undertaken to admit them on their return. The fire shone red and bright, as it sank calmly away, and the time-piece and clock on the stairs had begun their nightly duet of ticking, the crickets chirped in the kitchen, and the Doctor sat alone. His book lay with unturned pages, as he sat musing, with eyes fixed on the fire, living over again his own life, the easy bright days of his youth, when, without much pains on his own part, the tendencies of his generous affectionate disposition, and the influences of a warm friendship, and an early attachment, had guarded him from evil—then the period when he had been perfectly happy, and the sobering power of his position had been gradually working on him; but though always religious and highly principled, the very goodness of his natural character preventing him from perceiving the need of self-control, until the shock that changed the whole tenor of his life, and left him, for the first time, sensible of his own responsibility, but, with inveterate habits of heedlessness and hastiness, that love alone gave him force to combat. He was now a far gentler man. His younger children had never seen, his elder had long since forgotten, his occasional bursts of temper, but he suffered keenly from their effects, especially as regarded some of his children. Though Richard's timidity had been overcome, and Tom's more serious failures had been remedied, he was not without anxiety, and had a strange unsatisfactory feeling as regarded Flora. He could not feel that he had fathomed her! She reminded him of his old Scottish father-in-law, Professor Mackenzie, whom he had never understood, nor, if the truth were known, liked. Her dealings with the Ladies' Committee were so like her grandfather's canny ways in a public meeting, that he laughed over them—but they were not congenial to him. Flora was a most valuable person; all that she undertook prospered, and he depended entirely on her for household affairs, and for the care of Margaret; but, highly as he esteemed her, he was a little afraid of her cool prudence; she never seemed to be in any need of him, nor to place any confi-

DR. MAY AND FLORA.

dence in him, and seemed altogether so much older and wiser than he could feel himself—pretty girl as she was—and very pretty were her fine blue eyes and clear skin, set off by her dark brown hair. There arose the vision of eyes as blue, skin as clear, but of light blonde locks, and shorter, rounder, more dove-like form, open simple loving face, and serene expression, that had gone straight to his heart, when he first saw Maggie Mackenzie making tea.

He heard the wheels, and went out to unbolt the door. Those were a pair for a father to be proud of—Norman, of fine stature, and noble looks, with his high brow, clear thoughtful eye, and grave intellectual eagle face, lighting into animation with his rare, sweet smile; and Flora, so tall and graceful, and in her white dress, picturesquely half-concealed by her mantle, with flowers in her hair, and a deepened colour in her cheek, was a fair vision, as she came in from the darkness.

'Well! was it a pleasant party?'

Norman related the circumstances, while his sister remained silently leaning against the mantel-piece, looking into the fire, until he took up his candle, and bade them good night. Dr. May was about to do the same, when she held out her hand. 'One moment, if you please, dear papa,' she said—'I think you ought to know it.'

'What, my dear?'

'Mr. George Rivers, papa—'

'Ha!' said Dr. May, beginning to smile. 'So that is what he is at, is it? But what an opportunity to take.'

'It was in the conservatory,' said Flora—a little hurt, as her father discovered by her tone. 'The music was going on, and I don't know that there could have been—'

'A better opportunity, eh?' said Dr. May, laughing; 'well, I should have thought it awkward; was he very much discomposed?'

'I thought,' said Flora, looking down and hesitating, 'that he had better come to you.'

'Indeed! so you shifted the ungracious office to me. I am very glad to spare you, my dear; but it was hard on him to raise his hopes.'

'I thought,' faltered Flora, 'that you could not disapprove—'

'Flora—' and he paused completely confounded, while his daughter was no less surprised at the manner in which her news was received. Each waited for the other to speak, and Flora turned away, resting her head against the mantel-piece.

'Surely,' said he, laying his hand on her shoulder, 'you do not mean that you like this man.'

'I did not think that you would be against it,' said Flora, in a choked voice, her face still averted.

'Heaven knows, I would not be against anything for your happiness, my dear,' he answered; 'but have you considered what it would be to spend your life with a man that has not three ideas; not a resource for occupying himself—a regular prey to *ennui*—one whom you could never respect!' He had grown more and more vehement—and Flora put her handkerchief to her eyes, for tears of actual disappointment were flowing.

'Come, come,' he said, touched, but turning it off by a smile, 'we will not talk of it any more to-night.—It is your first offer, and you are flattered, but we know

> "Colours seen by candle-light,
> Will not bear the light of day."

There, good night, Flora, my dear—we will have a *tête à tête* in the study before breakfast, when you have had time to look into your own mind.'

He kissed her affectionately, and went up-stairs with her, stopping at her door to give her another embrace, and to say, 'Bless you, my dear child, and help you to come to a right decision—'

Flora was disappointed. She had been too highly pleased at her conquest to make any clear estimation of the prize, individually considered. Her vanity magnified her achievement, and she had come home in a flutter of pleasure, at having had such a position in society offered to her, and expecting that her whole family would share her triumph. Gratified by George Rivers's admiration, she regarded him with favour and complacency; and her habit of considering herself as the most sensible person in her sphere, made her so regard his appreciation of her, that she was blinded to his inferiority. It must be allowed, that he was less dull with her than with most others.

And, in the midst of her glory, when she expected her father to be delighted and grateful—to be received as a silly girl, ready to accept any proposal, her lover spoken of with scorn, and the advantages of the match utterly passed over, was almost beyond endurance. A physician, with eleven children dependent on his practice, to despise an offer from the heir of such a fortune! But that was his customary romance! She forgave him, when it occurred to her that she was too important, and valuable, to be easily spared; and a tenderness thrilled through her, as she looked at the sleeping Margaret's pale face, and thought of surrendering her and little Daisy to Ethel's keeping. And what would become of the housekeeping? She decided, however, that feelings must not sway her—out of six sisters some must marry, for the good of the rest. Blanche and Daisy should come and stay with her, to be formed by the best society; and, as to poor dear

Ethel, Mrs. Rivers would rule the Ladies' Committee for her with a high hand, and, perhaps, provide Cocksmoor with a school at her sole expense. What a useful admirable woman she would be! The Doctor would be the person to come to his senses in the morning, when he remembered Abbotstoke, Mr. Rivers, and Meta.

So Flora met her father, the next morning, with all her ordinary composure, in which he could not rival her, after his sleepless, anxious night. His looks of affectionate solicitude disconcerted what she had intended to say, and she waited, with downcast eyes, for him to begin.

'Well, Flora,' he said, at last, 'have you thought?'

'Do you know any cause against it?' said Flora, still looking down.

'I know almost nothing of him. I have never heard anything of his character, or conduct. Those would be a subject of enquiry, if you wish to carry this on—'.

'I see you are averse,' said Flora. 'I would do nothing against your wishes—'

'My wishes have nothing to do with it,' said Dr. May. 'The point is—that I must do right, as far as I can, as well as try to secure your happiness; and I want to be sure that you know what you are about.'

'I know he is not clever,' said Flora; 'but there may be many solid qualities without talent.'

'I am the last person to deny it; but where are these solid qualities? I cannot see the recommendation!'

'I place myself in your hands,' said Flora, in a submissive tone, which had the effect of making him lose patience.

'Flora, Flora! why will you talk as if I were sacrificing you to some dislike or prejudice of my own! Don't you think I should only rejoice, to have such a prosperous home offered to you, if only the man were worthy?'

'If you do not think him so, of course, there is an end of it,' said Flora, and her voice showed suppressed emotion.

'It is not what I think, in the absence of proof, but what you think, Flora. What I want you to do is this—to consider the matter fairly. Compare him with—I'll not say with Norman—but with Richard, Alan, Mr. Wilmot. Do you think you could rely on him—come to him for advice?' (Flora never did come to any one for advice.) 'Above all—do you think him likely to be a help, or a hindrance, in doing right?'

'I think you underrate him,' said Flora, steadily; 'but, of course, if you dislike it—though, I think, you would change your mind, if you knew him better—'

'Well!' he said, as if to himself, 'it is not always the most worthy—' then continued, 'I have no dislike to him. Perhaps I may find that you are right. Since your mind is made up, I will do this: first, we must be assured of his father's consent, for they may very fairly object, since, what I can give you, is a mere nothing to them. Next, I shall find out what character he bears in his regiment, and watch him well myself; and, if nothing appear seriously amiss, I will not withhold my consent. But, Flora, you should still consider whether he shows such principle, and right feeling, as you can trust to.'

'Thank you, papa. I know you will do all that is kind.'

'Mind, you must not consider it an engagement, unless all be satisfactory.'

'I will do as you please.'

Ethel perceived that something was in agitation, but the fact did not break upon her till she came to Margaret, after the school-room reading, and heard Dr. May declaiming away, in the vehement manner, that always relieved him.

'Such a cub!' These were the words that met her ear; and she would have gone away, but he called her—'Come in, Ethel; Margaret says, you guessed at this affair!'

'At what affair!' exclaimed Ethel. 'Oh, it is about Flora. Poor man; has he done it?'

'Poor! He is not the one to be pitied!' said her father.

'You don't mean that she likes him?'

'She does though! A fellow with no more brains than a turnip lantern!'

'She does not mean it?' said Ethel.

'Yes she does! Very submissive, and proper spoken, of course, but bent on having him; so there is nothing left for me but to consent—provided Mr. Rivers does, and he should turn out not to have done anything outrageous; but there's no hope of that —he has not the energy. What can possess her? What can she see to admire?'

'He is good-natured,' said Margaret, 'and rather good-look-ing—'

'Flora has more sense. What on earth can be the attraction?'

'I am afraid it is partly the grandeur—' said Ethel.

She broke off short, quite dismayed at the emotion she had excited. Dr. May stepped towards her, almost as if he could have shaken her.

'Ethel!' he cried, 'I won't have such motives ascribed to your sister!'

Ethel tried to recollect what she had said that was so shocking, for the idea of Flora's worldly motives was no novelty to her. They had appeared in too many instances ; and, though frightened at his anger, she stood still, without unsaying her words.

Margaret began to explain away. 'Ethel did not mean, dear papa—'

'No,' said Dr. May, his passionate manner giving way to dejection. 'The truth is, that I have made home so dreary, that my girls are ready to take the first means of escaping.'

Poor Margaret's tears sprang forth, and, looking up imploringly, she exclaimed, 'Oh, papa, papa! it was no want of happiness! I could not help it. You know he had come before—'

Any reproach to her had been entirely remote from his thoughts, and he was at once on his knee beside her, soothing and caressing, begging her pardon, and recalling whatever she could thus have interpreted.

Meanwhile, Ethel stood unnoticed and silent, making no outward protestation, but with lips compressed, as in her heart of hearts, she passed the resolution—that her father should never feel this pain on her account. Leave him who might, she would never forsake him; nothing but the will of Heaven should part them. It might be hasty and venturesome. She knew not what it might cost her; but, where Ethel had treasured her resolve to work for Cocksmoor, there she also laid up her secret vow—that no earthly object should be placed between her and her father.

The ebullition of feeling seemed to have restored Dr. May's calmness, and he rose, saying, 'I must go to my work; the man is coming here this afternoon.'

'Where shall you see him?' Margaret asked.

'In my study, I suppose. I fear there is no chance of Flora's changing her mind first. Or do you think one of you could talk to her, and get her fairly to contemplate the real bearings of the matter—' and with these words he left the room.

Margaret and Ethel glanced at each other; and both felt the impenetrability of Flora's nature, so smooth, that all thrusts glided off.

'It will be of no use,' said Ethel ; 'and, what is more, she will not have it done.'

'Pray try; a few of your forcible words would set it in a new light.'

'Why! Do you think she will attend to me, when she has not chosen to heed papa?' said Ethel, with an emphasis of incredulity. 'No; whatever Flora does, is done deliberately, and unalterably.'

'Still, I don't know whether it is not our duty,' said Margaret.

'More yours than mine,' said Ethel.

Margaret flushed up. 'Oh, no, I cannot!' she said, always timid, and slightly defective in moral courage. She looked so nervous and shaken by the bare idea of a remonstrance with Flora, that Ethel could not press her; and, though convinced that her representation would be useless, she owned that her conscience would rest better, after she had spoken. 'But there is Flora, walking in the garden with Norman,' she said. 'No doubt, he is doing it.'

So Ethel let it rest, and attended to the children's lessons, during which Flora came into the drawing-room, and practised her music, as if nothing had happened.

Before the morning was over, Ethel contrived to visit Norman, in the dining-room, where he was wont to study, and asked him whether he had made any impression on Flora.

'What impression do you mean?'

'Why, about this concern,' said Ethel; 'this terrible man, that makes papa so unhappy.'

'Papa unhappy! Why, what does he know against him? I thought the Riverses were his peculiar pets.'

'The Riverses! As if, because one liked the sparkling stream, one must like a muddy ditch.'

'What harm do you know of him?' said Norman, with much surprise, and anxiety, as if he feared that he had been doing wrong, in ignorance.

'Harm! Is he not a regular oaf?'

'My dear Ethel, if you wait to marry till you find some one as clever as yourself, you will wait long enough.'

'I don't think it right for a woman to marry a man decidedly her inferior.'

'We have all learnt to think much too highly of talent,' said Norman, gravely.

'I don't care for mere talent—people are generally more sensible without it; but, one way or other, there ought to be superiority on the man's side.

'Well, who says there is not?'

'My dear Norman! Why, this George Rivers is really below the average! you cannot deny that! Did you ever meet any one so stupid?'

'Really!' said Norman, considering; and speaking very innocently, 'I cannot see why you think so. I do not see that he is at all less capable of sustaining a conversation than Richard.'

Ethel sat down, perfectly breathless with amazement and indignation.

Norman saw that he had shocked her very much. 'I do not mean,' he said, 'that we have not much more to say to Richard; all I meant to say was, merely as to the intellect.'

'I tell you,' said Ethel, 'it is not the intellect. Richard! why, you know how we respect and look up to him. Dear old Ritchie! with his goodness, and earnestness, and right judgment—to compare him to that man! Norman! Norman! I never thought it of you!'

'You do not understand me, Ethel. I only cited Richard, as a person who proves how little cleverness is needed to insure respect.'

'And, I tell you, that cleverness is not the point.'

'It is the only objection you have put forward.'

'I did wrong,' said Ethel. 'It is not the real one. It is earnest goodness that one honours in Richard. Where do we find it in this man? who has never done anything but yawn over his self-indulgence.'

'Now, Ethel, you are working yourself up into a state of foolish prejudice. You, and papa, have taken a dislike to him; and you are overlooking a great deal of good safe sense, and right thinking. I know his opinions are sound, and his motives right. He has been under-educated, we all see, and is not very brilliant or talkative; but I respect Flora for perceiving his solid qualities.'

'Very solid and weighty, indeed!' said Ethel, ironically. 'I wonder if she would have seen them in a poor Curate!'

'Ethel! you are allowing yourself to be carried, by prejudice, a great deal too far. Are such imputations to be made, wherever there is inequality of means? It is very wrong! very unjust!'

'So papa said,' replied Ethel, as she looked sorrowfully down. 'He was very angry with me for saying so. I wish I could help feeling as if that were the temptation.'

'You ought,' said Norman. 'You will be sorry, if you set yourself and him against it.'

'I only wish you to know what I feel; and, I think, Margaret and papa do,' said Ethel, humbly, 'and then you will not think us more unjust than we are. We cannot see anything so agreeable or suitable in this man, as to account for Flora's liking, and we do not feel convinced of his being good for much. That makes papa greatly averse to it, though he does not know any positive reason for refusing; and we cannot feel certain that she is doing quite right, or for her own happiness.'

'You will be convinced,' said Norman, cheerfully. 'You will find out the good that is under the surface, when you have seen more of him. I have had a good deal of talk with him.'

A good deal of talk *to* him would have been more correct, if Norman had but been aware of it. He had been at the chief expense of the conversation with George Rivers, and had taken the sounds of assent, which he obtained, as evidences of his appreciation of all his views. Norman had been struggling so long against his old habit of looking down on Richard, and exalting intellect; and had seen, in his Oxford life, so many ill-effects of the knowledge that puffeth up, that he had come to have a certain respect for dulness, *per se*, of which George Rivers easily reaped the benefit, when surrounded by the halo which everything at Abbotstoke Grange bore in the eyes of Norman.

He was heartily delighted at the proposed connexion, and his genuine satisfaction not only gratified Flora, and restored the equanimity that had been slightly disturbed by her father, but it also reassured Ethel and Margaret, who could not help trusting in his judgment, and began to hope that George might be all he thought him.

Ethel, finding that there were two ways of viewing the gentleman, doubted whether she ought to express her opinion. It was Flora's disposition, and the advantages of the match, that weighed most upon her; and, in spite of her surmise having been treated as so injurious, she could not rid herself of the burthen.

Dr. May was not so much consoled by Norman's opinion as Ethel expected. The corners of his mouth curled up a little with diversion, and though he tried to express himself glad, and confident in his son's judgment, there was the same sort of involuntary lurking misgiving, with which he had accepted Sir Matthew Fleet's view of Margaret's case.

There was no danger that Dr. May would not be kind and courteous to the young man himself. It was not his fault if he were a dunce, and Dr. May perceived that his love for Flora was real, though clumsily expressed. He explained that he could not sanction the engagement till he should be better informed of the young gentleman's antecedents; this was, as George expressed it, a great nuisance, but his father agreed that it was quite right, in some doubt, perhaps, as to how Dr. May might be satisfied.

CHAPTER VII.

' Ye cumbrous fashions, crowd not on my head,
    Mine be the chip of purest white,
    Swan-like ; and, as her feathers light,
    When on the still wave spread ;
    And let it wear the graceful dress
    Of unadorned simpleness.'

CATHERINE FANSHAWE'S PARODY ON GRAY.

NOTHING transpired to the discredit of Lieutenant Rivers. He
had spent a great deal of money, but chiefly for want of something else to do, and, though he was not a subject for high praise,
there was no vice in him—no more than in an old donkey—as
Dr. May declared, in his concluding paroxysm of despair, on finding that, though there was little to reconcile him to the engagement, there was no reasonable ground for thwarting his daughter's
wishes.   He argued the matter once more with her, and, finding
her purpose fixed, he notified his consent, and the rest of the family
were admitted to a knowledge of the secret which they had never
suspected.

Etheldred could not help being gratified with the indignation
it excited. With one voice, Mary and Blanche declared that they
would never give up the title of " the detestable," and would not
make him any presents ; certainly, not watch-chains! Miss Bracy,
rather alarmed, lectured them just enough to make them worse ;
and Margaret, overhearing Blanche instructing Aubrey in her own
impertinences, was obliged to call her to her sofa, and assure her
that she was unkind to Flora, and that she must consider Mr.
George Rivers as her brother.

' Never my brother like Harry!' exclaimed Mary, indignantly.

' No, indeed; nor like Alan !' exclaimed Blanche.   ' And I
won't call him George, I am determined, if it is ever so !'

' It will not matter to him what such little girls call him,' said
Margaret.

Blanche was so annihilated, that the sound of a carriage, and
of the door bell, was a great satisfaction to her.

Meta Rivers came flying into the room, her beautiful eyes
dancing, and her cheeks glowing with pleasure, as, a little timidly,
she kissed Margaret ; while Ethel, in a confused way, received
Mr. Rivers, in pain for her own cold, abrupt manner, in contrast
with his gentle, congratulating politeness.

Meta asked, blushing, and with a hesitating voice, for their dear
Flora ; Mary offered to call her, but Meta begged to go herself,
and thus was spared the awkwardness that ensued.   Ethel was
almost vexed with herself, as ungrateful, when she saw Mr. Rivers

so mildly kind, and so delighted, with the bland courtesy that seemed fully conscious of the favour that Flora had conferred on his son, and thankful to the Mays for accepting him.

Margaret answered with more expression of gratification, than would have been sincere in Ethel; but it was a relief, when Flora and Meta came in together, as pretty a contrast as could be seen; the little dark-eyed fairy, all radiant with joy, clinging to the slender waist of Flora, whose quiet grace, and maidenly dignity, were never more conspicuous, than, as with a soft red mantling in her fair cheek, her eyes cast down, but with a simple, unaffected warmth of confidence and gratitude, she came forward to receive Mr. Rivers's caressing affectionate greeting.

Stiffness was over when she came in, and Dr. May, who presently made his appearance, soon was much more at his ease than could have been hoped, after his previous declarations that he should never be able to be moderately civil about it to Mr. Rivers. People of ready sympathy, such as Dr. May and Margaret, have a great deal of difficulty with their sincerity spared them, by being carried along with the feelings of others. Ethel could not feel the same, and was bent on avoiding any expression of opinion; she hoped that Meta's ecstasies would all be bestowed upon her future sister-in-law; but Meta was eager for an interview with Ethel herself, and, as usual, gained her point.

'Now then, you are property of my own!' she cried. 'May I not take you all for sisters?'

Ethel had not thought of this as a convenience of the connection, and she let Meta kiss her, and owned that it was very nice.

'Ethel,' said Meta, 'I see, and I wanted to talk to you. You don't think poor George good enough for Flora.'

'I never meant to show it,' said Ethel.

'You need not mind,' said Meta, smiling; 'I was very much surprised myself, and thought it all a mistake. But I am so very glad, for I know it will make such a difference to him, poor fellow! I should like to tell you all about him, for no one else can very well, and you will like him better, perhaps. You know my grandfather made his own fortune, and you would think some of our relations very queer. My aunt Dorothy once told me all about it —papa was made to marry the partner's daughter, and I fancy she could not have been much of a lady. I don't think he could have been very happy with her, but she soon died, and left him with this one son, whom those odd old aunts brought up their own way. By-and-by, you know, papa came to be in quite another line of society, but when he married again, poor George had been so spoilt by these aunts, and was so big, and old, that my mother did not know what to make of him.'

'A great lubberly boy,' Ethel said, rather repenting the next moment.

'He is thirteen years older than I am,' said Meta, 'and you see it has been hard on him altogether; he had not the education that papa would have given him if he had been born later; and he can't remember his mother, and has always been at a loss when with clever people. I never understood it till within the last two or three years, nor knew how trying it must be to see such a little chit as me made so much of—almost thrusting him aside. But you cannot think what a warm-hearted good fellow he is—he has never been otherwise than so very kind to me, and he was so very fond of his old aunt. Hitherto, he has had such disadvantages, and no real, sensible woman, has taken him in hand; he does not care for papa's tastes, and I am so much younger, that I never could get on with him at all, till this time; but I do know that·he has a real good temper, and all sorts of good qualities, and that he only needs to be led right, to go right. Oh! Flora may make anything of him, and we are so thankful to her for having found it out!'

'Thank you for telling me,' said Ethel. 'It is much more satisfactory to have no misunderstanding.'

Meta laughed, for Ethel's sham was not too successful; she continued, 'dear Dr. May, I thought he would think his beautiful Flora not exactly matched—but tell him, Ethel, for if he once is sorry for poor George, he will like him. And it will really be the making of George, to be thrown with him and your brothers. Oh! we are so glad! But I won't tease you to be so.'

'I can like it better now,' said Ethel. 'You know Norman thinks very highly of your brother, and declares that it will all come out by-and-by.'

Meta clapped her hands, and said that she should tell her father, and Ethel parted with her, liking *her*, at least, better than ever. There was a comical scene between her and the Doctor, trying to define what relations they should become to each other, which Ethel thought did a good deal to mollify her father.

The history of George's life did more; he took to pitying him, and pity was, indeed, akin to love in the good Doctor's mind. In fact, George was a man who could be liked, when once regarded as a belonging—a necessity, not a choice; for it was quite true that there was no harm in him, and a great deal of good nature. His constant kindness, and evident liking for Margaret, stood him in good stead; he made her a sort of confidante, bestowing on her his immeasurable appreciation of Flora's perfections, and telling her how well he was getting on with 'the old gentleman'—a name under which she failed to recognise her father.

As to Tom, he wrote his congratulations to Ethel, that she might make a wedding present of her Etruscan vases, the Cupids on which must have been put there by anticipation. Richard heard none of the doubts, and gave kind, warm congratulations, promising to return home for the wedding; and Mary and Blanche no sooner heard a whisper about bridesmaids, than all their opposition faded away, in a manner that quite scandalized Ethel, while it set Margaret on reminiscences of her having been a six-year old bridesmaid to Flora's godmother, Mrs. Arnott.

As to the gossip in the town, Ethel quite dreaded the sight of every one without Flora to protect her, and certainly, Flora's unaffected, quiet manner, was perfection, and kept off all too forward congratulations, while it gratified those whom she was willing to encourage.

There was no reason for waiting, and Mr. Rivers was as impatient as his son, so an understanding arose that the wedding should take place near the end of the Christmas holidays.

Flora showed herself sensible and considerate. Always open-handed, her father was inclined to do everything liberally, and laid no restrictions on her preparations, but she had too much discretion to be profuse, and had a real regard for the welfare of the rest. She laughed with Ethel at the anticipations of the Stoneborough ladies that she must be going to London, and, at the requests, as a great favour, that they might be allowed the sight of her *trousseau*. Her wedding-dress, white silk, with a white cashmere mantle, was, indeed, ordered from Meta's London dressmaker; but, for the rest, she contented herself with an expedition to Whitford, accompanied by Miss Bracy and her two enchanted pupils, and there laid in a stock of purchases, unpretending and in good taste, aiming only at what could be well done, and not attempting the decorative wardrobe of a great lady. Ethel was highly amused when the Miss Andersons came for their inspection, to see their concealed disappointment at finding no under garments trimmed with Brussels lace, nor pocket handkerchiefs all open-work, except a centre of the size of a crown-piece, and the only thing remarkable, was Margaret's beautiful marking in embroidery. There was some compensation in the costly wedding presents—Flora had reaped a whole harvest from friends of her own, grateful patients of her father, and the whole Rivers and Langdale connection; but, in spite of the brilliant uselessness of most of these, the young ladies considered themselves ill used, thought Dr. May never would have been shabby, and were of opinion that, when Miss Ward had married her father's surgical pupil, her outfit had been a far more edifying spectacle.

The same moderation influenced Flora's other arrangements. Dr. May was resigned to whatever might be thought most proper, stipulating only that he should not have to make a speech; but Flora felt that, in their house, a grand breakfast would be an unsuccessful and melancholy affair. If the bride had been any one else, she could have enjoyed making all go off well, but, under present circumstances, it would be great pain to her father and Margaret, a misery to Ethel, and something she dared not think of to the guests. She had no difficulty in having it dispensed with. George was glad to avoid 'a great nuisance.' Mr. Rivers feared the fatigue, and, with his daughter, admired Flora for her amiability, and, as to the home party, no words could express their gratitude to her for letting them off. Mary and Blanche did, indeed, look rather blank, but Blanche was consoled, by settling with Hector, the splendours in store for Alan and Margaret, and Mary cared the less, as there would be no Harry to enjoy the fun.

The bride-maiden's glory was theirs by right, though Ethel was an unsatisfactory chief, for such as desired splendour. She protested against anything incongruous with January, or that could not be useful afterwards, and Meta took her part, laughing at the cruel stroke they were preparing for Bellairs. Ethel begged for dark silks and straw bonnets, and Flora said that she had expected to hear of brown stuff and grey duffle, but owned that they had better omit the ordinary muslin garb in the heart of winter. The baby bridesmaid was, at last, the chief consideration. Margaret suggested how pretty she and Blanche would look in sky-blue merino, trimmed with swan's-down. Meta was charmed with the idea, and though Ethel stuck out her shoulder-blades and poked out her head, and said she should look like the ugly duckling, she was clamorously reminded that the ugly duckling ended by being a swan, and promised that she should be allowed a bonnet of a reasonable size, trimmed with white, for Mr. Rivers' good taste could endure, as little as Dr. May's sense of propriety, the sight of a daughter without shade to her face. Ethel, finally, gave in, on being put in mind that her papa had a *penchant* for swan's-down; and, on Margaret's promising to wear a dress of the same as theirs.

Ethel was pleased and satisfied by Flora's dislike of parade, and attention to the feelings of all. Passing over the one great fact; the two sisters were more of one mind than usual, probably because all latent jealousy of Ethel had ceased in Flora's mind. Hitherto, she had preferred the being the only practically useful person in the family, and had encouraged the idea of Ethel's *gaucherie;* but now she desired to render her sister able to take her place, and did all in her power to put her in good heart.

For Etheldred was terrified at the prospect of becoming responsible housekeeper. Margaret could only serve as an occasional reference. Her morning powers became too uncertain to be depended on for any regular, necessary duty, and it would have oppressed her so much to order the dinners, which she never saw, that, though she offered to resume the office, Flora would not hear of Ethel's consenting. If it were her proper business, Ethel supposed she could do it, but another hour of her leisure was gone, and what would become of them all, with her, a proverb for heedlessness, and ignorance of ordinary details. She did not know that these were more proverbial than actual, and, having a bad name, she believed in it herself. However, Flora made it her business to persuade her, that her powers were as good for household matters, as for books, or Cocksmoor; instructed her in her own methodical plans, and made her keep house for a fortnight, with so much success, that she began to be hopeful.

In the attendance on Margaret, the other great charge, old nurse was the security; and Ethel, who had felt herself much less unhandy than before, was to succeed to the abode in her room—Blanche being promoted, from the nursery, to the old attic. 'And,' said Flora, consolingly, 'if dear Margaret ever should be ill, you may reckon on me.'

Miss Flora May made her last appearance at the Ladies' Committee, to hear the reply from the Principal of the College. It was a civil letter, but declined taking any steps in the matter, without more certain intelligence of the wishes of the incumbent of the parish, or of the holders of the land in question.

The Ladies abused all Colleges—as prejudiced old Bodies, and feared that it would be impossible to ask Mrs. Perkinson's niece to take the school, while there was neither room nor lodging. So Miss Rich recorded the correspondence, and the vote of censure, by which it was to be hoped the Ladies' Committee of Market Stoneborough, inflicted a severe blow on the Principal and Fellows of M—— College.

'Never mind, Ethel,' said Flora. 'I shall meet Sir Henry Walkinghame in London, and will talk to him. We shall yet astonish the Muses. If we can get the land without them, we shall be able to manage it our own way, without obligations.'

'You forget the money!'

'We will keep them from dissipating it—or that might be no harm! A hundred pounds will be easily found, and we should then have it in our own hands. Besides, you know, I don't mean to give up. I shall write a polite note to Mrs. Ledwich, begging to subscribe on my own account, and to retain my seat! and you will see what we shall do.'

'You mean to come down with the external authority,' said Ethel, smiling.

'True! and though my driving in with a pair of horses may make little difference to you, Ethel, depend upon it, Mrs. Ledwich will be the more amenable. Whenever I want to be particularly impressive, I shall bring in that smelling-bottle, with the diamond stopper that won't come out, and you will find that carries all before it.'

'A talisman!' said Ethel, laughing. 'But I had rather they yielded to a sense of right!'

'So had I,' said Flora. 'Perhaps you will rule them that way?'

'Not I,' cried Ethel, terrified.

'Then you must come to me, and secondary motives. Seriously—I do mean that George should do something for Stoneborough; and, in a position of influence, I hope to be able to be useful to my poor old town. Perhaps we shall have the Minster restored.'

Flora did wish it. She did love Stoneborough, and was sincerely interested for Cocksmoor. She thought she worked earnestly for them, and that her situation would be turned to their profit; but there was something for which she worked more earnestly. Had Flora never heard of the two masters, whom we cannot serve at the same time?

Richard came home for 'a Parson's week,' so as to include the wedding. He looked very fresh and youthful; but his manner, though still gentle and retiring, had lost all that shrinking diffidence, and had, now, a very suitable grave composure. Everybody was delighted to have him; and Ethel, more than any one, except Margaret. What floods of Cocksmoor histories were poured upon him; and what comparing of notes about his present school-children! He could not enter into the refinements of her dread of the Ladies' Committee, and thought she might be thankful if the school were built by any proper means; for, if Cherry Elwood were retained, and the ladies prevented from doing harm, he did not understand why Ethel should wish to reject all assistance, that did not come in a manner she admired. He never would comprehend—so Ethel gave it up—feared she was again jealous and self-sufficient, and contented herself with the joy that his presence produced at Cocksmoor where the children smiled, blushed, and tittered with ecstasy whenever he even looked at one of them.

Richard was not allowed to have a Sunday of rest. His father apologised for having made an engagement for him—as Mr. Ramsden was unwell, and the school Clergy were all absent, so that he could do no otherwise than assist in the service. Richard coloured, and said that he had brought no sermon; and he was, in fact, deprived of much of his sisters' company, for composition was not easy to him, and the quantity of time he spent on it, quite alarmed Norman and Ethel, who both felt rather nervous on the Sunday morning, but agreed that preaching was not everything.

Ethel could not see well, as far as the reading desk, but she saw her father glance up, take off his spectacles, wipe them, and put them away; and she could not be displeased, though she looked reproof at Blanche's breathless whisper, 'Oh, he looks so nice!' Those white folds did truly suit well, with the meek, serious expression of the young Deacon's fair face, and made him, as his sisters afterwards said, like one of the solemnly peaceful angel-carvings of the earlier ages.

His voice was sweet and clear, and his reading full of quiet simplicity and devotion, such as was not often heard by that congregation, who were too much used, either to carelessness, or to pomposity. The sermon made his brother and sister ashamed of their fears. It was an exposition of the Gospel for the day, practical and earnest, going deep, and rising high, with a clearness and soberness, yet with a beauty and elevation, such as Norman and Ethel had certainly not expected—or, rather, they forgot all their own expectations, and Richard himself, and only recollected their own hearts, and the great future before them.

Even Blanche and Aubrey told Margaret a great deal about it, and declared that, if Richard preached every Sunday, they should like going to church much better.

When Dr. May came in, some time after, he was looking much pleased. 'So, Mr. Ritchie,' he said, 'you have made quite a sensation—every one shaking me by the hand, and thanking me for my son's sermon. You will be a popular preacher at last!'

Richard blushed distressfully, and quoted the saying, that it would be the true comfort to hear that people went home, thinking of themselves, rather than of the sermon. This put an end to the subject; but the Doctor went over it again, most thoroughly, with his other children, who were greatly delighted.

Flora's last home Sunday! She was pale and serious, evidently feeling much, though seeking no *tête-à-têtes*, and chiefly engrossed with waiting on Margaret, or fondling little Gertrude. No one saw the inside of her mind—probably she did not herself. On the outside was a very suitable pensiveness, and affection for all that she was leaving. The only one in the family to whom she talked much, was Norman, who continued to see many perfections in George, and contrived, by the force of his belief, to impress the same on the others; and to make them think his great talent for silence, such a proof of his discretion, that they were not staggered, even by his shy blundering exclamation, that his wedding would be a great nuisance—a phrase which, as Dr. May observed, was, to him, what *Est il possible* was to his namesake of Denmark.

Nobody wished for any misgivings, so Richard was never told of any, though there was a careful watch kept, to see what were his first impressions. None transpired, except something about good-nature, but it was shrewdly believed that Richard and George, being much alike in shy unwillingness to speak, had been highly satisfied with the little trouble they had caused to each other, and so had come to a *tacit* esteem.

There was very little bustle of preparation. Excepting the packing, everything went on much as usual, till the Thursday morning, and then the children were up early, refreshing the Christmas hollies, and working up their excitement, only to have it damped by the suppressed agitation of their elders at the breakfast-table.

Dr. May did not seem to know what he was about; and Flora looked paler and paler. She went away before the meal was over, and when Ethel went to the bed-room, shortly after, she found that she had fairly broken down, and was kneeling beside Margaret's sofa, resting her head on her sister's bosom, and sobbing—as Ethel had never seen her weep, except on that dreadful night, after their mother's death.

In a person ordinarily of such self-command as Flora, weeping was a terrible thing, and Margaret was much distressed and alarmed; but the worst had passed before Ethel came up, and Flora was able to speak. 'Oh! Margaret! I cannot leave you! Oh! how happy we have been—'

'You are going to be happier, we trust, dearest,' said Margaret, fondly.

'Oh! what have I done? It is not worth it!'

Ethel thought she caught those words, but no more; Mary's step was heard, and Flora was on her feet instantly, composing herself rapidly. She shed no more tears, but her eyelids were very heavy, and her face softened in a manner that, though she was less pretty than usual, was very becoming under her bridal veil. She recovered calmness, and even cheerfulness, while reversing the usual order of things, and dressing her bridesmaids, who would never have turned out fit to be seen, but for the exertions of herself, Margaret, and Miss Bracy. Ethel's long Scotch bones, and Mary's round, dumpy shapelessness, were, in their different ways, equally hard to overcome; and the one was swelled out with a fabulous number of petticoats, and the other pinched in, till she gasped and screamed for mercy, while Blanche and Gertrude danced about, beautiful to behold, under their shady hats; and presently, with a light tap at the door, Meta Rivers stepped in, looking so pretty, that all felt, that to try to attain to such an appearance was vain.

Timid in her affection, she hardly dared to do more than kiss them, and whisper her pretty caressing words to each. There was no more time—Dr. Hoxton's carriage was come to take up the bride.

Ethel did as she was told, without much volition of her own; and she quitted the carriage, and was drawn into her place by Norman, trusting that Meta would not let her do wrong, and relieved that, just in front of her, were the little ones, over whose head she could see her father, with Flora's veiled bending figure.

That pause, while the procession was getting into order, the slow movement up the centre aisle, the week-day atmosphere of the church, brought back to her thoughts a very different time, and one of those strange echoings on the mind, repeated in her ears the words—'For man walketh in a vain shadow, and disquieteth himself in vain—'

There was a little pause—George did not seem to be forthcoming, and Meta turned round, rather uneasily, and whispered something about his having been so nervous. However, there he was, looking exceedingly red, and very sheepish, and disposed to fall back on his best man, Norman, whose countenance was at the brightest—and almost handsome.

Dr. Hoxton performed the ceremony, 'assisted by' Richard. It had been Flora's choice; and his loud, sonorous voice was thought very impressive. Blanche stood nearest, and looked happy and important, with Flora's glove. Gertrude held Mary's hand, and gazed straight up into the fretted roof, as if that were to her the chief marvel. Ethel stood and knelt, but did not seem, to herself, to have the power of thinking or feeling. She saw and heard—that was all; she could not realize.

They drew her forward, when it was over, to sign her name, as witness. She took up the pen, looked at the Flora May, written for the last time, and found her hand so trembling, that she said, half smiling, that she could not write. Mary was only too well pleased to supply the deficiency. Dr. May looked at her anxiously, and asked whether she felt overcome.

'No, papa. I did not know my hand was shaky.'

He took it into his, and pressed it. Ethel knew, then, how much had been undeveloped in her own mind, catching it, as it were, from his touch and look. The thought of his past joy—the sad fading of hope for Margaret—the fear and doubt for their present bride—above all, the sense that the fashion of this world passeth away; and that it is not the outward scene, but our bearing in it, that is to last for ever.

The bells struck up, each peal ending with a crash, that gave Ethel some vague idea of fatality; and they all came back to the house, where Margaret was ready, in the drawing-room, to receive them, looking very pretty, in her soft blue dress, which especially became her fair complexion, and light brown hair. Ethel did not quite like the pink colour on her cheeks, and feared that she had been shaken by Flora's agitation, in the morning; but she was very calm and bright, in the affectionate greeting with which she held out her hands to the bride and bridegroom, as they came in.

Mr. Rivers and Meta were the only guests, and, while Meta was seized by the children, Margaret lay talking to Mr. Rivers, George standing upright and silent behind her sofa, like a sentinel. Flora was gone to change her dress, not giving way, but nervous and hurried, as she reiterated parting directions about household comforts to Ethel, who stood by the toilette-table, sticking a pin into the pincushion and drawing it out again, as if solely intent on making it always fit into the same hole, while Mary dressed Flora, packed, flew about, and was useful.

As they came down-stairs, Ethel found that Flora was trembling from head to foot, and leaning on her; Dr. May stood at the foot of the stairs, and folded his daughter in a long embrace; Flora gave herself up to it as if she would never bear to leave it. Did a flash come over her then, what the father was, whom she had held cheaply? what was the worth of that for which she had exchanged such a home? She spoke not a word, she only clung tightly—if her heart failed her—it was too late. 'Bless you! my child!' he said, at last. 'Only be what your mother was!'

A coming tread warned them to part. There was a tray of luncheon for the two who were about to depart, and the great snow-white cake was waiting for Flora to cut it. She smiled, accomplished that feat steadily, and Norman continuing the operation, Aubrey guided Gertrude in handing round the slices.

George did full justice thereto, as well as to the more solid viands. Flora could taste nothing, but she contrived to smile and say it was too early. She was in haste to have it over now, and, as soon as George had finished, she rose up, still composed and resolved, the last kisses were given—Gertrude was lifted up to her, after she was in the carriage for the very last, when George proposed to run away with her also, whereupon Daisy kicked and screamed, and was taken back in haste. The door was shut, and they drove off, bound for the Continent, and then Mary, as if the contingency of losing Flora had only for the first time occurred to her as the consequence of the wedding, broke out into a piteous fit of sobbing—rather too unrestrained, considering her fourteen years.

Poor Mary, she was a very child still! They pulled her into the study, out of the way of Mr. Rivers, and Meta had no sooner said how Flora would soon come home and live at the Grange, and talked of the grand school-feast, to which she was at once going to take her friends, than the round rosy face drew out of its melancholy puckers into smiles, as Mary began to tell the delight caused by the invitations which she had conveyed. That was to be a feast indeed—all the Abbotstoke children—all Flora's class at Stoneborough, and as many Cocksmoor scholars as could walk so far, were to dine on Christmas fare, at one o'clock, at the Grange, and Meta was in haste to be at home to superintend the feast.

Mary, Blanche, and Aubrey went with her, under the keeping of Miss Bracy, the boys were to follow. She had hoped for Ethel, but on looking at her, ceased her coaxing importunity.

'I see,' she said, kindly; 'even school children will not be so good for you as peace.'

'Thank you,' said Ethel, 'I should like to be quiet till the evening, if you will let me off. It is very kind in you.'

'I ought to know how to pity you,' said Meta, 'I who have gained what you have lost.'

'I want to think too,' said Ethel. 'It is the beginning to me of a new life, and I have not been able to look at it yet.'

'Besides, Margaret will want you. Poor Margaret—has it been very trying to her?'

'I fear so, but I shall keep out of the way, and leave her to a quiet afternoon with Richard. It will be the greatest treat to those two to be together.'

'Very well, I will carry off the children, and leave the house quiet.'

And quiet it was in another hour—Gertrude walking with the nurses, Dr. May gone to his patients, and all the rest at Abbotstoke, except Richard and Margaret down-stairs; and Ethel, who while arranging her properties in her new room, had full leisure to lay out before herself the duties that had devolved on her, and to grapple with them. She recalled the many counsels that she had received from Flora, and they sounded so bewildering, that she wished it had been Conic sections, and then she looked at a Hebrew grammar that Norman had given her, and gave a sigh as she slipped it into the shelf of the seldom used. She looked about the room, cleared out the last piece of brown paper, and burnt the last torn envelope, that no relic of packing and change might distress Margaret's eyes for order—then feeling at once desolate and intrusive, she sat down in Flora's fire-side chair, opened her desk, and took out her last time-table. She looked at it for some minutes, laid it aside, and rising, knelt down. Again seating herself, she resumed her paper, took a blank one, ruled it, and wrote her rules for each hour of each day in the week. That first hour after breakfast, when hitherto she had been free, was one sacrifice —it must go now, to ordering dinner, seeing after stores, watching over the children's clothes, and the other nondescripts, which, happily for her, Flora had already reduced to method. The other loss was the spare time between the walk and tea; she must not spend that in her own room now, or there would be no one to sit with Margaret, or keep the little ones from being troublesome to her. Ethel had often had to give up this space before, when Flora went out in the evening, and she had seldom felt otherwise than annoyed. Give it up for good! that was the cure for temper, but it had been valuable as something of her own! She would have been thankful could she have hoped to keep regularly to her own rules, but that she knew was utterly improbable—boys, holidays, callers, engagements, Dr. May, would all conspire to turn half her days upside down, and Cocksmoor itself must often depend not only on the weather, but on home doings. Two or three notes she wrote at the foot of her paper.

' N.B.—These are a standard—not a bed of Procrustes.

    Musts—To be first consulted. *Mays*—last. Ethel May's last of all.

    If I cannot do everything—omit the self-chosen.

    Mem.—Neither hurry when it depends on myself, nor fidget when it depends on others.

    Keep a book going, to pacify myself.'

Her rules drawn up, Ethel knelt once more. Then she drew a long sigh, and wondered where Flora was; and next, as she was fairly fagged, mind and body, she threw herself back in the arm-chair, took up a railway novel that Hector had brought home, and which they had hidden from the children, and repaired herself with the luxury of an idle reading.

Margaret and Richard likewise spent a peaceful, though pensive afternoon. Margaret had portions of letters from Alan to read to him, and a consultation to hold. The hope of her full recovery had so melted away, that she had, in every letter, striven to prepare Mr. Ernescliffe for the disappointment, and each that she received in return was so sanguine and affectionate, that the very fondness was as much grief as joy. She could not believe that he took in the true state of the case, or was prepared to perceive that she could never be his wife, and she wanted Richard to write one of his clear, dispassionate statements, such as carried full conviction, and to help to put a final end to the engagement.

'But why,' said Richard—'why should you wish to distress him?'

'Because I cannot bear that he should be deceived, and should feed on false hopes. Do you think it right, Richard?'

'I will write to him, if you like,' said Richard; 'but I think he must pretty well know the truth from all the letters to Harry and to himself.'

'It would be so much better for him, to settle his mind at once,' said Margaret.

'Perhaps he would not think so—'

There was a pause, while Margaret saw that her brother was thinking. At last, he said, 'Margaret, will you pardon me? I do think that this is a little restlessness. The truth has not been kept from him, and I do not see that we are called to force it on him. He is sensible and reasonable, and will know how to judge when he comes home.'

'It was to try to save him the pang,' murmured Margaret.

'Yes; but it will be worse far away than near. I do not mean that we should conceal the fact, but you have no right to give him up before he comes home. The whole engagement was for the time of his voyage.'

'Then you think I ought not to break it off before his return?'

'Certainly not.'

'It will be pain spared—unless it should be worse by-and-by.'

'I do not suppose we ought to look to by-and-by,' said Richard.

'How so?'

'Do the clearly right thing for the present, I mean,' he said, 'without anxiety for the rest. How do we—any of us—know what may be the case in another year?'

'Do not flatter me with hopes,' said Margaret, sadly smiling; 'I have had too many of them.'

'No,' said Richard; 'I do not think you will ever get well. But so much may happen—'

'I had rather have my mind made up once for all, and resign myself,' said Margaret.

'His will is sometimes that we should be uncertain,' said Richard.

'And that is the most trying,' said Margaret.

'Just so—' and he paused tenderly.

'I feel how much has been right,' said Margaret. 'This wedding has brought my real character before me. I feel what I should have been. You have no notion how excited and elated I can get about a little bit of dress out of the common way for myself, or others,' said she, smiling—'and then all the external show and things belonging to station—I naturally care much more for them than even Flora does. Ethel would bear all those things as if they did not exist—I could not.'

'They would be a temptation?'

'They would once have been. Yes, they would now,' said Margaret. 'And government, and management, and influence—you would not guess what dreams I used to waste on them, and now here am I set aside from it all, good for nothing but for all you dear ones to be kind to.'

'They would not say so,' said Richard, kindly.

'Not say it, but I feel it. Papa and Ethel are all the world to each other—Richard, I may say it to you—There has been only one thing more hard to bear than that—Don't suppose there was a moment's neglect, or disregard; but when first I understood that Ethel could be more to him than I—then I could not always feel rightly. It was the punishment for always wanting to be first.'

'My father would be grieved that you had the notion. You should not keep it.'

'He does not know it is so,' said Margaret; 'I am his first care, I fear, his second grief; but it is not in the nature of things that Ethel should not be more his comfort and companion. Oh! I am glad it was not she who married! What shall we do when she goes?'

This came from Margaret's heart, so as to show that, if there had once been a jealous pang of mortification, it had been healed by overflowing, unselfish affection, and humility.

They went off to praise Ethel, and thence to praise Norman, and the elder brother and sister, who might have had some jealousy of the superiority of their juniors, spent a good happy hour in dwelling on the shining qualities they loved so heartily.

And Richard was drawn into talking of his own deeper thoughts, and Margaret had again the comfort of clerical counsel—and now from her own most dear brother! So they sat till darkness closed in, when Ethel came down, bringing Gertrude and her great favour, very full of chatter, only not quite sure whether she had been bride, bridemaid, or bridegroom.

The school-room set, with Tom and Aubrey, came home soon
after, and tongues went fast with stories of roast-beef, plum-
pudding, and blind-man's buff. How the dear Meta had sent a
cart to Cocksmoor to bring Cherry herself, and how many slices
everybody had eaten, and how the bride's health had been drunk
by the children in real wine, and how they had all played,
Norman and all, and how Hector had made Blanche bold enough
to extract a raisin from the flaming snap-dragon.—It was not
half told when Dr. May came home, and Ethel went up to dress
for her dinner at Abbotstoke, Mary following to help her, and
continue her narration, which bade fair to entertain Margaret
the whole evening.

Dr. May, Richard, and Ethel, had a comfortable dark drive to
the Grange, and, on arriving, found Hector deep in 'Wild Sports
of the West,' while Norman and Meta were sitting over the fire
talking, and Mr. Rivers was resting in his library.

And when Ethel and Meta spent the time before the gentlemen
came in from the dining-room, in a happy *tête-à-tête*, Ethel learnt
that the fire-light dialogue had been the pleasantest part of the
whole day, and that Meta had had confided to her the existence
of Decius Mus—a secret which Ethel had hitherto considered as
her own peculiar property, but she supposed it was a pledge of
the sisterhood, which Meta professed with all the house of May.

CHAPTER VIII.

' The rest all accepted the kind invitation,
And much bustle it caused in the plumed creation;
Such ruffling of feathers, such pruning of coats,
Such chirping, such whistling, such clearing of throats,
Such polishing bills, and such oiling of pinions,
Had never been known in the biped dominions.'—PEACOCK AT HOME.

ETHELDRED was thankful for that confidence to Meta Rivers, for
without it, she would hardly have succeeded in spurring Norman
up to give the finishing touches to Decius, and to send him in. If
she talked of the poem as the devotion of Decius, he was willing
enough, and worked with spirit, for he liked the ideas, and enjoyed
the expressing them, and trying to bring his lines to his notion of
perfection, but if she called it the 'Newdigate,' or the 'Prize
Poem,' and declared herself sure it would be successful, he yawned,
slackened, leant back in his chair, and began to read other people's
poetry, which Ethel was disrespectful enough not to think nearly
as good as his own.

It was completed at last, and Ethel stitched it up with a narrow red and white ribbon—the Balliol colours; and set Meta at him till a promise was extorted that he would send it in.

And, in due time, Ethel received the following note:

'MY DEAR ETHEL—My peacock bubble has flown over the house. Tell them all about it. Your affectionate, N. W. M.'

They were too much accustomed to Norman's successes to be extraordinarily excited; Ethel would have been much mortified if the prize had been awarded to any one else, but, as it was, it came rather as a matter of course. The Doctor was greatly pleased, and said he should drive round by Abbotstoke to tell the news there, and then laughed beyond measure to hear that Meta had been in the plot, saying, he should accuse the little hummingbird of being a magpie, stealing secrets.

By this time, the bride and bridegroom were writing that they thought of soon returning—they had spent the early spring at Paris, had wandered about in the south of France, and now were at Paris again. Flora's letters were long, descriptive, and affectionate, and she was eager to be kept fully informed of everything at home. As soon as she heard of Norman's success, she wrote a whole budget of letters, declaring that she and George would hear of no refusal; they were going to spend a fortnight at Oxford for the Commemoration, and must have Meta and Ethel with them to hear Norman's poem in the theatre.

Dr. May, who already had expressed a hankering to run up for the day, and take Ethel with him, was perfectly delighted at the proposal, and so was Mr. Rivers, but the young ladies made many demurs. Ethel wanted Mary to go in her stead, and had to be told that this would not be by any means the same to the other parties—she could not bear to leave Margaret; it was a long time since there had been letters from the Alcestis, and she did not like to miss being at home when they should come; and Meta, on her side, was so unwilling to leave her father, that, at last, Dr. May scolded them both for a pair of conceited, self-important damsels, who thought nothing could go on without them; and next, compared them to young birds, obliged to be shoved by force into flying.

Meta consented first, on condition that Ethel would; and Ethel found that her whole house would be greatly disappointed if she refused, so she proceeded to be grateful, and then discovered how extremely delightful the plan was. Oxford, of which she had heard so much, and which she had always wished to see! And Norman's glory—and Meta's company—nay, the very holiday, and going from home, were charms enough for a girl of eighteen, who had never been beyond Whitford in her life.

Besides, to crown all, papa promised that, if his patients would behave well, and not want him too much, he would come up for the one great day.

Mr. and Mrs. George Rivers came to Abbotstoke to collect their party. They arrived by a railroad, whose station was nearer to Abbotstoke than to Stoneborough, therefore, instead of their visiting the High-street by the way, Dr. May, with Ethel, and Mary, were invited to dine at the Grange, the first evening—a proposal, at least, as new and exciting to Mary, as was the journey to Oxford, to her sister.

The two girls went early, as the travellers had intended to arrive before luncheon, and, though Ethel said few words, but let Mary rattle on with a stream of conjectures and questions, her heart was full of longings for her sister, as well as of strange doubts and fears, as to the change that her new life might have made in her.

'There! there!' cried Mary. 'Yes! it is Flora! Only she has her hair done in a funny way!'

Flora and Meta were both standing on the steps before the conservatory, and Mary made but one bound before she was hugging Flora. Ethel kissed her without so much violence, and then saw that Flora was looking very well and bright, more decidedly pretty and elegant than ever, and with certainly no diminution of affection; it was warmer, though rather more patronizing.

'How natural you look!' was her first exclamation, as she held Mary's hand, and drew Ethel's arm into hers. 'And how is Margaret?'

'Pretty well—but the heat makes her languid—'

'Is there any letter yet?'

'No—'

'I do not see any cause for alarm—letters are so often detained, but, of course, she will be anxious.—Has she had pain in the back again.'

'Sometimes, but summer always does her good—'

'I shall see her to-morrow—and the Daisy—How do you all get on? Have you broken down yet, Ethel?'

'Oh! we do go on,' said Ethel, smiling; 'the worst thing I have done was expecting James to dress the salads with lamp-oil.'

'A Greenland salad! But don't talk of oil—I have the taste still in my mouth after the Pyrennean cookery! Oh! Ethel, you would have been wild with delight in those places!'

'Snowy mountains! Are they not like a fairy-dream to you now? You must have felt at home, as a Scotchwoman's daughter.'

'Think of the peaks in the sunrise! Oh! I wanted you in the

pass of Roncevalles, to hear the echo of Roland's horn. And we saw the cleft made by Roland's sword in the rocks.'

'Oh! how delightful—and Spain too!'

'Aye, the Isle of Pheasants, where all the conferences took place.'

'Where Louis XIV. met his bride, and François I. sealed his treason with his empty flourish—'

'Well, don't let us fight about François I. now; I want to know how Tom likes Eton.'

'He gets on famously. I am so glad he is in the same house with Hector.'

'Mr. Ramsden—how is he?'

'No better—he has not done any duty for weeks. Tomkins and his set want to sell the next presentation, but papa hopes to stave that off, for there is a better set than usual in the Town Council this year.'

'Cocksmoor? And how are our friends the Muses? I found a note from the secretary telling me that I am elected again. How have they behaved?'

'Pretty well,' said Ethel. 'Mrs. Ledwich has been away, so we have had few meetings, and have been pretty quiet, except for an uproar about the mistress beating that Franklin's girl— and what do you think I did, Flora? I made bold to say the woman should show her to papa, to see if she had done her any harm, and he found that it was all a fabrication from one end to the other. So it ended in the poor girl being expelled, and Mary and I have her twice a week, to see if there is any grace in her.'

'To reward her!' said Flora. 'That is always your way—'

'Why, one cannot give the poor thing quite up,' said Ethel.

'You will manage the ladies at last!' cried Flora.

'Not while Mrs. Ledwich is there!'

'I'll cope with her! But, come, I want you in my room—'

'May not I come?' said Meta. 'I must see when—'

Flora held up her hand, and, while signing invitation, gave an arch look to Meta to be silent. Ethel here bethought herself of enquiring after Mr. Rivers, and then for George.

Mr. Rivers was pretty well—George, quite well, and somewhere in the garden; and Meta said that he had such a beard that they would hardly know him; while Flora added that he was delighted with the Oxford scheme.

Flora's rooms had been, already, often shown to her sisters, when Mr. Rivers had been newly furnishing them, with every luxury and ornament that taste could devise. Her dressing-room, with the large bay window, commanding a beautiful view of Stoneborough, and filled, but not crowded, with every sort of choice article, was a perfect exhibition to eyes unaccustomed to such varieties.

Mary could have been still amused by the hour, in studying the devices and ornaments on the shelves and chiffonieres; and Blanche had romanced about it, to the little ones, till they were erecting it into a mythical palace.

And Flora, in her simple, well-chosen dress, looked, and moved, as if she had been born and bred in the like.

There were signs of unpacking about the room—Flora's dressing-case on the table, and some dresses lying on the sofa and ottoman.

Mary ran up to them eagerly, and exclaimed at the beautiful shot blue-and-white silk.

'Paris fashions?' said Ethel, carelessly.

'Yes; but I don't parade my own dresses here,' said Flora.

'Whose are they, then? Your commissions, Meta?'

'No!' and Meta laughed heartily.

'Your French maid's, then?' said Ethel. 'I dare say she dresses quite as well; and the things are too really pretty and simple for an English maid's taste.'

'I am glad you like them,' said Flora, maliciously. 'Now, please to be good.'

'Who are they for, then?' said Ethel, beginning to be frightened.

'For a young lady, whose brother has got the Newdigate prize, and who is going to Oxford.'

'Me! Those! But I have not got four backs,' as Ethel saw Meta in fits of laughing, and Flora making affirmative signs. Mary gave a ponderous spring of ecstasy.

'Come!' said Flora, 'you may as well be quiet. Whatever you may like, I am not going to have the Newdigate prizeman shown as brother to a scare-crow. I knew what you would come to, without me to take care of you. Look at yourself in the glass.'

'I'm sure I see no harm in myself,' said Ethel, turning towards the pier-glass, and surveying herself—in a white muslin, made high, a black silk mantle, and a brown hat. She had felt very respectable when she set out, but she could not avoid a lurking conviction that, beside Flora and Meta, it had a scanty, school-girl effect. 'And,' she continued, quaintly, 'besides, I have *really* got a new gown on purpose—a good useful silk, that papa chose at Whitford—just the colour of a copper tea-kettle, where it turns purple.'

'Ethel! you will kill me!' said Meta, sinking back on the sofa.

'And, I suppose,' continued Flora, 'that you have sent it to Miss Broad's, without any directions, and she will trim it with flame-coloured gimp, and glass buttons; and, unless Margaret catches you, you will find yourself ready to set the Thames on fire. No, my dear tea-kettle, I take you to Oxford on my own terms, and you had better submit, without a fuss, and be thankful it is no worse. George wanted me to buy you a white brocade, with a perfect flower-garden on it, that you could have examined with a microscope. I was obliged to let him buy that lace mantle, to make up to him. Now then, Meta, the scene opens, and discovers—'

Meta opened the folding-doors into Flora's bed-room, and thence came forward Bellairs and a little brisk Frenchwoman, whom Flora had acquired at Paris. The former, who was quite used to adorning Miss Ethel against her will, looked as amused as her mistresses; and, before Ethel knew what was going on, her muslin was stripped off her back, and that instrument of torture, a half-made body, was being tried upon her. She made one of her most wonderful grimaces of despair, and stood still! The dresses were not so bad after all; they were more tasteful than costly, and neither in material nor ornament were otherwise than suitable to the occasion, and the wearer. It was very kind and thoughtful of Flora—that she could not but feel—nothing had been forgotten, but when Ethel saw the mantles, the ribbons, the collars, the bonnet, all glistening with the French air of freshness and grace, she began to feel doubts and hesitations, whether she ought to let her sister go to such an expense on her account, and privately resolved that the accepting thanks should not be spoken, till she should have consulted her father.

In the mean time, she could only endure, be laughed at by her elders, and entertained by Mary's extreme pleasure in her array. Good Mary—it was more than any comedy to her; she had not one moment's thought of herself, till, when Flora dived into her box, produced a pair of bracelets, and fastened them on her comfortable plump arms, her eyes grew wide with wonder, and she felt, at least, two stages nearer womanhood.

Flora had omitted no one. There was a Paris present for every servant at home, and a needle-case even for Cherry Elwood, for which Ethel thanked her with a fervency wanting in her own case.

She accomplished consulting her father on her scruples, and he set her mind at rest. He knew that the outlay was a mere trifle to the Riverses, and was greatly pleased and touched with the affection that Flora showed ; so he only smiled at Ethel's doubts, and dwelt with heartfelt delight on the beautiful print, that she had brought him from Ary Scheffer's picture of the Great Consoler.

Flora was in her glory. To be able to bestow benefits on those whom she loved, had been always a favourite vision, and she had the full pleasure of feeling how much enjoyment she was causing. They had a very pleasant evening ; she gave interesting accounts of their tour, and by her appeals to her husband, made him talk also. He was much more animated and agreeable than Ethel had ever seen him, and was actually laughing, and making Mary laugh heartily with his histories of the inns in the Pyrenees. Old Mr. Rivers looked as proud and happy as possible, and was quite young and gay, having evidently forgotten all his maladies, in paying elaborate attention to his daughter-in-law.

Ethel told Margaret, that night, that she was quite satisfied about Flora—she was glad to own that she had done her injustice, and that Norman was right in saying there was more in George Rivers than met the eye.

The morning spent at home was equally charming. Flora came back, with love strengthened by absence. She was devoted to Margaret—caressing to all; she sat in her old places; she fulfilled her former offices; she gratified Miss Bracy, by visiting her in the school-room, and talking of French books; and won golden opinions, by taking Gertrude in her hand, and walking to Minster-street, to call on Mrs. Hoxton, as in old times, and take her the newest foreign device of working to kill time.

So a few days passed merrily away, and the great journey commenced. Ethel met the Abbotstoke party at the station, and, with a parting injunction to her father, that he was to give all his patients a sleeping potion, that they might not miss him, she was carried away from Stoneborough.

Meta was in her gayest mood ; Ethel full of glee and wonder, for once beyond Whitford, the whole world was new to her; Flora more quiet, but greatly enjoying their delight, and George not saying much, but smiling under his beard, as if well pleased to be so well amused with so little trouble.

He took exceeding care of them, and fed them with everything he could make them eat at the Swindon station, asking for impossible things, and wishing them so often to change for something better, that, if they had been submissive, they would have had no luncheon at all; and, as it was, Flora was obliged to whisk into the carriage with her last sandwich in her hand.

'I am the more sorry,' said he, after grumbling at the allotted ten minutes, 'as we shall dine so late. You desired Norman to bring any friend he liked, did you not, Flora?'

'Yes, and he spoke of bringing our old friend, Charles Cheviot, and Mr. Ogilvie,' said Flora.

'Mr. Ogilvie!' said Ethel, 'the Master of Glenbracken! Oh! I am so glad. I have wanted so much to see him!'

'Ah! he is a great hero of yours,' said Flora.

'Do you know him?' said Meta.

'No; but he is a great friend of Norman's, and a Scottish cousin —Norman Ogilvie. Norman has his name from the Ogilvies.'

'Our grandmother, Mrs. Mackenzie, was a daughter of Lord Glenbracken,' said Flora.

'This man might be called the Master of Glenbracken at home,' said Ethel. 'It is such a pretty title, and there is a beautiful history belonging to them. There was a Master of Glenbracken who carried James IV.'s standard at Flodden, and would not yield, and was killed with it wrapped round his body, and the Lion was dyed with his blood. Mamma knew some scraps of a ballad about him. Then they were out with Montrose, and had their castle burnt by the Covenanters, and since that they have been Jacobites, and one barely escaped being beheaded at Carlisle! I want to hear the rights of it! Norman is to go, some time or other, to stay at Glenbracken!'

'Yes,' said Flora, 'coming down to times present, this young heir seems worthy of his race. They are pattern people—have built a Church, and have all their tenantry in excellent order. This is the only son, and very good and clever—he preferred going to Balliol, that he might work; but he is a great sportsman, George,' added she; 'you will get on with him very well, about fishing, and grouse shooting, I dare say.'

Norman met them at the station, and there was great excitement at seeing his long nose under his college cap. He looked rather thin and worn, but brightened at the sight of the party. After the question—whether there had been any letters from Harry? he asked whether his father were coming?—and Ethel thought he seemed nervous at the idea of this addition to his audience. He saw them to their hotel, and, promising them his two guests, departed.

Ethel watched collegiate figures passing in the street, and recollected the grey buildings, just glimpsed at in her drive—it was dreamy and confused, and she stood musing, not discovering that it was time to dress, till Flora and her Frenchwoman came in, and laid violent hands on her.

The effect of their manipulations was very successful. Ethel was made to look well-dressed, and, still more, distinguished. Her height told well, when her lankiness was overcome, and her hair was disposed so as to set off her features to advantage. The glow of amusement and pleasure did still more for her; and Norman, who was in the parlour when the sisters appeared, quite started with surprise and satisfaction at her aspect.

'Well done, Flora!' he said. 'Why! I have been telling Ogilvie that one of my sisters was very plain!'

'Then I hope we have been preparing an agreeable surprise for him,' said Flora. 'Ethel is very much obliged to you. By-the-by,' she said, in her universal amity, 'I must ask Harvey Anderson to dinner one of these days?'

Norman started—and his face said, 'Don't.'

'O, very well; it is as you please. I thought it would please Stoneborough, and that Edward was a *protégé* of yours. What has he been doing? Did we not hear he had been distinguishing himself? Dr. Hoxton was boasting of his two scholars.'

'Ask him,' said Norman, hurriedly. 'At least,' said he, 'do not let anything from me prevent you.'

'Has he been doing anything wrong?' reiterated Flora.

'Not that I know of,' was the blunt answer; and, at the same instant, Mr. Ogilvie arrived. He was a pleasant, high-bred looking gentleman, brown-complexioned, and dark-eyed, with a brisk and resolute cast of countenance, that, Ethel thought, might have suited the Norman of Glenbracken, who died on the ruddy Lion of Scotland, and speaking with the very same slight degree of Scottish intonation as she remembered in her mother, making a most home-like sound in her ears.

Presently, the rest of their own party came down, and, soon after, Charles Cheviot appeared, looking as quiet, and tame, as he used to be in the school-boy days, when Norman would bring him home, and he used to be too shy to speak a word.

However, he had learnt the use of his tongue by this time, though it was a very soft one; and he stood by Ethel, asking many questions about Stoneborough, while something apparently very spirited and amusing, was going on between the others.

The dinner went off well—there were few enough for the conversation to be general. The young men began to strike out sparks of wit against each other—Flora put in a word or two—Ethel grew so much interested in the discussion, that her face lighted up, and she joined in it, as if it had been only between her father and brother—keen, clear, and droll. After that, she had her full share in the conversation, and enjoyed it so much that, when she left the dinner-table, she fetched her writing-case, to sketch the colloquy for Margaret and her father.

Flora exclaimed at her, for never allowing any one to think of rest. Meta said she should like to do the same, but it was impossible now; she did not know how she should ever settle down to write a letter. Ethel was soon interrupted; the gentlemen entered, and Mr. Ogilvie came to the window where she was sitting, and began to tell her how much obliged to her he and his College were, for having insisted on her brother sending in his poem. 'Thanks are due, for our being spared an infliction next week,' he said.

'Have you seen it?' she asked, and she was amused by the quick negative movement of his head.

'I read my friend's poems? But our lungs are prepared! Will you give me my cue—it is of no use to ask him when we are to deafen you. One generally knows the crack passages—something beginning with "O woman!" but it is well to be in readiness—if you would only forewarn me of the telling hits?'

'If they cannot tell themselves,' said Ethel, smiling, 'I don't think they deserve the name.'

'Perhaps you think what does tell on the undergraduates, collectively, is not always what ought to tell on them.'

'I don't know. I dare say the same would not be a favourite with them and with me.'

'I should like to know which are your favourites. No doubt you have a copy here—made by yourself—' and he looked towards her paper-case.

There was the copy, and she took it out, peering to see whether Norman were looking.

'Let me see,' he said, as she paused to open the MS., 'he told me the thoughts were more yours than his own.'

'Did he? That was not fair. One thought was an old one, long ago talked over between us; the rest is all his own.'

Here Mr. Ogilvie took the paper, and Ethel saw his countenance show evident tokens of surprise and feeling.

'Yes,' he said, presently, 'May goes deep—deeper than most men—though I doubt whether they will applaud this.'

'I should like it better if they did not,' said Ethel. 'It is rather to be felt than shouted at.'

'And I don't know how the world would go on if it were felt. Few men would do much without the hope of fame,' said Norman Ogilvie.

'Is it the question what they *would* do ?' said Ethel.

'So you call fame a low motive ? I see where your brother's philosophy comes from.'

'I do not call it a low motive—' Her pause was expressive.

'Nor allow that the *Non omnis moriar* of Horace has in it something divine ?'

'For a heathen—yes.'

'And pray, what would you have the moving spring ?'

'Duty.'

'Would not that end in, " Mine be a cot, beside the rill ?" ' said he, with an intonation of absurd sentiment.

'Well, and suppose an enemy came, would not duty prompt the Hay with the yoke—or Winkelried on the spears ?'

'Nay, why not—" It is my duty to take care of Lucy." '

'Then Lucy ought to be broken on her own wheel.'

'Not at all ! It is Lucy's duty to keep her Colin from running into danger.'

'I hope there are not many Lucies who would think so.'

'I agree with you.   Most would rather have Colin killed than disgraced.'

'To be sure !' then, perceiving a knowing twinkle, as if he thought she had made an admission, she added, ' but what is disgrace ?'

'Some say it is misfortune,' said Mr. Ogilvie.

'Is it not failure in duty ?' said Ethel.

'Well !'

'Colin's first duty is to his king and country.   If he fail in that, he is disgraced, in his own eyes, before Heaven, and men. If he does it, there is a reward, which seems to me a better, more powerful motive for Lucy to set before him than, " My dear, I hope you will distinguish yourself," when, the fact is,

> " England has forty thousand men,
> We trust, as good as he." '

' " Victory or Westminster Abbey !" is a tolerable war cry,' said Mr. Ogilvie.

'Not so good as " England expects every man to do his duty." That serves for those who cannot look to Westminster Abbey.'

'Ah ! you are an English woman !'

'Only by halves.   I had rather have been the Master of Glenbracken at Flodden than King James, or—' for she grew rather ashamed of having been impelled to utter the personal allusion, ' better to have been the Swinton or the Gordon at Homildon, than all the rest put together.'

'I always thought Swinton a pig-headed old fellow, and I

have little doubt that my ancestor was a young ruffian,' coolly answered the Master of Glenbracken.

'Why?' was all that Ethel could say in her indignation.

'It was the normal state of Scottish gentlemen,' he answered.

'If I thought you were in earnest, I should say you did not deserve to be a Scot.'

'And so you wish to make me out a fause Scot!'

'Ogilvie!' called Norman, 'are you fighting Scottish and English battles with Ethel there? We want you to tell us which will be the best day for going to Blenheim.'

The rest of the evening was spent in arranging the programme of their lionizing, in which it appeared that the Scottish cousin intended to take his full share. Ethel was not sorry, for he interested her much, while provoking her. She was obliged to put out her full strength in answering him, and felt, at the same time, that he was not making any effort in using the arguments that puzzled her—she was in earnest, while he was at play; and, though there was something teasing in this, and she knew it partook of what her brothers called chaffing, it gave her that sense of power on his side, which is always attractive to women. With the knowledge, that through Norman, she had of his real character, she understood that half, at least, of what he said, was jest; and the other half was enough in earnest to make it exciting to argue with him.

CHAPTER IX.

'While I, thy dearest, sat apart,
And felt thy triumphs were as mine,
And loved them more that they were thine.'—TENNYSON.

THAT was a week of weeks; the most memorable week in Ethel's life, spent in indefatigable sight-seeing. College Chapels, Bodleian Library, Taylor Gallery, the Museum, all were thoroughly studied, and, if Flora had not dragged the party on, in mercy to poor George's patience, Ethel would never have got through a day's work.

Indeed, Mr. Ogilvie, when annoyed at being hurried in going over Merton Chapel with her, was heard to whisper that he acted the part of policeman, by a perpetual 'move on;' and as Ethel recollected the portly form and wooden face of the superintendent at Stoneborough, she was afraid that the comparison would not soon be forgotten. Norman Ogilvie seemed to consider himself bound to their train as much as his namesake, or, as on the second morning, Norman reported his reasoning, it was that a man must walk about with somebody in Commemoration week,

and that it was a comfort to do so with ladies who wore their
bonnets upon their heads, instead of, like most of those he met,
reminding him of what Cock Robin said to Jenny Wren in that
matrimonial quarrel, when

> 'Robin, he grew angry,
> Hopped upon a twig—'

Flora was extremely delighted, and, in matronly fashion, told
her sister that people were always respected and admired who
had the strength of mind to resist unsuitable customs.   Ethel
laughed in answer, and said, she thought it would take a great
deal more strength of mind to go about with her whole visage
exposed to the universal gaze; and, woman like, they had a
thorough gossip over the evils of the 'back-sliding' head-gear.

Norman had retreated from it into the window, when Flora
returned to the charge about Harvey Anderson.   She had been
questioning their old friend Mr. Everard, and had learnt from him
that the cause of the hesitation, with which his name had been
received, was that he had become imbued with some of the Ration-
alistic ideas current in some quarters.   He seldom met Norman
May without forcing on him debates, which were subjects of great
interest to the hearers, as the two young men were considered as
the most distinguished representatives of their respective causes,
among their own immediate contemporaries.   Norman's powers
of argument, his eloquence, readiness, and clearness, were thought
to rank very high, and, in the opinion of Mr. Everard, had been
of great effect in preventing other youths from being carried
away by the specious brilliancy of his rival.

Ethel valued this testimony far above the Newdigate prize, and
she was extremely surprised by hearing Flora declare her intention
of still asking Mr. Anderson to dinner, only consulting her brother
as to the day.

'Why, Flora! ask him! Norman—'

Norman had turned away with the simple answer, 'any day.'

'Norman is wiser than you are, Ethel,' said Flora.   'He
knows that Stoneborough would be up in arms at any neglect
from us to one of the Andersons, and, considering the rivalship,
it is the more graceful and becoming.'

'I do not think it right,' said Ethel, stoutly; 'I believe that
a line ought to be drawn, and that we ought not to associate
with people who openly tamper with their faith.'

'Never fear,' smiled Flora; 'I promise you that there shall be
no debates at *my* table.'

Ethel felt the force of the pronoun, and, as Flora walked out
of the room, she went up to Norman, who had been resting his
brow against the window.

'It is vain to argue with her,' she said; 'but, Norman, do not you think it is clearly wrong to seek after men who desert and deny—'

She stopped short, frightened at his pale look.

He spoke in a clear low tone, that seemed to thrill her with a sort of alarm. 'If the secrets of men's hearts were probed, who could cast the first stone?'

'I don't want to cast stones,' she began; but he made a gesture as if he would not hear, and, at the same moment, Mr. Ogilvie entered the room.

Had Ethel been at home, she would have pondered much over her brother's meaning—here she had no leisure. Not only was she fully occupied with the new scenes around, but her Scottish cousin took up every moment open to conversation. He was older than Norman, and had just taken his degree, and he talked with that superior *aplomb*, which a few years bestow at their time of life, without conceit, but more hopeful and ambitious, and with higher spirits than his cousin.

Though industrious and distinguished, he had not avoided society or amusement, was a great cricketer and tennis-player, one of the 'eight' whose success in the boat-races was one of Norman's prime interests, and he told stories of frolics that reminded Ethel of her father's old Cambridge adventures.

He was a new variety in her eyes, and entertained her greatly. Where the bounds of banter ended, was not easy to define, but whenever he tried a little mystification, she either entered merrily into the humour, or threw it over with keen wit that he kept constantly on the stretch. They were always discovering old, unexpected bits of knowledge in each other, and a great deal more accordance in views and opinions than appeared on the surface, for his enthusiasm usually veiled itself in persiflage on hers, though he was too good and serious at heart to carry it too far.

At Blenheim, perhaps, he thought he had given an overdose of nonsense, and made her believe, as Meta really did, that the Duchess Sarah was his model woman; for as they walked in the park in search of Phœbe Mayflower's well, he gathered a fern leaf, to show her the Glenbracken badge, and talked to her of his home, his mother, and his sister Marjorie, and the little Church in the rocky glen. He gave the history of the stolen meetings of the little knot of Churchmen during the days of persecution, and showed a heart descended straight from the Ogilvie who was 'out with Montrose,' now that the upper structure of Young England was for a little while put aside.

After this, she took his jokes much more coolly, and made thrusts beneath them, which he seemed to enjoy, and caused him to unfold himself the more. She liked him all the better for finding that he thought Norman had been a very good friend to him, and that he admired her brother heartily, watching tenderly over his tendencies to make himself unhappy. He confided to her that, much as he rejoiced in the defeats of Anderson, he feared that the reading and thought consequent on the discussions, had helped to overstrain Norman's mind, and he was very anxious to carry him away from all study and toil, and make his brains rest, and his eyes delight themselves upon Scottish mountains.

Thereupon came vivid descriptions of the scenery, especially his own glen with the ruined tower, and ardent wishes that his cousin Ethel could see them also, and know Marjorie. She could quite echo the wish, Edinburgh and Loch Katrine had been the visions of her life, and now that she had once taken the leap and left home, absence did not seem impossible, and, with a start of delight, she hailed her own conviction that he intended his mother to invite the party to Glenbracken.

After Norman's visit, Mr. Ogilvie declared that he must come home with him and pay his long-promised visit to Stoneborough. He should have come long ago. He had been coming last winter, but the wedding had prevented him; he had always wished to know Dr. May, whom his father well remembered, and now nothing should keep him away!

Flora looked on amused and pleased at Ethel's development—her abruptness softened into piquancy, and her countenance so embellished, that the irregularity only added to the expressiveness. There was no saying what Ethel would come to! She had not said that she would not go to the intended ball, and her grimaces at the mention of it were growing fainter every day.

The discussion about Harvey Anderson was never revived; Flora sent the invitation without another word—he came with half-a-dozen other gentlemen—Ethel made him a civil greeting, but her head was full of boats and the procession day, about which Mr. Ogilvie was telling her, and she thought of him no more.

'A lucky step!' thought Flora. 'A grand thing for Ethel—a capital connection for us all. Lady Glenbracken will not come too much into my sphere either. Yes, I am doing well by my sisters.'

It would make stay-at-home people giddy to record how much pleasure, how much conversation and laughter were crowded into those ten days, and with much thought and feeling beside them, for these were not girls on whom grave Oxford could leave no impression but one of gaiety.

The whole party was very full of merriment. Norman May, especially, on whom Flora contrived to devolve that real leadership of conversation that should rightly have belonged to George Rivers, kept up the ball with wit and drollery far beyond what he usually put forth; enlivened George into being almost an agreeable man, and drew out little Meta's vivacity into sunny sparkles.

Meta generally had Norman for her share, and seemed highly contented with his lionizings, which were given much more quietly and copiously than those which his cousin bestowed upon his sister. Or if there were anything enterprising to be done, any tower to be mounted, or anything with the smallest spice of danger in it, Meta was charmed, and with her lightness and airiness of foot and figure, and perfectly feminine ways, showed a spirit of adventure that added to the general diversion. But if she were to be helped up or down anywhere, she certainly seemed to find greater security in Norman May's assistance, though it was but a feather-like touch that she ever used to aid her bounding step.

Both as being diffident, and, in a manner at home, Norman was not as constantly her cavalier as was Mr. Ogilvie to his sister; and, when supplanted, his wont was either to pioneer for Flora, or, if she did not need him, to walk alone, grave and abstracted. There was a weight on his brow, when nothing was going on to drive it away, and whether it were nervousness as to the performance in store for him, anxiety about Harry, or, as Mr. Ogilvie said, too severe application; some burthen hung upon him, that was only lightened for the time by his participation in the enjoyment of the party.

On Sunday evening, when they had been entering into the almost vision-like delight of the choicest of music, and other accompaniments of Church service, they went to walk in Christchurch meadows. They had begun altogether by comparing feelings—Ethel wondering whether Stoneborough Minster would ever be used as it might be, and whether, if so, they should be practically the better for it; and proceeding with metaphysics on her side, and satire on Norman Ogilvie's, to speculate whether that which is, is best, and the rights and wrongs of striving for change and improvements, what should begin from above, and what from beneath—with illustrations often laughter-moving, though they were much in earnest, as the young heir of Glenbracken looked into his future life.

Flora had diverged into wondering who would have the living after poor old Mr. Ramsden, and walked, keeping her husband amused with instances of his blunders.

Meta, as with Norman she parted from the rest, thought her own dear Abbotstoke Church, and Mr. Charles Wilmot, great subjects for content and thanksgiving, though it was a wonderful treat to see and hear such as she had enjoyed to-day; and she thought it was a joy, to carry away abidingly, to know that praise and worship, as near perfection as this earth could render them, were being offered up.

Norman understood her thought, but responded by more of a sigh than was quite comfortable.

Meta went on with her own thoughts, on the connection between worship and good works, how the one leads to the other, and how praise, with pure lips, is, after all, the great purpose of existence. —Her last thought she spoke aloud.

'I suppose everything, our own happiness and all, are given to us to turn into praise,' she said.

'Yes—' echoed Norman; but as if his thoughts were not quite with hers, or rather in another part of the same subject; then recalling himself, 'Happy such as can do so.'

'If one only could—' said Meta.

'You can—don't say otherwise,' exclaimed Norman; 'I know, at least, that you and my father can.'

'Dr. May does so, more than any one I know,' said Meta.

'Yes,' said Norman, again; 'it is his secret of joy. To him, it is never, "I am half sick of shadows."'

'To him they are not shadows, but foretastes,' said Meta.

Silence again; and when she spoke, she said, 'I have always thought it must be such a happiness to have power of any kind that can be used in direct service, or actual doing good.'

'No,' said Norman. 'Whatever becomes a profession, becomes an unreality.'

'Surely not, in becoming a duty,' said Meta.

'Not for all,' he answered; 'but where the fabric erected by ourselves, in the sight of the world, is but an outer case, a shell of mere words, blown up for the occasion, strung together as mere language; then, self-convicted, we shrink within the husk, and feel our own worthlessness and hypocrisy.'

'As one feels in reproving the school children for behaving ill at Church?' said Meta.

'You never felt anything approaching to it!' said Norman. 'To know oneself to be such a deception, that everything else seems a delusion too!'

'I don't know whether that is metaphysical,' said Meta, 'but I am sure I don't understand it. One must know oneself to be worse than one knows any one else to be.'

'I could not wish you to understand,' said Norman; and yet he seemed impelled to go on; for, after a hesitating silence, he added,

'When the wanderer in the desert fears that the spring is but a mirage; or when all that is held dear is made hazy or distorted by some enchanter, what do you think are the feelings, Meta?'

'It must be dreadful,' she said, rather bewildered; 'but he may know it is a delusion, if he can but wake. Has he not always a spell, a charm?—'

'What is the spell?' eagerly said Norman, standing still.

'Believe—' said Meta, hardly knowing how she came to choose the words.

'I believe!' he repeated. 'What—when we go beyond the province of reason—human, a thing of sense after all! How often have I so answered. But Meta, when a man has been drawn, in self-sufficient security, to look into a magic mirror, and cannot detach his eyes from the confused, misty scene—where all that had his allegiance appears shattered, overthrown, like a broken image, or at least unable to endure examination, then—'

'O Norman, is that the trial to any one here? I thought old Oxford was the great guardian nurse of truth! I am sure she cannot deal in magic mirrors or such frightful things. Do you know you are talking like a very horrible dream?'

'I believe I am in one,' said Norman

'To be sure you are. Wake!' said Meta, looking up, smiling in his face. 'You have read yourself into a maze, that's all—what Mary calls, muzzling your head; you don't really think all this, and when you get into the country, away from books, you will forget it. One look at our dear old purple Welsh hills will blow away all the mists!'

'I ought not to have spoken in this manner,' said Norman, sadly. 'Forget it, Meta.'

'Forget it! Of course I will. It is all nonsense, and meant to be forgotten,' said Meta, laughing. 'You will own that it is by-and-by.'

He gave a deep sigh.

'Don't think I am unfeeling,' she said; 'but I know it is all a fog up from books, books, books—I should like to drive it off with a good fresh gust of wind! Oh! I wish those yellow lilies would grow in our river!'

Meta talked away gaily for the rest of the walk. She was anything but unfeeling, but she had a confidence in Norman that forbade her to see anything here but one of his variations of spirits, which always sank in the hour of triumph. She put forth her brightness to enliven him, and, in their subsequent *tête-à-têtes*, she avoided all that could lead to a renewal of this conversation. Ethel would not have rested till it had been fought out. Meta thought it so imaginary, that it had better die for want of the aliment of words; certainly, hers could not reach an intellect like his, and she would only soothe and amuse him. Dr. May, mind-curer, as well as body-curer, would soon be here, to put the climax to the general joy, and watch his own son.

He did arrive; quite prepared to enjoy, giving an excellent account of both homes; Mr. Rivers very well, and the Wilmots taking care of him, and Margaret as comfortable as usual, Mary making a most important and capable little housekeeper, Miss Bracy as good as possible. He talked as if they had all flourished the better for Ethel's absence, but he had evidently missed her greatly, as he showed, without knowing it, by his instant eager-ness to have her to himself. Even Norman, prizeman as he was, was less wanted. There was proud affection, eager congratula-tion, for him, but it was Ethel to whom he wanted to tell every-thing that had passed during her absence—whom he treated as if they were meeting after a tedious separation.

They dined rather early, and went out afterwards, to walk down the High Street to Christ Church Meadow. Norman and Ethel had been anxious for this; they thought it would give their father the best idea of the *tout ensemble* of Oxford, and were not without hopes of beating him by his own confession, in that standing fight between him and his sons, as to the beauties of Oxford and Cambridge—a fight in which, hitherto, they had been equally matched, neither partisan having seen the rival University.

Flora stayed at home; she owned herself fairly tired by her arduous duties of following the two young ladies about, and was very glad to give her father the keeping of them. Dr. May held out his arm to Ethel—Mr. Ogilvie secured his peculiar property. Ethel could have preferred that it should be otherwise—Norman would have no companion but George Rivers; how bored he would be!

All through the streets, while she was telling her father the names of the buildings, she was not giving her whole attention; she was trying to guess, from the sounds behind, whether Mr. Ogilvie were accompanying them. They entered the meadows—Norman turned round, with a laugh, to defy the Doctor to talk of the Cam, on the banks of the Isis. The party stood still—the other two gentlemen came up. They amalgamated again—all the Oxonians conspiring to say spiteful things of the Cam, and Dr. May making a spirited defence, in which Ethel found herself impelled to join.

In the wide gravelled path they proceeded in threes; George

attached himself to his sister and Norman. Mr. Ogilvie came to Ethel's other side, and began to point out all the various notabilities. Ethel was happy again; her father was so much pleased and amused with him, and he with her father, that it was a treat to look on.

Presently, Dr. May, as usual, always meeting with acquaintances, fell in with a county neighbour, and Ethel had another pleasant aside, until her father claimed her, and Mr. Ogilvie was absorbed among another party, and lost to her sight.

He came to tea, but, by that time, Dr. May had established himself in the chair which had, hitherto, been appropriated to her cousin—a chair that cut her nook off from the rest of the world, and made her the exclusive possession of the occupant. There was a most interesting history for her to hear, of a meeting with the Town Council, which she had left pending, when Dr. May had been battling to save the next presentation of the living from being sold.

Few subjects could affect Ethel more nearly, yet she caught herself missing the thread of his discourse in trying to hear what Mr. Ogilvie was saying to Flora about a visit to Glenbracken.

The time came for the two Balliol men to take their leave. Norman May had been sitting very silent all the evening, and Meta, who was near him, respected his mood. When he said good-night, he drew Ethel outside the door. 'Ethel,' he said, 'only one thing: do ask my father not to put on his spectacles to-morrow.'

'Very well,' said Ethel, half smiling; 'Richard did not mind them.'

'Richard has more humility—I shall break down if he looks at me! I wish you were all at home.'

'Thank you.'

The other Norman came out of the sitting-room at the moment, and heard the last words.

'Never mind,' said he to Ethel, 'I'll take care of him. He shall comport himself as if you were all at Nova Zembla. A pretty fellow to talk of despising fame, and then get a fit of stage-fright!'

'Well, good-night,' said Norman, sighing. 'It will be over to-morrow, only remember the spectacles.'

Dr. May laughed a good deal at the request, and asked if the rest of the party were to be blindfolded. Meta wondered that Ethel should have mentioned the request so publicly; she was a good deal touched by it, and she thought Dr. May ought to be so.

Good-night was said, and Dr. May put his arm round Ethel,

and gave her the kiss that she had missed for seven nights. It was very homelike, and it brought a sudden flash of thought across Ethel. What had she been doing? She had been impatient of her father's monopoly of her!

She parted with Flora, and entered the room she shared with Meta, where Bellairs waited to attend her little mistress. Few words passed between the two girls, and those chiefly on the morrow's dress. Meta had some fixed ideas—she should wear pink—Norman had said he liked her pink bonnet, and then she could put down her white veil, so that he could be certain that she was not looking; Ethel vaguely believed Flora meant her to wear—something—

Bellairs went away, and Meta gave expression to her eager hope that Norman would go through it well. If he would only read it, as he did last Easter to her and Ethel.

'He will,' said Ethel. 'This nervousness always wears off when he comes to the point, and he warms with his subject.'

'Oh! but think of all the eyes looking at him!'

'Ours are all that he really cares for, and he will think of none of them when he begins. No, Meta, you must not encourage him in it. Papa says, if he did not think it half-morbid—the result of *the* shock to his nerves—he should be angry with it as a sort of conceit!'

'I should have thought *that* the last thing to be said of Norman!' said Meta, with a little suppressed indignation.

'It was once in his nature,' said Ethel; 'and I think it is the fault he most beats down. There was a time, before you knew him, when he would have been vain and ambitious.'

'Then it is as they say, conquered faults grow to be the opposite virtues!' said Meta. 'How very good he is, Ethel; one sees it more when he is with other people, and one hears all these young men's stories!'

'Everything Norman does not do, is not therefore wrong,' said Ethel, with her usual lucidity of expression.

'Don't you like him the better for keeping out of all these follies?'

'Norman does not call them so, I am sure.'

'No, he is too good to condemn—'

'It is not only that,' said Ethel. 'I know papa thinks that the first grief, coming at his age, and in the manner it did, checked and subdued his spirits, so that he has little pleasure in those things. And he always meant to be a Clergyman, which acted as a sort of Consecration on him; but many things are innocent, and I do believe papa would like it better, if Norman were less grave.'

'Yes,' said Meta, remembering the Sunday talk, 'but still, he would not be all he is—so different from others—'

'Of course, I don't mean less good, only less grave,' said Ethel, 'and certainly less nervous. But, perhaps, it is a good thing; dear mamma thought his talents would have been a greater temptation than they seem to be, subdued as he has been. I only meant, that you must not condemn all that Norman does not do. Now, good-night.'

Very different were the feelings with which those two young girls stretched themselves in their beds that night. Margaret Rivers's innocent, happy little heart was taken up in one contemplation. Admiration, sympathy, and the exultation for him, which he would not feel for himself, drew little Meta entirely out of herself—a self that never held her much. She was proud of the slender thread of connexion between them; she was confident that his vague fancies were but the scruples of a sensitive mind; and, as she fell sound asleep, she murmured broken lines of Decius, mixed with promises not to look.

Etheldred heard them, for there was no sleep for her. She had a parley to hold with herself, and to accuse her own feelings of having been unkind, ungrateful, undutiful towards her father. What had a fit of vanity brought her to? that she should have been teased by what would naturally have been her greatest delight! her father's pleasure in being with her. Was this the girl who had lately vowed within herself that her father should be her first earthly object?

At first, Ethel blamed herself for her secret impatience, but another conviction crossed her, and not an unpleasing one, though it made her cheeks tingle with maidenly shame, at having called it up. Throughout this week, Norman Ogilvie had certainly sought her out. He had looked disappointed this evening—there was no doubt that he was attracted by her—by her, plain, awkward Ethel! Such a perception assuredly never gave so much pleasure to a beauty as it did to Ethel, who had always believed herself far less good-looking than she really was. It was a gleam of delight, and, though she set herself to scold it down, the conviction was elastic, and always leapt up again.

That resolution came before her, but it had been unspoken; it could not be binding, and, if her notion were really right, the misty brilliant future of mutual joy dazzled her! But there was another side: her father oppressed and lonely, Margaret ill and pining, Mary, neither companion nor authority, the children running wild; and she, who had mentally vowed never to forsake her father, far away, enjoying her own happiness. 'Ah! that resolve had seemed easy enough when it was made, when, thought Ethel, ' I fancied no one could care for me! Shame on me! Now is the time to test it! I must go home with papa.'

It was a great struggle—on one side there was the deceitful guise of modesty, telling her it was absurd to give so much importance to the kindness of the first cousin with whom she had ever been thrown; there was the dislike to vex Flora to make a discussion, and break up the party. There was the desire to hear the concert, to go to the breakfast at —— College, to return round by Warwick Castle, and Kenilworth, as designed. Should she lose all this for a mere flattering fancy. She, who had laughed at Miss Boulder, for imagining every one who spoke to her was smitten. What reason could she assign? It would be simply ridiculous, and unkind—and it was so very pleasant. Mr. Ogilvie would be too wise to think of so incongruous a connexion, which would be so sure to displease his parents. It was more absurd than ever to think of it. The heir of Glenbracken, and a country physician's daughter!

That was a candid heart which owned that its own repugnance to accept this disparity as an objection, was an additional evidence that she ought to flee from further intercourse. She believed that no harm was done yet; she was sure that she loved her father better than anything else in the world, and whilst she did so, it was best to preserve her heart for him. Widowed as he was, she knew that he would sorely miss her, and that for years to come, she should be necessary at home. She had better come away while it would cost only a slight pang, for that it was pain to leave Norman Ogilvie, was symptom enough of the need of not letting her own silly heart go further. However it might be with him, another week would only make it worse with her.

' I will go home with papa!' was the ultimatum reached by each chain of mental reasonings, and borne in after each short prayer for guidance, as Ethel tossed about listening to the perpetual striking of all the Oxford clocks, until daylight had begun to shine in; when she fell asleep, and was only waked by Meta, standing over her with a sponge, looking very mischievous, as she reminded her of their appointment with Dr. May, to go to the early service in New College Chapel.

The world looked different that morning with Ethel, but the determination was fixed, and the service strengthened it. She was so silent during the walk, that her companions rallied her, and they both supposed she was anxious about Norman; but taking her opportunity, when Meta was gone to prepare for breakfast, she rushed, in her usual way, into the subject.

'Papa,' if you please, I should like to go home to-morrow with you.'

'Eh?' said the Doctor, amazed. 'How is this? I told you that Miss Bracy and Mary are doing famously.'

'Yes, but I had rather go back.'

'Indeed!' and Dr. May looked at the door, and spoke low. 'They make you welcome, I hope—'

'Oh! yes, nothing can be kinder.'

'I am glad to hear it. This Rivers *is* such a lout, that I could not tell how it might be. I did not look to see you turn homesick all at once.'

Ethel smiled. 'Yes, I have been very happy; but please, papa, ask no questions—only take me home.'

'Come! it is all a homesick fit, Ethel—never fear the ball. Think of the concert. If it were not for that poor baby of Mrs. Larkins, I should stay myself to hear Sontag again. You won't have such another chance.'

'I know, but I think I ought to go—'

George came in, and they could say no more. Both were silent on the subject at breakfast, but when afterwards Flora seized on Ethel, to array her for the theatre, she was able to say, 'Flora, please don't be angry with me—you have been very kind to me, but I mean to go home with papa to-morrow.'

'I declare!' said Flora, composedly, 'you are as bad as the children at the Infant School, crying to go home the instant they see their mothers!'

'No, Flora, but I must go. Thank you for all this pleasure, but I shall have heard Norman's poem, and then I must go.'

Flora turned her round, looked in her face kindly, kissed her, and said, 'My dear, never mind, it will all come right again—only, don't run away.'

'What will come right?'

'Any little misunderstanding with Norman Ogilvie.'

'I don't know what you mean,' said Ethel, becoming scarlet.

'My dear, you need not try to hide it. I see that you have got into a fright. You have made a discovery, but that is no reason for running away.'

'Yes it is!' said Ethel firmly, not denying the charge, though reddening more than ever at finding her impression confirmed.

'Poor child! she is afraid!' said Flora, tenderly; 'but I will take care of you, Ethel. It is everything delightful. You are the very girl for such a *héros de Roman*, and it has embellished you more than all my Paris fineries.'

'Hush, Flora! We ought not to talk in this way, as if—'

'As if he had done more than walk with, and talk with, nobody else! How he did hate papa, last night. I had a great mind to call papa off, in pity to him.'

'Don't, Flora. If there were anything in it, it would not be proper to think of it, so I am going home to prevent it.' The words were spoken with averted face, and heaving breath.

'Proper?' said Flora. 'The Mays are a good old family, and our own grandmother was an honourable Ogilvie herself. A Scottish Baron, very poor, too, has no right to look down—'

'They shall not look down. Flora, it is of no use to talk. I cannot be spared from home, and I will not put myself in the way of being tempted to forsake them all.'

'Tempted!' said Flora, laughing. 'Is it such a wicked thing?'

'Not in others, but it would be wrong in me, with such a state of things as there is at home.'

'I do not suppose he would want you for some years to come. He is only two-and-twenty. Mary will grow older.'

'Margaret will either be married, or want constant care. Flora, I will not let myself be drawn from them.'

'You may think so now; but it would be for their real good to relieve papa of any of us. If we were all to think as you do, how should we live? I don't know—for papa told me there will be barely ten thousand pounds, besides the houses, and what will that be among ten? I am not talking of yourself, but think of the others!'

'I know papa will not be happy without me, and I will not leave him,' repeated Ethel, not answering the argument.

Flora changed her ground, and laughed. 'We are getting into the heroics,' she said, 'when it would be very foolish to break up our plans, only because we have found a pleasant cousin. There is nothing serious in it, I dare say. How silly of us to argue on such an idea!'

Meta came in before Flora could say more, but Ethel, with burning cheeks, repeated, 'It will be safer!'

Ethel had, meantime, been dressed by her sister; and, as Bellairs came to adorn Meta, and she could have no solitude, she went down-stairs, thinking she heard Norman's step, and hoping to judge of his mood.

She entered the room with an exclamation—'O Norman!'

'At your service!' said the wrong Norman, looking merrily up, from behind a newspaper.

'Oh, I beg your pardon; I thought—'

'Your thoughts were quite right,' he said, smiling. 'Your brother desires me to present his respects to his honoured family, and to inform them that his stock of assurance is likely to be diminished by the pleasure of their company this morning.'

'How is he?' asked Ethel, anxiously.

'Pretty fair. He has blue saucers round his eyes, as he had before he went up for his little go.'

'Oh, I know them,' said Ethel.

'Very odd,' continued her cousin; 'when the end always is, that he says he has the luck of being set on in the very place he knows best. But, I think it has expended itself in a sleepless night, and I have no fears, when he comes to the point.'

'What is he doing?'

'Writing to his brother Harry. He said it was the day for the Pacific mail, and that Harry's pleasure would be the best of it.'

'Ah!' said Ethel, glancing towards the paper, 'Is there any naval intelligence?'

He looked; and while she was thinking whether she ought not to depart, he exclaimed, in a tone that startled her, 'Ha! No. Is your brother's ship the Alcestis?'

'Yes! Oh, what?'

'Nothing then, I assure you. See, it is merely this—she has not come into Sydney so soon as expected, which you knew before. That is all.'

'Let me see,' said the trembling Ethel.

It was no more than an echo of their unconfessed apprehensions, yet it seemed to give them a body; and Ethel's thoughts flew to Margaret. Her going home would be absolutely necessary now. Mr. Ogilvie kindly began to talk away her alarm, saying that there was still no reason for dread, mentioning the many causes that might have delayed the ship, and reassuring her greatly.

'But Norman!' she said.

'Ah! true. Poor May! He will break down to a certainty, if he hears it. I will go at once, and keep guard over him, lest he should meet with this paper. But, pray don't be alarmed. I assure you there is no cause. You will have letters to-morrow.'

Ethel would fain have thrown off her finery and hurried home at once, but no one regarded the matter as she did. Dr. May agreed with Flora, that it was no worse than before, and though they now thought Ethel's return desirable, on Margaret's account, it would be better not to add to the shock by a sudden arrival, especially as they took in no daily paper at home. So the theatre was not to be given up, nor any of the subsequent plans, except so far as regarded Ethel; and, this agreed, they started for the scene of action.

They were hardly in the street before they met the ubiquitous

Mr. Ogilvie, saying, that Cheviot, Norman's prompter, was aware of the report, and was guarding him, while he came to escort the ladies, through what he expressively called 'the bear fight.' Ethel resolutely adhered to her father, and her cousin took care of Meta, who had been clinging in a tiptoe manner to the point of her brother's high elbow, looking as if the crowd might easily brush off such a little fly, without his missing her.

Inch by inch, a step at a time, the ladies were landed in a crowd of their own sex, where Flora bravely pioneered—they emerged on their benches, shook themselves out, and seated themselves. There was the swarm of gay ladies, around them, and beneath the area, fast being paved with heads, black, brown, grey, and bald, a surging living sea, where Meta soon pointed out Dr. May and George; the mere sight of such masses of people was curious and interesting, reminding Ethel of Cherry Elwood having once shocked her by saying the Whitmonday club was the most beautiful sight in the whole year. And above! that gallery of trampling undergraduates, and more than trampling! Ethel and Meta could, at first, have found it in their hearts to be frightened at those thundering shouts, but the young ladies were usually of opinions so similar, that the louder grew the cheers, the more they laughed and exulted, so carried along, that no cares could be remembered.

Making a way through the thronged area, behold the procession of scarlet Doctors, advancing through the midst, till the red and black Vice-Chancellor sat enthroned in the centre, and the scarlet line became a semicircle, dividing the flower-garden of ladies from the black mass below.

Then came the introduction of the honorary Doctors, one by one, with the Latin speech, which Ethel's companions unreasonably required her to translate to them, while she was using all her ears to catch a word or two, and her eyes to glimpse at the features of men of note.

By-and-by, a youth made his appearance in the rostrum, and a good deal of Latin ensued, of which Flora hoped Ethel was less tired of than she was. In time, however, Meta saw the spectacles removed, and George looking straight up, and she drew down her veil, and took hold of Flora's hand, and Ethel flushed like a hot coal. Nevertheless, all contrived to see a tall figure, with face much flushed, and hands moving nervously! The world was tired, and people were departing, so that the first lines were lost, perhaps a satisfaction to Norman, but his voice soon cleared and became louder, his eyes lighted, and Ethel knew the 'funny state' had come to his relief—people's attention was arrested— there was no more going away—

It was well that Norman was ignorant of the fears for Harry, for four lines had been added since Ethel had seen the poem, saying how self-sacrifice sent forth the sailor-boy from home, to the lone watch, the wave and storm, his spirit rising high, ere manhood braced his form.

Applause did not come where Ethel had expected it; and, at first, there was silence at the close, but, suddenly, the acclamations rose with deafening loudness, though hardly what greets some poems with more to catch the popular ear.

Ethel's great excitement was over, and presently she found herself outside of the theatre, a shower falling, and an umbrella held over her by Mr. Ogilvie, who was asking her if it was not admirable, and declaring the poem might rank with Heber's Palestine, or Milman's Apollo.

They were bound for a great luncheon at one of the Colleges, where Ethel might survey the Principal with whom Miss Rich had corresponded. Mr. Ogilvie sat next to her, told her all the names, and quizzed the dignitaries, but she had a sense of depression, and did not wish to enter into the usual strain of banter. He dropped his lively tone, and drew her out about Harry, till she was telling eagerly of her dear sailor brother, and found him so sympathizing and considerate, that she did not like him less; though she felt her intercourse with him a sort of intoxication, that would only make it the worse for her by-and-by.

During that whole luncheon, and their walk through the gardens, where there was a beautiful horticultural show, something was always prompting her to say, while in this quasi-privacy, that she was on the eve of departure, but she kept her resolution against it—she thought it would have been an unwarrantable experiment.

When they returned to their inn, they found Norman looking fagged, but relieved, half-asleep on the sofa, with a novel in his hand. He roused himself as they came in, and, to avoid any compliments on his own performance, began—'Well, Ethel, are you ready for the ball?'

'We shall spare her the ball,' said Dr. May; 'there is a report about the Alcestis, in the newspaper, that may make Margaret uncomfortable, and this good sister will not stay away from her.'

Norman started up, crying, 'What, papa?'

'It is a mere nothing in reality,' said Dr. May, 'only what we knew before;' and he showed his son the paragraph, which Norman read as a death warrant—the colour ebbed from his lips and cheeks—he trembled so, that he was obliged to sit down, and, without speaking, he kept his eyes fixed on the words,

'Serious apprehensions are entertained with regard to H. M. S. Alcestis, Captain Gordon—'

'If you had seen as many newspaper reports come to nothing, as I have, you would not take this so much to heart,' said Dr. May. 'I expect to hear that this very mail has brought letters.'

And Meta added that, at luncheon, she had been seated next to one of the honorary doctors—a naval captain—who had been making discoveries in the South Sea, and that he had scouted the notion of harm befalling the Alcestis, and given all manner of reassuring suppositions as to her detention, adding besides, that no one believed the Australian paper, whence the report was taken. He had seen the Alcestis, knew Captain Gordon, and spoke of him as one of the safest people in the world. Had his acquaintance extended to lieutenants and midshipmen, it would have been perfect—as it was, the tidings brought back the blood to Norman's cheek, and the light to his eye.

'When do we set off?' was Norman's question.

'At five,' said Ethel. 'You mean it, papa?'

'I did intend it if I had gone alone, but I shall not take you till eight; nor you, Norman, at all.'

Norman was bent on returning, but his father and Flora would not hear of it. Flora could not spare him, and Dr. May was afraid of the effect of anxiety on nerves and spirits so sensitive. While this was going on, Mr. Ogilvie looked at Ethel in consternation, and said, 'Are you really going home?'

'Yes, my eldest sister must not be left alone when she hears this.'

He looked down—Ethel had the resolution to walk away. Flora could not give up the ball, and Meta found that she must go; but both the Normans spent a quiet evening with Dr. May and Ethel. Norman May had a bad headache, which he was allowed to have justly earned; Dr. May was very happy reviving all his Scottish recollections, and talking to young Ogilvie about Edinburgh.—Once, there was a private consultation. Ethel was provoked and ashamed at the throbs that it *would* excite. What! on a week's acquaintance?—

When alone with her father, she began to nerve herself for something heroic, and great was her shame when she heard only of her cousin's kind consideration for her brother, whom he wished to take home with him, and thence to see the Highlands, so as to divert his anxiety for Harry, as well as to call him off from the studies with which he had this term overworked himself even more than usual. Dr. May had given most grateful consent, and he spoke highly in praise of the youth; but there was no more to come, and Ethel could have beaten herself for the moment of anticipation.

Meta came home, apologizing for wakening Ethel—but Ethel had not been asleep. The ball had not, it seemed, been as charming to her as most events were, and Ethel heard a sigh, as the little lady lay down in her bed.

Late as it was when she went to rest, Meta rose to see the travellers off—she sent hosts of messages to her father, and wished she might go with them. George and Flora were not visible, and Dr. May was leaving messages for them, and for Norman, in her charge, when the two Balliol men walked in.

Ethel had hoped it was over, yet she could not be sorry that the two youths escorted them to the station, and, as Ethel was placed in the carriage, she believed that she heard something of never forgetting—happiest week—but in the civilities which the other occupant of the carriage was offering for the accommodation of their lesser luggage, she lost the exact words, and the last she heard were, 'Good bye—I hope you will find letters at home.'

CHAPTER X.

'True to the kindred points of heaven and home.'—WORDSWORTH.

ETHELDRED'S dream was over. She had wakened to the inside of a Great Western carriage, her father beside her, and opposite a thin, foreign-looking gentleman. Her father, to whom her life was to be devoted! She looked at his profile, defined against the window, and did not repent. In a sort of impulse to do something for him, she took his hat from his hand, and was going to dispose of it in the roof, when he turned, smiling his thanks, but saying, 'it was not worth while—this carriage was a very transitory resting-place.'

The stranger at that moment sprang to his feet, exclaiming, 'Dick himself!'

'Spencer! old fellow, is it you?' cried Dr. May, in a voice of equal amazement and joy, holding out his hand, which was grasped and wrung with a force that made Ethel shrink for the poor maimed arm.

'Ha! what is amiss with your arm?' was the immediate question. Three technical words were spoken in a matter of fact way, as Dr. May replaced his hand in his bosom, and then, with an eager smile, said, 'Ethel, here! You have heard of him!'

Ethel had indeed, and gave her hand cordially, surprised by

the bow and air of deferential politeness with which it was received, like a favour, while Dr. Spencer asked her whether she had been staying in Oxford.

'Aye, and what for, do you think?' said Dr. May, joyously.

'You don't say that was your son who held forth yesterday! I thought his voice had a trick of yours—but then I thought you would have held by old Cambridge.'

'What could I do?' said Dr. May, deprecatingly; 'the boy would go and get a Balliol scholarship—'

'Why! the lad is a genius! a poet—no mistake about it! but I scarcely thought you could have one of such an age.'

'Of his age! His brother is in Holy Orders—one of his sisters is married. There's for you, Spencer!'

'Bless me, Dick! I thought myself a young man!'

'What! with hair of that colour?' said Dr. May, looking at his friend's milk-white locks.

'Bleached by that frightful sickly season at Poonshedagore, when I thought I was done for. But you! you—the boy of the whole lot! You think me very disrespectful to your father,' added he, turning to Ethel, 'but you see what old times are.'

'I know,' said Ethel, with a bright look.

'So you were in the theatre, yesterday,' continued Dr. May; 'but there is no seeing any one in such a throng. How long have you been in England?'

'A fortnight. I went at once to see my sister, at Malvern; there I fell in with Rudden, the man I was with in New Guinea. He was going up to be made an honorary Doctor, and made me come with him.'

'And where are you bound for?' as the train showed signs of a halt.

'For London: I meant to hunt up Mat Fleet, and hear of you, and other old friends.'

'Does he expect you?'

'No one expects me. I am a regular vagabond.'

'Come home with us,' said Dr. May, laying his hand on his arm. 'I cannot part with you so soon. Come, find your luggage. Take your ticket for Gloucester.'

'So suddenly. Will it not be inconvenient?' said he, looking tempted, but irresolute.

'O no, no; pray come!' said Ethel, eagerly. 'We shall be so glad.'

He looked his courteous thanks, and soon was with them *en route* for Stoneborough.

Ethel's thoughts were diverted from all she had left at

Oxford. She could not but watch those two old friends. She knew enough of the traveller to enter into her father's happiness, and to have no fears of another Sir Matthew.

They had been together at Stoneborough, at Cambridge, at Paris, at Edinburgh, always linked in the closest friendship; but, by Dr. May's own account, his friend had been the diligent one of the pair, a bright compound of principle and spirit, and highly distinguished in all his studies, and Dr. May's model of perfection. Their paths had since lain far apart, and they had not seen each other, since, twenty-six years ago, they had parted in London—the one to settle at his native town, while the other accepted a situation as travelling physician. On his return, he had almost sacrificed his life, by self-devoted attendance on a fever-stricken emigrant-ship. He had afterwards received an appointment in India, and there the correspondence had died away, and Dr. May had lost traces of him, only knowing that, in a visitation of cholera, he had again acted with the same carelessness of his own life, and a severe illness, which had broken up his health, had occasioned him to relinquish his post.

It now appeared that he had thought himself coming home ever since. He had gone to recruit, in the Himalayas, and had become engrossed in scientific observations on their altitudes, as well as investigations in natural history. Going to Calcutta, he had fallen in with a party about to explore the Asiatic islands, and he had accompanied them, as well as going on an expedition into the interior of Australia. He had been employed in various sanitary arrangements there, and in India, and had finally worked his way slowly home, overland, visiting Egypt and Palestine, and refreshing his memory with every Italian, German, or French Cathedral, or work of art, that had delighted him in early days.

He was a slight, small man, much sun-burnt, nearly bald, and his hair snowy, but his eyes were beautiful, very dark, soft, and smiling, and yet their gaze peculiarly keen and steady, as if ready for any emergency, and his whole frame was full of alertness and vigour. His voice was clear and sweet, and his manner most refined and polished; indeed, his courtesy to Ethel, whenever there was a change of carriage, was so exemplary, that she understood it as the effect on a chivalrous mind, of living where a lady was a rare and precious article. It frightened Ethel a little at first, but, before the end of the journey, she had already begun to feel, towards him, like an old friend—one of those inheritances, who are so much valued and loved, like a sort of uncles-in-friendship. She had an especial grateful honour for the delicate tact which asked no questions, as she saw his eye often falling anxiously on her father's left hand, where the wedding-ring shone upon the little finger.

There was talk enough upon his travels, on public changes, and on old friends; but, after those first few words, home had never been mentioned.

When, at five o'clock, the engine blew its whistle, at the old familiar station, Dr. May had scarcely put his head out before Adams hastened up to him with a note.

'All well at home?'

'Yes, sir. Miss Margaret sent up the gig.'

'I must go at once,' said Dr. May, hastily—'the Larkins' child is worse. Ethel, take care of him, and introduce him. Love to Margaret. I'll be at home before tea.'

He was driven off at speed, and Ethel proposed to walk home. Dr. Spencer gave her his arm, and was silent; but presently said, in a low, anxious voice, 'My dear, you must forgive me, I have heard nothing for many years. Your mother—'

'It was an accident,' said Ethel, looking straight before her. 'It was when papa's arm was hurt. The carriage was overturned.'

'And—' repeated Dr. Spencer, earnestly.

'She was killed on the spot,' said Ethel, speaking shortly, and abruptly. If she was to say it at all, she could not do so otherwise.

He was dreadfully shocked—she knew it by the shudder of his arm, and a tight, suppressed groan. He did not speak, and Ethel, as if a relief from the silence must be made, said what was not very consoling, and equally blunt, 'Margaret had some harm done to her spine—she cannot walk.'

He did not seem to hear, but walked on, as in a dream, where Ethel guided him, and she would not interrupt him again.

They had just passed Mr. Bramshaw's office, when a voice was heard behind, calling, 'Miss Ethel! Miss Ethel!' and Edward Anderson, now articled to Mr. Bramshaw, burst out, pen in hand, and looking shabby and inky.

'Miss Ethel!' he said, breathlessly, 'I beg your pardon, but have you heard from Harry?'

'No!' said Ethel. 'Have they had that paper at home?'

'Not that I know of,' said Edward. 'My mother wanted to send it, but I would not take it—not while Dr. May was away.'

'Thank you—that was very kind of you.'

'And oh! Miss Ethel, do you think it is true?'

'We hope not,' said Ethel, kindly—'we saw a Captain at Oxford who thought it not at all to be depended on.'

'I am so glad,' said Edward; and, shaking hands, he went

back to his high stool, Ethel feeling that he deserved the pains that Norman had taken to spare and befriend him. She spoke to her companion in explanation. 'We are very anxious for news of my next brother's ship, Alcestis, in the Pacific—'

'More!' exclaimed poor Dr. Spencer, almost overpowered; 'Good Heavens! I thought May, at least, was happy!'

'He is not unhappy,' said Ethel, not sorry that they had arrived at the back entrance of the shrubbery.

'How long ago was this?' said he, standing still, as soon as they had passed into the garden.

'Four years, next October. I assure you, his spirits are almost always good.'

'When I was at Adelaide, little thinking!' he sighed, then recollecting himself. 'Forgive me, I have given you pain.'

'No,' she said, 'or rather, I gave you more.'

'I knew her—' and there he broke off, paused for a minute, then collecting himself, seemed resolutely to turn away from the subject, and said, walking on, 'This garden is not much altered.'

At that moment, a little shrill voice broke out in remonstrance among the laurels—'But you know, Daisy, you are the captain of the forty thieves!'

'A startling announcement!' said Dr. Spencer, looking at Ethel, and the next two steps brought them in view of the play-place in the laurels, where Aubrey lay on the ground, feigning sleep, but keeping a watchful eye over Blanche, who was dropping something into the holes of inverted flower-pots, Gertrude dancing about in a way that seemed to have called for the reproof of the more earnest actors.

'Ethel! Ethel!' screamed the children with one voice; and, while the two girls stood in shyness at her companion, Aubrey had made a dart at her neck, and hung upon her, arms, legs, body and all, like a wild cat.

'That will do! that will do, old man—let go! Speak to Dr. Spencer, my dear.'

Blanche did so demurely, and asked where was papa?'

'Coming, as soon as he has been to Mrs. Larkins's poor baby.'

'George Larkins has been here,' said Aubrey. 'And I have finished *Vipera et lima*, Ethel, but Margaret makes such false quantities!'

'What is your name, youngster?' said Dr. Spencer, laying his hand on Aubrey's head.

'Aubrey Spencer May,' was the answer.

'Hey day! where did you steal my name?' exclaimed Dr. Spencer, while Aubrey stood abashed at so mysterious an accusation.

'Oh!' exclaimed Blanche, seizing on Ethel, and whispering, 'Is it really the boy that climbed the market-cross?'

'You see your fame lives here,' said Ethel, smiling, as Dr. Spencer evidently heard.

'He was a little boy!' said Aubrey, indignantly, looking at the grey-haired man.

'There!' said Ethel, to Dr. Spencer.

'The tables turned!' he said, laughing heartily. 'But do not let me keep you—You would wish to prepare your sister for a stranger, and I shall improve my acquaintance here. Where are the forty thieves?'

'I am all of them,' said the innocent, daisy-faced Gertrude; and Ethel hastened towards the house, glad of the permission granted by his true good-breeding.

There was a shriek of welcome from Mary, who sat working beside Margaret. Ethel was certain that no evil tidings had come to her elder sister, so joyous was her exclamation of wonder and rebuke to her home-sick Ethel. 'Naughty girl! running home at once! I did think you would have been happy there!'

'So I was,' said Ethel, hastily; 'but whom do you think I have brought home?' Margaret flushed with such a pink, that Ethel resolved never to set her guessing again, and hurried to explain; and having heard that all was well, and taken her house-keeping measures, she proceeded to fetch the guest; but Mary, who had been unusually silent all this time, ran after her, and checked her.

'Ethel, have you heard?' she said.

'Have you?' said Ethel.

'George Larkins rode in this morning to see when papa would come home, and he told me. He said I had better not tell Margaret, for he did not believe it.'

'And you have not! That is very good of you, Mary.'

'Oh! I am glad you are come! I could not have helped telling, if you had been away a whole week! But, Ethel, does papa believe it?' Poor Mary's full lip swelled, and her eyes swam, ready to laugh or weep, in full faith in her sister's answer.

Ethel told of Meta's captain, and the smile predominated, and settled down into Mary's usual broad beamy look, like a benignant rising sun on the sign of an inn, as Ethel praised her warmly for a fortitude and consideration of which she had not thought her capable.

Dr. Spencer was discovered full in the midst of the comedy of the forty thieves, alternating, as required, between the robber-captain and the ass, and the children in perfect ecstasies with him.

They all followed in his train to the drawing-room, and were so clamorous, that he could have no conversation with Margaret. He certainly made them so, but Ethel, remembering what a blow her disclosures had been, thought it would be only a kindness to send Aubrey to show him to his room, where he might have some peace.

She was not sorry to be very busy, so as to have little time to reply to the questions on the doings at Oxford, and the cause of her sudden return; and yet it would have been a comfort to be able to sit down to understand herself, and recal her confused thoughts. But solitary reflection was a thing only to be hoped for in that house in bed, and Ethel was obliged to run up and down, and attend to everybody, under an undefined sense that she had come home to a dull, anxious world of turmoil.

Margaret seemed to guess nothing, that was one comfort; she evidently thought that her return was fully accounted for by the fascination of her papa's presence in a strange place. She gave Ethel no credit for the sacrifice, naturally supposing that she could not enjoy herself away from home. Ethel did not know whether to be glad or not; she was relieved, but it was flat. As to Norman Ogilvie, one or two inquiries whether she liked him, and if Norman were going to Scotland with him, were all that passed, and it was very provoking to be made so hot and conscious by them.

She could not begin to dress till late, and while she was un-packing, she heard her father come home, among the children's loud welcomes, and go to the drawing-room. He presently knocked at the door between their rooms.

'So Margaret does not know?' he said.

'No, Mary has been so very good,' and she told what had passed.

'Well done, Mary, I must tell her so. She is a good girl on a pinch, you see!'

'And we don't speak of it now? Or will it hurt Margaret more to think we keep things from her?'

'That is the worst risk of the two. I have seen great harm done in that way. Mention it, but without seeming to make too much of it.'

'Won't you, papa?'—

'You had better—It will seem of less importance. I think nothing of it myself—'

Nevertheless, Ethel saw that he could not trust himself to broach the subject to Margaret.

'How was the Larkins' baby?'

'Doing better. What have you done with Spencer?'

'I put him into Richard's room. The children were eating him up! He is so kind to them.'

'Aye! I say, Ethel, that was a happy consequence of your coming home with me.'

'What a delightful person he is!'

'Is he not? A true knight errant, as he always was. I could not tell you what I owed to him as a boy—all my life, I may say—Ethel,' he added, suddenly, 'we must do our best to make him happy here. I know it now—I never guessed it *then*, but one is very hard and selfish when one is happy—'

'What do you mean, papa?'

'I see it now,' continued Dr. May, incoherently; 'the cause of his wandering life—advantages thrown aside. He! the most worthy. Things I little heeded at the time have come back on me! I understand why he banished himself!'

'Why?' asked Ethel, bewildered.

'She never had an idea of it; but I might have guessed from what fell from him unconsciously, for not a word would he have said—nor did he say, to show how he sacrificed himself!'

'Who was it? Aunt Flora?' said Ethel, beginning to collect his meaning.

'No, Ethel, it was your own dear mother! You will think this another romantic fancy of mine, but I am sure of it.'

'So am I,' said Ethel.

'How—what? Ah! I remembered, after we parted, that he might know nothing—'

'He asked me,' said Ethel.

'And how did he bear it?'

Ethel told, and the tears filled her father's eyes. 'It was wrong and cruel in me to bring him home unprepared! and then to leave it to you. I always forget other people's feelings. Poor Spencer! And now, Ethel, you see what manner of man we have here, and how we ought to treat him.'

'Indeed I do!'

'The most unselfish—the most self-sacrificing—' continued Dr. May. 'And to see what it all turned on! I happened to have this place open to me—the very cause, perhaps, of my having taken things easy—and so the old Professor threw opportunities in my way; while Aubrey Spencer, with every recommendation that man could have, was set aside, and exiled himself, leaving the station, and all he might so easily have gained. Ah, Ethel, Sir Matthew Fleet never came near him in ability. But not one word to interfere with me, would he say, and—how I have longed to meet him again, after parting in my selfish, unfeeling gladness ; and now I have nothing to do for him, but show him how little I was to be trusted with her.'

Ethel never knew how to deal with these occasional bursts of grief, but she said that she thought Dr. Spencer was very much pleased to have met with him, and delighted with the children.

'Ah ! well, you are *her* children,' said Dr. May, with his hand on Ethel's shoulder.

So they went down-stairs, and found Mary making tea ; and Margaret, fearing Dr. Spencer was overwhelmed with his young admirers—for Aubrey and Gertrude were one on each knee, and Blanche standing beside him, inflicting on him a catalogue of the names and ages of all the eleven.

'Ethel has introduced you, I see,' said Dr. May.

'Aye, I assure you, it was an alarming introduction. No sooner do I enter your garden, than I hear that I am in the midst of the Forty Thieves. I find a young lady putting the world to death, after the fashion of Hamlet—and, looking about to find what I have lost, I find this urchin has robbed me of my name—a property I supposed was always left to unfortunate travellers, however small they might be chopped themselves.'

'Well, Aubrey boy, will you make restitution ?'

'It is my name,' said Aubrey, positively ; for, as his father added, ' He is not without dread of the threat being fulfilled, and himself left to be that Anon, who, Blanche says, writes so much poetry.'

Aubrey privately went to Ethel, to ask her if this were possible ; and she had to reassure him, by telling him that they were ' only in fun.'

It was fun with a much deeper current though ; for Dr. Spencer was saying, with a smile, between gratification and sadness, ' I did not think my name would have been remembered here so long.'

'We had used up mine, and the grandfathers', and the uncles', and began to think we might look a little further a-field,' said Dr. May. 'If I had only known where you were, I would have asked you to be the varlet's godfather ; but I was much afraid you were nowhere in the land of the living.'

'I have but one godson, and he is coffee-coloured ! I ought to have written ; but, you see, for seven years I thought I was coming home.'

Aubrey had recovered sufficiently to observe to Blanche, ' that was almost as bad as Ulysses,' which, being overheard and repeated, led to the information that he was Ethel's pupil, whereupon Dr. Spencer began to inquire after the school, and to exclaim at his friend for having deserted it in the person of Tom. Dr. May looked convicted, but said it was all Norman's fault; and Dr. Spencer, shaking his head at Blanche, opined that the young gentleman was a great innovator, and that he was sure he was at the bottom of the pulling down the Market Cross, and the stopping up Randall's Alley—iniquities of the 'nasty people,' of which she already had made him aware.

'Poor Norman, he suffered enough anent Randall's Alley,' said Dr. May; 'but as to the Market Cross, that came down a year before he was born.'

'It was the Town Council!' said Ethel.

'One of the ordinary stultifications of Town Councils?—'

'Take care, Spencer,' said Dr. May. 'I am a Town Councilman myself—'

'You, Dick!' and he turned with a start of astonishment, and went into a fit of laughing, re-echoed by all the young ones, who were especially tickled by hearing, from another, the abbreviation that had, hitherto, only lived in the favourite expletive, 'As sure as my name is Dick May.'

'Of course,' said Dr. May. '"Dost thou not suspect my place? Dost thou not suspect my years? One that hath two gowns, and everything handsome about him!"'

His friend laughed the more, and they betook themselves to the College stories, of which the quotation from Dogberry seemed to have reminded them.

There was something curious and affecting in their manner to each other. Often it was the easy bantering familiarity of the two youths they had once been together, with somewhat of elder brotherhood on Dr. Spencer's side—and of looking up on Dr. May's—and just as they had recurred to these terms, some allusion would bring back to Dr. Spencer, that the heedless, high-spirited 'Dick,' whom he had always had much ado to keep out of scrapes, was a householder, a man of weight and influence; a light which would at first strike him as most ludicrous, and then mirth would end in a sigh, for there was yet another aspect! After having thought of him so long as the happy husband of Margaret Mackenzie, he found her place vacant, and the trace of deep grief apparent on the countenance, once so gay—the oppression of anxiety marked on the brow, formerly so joyous, the merriment almost more touching than gravity would have been, for the former nature seemed rather shattered than altered. In merging towards this side, there was a tender respect in Dr. Spencer's manner that was most beautiful, though this evening such subjects were scrupulously kept at the utmost distance, by the constant interchange of new and old jokes and stories.

Only when bed-time had come, and Margaret had been carried off—did a silence fall on the two friends, unbroken till Dr. May rose and proposed going up-stairs. When he gave his hand to wish good night, Dr. Spencer held it this time most carefully, and said, 'Oh, May! I did not expect this!'

'I should have prepared you,' said his host, 'but I never recollected that you knew nothing—'

'I had dwelt on your happiness!'

'There never were two happier creatures for twenty-two years,' said Dr. May, his voice low with emotion. 'Sorrow spared her! Yes, think of her always in undimmed brightness—always smiling as you remember her—She was happy. She is,' he concluded. His friend had turned aside and hidden his face with his hand, then looked up for a moment, 'And you, Dick,' he said, briefly.

'Sorrow spared her,' was Dr. May's first answer. 'And hers are very good children!'

There was a silence again, ending in Dr. May's saying, 'What do you think of my poor girl?'

They discussed the nature of the injury: Dr. Spencer could not feel otherwise than that it was a very hopeless matter. Her father owned that he had thought so from the first, and had wondered at Sir Matthew Fleet's opinion. His subdued tone of patience and resignation, struck his guest above all, as changed from what he had once been.

'You have been sorely tried,' he said, when they parted at his room door.

'I have received much good!' simply answered Dr. May. 'Good night! I am glad to have you here—if you can bear it.'

'Bear it? Dick! how like that girl is to you! She is yourself!'

'Such a self as I never was! Good-night.'

Ethel overcame the difficulty of giving the account of the newspaper alarm, with tolerable success, by putting the story of Meta's conversation foremost. Mragaret did not take it to heart as much as she had feared, nor did she appear to dwell on it afterwards. The truth was perhaps that Dr. Spencer's visit was to every one more of an excitement and amusement than it was to Ethel. Not that she did not like him extremely, but after such a week as she had been spending, the home-world seemed rather stale and unprofitable.

Miss Bracy relapsed into a state of 'feelings,' imagining perhaps that Ethel had distrusted her capabilities, and therefore returned; or as Ethel herself sometimes feared, there might be an irritability in her own manner that gave cause of annoyance. The children were inclined to be riotous with their new friend, who made much of them continually, and especially patronized Aubrey; Mary was proud of showing how much she had learnt to do for Margaret in her sister's absence; Dr. May was so much taken up with his friend, that Ethel saw less of him than usual, and she began to believe that it had been all a mistake that every one was so dependent on her, for, in fact, they did much better without her.

Meantime, she heard of the gaieties which the others were enjoying, and she could not feel heroic when they regretted her. At the end of a week, Meta Rivers was escorted home from Warwick by two servants, and came to Stoneborough, giving a lively description of all the concluding pleasures, but declaring that Ethel's departure had taken away the zest of the whole, and Mr. Ogilvie had been very disconsolate. Margaret had not been prepared to hear that Mr. Ogilvie had been so constant a companion, and was struck by finding that Ethel had passed over one who had evidently been so great an ingredient in the delights of the expedition. Meta had, however, observed nothing—she was a great deal too simple and too much engrossed for such notions to have crossed her mind; but Margaret inferred something, and hoped to learn more when she should see Flora. This would not be immediately. George and his wife were gone to London, and thence intended to pay a round of visits; and Norman had accompanied his namesake to Glenbracken.

Ethel fought hard with her own petulance and sense of tedium at home, which was, as she felt, particularly uncalled for at present; when Dr. Spencer was enlivening them so much. He was never in the way, he was always either busy in the dining room in the morning with books and papers, or wandering about his old school-boy haunts in the town, or taking Adams' place, and driving out Dr. May, or sometimes joining the children in a walk, to their supreme delight. His sketches, for he drew most beautifully, were an endless pleasure to Margaret, with his explanations of them—she even tried to sit up to copy them, and he began to teach Blanche to draw. The evenings, when there was certain to be some entertaining talk going on between the two Doctors, were very charming, and Margaret seemed quite revived by seeing her father so happy with his friend. Ethel knew she ought to be happy also, and if attention could make her so, she had it, for kind and courteous as Dr. Spencer was to all, she seemed to have a double charm for him. It was as if he found united in her the quaint *brusquerie*, that he had loved in her father, with somewhat of her mother; for though Ethel had less personal resemblance to Mrs. May than any other of the family, Dr. Spencer transferred to her much of the chivalrous distant devotion, with which he had regarded her mother. Ethel was very little conscious of it, but he was certainly her sworn knight, and there was an eagerness in his manner of performing every little service for her, a deference in his way of listening to her, over and above his ordinary polish of manner.

Ethel lighted up, and enjoyed herself when talking was going on—her periods of *ennui* were when she had to set about any home employment—when Aubrey's lessons did not go well—when she wanted to speak to her father, and could not catch him; and even when she had to go to Cocksmoor.

She did not seem to make any progress there—the room was very full, and very close, the children were dull, and she began to believe she was doing no good—it was all a weariness. But she was so heartily ashamed of her feelings, that she worked the more vehemently for them, and the utmost show that they outwardly made was, that Margaret thought her less vivacious than her wont, and she was a little too peremptory at times with Mary and Blanche. She had so much disliked the display that Flora had made about Cocksmoor, that she had imposed total silence on it upon her younger sisters, and Dr. Spencer had spent a fortnight at Stoneborough without being aware of their occupation; when there occurred such an extremely sultry day, that Margaret remonstrated with Ethel on her intention of broiling herself and Mary by walking to Cocksmoor, when the quicksilver stood at 80° in the shade.

Ethel was much inclined to stay at home, but she did not know whether this was from heat or from idleness, and her fretted spirits took the turn of determination—so she posted off at a galloping pace, that her brothers called her ' Cocksmoor speed,' and Mary panted by her side, humbly petitioning for the plantation path, when she answered, ' that it was as well to be hot in the sun as in the shade.'

The school-room was unusually full, all the haymaking mothers made it serve as an infant school, and though as much window was opened as there could be, the effect was not coolness. Nevertheless, Ethel sat down and gathered her class round her, and she had just heard the chapter once read, when there was a little confusion, a frightened cry of ' Ethel !' and before she could rise to her feet—a flump upon the floor—poor Mary had absolutely fainted dead away.

Ethel was much terrified, and very angry with herself; Mary

was no light weight, but Mrs. Elwood coming at their cry, helped Ethel to drag her into the outer room, where she soon began to recover, and to be excessively puzzled as to what had happened to her. She said the sea was roaring, and where was Harry? and then she looked much surprised to find herself lying on Mrs. Elwood's damp flags—a circumstance extremely distressing to Mrs. Elwood, who wanted to carry her up-stairs into Cherry's room, very clean and very white, but with such a sun shining full into it!

Ethel lavished all care, and reproached herself greatly, though to be sure nothing had ever been supposed capable of hurting Mary, and Mary herself protested that nothing at all had ailed her till the children's voices began to sound funny, and turned into the waves of the sea, and therewith poor Mary burst into a great flood of tears, and asked whether Harry would ever come back. The tears did her a great deal of good, though not so much as the being petted by Ethel, and she soon declared herself perfectly well; but Ethel could not think of letting her walk home, and sent off a boy—who she trusted would not faint—with a note to Margaret, desiring her to send the gig, which fortunately was at home to-day.

Mary had partaken of some of Mrs. Elwood's tea, which, though extremely bitter, seemed a great cordial, and was sitting, quite revived, in the arbour at the door, when the gig stopped, and Dr. Spencer walked in.

' Well, and how are you?'

'Quite well, now, thank you. Was Margaret frightened? Why did you come?'

' I thought it would make her happier, as your father was not at home. Here, let me feel your pulse. Do you think no one is a doctor but your papa? There's not much the matter with you, however. Where is Ethel?'

' In the school,' and Mary opened the door. Dr. Spencer looked in, as Ethel came out, and his face put her in mind of Norman's look.

'No wonder!' was all he said.

Ethel was soon satisfied that he did not think Mary ill. In fact, he said fainting was the most natural and justifiable measure, under the circumstances. ' How many human creatures do you keep there?' he asked.

'Forty-seven to-day,' said Mary, proudly.

'I shall indict you for cruelty to animals! I think I have known it hotter at Poonshedagore, but there we had punkahs!'

' It was very wrong of me,' said Ethel. ' I should have

thought of poor Mary, in that sunny walk, but Mary never complains.'

'Oh, never mind,' said Mary, 'it did not hurt.'

'I'm not thinking of Mary,' said Dr. Spencer, 'but of the wretched beings you are leaving shut up there. I wonder what the mercury would be there.'

'We cannot help it,' said Mary. 'We cannot get the ground.'

And Mary having been voted into the seat of honour and comfort, by his side, in the carriage, told her version of Cocksmoor and the Committee; while Ethel sat up in the little narrow seat behind, severely reproaching herself for her want of consideration towards one so good and patient as Mary, who proved to have been suffering far more on Harry's account than they had guessed, and who was so simple and thoroughgoing in doing her duty. This was not being a good elder sister, and, when they came home, she confessed it, and showed so much remorse, that poor Mary was quite shocked, and cried so bitterly, that it was necessary to quit the subject.

'Ethel, dearest,' said Margaret, that night, after they were in bed, 'is there anything the matter?'

'No, nothing, but that Oxford has spoilt me,' said Ethel, resolutely. 'I am very cross and selfish!'

'It will be better by-and-by,' said Margaret, 'if only you are sure you have nothing to make you unhappy.'

'Nothing,' said Ethel. She was becoming too much ashamed of her fancy to breathe one word about it, and she had spoken the truth. Pleasure *had* spoilt her.

'If only we could do something for Cocksmoor!' she sighed, presently, 'with that one hundred and fifty pounds lying idle.'

Margaret was very glad that her thoughts were taking this channel, but it was not a promising one, for there seemed to be nothing practicable, present or future. The ground could not be had—the pig would not get over the stile—the old woman could not get home to-night. Cocksmoor must put up with its present school, and Mary must not be walked to death.

Or, as Ethel drew her own moral, sacrifice must not be selfish. One great resolution that has been costly, must not blunt us in the daily details of life.

CHAPTER XI.

'If to do were as easy as to know what were good to do, Chapels had been Churches, and poor men's cottages, princes' palaces.'—MERCHANT OF VENICE.

'DICK,' said Dr. Spencer, as the friends sat together in the evening, after Mary's swoon, 'you seem to have found an expedient for making havoc among your daughters.'

'It does not hurt them,' said Dr. May, carelessly.

'Pretty well, after the specimen of to-day.'

'That was chance.'

'If you like it, I have no more to say; but I should like to make you sit for two hours in such a temperature. If they were mine—'

'Very fine talking, but I would not take the responsibility of hindering the only pains that have ever been taken with that unlucky place. You don't know that girl Ethel. She began at fifteen, entirely of her own accord, and has never faltered. If any of the children there are saved from perdition, it is owing to her, and I am not going to be the man to stop her. They are strong, healthy girls, and I cannot see that it does them any harm—rather good.'

'Have you any special predilection for a room eight feet by nine?'

'Can't be helped. What would you have said if you had seen the last?'

'What is this about one hundred and fifty pounds in hand?'

'The ladies here chose to have a fancy fair, the only result of which, hitherto, has been the taking away my Flora. There is the money, but the land can't be had.'

'Why not?'

'Tied up between the Drydale Estate and —— College, and in the hands of the quarrymaster, Nicolson. There was an application made to the College, but they did not begin at the right end.'

'Upon my word, Dick, you take it easy!' cried his friend, rather indignantly.

'I own I have not stirred in the matter,' said Dr. May. 'I knew nothing would come to good under the pack of silly women that our schools are ridden with—' and, as he heard a sound a little like 'pish!' he continued, 'and that old Ramsden, it is absolutely useless to work with such a head—or no head. There's nothing for it, but to wait for better times, instead of setting up independent, insubordinate action.'

'You are the man to leave venerable abuses undisturbed!'

'The cure is worse than the disease!'

'There spoke the Corporation!'

'Ah! it was not the way you set to work in Poonshedagore.'

'Why, really, when the venerable abuses consisted of Hindoos praying to their own three-legged stools, and keeping sacred monkeys in honour of the ape Hanyuman, it was a question whether one could be a Christian oneself, and suffer it undisturbed. It was coming it too strong, when I was requested to lend my own step-ladder for the convenience of an exhibition of a devotee, swinging on hooks in his sides.'

Dr. Spencer had, in fact, never rested till he had established a mission in his former remote station; and his brown godson, once a Brahmin, now an exemplary Clergyman, traced his conversion to the friendship, and example, of the English physician.

'Well, I have lashed about me at abuses in my time,' said Dr. May.

'I dare say you have, Dick!' and they both laughed—the inconsiderate way was so well delineated.

'Just so,' replied Dr. May; and I made enemies enough to fetter me now. I do not mean that I have done right—I have not; but there is a good deal on my hands, and I don't write easily. I have been slower to take up new matters than I ought to have been.'

'I see, I see!' said Dr. Spencer, rather sorry for his implied reproach, 'but must Cocksmoor be left to its fate, and your gallant daughter to hers?'

'The Vicar won't stir. He is indolent enough by nature, and worse with gout; and I do not see what good I could do. I once offended the tenant, Nicolson, by fining him, for cheating his unhappy labourers, on the abominable truck system; and he had rather poison me, than do anything to oblige me. And, as to the copyholder, he is a fine gentleman, who never comes near the place, nor does anything for it.'

'Who is he?'

'Sir Henry Walkinghame.'

'Sir Henry Walkinghame! I know the man. I found him in one of the caves at Thebes, among the mummies, laid up with a fever, nearly ready to be a mummy himself! I remember bleeding him—irregular, was not it? but one does not stand on ceremony in Pharaoh's tomb. I got him through with it; we came up the Nile together, and the last I saw of him was at Alexandria. He is your man! something might be done with him!'

'I believe Flora promises to ask him, if she should ever meet him in London, but he is always away. If ever we should be happy enough to get an active incumbent, we shall have a chance.'

Two days after, Ethel came down equipped for Cocksmoor. It was as hot as ever, and Mary was ordered to stay at home, being somewhat pacified by a promise that she should go again as soon as the weather was fit for anything but a salamander.

Dr. Spencer was in the hall, with his bamboo, his great Panama hat, and grey loose coat, for he entirely avoided, except on Sundays, the medical suit of black. He offered to relieve Ethel of her bag of books.

'No thank you.' (He had them by this time.) 'But I am going to Cocksmoor.'

'Will you allow me to be your companion?'

'I shall be very glad of the pleasure of your company, but I am not in the least afraid of going alone,' said she, smiling, however, so as to show that she was glad of such pleasant company. 'I forewarn you, though, that I have business there.'

'I will find occupation.'

'And you must promise not to turn against me. I have undergone a great deal already about that place. Norman was always preaching against it, and now that he has become reasonable, I can't have papa set against it again—besides, he would mind you more.'

Dr. Spencer promised to do nothing but what was quite reasonable. Ethel believed that he accompanied her merely because his gallantry would not suffer her to go unescorted, and she was not sorry, for it was too long a walk for solitude to be very agreeable, when strange waggoners might be on the road, though she had never let them be 'lions in the path.'

The walk was as pleasant as a scorching sun would allow, and by the time they arrived at the scattered cottages, Ethel had been drawn into explaining many of her Cocksmoor perplexities.

'If you could get the land granted, where should you choose to have it?' he asked. 'You know it will not do to go and say, "Be pleased to give me a piece of land," without specifying what, or you might chance to have one at the Land's End.'

'I see, that was one of the blunders,' said Ethel. 'But I had often thought of this nice little square place, between two gardens, and sheltered by the old quarry.'

'Ha! hardly space enough, I should say,' replied Dr. Spencer, stepping it out. 'No, that won't do, so confined by the quarry Let us look further.'

A surmise crossed Ethel. Could he be going to take the work on himself, but that was too wild a supposition—she knew he had nothing of his own, only a moderate pension from the East India Company.

'What do you think of this?' he said, coming to the slope of a knoll, commanding a pretty view of the Abbotstoke woods, clear from houses, and yet not remote from the hamlet. She agreed that it would do well, and he kicked up a bit of turf and pryed into the soil, pronouncing it dry, and fit for a good foundation. Then he began to step it out, making a circuit that amazed her; but he said, 'It is of no use to do it at twice. Your school can be only the first step towards a Church, and you had better have room enough at once. It will serve as an endowment in the meantime.'

He would not let her remain in the sun, and she went into school. She found him, when she came out, sitting in the arbour, smoking a cigar—rather a shock to her feelings, though he threw it away the instant she appeared, and she excused him for his foreign habits.

In the evening, he brought down a traveller's case of instruments, and proceeded to draw a beautiful little map of Cocksmoor, where it seemed that he had taken all his measurements whilst she was in school. He ended by an imaginary plan and elevation for the school, with a pretty oriel window and bell-gable, that made Ethel sigh with delight at the bare idea.

Next day he vanished after dinner, but this he often did; he used to say he must go and have a holiday of smoking—he could not bear too much civilised society. He came back for tea, however, and had not sat down long before he said, 'Now, I know all about it. I shall pack up my goods, and be off for Vienna to-morrow.'

'To Vienna!' was the general and dolorous outcry; and Gertrude laid hold of him, and said he should not go.

'I am coming back,' he said, 'if you will have me. The College holds a Court at Fordholm, on the 3rd, and on the last of this month I hope to return.'

'College! Court! What are you going to do at Vienna? Where have you left your senses?' asked Dr. May.

'I find Sir Henry Walkinghame is there. I have been on an exploring expedition to Drydale, found out his man of business, and where he is to be written to. The College holds a Court at Fordholm, and I hope to have our business settled.'

Ethel was too much confounded to speak. Her father was exclaiming on the shortness of the time.

'Plenty of time,' said Dr. Spencer, demonstrating that he should be able to travel comfortably, and have four days to spare at Vienna—a journey which he seemed to think less of than did Dr. May of going to London.

As to checking him, of that there was no possibility, nor, indeed, notion, though Ethel did not quite know how to believe in it, nor that the plan could come to good. Ethel was much better by this time: by her vigorous efforts, she had recovered her tone of mind and interest in what was passing; and though, now and then, Norman's letters, carrying sentences of remembrance, made her glow a little, she was so steady to her resolution that she averted all traffic in messages through her brother's correspondence, and, in that fear, allowed it to lapse into Margaret's hands more than she had ever done. Indeed, no one greatly liked writing from home, it was heartless work to say always, 'No news from the Alcestis,' and yet they all declared they were not anxious.

Hector Ernescliffe knelt a great while beside Margaret's sofa, on the first evening of his holidays, and there was a long low-voiced talk between them. Ethel wished that she had warned him off, for Margaret looked much more harassed and anxious, after having heard the outpouring of all that was on his mind.

Dr. Spencer thought her looking worse, when he came, as come he did, on the appointed day. He had brought Sir Henry Walkinghame's full consent to the surrender of the land; drawn up in such a form as could be acted upon, and a letter to his man of business. But Nicolson! He was a worse dragon nearer home, hating all schools—especially hating Dr. May.

However, said Dr. Spencer, in eastern form, 'Have I encountered Rajahs, and smoked pipes with three-tailed Pachas, that I should dread the face of the father of quarrymen.'

What he did with the father of quarrymen was not known; whether he talked him over, or bought him off—Margaret hoped the former, Dr. May feared the latter—the results were certain. Mr. Nicolson had agreed that the land should be given up.

The triumphant Dr. Spencer sat down to write a statement to be shown to the College authorities when they should come to hold their Court.

'The land must be put into the hands of trustees,' he said. 'The incumbent, of course?'

'Then yourself; and we must have another. Your son-in-law?'

'You, I should think,' said Dr. May.

'I! Why, I am going.'

'Going, but not gone,' said his friend.

'I must go! I tell you, Dick; I must have a place of my own to smoke my pipe in.'

'Is that all?' said Dr. May. 'I think you might be accommodated here, unless you wished to be near your sister.'

'My sister is always resorting to watering-places. My nieces do nothing but play on the piano. No, I shall perhaps go off to America, the only place I have not seen yet, and I more than half engaged to go and help at Poonshedagore.'

'Better order your coffin, then,' muttered Dr. May.

'I shall try lodgings in London, near the old Hospital, perhaps —and go and turn over the British Museum library.'

'Look you here, Spencer, I have a much better plan. Do you know that scrap of a house of mine, by the back gate, just big enough for you and your pipe? Set up your staff there. Ethel will never get her school built without you.'

'Oh! that would be capital!' cried Ethel.

'It would be the best speculation for me. You would pay rent, and the last old woman never did,' continued Dr. May. 'A garden the length of this one—'

'But I say—I want to be near the British Museum.'

'Take a season-ticket, and run up once a week.'

'I shall teach your boys to smoke!'

'I'll see to that!'

'You have given Cocksmoor one lift,' said Ethel, 'and it will never go on without you.'

'It is such a nice house!' added the children, in chorus; 'it would be such fun to have you there.'

'Daisy will never be able to spare her other Doctor,' said Margaret, smiling.

'Run to Mrs. Adams, Tom, and get the key,' said Dr. May.

There was a putting on of hats and bonnets, and the whole party walked down the garden to inspect the house—a matter of curiosity to some—for it was where the old lady had resided on whom Harry had played so many tricks, and the subject of many myths hatched between him and George Larkins.

It was an odd, little narrow slip of a house, four stories, of two rooms all the way up, each with a large window, with a marked white eye-brow. Dr. May eagerly pointed out all the conveniences, parlour, museum, smoking den, while Dr. Spencer listened, and answered doubtfully; and the children's clamorous anxiety seemed to render him the more silent.

Hector Ernescliffe discovered a jack-daw's nest in the chimney, whereupon the whole train rushed off to investigate, leaving the two Doctors and Ethel standing together in the empty parlour, Dr. May pressing, Dr. Spencer raising desultory objections; but so evidently against his own wishes, that Ethel said, 'Now, indeed, you must not disappoint us all.'

'No,' said Dr. May, 'it is a settled thing.'

'No, no, thanks, thanks to you all, but it cannot be. Let me go—' and he spoke with emotion. 'You are very kind, but it is not to be thought of.'

'Why not?' said Dr. May. 'Spencer, stay with me—,' and he spoke with a pleading, almost dependent air, 'Why should you go?'

'It is of no use to talk about it. You are very kind, but it will not do to encumber you with a lone man, growing old.'

'We have been young together,' said Dr. May.

'And you must not leave papa,' said Ethel.

'No,' said Dr. May. 'Trouble may be at hand. Help us through with it. Remember, these children have no uncles.'

'You will stay?' said Ethel.

He made a sign of assent—he could do no more, and, just then, Gertrude came trotting back, so exceedingly smutty, as to call every one's attention. Hector had been shoving Tom half-way up the chimney, in hopes of reaching the nest; and the consequences of this amateur chimney-sweeping had been a plentiful bespattering of all the spectators with soot, that so greatly distressed the young ladies, that Mary and Blanche had fled away from public view.

Dr. Spencer's first act of possession was, to threaten to pull Tom down by the heels, for disturbing *his* jackdaws, whereupon there was a general acclamation; and Dr. May began to talk of marauding times, when the jackdaws in the Minster tower had been harried.

'Ah!' said Dr. Spencer, as Tom emerged, blacker than the outraged jackdaws, and half choked, 'what do you know about jackdaws' nests? You that are no Whichcote scholars.'

'Don't we?' cried Hector, 'when there is a jackdaw's nest in Eton Chapel, twenty feet high.'

'Old Grey made that!' said Tom, who usually acted the part of *esprit fort* to Hector's credulity.

'Why, there is a picture of it in Jesse's book,' said Hector.

'But may not we get up on the roof, to see if we can get at the nest, papa?' said Tom.

'You must ask Dr. Spencer. It is his house.'

Dr. Spencer did not gainsay it, and proceeded even to show the old Whichcote spirit, by leading the assault, and promising to take care of Aubrey, while Ethel retained Gertrude, and her father too; for Dr. May had such a great inclination to scramble up the ladder after them, that she, thinking it a dangerous experiment for so helpless an arm, was obliged to assure him that it would create a sensation among the gossiphood of Stoneborough, if their physician were seen disporting himself on the top of the house.

'Ah! I'm not a physician unattached, like him,' said Dr. May, laughing. 'Hollo! have you got up, Tom? There's a door up there. I'll show you—'

'No, don't papa. Think of Mrs. Ledwich; and asking her to see two trustees up there!' said Ethel.

'Ah! Mrs. Ledwich; what is to be done with her, Ethel?'

'I am sure I can't tell. If Flora were but at home, she would manage it.'

'Spencer can manage anything!' was the answer. 'That was the happiest chance imaginable that you came home with me, and so we came to go by the same train.'

Ethel was only afraid that time was being cruelly wasted; but the best men, and it is emphatically the best that generally are so—have the boy strong enough, on one side or other of their natures, to be a great provocation to womankind; and Dr. Spencer did not rest from his pursuit till the brood of the jackdaws had been discovered, and two grey-headed nestlings kidnapped, which were destined to a wicker cage, and education. Little Aubrey was beyond measure proud, and was suggesting all sorts of outrageous classical names for them, till politely told by Tom that he would make them as great prigs as himself, and that their names should be nothing but Jack and Jill.

'There's nothing for it but for Aubrey to go to school,' cried Tom, sententiously turning round to Ethel.

'Aye, to Stoneborough,' said Dr. Spencer.

Tom coloured, as if sorry for his movement, and hastened away to make himself sufficiently clean to go in quest of a prison for his captives.

Dr. Spencer began to bethink him of the paper that he had been so eagerly drawing up, and looking at his own begrimed hands, asked Ethel whether she would have him for a trustee.

'Will the other eight ladies?' said Ethel, 'that's the point.'

'Ha, Spencer! you did not know what you were undertaking. Do you wish to be let off?' said Dr. May.

'Not I,' said the undaunted Doctor. 'Come, Ethel, let us hear what should be done.'

'There's no time,' said Ethel, bewildered. 'The Court will be only on the day after to-morrow.'

'Ample time!' said Dr. Spencer, who seemed ready to throw himself into it with all his might. 'What we have to do is this. The ladies to be propitiated are—'

'Nine Muses, to whom you will have to act Apollo,' said Dr. May, who, having put his friend into the situation, had a mischievous delight in laughing at him, and watching what he would do.

'One and two, Ethel, and Mrs. Rivers!'

'Rather eight and nine,' said Ethel, 'though Flora may be somebody now.'

'Seven then,' said Dr. Spencer. 'Well then, Ethel, suppose we set out on our travels this afternoon. Visit these ladies, get them to call a meeting to-morrow, and sanction their three trustees.'

'You little know what a work it is to call a meeting, or how many notes Miss Rich sends out before one can be accomplished.'

'Faint heart—you know the proverb, Ethel, *Allons*. I'll call on Mrs. Ledwich.'

'Stay,' said Dr. May. 'Let Ethel do that, and ask her to tea, and we will show her your drawing of the school.'

So the remaining ladies were divided—Ethel was to visit Miss Anderson, Miss Boulder, and Mrs. Ledwich; Dr. Spencer, the rest, and a meeting, if possible, be appointed for the next day.

Ethel did as she was told, though rather against the grain, and her short, abrupt manner, was excused the more readily, that Dr. Spencer had been a subject of much mysterious speculation in Stoneborough, and to gain any intelligence respecting him was a great object; so that she was extremely welcome, wherever she called.

Mrs. Ledwich promised to come to tea, and instantly prepared to walk to Miss Rich, and authorize her to send out the notes of summons to the morrow's meeting. Ethel offered to walk with her, and found Mrs. and Miss Rich in a flutter, after Dr. Spencer's call; the daughter just going to put on her bonnet and consult Mrs. Ledwich, and both extremely enchanted with Dr. Spencer, who 'would be such an acquisition.'

The hour was fixed and the notes sent out, and Ethel met Dr. Spencer at the garden gate.

'Well!' he said, smiling, 'I think we have fixed them off—have not we?'

'Yes; but is it not heartless that everything should be done through so much nonsense?'

'Did you ever hear why the spire of Ulm Cathedral was never finished?' said Dr. Spencer.

'No; why not?'

'Because the citizens would accept no help from their neighbours.'

'I am glad enough of help when it comes in the right way, and from good motives.'

'There are more good motives in the world than you give people credit for, Ethel. You have a good father, good sense, and a good education; and you have some perception of the system by which things like this should be done. Unfortunately, the system is in bad hands here, and these good ladies have been left to work for themselves, and it is no wonder that there is plenty of little self-importance, nonsense, and the like, among them; but for their own sakes we should rather show them the way, than throw them overboard.'

'If they will be shown,' said Ethel.

'I can't say they seemed to me so very formidable,' said Dr. Spencer, 'gentle little women.'

'Oh! it is only Mrs. Ledwich that stirs them up. I hope you are prepared for that encounter.'

Mrs. Ledwich came to tea, sparkling with black bugles, and was very patronizing and amiable. Her visits were generally subjects of great dread, for she talked unceasingly, laid down the law, and overwhelmed Margaret with remedies; but to-night Dr. Spencer took her in hand. It was not that he went out of his ordinary self, he was always the same simple mannered, polished gentleman; but it was this that told—she was evidently somewhat in awe of him—the refinement kept her in check. She behaved very quietly all the evening, admired the plans, consented to everything, and was scarcely Mrs. Ledwich!

'You will get on now, Ethel,' said Dr. May, afterwards. 'Never fear but that he will get the Ladies' Committee well in hand.'

'Why do you think so, papa?'

'Never you fear—'

That was all she could extract from him, though he looked very arch.

The Ladies' Committee accepted of their representatives with full consent; and the indefatigable Dr. Spencer next had to hunt up the fellow trustee. He finally contrived to collect every one he wanted at Fordholm, the case was laid before the College— the College was propitious, and, by four o'clock in the evening, Dr. Spencer laid before Ethel the promise of the piece of land.

Mary's joy was unbounded, and Ethel blushed, and tried to thank. This would have been the summit of felicity a year ago, and she was vexed with herself for feeling that though land and money were both in such safe hands, she could not care sufficiently to feel the ecstasy the attainment of her object would once have given to her. Then she would have been frantic with excitement, and heedless of everything; now she took it so composedly as to annoy herself.

'To think of that one week at Oxford having so entirely turned this head of mine!'

Perhaps it was the less at home, because she had just heard that George and Flora had accepted an invitation to Glenbracken, but though the zest of Cocksmoor might be somewhat gone, she called herself to order, and gave her full attention to all that was planned by her champion.

Never did man plunge into business more thoroughly than he, when he had once undertaken it. He was one of those men who, from gathering particulars of every practical matter that comes under their notice, are able to accomplish well whatever they set their hand to; and building was not new to him, though his former subjects—a Church and Mission station in India— bore little resemblance to the present.

He bought a little round dumpling of a white pony, and trotted all over the country in search of building materials and builders, he discovered trees in distant timber-yards, he brought home specimens of stone, one in each pocket, to compare and analyse, he went to London to look at model schools, he drew plans each more neat and beautiful than the last, he compared builders' estimates, and wrote letters to the National Society, so as to be able to begin in the spring.

In the mean time he was settling himself, furnishing his new house with great precision and taste. He would have no assist- ance in his choice, either of servants or furniture, but made numerous journeys of inspection to Whitford, to Malvern, and to London, and these seemed to make him the more content with Stoneborough. Sir Matthew Fleet had evidently chilled him, and as he found his own few remaining relations uncongenial, he became the more ready to find a resting-place in the grey old town, the scene of his school life, beside the friend of his youth, and the children of her, for whose sake he had never sought a home of his own. Though he now and then talked of seeing America, or of going back to India, in hopes of assisting his beloved mission at Poonshedagore; these plans were fast dying away, as he formed habits and attachments, and perceived the sphere of usefulness open to him.

It was a great step when his packages arrived, and his beautiful Indian curiosities were arranged, making his drawing-room as pretty a room as could anywhere be seen; in readiness, as he used to tell Ethel, for a grand tea-party for all the Ladies' Committee, when he should borrow her and the best silver tea-pot to preside. Moreover he had a chemical apparatus, a telescope, and microscope, of great power, wherewith he tried experiments that were the height of felicity to Tom and Ethel, and much interested their father. He made it his business to have full occupation for himself, with plans, books, or correspondence, so as not to be a charge on the hands of the May family, with whom he never spent an evening without special and earnest invitation.

He gave attendance at the hospital on alternate days, as well as taking off Dr. May's hands such of his gratuitous patients as were not averse to quit their old Doctor, and could believe in a physician in shepherd's plaid, and Panama hat. Exceedingly sociable, he soon visited every one far and wide, and went to every sort of party, from the grand dinners of the 'county families,' to the tea drinkings of the Stoneborough ladies, a welcome guest at all, and enjoying each in his own way. English life was so new to him that he entered into the little accessories with the zest of a youth; and there seemed to be a curious change between the two old fellow students, the elder and more staid of former days having come back with unencumbered freshness to enliven his friend, just beginning to grow aged under the wear of care and sorrows.

It was very droll to hear Dr. May laughing at Dr. Spencer's histories of his adventures, and at the new aspects in which his own well-trodden district appeared to travelled eyes; and not less amusing was Dr. Spencer's resolute defence of all the Nine Muses, generally and individually.

He certainly had no reason to think ill of them. As one woman, they were led by him, and conformed their opinions. The only seceder was Louisa Anderson, who had her brother for her oracle; and, indeed, the more youthful race, to whom Harvey was the glass of fashion, uttered disrespectful opinions as to the Doctor's age, and would not accede to his being, as Mrs. Ledwich declared, 'much younger than Dr. May.'

Harvey Anderson had first attempted patronage, then argument, with Dr. Spencer, but found him equally impervious to both. 'Very clever, but an old world man,' said Harvey. 'He has made up his bundle of prejudices.'

'Clever sort of lad!' said Dr. Spencer, 'a cool hand, but very shallow—'

Ethel wondered to hear thus lightly disposed of, the powers of argument that had been thought fairly able to compete with Norman, and which had taxed him so severely. She did not know how differently abstract questions appear to a mature mind, confirmed in principle by practice; and to one young, struggling in self-formation, and more used to theories than to realities.

CHAPTER XII.

' The heart may ache, but may not burst ;
Heaven will not leave thee, nor forsake.'—CHRISTIAN YEAR.

HECTOR and Tom finished their holidays by a morning's shooting at the Grange, Dr. May promising to meet them, and let them drive him home.

Meta was out, when he arrived; and, repairing to the library, he found Mr. Rivers sitting by a fire, though it was early in September, with the newspaper before him, but not reading. He looked depressed, and seemed much disappointed at having heard that George and Flora had accepted some further invitations in Scotland, and did not intend to return for another month. Dr. May spoke cheerfully of the hospitality and kindness they had met, but failed to enliven him, and, as if trying to assign some cause for his vexation, he lamented over fogs and frosts, and began to dread an October in Scotland for Flora, almost as if it were the Arctic regions.

He grew somewhat more animated in praising Flora, and speaking of the great satisfaction he had in seeing his son married to so admirable a person. He only wished it could be the same with his daughter.

'You are a very unselfish father,' said Dr. May. ' I cannot imagine you without your little fairy.'

'It would be hard to part,' said Mr. Rivers, sighing; ' yet I should be relieved to see her in good hands, so pretty and engaging as she is, and something of an heiress. With our dear Flora, she is secure of a happy home when I am gone, but still I should be glad to have seen—,' and he broke off thoughtfully.

'She is so sensible, that we shall see her make a good choice,' said Dr. May, smiling; ' that is, if she choose at all, for I do not know who is worthy of her.'

'I am quite indifferent as to fortune,' continued Mr. Rivers. ' She will have enough of her own.'

'Enough not to be dependent, which is the point,' said Dr. May, ' though I should have few fears for her any way.'

'It would be a comfort,' harped on Mr. Rivers, dwelling on the subject, as if he wanted to say something, ' if she were only safe with a man who knew how to value her, and make her happy. Such a young man as your Norman, now—I have often thought—'

Dr. May would not seem to hear, but he could not prevent himself from blushing as crimson as if he had been the very Norman, as he answered, going on with his own speech, as if Mr. Rivers's had been unmade: 'She is the brightest little creature under the sun, and the sparkle is down so deep within, that however it may turn out, I should never fear for her happiness.'

'Flora is my great reliance,' proceeded Mr. Rivers. 'Her aunt, Lady Leonora, is very kind, but somehow she does not seem to suit with Meta.'

O ho, thought the Doctor, have you made that discovery, my good friend?

The voices of the two boys were heard in the hall, explaining their achievements to Meta, and Dr. May took his departure, Hector driving him, and embarking in a long discourse on his own affairs, as if he had quite forgotten that the Doctor was not his father, and going on emphatically, in spite of the absence of mind now and then betrayed by his auditor, who, at Dr. Spencer's door, exclaimed, 'Stop, Hector, let me out here—thank you;' and presently brought out his friend into the garden, and sat down on the grass, talking low, and earnestly, over the disease with which Mr. Rivers had been so long affected; for though Dr. May could not perceive any positively unfavourable symptom, he had been rendered vaguely uneasy by the unusual heaviness and depression of manner. So long did they sit conversing, that Blanche was sent out, primed with an impertinent message, that two such old Doctors ought to be ashamed of themselves for sitting so late in the dew.

Dr. Spencer was dragged in to drink tea, and the meal had just been merrily concluded, when the door-bell rang, and a message was brought in. 'The carriage from the Grange, sir—Miss Rivers would be much obliged if you would come directly.'

'There!' said Dr. May, looking at Dr. Spencer, as if to say I told you so; in the first triumph of professional sagacity; but the next moment exclaiming, 'Poor little Meta!' he hurried away.

A gloom fell on those who remained, for, besides their sympathy for Meta, and their liking for her kind old father, there was that one unacknowledged heartache, which, though in general bravely combated, lay in wait always ready to prey on them. Hector stole round to sit by Margaret, and Dr. Spencer muttered, 'this will never do,' and sent Tom to fetch some papers lying on his table, whence he read them some curious accounts that he had just received from his Missionary friends in India.

They were interested, but in a listening mood, that caused a universal start when the bell again sounded. This time, James reported that the servant from the Grange said his master was very ill—he had brought a letter to post for Mr. George Rivers, and here was a note for Miss Ethel. It was the only note Ethel had ever received from her father, and only contained these few words:—

'DEAR E.—I believe this attack will be the last. Come to Meta, and bring my things.
'R. M.'

Ethel put her hands to her forehead. It was as if she had been again plunged into the stunned dream of misery of four years ago, and her sensation was of equal bewilderment and uselessness, but it was but for a moment—the next she was in a state of over bustle and eagerness. She wanted to fly about and hasten to help Meta, and could hardly obey the word and gesture by which Margaret summoned her to her side.

'Dear Ethel, you must calm yourself, or you will not be of use.'

'I? I can't be of any use! Oh! if you could go! If Flora were but here! But I must go, Margaret.'

'I will put up your father's things,' said Dr. Spencer, in a soothing tone. 'The carriage cannot be ready in a moment, so that there will be full time.'

Mary and Miss Bracy prepared Ethel's own goods, which she would otherwise have forgotten; and Margaret, meanwhile, detained her by her side, trying to calm and encourage her with gentle words of counsel, that might hinder her from giving way to the flurry of emotion that had seized her, and prevent her from thinking herself certain to be useless.

Adams was to drive her thither in the gig, and it presently came to the door. Dr. Spencer wrapped her up well in cloaks and shawls, and spoke words of kindly cheer in her ear as she set off. The fresh night air blew pleasantly on her, the stars glimmered in full glory over her head, and now and then her eye was caught by the rocket-like track of a shooting-star. Orion was rising slowly far in the east, and bringing to her mind the sailor-boy under the southern sky; if, indeed, he were not where sun and stars no more are the light. It was strange that the thought came more as soothing than as acute pain; she could bear to think of him thus in her present frame, as long as she had not to talk of him. Under those solemn stars, the Life Everlasting seemed to overpower the sense of this mortal life, and Ethel's agitation was calmed away.

The old cedar-tree stood up in stately blackness against the sky, and the lights in the house glanced behind it. The servants looked rather surprised to see Ethel, as if she were not expected, and conducted her to the great drawing-room, which looked the more desolate and solitary, from the glare of lamplight, falling on the empty seats which Ethel had lately seen filled with a glad, home party. She was looking round, thinking whether to venture up to Meta's room, and there summon Bellairs, when Meta came gliding in, and threw her arms round her. Ethel could not speak, but Meta's voice was more cheerful than she had expected. 'How kind of you, dear Ethel!'

'Papa sent for me,' said Ethel.

'He is so kind! Can Margaret spare you?'

'Oh, yes! but you must leave me. You must want to be with him.'

'He never lets me come in when he has these attacks,' said Meta. 'If he only would! But will you come up to my room? That is nearer.'

'Is papa with him?'

'Yes.'

Meta wound her arms round Ethel, and led her up to her sitting-room, where a book lay on the table. She said that her father had seemed weary and torpid, and had sat still until almost their late dinner hour, when he seemed to bethink himself of dressing, and had risen. She thought he walked weakly, and rather tottering, and had run to make him lean on her, which he did, as far as his own room door. There he had kissed her, and thanked her, and murmured a word like blessing. She had not, however, been alarmed, until his servant had come to tell her that he had another seizure.

Ethel asked whether she had seen Dr. May since he had been with her father. She had; but Ethel was surprised to find that she had not taken in the extent of his fears. She had become so far accustomed to these attacks, that, though anxious and distressed, she did not apprehend more than a few days' weakness, and her chief longing was to be of use. She was speaking cheerfully of beginning her nursing to-morrow, and of her great desire that her papa would allow her to sit up with him, when there was a slow, reluctant movement of the lock of the door, and the two girls sprang to their feet, as Dr. May opened it; and Ethel read his countenance at once.

Not so Meta. 'How is he? May I go to him?' cried she.

'Not now, my dear,' said Dr. May, putting his hand on her shoulder, in a gentle, detaining manner, that sent a thrill of trembling through her frame, though she did not otherwise move.

She only clasped her hands together, and looked up into his face. He answered the look. 'Yes, my dear, the struggle is over.'

Ethel came near, and put her arm round Meta's waist, as if to strengthen her, as she stood quite passive, and still.

Dr. May seemed to think it best that all should be told; but, though intently watching Meta, he directed his words to his own daughter. 'Thank Heaven, it has been shorter, and less painful, than I had dared to hope.'

Meta tried to speak, but could not bring out the words, and, with an imploring look at Ethel, as if to beg her to make them clear for her, she inarticulately murmured, 'Oh! why did not you call me!'

'I could not. He would not let me. His last conscious word to me was not to let you see him suffer.'

Meta wrung her clasped hands together in mute anguish. Dr. May signed to Ethel to guide her back to the sofa, but the movement seemed so far to rouse her, that she said, 'I should like to go to bed.'

'Right—the best thing,' said Dr. May; and he whispered to Ethel, 'go with her, but don't try to rouse her—don't talk to her. Come back to me, presently.'

He did not even shake hands with Meta, nor wish her good-night, as she disappeared into her own room.

Bellairs undressed her, and Ethel stood watching, till the young head, under the load of sorrow, so new to it, was laid on the pillow. Bellairs asked her if she would have a light.

'No, no, thank you—the dark and alone. Good-night,' said Meta.

Ethel went back to the sitting-room, where her father was standing at the window, looking out into the night. He turned as she came in, folded her in his arms, and kissed her forehead. 'And how is the poor little dear?' he asked.

'The same,' said Ethel. 'I can't bear to leave her alone, and to have said nothing to comfort her.'

'It is too soon as yet,' said Dr. May—'her mind has not taken it in. I hope she will sleep all night, and have more strength to look at it when she wakens.'

'She was utterly unprepared.'

'I could not make her understand me,' said Dr. May.

'And, oh, papa, what a pity she was not there!'

'It was no sight for her, till the last few minutes; and his whole mind seemed bent on sparing her. What tenderness it has been.'

'Must we leave her to herself all night?'

'Better so,' said Dr. May. 'She has been used to loneliness; and to thrust companionship on her would be only harassing.'

Ethel, who scarcely knew what it was to be alone, looked as if she did not understand.

'I used to try to force consolation on people,' said Dr. May, 'but I know, now, that it can only be done by following their bent.'

'You have seen so many sorrows,' said Ethel.

'I never understood till I felt,' said Dr. May. 'Those few first days were a lesson.'

'I did not think you knew what was passing,' said Ethel.

'I doubt whether any part of my life is more distinctly before me than those two days,' said Dr. May. 'Flora coming in and out, and poor Alan sitting by me; but I don't believe I had any will. I could no more have moved my mind than my broken arm; and I verily think, Ethel, that, but for that merciful torpor, I should have been frantic. It taught me never to disturb grief.'

'And what shall we do?'

'You must stay with her till Flora comes. I will be here as much as I can. She is our charge, till they come home. I told him, between the spasms, that I had sent for you, and he seemed pleased.'

'If only I were anybody else!'

Dr. May again threw his arm round her, and looked into her face. He felt that he had rather have her, such as she was, than anybody else; and, together, they sat down, and talked of what was to be done, and what was best for Meta, and of the solemnity of being in the house of death. Ethel felt and showed it so much, in her subdued, awe-struck manner, that her father felt checked whenever he was about to return to his ordinary manner, familiarized, as he necessarily was, with the like scenes. It drew him back to the thought of their own trouble, and their conversation recurred to those days, so that each gained a more full understanding of the other, and they at length separated, certainly with the more peaceful and soft feelings for being in the abode of mourning.

Bellairs promised to call Ethel, to be with her young lady as early as might be, reporting that she was sound asleep. And sleep continued to shield her till past her usual hour, so that Ethel was up, and had been with Dr. May, before she was summoned to her, and then she found her half-dressed, and hastening that she might not make Dr. May late for breakfast, and in going to his patients. There was an elasticity in the happily constituted young mind that could not be entirely struck down, nor deprived of power of taking thought for others. Yet her eyes looked wandering, and unlike themselves, and her words, now and then, faltered, as if she was not sure what she was doing or saying. Ethel told her not to mind—Dr. Spencer would take care of the patients; but she did not seem to recollect, at first, who Dr. Spencer was, nor to care for being reminded.

Breakfast was laid out in the little sitting-room. Ethel wanted to take the trouble off her hands, but she would not let her. She sat behind her urn, and asked about tea or coffee, quite accurately, in a low, subdued voice, that nearly overcame Dr. May. When the meal was over, and she had rung the bell, and risen up, as if to her daily work, she turned round, with that piteous, perplexed air, and stood for a moment, as if confused.

'Cannot we help you?' said Ethel.

'I don't know. Thank you. But, Dr. May, I must not keep you from other people—'

'I have no one to go to this morning,' said Dr. May. 'I am ready to stay with you, my dear.'

Meta came closer to him, and murmured, 'Thank you!'

The breakfast things had, by this time, been taken away, and Meta, looking to see that the door had shut for the last time, said, in a low voice, 'Now tell me—'

Dr. May drew her down, to sit on the sofa beside him, and, in his soft, sweet voice, told her all that she wished to learn of her father's last hours, and was glad to see showers of quiet wholesome tears drop freely down, but without violence, and she scarcely attempted to speak. There was a pause at the end, and then she said, gently, 'Thank you, for it all. Dear papa!' And she rose up, and went back to her room.

'She has learnt to dwell apart,' said Dr. May, much moved.

'How beautifully she bears up!' said Ethel.

'It has been a life which, as she has used it, has taught her strength and self-dependence in the midst of prosperity.'

'Yes,' said Ethel, 'she has trained herself by her dread of self-indulgence, and seeking after work. But oh! what a break up it is for her! I cannot think how she holds up. Shall I go to her?'

'I think not. She knows the way to the only Comforter. I am not afraid for her after those blessed tears.'

Dr. May was right; Meta presently returned to them, in the same gentle subdued sadness, enfolding her, indeed, as a flower weighed down by mist, but not crushing nor taking away her powers. It was as if she were truly upheld; and thankful to her friends as she was, she did not throw herself on them in utter dependence or self-abandonment.

She wrote needful letters, shedding many tears over them, and often obliged to leave off to give the blinding weeping its course, but refusing to impose any unnecessary task upon Dr. May's lame arm. All that was right she strove to do; she saw Mr. Charles Wilmot, and was refreshed by his reading to her, and when Dr. May desired it, she submissively put on her bonnet, and took several turns with Ethel in the shrubbery, though it made her cry heartily to look into the down-stairs rooms. And she lay on the sofa at last, owning herself strangely tired, she did not know why, and glad that Ethel should read to her. By-and-by, she went to dress for the evening, and came back, full of the tidings that one of the children in the village had been badly burnt. It occupied her very much—she made Ethel promise to go and see about her to-morrow, and sent Bellairs at once with every comfort that she could devise.

On the whole, those two days were to Ethel a peaceful and comfortable time. She saw more than usual of her father, and had such conversations with him as were seldom practicable at home, and that chimed in with the unavowed care which hung on their minds; while Meta was a most sweet and loving charge, without being a burthen, and often saying such beautiful things in her affectionate resignation, that Ethel could only admire and lay them up in her mind. Dr. May went backwards and forwards, and brought good accounts of Margaret and fond messages; he slept at the Grange each night, and Meta used to sit in her corner of the sofa and work, or not, as best suited her, while she listened to his talk with Ethel, and now and then herself joined.

George Rivers' absence was a serious inconvenience in all arrangements; but his sister dreaded his grief as much as she wished for his return; and often were the posts and the journeys reckoned over, without a satisfactory conclusion, as to when he could arrive from so remote a part of Scotland.

At last, as the two girls had finished their early dinner, the butler brought in word that Mr. Norman May was there. Meta at once begged that he would come in, and Ethel went into the hall to meet him. He looked very wan, with the dark rings round his eyes a deeper purple than ever, and he could hardly find utterance to ask 'How is she?'

'As good and sweet as she can be,' said Ethel, warmly; but no more, for Meta herself had come to the dining-room door, and was holding out her hand. Norman took it in both his, but could not speak; Meta's own soft voice was the first. 'I thought you would come—he was so fond of you.'

Poor Norman quite gave way, and Meta was the one to speak

gentle words of soothing. 'There is so much to be thankful for,' she said. 'He has been spared so much of the suffering Dr. May feared for him; and he was so happy about George.'

Norman made a great effort to recover himself. Ethel asked for Flora and George. It appeared that they had been on an excursion when the first letter arrived at Glenbracken, and thus had received both together in the evening, on their return. George had been greatly overcome, and they had wished to set off instantly; but Lady Glenbracken would not hear of Flora's travelling night and day, and it had at length been arranged that Norman Ogilvie should drive Norman across the country that evening, to catch the mail for Edinburgh, and he had been on the road ever since. George was following with his wife more slowly, and would be at home to-morrow evening. Meantime, he sent full authority to his father-in-law to make arrangements.

Ethel went to see the burnt child, leaving Meta to take her walk in the garden under Norman's charge. He waited on her with a sort of distant reverence for a form of grief, so unlike what he had dreaded for her, when the first shock of the tidings had brought back to him the shattered bewildered feelings to which he dared not recur.

To dwell on the details was, to her, a comfort, knowing his sympathy and the affection there had been between him and her father; nor had they parted in such absolute brightness, as to make them unprepared for such a meeting as the present. The cloud of suspense was brooding lower and lower over the May family, and the need of faith and submission was as great with them as with the young orphan herself. Norman said little, but that little was so deep and fervent, that after a time, Meta could not help saying, when Ethel was seen in the distance, and their talk was nearly over—'Oh! Norman, these things are no mirage.'

'It is the world that is the mirage,' he answered.

Ethel came up, and Dr. May also, in good time for the post. He was obliged to become very busy, using Norman for his secretary, till he saw his son's eyes so heavy, that he remembered the two nights that he had been up, and ordered him to go home, and go to bed as soon as tea was over.

'May I come back to-morrow?'

'Why—yes—I think you may. No, no,' he added, recollecting himself, 'I think you had better not,' and he did not relent, though Norman looked disappointed.

Meta had already expressed her belief that her father would be buried at the suburban Church, where lay her mother; and Dr. May, having been desired to seek out the will and open it, found it was so; and fixed the day and hour with Meta, who was as submissive and reasonable as possible, though much grieved that he thought she could not be present.

Ethel, after going with Meta to her room at night, returned as usual to talk matters over with him, and again say how good Meta was.

'And I think Norman's coming did her a great deal of good,' said Ethel.

'Ha! yes,' said the Doctor, thoughtfully.

'She thinks so much of Mr. Rivers having been fond of him.'

'Yes,' said the Doctor, 'he was. I find, in glancing over the will, which was newly made on Flora's marriage, that he has remembered Norman—left him 100*l.* and his portfolio of prints from Raffaelle.'

'Has he, indeed? how very kind—how much Norman will value it.'

'It is remarkable,' said Dr. May, and then, as if he could not help it, told Ethel what Mr. Rivers had said of his wishes with regard to his daughter. Ethel blushed and smiled, and looked so much touched and delighted, that he grew alarmed and said, 'You know, Ethel, this must be as if it never had been mentioned.'

'What! you will not tell Norman?'

'No, certainly not, unless I see strong cause. They are very fond of each other, certainly, but they don't know, and I don't know, whether it is not like brother and sister. I would not have either of them guess at this, or feel bound in any way. Why, Ethel! she has thirty thousand pounds, and I don't know how much more.'

'Thirty thousand!' said Ethel, her tone, one of astonishment, while his had been almost of objection.

'It would open a great prospect,' continued Dr. May, complacently, 'with Norman's talents, and such a lift as that, he might be one of the first men in England, provided he had nerve and hardness enough, which I doubt.'

'He would not care for it,' said Ethel.

'No; but the field of usefulness—but what an old fool I am, after all my resolutions not to be ambitious for that boy; to be set a going by such a thing as this! Still Norman is something out of the common way. I wonder what Spencer thinks of him.'

'And you never mean them to hear of it?'

'If they settle it for themselves,' said Dr. May, 'that sanction will come in to give double value to mine—or if I should see poor Norman hesitating as to the inequality, I might smooth the way; but you see, Ethel, this puts us in a most delicate situation towards this pretty little creature. What her father wanted, was only to guard her from fortune-hunters, and if she should marry suitably elsewhere,—why—we will be contented.'

'I don't think I should be,' said Ethel.

'She is the most winning of hummingbirds, and what we see of her now, gives one double confidence in her. She is so far from the petted helpless girl, that he, poor man, would fain have made her! And she has a bright, brave temper and elastic spirits that would be the very thing for him, poor boy, with that morbid sensitiveness—he would not hurt her, and she would brighten him. It would be a very pretty thing—but we must never think about it again.'

'If we can help it,' said Ethel.

'Ah! I am sorry I have put it into your head too. We shall not so easily be unconscious now, when they talk about each other in the innocent way they do. We have had a lesson against being pleased at match-making!' But turning away from the subject, 'You shall not lose your Cocksmoor income, Ethel—'

'I had never thought of that. You have taken no fees here since we have been all one family.'

'Well, he has been good enough to leave me £500, and Cocks-moor can have the interest, if you like.'

'Oh, thank you, papa.'

'It is only its due, for I suppose that is for attendance. Per-sonally, to myself, he has left that beautiful Claude which he knew I admired so much. He has been very kind! But, after all, we ought not to be talking of all this—I should not have known it, if I had not been forced to read the will. Well, so we are in Flora's house, Ethel! I wonder how poor, dear, little Meta will feel the being a guest here, instead of the mistress. I wish that boy were three or four years older! I should like to take her straight home with us—I should like to have her for a daughter—I shall always look on her as one.'

'As a Daisy!' said Ethel.

'Don't talk of it!' said Dr. May, hastily; 'this is no time for such things. After all, I am glad that the funeral is not here— Flora and Meta might be rather overwhelmed with those three incongruous sets of relations. By their letters, these Riverses must be quite as queer a lot as George's relations. After all, if we have nothing else, Ethel, we have the best of it, in regard to such relations as we have.'

'There is Lord Cosham,' said Ethel.

'Yes, he is Meta's guardian, as well as her brother; but he could not have her to live with him. She must depend upon Flora. But we shall see—'

Ethel felt confident that Flora would be very kind to her little sister-in-law, and yet one of those gleams of doubt crossed her, whether Flora would not be somewhat jealous of her own authority.

Late the next evening, the carriage drove to the door, and George and Flora appeared in the hall. Their sisters went out to meet them, and George folded Meta in his arms, and kissing her again and again, called her his poor, dear, little sister, and wept bitterly, and even violently. Flora stood beside Ethel, and said, in a low voice, that poor George felt it dreadfully, and then came forward, touched him gently, and told him that he must not overset Meta; and, drawing her from him, kissed her, and said what a grievous time this had been for her, and how sorry they had been to leave her so long, but they knew she was in the best hands.

'Yes, I should have been so sorry you had been over-tired. I was quite well off,' said Meta.

'And you must look on us as your home,' added Flora.

How can she? thought Ethel. This is taking possession, and making Meta a guest already!

However, Meta did not seem so to feel it—she replied by caresses, and turned again to her brother. Poor George was by far the most struck down of all the mourners, and his whole demeanour gave his new relations a much warmer feeling towards him than they could ever have hoped to entertain. His gentle, refined father had softly impressed his duller nature; and his want of attention, and many extravagances, came back upon him acutely now, in his changed home. He could hardly bear to look at his little orphan sister, and lavished every mark of fondness upon her; nor could he endure to sit at the bottom of his table; but when they had gone in to dinner, he turned away from the chair, and hid his face. He was almost like a child in his want of self-restraint; and with all Dr. May's kind soothing manner, he could not bring him to attend to any of the necessary questions as to arrangements, and was obliged to refer to Flora, whose composed good sense was never at fault.

Ethel was surprised to find that it would be a great distress to Meta to part with her until the funeral was over, though she would hardly express a wish, lest Ethel should be needed at home. As soon as Flora perceived this, she begged her sister to stay, and again Ethel felt unpleasantly that Meta might have seen, if she had chosen, that Flora took the invitation upon herself.

So, while Dr. May, with George, Norman, and Tom, went to London, she remained, though not exactly knowing what good she was doing, unless by making the numbers rather less scanty;

but both sisters declared her to be the greatest comfort possible; and when Meta shut herself up in her own room, where she had long learnt to seek strength in still communing with her own heart, Flora seemed to find it a relief to call her sister to hers, and talk over ordinary subjects, in a tone that struck on Ethel's ear as a little incongruous—but then Flora had not been here from the first, and the impression could not be as strong. She was very kind, and her manner, when with others, was perfect, from its complete absence of affectation; but, alone with Ethel, there was a little complacency sometimes betrayed, and some curiosity whether her father had read the will. Ethel allowed what she had heard of the contents to be extracted from her, and it certainly did not diminish Flora's secret satisfaction at being 'somebody.'

She told the whole history of her visits; first, how cordial Lady Leonora Langdale had been, and then, how happy she had been at Glenbracken. The old Lord and Lady, and Marjorie, all equally charming in their various ways; and Norman Ogilvie, so good a son, and so highly thought of in his own country.

'Did I tell you, Ethel, that he desired to be remembered to you?'

'Yes, you said so.'

'What has Coralie done with it?' continued Flora, seeking in her dressing-case. 'She must have put it away with my brooches. Oh, no, here it is. I had been looking for Cairn-gorm specimens in a shop, saying I wanted a brooch that you *would* wear, when Norman Ogilvie came riding after the carriage, looking quite hot and eager! He had been to some other place, and hunted this one up. Is it not a beauty?'

It was one of the round Bruce brooches, of dark pebble, with a silver fern-leaf lying across it, the dots of small Cairn-gorm stones. 'The Glenbracken badge, you know,' continued Flora.

Ethel twisted it about in her fingers, and said, 'Was not it meant for you?'

'It was to oblige me, if you choose so to regard it,' said Flora, smiling. 'He gave me no injunctions; but, you see, you must wear it now. I shall not wear coloured brooches for a year.'

Ethel sighed. She felt as if her black dress ought, perhaps, to be worn for a nearer cause. She had a great desire to keep that Glenbracken brooch; and surely it could not be wrong. To refuse it would be much worse, and would only lead to Flora's keeping it, and not caring for it.

'Then it is your present, Flora?'

'If you like better to call it so, my dear. I find Norman Ogilvie is going abroad in a few months. I think we ought to ask him here on his way.'

'Flora! I wish you would not talk about such things!'

'Do you really and truly, Ethel?'

'Certainly not, at such a time as this,' said Ethel.

Flora was checked a little, and sat down to write to Marjorie Ogilvie. 'Shall I say you like the brooch, Ethel?' she asked, presently.

'Say what is proper,' said Ethel, impatiently. 'You know what I mean, in the fullest sense of the word.'

'Do I?' said Flora.

'I mean,' said Ethel, 'that you may say, simply and rationally, that I like the thing, but I *won't* have it said as a message, or that I take it as his present.'

'Very well,' said Flora, 'the whole affair is simple enough, if you would not be so conscious, my dear.'

'Flora! I can't stand your calling me my dear!'

'I am very much obliged to you,' said Flora, laughing, more than she would have liked to be seen, but recalled by her sister's look. Ethel was sorry at once. 'Flora, I beg your pardon, I did not mean to be cross, only please don't begin about that—Indeed, I think you had better leave out about the brooch altogether. No one will wonder at your passing it over in such a return as this.'

'You are right,' said Flora, thoughtfully.

Ethel carried the brooch to her own room, and tried to keep herself from speculating what had been Mr. Ogilvie's views in procuring it, and whether he remembered showing her, at Woodstock, which sort of fern was his badge, and how she had abstained from preserving the piece shut up in her guide-book.

Meta's patient sorrow was the best remedy for proneness to such musings. How happy poor little Meta had been! The three sisters sat together that long day, and Ethel read to the others, and by-and-by went to walk in the garden with them, till, as Flora was going in, Meta asked, 'Do you think it would be wrong for me to cross the park to see that little burnt girl, as Mr. Wilmot is away to-day, and she has no one to go to her?'

Flora could see no reason against it, and Meta and Ethel left the garden, and traversed the green park, in its quiet home beauty, not talking much, except that Meta said, 'Well! I think there is quite as much sweetness, as sadness, in this evening.'

'Because of this calm autumn sunset beauty?' said Ethel. 'Look at the golden light coming in under the branches of the trees.'

'Yes,' said Meta, 'one cannot help thinking how much more beautiful it must be—'

PART II.   I I

The two girls said no more, and came to the cottage, where so much gratitude was expressed at seeing Miss Rivers, that it was almost too much for her. She left Ethel to talk, and only said a few soft little words to her sick scholar, who seemed to want her voice and smile to convince her that the small mournful face under all that black crape, belonged to her own dear bright teacher.

'It is odd,' said Meta, as they went back; 'it is seeing other people that makes one know it is all sad and altered—it seems so bewildering, though they are so kind.'

'I know what you mean,' said Ethel.

'One ought not to wish it to go on, because there are other people and other duties,' said Meta, 'but quietness is so peaceful. Do you know, Ethel, I shall always think of those two first days, before anybody came, with you and Dr. May, as something very —very—precious,' she said, at last, with the tears rising.

'I am sure I shall,' said Ethel.

'I don't know how it is, but there is something even in this affliction that makes it like—a strange sort of happiness,' said Meta, musingly.

'I know what it is!' said Ethel.

'That He is so very good?' said Meta, reverently.

'Yes,' said Ethel, almost rebuked for the first thought, namely, that it was because Meta was so very good.

'It does make one feel more confidence,' said Meta.

' " It is good for me to have been in trouble," ' repeated Ethel.

'Yes,' said Meta. 'I hope it is not wrong or unkind in me to feel it, for I think dear papa would wish it; but I do not feel as if— miss him always as I shall—the spring of life were gone from me. I don't think it can, for I know no more pain or trouble can reach him, and there is—don't you think, Ethel, that I may think so? —especial care for the orphan, like a compensation. And there is hope and work here. And I am very thankful! How much worse it would have been, if George had not been married! Dear Flora! Will you tell her, Ethel, how really I do wish her to take the command of me. Tell her it will be the greatest kindness in the world to make me useful to her.'

'I will,' said Ethel.

'And please tell her that I am afraid I may forget, and take upon me, as if I were still lady of the house. Tell her I do not mean it, and I hope that she will check it.'

'I think there is no fear of her forgetting that,' said Ethel, regretting the words before they were out of her mouth.

'I hope I shall not,' said Meta. 'If I do, I shall drive myself away to stay with Aunt Leonora, and I don't want to do that at all. So please to make Flora understand that she is head, and I am ready to be hand and foot;' and Meta's bright smile shone out, with the pleasure of a fresh and loving service.

Ethel understood the force of her father's words, that it was a brave, vigorous spirit.

Dr. May came back with George, and stayed to dinner, after which he talked over business with Flora, whose sagacity continually amazed him, and who undertook to make her husband understand, and do what was needed.

Meta meanwhile cross-questioned her brother on the pretty village, by the Thames, of which she had a fond, childish remembrance, and heard from him of the numerous kind messages from all her relations. There were various invitations, but George repeated them unwillingly.

'You won't go, Meta,' he said. 'It would be a horrid nuisance to part with you.'

'As long as you think so, dear George.—When I am in your way, or Flora's—'

'That will never be! I say, Flora, will she ever be in our way?'

'No, indeed! Meta and I understand that,' said Flora, looking up. 'Well, I suppose Bruce can't be trusted to value the books and prints—'

Dr. May thought it a great relief that Meta had a home with Flora, for, as he said to Ethel, as they went home together, 'Certainly, except Lord Cosham, I never saw such an unpresentable crew as their relations. You should have heard the boys afterwards! There was Master Tom turning up his Eton nose at them, and pronouncing that there never were such a set of snobs, and Norman taking him to task as I never heard him do before—telling him that he would never have urged his going to Eton, if he had thought it would make him despise respectable folks, probably better than himself, and that this was the last time in the world for such observations—whereat poor Tommy was quite annihilated; for a word from Norman goes further with him, than a lecture from any one else.'

'Well, I think Norman was right as to the unfitness of the time.'

'So he was. But we had a good deal of them, waiting in the inn parlour. People make incongruities when they will have such things done in state. It could not be helped here, to be sure; but I always feel, at a grand undertaker's display like this, that, except the service itself, there is little to give peace or soothing. I hate what makes a talk! Better be little folk.'

'One would rather think of our own dear cloister, and those who cared so much,' said Ethel.

'Ah! you are happy to be there!' said Dr. May. 'But it all comes to the same—' Pausing, he looked from the window—then signed to Ethel, to do the same—Orion glittered in the darkness.

'One may sleep sound without the lullaby,' said Dr. May, 'and the waves—'

'Oh! don't, papa. You don't give up hope!'

'I believe we ought, Ethel. Don't tell her, but I went to the Admiralty to-day.'

'And what did you hear there?'

'Great cause for fear—but they do not give up. My poor Margaret! But those stars tell us they are in the same Hand.'

CHAPTER XIII.

'Shall I sit alone in my chamber,
    And set the chairs by the wall,
While you sit with lords and princes,
    Yet have not a thought at all?

'Shall I sit alone in my chamber,
    And duly the table lay,
Whilst you stand up in the diet,
    And have not a word to say?'—OLD DANISH BALLAD.

'O NORMAN, are you come already?' exclaimed Margaret, as her brother opened the door, bringing in with him the crisp breath of December.

'Yes, I came away directly after collections. How are you, Margaret?'

'Pretty brave, thank you;' but the brother and sister both read on each other's features, that the additional three months of suspense had told. There were traces of toil and study on Norman's brow, the sunken look about his eyes, and the dejected outline of his cheek, Margaret knew betokened discouragement; and though her mild serenity was not changed, she was almost transparently thin and pale. They had long ago left off asking whether there were tidings, and seldom was the subject adverted to, though the whole family seemed to be living beneath a dark shadow.

'How is Flora?' he next asked.

'Going on beautifully, except that papa thinks she does too much in every way. She declares that she shall bring the baby to show me in another week, but I don't think it will be allowed.'

'And the little lady prospers?'

'Capitally, though I get rather contradictory reports of her. First, papa declared her something surpassing—exactly like Flora, and so I suppose she is; but Ethel and Meta will say nothing for her beauty, and Blanche calls her a fright. But papa is her devoted admirer—he does so enjoy having a sort of property again in a baby.'

'And George Rivers?' said Norman, smiling.

'Poor George! he is very proud of her in his own way. He has just been here with a note from Flora, and actually talked! Between her and the election, he is wonderfully brilliant.'

'The election? Has Mr. Esdaile resigned?'

'Have you not heard? He intends it, and George himself is going to stand. The only danger is, that Sir Henry Walking-hame should think of it.'

'Rivers in parliament! Well, sound men are wanted.'

'Fancy—Flora, our member's wife. How well she will become her position.'

'How soon is it likely to be?'

'Quickly, I fancy. Dr. Spencer, who knows all kinds of news (papa says he makes a scientific study of gossip, as a new branch of comparative anatomy), found out from the Clevelands, that Mr. Esdaile meant to retire, and happened to mention it the last time that Flora came to see me. It was like firing a train. You would have wondered to see how it excited her, who usually shows her feelings so little. She has been so much occupied with it, and so anxious that George should be ready to take the field at once, that papa was afraid of its hurting her, and Ethel comes home declaring that the election was more to her than her baby.'

'Ethel is apt to be a little hard on Flora. They are too unlike to understand each other.'

'Ethel is to be godmother, though; and Flora means to ask Mr. Ogilvie to come and stand.'

'I think he will be gone abroad, or I should have asked him to fulfil his old promise of coming to us.'

'I believe he must be lodged here, if he should come. Flora will have her house full, for Lady Leonora is coming. The baby is to be called after her.'

'Indeed!' exclaimed Norman.

'Yes: I thought it unnecessary, as she is not George's aunt, but Flora is grateful to her for much kindness, and she is coming to see Meta. I am afraid papa is a little hurt, that any name but one should have been chosen '

'Has Meta been comfortable?'

'Dear little thing! Every one says how beautifully she has behaved. She brought all her housekeeping books to Flora at once, and only begged to be made helpful in whatever way might be most convenient. She explained, what we never knew before, how she had the young maids in to read with her, and asked leave to go on. Very few could have been set aside so simply and sweetly in their own house.'

'Flora was sensible of it, I hope.'

'O yes. She took the management of course; but Meta is charmed with her having the girls in from the village, in turn, to help in the scullery. They have begun family prayers, too, and George makes the stable-men go to Church—a matter which had been past Meta, as you may guess, though she had been a wonderful little manager, and Flora owned herself quite astonished.'

'I wonder only at her being astonished.'

'Meta owned to Ethel that what had been worst of all to her was the heart sinking, at finding herself able to choose her occupations, with no one to accommodate them to. But she would not give way—she set up more work for herself at the school, and has been talking of giving singing lessons at Cocksmoor; and she forced herself to read, though it was an effort. She has been very happy lately in nursing Flora.'

'Is Ethel there?'

'No; she is, as usual, at Cocksmoor. There are great councils about sending Cherry to be trained for her new school.'

'Would Flora be able to see me, if I were to ride over to the Grange?'

'You may try; and if papa is not there, I dare say she will.'

'At least, I shall see Meta, and she may judge. I want to see Rivers, too, so I will ask if the bay is to be had. Ah! you have the Claude, I see.'

'Yes; it is too large for this room; but papa put it here that I might enjoy it, and it is almost a companion. The sky improves so in the sunset light.'

Norman was soon at Abbotstoke; and, as he drew his rein, Meta's bright face nodded to him from Flora's sitting-room window; and, as he passed the conservatory, the little person met him, with a summons, at once, to his sister.

He found Flora on the sofa, with a table beside her, covered with notes and papers. She was sitting up writing; and, though somewhat pale, was very smiling and animated.

'Norman, how kind to come to me the first thing!'

'Margaret encouraged me to try whether you would be visible.'

'They want to make a regular prisoner of me,' said Flora, laughing. 'Papa is as bad as the old nurse! But he has not been here to-day, so I have had my own way. Did you meet George?'

'No; but Margaret said he had been with her.'

'I wish he would come. We expect the second post to bring the news that Mr. Esdaile has accepted the Chiltern Hundreds. If he found it so, he meant to go and talk to Mr. Bramshaw; for, though he is so dull, we must make him agent.'

'Is there any danger of opposition?'

'None at all, if we are soon enough in the field. Papa's name will secure us; and there is no one else on the right side to come forward, so that it is an absolute rescue of the seat.'

'It is the very moment when men of principle are most wanted,' said Norman. 'The questions of the day are no light matters; and it is an immense point to save Stoneborough from being represented by one of the Tomkins' set.'

'Exactly so,' said Flora. 'I should feel it a crime to say one word to deter George, at a time when every effort must be made to support the right cause. One must make sacrifices when the highest interests are at stake.'

Flora seemed to thrive upon her sacrifice—she had never appeared more brilliant and joyous. Her brother saw, in her, a Roman matron; and the ambition that was inherent in his nature, began to find compensation for being crushed, as far as regarded himself, by soaring for another. He eagerly answered that he fully agreed with her, and that she would never repent urging her husband to take on himself the duties incumbent on all who had the power.

Highly gratified, she asked him to look at a copy of George's intended address, which was lying on the table. He approved of the tenor, but saw a few phrases susceptible of a better point. 'Give it,' she said, putting a pen into his hand; and he began to interline and erase her fair manuscript, talking earnestly, and working up himself and the address at the same time, till it had grown into a composition far superior to the merely sensible affair it had been. Eloquence and thought were now in the language and substance—and Flora was delighted.

'I have been very disrespectful to my niece all this time,' said Norman, descending from the clouds of patriotism.

'I do not mean to inflict her mercilessly on her relations,' said Flora; 'but I should like you to see her. She is so like Blanche.'

The little girl was brought in, and Flora made a very pretty young mother, as she held her in her arms, with so much graceful pride. Norman was perfectly entranced—he had never seen his sister so charming or so admirable, between her delight in her infant, and her self-devotion to the good of her husband and her country—acting so wisely, and speaking so considerately; and praising her dear Meta with so much warmth. He would never have torn himself away, had not the nurse hinted that Mrs. Rivers had had too much excitement and fatigue already to-day; and, besides, he suspected that he might find Meta in the drawing-room, where he might discuss the whole with her, and judge for himself of her state of spirits.

Flora's next visitor was her father, who came as the twilight was enhancing the comfortable red brightness of the fire. He was very happy in these visits—mother and child had both prospered so well, and it was quite a treat to be able to expend his tenderness on Flora. His little grandchild seemed to renew his own happy days, and he delighted to take her from her mother, and fondle her. No sooner was the baby in his arms, than Flora's hands were busy among the papers, and she begged him to ring for lights.

'Not yet,' he said. 'Why can't you sit in the dark, and give yourself a little rest?'

'I want you to hear George's address. Norman has been looking at it, and I hope you will not think it too strong;' and she turned, so that the light might fall on the paper.

'Let me see,' said Dr. May, holding out his hand for it.

'This is a rough copy, too much scratched for you to make out.'

She read it accordingly, and her father admired it exceedingly —Norman's touches, above all; and Flora's reading had dovetailed all so neatly together that no one knew where the joins were. 'I will copy it fairly,' she said, 'if you will show it to Dr. Spencer, and ask whether he thinks it too strong. Mr. Dodsley, too; he would be more gratified if he saw it first, in private, and thought himself consulted.'

Dr. May was dismayed at seeing her take up her pen, make a desk of her blotting-book, and begin her copy by firelight.

'Flora, my dear,' he said, 'this must not be. Have I not told you that you must be content to rest?'

'I did not get up till ten o'clock, and have been lying here ever since.'

'But what has this head of yours been doing? Has it been resting for ten minutes together? Now, I know what I am saying, Flora—I warn you, that if you will not give yourself needful quiet now, you will suffer for it by-and-by.'

Flora smiled, and said, 'I thought I had been very good. But, what is to be done when one's wits will work, and there is work for them to do?'

'Is not there work enough for them here?' said Dr. May, looking at the babe. 'Your mother used to value such a retirement from care.'

Flora was silent for a minute, then said, 'Mr. Esdaile should have put off his resignation to suit me. It is an unfortunate time for the election.'

'And you can't let the election alone?'

She shook her head, and smiled a negative, as if she would, but that she was under a necessity.

'My dear, if the election cannot go on without you, it had better not go on at all.'

She looked very much hurt, and turned away her head.

Her father was grieved. 'My dear,' he added, 'I know you desire to be of use, especially to George; but do you not believe that he would rather fail, than that you, or his child, should suffer?'

No answer.

'Does he stand by his own wish, or yours, Flora?'

'He wishes it. It is his duty,' said Flora, collecting her dignity.

'I can say no more, except to beg him not to let you exert yourself.'

Accordingly, when George came home, the Doctor read him a lecture on his wife's over-busy brain; and was listened to, as usual, with gratitude and deference. He professed that he only wished to do what was best for her, but she never would spare herself; and, going to her side, with his heavy, fond solicitude, he made her promise not to hurt herself, and she laughed and consented.

The promise was easily given, for she did not believe she was hurting herself; and, as to giving up the election, or ceasing secretly to prompt George, that was absolutely out of the question. What could be a greater duty than to incite her husband to usefulness?

Moreover it was but proper to invite Meta's aunt and cousin to see her, and to project a few select dinners for their amusement, and the gratification of her neighbours. It was only grateful and cousinly likewise, to ask the 'Master of Glenbracken;' and as she saw the thrill of colour on Ethel's cheeks, at the sight of the address to the Honorable Norman Ogilvie, she thought herself the best of sisters. She even talked of Ogilvie as a second Christian name, but Meta observed that old aunt Dorothy would call it

Leonorar Rogilvie Rivers, and thus averted it, somewhat to Ethel's satisfaction.

Ethel scolded herself many times for wondering whether Mr. Ogilvie would come. What was it to her? Suppose he should; suppose the rest. What a predicament! How unreasonable and conceited, even to think of such a thing, when her mind was made up. What could result, save tossings to and fro, a passing gratification set against infinite pain, and strife with her own heart, and with her father's unselfishness! Had he but come before Flora's marriage! No; Ethel hated herself for the wish that arose for the moment. Far better he should keep away, if, perhaps, without the slightest inclination towards her, his mere name could stir up such a tumult—all, it might be, founded in vanity. Rebellious feelings and sense of tedium had once been subdued—why should they be roused again?

The answer came. Norman Ogilvie was setting off for Italy, and regretted that he could not take Abbotstoke on his way. He desired his kind remembrances and warm Christmas wishes to all his cousins.

If Ethel breathed more freely, there was a sense that tranquillity is uninteresting. It was, it must be confessed, a flat end to a romance, that all the permanent present effect was a certain softening, and a degree more attention to her appearance; and after all, this might, as Flora averred, be ascribed to the Paris outfit having taught her to wear clothes; as well as to that which had awakened the feminine element, and removed that sense of not being like other women, which sometimes hangs painfully about girls who have learnt to think themselves plain or awkward.

There were other causes why it should be a dreary winter to Ethel, under the anxiety that strengthened by duration, and the strain of acting cheerfulness for Margaret's sake. Even Mary was a care. Her round rosy childhood had worn into height and sallowness, and her languor and indifference fretted Miss Bracy, and was hunted down by Ethel, till Margaret convinced her that it was a case for patience and tenderness, which, thenceforth, she heartily gave, even encountering a scene with Miss Bracy, who was much injured by the suggestion that Mary was oppressed by perspective. Poor Mary, no one guessed the tears nightly shed over Harry's photograph.

Nor could Ethel quite fathom Norman. He wore the dispirited, burthened expression that she knew too well, but he would not, as formerly, seek relief in confidence to her, shunning the being alone with her, and far too much occupied to offer to walk to Cocksmoor. When the intelligence came that good old Mr.

Wilmot of Settlesham had peacefully gone to his rest, after a short and painless illness, Tom was a good deal affected in his peculiar silent and ungracious fashion; but Norman did not seek to talk over the event, and the feelings he had entertained two years ago —he avoided the subject, and threw himself into the election matters with an excitement foreign to his nature.

He was almost always at Abbotstoke, or attending George Rivers at the committee-room at the Swan, talking, writing, or consulting, concocting squibs, and perpetrating *bon mots*, that were the delight of friends and the confusion of foes. Flora was delighted, George adored him, Meta's eyes danced whenever he came near, Dr. Spencer admired him, and Dr. Hoxton prophesied great things of him; but Ethel did not feel as if he were the veritable Norman, and had an undefined sensation of discomfort when she heard his brilliant repartees, and the laughter with which he accompanied them, so unlike his natural rare and noiseless laugh. She knew it was false excitement, to drive away the suspense that none dared to avow, but which did not press on them the less heavily, for being endured in silence. Indeed, Dr. May could not help now and then giving way to outbursts of despondency, of which his friend, Dr. Spencer, who made it his special charge to try to lighten his troubles, was usually the kind recipient.

And though the bustle of the election was incongruous, and seemed to make the leaden weight the more heavy, there was a compensation in the tone of feeling that it elicited, which gave real and heartfelt pleasure.

Dr. May had undergone numerous fluctuations of popularity. He had always been the same man, excellent in intention, though hasty in action, and heeding neither praise nor censure; and while the main tenor of his course never varied, making many deviations by flying to the reverse of the wrong most immediately before him; still his personal character gained esteem every year; and though sometimes his merits, and sometimes his failings, gave violent umbrage, he had steadily risen in the estimation of his fellow-townsmen, as much as his own inconsistencies and theirs would allow, and every now and then was the favourite with all, save with the few who abused him for tyranny, because he prevented them from tyrannizing.

He was just now on the top of the wave, and his son-in-law had nothing to do but to float in on the tide of his favour. The opposite faction attempted a contest, but only rendered the triumph more complete, and gave the gentlemen the pleasure of canvassing, and hearing, times without number, that the constituents only wished the candidate were Dr. May himself. His sons and daughters were full of exultation—Dr. Spencer, much struck, rallied 'Dick' on his influence—and Dr. May, the drops of warm emotion trembling on his eye-lashes, smiled, and bade his friend see him making a Church-rate.

The addresses and letters that came from the Grange were so admirable, that Dr. May often embraced Norman's steady opinion, that George was a very wise man. If Norman was unconscious how much he contributed to these compositions, he knew far less how much was Flora's. In his ardour he crammed them both, and conducted George when Flora could not be at his side. George himself was a personable man, wrote a good bold hand, would do as he was desired, and was not easily put out of countenance; he seldom committed himself by talking; and when a speech was required, was brief, and to the purpose. He made a very good figure; and, in the glory of victory, Ethel herself began to grow proud of him, and the children's great object in life was to make the jackdaws cry, 'Rivers for ever!'

Flora had always declared that she would be at Stoneborough for the nomination. No one believed her, until three days before, she presented herself and her daughter before the astonished Margaret, who was too much delighted to be able to scold. She had come away on her own responsibility, and was full of triumph. To come home in this manner, after having read 'Rivers for ever!' on all the dead walls, might be called that for which she had lived. She made no stay—she had only come to show her child, and establish a precedent for driving out, and Margaret had begun to believe the apparition a dream, when the others came in, some from Cocksmoor, others from the committee-room at the Swan.

'So she brought the baby,' exclaimed Ethel. 'I should have thought she would not have taken her out before her Christening.'

'Ethel,' said Dr. Spencer, 'permit me to make a suggestion. When relations live in the same neighbourhood, there is no phrase to be more avoided than "I should have thought—"'

The nomination-day brought Flora, Meta, baby and all to be very quiet, as was said; but how could that be? when every boy in the house was frantic, and the men scarcely less so. Aubrey and Gertrude, and the two jackdaws, each had a huge blue and orange rosette, and the two former went about roaring 'Rivers for ever!' without the least consideration for the baby, who would have been decked in the same manner, if Ethel would have heard of it without indignation, at her wearing any colour before her Christening white; as to Jack and Jill, though they *could* say their lesson, they were too much distressed by their ornaments to do aught but lurk in corners, and strive to peck them off.

Flora comported herself in her usual quiet way, and tried to talk of other things, though a carnation spot in each cheek showed her anxiety and excitement. She went with her sisters to look out from Dr.Spencer's windows toward the Town Hall. Her husband gave her his arm as they went down the garden, and Ethel saw her talking earnestly to him, and pressing his arm with her other hand to enforce her words, but if she did tutor him, it was hardly visible, and he was very glad of whatever counsel she gave.

She spoke not a word after the ladies were left with Aubrey, who was in despair at not being allowed to follow Hector and Tom, but was left, as his prematurely classical mind expressed it, like the Gaulish women with the impedimenta in the marshes— whereas Tom had added insult to injury, by a farewell to 'Jack among the maidens.'

Meta tried to console him, by persuading him that he was their protector, and he began to think there was need of a guard, when a mighty cheer caused him to take refuge behind Ethel. Even when assured that it was anything but terrific, he gravely declared that he thought Margaret would want him, but—he could not cross the garden without Meta to protect him.

She would not allow any one else to relieve her from the doughty champion, and thereby she missed the spectacle. It might be that she did not regret it, for though it would have been unkind to refuse to come in with her brother and sister, her wound was still too fresh for crowds, turmoil, and noisy rejoicing to be congenial. She did not withdraw her hand, which Aubrey squeezed harder at each resounding shout, nor object to his conducting her to see his museum in the dark corner of the attics, most remote from the tumult.

The loss was not great. The others could hear nothing distinctly, and see only a wilderness of heads; but the triumph was complete. Dr. May had been cheered enough to satisfy even Hector; George Rivers had made a very fair speech, and hurrahs had covered all deficiencies; Hector had shouted till he was as hoarse as the jackdaws; the opposite candidate had never come forward at all; Tomkins was hiding his diminished head; and the gentlemen had nothing to report but success, and were in the highest spirits.

By-and-by Blanche was missing, and Ethel, going in quest of her, spied a hem of blue merino peeping out under all the cloaks in the hall cupboard, and found ·the poor little girl sobbing in such distress, that it was long before any explanation could be extracted, but at last it was revealed—when the door had been shut, and they stood in the dark, half stifled among the cloaks, that George's spirits had taken his old facetious style with Blanche, and in the very hearing of Hector! The misery of such jokes to a sensitive child, conscious of not comprehending their scope, is incalculable, and Blanche having been a baby-coquette was the more susceptible. She hid her face again from the very sound of her own confession, and resisted Ethel's attempts to draw her out of the musty cupboard, declaring that she could never see either of them again. Ethel, in vain, assured her that George was gone to the dinner at the Swan; nothing was effectual but being told that, for her to notice what had passed, was the sure way to call Hector's attention thereto, when she bridled, emerged, and begged to know whether she looked as if she had been crying. Poor child, she could never again be unconscious, but, at least, she was rendered peculiarly afraid of a style of notice, that might otherwise have been a temptation.

Ethel privately begged Flora to hint to George to alter his style of wit, and the suggestion was received better than the blundering manner deserved; Flora was too exulting to take offence, and her patronage of all the world was as full-blown as her lady-like nature allowed. Ethel, she did not attempt to patronize, but she promised all the sights of London to the children, and masters to Mary and Blanche, and she perfectly overwhelmed Miss Bracy with orphan asylums for her sisters. She would have liked nothing better than dispersing cards, with Mrs. Rivers prominent among the recommenders of the case.

'A fine coming out for you, little lady,' said she to her baby, when taking leave that evening. 'If it was good luck for you to make your first step in life upwards, what is this?'

'*Excelsior?*' said Ethel, and Flora smiled, well-pleased, but she had not caught half the meaning. 'May it be the right *excelsior*,' added Ethel, in a low voice, that no one heard, and she was glad they did not. They were all triumphant, and she could not tell why she had a sense of sadness, and thought of Flora's story long ago, of the girl who ascended Mont Blanc, and for what?

All she had to do at present was to listen to Miss Bracy, who was sure that Mrs. Rivers thought Mary and Blanche were not improved, and was afraid she was ungrateful for all the intended kindness to her sister.

Ethel had more sympathy here, for she had thought that Flora was giving herself airs, and she laughed and said her sister was pleased to be in a position to help her friends; and tried to turn it off, but ended by stumbling into allowing that prosperity was apt to make people over lavish of offers of kindness.

'Dear Miss Ethel, you understand so perfectly. There is no one like you!' cried Miss Bracy, attempting to kiss her hand.

If Ethel had not spoken rightly of her sister, she was sufficiently punished.

What she did was to burst into a laugh, and exclaim, 'Miss Bracy! Miss Bracy! I can't have you sentimental. I am the worst person in the world for it.'

'I have offended. You cannot feel with me!'

'Yes, I can, when it is sense; but please don't treat me like a heroine. I am sure there is quite enough in the world that is worrying, without picking shades of manner to pieces. It is the sure way to make an old crab of me, and so I am going off. Only, one parting piece of advice, Miss Bracy—read "Frank Fairlegh," and put everybody out of your head.'

And thinking she had been savage about her hand, Ethel turned back, and kissed the little governess's forehead, wished her good-night, and ran away.

She had learnt that, to be rough and merry, was the best way of doing Miss Bracy good in the end; and so she often gave herself the present pain of knowing that she was being supposed careless and hard-hearted; but the violent affection for her proved that the feeling did not last.

Ethel was glad to sit by the fire at bed-time, and think over the day, outwardly so gay, inwardly so fretting and perplexing.

It was the first time that she had seen much of her little niece. She was no great baby-handler, nor had she any of the phrases adapted to the infant mind; but that pretty little serene blue-eyed girl had been her chief thought all day, and she was abashed by recollecting how little she had dwelt on her own duties as her sponsor, in the agitations excited by the doubts about her coadjutor.

She took out her Prayer-book, and read the service for Baptism, recollecting the thoughts that had accompanied her youngest sister's orphaned Christening, 'The vain pomp and glory of the world, and all covetous desires of the same.' They seemed far enough off then, and now—poor little Leonora!

Ethel knew that she judged her sister hardly; yet she could not help picturing to herself the future—a young lady, trained for fashionable life, serious teaching not omitted, but right made the means of rising in the world; taught to strive secretly, but not openly, for admiration—a scheming for her marriage—a career like Flora's own. Ethel could scarcely feel that it would not be a mockery to declare, on her behalf, that she renounced the world. But, alas! where was not the world? Ethel blushed as having censured others, when, so lately, she had herself been oblivious of the higher duty. She thought of the prayer, including every Christian in holy and loving intercession—'I pray not that Thou wouldest take them out of the world, but that Thou wouldest keep them from the evil.'

'Keep her from the evil—that shall be my prayer for my poor little Leonora. His Grace can save her, were the surrounding evil far worse than ever it is likely to be. The intermixture with good is the trial, and is it not so everywhere—ever since the world and the Church have seemed fused together? But she will soon be the child of a Father who guards His own; and, at least, I can pray for her, and her dear mother. May I only live better, that so I may pray better, and act better, if ever I should have to act.'

There was a happy family gathering on the New Year's Day, and Flora, who had kindly felt her way with Meta, finding her not yet ready to enjoy a public festivity for the village, added a supplement to the Christmas beef; that a second dinner might be eaten at home, in honour of Miss Leonora Rivers.

Lady Leonora was highly satisfied with her visit, which impressed her far more in favour of the Abbotstoke neighbourhood than in the days of poor old Mr. Rivers. Flora knew every one, and gave little select dinner parties, which, by her good management, even George, at the bottom of the table, could not make heavy. Dr. Spencer enjoyed them greatly, and was an unfailing resource for conversation; and as to the Hoxtons, Flora felt herself amply repaying the kindness she had received in her young lady days, when she walked down to the dining-room with the portly head master, or saw his good lady sit serenely admiring the handsome rooms. 'A very superior person, extremely pleasing and agreeable,' was the universal verdict on Mrs. Rivers. Lady Leonora struck up a great friendship with her, and was delighted that she meant to take Meta to London. The only fault that could be found with her was that she had so many brothers; and Flora, recollecting that her Ladyship mistrusted those brothers, avoided encouraging their presence at the Grange, and took every precaution against any opening for the suspicion that she threw them in the way of her little sister-in-law.

Nor had Flora forgotten the Ladies' Committee, or Cocksmoor. As to the Muses, they gave no trouble at all. Exemplary civilities about the chair passed between the Member's lady and Mrs. Ledwich, ending in Flora's insisting that priority in office should prevail, feeling that she could well afford to yield the post of honour, since anywhere she was the leader. She did not know how much more conformable the ladies had been ever since they had known Dr. Spencer's opinion; and yet he only believed that they were grateful for good advice, and went about among them, easy, good-natured, and utterly unconscious, that for him, sparkled Mrs. Ledwich's bugles, and for him waved every spinster's ribbon, from Miss Rich down to Miss Boulder.

The point carried by their united influence was Charity Elwood's being sent for six months' finish at the Diocesan Training School; while a favourite pupil teacher from Abbot-stoke took her place at Cocksmoor.

Dr. Spencer looked at the Training School, and talked Mrs. Ledwich into magnanimous forgiveness of Mrs. Elwood. Cherry dreaded the ordeal, but she was willing to do anything that was thought right, and likely to make her fitter for her office.

CHAPTER XIV.

'Twas a long doubt; we never heard
Exactly how the ship went down.'—ARCHER GURNEY.

THE tidings came at last, came when the heart-sickness of hope deferred had faded into the worse heart-sickness of fear deferred, and when spirits had been fain to rebel, and declare that they would be almost glad to part with the hope that but kept alive despair.

The Christmas holidays had come to an end, and the home party were again alone, when, early in the forenoon, there was a tap at the drawing-room door, and Dr. Spencer called, 'Ethel, can you come and speak to me?'

Margaret started as if those gentle tones had been a thunder-clap. 'Go! go, Ethel,' she said, 'don't keep me waiting.'

Dr. Spencer stood in the hall with a newspaper in his hand. Ethel said, 'Is it?' and he made a sorrowful gesture.

'Both?' she asked.

'Both,' he repeated. 'The ship burnt—the boat lost.'

'Ethel, come!' hoarsely called Margaret.

'Take it,' said Dr. Spencer, putting the paper into her hand; 'I will wait.'

She obeyed. She could not speak, but kneeling down by her sister, they read the paragraph together; Ethel, with one eye on the words, the other on Margaret.

No doubt was left. Captain Gordon had returned, and this was his official report. The names of the missing stood below, and the list began thus—

Lieutenant A. H. Ernescliffe.
Mr. Charles Owen, Mate.
Mr. Harry May, Midshipman.

The Alcestis had taken fire on the 12th of April of the former year. There had been much admirable conduct, and the intrepid coolness of Mr. Ernescliffe was especially recorded. The boats had been put off without loss, but they were scantily provisioned, and the nearest land was far distant. For five days the boats kept together, then followed a night of storms, and, when morning dawned, the second cutter, under command of Mr. Ernescliffe, had disappeared. There could be no doubt that she had sunk, and the captain could only record his regrets for the loss the service had experienced in the three brave young officers and their gallant seamen. After infinite toil and suffering, the captain, with the other boats' crews, had reached Tahiti, whence they had made their way home.

'O Margaret, Margaret!' cried Ethel.

Margaret raised herself, and the colour came into her face. 'I did not write the letter!' she said.

'What letter?' said Ethel, alarmed.

'Richard prevented me. The letter that would have parted us. Now all is well.'

'All is well, I know, if we could but feel it.'

'He never had the pain. It is unbroken!' continued Margaret, her eyes brightening, but her breath, in long-drawn gasps that terrified Ethel into calling Dr. Spencer.

Mary was standing before him, with bloodless face and dilated eyes; but, as Ethel approached, she turned and rushed up-stairs.

Dr. Spencer entered the drawing-room with Ethel, who tried to read his face as he saw Margaret—restored, as it seemed, to all her girlish bloom, and her eyes sparkling as they were lifted up, far beyond the present scene. Ethel had a moment's sense that his expression was as if he had seen a death-blow struck, but it was gone in a moment, as he gently shook Margaret by the hand, and spoke a word of greeting, as though to recal her.

'Thank you,' she said, with her own grateful smile.

'Where is your father?' he asked of Ethel.

'Either at the hospital, or at Mr. Ramsden's,' said Ethel, with a ghastly suspicion, that he thought Margaret in a state to require him.

'Papa!' said Margaret. 'If he were but here! But—ah! I had forgotten.'

She turned aside her head, and hid her face. Dr. Spencer signed Ethel nearer to him. 'This is a more natural state,' he said. 'Don't be afraid for her. I will find your father, and bring him home.' Pressing her hand he departed.

Margaret was weeping tranquilly—Ethel knelt down beside

her, without daring at first to speak, but sending up intense
mental prayers to Him, who alone could bear her or her dear
father through their affliction. Then she ventured to take her
hand, and Margaret returned the caress, but began to blame
herself for the momentary selfishness that had allowed her
brother's loss and her father's grief to have been forgotten in
her own.—Ethel's 'oh! no! no!' did not console her for this
which seemed the most present sorrow, but the flow of tears was
so gentle, that Ethel trusted that they were a relief. Ethel
herself seemed only able to watch her, and to fear for her father,
not to be able to think for herself.

The front door opened, and they heard Dr. May's step hesitating in the hall, as if he could not bear to come in.

'Go to him!' cried Margaret, wiping off her tears.

Ethel stood a moment in the door-way, then sprang to him,
and was clasped in his arms.

'You know it?' he whispered.

'Dr. Spencer told us. Did not you meet him?'

'No. I read it at Bramshaw's office. How—' He could
not say the words, but he looked towards the room, and wrung
the hand he held.

'Quiet. Like herself. Come.'

He threw one arm round Ethel, and laid his hand on her head,
'How much there is to be thankful for!' he said, then advancing,
he hung over Margaret, calling her his own poor darling.

'Papa, you must forgive me. You said, sending him to sea
was giving him up.'

'Did I? Well, Margaret, he did his duty. That is all we
have to live for. Our yellow-haired laddie made a gallant
sailor, and—'

Tears choked his utterance—Margaret gently stroked his hand.

'It falls hard on you, my poor girl,' he said.

'No, papa,' said Margaret, 'I am content and thankful. He
is spared pain and perplexity.'

'You are right, I believe,' said Dr. May. 'He would have
been grieved not to find you better.'

'I ought to grieve for my own selfishness,' said Margaret.
'I cannot help it! I cannot be sorry the link is unbroken, and
that he had not to turn to any one else.'

'He never would!' cried Dr. May, almost angrily.

'I tried to think he ought,' said Margaret. 'His life would
have been too dreary. But it is best as it is.'

'It must be,' said the Doctor. 'Where are the rest, Ethel?
Call them all down.'

Poor Mary, Ethel felt as if she had neglected her! She found her hanging over the nursery fire, alternating with old nurse in fond reminiscences of Harry's old days, sometimes almost laughing at his pranks, then crying again, while Aubrey sat between them, drinking in each word.

Blanche and Gertrude came from the school-room, where Miss Bracy seemed to have been occupying them, with much kindness and judgment. She came to the door to ask Ethel anxiously for the Doctor and Miss May, and looked so affectionate and sympathizing, that Ethel gave her a hearty kiss.

'Dear Miss Ethel! if you can only let me help you.'

'Thank you,' said Ethel with all her heart, and hurried away.

Nothing was more in favour of Miss Bracy, than that there should be a hurry. Then she could be warm, and not morbid.

Dr. May gathered his children round him, and took out the great Prayer-book. He read a Psalm and a prayer from the Burial Service, and the sentence for funerals at sea. Then he touched each of their heads, and, in short broken sentences, gave thanks for those still left to him, and for the blessed hope they could feel for those who were gone; and he prayed that they might so follow in their footsteps, as to come to the same Holy place, and in the meantime realize the Communion of Saints. Then they said the Lord's Prayer, he blessed them, and they arose.

'Mary, my dear,' he said, 'you have a photograph.'

She put the case into his hands, and ran away.

He went to the study, where he found Dr. Spencer awaiting him.

'I am only come to know where I shall go for you.'

'Thank you, Spencer. Thank you for taking care of my poor girls.'

'They took care of themselves. They have the secret of strength.'

'They have—' He turned aside, and burst out, 'Oh, Spencer! you have been spared a great deal. If you missed a great deal of joy, you have missed almost as much sorrow!' And, covering his face, he let his grief have a free course.

'Dick! dear old Dick, you must bear up. Think what treasures you have left.'

'I do. I try to do so,' said poor Dr. May; 'but, Spencer, you never saw my yellow-haired laddie, with his lion look! He was the flower of them all! Not one of these other boys came near him in manliness, and with such a loving heart! An hour ago, I thought any certainty would be gain, but now I would give a lifetime to have back the hope that I might see my boy's face again! O, Spencer! this is the first time I could rejoice that his mother is not here!'

'She would have been your comforter,' sighed his friend, as he felt his inability to contend with such grief.

'There, I can be thankful,' Dr. May said, and he looked so. 'She has had her brave loving boy with her all this time, while we little thought—but there are others. My poor Margaret—

'Her patience *must* be blessed,' said Dr. Spencer. 'I think she will be better. Now that the suspense no longer preys on her, there will be more rest.'

'Rest,' repeated Dr. May, supporting his head on his hand; and, looking up dreamily—'there remaineth a rest—'

The large Bible lay beside him, on the table, and Dr. Spencer thought that he would find more rest there than in his words. Leaving him, therefore, his friend went to undertake his day's work, and learn, once more, in the anxious inquiries, and saddened countenances of the patients and their friends, how great an amount of love and sympathy Dr. May had won by his own warmth of heart. The patients seemed to forget their complaints in sighs for their kind Doctor's troubles; and the gouty Mayor of Stoneborough kept Dr. Spencer half an hour to listen to his recollections of the bright-faced boy's droll tricks, and then to the praises of the whole May family, and especially of the mother.

Poor Dr. Spencer! he heard her accident described so many times in the course of the day, that his visits were one course of shrinking and suffering; and his only satisfaction was in knowing how his friend would be cheered, by hearing of the universal feeling for him and his children.

Ethel wrote letters to her brothers; and Dr. May added a few lines, begging Richard to come home, if only for a few days. Margaret would not be denied writing to Hector Ernescliffe, though she cried over her letter so much, that her father could almost have taken her pen away; but she said it did her good.

When Flora came in the afternoon, Ethel was able to leave Margaret to her, and attend to Mary, with whom Miss Bracy's kindness had been inefficacious. If she was cheered for a few minutes, some association, either with the past, or the vanished future, soon set her off sobbing again. 'If I only knew where dear, dear Harry is lying,' she sobbed, 'and that it had not been very bad indeed, I could bear it better.'

The ghastly uncertainty was too terrible for Ethel to have borne to contemplate it. She knew that it would haunt their pillows, and she was trying to nerve herself by faith.

'Mary,' she said, 'that is the worst; but, after all, God willed that we should not know. We must bear it like His good children. It makes no difference to them now—'

'I know,' said Mary, trying to check her sobs.

'And, you know, we are all in the same keeping. The sea is a glorious great pure thing, you know, that man cannot hurt or defile. It seems to me,' said Ethel, looking up, 'as if resting there was like being buried in our Baptism-tide over again, till the great new Birth. It must be the next best place to a church-yard. Any where, they are as safe as among the daisies in our own Cloister.'

'Say it again—what you said about the sea,' said Mary, more comforted than if Ethel had been talking *down* to her.

By-and-by, Ethel discovered that the sharpest trouble to the fond simple girl, was the deprivation of her precious photograph. It was like losing Harry over again, to go to bed without it, though she would not for the world seem to grudge it to her father.

Ethel found an opportunity of telling him of this distress, and it almost made him smile. 'Poor Mary,' he said, 'is she so fond of it? It is rather a libel than a likeness.'

'Don't say so to her, pray, papa. It is all the world to her. Three strokes on paper would have been the same, if they had been called by his name.'

'Yes; a loving heart has eyes of its own, and she is a dear good girl!'

He did not forget to restore the treasure with gratitude pro-portionate to what the loan had cost Mary. With a trembling voice, she proffered it to him for the whole day, and every day, if she might only have it at night; and she even looked blank when he did not accept the proposal.

'It is exactly like—' said she.

'It can't help being so, in a certain sense,' he answered, kindly, 'but, after all, Mary dear, he did not pout out his chin in that way.'

Mary was somewhat mortified, but she valued her photograph more than ever, because no one else would admire it, except Daisy, whom she had taught to regard it with unrivalled vene-ration.

A letter soon arrived from Captain Gordon, giving a fuller account of the loss of his ship, and of the conduct of his officers, speaking in the highest terms of Alan Ernescliffe, for whom he said he mourned as for his own son, and, with scarcely less warmth, of Harry, mentioning the high esteem all had felt for the boy, and the good effect which the influence of his high and truthful spirit had produced on the other youngsters, who keenly regretted him.

Captain Gordon added that the will of the late Captain Ernescliffe had made him guardian of his sons, and that he believed poor Alan had died intestate. He should therefore take upon himself the charge of young Hector, and he warmly thanked Dr. May and his family for all the kindness that the lad had received.

Though the loss of poor Hector's visits was regretted, it was, on the whole, a comforting letter, and would give still more comfort in future time.

Richard contrived to come home through Oxford and see Norman, whom he found calm, and almost relieved by the cessation from suspense; not inclined, as his father had feared, to drown sorrow in labour, but regarding his grief as an additional call to devote himself to ministerial work. In fact, the blow had fallen when he first heard the rumour of danger, and could not recur with the same force.

Richard was surprised to find that Margaret was less cast down than he could have dared to hope. It did not seem like an affliction to her. Her countenance wore the same gentle smile, and she was as ready to participate in all that passed, finding sympathy for the little pleasures of Aubrey and Gertrude, and delighting in Flora's baby; as well as going over Cocksmoor politics with a clearness and accuracy that astonished him, and asking questions about his parish and occupations, so as fully to enjoy his short visit, which she truly called the greatest possible treat.

If it had not been for the momentary consternation that she had seen upon Dr. Spencer's face, Ethel would have been perfectly satisfied; but she could not help sometimes entertaining a dim fancy that this composure came from a sense that she was too near Alan to mourn for him. Could it be true that her frame was more wasted, that there was less capability of exertion, that her hours became later in the morning, and that her nights were more wakeful? Would she fade away? Ethel longed to know what her father thought, but she could neither bear to inspire him with the apprehension, nor to ask Dr. Spencer's opinion, lest she should be confirmed in her own.

The present affliction altered Dr. May more visibly than the death of his wife, perhaps, because there was not the same need of exertion. If he often rose high in faith and resignation, he would also sink very low under the sense of bereavement and disappointment. Though Richard was his stay, and Norman his pride, there was something in Harry more congenial to his own temper, and he could not but be bowed down by the ruin of such bright hopes. With all his real submission, he was weak, and gave way to outbursts of grief, for which he blamed himself as unthankful; and his whole demeanour was so saddened and depressed, that Ethel and Dr. Spencer consulted mournfully over him, whenever they walked to Cocksmoor together.

This was not as often as usual, though the walls of the school were rising, for Dr. Spencer had taken a large share of his friend's work for the present, and both physicians were much occupied by the condition of Mr. Ramsden, who was fast sinking, and, for some weeks, seemed only kept alive by their skill. The struggle ended at last, and his forty years' cure of Stoneborough was closed. It made Dr. May very sad—his affections had tendrils for anything that he had known from boyhood; and though he had often spoken strong words of the Vicar, he now sat sorrowfully moralizing, and making excuses. 'People in former times had not so high an estimate of pastoral duty—poor Mr. Ramsden had not much education—he was already old when better times came in—he might have done better in a less difficult parish with better laity to support him, &c.' Yet after all, he exclaimed with one of his impatient gestures, 'Better have my Harry's seventeen years than his sixty-seven!'

'Better improve a talent than lay it by,' said Ethel.

'Hush! Ethel. How do you know what he may have done? If he acted up to his own standard, he did more than most of us.'

'Which is best,' said Ethel, 'a high standard not acted up to, or a lower one fulfilled?'

'I think it depends on the will,' said Margaret.

'Some people are angry with those whose example would show that there is a higher standard,' said Ethel.

'And,' said Margaret, 'some who have the high one set before them, content themselves with knowing that it cannot be fully attained, and will not try.'

'The standard is the effect of early impression,' said Dr. May. 'I should be very sorry to think it could not be raised.'

'Faithful in a little—' said Ethel. 'I suppose all good people's standard is always going higher.'

'As they comprehend more of absolute perfection,' said Margaret.

CHAPTER XV.

'The city's golden spire it was,
    When hope and health were strongest;
But now it is the church-yard grass,
    We look upon the longest.'—E. B. BROWNING.

A DISINCLINATION for exertion or going into public hung upon
Dr. May, but he was obliged to rouse himself to attend the Town
Council meeting, which was held a few days after the Vicar's
funeral, to decide on the next appointment. If it had depended
on himself alone, his choice would have been Mr. Edward Wilmot, whom the death of his good old father had uprooted from
Settlesham; and the girls had much hope, but he was too much
out of spirits to be sanguine. He said that he should only hear
a great deal of offensive stuff from Tomkins the brewer; and that,
in the desire to displease nobody, the votes should settle down
on some nonentity, was the best which was likely to happen.
Thus, grumbling, he set off, and his daughters watched anxiously
for his return. They saw him come through the garden with a
quick, light step, that made them augur well, and he entered the
room with the corners of his mouth turning up. 'I see,' said
Ethel, 'it is all right.'

'They were going to have made a very absurd choice.'

'But you prevented it? Who was it?'

'Ah! I told you Master Ritchie was turning out a popular
preacher.'

'You don't mean that they chose Richard!' cried Margaret,
breathlessly.

'As sure as my name is Dick May, they did, every man of
them, except Tomkins, and even he held his tongue; I did not
think it of them,' said the Doctor, almost overcome; 'but there
is much more goodness of heart in the world than one gives it
credit for.'

And good Dr. May was not one to give the least credit for all
that was like himself.

'But it was Richard's own doing,' he continued. 'Those sermons made a great impression, and they love the boy, because he
has grown up among them. The old Mayor waddled up to me,
as I came in, telling me that they had been talking it over, and
they were unanimously agreed that they could not have a parson
they should like better than Mr. Richard.'

'Good old Mr. Dodsley! I can see him!' cried Ethel.

'I expected it so little, that I thought he meant some Richards; but no, he said Mr. Richard May, if he had nothing better

in view—they liked him, and knew he was a very steady, good
young gentleman, and if he took after his fathers that went
before him—and they thought we might like to have him settled
near!'

'How very kind!' said Margaret, as the tears came. 'We
shall love our own townsfolk better than ever!'

'I always told you so, if you would but believe it. They have
warm, sound hearts, every one of them! I declare, I did not
know which way to look, I was so sorry to disappoint them.'

'Disappoint them!' cried Margaret, in consternation.

'I was thinking,' said Ethel. 'I do not believe Richard would
think himself equal to this place in such a state as it is. He is
so diffident.'

'Yes,' said Dr. May, 'if he were ten or twelve years older, it
would be another thing; but here, where everything is to be done,
he would not bring weight or force enough. He would only work
himself to death, for individuals, without going to the root.
Margaret, my darling, I am very sorry to have disappointed you
so much—it would have been as great a pleasure as we could
have had in this world to have the lad here—'

'And Cocksmoor,' sighed Ethel.

'I shall be grateful all my life to those good people for thinking of it,' continued the Doctor; 'but look you here, it was my
business to get the best man chosen in my power, and, though as
to goodness, I believe the dear Ritchie has not many equals; I
don't think we can conscientiously say he would be, at present,
the best Vicar for Stoneborough.'

Ethel would not say no, for fear she should pain Margaret.
'Besides,' continued Dr. May, 'after having staved off the sale
of the presentation as a sin, it would hardly have been handsome
to have let my own son profit by it. It would have seemed as
if we had our private ends, when Richard helped poor old Mr.
Ramsden.'

Margaret owned this, and Ethel said Richard would be glad
to be spared the refusal.

'I was sure of it. The poor fellow would have been perplexed
between the right and consideration for us. A Vicar here ought
to carry things with a high hand, and that is hardest to do at a
man's own home, especially for a quiet lad like him.'

'Yes, papa, it was quite right,' said Margaret, recovering herself; 'it has spared Richard a great deal.'

'But are we to have Mr. Wilmot?' said Ethel. 'Think of our
not having heard!'

'Aye. If they would not have had Wilmot, or a man of his

calibre, perhaps I might have let them offer it to Richard. I almost wish I had.—With help, and Ethel—'

'No, no! papa,' said Margaret. 'You are making me angry with myself for my folly. It is much better for Richard himself, and for us all, as well as the town. Think how long we have wished for Mr. Wilmot!'

'He will be in time for the opening of Cocksmoor school!' cried Ethel. 'How did you manage it?'

'I did not manage at all,' said the Doctor. 'I told them exactly my mind, that Richard was not old enough for such arduous work; and though no words could tell how obliged I was, if they asked me who was the best man for it I knew, I should say Edward Wilmot, and I thought he deserved something from us, for the work he did gratis, when he was second master. Tomkins growled a little, but, fortunately, no one was prepared with another proposal, so they all came round, and the Mayor is to write by this evening's post, and so shall I. If we could only have given Richard a dozen more years!'

Margaret was somewhat comforted to find that the sacrifice had cost her father a good deal; she was always slightly jealous for Richard, and now that Alan was gone, she clung to him more than ever. His soft calm manner supported her more than any other human comforter, and she always yearned after him when absent, more than for all the other brothers; but her father's decision had been too high-minded for her to dare to wish it recalled, and she could not but own that Richard would have had to undergo more toil and annoyance, than perhaps his health would have endured.

Flora had discontinued comments to her sisters, on her father's proceedings, finding that observations mortified Margaret, and did not tend to peace with Ethel; but she told her husband that she did not regret it much, for Richard would have exhausted his own income, and his father's likewise, in paying Curates, and raising funds for charities. She scarcely expected Mr. Edward Wilmot to accept the offer, aware as he was, of the many disadvantages he should have to contend with, and unsuccessful as he had been in dealing with the Ladies' Committee.

However, Mr. Wilmot signified his thankful acceptance, and, in due time, his familiar tap was heard at the drawing-room door, at tea-time, as if he had just returned after the holidays. He was most gladly welcomed, and soon was installed in his own place, with his god-daughter, Mary, blushing with pleasure at pouring out his coffee.

'Well, Ethel, how is Cocksmoor? How like old times!'

'Oh!' cried Ethel, 'we are so glad you will see the beginning of the school!'

'I hear you are finishing Cherry Elwood, too.'

'Much against Ethel's will,' said Margaret; 'but we thought Cherry not easily spoilt. And Whitford school seems to be in very good order. Dr. Spencer went and had an inspection of it, and conferred with all the authorities.'

'Ah! we have a jewel of a parishioner for you,' said Dr. May. 'I have some hopes of Stoneborough now.'

Mr. Wilmot did not look too hopeful, but he smiled, and asked after Granny Hall, and the children.

'Polly grew up quite civilized,' said Ethel. 'She lives at Whitford, with some very respectable people, and sends Granny presents, which make her merrier than ever. Last time it was a bonnet, and Jenny persuaded her to go to church in it, though she said, what she called the moon of it, was too small.'

'How do the people go on?'

'I cannot say much for them. It is disheartening. We really have done nothing. So very few go to Church regularly.'

'None at all went in my time,' said Mr. Wilmot.

'Elwood always goes,' said Mary, 'and Taylor; yes, and Sam Hall, very often, and many of the women, in the evening, because they like to walk home with the children.'

'The children? the Sunday scholars?'

'Oh! every one, that is big enough, comes to school now, here on Sunday. If only the teaching were better—'

'Have you sent out any more pupils to service?'

'Not many. There is Willie Brown, trying to be Dr. Spencer's little groom,' said Ethel.

'But I am afraid it will take a great deal of the Doctor's patience to train him,' added Margaret.

'It is hard,' said Dr. May. 'He did it purely to oblige Ethel; and, I tell her, when he lames the pony, I shall expect her to buy another for him, out of the Cocksmoor funds.'

Ethel and Mary broke out in a chorus of defence of Willie Brown.

'There was Ben Wheeler,' said Mary, 'who went to work in the quarries; and the men could not teach him to say bad words, because the young ladies told him not.'

'The young ladies have not quite done nothing,' said Dr. May, smiling.

'These are only little stray things, and Cherry has done the chief of them,' said Ethel. 'Oh! it is grievously bad still,' she added, sighing. 'Such want of truth, such ungoverned tongues and tempers, such godlessness altogether! It is only surface-work, taming the children at school, while they have such homes; and their parents—even if they do come where they might learn better, are always liable to be upset, as they call it—turned out of their places in church, and they will not run the chance.'

'The church must come to them,' said Mr. Wilmot. 'Could the school be made fit to be licensed for service?'

'Ask our architect,' said Dr. May. 'There can be little doubt.'

'I have been settling that I must have a curate specially for Cocksmoor,' said Mr. Wilmot. 'Can you tell me of one, Ethel —or perhaps Margaret could?'

Margaret could only smile faintly, for her heart was beating.

'Seriously,' said Mr. Wilmot, turning to Dr. May, 'do you think Richard would come and help us here?'

'This seems to be his destiny,' said the Doctor, smiling, 'only it would not be fair to tell you, lest you should be jealous —that the Town Council had a great mind for him.'

The matter was explained, and Mr. Wilmot was a great deal more struck by Dr. May's conduct, than the good Doctor thought it deserved. Every one was only too glad that Richard should come as Cocksmoor curate; and, though the stipend was very small—since Mr. Wilmot meant to have other assistance— yet, by living at home, it might be feasible.

Margaret's last words that night to Ethel were, 'The last wish I had dared to make is granted!'

Mr. Wilmot wrote to Richard, who joyfully accepted his proposal, and engaged to come home as soon as his present Rector could find a substitute.

Dr. Spencer was delighted, and, it appeared, had already had a view to such possibilities in designing the plan of the school.

The first good effect of Mr. Wilmot's coming was, that Dr. Spencer was cured of the vagrant habits of going to church at Abbotstoke or Fordholm, that had greatly concerned his friend, Dr. May, who could never get any answer from him except that he was not a Town Councillor, and, as to example, it was no way to set that to sleep through the sermon.

To say that Dr. May never slept under the new dynasty would be an over-statement, but slumber certainly prevailed in the Minster to a far less degree than formerly. One cause might be that it was not shut up unaired from one Sunday to another, but that the chime of the bells was no longer an extraordinary sound on a week-day. It was at first pronounced that time could not be found for going to Church on week-days without neglecting other things, but Mary, who had lately sat very loose to the school-room, began gradually to slip down to Church whenever the Service was neither too early nor too late; and Gertrude was often found trotting by her side—going to mamma, as the little Daisy called it, from some confusion between the Church and the Cloister, which Ethel was in no hurry to disturb.

Lectures in Lent filled the Church a good deal, as much perhaps from the novelty as from better motives, and altogether there was a renewal of energy in parish work. The poor had become so little accustomed to pastoral care, that the doctors and the district visitors were obliged to report cases of sickness to the clergy, and vainly tried to rouse the people to send of their own accord. However, the better leaven began to work, and, of course, there was a ferment, though less violent than Ethel had expected.

Mr. Wilmot set more cautiously to work than he had done in his younger days, and did not attack prejudices so openly, and he had an admirable assistant in Dr. Spencer. Every one respected the opinion of the travelled Doctor, and he had a courteous clever process of the reduction to the absurd, which seldom failed to tell, while it never gave offence. As to the Ladies' Committee, though there had been expressions of dismay, when the tidings of the appointment first went abroad, not one of the whole ' Aonian choir' liked to dissent from Dr. Spencer, and he talked them over, individually, into a most conformable state, merely by taking their compliance for granted, and showing that he deemed it only the natural state of things, that the Vicar should reign over the charities of the place.

The Committee was not dissolved—that would have been an act of violence—but it was henceforth subject to Mr. Wilmot, and he and his curates undertook the religious instruction in the week, and chose the books—a state of affairs brought about with so much quietness, that Ethel knew not whether Flora, Dr. Spencer, or Mr. Wilmot, had been the chief mover.

Mrs. Ledwich was made treasurer of a new coal club, and Miss Rich keeper of the lending library, occupations which delighted them greatly; and Ethel was surprised to find how much unity of action was springing up, now that the period was over, of each ' doing right in her own eyes.'

' In fact,' said Dr. Spencer, ' when women have enough to do, they are perfectly tractable.'

The Cocksmoor accounts were Ethel's chief anxiety. It seemed as if now there might be a school-house, but with little income to depend upon, since poor Alan Ernescliffe's annual £10 was at an end. However, Dr. May leant over her, as she was puzzling over her pounds shillings and pence, and laid a cheque upon her desk. She looked up in his face. 'We must make Cocksmoor Harry's heir,' he said.

By-and-by it appeared that Cocksmoor was not out of Hector Ernescliffe's mind. The boy's letters to Margaret had been brief, matter-of-fact, and discouraging, as long as the half-year lasted, and there was not much to be gathered about him from Tom, on his return for the Easter holidays, but soon poor Hector wrote a long dismal letter to Margaret.

Captain Gordon had taken him to Maplewood, where the recollection of his brother, and the happy hopes with which they had taken possession, came thronging upon him. The house was forlorn, and the corner that had been unpacked for their reception, was as dreary a contrast to the bright home at Stoneborough, as was the dry stern Captain, to the fatherly warm-hearted Doctor. Poor Hector had little or nothing to do, and the pleasure of possession had not come yet; he had no companion of his own age, and bashfulness made him shrink with dislike from introduction to his tenants and neighbours.

There was not an entertaining book in the house, he declared; and the Captain snubbed him if he bought anything he cared to read. The Captain was always at him to read musty old improving books, and talking about the position he would occupy! The evenings were altogether unbearable; and if it were not for rabbit shooting now, and the half-year soon beginning again, Hector declared he should be ready to cut and run, and leave Captain Gordon and Maplewood to each other—and very well matched too! He was nearly in a state of mind to imitate that unprecedented boy, who wrote a letter to the *Times*, complaining of extra weeks.

As to Cocksmoor, Ethel must not think it forgotten; he had spoken to the Captain about it, and the old wooden-head had gone and answered that it was not incumbent on him, that Cocksmoor had no claims upon him, and he could not make it up out of his allowance; for the old fellow would not give him a farthing more than he had before, and had said that was too much.

There was a great blur over the words 'wooden-head,' as if Hector had known that Margaret would disapprove, and had tried to scratch it out. She wrote all the consolation in her power, and exhorted him to patience, apparently without much effect. She would not show his subsequent letters, and the reading and answering them fatigued her so much, that Hector's writing was an unwelcome sight at Stoneborough. Each letter, as Ethel said, seemed so much taken out of her, and she begged her not to think about them.

'Nothing can do me much good or harm, now,' said Margaret; and seeing Ethel's anxious looks—'Is it not my greatest comfort that Hector can still treat me as his sister, or, if I can only be of any use in keeping him patient? Only think of the danger of a boy, in his situation, being left without sympathy!'

There was nothing more to be said. They all felt it was good for them that the building at Cocksmoor gave full occupation to thoughts and conversation; indeed, Tom declared they never walked in any other direction, nor talked of anything else, and that without Hector or George Rivers, he had nobody to speak to! However, he was a good deal tranquillised by an introduction to Dr. Spencer's laboratory, where he compounded mixtures that Dr. Spencer promised should do no more harm than was reasonable, to himself or any one else. Ethel suspected that, if Tom had chanced to singe his eyebrows, his friend would not have regretted a blight to his nascent coxcombry, but he was far too careful of his own beauty to do any such thing.

Richard was set at liberty just before Easter, and came home to his new charge. He was aware of what had taken place, and heartily grateful for the part his father had taken. To work at Cocksmoor, under Mr. Wilmot, and to live at home, was felicity; and he fitted at once into his old place, and resumed all the little home services for which he had been always famed. Ethel was certain that Margaret was content, when she saw her brother bending over her, and the sense of reliance and security that the presence of the silent Richard imparted to the whole family, was something very peculiar, especially as they were so much more active and demonstrative than he was.

Mr. Wilmot put him at once in charge of the hamlet. The inhabitants were still a hard, rude, unpromising race, and there were many flagrant evils amongst them, but the last few years had not been without some effect—some were less obdurate, a few really touched, and, almost all, glad of instruction for their children. If Ethel's perseverance had done nothing else, it had, at least, been a witness, and her immediate scholars showed the influence of her lessons.

————

CHAPTER XVI.

'Then out into the world, my course I did determine;
 Though, to be rich was not my wish, yet to be great was charming.
 My talents they were not the worst, nor yet my education;
 Resolved was I, at least to try, to mend my situation.'—BURNS.

IN the meantime, the Session of Parliament had begun, and the Rivers' party had, since February, inhabited Park Lane. Meta had looked pale and pensive, as she bade her friends, at Stoneborough, good-bye; but only betrayed that she had rather have stayed at home, by promising herself great enjoyment in meeting them again at Easter.

Flora was, on the other hand, in a state of calm patronage, that betokened perfect satisfaction. She promised wonders for Miss Bracy's sisters—talked of inviting Mary and Blanche to see sights and take lessons; and undertook to send all the apparatus needed by Cocksmoor school; and she did, accordingly, send down so many wonderful articles, that Curate and school-mistress were both frightened; Mrs. Taylor thought the easels were new-fashioned instruments of torture; and Ethel found herself in a condition to be liberal to Stoneborough National School.

Flora was a capital correspondent, and made it her business to keep Margaret amused, so that the home-party were well informed of the doings of each of her days—and very clever her descriptions were. She had given herself a dispensation from general society until after Easter; but, in the meantime, both she and Meta seemed to find great enjoyment in country rides and drives, and in quiet little dinners at home, to George's agreeable political friends. With the help of two such ladies as Mrs. and Miss Rivers, Ethel could imagine George's house pleasant enough to attract clever people; but she was surprised to find how full her sister's letters were of political news.

It was a period when great interests were in agitation; and the details of London talk and opinions were extremely welcome. Dr. Spencer used to come in to ask after 'Mrs. Rivers's Intelligencer;' and, when he heard the lucid statements, would say, she ought to have been a 'special correspondent.' And her father declared that her news made him twice as welcome to his patients; but her cleverest sentences always were prefaced with 'George says,' or 'George thinks,' in a manner that made her appear merely the dutiful echo of his sentiments.

In an early letter, Flora mentioned how she had been reminded of poor Harry, by finding Miss Walkinghame's card. That lady lived with her mother at Richmond, and, on returning the visit, Flora was warmly welcomed by the kind old Lady Walkinghame, who insisted on her bringing her baby and spending a long day. The sisters-in-law had been enchanted with Miss Walkinghame, whose manners, wrote Flora, certainly merited papa's encomium.

On the promised 'long day,' they found an unexpected addition to the party, Sir Henry Walkinghame, who had newly returned from the Continent. 'A fine-looking, agreeable man, about five-and thirty,' Flora described him, 'very lively and entertaining.

He talked a great deal of Dr. Spencer, and of the life in the caves at Thebes; and he asked me whether that unfortunate place, Cocksmoor, did not owe a great deal to me, or to one of my sisters. I left Meta to tell him that story, and they became very sociable over it.'

A day or two after—'Sir Henry Walkinghame has been dining with us. He has a very good voice, and we had some delightful music in the evening.'

By-and-by, Sir Henry was the second cavalier, when they went to an oratorio, and Meta's letter overflowed with the descriptions she had heard from him of Italian Church music. He always went to Rome for Easter, and had been going as usual, this spring, but he lingered, and, for once, remained in England, where he had only intended to spend a few days on necessary business.

The Easter recess was not spent at the Grange, but at Lady Leonora's pretty house in Surrey. She had invited the party in so pressing a manner that Flora did not think it right to decline. Meta expressed some disappointment at missing Easter among her school-children, but she said a great deal about the primroses and the green corn-fields and nightingales—all which Ethel would have set down to her trick of universal content, if it had not appeared that Sir Henry was there too, and shared in all the delicious rides.

'What would Ethel say,' wrote Flora, 'to have our little Meta as Lady of the Manor at Cocksmoor? He has begun to talk about Drydale, and there are various suspicious circumstances that Lady Leonora marks with the eyes of a discreet dowager. It was edifying to see how, from smiles, we came to looks, and by-and-by to confidential talks, which have made her entirely forgive me for having so many tall brothers. Poor dear old Mr. Rivers! Lady Leonora owns that it was the best thing possible for that sweet girl that he did not live any longer to keep her in seclusion; it is so delightful to see her appreciated as she deserves, and with her beauty and fortune she might make any choice she pleases. In fact, I believe Lady Leonora would like to look still higher for her, but this would be mere ambition, and we should be far better satisfied with such a connection as this, founded on mutual and increasing esteem, with a man so well suited to her, and fixing her so close to us. You must not, however, launch out into an ocean of possibilities, for the good aunt has only infected me with the castle-building propensities of chaperons, and Meta is perfectly unconscious, looking on him as too hopelessly middle-aged, to entertain any such evil designs, avowing freely that she likes him, and treating him very nearly as she does papa. It is my business to keep "our aunt," who, between ourselves, has, below the surface, the vulgarity of nature that high-breeding cannot eradicate, from startling the little hummingbird, before the net has been properly twined round her bright little heart. As far as I can see, he is much smitten, but very cautious in his approaches, and he is wise.'

Margaret did not know what dismay she conveyed, as she handed this letter to her sister. There was no rest for Ethel till she could be alone with her father. 'Could nothing prevent it? Could not Flora be told of Mr. Rivers' wishes?' she asked.

'His wishes would have lain this way.'

'I do not know that.'

'It is no concern of ours. There is nothing objectionable here, and though I can't say it is not a disappointment, it ought not to be. The long and short of it is, that I never ought to have told you anything about it.'

'Poor Norman!'

'Absurd! The lad is hardly one-and-twenty. Very few marry a first love.' (Ah, Ethel!) 'Poor old Rivers only mentioned it as a refuge from fortune-hunters, and it stands to reason that he would have preferred this. Any way, it is awkward for a man with empty pockets to marry an heiress, and it is wholesomer for him to work for his living. Better that it should be out of his head at once, if it were there at all. I trust it was all our fancy. I would not have him grieved now for worlds, when his heart is sore.'

'Somehow,' said Ethel, 'though he is depressed and silent, I like it better than I did last Christmas.'

'Of course, when we were laughing out of the bitterness of our hearts,' said Dr. May, sighing. 'It is a luxury to let oneself alone to be sorrowful.'

Ethel did not know whether she desired a *tête-à-tête* with Norman or not. She was aware that he had seen Flora's letter, and she did not believe that he would ever mention the hopes that must have been dashed by it; or, if he should do so, how could she ever guard her father's secret? At least, she had the comfort of recognising the accustomed Norman in his manner, low-spirited, indeed, and more than ever dreamy and melancholy, but not in the unnatural and excited state that had made her unhappy about him. She could not help telling Dr. Spencer, that this was much more the real brother.

'I dare say,' was the answer, not quite satisfactory in tone.

'I thought you would like it better.'

'Truth is better than fiction, certainly. But I am afraid he has a tendency to morbid self-contemplation, and you ought to shake him out of it.'

'What is the difference between self-contemplation and self-examination?'

'The difference between your brother and yourself. Ah! you think that no answer. Will you have a medical simile? Self-examination notes the symptoms and combats them; self-contemplation does as I did when I was unstrung by that illness at Poonshedagore, and was always feeling my own pulse. It dwells on them, and perpetually deplores itself. Oh dear! this is no better—what a wretch I am! It is always studying its deformities in a moral looking-glass.'

'Yes, I think poor Norman does that, but I thought it right and humble.'

'The humility of a self-conscious mind. It is the very reverse of your father, who is the most really humble man in existence.'

'Do you call self-consciousness a fault?'

'No. I call it a misfortune. In the vain, it leads to prudent vanity; in the good, to a painful effort of humility.'

'I don't think I quite understand what it is.'

'No, and you have so much of your father in you, that you never will. But take care of your brother, and don't let his brains work.'

How Ethel was to take care of him she did not know; she could only keep a heedful eye on him, and rejoice when he took Tom out for a long walk—a companion certainly not likely to promote the working of the brain—but though it was in the opposite direction to Cocksmoor, Tom came home desperately cross, snubbed Gertrude, and fagged Aubrey; but, then, as Blanche observed, perhaps that was only because his trousers were splashed.

In her next solitary walk to Cocksmoor, Norman joined Ethel. She was gratified, but she could not think of one safe word worth saying to him, and for a mile they preserved an absolute silence, until the first began, 'Ethel, I have been thinking—'

'That you have!' said she, between hope and dread, and the thrill of being again treated as his friend.

'I want to consult you. Don't you think now that Richard is settled at home, and if Tom will study medicine, that I could be spared?'

'Spared!' exclaimed Ethel. 'You are not much at home.'

'I meant more than my present absences. It is my earnest wish—' he paused, and the continuation took her by surprise. 'Do you think it would give my father too much pain to part with me as a Missionary to New Zealand?'

She could only gaze at him in mute amazement.

'Do you think he could bear it?' said Norman, hastily.

'He would consent,' she replied. 'O Norman, it is the most glorious thing man can do! How I wish I could go with you!'

'Your mission is here,' said Norman, affectionately.

'I know it is—I am contented with it,' said Ethel; 'but oh! Norman, after all our talks about races and gifts, you have found the more excellent way.'

'Hush! Charity finds room at home, and mine are not such unmixed motives as yours.'

She made a sound of inquiry.

'I cannot tell you all. Some you *shall* hear. I am weary of this feverish life of competition and controversy—'

'I thought you were so happy with your Fellowship. I thought Oxford was your delight.'

'She will always be nearer my heart than any place, save this. It is not her fault that I am not like the simple and dutiful, who are not fretted or perplexed.'

'Perplexed?' repeated Ethel.

'It is not so now,' he replied. 'God forbid! But where better men have been led astray, I have been bewildered; till, Ethel, I have felt as if the ground were slipping from beneath my feet, and I have only been able to hide my eyes, and entreat that I might know the truth.'

'You knew it!' said Ethel, looking pale, and gazing searchingly at him.

'I did, I *do;* but it was a time of misery when, for my presumption, I suppose, I was allowed to doubt whether it were the truth.'

Ethel recoiled, but came nearer, saying, very low, 'It is past.'

'Yes, thank Him who is Truth. You all saved me, though you did not know it.'

'When was this?' she asked, timidly.

'The worst time was before the Long Vacation. They told me I ought to read this book, and that. Harvey Anderson used to come primed with arguments. I could always overthrow them, but when I came to glory in doing so, perhaps I prayed less. Any way, they left a sting. It might be, that I doubted my own sincerity, from knowing that I had got to argue, chiefly because I liked to be looked on as a champion.'

Ethel saw the truth of what her friend had said of the morbid habit of self-contemplation.

'I read, and I mystified myself. The better I talked, the more my own convictions failed me; and, by the time you came up to Oxford, I knew how you would have shrunk from him who was your pride, if you could have seen into the secrets beneath.'

Ethel took hold of his hand. 'You seemed bright,' she said.

'It melted like a bad dream before—before the hummingbird, and with my father. It was weeks ere I dared to face the subject again.'

'How could you? Was it safe?'

'I could not have gone on as I was. Sometimes the sight of my father, or the mountains and lakes in Scotland, or—or—things at the Grange, would bring peace back; but there were dark hours, and I knew that there could be no comfort till I had examined and fought it out.'

'I suppose examination was right,' said Ethel, 'for a man, and defender of the faith. I should only have tried to pray the terrible thought away. But I can't tell how it feels.'

'Worse than you have power to imagine,' said Norman, shuddering. 'It is over now. I worked out their fallacies, and went over the reasoning on our side.'

'And prayed—' said Ethel.

'Indeed I did; and the confidence returned, firmer, I hope, than ever. It had never gone for a whole day.'

Ethel breathed freely. 'It was life or death,' she said, 'and we never knew it!'

'Perhaps not; but I know your prayers were angel-wings ever round me. And far more than argument, was the thought of my father's heart-whole Christian love and strength.'

'Norman, you believed, all the time, with your heart. This was only a bewilderment of your intellect.'

'I think you are right,' said Norman. 'To me the doubt was cruel agony—not the amusement it seems to some.'

'Because our dear home has made the truth, our joy, our union,' said Ethel. 'And you are sure the cloud is gone, and for ever?' she still asked, anxiously.

He stood still. 'For ever, I trust,' he said. 'I hold the faith of my childhood in all its fulness as surely as—as ever I loved my mother and Harry.'

'I know you do,' said Ethel. 'It was only a bad dream.'

'I hope I may be forgiven for it,' said Norman. 'I do not know how far it was sin. It was gone so far as that my mind was convinced last Christmas, but the shame and sting remained. I was not at peace again till the news of this spring came, and brought, with the grief, this compensation—that I could cast behind me and forget the criticisms and doubts that those miserable debates had connected with sacred words.'

'You will be the sounder for having fought the fight,' said Ethel.

'I do not dread the like shocks,' said her brother, 'but I long to leave this world of argument and discussion. It is right that there should be a constant defence and battle, but I am not fit for it. I argue for my own triumph, and, in heat and harassing, devotion is lost. Besides, the comparison of intellectual power has been my bane all my life.'

'I thought "praise was your penance here."'

'I would fain render it so, but—in short, I must be away from it all, and go to the simplest, hardest work, beginning from the rudiments, and forgetting subtle arguments.'

'Forgetting yourself,' said Ethel.

'Right. I want to have no leisure to think about myself,' said Norman. 'I am never so happy as at such times.'

'And you want to find work so far away?'

'I cannot help feeling drawn towards those Southern seas. I am glad you can give me good speed. But what do you think about my father?'

Ethel thought and thought. 'I know he would not hinder you,' she repeated.

'But you dread the pain for him? I had talked to Tom about taking his profession; but the poor boy thinks he dislikes it greatly, though, I believe, his real taste lies that way, and his aversion only arises from a few grand notions he has picked up, out of which I could soon talk him.'

'Tom will not stand in your place,' said Ethel.

'He will be more equable and more to be depended upon,' said Norman. 'None of you appreciate Tom. However, you must hear my alternative. If you think my going would be too much grief for papa, or if Tom be set against helping him in his practice, there is an evident leading of Providence, showing that I am unworthy of this work. In that case I would go abroad, and throw myself at once, with all my might, into the study of medicine, and get ready to give my father some rest. It is a shame that all his sons should turn away from his profession.'

'I am more than ever amazed!' cried Ethel. 'I thought you detested it. I thought papa never wished it for you. He said you had not nerve.'

'He was always full of the tenderest consideration for me,' said Norman. 'With Heaven to help him, a man may have nerve for whatever is his duty.'

'How he would like to have you to watch and help! But New Zealand would be so glorious!'

'Glory is not for me,' said Norman. 'Understand, Ethel, the choice is New Zealand, or going at once—at once, mind—to study at Edinburgh or Paris.'

'New Zealand at once?' said Ethel.

'I suppose I must stay for Divinity lectures, but my intention must be avowed,' said Norman, hastily. 'And, now, will you sound my father? I cannot.'

'I can't sound,' said Ethel. 'I can only do things point-blank.'

'Do then,' said Norman, 'any way you can! Only let me know which is best for him. You get all the disagreeable things to do, good old Unready one,' he added, kindly. 'I believe you are the one who would be shoved in front, if we were obliged to face a basilisk.'

The brightness that had come over Norman, when he had discharged his cares upon her, was encouragement enough for Ethel. She only asked how much she was to repeat of their conversation?

'Whatever you think best. I do not want to grieve him, but he must not think it fine in me.'

Ethel privately thought that no power on earth could prevent him from doing that.

It was not consistent with cautious sounding, that Norman was always looking appealingly towards her; and, indeed, she could not wait long with such a question on her mind. She remained with her father in the drawing-room, when the rest were gone up-stairs, and, plunging at once into the matter, she said, 'Papa, there is something that Norman cannot bear to say to you himself.'

'Hummingbirds to wit?' said Dr. May.

'No, indeed, but he wants to be doing something at once. What should you think of—of—there are two things; one is—going out as a missionary—'

'Hummingbirds in another shape,' said the Doctor, startled, but smiling, so as to pique her.

'You mean to treat it as a boy's fancy!' said she.

'It is rather suspicious,' he said. 'Well, what is the other of his two things?'

'The other is, to begin studying medicine at once, so as to help you.'

'Hey day!' cried Dr. May, drawing up his tall vigorous figure, 'does he think me so very ancient and superannuated?'

What could possess him to be so provoking and unsentimental to-night? Was it her own bad management? She longed to put an end to the conversation, and answered, 'No, but he thinks it hard that none of your sons should be willing to relieve you.'

'It won't be Norman,' said Dr. May. 'He is not made of the stuff. If he survived the course of study, every patient he lost, he would bring himself in guilty of murder, and there would soon be an end of him!'

'He says that a man can force himself to anything that is his duty.'

'This is not going to be his duty, if I can make it otherwise. What is the meaning of all this? No, I need not ask, poor boy, it is what I was afraid of!'

'It is far deeper,' said Ethel; and she related great part of what she had heard in the afternoon. It was not easy to make her father listen—his line was to be positively indignant, rather than compassionate, when he heard of the doubts that had assailed poor Norman. 'Foolish boy, what business had he to meddle with those accursed books, when he knew what they were made of—it was tasting poison, it was running into temptation! He had no right to expect to come out safe—' and then he grasped tightly hold of Ethel's hands, and, as if the terror had suddenly flashed on him, asked her, with dilated eye and trembling voice, whether she were sure that he was safe, and held the faith!

Ethel repeated his asseveration, and her father covered his face with his hands in thanksgiving.

After this, he seemed somewhat inclined to hold poor Oxford in horror, only, as he observed, it would be going out of the frying-pan into the fire, to take refuge at Paris—a recurrence to the notion of Norman's medical studies, that showed him rather enticed by the proposal.

He sent Ethel to bed, saying, he should talk to Norman and find out what was the meaning of it, and she walked up-stairs, much ashamed of having so ill-served her brother, as almost to have made him ridiculous.

Dr. May and Norman never failed to come to an understanding, and after they had had a long drive into the country together, Dr. May told Ethel that he was afraid, of what he ought not to be afraid of, that she was right, that the lad was very much in earnest now, at any rate, and if he should continue in the same mind, he hoped he should not be so weak as to hold him from a blessed work.

From Norman, Ethel heard the warmest gratitude for his father's kindness. Nothing could be done yet, he must wait patiently for the present, but he was to write to his uncle, Mr. Arnott, in New Zealand, and, without pledging himself, to make inquiries as to the mission; and, in the meantime, return to Oxford, where, to his other studies, he was to add a course of medical lectures, which, as Dr. May said, would do him no harm, would occupy his mind, and might turn to use wherever he was.

Ethel was surprised to find that Norman wrote to Flora an expression of his resolution, that, if he found he could be spared from assisting his father as a physician, he would give himself up to the mission in New Zealand. Why should he tell any one so unsympathetic as Flora, who would think him wasted in either case?

CHAPTER XVII.

'Do not fear: Heaven is as near,
By water, as by land.'—LONGFELLOW.

THE fifth of May was poor Harry's eighteenth birthday, and, as usual, was a holiday. Etheldred privately thought his memory more likely to be respected, if Blanche and Aubrey were employed, than if they were left in idleness; but Mary would have been wretched, had the celebration been omitted, and a leisure day was never unwelcome.

Dr. Spencer carried off Blanche and Aubrey for a walk, and Ethel found Mary at her great resort—Harry's cupboard— dusting and arranging his books, and the array of birthday gifts, to which, even to-day, she had not failed to add the marker that had been in hand at Christmas. Ethel entreated her to come down, and Mary promised, and presently appeared, looking so melancholy, that, as a sedative, Ethel set her down to the basket of scraps to find materials for a tippet for some one at Cocksmoor, intending, as soon as Margaret should be dressed, to resign her morning to the others, invite Miss Bracy to the drawing-room, and read aloud.

Gertrude was waiting for her walk, till nurse should have dressed Margaret, and was frisking about the lawn, sometimes looking in at the drawing-room window at her sisters, sometimes chattering to Adams at his work, or laughing to herself and the flowers, in that overflow of mirth, that seemed always bubbling up within her.

She was standing in rapt contemplation of a pear-tree in full blossom, her hands tightly clasped behind the back, for greater safety from the temptation, when, hearing the shrubbery-gate open, she turned, expecting to see her papa, but was frightened at the sight of two strangers, and began to run off at full speed.

'Stop! Blanche! Blanche, don't you know me?' The voice

was that tone of her brother's, and she stood and looked, but it came from a tall, ruddy youth, in a shabby rough blue coat, followed by a grizzled old seaman. She was too much terrified and perplexed even to run.

'What's the matter? Blanche, it is I! Why, don't you know me—Harry?'

'Poor brother Harry is drowned,' she answered; and, with one bound, he was beside her, and, snatching her up, devoured her with kisses.

'Put me down—put me down, please,' was all she could say.

'It is not Blanche! What? the little Daisy, I do believe!'

'Yes, I am Gertrude, but please let me go;' and, at the same time, Adams hurried up, as if he thought her being kidnapped, but his aspect changed at the glad cry, 'Ha! Adams! how are you? Are they all well?'

'Tisn't never Master Harry! Bless me!' as Harry's hand gave him sensible proof; 'when we had given you up for lost!'

'My father well?' Harry asked, hurrying the words one over the other.

'Quite well, sir, but he never held up his head since he heard it, and poor Miss Mary has so moped about. If ever I thought to see the like—'

'So they did not get my letter, but I can't stop. Jennings will tell you—Take care of him. Come, Daisy—' for he had kept her unwilling hand all the time. 'But what's that for?' pointing to the black ribbons, and, stopping short, startled.

'Because of poor Harry,' said the bewildered child.

'O that's right!' cried he, striding on, and dragging her in a breathless run, as he threw open the well-known doors; and, she escaping from him, hid her face in Mary's lap, screaming, 'He says he is Harry! he says he is not drowned!'

At the same moment Ethel was in his arms, and his voice was sobbing, 'Ethel! Mary! home! Where's papa?' One moment's almost agonizing joy in the certainty of his identity! but ere she could look or think, he was crying 'Mary! O Ethel, see—'

Mary had not moved, but sat as if turned to stone, with breath suspended, wide-stretched eyes, and death-like cheeks. Ethel sprang to her—'Mary, Mary dear, it is Harry! It is himself! Don't you see? Speak to her, Harry.'

He seemed almost afraid to do so, but, recovering himself, exclaimed, 'Mary, dear old Polly, here I am! O, won't you speak to me?' he added, piteously, as he threw his arm round her and kissed her, startled at the cold touch of her cheek.

The spell seemed broken, and, with a wild hoarse shriek that rang through the house, she struggled to regain her breath, but it would only come in painful, audible catches, as she held Harry's hand convulsively.

'What have I done?' he exclaimed, in distress.

'What's this! Who is this frightening my dear?' was old nurse's exclamation, as she and James came, at the outcry.

'O nurse, what have I done to her?' repeated Harry.

'It is joy—it is sudden joy!' said Ethel. 'See, she is better now—'

'Master Harry! Well, I never!' and James, with one wring of the hand, retreated, while old nurse was nearly hugged to death, declaring all the time that he didn't ought to have come in such a way, terrifying every one out of their senses! and as for poor Miss May—'

'Where is she?' cried Harry, starting at the sight of the vacant sofa.

'Only up-stairs,' said Ethel; 'but where's Alan? Is not he come?'

'Oh! Ethel, don't you know?' His face told but too plainly.

'Nurse! nurse, how *shall* we tell her?' said Ethel.

'Poor dear!' exclaimed nurse, sounding her tongue on the roof of her mouth. 'She'll never abear it without her papa. Wait for him, I should say. But bless me, Miss Mary, to see you go on like that, when Master Harry is come back such a bonny man!'

'I'm better now,' said Mary, with an effort. 'Oh! Harry, speak to me again.'

'But Margaret!' said Ethel, while the brother was holding Mary in his embrace, and she lay tremulous with the new ecstasy, upon his breast—'but Margaret. Nurse, you must go up, or she will suspect. I'll come, when I can speak quietly— Oh! poor Margaret! If Richard would but come in!'

Ethel walked up and down the room, divided between a tumult of joy, grief, dread, and perplexity.—At that moment a little voice said at the door, 'Please, Margaret wants Harry to come up directly.'

They looked one upon another in consternation. They had never thought of the child, who, of course, had flown up at once with the tidings.

'Go up, Miss Ethel,' said nurse.

'Oh, nurse! I can't be the first. Come, Harry, come.'

Hand-in-hand they silently ascended the stairs, and Ethel pushed open the door. Margaret was on her couch, her whole form and face in one throb of expectation.

She looked into Harry's face—the eagerness flitted like sunshine on the hill-side before a cloud, and, without a word, she held out her arms.

He threw himself on his knees, and her fingers were clasped among his thick curls, while his frame heaved with suppressed sobs—'Oh! if he could only have come back to you.'

'Thank God!' she said, then slightly pushing him back, she lay holding his hand in one of hers, and resting the other on his shoulder, and gazing in silence into his face. Each was still— she was gathering strength—he dreaded word or look.

'Tell me how and where?' she said at last.

'It was in the Loyalty Isles; it was fever—the exertions for us. His head was lying here,' and he pointed to his own breast. 'He sent his love to you—he bade me tell you there would be meeting by-and-by, in the haven where he would be. I laid his head in the grave—under the great palm—I said some of the prayers—there are Christians round it.'

He said this in short disconnected phrases, often pausing to gather voice, but forced to resume, by her inquiring looks, and pressure of his hand.

She asked no more. 'Kiss me,' she said, and when he had done so, 'Thank you; go down, please, all of you. You have brought great relief. Thank you. But I can't talk yet. You shall tell me the rest by-and-by.'

She sent them all away, even Ethel, who would have lingered. 'Go to him, dearest. Let me be alone. Don't be uneasy. This is peace—but go.'

Ethel found Mary and Harry interlaced into one moving figure, and Harry greedily asking for his father and Norman, as if famishing for the sight of them. He wanted to set out to seek the former in the town, but his movements were too uncertain, and the girls clung to the newly-found, as if they could not trust him away from them. They wandered about, speaking, all three at random, without power of attending to the answers. It was enough to see him and touch him; they could not yet care where he had been.

Dr. May was in the midst of them ere they were aware. One look, and he flung his arms round his son; but, suddenly letting him go, he burst away, and banged his study door. Harry would have followed.

'No, don't,' said Ethel; then, seeing him disappointed, she came nearer, and murmured, 'He entered into his chamber, and—'

Harry silenced her with another embrace; but their father was with them again, to verify that he had really seen his boy, and ask, alas! whether Alan were with Margaret. The brief sad answer sent him to see how it was with her. She would not let him stay; she said it was infinite comfort, and joy was coming, but she would rather be still, and not come down till evening.

Perhaps others would fain have been still, could they have borne an instant's deprivation of the sight of their dear sailor, while greetings came thickly on him. The children burst in, having heard a report in the town, and Dr. Spencer waited at the door for the confirmation; but when Ethel would have flown out to him, he waved his hand, shut the door, and hurried away, as if a word to her would have been an intrusion.

The brothers had been summoned by a headlong apparition of Will Adams in Cocksmoor school, shouting that Master Harry was come home; and Norman's long legs out-speeding Richard, had brought him back flushed, and too happy for one word, while, 'Well, Harry,' was Richard's utmost, and his care for Margaret seemed to overpower everything else, as he went up, and was not so soon sent away.

Words were few down-stairs. Blanche and Aubrey agreed that they thought people would have been much happier; but, in fact, the joy was oppressive from very newness. Ethel roamed about, she could not sit still without feeling giddy, in the strangeness of the revulsion. Her father sat, as if a word would break the blest illusion; and Harry stood before each of them in turn, as if about to speak, but turned his address into a sudden caress, or blow on the shoulder, and tried to laugh. Little Gertrude, not understanding the confusion, had taken up her station under the table, and peeped out from beneath the cover.

There was more composure as they sat at dinner, and yet there was very little talking or eating. Afterwards, Dr. May and Norman exultingly walked away, to show their Harry to Dr. Spencer and Mr. Wilmot; and Ethel would gladly have tried to calm herself, and recover the balance of her mind, by giving thanks where they were due, but she did not know what to do with her sisters. Blanche was wild, and Mary still in so shaky a state of excitement, that she went off into mad laughing, when Blanche discovered that they were in mourning for Harry.

Nothing would satisfy Blanche but breaking in on Margaret, and climbing to the top of the great wardrobe to disinter the coloured raiment, beseeching that each favourite might be at once put on to do honour to Harry. Mary chimed in with her, in begging for the wedding merinos—would not Margaret wear her beautiful blue?

'No, my dear, I cannot,' said Margaret, gently.

Mary looked at her, and was again in a flood of tears, incoherently protesting, together with Ethel, that they would not change.

'No, dears,' said Margaret. 'I had rather you did so. You must not be unkind to Harry. He will not think I do not welcome him. I am only too glad that Richard would not let my impatience take away my right to wear this.'

Ethel knew that it was for life.

Mary could not check her tears, and *would* go on making heroic protests against leaving off her black, sobbing the more at each. Margaret's gentle caresses seemed to make her worse; and Ethel, afraid that Margaret's own composure would be overthrown, exclaimed, 'How can you be so silly? Come away!' and rather roughly pulled her out of the room, when she collapsed entirely at the top of the stairs, and sat crying helplessly.

'I can't think what's the use of Harry's coming home,' Gertrude was heard saying to Richard. 'It is very disagreeable;' whereat Mary relapsed into a giggle, and Ethel felt frantic.

'Richard! Richard, what *is* to be done with Mary? She can't help it, I believe; but this is not the way to treat the mercy that—'

'Mary had better go and lie down in her own room,' said Richard, tenderly and gravely.

'O, please! please!' began Mary, 'I shall not see him when he comes back!'

'If you can't behave properly when he does come,' said Richard, 'there is no use in being there.'

'Remember, Ritchie,' said Ethel, thinking him severe, 'she has not been well this long time.'

Mary began to plead; but, with his own pretty persuasive manner, he took her by the hand, and drew her into his room; and when he came down, after an interval, it was to check Blanche, who would have gone up to interrupt her with queries about the perpetual blue merino. He sat down with Blanche on the staircase window-seat, and did not let her go till he had gently talked her out of flighty spirits into the soberness of thankfulness.

Ethel, meanwhile, had still done nothing but stray about, long for loneliness, find herself too unsteady to finish her letters to Flora and Tom; and while she tried to make Gertrude think Harry a pleasant acquisition, she hated her own wild heart, that could not rejoice, or give thanks aright.

By-and-by, Mary came down, with her bonnet on, quite quiet now. 'I am going to Church with Ritchie,' she said. Ethel caught at the notion, and it spread through the house. Dr. May, who just then came in with his two sons, looked at Harry, saying,

'What do you think of it? Shall we go, my boy?' And Harry, as soon as he understood, declared that he should like nothing better. It seemed what they all needed; even Aubrey and Gertrude begged to come; and, when the solemn old Minster was above their heads, and the hallowed stillness around them, the tightened sense of half-realized joy began to find relief in the chant of glory. The voices of the sanctuary, ever uplifting notes of praise, seemed to gather together and soften their emotions; and agitation was soothed away, and all that was oppressive and tumultuous gave place to sweet peace and thankfulness. Ethel dimly remembered the like sense of relief, when her mother had hushed her wild ecstasy, while sympathising with her joy. Richard could not trust his voice, but Mr. Wilmot offered the special thanksgiving.

Harry was, indeed, 'at home,' and his tears fell fast over his book, as he heard his father's 'Amen,' so fervent and so deep; and he gazed up and around, with fond and earnest looks, as thoughts and resolutions, formed there of old, came gathering thick upon him. And there little Gertrude seemed first to accept him. She whispered to her papa, as they stood up to go away, that it was very good in God Almighty to have sent Harry home; and, as they left the Cloister, she slipped into Harry's hand a daisy from the grave—such a gift as she had never carried to any one else, save her father and Margaret, and she shrank no longer from being lifted up in his arms, and carried home through the twilight street.

He hurried into the drawing-room, and was heard declaring that all was right, for Margaret was on the sofa; but he stopped short, grieved at her altered looks. She smiled as he stooped to kiss her, and then made him stand erect, and measure himself against Norman, whose height he had almost reached. The little curly midshipman had come back, as nurse said, 'a fine-growed young man,' his rosy cheeks, brown and ruddy, and his countenance—

'You are much more like papa and Norman than I thought you would be,' said Margaret.

'He has left his snub nose and yellow locks behind,' said his father; 'though the shaggy mane seems to remain. I believe lions grow darker with age—So there stand June and July together again?'

Dr. May walked backwards to look at them. It was good to see his face!

'I shall see Flora and Tom to-morrow!' said Harry, after nodding with satisfaction, as they all took their wonted places.

'Going!' exclaimed Richard.

'Why, don't you know,' said Ethel; 'it is current in the nursery that he is going to be tried by court-martial for living with the King of the Cannibal islands.'

'Aubrey says he had a desert island, with Jennings for his man Friday,' said Blanche.

'Harry,' said little Gertrude, who had established herself on his knee, 'did you really poke out the giant's eye with the top of a fir-tree?'

'Who told you so, Daisy?' was the general cry; but she became shy, and would not answer more than by a whisper about Aubrey, who indignantly declared that he never said so, only Gertrude was so foolish, that she did not know Harry from Ulysses.

'After all,' said Ethel, 'I don't think our notions are much more defined. Papa and Norman may know more, but we have heard almost nothing. I have been waiting to hear more to close up my letters to Flora and Tom. What a shame that has not been done!'

'I'll finish,' said Mary, running to the side-table.

'And tell her I'll be there to-morrow,' said Harry. 'I must report myself, and what fun to see Flora a member of parliament! Come with me, June, I'll be back next day. I wish you all would come.'

'Yes, I must come with you,' said Norman. 'I shall have to go to Oxford on Thursday—' and very reluctant he looked. 'Tell Flora I am coming, Mary.'

'How did you know that Flora was a married lady?' asked Blanche, in her would-be grown up manner.

'I heard that from Aunt Flora. A famous lot of news I picked up there!'

'Aunt Flora!'

'Did you not know he had been at Auckland?' said Dr. May.

'Aunt Flora had to nurse him well after all he had undergone. Did you not think her very like mamma, Harry?'

'Mamma never looked half so old!' cried Harry, indignantly. 'Flora was five years younger!'

'She has got her voice and way with her,' said Harry; 'but you will soon see. She is coming home soon.'

There was a great outcry of delight.

'Yes, there is some money of uncle Arnott's that must be looked after, but he does not like the voyage, and can't leave his office, so perhaps Aunt Flora may come alone. She had a great mind to come with me, but there was no good berth for her in this schooner, and I could not wait for another chance. I can't think what possessed the letters not to come! She would not write by the first packet because I was so ill, but we both wrote by the next, and I made sure you had them, or I would have written before I came.'

The words were not out of his mouth, before the second post was brought in, and there were two letters from New Zealand! What would they not have been yesterday? Harry would have burnt his own, but the long closely-written sheets were eagerly seized, as affording the best hope of understanding his adventures, as it had been written at intervals from Auckland, and the papers, passing from one to the other, formed the text for interrogations on further details, though much more was gleaned incidentally in *tête-à-têtes*, by Margaret, Norman, or his father, and no one person ever heard the whole connectedly from Harry himself.

' What was the first you knew of the fire, Harry ?' asked Dr. May, looking up from the letter.

'Owen shaking me awake; and I thought it was a hoax,' said Harry. 'But it was true enough, and when we got on deck, there were clouds of smoke coming up the main hatchway.'

Margaret's eyes were upon him, and her lips formed the question, ' And he ?'

' He met us, and told us to be steady—but there was little need for that! Every man there was as cool and collected as if it had been no more than the cook's stove, and we should have scorned to be otherwise! He put his hand on my shoulder, and said, " Keep by me," and I did.'

' Then there was never much hope of extinguishing the fire ?'

'No—if you looked down below the forecastle it was like a furnace, and though the pumps were at work, it was only to gain time while the boats were lowered. The First Lieutenant told off the men, and they went down the side without one word, only shaking hands with those that were left.'

'Oh! Harry! what were you thinking of ?' cried Blanche.

' Of the powder,' said Harry.

Ethel thought there was more in that answer than met the ear, and that Harry, at least, had thought of the powder to-night at Church.

' Mr. Ernescliffe had the command of the second cutter. He asked to take me with him, I was glad enough, and Owen—he is a mate, you know—went with us.'

As to telling how he felt when he saw the good ship Alcestis blown to fragments, that was past Harry, and all but Blanche were wise enough not to ask. She had by way of answer, ' Very glad to be safe out of her.'

Nor was Harry willing to dwell on the subsequent days, when

the unclouded sun had been a cruel foe: and the insufficient stores
of food and water did, indeed, sustain life, but a life of extreme
suffering. What he told was of the kindness that strove to save
him, as the youngest, from all that could be spared him. 'If I
dropped asleep at the bottom of the boat, I was sure to find some
one shading me from the sun. If there was an extra drop of
water, they wanted me to have it.'

'Tell me their names, Harry!' cried Dr. May. 'If ever I
meet one of them!'

'But the storm, Harry, the storm?' asked Blanche. 'Was that
not terrible?'

'Very comfortable at first, Blanche,' was the answer. 'Oh!
that rain!'

'But when it grew so very bad?'

'We did not reck much what happened to us,' said Harry. 'It
could not be worse than starving. When we missed the others
in the morning, most of us thought them the best off.'

Mary could not help coming round to kiss him, as if eyes alone
were not enough to satisfy her that here he was.

Dr. May shuddered, and went on reading, and Margaret drew
Harry down to her, and once more by looks, craved for more
minute tidings.

'All that you can think,' murmured Harry; 'the very life and
soul of us all—so kind, and yet discipline as perfect as on board.
But don't now, Margaret—'

The tone of the *don't*, the reddening cheek, liquid eye, and
heaving chest, told enough of what the Lieutenant had been to
one, at least, of the desolate boat's crew.

'Oh! Harry, Harry! I can't bear it,' exclaimed Mary. 'How
long did it last? How did it end?'

'Fifteen days,' said Harry. 'It was time it should end, for
all the water we had caught in the storm, was gone—we gave
the last drop to Jones, for we thought him dying—one's tongue
was like a dry sponge.'

'How did it end?' repeated Mary, in an agony.

'Jennings saw a sail. We thought it all a fancy of weakness, but 't was true enough, and they saw our signal of distress!'

The vessel proved to be an American whaler, which had just
parted with her cargo to a homeward-bound ship, and was going
to refit, and take in provisions and water at one of the Melanesian
islands, before returning for further captures. The master was a
man of the shrewd, hard money-making cast; but, at the price
of Mr. Ernescliffe's chronometer, and of the services of the

sailors, he undertook to convey them where they might fall in with packets bound for Australia.

The distressed Alcestes at first thought themselves in paradise, but the vessel, built with no view, save to whales, and, with a considerable reminiscence of the blubber lately parted with, proved no wholesome abode, when overcrowded, and in the tropics! Mr. Ernescliffe's science, resolution, and constancy, had saved his men so far; but with the need for exertion, his powers gave way, and he fell a prey to a return of the fever, which had been his introduction to Dr. May.

'There he was,' said Harry, 'laid up in a little bit of a stifling cabin, just like an oven; without the possibility of a breath of air! The skin-flint skipper carried no medicine; the water, shocking stuff it was, was getting so low, that there was only a pint a day served out to each, and though all of us Alcestes clubbed every drop we could spare for him—it was bad work! Owen and I never were more glad in our lives than when we heard we were to cast anchor at the Loyalty isles! Such a place as it was! You little know what it was to see anything green! and there was this isle fringed down close to the sea with cocoa-nut trees! and the bay as clear!—you could see every shell, and wonderful fishes swimming in it! Well, every one was for going ashore, and some of the natives swam out to us, and brought things in their canoes, but not many; it is not encouraged by the mission, nor by David—for those Yankee traders are not the most edifying society—and the crew vowed they were cannibals, and had eaten a man three years ago, so they all went ashore armed.'

'You stayed with him,' said Margaret.

'Aye, it was my turn, and I was glad enough to have some fresh fruit and water for him, but he could not take any notice of it. Did not I want you, papa? Well, by-and-by, Owen came back, in a perfect rapture with the place and the people, and said it was the only hope for Mr. Ernescliffe, to take him on shore—'

'Then you did really go amongst the cannibals!' exclaimed Blanche.

'That is all nonsense,' said Harry. 'Some of them may once have been, and I fancy the heathens might not mind a bit of "long pig" still; but these have been converted by the Samoans.'

The Samoans, it was further explained, are the inhabitants of the Navigator islands, who, having been converted by the Church Missionary Society, have sent out great numbers of most active and admirable teachers among the scattered islands, braving martyrdom and disease, never shrinking from their work, and, by teaching and example, preparing the way for fuller doctrine than they can yet impart. A station of these devoted men had for some years been settled in this island, and had since been visited by the missions of Newcastle and New Zealand. The young chief, whom Harry called David, and another youth, had spent two summers under instruction at New Zealand, and had been baptized. They were spending the colder part of the year at home, and hoped shortly to be called for by the mission-ship to return, and resume their course of instruction.

Owen had come to an understanding with the chief, and the Samoans, and had decided on landing his Lieutenant, and it was accordingly done, with very little consciousness, on the patient's part. Black figures, with woolly mop-heads, and sometimes decorated with whitewash of lime, crowded round to assist in the transport of the sick man through the surf; and David himself, in a white European garb, met his guests, with dignified manners that would have suited a prince of any land, and conducted them through the grove of palms, interspersed with white huts, to a beautiful house consisting of a central room, with many others opening from it, floored with white coral lime, and lined with soft shining mats of Samoan manufacture. This, Harry learnt, had been erected by them in hopes of an English Missionary taking up his abode amongst them.

They were a kindly people, and had shown hospitality to other Englishmen, who had less appreciated it than these young officers could. They lavished every kindness in their power upon them, and Mr. Ernescliffe, at first, revived so much, that he seemed likely to recover.

But the ship had completed her repairs, and was ready to sail. The two midshipmen thought it would be certain death to their Lieutenant to bring him back to such an atmosphere; 'and so,' continued Harry's letter to his father, 'I thought there was nothing for it, but for me to stay with him, and that you would say so. I got Owen to consent, after some trouble, as we were sure to be fetched off one time or another. We said not a word to Mr. Ernescliffe, for he was only sensible now and then, so that Owen had the command. Owen made the skipper leave me a pistol and some powder, but I was ashamed David should know it, and stowed it away. As to the quarter-master, old Jennings, whose boy you remember we picked up at the Roman camp, he had not forgotten that, and when we were shaking hands and wishing good-bye, he leapt up, and vowed 'he would never leave the young gentleman that had befriended his boy, to be eaten up by them black savage niggers. If they made roast-pork of Mr. May, he would be eaten first, though he reckoned they would find him a tougher morsel.' I don't think Owen was sorry he volunteered, and no words can tell what a blessing the good old fellow was to us both.

'So there we stayed, and, at first, Mr. Ernescliffe seemed mending. The delirium went off, he could talk quite clearly and comfortably, and he used to lie listening, when David and I had our odd sort of talks. I believe, if you had been there, or we could have strengthened him any way, he might have got over it; but he never thought he should, and he used to talk to me about all of you, and said Stoneborough had been the most blessed spot in his life; he had never had so much of a home, and that sharing our grief, and knowing you, had done him great good, just when he might have been getting elated. I cannot recollect it all, though I tried hard, for Margaret's sake, but he said Hector would have a great deal of temptation, and he hoped you would be a father to him, and Norman an elder brother. You would not think how much he talked of Cocksmoor, about a Church being built there, as Ethel wished, and little Daisy laying the first stone. I remember one night, I don't know whether he was quite himself, for he looked full at me with his eyes, that had grown so large, till I did not know what was coming, and he said, "I have seen a church built by a sailor's vow; the roof was like the timbers of a ship—that was right. Mind, it is so. That is the ship that bears through the waves; there is the anchor that enters within the veil." I believe that was what he said. I could not forget that—he looked at me so; but much more he said, that I dimly remember, and chiefly about poor dear Margaret. He bade me tell her—his own precious pearl, as he used to call her—that he was quite content, and believed it was best for her and him both, that all should be thus settled, for they did not part for ever, and he trusted—but I can't write all that.' (There was a great tear-blot just here.) 'It is too good to recollect anywhere but at Church. I have been there to-day, with my uncle and aunt, and I thought I could have told it when I came home, but I was too tired to write then, and now I don't seem as if it could be written anyhow. When I come home, I will try to tell Margaret. The most part was about her, only what was better seemed to swallow that up.'

The narrative broke off here, but had been subsequently resumed. 'For all Mr. Ernescliffe talked as I told you, he was so quiet and happy, that I made sure he was getting well, but Jennings did not; and there came an old heathen native once to see us, who asked why we did not bury him alive, because he got no better, and gave trouble. At last, one night—it was the third of August—he was very restless, and could not breathe, nor lie easily; I lifted him up in my arms, for he was very light and thin, and tried to make him more comfortable. But presently he said, 'Is it you, Harry? God bless you;' and in a minute, I knew he was dead. You will tell Margaret all about it. I don't think she can love him more than I did; and she did not half know him, for she never saw him on board, nor in all that dreadful time, nor in his illness. She will never know what she has lost.'

There was another break here, and the story was continued.

'We buried him the next day, where one could see the sea, close under the great palm, where David hopes to have a Church one of these days. David helped us, and said the Lord's Prayer and the Glory with us there. I little thought, when I used to grumble at my two verses of the Psalms every day, when I should want the ninetieth, or how glad I should be to know so many by heart, for they were such a comfort to Mr. Ernescliffe.

'David got us a nice bit of wood, and Jennings carved the Cross, and his name, and all about him. I should have liked to have done it, but I knocked up after that. Jennings thinks I had a sun-stroke. I don't know, but my head was so bad, whenever I moved, that I thought only Jennings would ever have come to tell you about it. Jennings looked after me as if I had been his own son; and there was David too, as kind as if he had been Richard himself—always sitting by, to bathe my forehead, or, when I was a little better, to talk to me, and ask me questions about his Christian teaching. You must not think of him like a savage, for he is my friend, and a far more perfect gentleman than I ever saw any one, but you, papa, holding the command over his people so easily and courteously, and then coming to me with little easy first questions about the Belief, and such things, like what we used to ask mamma. He liked nothing so well as for me to tell him about King David; and we had learnt a good deal of each other's languages by that time. The notion of his heart—like Cocksmoor to Ethel—is, to get a real English mission, and have all his people Christians. Ethel talked of good kings being Davids to their line; I think that is what he will be, if he lives; but those islanders have been dying off since Europeans came among them.'

But Harry's letter could not tell what he confessed, one night, to his father, the next time he was out with him by star-light, how desolate he had been, and how he had yearned after his home, and, one evening, he had been utterly overcome by illness and loneliness, and had cried most bitterly and uncontrollably; and, though Jennings thought it was for his friend's death, it really was homesickness, and the thought of his father and Mary. Jennings had helped him out to the entrance of the hut, that the cool night air might refresh his burning brow. Orion shone clear and bright, and brought back the night when they had chosen the starry hunter as his friend. 'It seemed,' he said, 'as if you all were looking at me, and smiling to me in the stars. And there was the Southern Cross upright, which was like the Minster to me; and I recollected it was Sunday morning at home, and knew you would be thinking about me. I was so glad you had let me be Confirmed, and be with you that last Sunday, papa, for it seemed to join me on so much the more; and when I thought of the words in Church, they seemed, somehow, to float on me so much more than ever before, and it was like the Minster, and your voice. I should not have minded dying so much after that.'

At last Harry's Black Prince had hurried into the hut with the tidings that his English father's ship was in the bay, and soon English voices again sounded in his ears, bringing the forlorn boy such warmth of kindness that he could hardly believe himself a mere stranger. If Alan could but have shared the joy with him!

He was carried down to the boat in the cool of the evening, and paused on the way, for a last farewell to the lonely grave under the palm tree—one of the many sailors' graves scattered from the tropics to the poles, and which might be the first seed in a 'God's acre' to that island, becoming what the graves of holy men of old are to us.

A short space more of kind care from his new friends, and his Christian Chief, and Harry awoke from a feverish doze at sounds that seemed so like a dream of home, that he was unwilling to break them by rousing himself, but they approved themselves as real, and he found himself in the embrace of his mother's sister.

And here Mrs. Arnott's story began, of the note that reached her in the early morning with tidings that her nephew had been picked up by the mission-ship, and how she and her husband had hastened, at once, on board.

'They sent me below to see a hero,' she wrote. 'What I saw was, a scarecrow sort of likeness of you, dear Richard; but, when he opened his eyes, there was our Maggie smiling at me. I suppose he would not forgive me for telling how he sobbed and cried, when he had his arms round my neck, and his poor aching head on my shoulder. Poor fellow, he was very weak, and I believe he felt, for the moment, as if he had found his mother.

'We brought him home with us, but when the next mail went, the fever was still so high, that I thought it would be only alarm to you to write, and I had not half a story either, though you may guess how proud I was of my nephew.'

Harry's troubles were all over from that time. He had thenceforth to recover under his aunt's motherly care, while talking endlessly over the home that she loved almost as well as he did. He was well more quickly than she had ventured to hope, and nothing could check his impatience to reach his home, not even the hopes of having his aunt for a companion. The very happiness he enjoyed with her only made him long the more ardently to be with his own family ; and he had taken his leave of her, and of his dear David, and sailed by the first packet leaving Auckland.

'I never knew what the old Great Bear was to me till I saw him again !' said Harry.

It was late when the elders had finished all that was to be heard at present, and the clock reminded them that they must part.

'And you go to-morrow ?' sighed Margaret.

'I must. Jennings has to go on to Portsmouth, and see after his son.'

'O, let me see Jennings !' exclaimed Margaret. 'May I not, papa ?'

Richard, who had been making friends with Jennings, whenever he had not been needed by his sisters that afternoon, went to fetch him from the kitchen, where all the servants, and all their particular friends, were listening to the yarn that made them hold their heads higher, as belonging to Master Harry.

Harry stepped forward, met Jennings, and said, aside, ' My sister, Jennings ; my sister that you have heard of.'

Dr. May had already seen the sailor, but he could not help addressing him again. ' Come in ; come in, and see my boy among us all. Without you, we never should have had him.'

'Make him come to me,' said Margaret, breathlessly, as the embarrassed sailor stood, sleeking down his hair ; and, when he had advanced to her couch, she looked up in his face, and put her hand into his great brown one.

'I could not help saying thank you,' she said.

'Mr. May, sir !' cried Jennings, almost crying, and looking round for Harry, as a sort of protector—'tell them, sir, please, it was only my duty—I could not do no less, and you knows it, sir,' as if Harry had been making an accusation against him.

'We know you could not,' said Margaret, ' and that is what we would thank you for, if we could. I know he—Mr. Ernescliffe—must have been much more at rest for leaving my brother with so kind a friend, and—'

'Please, miss, don't say no more about it. Mr. Ernescliffe was as fine an officer as ever stepped a quarter-deck, and Mr. May here won't fall short of him ; and was I to be after leaving the like of them to the mercy of the black fellows—that was not so bad neither? If it had only pleased God that we had brought them both back to you, miss; but, you see, a man can't be everything at once, and Mr. Ernescliffe was not so stout as his heart.'

'You did everything, we know—' began Dr. May.

''Twas a real pleasure,' said Jennings, hastily, 'for two such real gentlemen as they was. Mr. May, sir, I beg your pardon if I say it to your face, never flinched, nor spoke a word of complaint, through it all; and, as to the other—'

'Margaret cannot bear this,' said Richard, coming near. 'It is too much.'

The sailor shook his head, and was retreating, but Margaret signed him to come near again, and grasped his hand. Harry followed him out of the room, to arrange their journey, and presently returned.

'He says he is glad he has seen Margaret; he says she is the right sort of stuff for Mr. Ernescliffe.'

Harry had not intended Margaret to hear, but she caught the words, smiled radiantly, and whispered, 'I wish I may be!'

CHAPTER XVIII.

MARGARET had borne the meeting much too well for her own good, and a wakeful night of palpitation was the consequence; but she would not allow any one to take it to heart, and declared that she should be ready to enjoy Harry by the time he should return, and, meantime, she should dwell on the delight of his meeting Flora.

No one had rested too soundly that night, and Dr. May had not been able to help looking in at his sleeping boy at five in the morning, to certify himself that he had not only figured his present bliss to himself, in his ten minutes' dream. And looking in again at half-past seven, he found Harry half-dressed, with his arm round Mary; laughing, almost sobbing, over the treasures in his cupboard, which he had newly discovered in their fresh order.

Dr. May looked like a new man that morning, with his brightened eye and bearing, as if there were a well-spring of joy within him, ready to brim over at once in tear and in smile, and finding an outlet in the praise and thanksgiving that his spirit chanted, and his face expressed, and in that sunny genial benevolence that must make all share his joy.

He was going to run over half the town—every one would like to hear it from him; Ethel and Mary must go to the rest—the old women in the almshouses, where lived an old cook who used to be fond of Harry—they should have a feast—all who were well enough in the hospital should have a tea-drinking—Dr. Hoxton had already granted a holiday to the school; every boy with whom they had any connection should come to dinner, and Edward Anderson should be asked to meet Harry on his return, because, poor fellow, he was so improved.

Dr. May was in such a transport of kind-hearted schemes, that he was not easily made to hear that Harry had not a sixpence wherewith to reach London.

Ethel, meanwhile, was standing beside her brother tendering to him some gold, as his last quarter.

'How did you get it, Ethel? do you keep the purse?'

'No, but papa took Cocksmoor in your stead, when—'

'Nonsense, Ethel,' said Harry; 'I don't want it. Have I not all my pay and allowance for the whole time I was dead? And as to robbing Cocksmoor—'

'Yes, keep it, Ethel,' said her father, 'do you think I would take it *now*, when if there were a thankoffering in the world!—And, by-the-by, your Cocksmoor children must have something to remember this by—'

Every one could have envied Norman, for travelling to London with Harry, but that he must proceed to Oxford in two days, when Harry would return to them. The station-master, thinking he could not do enough for the returned mariner, put the two brothers into the *coupé*, as if they had been a bridal couple, and they were very glad of the privacy, having, as yet, hardly spoken to each other, when Harry's attention was dispersed among so many.

Norman asked many questions about the mission work in the southern hemisphere, and ended by telling his brother of his design, which met with Harry's hearty approbation.

'That's right, old June. There's nothing they want so much, as such as you. How glad my aunt will be! Perhaps you will see David! Oh! if you were to go out to the Loyalty group!'

'Very possibly I might,' said Norman.

'Tell them you are my brother, and how they will receive you. I can see the mop-heads they will dress in honour of you, and what a feast of pork and yams you will have to eat! But there is plenty of work among the Maoris for you—they want a clergyman terribly at the next village to my uncle's place. I say, Norman, it will go hard if I don't get a ship bound for the Pacific, and come and see you.'

'I shall reckon on you. That is if I have not to stay to help my father.'

'To be sure,' exclaimed Harry; 'I thought you would have stayed at home, and married little Miss Rivers!'

Thus broadly and boyishly did he plunge into that most tender subject, making his brother start and wince, as if he had touched a wound.

'Nonsense!' he cried, almost angrily.

'Well! you used to seem very much smitten, but so, to be sure, were some of the Alcestes with the young ladies at Valparaiso. How we used to roast Owen about that Spanish Donna, and he was as bad at Sydney about the young lady, whose father, we told him, was a convict though he kept such a swell carriage. He had no peace about his father-in-law, the house-breaker! Don't I remember how you pinched her hand the night you were righted!'

'You know nothing about it,' said Norman, shortly. 'She is far beyond my reach.'

'A fine lady? Ha? Well, I should have thought you as good as Flora, any day,' said Harry, indignantly.

'She is what she always was,' said Norman, anxious to silence him; 'but it is unreasonable to think of it. She is all but engaged to Sir Henry Walkinghame.'

'Walkinghame!' cried the volatile sailor. 'I have half a mind to send in my name to Flora as Miss Walkinghame!' and he laughed heartily over that adventure, ending, however, with a sigh, as he said, 'It had nearly cost me a great deal! But tell me, Norman, how has that Meta, as they called her, turned out? I never saw anything prettier or nicer than she was that day of the Roman encampment, and I should be sorry if that fine fashionable aunt of hers, had made her stuck-up and disdainful.'

'No such thing,' said Norman.

'Ha!' said Harry to himself, 'I see how it is! She has gone and made poor old June unhappy, with her scornful airs—a little impertinent puss!—I wonder Flora does not teach her better manners.'

Norman, meanwhile, as the train sped over roofs, and among chimneys, was reproaching himself for running into the fascination of her presence, and then recollecting that her situation, as well as his destiny, both guaranteed that they could meet only as friendly connections.

No carriage awaited them at the station, which surprised Norman, till he recollected that the horses had probably been out all day, and it was eight o'clock. Going to Park Lane in a cab, the brothers were further surprised to find themselves evidently not expected. The butler came to speak to them, saying that Mr. and Mrs. Rivers were gone out to dinner, but would return, probably, at about eleven o'clock. He conducted them up-stairs, Harry following his brother, in towering vexation and disappointment, trying to make him turn to hear that they would go directly —home—to Eton—anywhere—why would he go in at all?

The door was opened, Mr. May was announced, and they were in a silk-lined *boudoir*, where a little slender figure in black started up, and came forward with outstretched hand.

'Norman!' she cried, 'how are you? Are you come on your way to Oxford?'

'Has not Flora had Mary's letter?'

'Yes, she said she had one. She was keeping it till she had time to read it.'

As she spoke, Meta had given her hand to Harry, as it was evidently expected; she raised her eyes to his face, and said, smiling, and blushing, 'I am sure I ought to know you, but I am afraid I don't.'

'Look again,' said Norman. 'See if you have ever seen him before.'

Laughing, glancing, and casting down her eyes, she raised them with a sudden start of joy, but colouring more deeply, said, 'Indeed, I cannot remember. I dare say I ought.'

'I think you see a likeness,' said Norman.

'O yes, I see,' she answered, faltering; but perceiving how bright were the looks of both, 'No? Impossible! Yes it is!'

'Yes, it is,' said both brothers with one voice.

She clasped her hands, and absolutely bounded with transport, then grasped both Harry's hands, and then Norman's, her whole countenance radiant with joy and sympathy beyond expression.

'Dear, dear Dr. May!' was her first exclamation. 'Oh! how happy you must all be! And Margaret?' She looked up at Norman, and came nearer. 'Is not Mr. Ernescliffe come?' she asked softly, and trembling.

'No,' was the low answer, which Harry could not bear to hear, and therefore walked to the window. 'No, Meta, but Margaret is much comforted about him. He died in great peace—in his arms—' as he signed towards his brother. And as Harry continued to gaze out on the stars of gas on the opposite side of the park, he was able to add a few of the particulars.

Meta's eyes glistened with tears, as she said, 'Perhaps it would have been too perfect if he had come; but oh, Norman! how good she is to bear it so patiently! And how gloriously he behaved! How can we make enough of him! And Flora out! how sorry she will be!'

'And she never opened Mary's letter,' said Harry, coming back to them.

'She little thought what it contained,' said Meta. 'Mary's letters are apt to bear keeping, you know, and she was so busy, that she laid it aside for a treat after the day's work. But there! inhospitable wretch that I am! you have had no dinner!'

A refection of tea and cold meat was preferred, and in her own pretty manner, Meta lavished her welcomes, trying to cover any pain given by Flora's neglect.

'What makes her so busy?' asked Harry, looking round on the beautifully furnished apartment, which, to many eyes besides those fresh from a Melanesian hut, might have seemed a paradise of luxurious ease.

'You don't know what an important lady you have for a sister,' said Meta, merrily.

'But tell me, what can she have to do? I thought you London ladies had nothing to do, but to sit with your hands before you entertaining company.'

Meta laughed heartily. 'Shall I begin at the beginning? I'll describe to-day then, and you must understand that this is what Tom would call a mild specimen—only one evening engagement. Though, perhaps, I ought to start from last night at twelve o'clock, when she was at the Austrian ambassador's ball, and came home at two, but she was up by eight—she always manages to get through her housekeeping matters before breakfast. At nine, breakfast, and baby—by-the-by, you have never inquired for our niece.'

'I have not come to believe in her yet,' said Harry.

'Seeing is believing,' said Meta; 'but no, I won't take an unfair advantage over her mamma—and she will be fast asleep—I never knew a child sleep as she does. So to go on with our day. The papers come, and Miss Leonora is given over to me; for you must know we are wonderful politicians. Flora studies all the debates till George finds out what he has heard in the House, and baby and I profit. Baby goes out walking, and the post comes. Flora always goes to the study with George, and writes, and does all sorts of things for him. She is the most useful wife in the world. At twelve, we had our singing lesson—'

'Singing lesson!' exclaimed Harry.

'Yes, you know she has a pretty voice, and she is glad to cultivate it. It is very useful at parties, but it takes up a great deal of time, and with all I can do to save her in note writing, the morning is gone directly. After luncheon, she had to ride with George, and came back in a hurry to make some canvassing calls about the orphan asylum, and Miss Bracy's sister. If we get her in at all, it will be by Flora's diplomacy. And there was shopping to do, and when we came in hoping for time for our letters, there were the Walkinghames, who stayed a long time, so that Flora could only despatch the most important notes, before George came in and wanted her. She was reading something for him all the time she was dressing, but, as I say, this is quite a quiet day.'

'Stop!' cried Harry, with a gesture of oppression, 'it sounds harder than cleaning knives, like aunt Flora! And what is an unquiet day like?'

'You will see, for we have a great evening party to-morrow.'

'Do you always stay at home?' asked Harry.

'Not always; but I do not go to large parties or balls this year,' said Meta, glancing at her deep mourning. 'I am very glad of a little time at home.'

'So you don't like it?'

'Oh, yes! it is very pleasant,' said Meta. 'It is so entertaining when we talk it over afterwards, and I like to hear how Flora is admired, and called the beauty of the season. I tell George, and we do so gloat over it together! There was an old French Marquis the other night, a dear old man, quite of the *ancien régime,* who said she was exactly like the portraits of Madame de Maintenon, and produced a beautiful miniature on a snuff-box, positively like that very pretty form of face of hers. The old man even declared that Mistress Rivers was worthy to be a Frenchwoman.'

'I should like to kick him!' amiably responded Harry.

'I hope you won't to-morrow! But don't let us waste our time over this; I want so much to hear about New Zealand.'

Meta was well read in Australasian literature, and drew out a great deal more information from Harry than Norman had yet heard. She made him talk about the Maori pah near his uncle's farm, where the Sunday services were conducted by an old gentleman tattooed elegantly in the face, but dressed like an English Clergyman; and tell of his aunt's troubles about the younger generation, whom their elders, though Christians themselves, could not educate, and who she feared would relapse into heathenism, for want of instruction, though with excellent dispositions.

'How glad you must be that you are likely to go!' exclaimed Meta to Norman, who had sat silently listening.

The sound of the door-bell was the first intimation that Harry's histories had occupied them until long past twelve o'clock.

'Now then!' cried Meta, springing forward, as if intending to meet Flora with the tidings, but checking herself, as if she ought not to be the first. There was a pause. Flora was hearing down-stairs, that Mr. Norman May and another gentleman had arrived; and, while vexed at her own omission, and annoyed at Norman bringing friends without waiting for permission, she was yet prepared to be courteous and amiable. She entered, in her rich black watered silk, deeply trimmed with lace, and with silver ornaments in her dark hair, so graceful and distinguished looking, that Harry stood suspended, hesitating, for an instant, whether he beheld his own sister, especially as she made a dignified inclination towards him, offering her hand to Norman, as she said, ' Meta has told you—' but there she broke off, exclaiming, ' Ha! is it possible! No, surely it cannot be—'

' Miss Walkinghame?' said the sailor, who had felt at home with her at the first word, and she flew into his great rough arms.

' Harry! this is dear Harry! our own dear sailor come back,' cried she, as her husband stood astonished; and, springing towards him, she put Harry's hand into his—' My brother Harry! our dear lost one.'

' Your—brother—Harry,' slowly pronounced George, as he instinctively gave the grasp of greeting—' your brother that was lost? Upon my word,' as the matter dawned fully on him, and he became eager, ' I am very glad to see you. I never was more rejoiced in my life.'

' When did you come? Have you been at home?' asked Flora.

' I came home yesterday—Mary wrote to tell you.'

' Poor dear old Mary! There's a lesson against taking a letter on trust. I thought it would be all Cocksmoor, and would wait for a quiet moment! How good to come to me so soon, you dear old shipwrecked mariner.'

' I was forced to come to report myself,' said Harry, ' or I could not have come away from my father so soon.'

The usual questions and their sad answers ensued, and while Flora talked to Harry, fondly holding his hand, Norman and Meta explained the history to George, who no sooner comprehended it, than he opined it must have been a horrid nuisance, and that Harry was a gallant fellow; then striking him over the shoulder, welcomed him home with all his kind heart, told him he was proud to receive him, and falling into a state of rapturous hospitality, rang the bell, and wanted to order all sorts of eatables and drinkables, but was sadly baffled to find him already satisfied.

There was more open joy than even at home, and Flora was supremely happy, as she sat between her brothers, listening and inquiring till far past one o'clock, when she perceived poor George dozing off, awakened every now and then by a great nod, and casting a wishful glance of resigned remonstrance, as if to appeal against sitting up all night.

The meeting at breakfast was a renewal of pleasure. Flora was proud and happy in showing off her little girl, a model baby, as she called her, a perfect doll for quietness, so that she could be brought in at Family Prayers; 'and,' said Flora, 'I am the more glad that she keeps no one away, because we can only have Evening Prayers on Sunday. It is a serious thing to arrange for such a household.'

'She is equal to anything,' said George.

The long file of servants marched in, George read soncrously, and Flora rose from her knees, highly satisfied at the impression produced upon her brothers.

'I like to have the baby with us at breakfast,' she said; 'it is the only time of day when we can be sure of seeing anything of her, and I like her nurse to have some respite. Do you think her grown, Norman?'

'Not very much,' said Norman, who thought her more inanimate and like a pretty little waxen toy, than when he had last seen her. 'Is she not rather pale?'

'London makes children pale. I shall soon take her home to acquire a little colour. You must know Sir Henry has bitten us with his yachting tastes, and as soon as we can leave London, we are going to spend six weeks with the Walkinghames at Ryde, and rival you, Harry I think Miss Leonora will be better at home, and so we must leave her there. Lodgings and irregularities don't suit people of her age.'

'Does home mean Stoneborough?' asked Norman.

'No. Old nurse has one of her deadly prejudices against Preston, and I would not be responsible for the consequences of shutting them up in the same nursery. Margaret would be distracted between them. No, miss, you shall make her a visit every day, and be fondled by your grandpapa.'

George began a conversation with Harry on nautical matters, and Norman tried to discover how Meta liked the yachting project, and found her prepared to think it charming. Hopes were expressed that Harry might be at Portsmouth, and a quantity of gay scheming ensued, with reiterations of the name of Walkinghame, while Norman had a sense of being wrapped in some grey mist, excluding him from participation in their enjoyments, and condemned his own temper, as frivolous, for being thus excited to discontent.

Presently he heard George insisting that he and Harry should return in time for the evening party; and, on beginning to refuse, was amazed to find Harry's only objection was on the score of lack of uniform.

'I don't want you in one, sir,' said Flora.

'I have only one coat in the world, besides this,' continued Harry, 'and that is all over tar.'

'George will see to that,' said Flora. 'Don't you think you would be welcome in matting, with an orange cowry round your neck?'

Norman, however, took a private opportunity of asking Harry if he was aware of what he was undertaking, and what kind of people they should meet.

'All English people behave much the same in a room,' said Harry, as if all society, provided it was not cannibal, were alike to him.

'I should have thought you would prefer finding out Forder in his chambers, or going to one of the theatres.'

'As you please,' said Harry; 'but Flora seems to want us, and I should rather like to see what sort of company she keeps.'

Since Harry was impervious to shyness, Norman submitted, and George took them to a wonderworker in cloth, who undertook that full equipments should await the young gentleman. Harry next despatched his business at the Admiralty, and was made very happy by tidings of his friend Owen's safe arrival in America.

Thence the brothers went to Eton, where home letters had been more regarded; and Dr. May having written to secure a holiday for the objects of their visit, they were met at the station by the two boys. Hector's red face and prominent light eyebrows were instantly recognised; but, as to Tom, Harry could hardly believe that the little, dusty, round-backed grub he had left, had been transformed into the well-made gentlemanlike lad before him, peculiarly trim and accurate in dress, even to the extent of as much foppery as Eton taste permitted.

Ten minutes had not passed before Tom, taking a survey of the new comer, began to exclaim at Norman, for letting him go about such a figure; and, before they knew what was doing, they had all been conducted into the shop of the 'only living man who knew how to cut hair.' Laughing and good-natured, Harry believed his hair was 'rather long,' allowed himself to be seated, and to be divested of a huge superfluous mass of sun-dried curls, which Tom, particularly resenting that 'rather long,' kept on taking up, and unrolling from their tight rings, to measure the number of inches.

'That is better,' said he, as they issued from the shop; 'but, as to that coat of yours, the rogue who made it should never make another. Where could you have picked it up?'

'At a shop at Auckland,' said Harry, much amused.

'Kept by a savage?' said Tom, to whom it was no laughing matter. 'See that seam!'

'Have done, May!' exclaimed Hector. 'He will think you a tailor's apprentice!'

'Or worse,' said Norman. 'Rivers's tailor kept all strictures to himself.'

Tom muttered that he only wanted Harry to be fit to be seen by the fellows.

'The fellows are not such asses as you!' cried Hector. 'You don't deserve that he should come to see you. If my—'

There poor Hector broke off. If his own only brother had been walking beside him, how would he not have felt? They had reached their tutor's house, and, opening his own door, he made an imploring sign to Harry to enter with him. On the table lay a letter from Margaret, and another which Harry had written to him from Auckland.

'Oh, Harry, you were with him,' he said; 'tell me all about him!'

And he established himself, with his face hidden on the table, uttering nothing, except 'Go on,' whenever Harry's voice failed in the narration. When something was said of 'all for the best,' he burst out, 'He might say so. I suppose one ought to think so. But is not it hard, when I had nobody but him? And there was Maplewood; and I might have been so happy there, with him and Margaret.'

'They say nothing could have made Margaret well,' said Harry.

'I don't care; he would have married her all the same, and we should have made her so happy at Maplewood. I hate the place! I wish it were at Jericho!'

'You are captain of the ship now,' said Harry, 'and you must make the best of it.'

'I can't. It will never be home. Home is with Margaret, and the rest of them.'

'So Alan said he hoped you would make it; and you are just like one of us, you know.'

'What's the use of that, when Captain Gordon will not let me go near you. Taking me to that abominable Maplewood last Easter, with half the house shut up, and all horrid! And he is as dry as a stick!'

'The Captain!' cried Harry, angrily. 'There's not a better

Captain to sail with in the whole navy, and your brother would be the first to tell you so! I'm not discharged yet, Hector— you had better look out what you say!'

'May be, he is the best to sail with, but that is not being the best to live with,' said the heir of Maplewood, disconsolately. 'Alan himself always said he never knew what home was, till he got to your father and Margaret.'

'So will you,' said Harry; 'why, my father is your master, or whatever you may call it.'

'No, Captain Gordon is my guardian.'

'Eh! what's become of the will, then?'

'What will?' cried Hector. 'Did Alan make one, after all?'

'Aye. At Valparaiso, he had a touch of fever; I went ashore to nurse him, to a merchant's, who took us in for love of our Scottish blood. Mr. Ernescliffe made a will there, and left it in his charge.'

'Do you think he made Dr. May my guardian?'

'He asked me whether I thought he would dislike it, and I told him, no.'

'That's right!' cried Hector. 'That's like dear old Alan! I shall get back to the Doctor and Margaret, after all. Mind you write to the Captain, Harry!'

Hector was quite inspirited and ready to return to the others, but Harry paused to express a hope that he did not let Tom make such a fool of himself as he had done to-day.

'Not he,' said Hector. 'He is liked as much as any one in the house—he has been five times sent up for good. See there in the Eton list! He is a real clever fellow.'

'Aye, but what's the good of all that, if you let him be a puppy?'

'Oh, he'll be cured. A fellow that has been a sloven always is a puppy for a bit,' said Hector, philosophically.

Norman was meantime taking Tom to task for these same airs, and, hearing it was from the desire to see his brother respectable —Stoneborough men never cared for what they looked like, and he must have Harry do himself credit.

'You need not fear,' said Norman. 'He did not require Eton to make him a gentleman. How now? Why, Tom, old man, you are not taking that to heart? That's all over long ago.'

For that black spot in his life had never passed out of the lad's memory, and it might be from the lurking want of self-respect that there was about him so much of self-assertion, in attention to trifles. He was very reserved, and no one except Norman had ever found the way to anything like confidence, and Norman had vexed him by the proposal he had made in the holidays.

He made no answer, but stood looking at Norman with an odd undecided gaze.

'Well, what now, old fellow?' said Norman, half fearing '*that*' might not be absolutely over. 'One would think you were not glad to see Harry.'

'I suppose he has made you all the more set upon that mad notion of yours,' said Tom.

'So far as making me feel that *that* part of the world has a strong claim on us,' replied Norman.

'I'm sure you don't look as if you found your pleasure in it,' cried Tom.

'Pleasure is not what I seek,' said Norman.

'What is the matter with you?' said Tom. 'You said I did not seem rejoiced—you look worse, I'm sure.' Tom put his arm on Norman's shoulder, and looked solicitously at him—demonstrations of affection very rare with him.

'I wonder which would really make you happiest, to have your own way, and go to these black villains?—'

'Remember, that but for others who have done so, Harry—'

'Pshaw,' said Tom, rubbing some invisible dust from his coat sleeve. 'If it would keep you at home, I would say I never would hear of doctoring.'

'I thought you had said so.'

'What's the use of my coming here, if I'm to be a country doctor?'

'I have told you I do not mean to victimize you. If you have a distaste to it, there's an end of it—I am quite ready.'

Tom gave a great sigh. 'No,' he said, 'if I must, I must; I don't mind the part of it that you do. I only hate the name of it, and the being tied down to a country place like that, while you go out thousands of miles off to these savages; but if it is the only thing to content you, I won't stand in your way. I can't bear your looking disconsolate.'

'Don't think yourself bound, if you really dislike the profession.'

'I don't,' said Tom. 'It is my free choice. If it were not for horrid sick people, I should like it.'

Promising! it must be confessed!

Perhaps Tom had expected Norman to brighten at once, but it was a fallacious hope. The gaining his point involved no pleasant prospect, and the young brother's moody devotion to him, suggested scruples whether he ought to exact the sacrifice, though, in his own mind, convinced that it was Tom's vocation; and knowing that would give him many of the advantages of an eldest son.

Eton fully justified Hector's declaration that it would not regard the cut of Harry's coat. The hero of a lost ship and savage isle, was the object of universal admiration and curiosity, and inestimable were the favours conferred by Hector and Tom in giving introductions to him, till he had shaken hands with half the school, and departed amid deafening cheers.

In spite of Harry, the day had been long and heavy to Norman, and though he chid himself for his depression, he shrank from the sight of Meta and Sir Henry Walkinghame together, and was ready to plead an aching head as an excuse for not appearing at the evening party; but, besides that this might attract notice, he thought himself bound to take care of Harry in so new a world, where the boy must be at a great loss.

'I say, old June,' cried a voice at his door, 'are you ready?'

'I have not begun dressing yet. Will you wait?'

'Not I. The fun is beginning.'

Norman heard the light foot scampering down-stairs, and prepared to follow, to assume the protection of him.

Music sounded as Norman left his room, and he turned aside to avoid the stream of company flowing up the flower-decked stairs, and made his way into the rooms through Flora's boudoir. He was almost dazzled by the bright lights, and the gay murmurs of the brilliant throng. Young ladies with flowers and velvet streamers down their backs, old ladies portly and bejewelled, gentlemen looking civil, abounded wherever he turned his eyes. He could see Flora's graceful head bending as she received guest after guest, and the smile with which she answered congratulations on her brother's return; but Harry he did not so quickly perceive, and he was trying to discover in what corner he might have hidden himself, when Meta stood beside him, asking whether their Eton journey had prospered, and how poor Hector was feeling at Harry's return?

'Where is Harry?' asked Norman. 'Is he not rather out of his element?'

'No, indeed,' said Meta, smiling. 'Why, he is the lion of the night!'

'Poor fellow, how he must hate it!'

'Come this way, into the front room. There, look at him—is it not nice to see him, so perfectly simple and at his ease, neither shy nor elated? And what a fine-looking fellow he is!'

Meta might well say so. The trim, well-knit broad-chested form, the rosy embrowned honest face, the shining light-brown curly locks, the dancing well-opened blue-eyes, and merry hearty smile showed to the best advantage, in array that even Tom would not have spurned, put on with naval neatness; and his attitude and manner were so full of manly ease, that it was no wonder that every eye rested on him with pleasure. Norman smiled at his own mistake, and asked who were the lady and gentleman conversing with him? Meta mentioned one of the most distinguished of English names, and shared his amusement in seeing Harry talking to them with the same frank unembarrassed ease, as when he had that morning shaken hands with their son, in the capacity of Hector Ernescliffe's fag. No one present inspired him with a tithe of the awe he felt for a post-captain—it was simply a pleasant assembly of good-natured folks, glad to welcome home a battered sailor, and of pretty girls, for whom he had a sailor's admiration, but without forwardness or presumption—all in happy grateful simplicity.

'I suppose you cannot dance?' said Flora, to him.

'I!' was Harry's interjection; and while she was looking round for a partner to whom to present him, he had turned to the young daughter of his new acquaintance, and had her on his arm, unconscious that George had been making his way to her.

Flora was somewhat uneasy, but the mother was looking on smiling, and expressed her delight in the young midshipman; and Mrs. Rivers, while listening gladly to his praises, watched heedfully, and was reassured to see that dancing was as natural to him as everything else; his steps were light as a feather, his movement all freedom and joy, without being boisterous, and his boyish chivalry as pretty a sight as any one could wish to see.

If the rest of the world enjoyed their dances a quarter as much as did 'Mr. May,' they were enviable people, and he contributed not a little to their pleasure, if merely by the sight of his blithe freshness, and spirited simplicity, as well as the general sympathy with his sister's joy, and the interest in his adventures. He would have been a general favourite, if he had been far less personally engaging; as it was, every young lady was in raptures at dancing with him, and he did his best to dance with them all; and to try to stir up Norman, who, after Meta had been obliged to leave him, and go to act her share of the part of hostess, had disposed of himself against a wall, where he might live out the night.

'Ha! June! what makes you stand sentry there? Come and dance, and have some of the fun! Some of those girls are the nicest partners in the world. There's that Lady Alice Something, with the dangling things in her hair, sitting down now—famous at a polka. Come along, I'll introduce you—it will do you good.'

'I know nothing of dancing,' said Norman, beginning to apprehend that he might be dragged off, as often he had been, to cricket or foot-ball, and by much the same means.

'Comes by nature, when you hear the music. Ha! what a delicious polka! Come along, or I must be off! She will be waiting for me, and she is the second prettiest girl here! Come!'

'I have been trying to make something of him, Harry,' said the ubiquitous Flora, 'but I don't know whether it is *mauvaise honte*, or headache.'

'I see! Poor old June!' cried Harry. 'I'll get you an ice at once, old fellow! Nothing like one for setting a man going!'

Before Norman could protest, Harry had flown off.

'Flora,' asked Norman, 'is—are the Walkinghames here?'

'Yes. Don't you see Sir Henry. That fine-looking man with the black moustache. I want you to know him. He is a great admirer of your prize poem, and of Dr. Spencer.'

Harry returning, administered his ice, and then darted off to excuse himself to his partner, by explanations about his brother, whom everybody must have heard of, as he was the cleverest fellow living, and had written the best prize poem ever heard at Oxford. He firmly believed Norman a much greater lion than himself.

Norman was forced to leave his friendly corner to dispose of the glass of his ice, and thus encountered Miss Rivers, of whom Sir Henry was asking questions about a beautiful collection of cameos, which Flora had laid out as a company trap.

'Here is Norman May,' said Meta—'he knows them better than I do. Do you remember which of these is the head of Diana, Norman?'

Having set the two gentlemen to discuss them, she glided away on fresh hospitable duties, while Norman repeated the comments that he had so enjoyed hearing from poor Mr. Rivers, hoping he was, at least, sparing Meta some pain, and wondering that Flora should have risked hurting her feelings by exposing these treasures to the general gaze.

If Norman were wearied by Sir Henry, it was his own fault, for the baronet was a very agreeable person, who thought a first-class man worth cultivation, so that the last half hour might have compensated for all the rest, if conversation were always the test.

'Why, Meta!' cried Harry, coming up to her, 'you have not once danced! We are a sort of brother and sister, to be sure, but that is no hindrance, is it?'

'No,' said Meta, smiling, 'thank you, Harry, but you must find some one more worthy. I do not dance this season; at least, not in public. When we get home, who knows what we may do?'

'You don't dance! Poor little Meta! And you don't go out! What a pity!'

'I had rather not work quite so hard,' said Meta. 'Think what good fortune I had by staying at home last night!'

'I declare!' exclaimed Harry, bewitched by the beaming congratulation of her look, 'I can't imagine why Norman had said you had turned into a fine lady! I can't see a bit of it!'

'Norman said I had turned into a fine lady!' repeated Meta. 'Why?'

'Never mind! *I* don't think so; you are just like papa's hummingbird, as you always were, not a bit more of a fine lady than any girl here, and I'm sure papa would say so. Only old June had got a bad headache, and is in one of his old dumps, such as I hoped he had left off. But he can't help it, poor fellow, and he will come out of it, by-and-by—so never mind. Hollo; why people are going away already. There's that girl without any one to hand her down-stairs.'

Away ran Harry, and presently the brothers and sisters gathered round the fire—George declaring that he was glad that nuisance was so well over, and Harry exclaiming, 'Well done, Flora! It was capital fun! I never saw a lot of prettier or more good-natured people in my life. If I am at home for the Stoneborough ball, I wonder whether my father will let me go to it.'

This result of Harry's successful *début* in high life struck his sister and Norman as so absurd that both laughed.

'What's the matter now?' asked Harry.

'Your comparing Flora's party to a Stoneborough ball,' said Norman.

'It is all the same, isn't it?' said Harry. 'I'm sure you are equally disgusted at both!'

'Much you know about it,' said Flora, patting him gaily. 'I'm not going to put conceit in that lion head of yours, but you were as good as an Indian prince to my party. Do you know to whom you have been talking so coolly?'

'Of course. You see, Norman, it is just as I told you. All civilized people are just alike when they get into a drawing-room.'

'Harry takes large views of the *Genus homo*,' Norman exerted himself to say. 'Being used to the black and brown species, he takes little heed of the lesser varieties.'

'It is enough for him that he does not furnish the entertainment in another way,' said Flora. 'But, good-night. Meta, you look tired.'

CHAPTER XIX.

'Let none, henceforward, shrink from daring dreams,
For earnest hearts shall find their dreams fulfilled.'—FOUQUÉ.

'I HAVE it!' began Harry, as he came down to breakfast. 'I
don't know how I came to forget it. The will was to be sent
home to Mr. Mackintosh's English partner. I'll go and overhaul
him this very morning. They won't mind my coming by a later
train, when there is such a reason.'

'What is his name? Where shall you find him?' asked Flora.

'I can't be sure; but you've a Navy List of that sort of cattle,
have not you, Flora? I'll hunt him up.'

Flora supposed he meant a Directory; and all possible South
American merchants having been overlooked, and the Mackin-
toshes selected, he next required a chart of London, and wanted
to attempt self-navigation, but was forced to accept of George's
brougham and escort; Flora would not trust him otherwise;
and Norman was obliged to go to Oxford at once, hurrying off
to his train before breakfast was over.

Flora might have trusted Harry alone. George contributed no
more than the dignity of his presence; and, indeed, would have
resigned the pursuit at the first blunder about the firm; and still
more when the right one had been found, but the partner proved
crusty, and would not believe that any such document was in his
hands. George was consenting to let it rest till Mr. Mackintosh
could be written to; but Harry, outrunning his management, and
regardless of rebuffs, fairly teased the old gentleman into a search,
as the only means of getting rid of the troublesome sailor.

In the midst of George's civil regrets at the fruitless trouble
they were causing, forth came a bundle of papers, and forth from
the bundle fell a packet, on which Harry pounced as he read,
'Will of Alan Halliday Ernescliffe, Esquire, of Maplewood, Shropshire, Lieutenant in H.M.S. Alcestis,' and, in the corner, the
executors' names, Captain John Gordon, of H.M.S. Alcestis; and
Richard May, Esquire, M.D., Market Stoneborough.

As if in revenge, the prudent merchant would not be induced
to entrust him with the document, saying he could not give it
up till he had heard from the executors, and had been certified
of the death of the testator. He withstood both the angry
gentlemen, who finally departed in a state of great resentment—
Harry declaring that the old landlubber would not believe that
he was his own father's son; and Mr. Rivers, no less incensed,

that the House of Commons had been insulted in his person, because he did not carry all before him.

Flora laughed at their story, and told them that she suspected that the old gentleman was in the right; and she laid plans for having Harry to teach them yachting at Ryde, while Harry declared he would have nothing to do with such trumpery.

Harry found his home in a sort of agony of expectation, for his non-arrival at the time expected had made his first appearance seem like an unsubstantial illusion, though Dr. May, or Mary and Aubrey, had been at the station at the coming in of each train. Margaret had recovered the effects of the first shock, and the welcome was far more joyous than the first had been, with the mixed sensations that were now composed, and showed little, outwardly, but gladness.

Dr. May took Flora's view of the case, and declared that, if Harry had brought home the will, he should not have opened it without his co-executor. So he wrote to the Captain, while Harry made the most of his time in learning his sisters over again. He spent a short time alone with Margaret every morning, patiently and gently allowing himself to be recalled to the sad recollections that were all the world to her. He kept Ethel and Mary merry with his droll desultory comments; he made Blanche keep up her dancing; and taught Gertrude to be a thorough little romp. As to Dr. May, his patients never were so well or so cheerful, till Dr. Spencer and Ethel suspected that the very sight of his looks brightened them—how could they help it? Dr. Spencer was as happy as a king in seeing his friend, freed from the heavy weight on his spirits; and, truly, it was goodly to watch his perfect look of content, as he leant on his lion-faced boy's arm, and walked down to the Minster, whither it seemed to have become possible to go on most evenings. Good Dr. May was no musician, but Mr. Wilmot could not regret certain tones that now and then burst out in the chanting, from the very bottom of a heart that assuredly sang with the full melody of thankfulness, whatever the voice might do.

Captain Gordon not only wrote but came to Stoneborough, whence Harry was to go with him to the court-martial, at Portsmouth.

The girls wondered that, after writing with so much warmth and affection, both of and to Harry, he met him without any demonstration of feeling; and his short peremptory manner removed all surprise that poor Hector had been so forlorn with him at Maplewood, and turned, with all his heart, to Dr. May. They were especially impressed at the immediate subsidence of all Harry's noise and nonsense, as if the drawing-room had been the quarter-deck of the Alcestis.

'And yet,' said Margaret, 'Harry will not hear a single word in dispraise of him. I do believe he loves him with all his heart.'

'I think,' said Ethel, 'that in a strong character, there is an exulting fear in looking up to a superior, in whose justice there is perfect reliance. It is a germ of the higher feeling.'

'I believe you are right,' said Margaret; 'but it is a serious thing for a man to have so little sympathy with those below him. You see how Hector feels it, and I now understand how it told upon Alan, and how papa's warmth was like a surprise to him.'

'Because Captain Gordon had to be a father to them, and that is more than a captain. I should not wonder if there were more similarity and fellow-feeling between him and Harry than there could be with either of them. Harry, though he has all papa's tenderness, is of a rougher sort that likes to feel itself mastered. Poor Hector! I wonder if he is to be given back to us.'

'Do you know—when—whether they will find out this morning?' said Margaret, catching her dress nervously, as she was moving away.

'Yes, I believe so. I was not to have told you, but—'

'There is no reason that it should do me any harm,' said Margaret, almost smiling, and looking as if she was putting a restraint on something she wished to say. 'Go down, dear Ethel—Aubrey will be waiting for you.'

Ethel went down to the difficult task of hearing Aubrey's lessons, while Harry was pretending to write to Mrs. Arnott, but, in reality, teaching Gertrude the parts of a ship, occasionally acting mast, for her to climb.

By-and-by, Dr. May came in. 'Margaret not down-stairs yet?' he said.

'She is dressed, but will not come down till the evening,' said Ethel.

'I'll go to her. She will be pleased. Come up, presently, Ethel. Or, where's Richard?'

'Gone out,' said Harry. 'What, is it anything left to her?'

'The best, the best!' said Dr. May. 'Ethel, listen—twenty thousand, to build and endow a Church for Cocksmoor!'

No need to bid Ethel listen. She gave a sort of leap in her chair, then looked almost ready to faint.

'My dear child,' said her father, 'this *is* your wish. I give you joy, indeed I do!'

Ethel drew his arm round her, and leant against him.

'My wish! my wish!' she repeated, as if questioning the drift of the words.

'I'm glad it is found!' cried Harry. 'Now I know why he talked of Cocksmoor, and seemed to rest in planning for it. You will mind the roof is as he said.'

'You must talk to Dr. Spencer about that,' said Dr. May. 'The Captain means to leave it entirely in our hands.'

'Dear Alan!' exclaimed Ethel. 'My wish! O yes, but how gained? Yet, Cocksmoor with a Church! I don't know how to be glad enough, and yet—'

'You shall read the sentence,' said Dr. May. '"In testimony of thankfulness for mercy vouchsafed to him here—" poor dear boy!'

'What does the Captain say?' asked Harry.

'He is rather astounded, but he owns that the estate can bear it, for old Halliday had saved a great deal, and there will be more before Hector comes of age.'

'And Hector?'

'Yes, we get him back. I am fellow-trustee with Captain Gordon; and as to personal guardianship, I fancy the Captain found he could not make the boy happy, and thinks you no bad specimen of our training.'

'Famous!' cried Harry. 'Hector will hurrah now! Is that all?'

'Except legacies to Captain Gordon, and some Scottish relations. But poor Margaret ought to hear it. Ethel, don't be long in coming.'

With all Ethel's reputation for bluntness, it was remarkable how her force of character made her always called for whenever there was the least dread of a scene.

She turned abruptly from Harry; and, going outside the window, tried to realize and comprehend the tidings, but all she could have time to discover was, that Alan's memory was dearer to her than ever, and she was obliged to hasten up-stairs.

Her father quitted the room by one door, as she entered by the other; she believed that it was to hide his emotion, but Margaret's fair wan face was beaming with the sweetest of congratulating smiles.

'I thought so,' she said, as Ethel came in. 'Dear Ethel, are you not glad?'

'I think I am,' said Ethel, putting her hands to her brow.

'You think!' exclaimed Margaret, as if disappointed.

'I beg your pardon,' said Ethel, with quivering lip. 'Dear Margaret, I am glad—don't you believe I am; but, somehow, it is harder to deal with joy than grief. It confuses one. Dear Alan—and then to have been set on it so long—to have prayed so for it, and to have it come in this way—by your—'

'Nay, Ethel, had he come home, it was his great wish to have done it. He used to make projects when he was here, but he

would not let me tell you, lest he should find duties at Maplewood—whereas this would have been his pleasure.'

'Dear Alan!' repeated Ethel. 'If you are so kind, so dear as
to be glad, Margaret, I think I shall be so presently.'

Margaret almost grudged the lack of the girlish outbreak of
rejoicing which would once have forgotten everything in the
ecstasy of the fulfilled vision. It did not seem to be what Alan
had intended; he had figured to himself unmixed joy, and she
wanted to see it, and something of the wayward impatience of
weakness throbbed at her heart, as Ethel paced the room, and
disappeared in her own curtained recess.

Presently she came back, saying, ' You are sure you are glad?'

'It would be strange, if I were not,' said Margaret. 'See,
Ethel, here are blessings springing up from what I used to think
had served for nothing but to bring him pain and grief. I am
so thankful that he could express his desire, and so grateful to
dear Harry for bringing it to light. How much better it is than
I ever thought it could be! He has been spared disappointment,
and surely the good that he will have done will follow him.'

'And you?' said Ethel, sadly.

'I shall lie here and wait,' said Margaret. 'I shall see the
plans, and hear all about it; and, oh!' her eyes lighted up,
'perhaps, some day, I may hear the bell.'

Richard's tap interrupted them. 'Had he heard?'

'I have.' The deepened colour in his cheek betrayed how
much he felt, as he cast an anxious glance towards Margaret
—an inquiring one on Ethel.

'She is so pleased,' was all Ethel could say.

'I thought she would be,' said Richard, approaching. 'Captain
Gordon seemed quite vexed that no special token of remembrance
was left to her.'

Margaret smiled in a peculiar way. 'If he only knew how
glad I am there was not.'

And Ethel knew that the Church was his token to Margaret,
and that any 'fading frail memorial' would have lessened the
force of the signification.

Ethel could speak better to her brother than to her sister.
'O Richard! Richard! Richard!' she cried, and a most unusual
thing with both, she flung her arms round his neck. 'It is
come at last! If it had not been for you, this would never
have been. How little likely it seemed, that dirty day, when
I talked wildly, and you checked me!'

'You had faith and perseverance,' said Richard, 'or—'

'You are right,' said Margaret, as Ethel was about to disclaim.
'It was Ethel's steadiness that brought it before Alan's mind,

If she had yielded, when we almost wished it, in the time of the distress about Mrs. Green, I do believe that all would have died away!'

'I didn't keep steady—I was only crazy. You and Ritchie and Mr. Wilmot—' said Ethel, half-crying; then, as if unable to stay, she exclaimed, with a sort of petulance, 'And there's Harry playing all sorts of rigs with Aubrey! I shan't get any more sense out of him to-day!'

And away she rushed to the wayfaring dust of her life of labour, to find Aubrey and Daisy half-way up the tulip tree, and Harry mischievously unwilling to help them down again, assuring her that such news deserved a holiday, and that she was growing a worse Tartar than Miss Winter. She had better let the poor children alone, put on her bonnet, and come with him to tell Mr. Wilmot.

Whereat Ethel was demurring, when Dr. May came forth, and declared he should take her himself.

Poor Mr. Wilmot laboured under a great burthen of gratitude, which no one would receive from him. Dr. May and Ethel repudiated thanks almost with terror; and, when he tried them with the Captain, he found very doubtful approval of the whole measure, so that Harry alone was a ready acceptant of a full meed of acknowledgment for his gallant extraction of the will.

No one was more obliged to him than Hector Ernescliffe, who wrote to Margaret that it would be very jolly to come *home* again, and that he was delighted that the Captain could not hinder either that or Cocksmoor Church. 'And as to Maplewood, I shall not hate it so much if that happens which I hope will happen.' Of which oracular sentence Margaret could make nothing.

The house of May felt more at their ease when the uncongenial Captain had departed, although he carried off Harry with him. There was the better opportunity for a tea-drinking consultation with Dr. Spencer and Mr. Wilmot, when Margaret lay on her sofa, looking better than for months past, and taking the keenest interest in every arrangement.

Dr. Spencer, whose bright eyes glittered at every mention of the subject, assumed that he was to be the architect, while Dr. May was assuring him that it was a maxim that no one unpaid could be trusted; and when he talked of beautiful German churches with pierced spires, declared that the building must not make too large a hole in the twenty thousand, at the expense of future curates, because Richard was the first.

'I'll be prudent, Dick,' said Dr. Spencer. 'Trust me not to rival the Minster.'

'We shall find work next for you there,' said Mr. Wilmot.

'Aye, we shall have May out of his family packing-box before many years are over his head.'

'Don't mention it,' said Dr. May; 'I know what I exposed myself to in bringing Wilmot here.'

'Yes,' said Dr. Spencer, 'we shall put you in the van when we attack the Corporation pen.'

'I shall hold by the good old cause. As if the galleries had not been there before you were born!'

'As if poor people had a right to sit in their own Church!' said Ethel.

'*Sit*, you may well say,' said Mr. Wilmot. 'As if any one could do otherwise, with those ingenious traps for hindering kneeling.'

'Well, well, I know the people must have room,' said Dr. May, cutting short several further attacks which he saw impending.

'Yes, you would like to build another blue gallery, blocking up another window, and with Richard May and Christopher Tomkins, Churchwardens, on it, in orange-coloured letters—the Rivers' colours. No disrespect to your father, Miss May, but, as a general observation, it is a property of Town Councillors to be conservative only where they ought not.'

'I brought you here to talk of building a Church, not of pulling one to pieces.'

Poor Dr. May, he knew it was inevitable and quite right, but his affectionate heart and spirit of perpetuity, which had an association connected with every marble cloud, green baize pew, and square-headed panel, anticipated tortures in the general sweep, for which his ecclesiastical taste and sense of propriety would not soon compensate.

Margaret spared his feelings by bringing the Cocksmoor subject back again; Dr. Spencer seemed to comprehend the ardour with which she pressed it on, as if it were very near her heart that there should be no delay. He said he could almost promise her that the first stone should be laid before the end of the summer, and she thanked him in her own warm sweet way, hoping that it would be while Hector and Harry were at home.

Harry soon returned, having gone through the Court Martial with the utmost credit, been patronized by Captain Gordon in an unheard-of manner, asked to dine with the Admiral, and promised to be quickly afloat again. Ere many days had passed, he was appointed to one of the finest vessels in the fleet, commanded by a captain to whom Captain Gordon had introduced him, and who 'seemed to have taken a fancy to him,' as he said. The Bucephalus, now the object of his pride, was refitting, and his sisters hoped to see a good deal of him before he should again sail. Besides, Flora would be at Ryde before the end of July.

It was singular that Ethel's vision should have been fulfilled simultaneously with Flora's having obtained a position so far beyond what could have been anticipated.

She was evidently extremely happy and valuable, much admired and respected, and with full exercise for the energy and cleverness, which were never more gratified than by finding scope for action. Her husband was devotedly attached to her, and was entirely managed by her; and though her good judgment kept her from appearing visibly in matters not pertaining to her own sphere, she was, in fact, his understanding. She read, listened, and thought for him, imbued him with her own views, and composed his letters for him; ruling his affairs both political and private, and undeniably making him fill a position which, without her, he would have left vacant; nor was there any doubt that he was far happier for finding himself of consequence, and being no longer left a charge upon his own hands. He seemed fully to suffice to her as a companion, although she was so far superior in power; for it was, perhaps, her nature to love best that which depended upon her, and gave her a sense of exercising protection; as she had always loved Margaret better than Ethel.

'Mrs. Rivers was an admirable woman.' So every one felt, and her youthful beauty and success in the fashionable world, made her qualities, as a wife and mistress of a household, the more appreciated. She never set aside her religious habits or principles, was an active member of various charitable associations, and found her experience of the Stoneborough Ladies' Committee applicable among far greater names. Indeed, Lady Leonora thought dear Flora Rivers' only fault, her over strictness, which encouraged Meta in the same, but there were points that Flora could not have yielded on any account, without failing in her own eyes.

She made time for everything, and though, between business and fashion, she seemed to undertake more than mortal could accomplish, it was all effected, and excellently. She did, indeed, sigh over the briefness of the time that she could bestow on her child or on home correspondence, and declared that she should rejoice in rest; but, at the same time, her achievements were a positive pleasure to her.

Meta, in the meantime, had been living passively on the most affectionate terms with her brother and sister, and though often secretly yearning after the dear old father, whose darling she had been, and longing for power of usefulness, she took it on trust that her present lot had been ordered for her, and was thankful,

PART II. O O

like the bird of Dr. May's fable, for the pleasures in her path—culling sweet morals, and precious thoughts out of book, painting or concert, occasions for Christian charities in each courtesy of society, and opportunities for cheerful self-denial and submission, whenever any little wish was thwarted.

So Norman said she had turned into a fine lady! It was a sudden and surprising intimation, and made a change in the usually bright and calm current of her thoughts. She was not aware that there had been any alteration in herself, and it was a revelation that set her to examine where she had changed—poor little thing! She was not angry, she did not resent the charge, she took it for granted that, coming from such a source, it must be true and reasonable—and what did it mean? Did they think her too gay, or neglectful of old friends? What had they been saying to Harry about her?

'Ah!' thought Meta, 'I understand it. I am living a life of ease and uselessness, and with his higher aims and nobler purposes, he shrinks from the frivolities among which I am cast. I saw his saddened countenance among our gaieties, and I know that to deep minds there is heaviness in the midst of display. He withdraws from the follies that have no charms for him, and I—ought I to be able to help being amused? I don't seek these things, but, perhaps, I ought to avoid them more than I do—If I could be quite clear what is right, I should not care what effort I made. But I was born to be one of those who have the trial of riches, and such blessed tasks are not my portion. But if he sees the vanities creeping into my heart, I should be grateful for that warning.'

So meditated Meta, as she copied one of her own drawings of the Grange, for her dear old governess, Mrs. Larpent, while each line and tint recalled the comments of her fond amateur father, and the scenery carried her home, in spite of the street sounds, and the scratching of Flora's pen, coursing over note paper. Presently, Sir Henry Walkinghame called, bringing a beautiful bouquet.

'Delicious,' cried Meta. 'See, Flora, it is in good time, for those vases were sadly shabby.'

She began at once to arrange the flowers, a task that seemed what she was born for, and the choice roses and geraniums acquired fresh grace as she placed them in the slender glasses and classic vases; but Flora's discerning eyes perceived some mortification on the part of the gentleman, and, on his departure, playfully reproached Meta for ingratitude.

'Did we not thank him? I thought I did them all due honour, actually using the Dresden bowl.'

'You little wretch! quite insensible to the sentiment of the thing.'

'Sentiment! One would think you had been reading about the language of flowers!'

'Whatever there was, poor Sir Henry did not mean it for the Dresden bowl, or Bohemian glass.'

'Flora! do pray tell me whether you are in fun?'

'You ridiculous child!' said Flora, kissing her earnest forehead, ringing the bell, and gathering up her papers, as she walked out of the room, and gave her notes to the servant.

'What does she mean? Is it play? O no, a hint would be far more like her. But I hope it is nonsense. He is very kind and pleasant, and I should not know what to do.'

Instances of his complaisance towards herself rose before her, so as to excite some warmth and gratitude. Her lonely heart thrilled at the idea of being again the best beloved, and her energetic spirit bounded at the thought of being no longer condemned to a life of idle ease. Still it was too new a light to her to be readily accepted, after she had looked on him so long, merely as a familiar of the house, attentive to her, because she fell to his share, when Flora was occupied. She liked him decidedly; she could possibly do more; but she was far more inclined to dread, than to desire, any disturbance of their present terms of intercourse.

'However,' thought she, 'I must see my way. If he should have any such thing in his head, to go on as we do now would be committing myself, and I will not do that, unless I am sure it is right. O papa! you would settle it for me! But I will have it out with Flora. She will find out what I cannot—how far he is a man for whom one ought to care. I do not think Norman liked him, but then Norman has so keen a sense of the world-touched. I suppose I am that! If any other life did but seem appointed for me, but one cannot tell what is thwarting providential leading, and if this be as good a man as—What would Ethel say? If I could but talk to Dr. May! But Flora I will catch, before I see him again, that I may know how to behave.'

Catching Flora was not the easiest thing in the world, among her multifarious occupations; but Meta was not the damsel to lose an opportunity for want of decision.

Flora saw what was coming, and was annoyed with herself for having given the alarm; but, after all, it must have come some time or other, though she had rather that Meta had been more involved first.

It should be premised that Mrs. Rivers had no notion of the degree of attachment felt by her brother for Meta; she only knew that Lady Leonora had a general distrust of her family, and she felt it a point of honour to promote no dangerous meetings, and to encourage Sir Henry—a connection who would be most valuable, both as conferring importance upon George in the county, and as being himself related to persons of high influence, whose interest might push on her brothers. Preferment for Richard; promotion for Harry; nay, diplomatic appointments for Tom, came floating before her imagination, even while she smiled at her Alnaschar visions.

But the tone of Meta, as she drew her almost forcibly into her room, showed her that she had given a great shock to her basket.

'Flora, if you would only give me a minute, and would tell me—'

'What?' asked Flora, not inclined to spare her blushes.

'Whether, whether you meant anything in earnest?'

'My dear little goose, did no one ever make an innocent joke in their lives before?'

'It was very silly of me,' said Meta; 'but you gave me a terrible fright.'

'Was it so very terrible, poor little bird?' said Flora, in commiseration. 'Well, then, you may safely think of him as a man tame about the house. It was much prettier of you not to appropriate the flowers, as any other damsel would have done.'

'Do you really and truly think—' began Meta; but, from the colour of her cheek, and the timid resolution of her tone, Flora thought it safest not to hear the interrogation, and answered, 'I know what he comes here for—it is only as a refuge from his mother's friend, old Lady Drummond, who would give the world to catch him for her daughters—that's all. Put my nonsense out of your head, and be yourself, my sweet one.'

Flora had never gone so near an untruth, as when she led Meta to believe this was the sole reason. But, after all, what did Flora herself *know* to the contrary?

Meta recovered her ease, and Flora marked, as weeks passed on, that she grew more accustomed to Sir Henry's attentions. A little while, and she would find herself so far bound by the encouragement she had given, that she could not reject him.

'My dear,' said George, 'when do you think of going down to take the baby to the Grange? She looks dull, I think.'

'Really, I think it is hardly worth while to go down *en masse*,' said Flora. 'These last debates may be important, and it is a bad time to quit one's post. Don't you think so?'

'As you please—the train is a great bore.'

'And we will send the baby down the last day before we go

to Ryde, with Preston and Butts to take care of her. We can't spare him to take them down, till we shut up the house. It is so much easier for us to go to Portsmouth from hence.'

The lurking conviction was, that one confidential talk with Ethel, would cause the hummingbird to break the toils that were being wound invisibly round her. Ethel and her father knew nothing of the world, and were so unreasonable in their requirements! Meta would consult them all, and all her scruples would awaken, and perhaps Dr. Spencer might be interrogated on Sir Henry's life abroad, where Flora had a suspicion that gossip had best not be raked up.

Not that she concealed anything positively known to her, or that she was not acting just as she would have done by her own child. She found herself happily married to one whom home notions would have rejected, and she believed Meta would be perfectly happy with a man of decided talent, honour, and unstained character, even though he should not come up to her father's or Ethel's standard.

If Meta were to marry as they would approve, she would have far to seek among 'desirable connections.' Meantime, was not Flora acting with exemplary judgment and self-denial?

So she wrote that she could not come home; Margaret was much disappointed, and so was Meta, who had looked to Ethel to unravel the tangles of her life.

'No, no, little Miss,' said Flora to herself; 'you don't talk to Ethel till your fate is irrevocable. Why, if I had listened to her, I should be thankful to be singing at Mrs. Hoxton's parties at this minute! and, as for herself, look at Norman Ogilvie! No, no, after six weeks' yachting—moonlight, sea, and sympathy— I defy her to rob Sir Henry of his prize! And, with Meta lady of Cocksmoor, even Ethel herself must be charmed!'

CHAPTER XX.

'We barter life for pottage, sell true bliss
For wealth or power, for pleasure or renown:
Thus, Esau-like, our Father's blessing miss,
Then wash with fruitless tears our faded crown.'—CHRISTIAN YEAR.

'PAPA, here is a message from Flora for you,' said Margaret, holding up a letter; 'she wants to know whom to consult about the baby.'

'Ha! what's the matter?'

Margaret read—'Will you ask papa whom I had better call in to see the baby. There does not seem to be anything positively

amiss, but I am not happy about her. There is a sleepiness
about her which I do not understand, and, when roused, she is
fretful, and will not be amused. There is a look in her eyes
which I do not like, and I should wish to have some advice for
her. Lady Leonora recommends Mr. ——, but I always distrust people who are very much the rage, and I shall send for no
one without papa's advice.'

'Let me see!' said Dr. May, startled, and holding out his
hand for the letter.—'A look about the eyes! I shall go up and
see her myself. Why has not she brought her home?'

'It would have been far better,' said Margaret.

'Sleepy and dull! She was as lively a child when they took
her away, as I ever saw. What! is there no more about her?
The letter is crammed with somebody's *fête*—vote of want of
confidence—debate last night. What is she about? She fancies she knows everything, and, the fact is, she knows no more
about infants—I could see that, when the poor little thing was
a day old!'

'Do you think there is cause for fear?' said Margaret,
anxiously.

'I can't tell. With a first child, one can't guess what may
be mamma's fancy, or what may be serious. But Flora is not too
fanciful, and I must see her for my own satisfaction. Let some
one write, and say I will come up to-morrow by the twelve o'clock
train—and mind she opens the letter.'

Dr. May kept his word, and the letter had evidently not been
neglected; for George was watching for him at the station, and
thanked him so eagerly for coming, that Dr. May feared that he
was indeed needed, and inquired anxiously.

'Flora is uneasy about her—she seems heavy, and cries when
she is disturbed,' replied George. 'Flora has not left her to-day,
and hardly yesterday.'

'Have you had no advice for her?'

'Flora preferred waiting till you should come.'

Dr. May made an impatient movement, and thought the way
long, till they were set down in Park Lane. Meta came to meet
them on the stairs, and said that the baby was just the same, and
Flora was in the nursery, and thither they hastily ascended.

'O papa! I am so glad you are come!' said Flora, starting up
from her low seat, beside the cradle.

Dr. May hardly paused to embrace his daughter, and she
anxiously led him to the cradle, and tried to read his expression,
as his eyes fell on the little face, somewhat puffed, but of a waxy
whiteness, and the breathing seeming to come from the lips.

' How long has she been so ?' he asked, in a rapid, professional manner.

' For about two or three hours. She was very fretful before, but I did not like to call in any one, as you were coming. Is it from her teeth ?' said Flora, more and more alarmed by his manner. ' Her complexion is always like that—she cannot bear to be disturbed'—added she, as the child feebly moaned, on Dr. May beginning to take her from her cradle ; but, without attending to the objection, he lifted her up, so that she lay as quietly as before, on his arm. Flora had trusted that hope and confidence would come with him ; but, on the contrary, every lurking misgiving began to rush wildly over her, as she watched his countenance, while he carried his little grand-daughter towards the light, studied her intently, raised her drooping eyelids, and looked into her eyes, scarcely eliciting another moan. Flora dared not ask a question, but looked on with eyes open, as it were, stiffened.

' This is the effect of opium !' were Dr. May's first words, breaking on all with startling suddenness ; but, before any one could speak, he added, ' We must try some stimulant, directly ;' then looking round the room, ' What have you nearest ?'

' Godfrey's cordial, sir,' quickly suggested the nurse.

' Aye—anything to save time—she is sinking for want of the drug that has—' he broke off to apportion the dose, and to hold the child in a position to administer it—Flora tried to give it—the nurse tried—in vain.

' Do not torment it further,' said the Doctor, as Flora would have renewed the trial—' it cannot be done. What have you all been doing ?' cried he, as, looking up, his face changed from the tender compassion with which he had been regarding his little patient, into a look of strong indignation, and one of his sentences of hasty condemnation broke from him, as it would not have done, had Flora been less externally calm. ' I tell you this child has been destroyed with opium !'

They all recoiled ; the father turned fiercely round on the nurse, with a violent exclamation, but Dr. May checked him. ' Hush ! This is no presence for the wrath of man.' The solemn tone seemed to make George shrink into an awestruck quiescence ; he stood motionless and transfixed, as if indeed conscious of some overwhelming presence.

Flora had come near, with an imploring gesture, to take the child in her own arms ; but Dr. May, by a look of authority, prevented it ; for, indeed, it would have been harassing and distressing the poor little sufferer again to move her, as she lay with feeble gasps on his arm.

So they remained, for what space no one knew—not one word was uttered—not a limb moved, and the street noises sounded far off.

Dr. May stooped his head closer to the babe's face, and seemed listening for a breath, as he once more touched the little wrist— he took away his finger, he ceased to listen, he looked up.

Flora gave one cry—not loud, not sharp, but 'an exceeding bitter cry'—she would have moved forward, but reeled, and her husband's arms supported her as she sank into a swoon.

'Carry her to her room,' said Dr. May. 'I will come'—and, when George had borne her away, he kissed the lifeless cheek, and reverently placed the little corpse in the cradle; but, as he rose from doing so, the sobbing nurse exclaimed, 'Oh! sir! oh! sir, indeed, I never did—'

'Never did what?' said Dr. May, sternly.

'I never gave the dear baby anything to do her harm,' cried Preston, vehemently.

'You gave her this,' said Dr. May, pointing to the bottle of Godfrey's Cordial.

He could say no more, for her master was hurrying back into the room. Anger was the first emotion that possessed him, and he hardly gave an answer to Dr. May's question about Flora. 'Meta is with her! Where is that woman? Have you given her up to the police?'

Preston shrieked and sobbed, made incoherent exclamations, and was much disposed to cling to the Doctor.

'Silence!' said Dr. May, lifting his hand, and assuming a tone and manner that awed them both, by reminding them that death was present in the chamber; and, taking his son-in-law out, and shutting the door, he said, in a low voice, 'I believe this is no case for the police—have mercy on the poor woman.'

'Mercy—I'll have no mercy on my child's murderer! You said she had destroyed my child.'

'Ignorantly.'

'I don't care for ignorance! She destroyed her—I'll have justice,' said George, doggedly.

'You shall,' said Dr. May, laying his hand on his arm; 'but it must be investigated, and you are in no state to investigate. Go down-stairs—do not do anything till I come to you.'

His peremptory manner imposed on George, who, nevertheless, turned round as he went, saying, with a fierce glare in his eyes, 'You will not let her escape.'

'No. Go down—be quiet.'

Dr. May returned to Preston, and had to assure her that Mr.

Rivers was not gone to call the police, before he could bring her to any degree of coherence. She regarded him as her only friend, and soon undertook to tell the whole truth, and he perceived that it was, indeed, the truth. She had not known that the cordial was injurious, deeming it a panacea against fretfulness, precious to nurses, but against which ladies always had a prejudice, and, therefore, to be kept secret. Poor little Leonora had been very fretful and uneasy when Flora's many avocations had first caused her to be set aside, and Preston had had recourse to the remedy which, lulling her successfully, was applied with less moderation and judgment than would have been shown by a more experienced person, till gradually the poor child became dependent on it for every hour of rest. When her mother, at last, became aware of her unsatisfactory condition, and spent her time in watching her, the nurse being prevented from continuing her drug, she was, of course, so miserable without it, that Preston had ventured on proposing it, to which Mrs. Rivers had replied with displeasure sufficient to prevent her from declaring how much she had previously given. Preston was in an agony of distress for her little charge, as well as of fear for herself, and could hardly understand what her error had been. Dr. May soon saw that, though not highly principled, her sorrow was sincere, and that she still wept bitterly over the consequences of her treatment, when he told her that she had nothing to fear from the law, and that he would protect her from Mr. Rivers.

Her confession was hardly over, when Meta knocked at the door, pale and frightened. 'Oh! Dr. May, do come to poor Flora! I don't know what to do, and George is in such a state!'

Dr. May made a sound of sorrow and perplexity, and Meta, as she went down before him, asked, in a low, horror-stricken whisper, 'Did Preston really—'

'Not knowingly,' said Dr. May. 'It is the way many children have gone; but I never thought—'

They had come to Flora's dressing-room. Her bed-room door was open, and George was pacing heavily up and down the length of both apartments, fiercely indignant. 'Well!' said he, advancing eagerly on Dr. May, 'has she confessed?'

'But Flora!' said Dr. May, instead of answering him.

Flora lay on her bed, her face hidden on her pillow, only now and then moaning.

'Flora! my poor, poor child!' said her father, bending down to raise her, and taking her hand.

She moved away, so as to bury her face more completely, but there was life in the movement, and he was sufficiently reassured on her situation to be able to attend to George, who was only impatient to rush off to take his revenge. He led him into the outer room, where Meta was waiting, and forced upon his unwilling conviction that it was no case for the law. The child had not been killed by any one dose, but had rather sunk from the want of stimulus, to which she had been accustomed. As to any pity for the woman, George would not hear of it. She was still, in his eyes, the destroyer of his child; and, when he found the law would afford him no vengeance, he insisted that she should be turned out of his house at once.

'George!' called a hollow voice from the next room, and, hurrying back, they saw Flora sitting up, and, as well as trembling limbs allowed, endeavouring to rise to her feet, while burning spots were in her cheeks. 'George, turn me out of the house too! If Preston killed her, I did!' and she gave a ghastly laugh.

George threw his arms round her, and laid her on her bed again, with many fond words, and strength which she had not power to withstand. Dr. May, in the meantime, spoke quickly to Meta, in the doorway. 'She must go. They cannot see her again; but has she any friends in London?'

'I think not.'

'Find out. She must not be sent adrift. Send her to the Grange, if nothing better offers. You must judge.'

He felt that he could confide in Meta's discretion and promptitude, and returned to the parents.

'Is she gone?' said George, in a whisper, which he meant should be unheard by his wife, who had sunk her face in her pillows again.

'Going. Meta is seeing to it.'

'And that woman gets off free!' cried George, 'while my poor little girl—' and, no longer occupied by the hope of retribution, he gave way to an overpowering burst of grief.

His wife did not rouse herself to comfort him, but still lay motionless, excepting for a convulsive movement, that passed over her frame at each sound from him, and her father felt her pulse bound at the same time with corresponding violence, as if each of his deep-drawn sobs were a mortal thrust. Going to him, Dr. May endeavoured to repress his agitation, and lead him from the room; but he could not, at first, prevail on him to listen or understand, still less to quit Flora. The attempt to force on him the perception that his uncontrolled sorrow was injuring her, and that he ought to bear up for her sake, only did further harm; for, when he rose up and tried to caress her, there was the same torpid, passive resistance, the same burying her face from the light, and the only betrayal of consciousness in the agonized throbs of her pulse.

He became excessively distressed at being thus repelled, and, at last, yielded to the impatient signals of Dr. May, who drew him into the next room, and, with brief, strong, though most affectionate and pitying words, enforced on him that Flora's brain —nay, her life, was risked, and that he must leave her alone to his care for the present. Meta coming back at the same moment, Dr. May put him in her charge, with renewed orders to impress on him how much depended on tranquillity.

Dr. May went back, with his soft, undisturbing, physician's footfall, and stood at the side of the bed, in such intense anxiety as those only can endure who know how to pray, and to pray in resignation and faith.

All was still in the darkening twilight; but the distant roar of the world surged without, and a gas-light shone flickering through the branches of the trees, and fell on the rich dress spread on the couch, and the ornaments on the toilette-table. There was a sense of oppression, and of being pursued by the incongruous world, and Dr. May sighed to silence all around, and see his poor daughter in the calm of her own country air; but she had chosen for herself, and here she lay, stricken down in the midst of the prosperity that she had sought.

He could hear every respiration, tightened and almost sobbing, and he was hesitating whether to run the risk of addressing her; when, as if it had occurred to her suddenly that she was alone and deserted, she raised up her head with a startled movement, but, as she saw him, she again hid her face, as if his presence were still more intolerable than solitude.

'Flora! my own, my dearest—my poor child! you should not turn from me. Do I not carry with me the like self-reproachful conviction?'

Flora let him turn her face towards him and kiss her forehead. It was burning, and he brought water and bathed it, now and then speaking a few fond, low, gentle words, which, though she did not respond, evidently had some soothing effect; for she admitted his services, still, however, keeping her eyes closed, and her face turned towards the darkest side of the room. When he went towards the door, she murmured, 'Papa!' as if to detain him.

'I am not going, darling. I only wanted to speak to George.'

'Don't let him come!' said Flora.

'Not till you wish it, my dear.'

George's step was heard; his hand was on the lock, and again Dr. May was conscious of the sudden rush of blood through all her veins. He quickly went forward, met him, and shut him out, persuading him, with difficulty, to remain outside, and giving him the occupation of sending out for an anodyne—since the best hope, at present, lay in encouraging the torpor that had benumbed her crushed faculties.

Her father would not even venture to rouse her to be undressed; he gave her the medicine, and let her lie still, with as little movement as possible, standing by till her regular breathings showed that she had sunk into a sleep; when he went into the other room and found that George had also forgotten his sorrows in slumber on the sofa, while Meta sat sadly presiding over the tea equipage.

She came up to meet him, her question expressed in her looks.

'Asleep,' he said; 'I hope the pulses are quieter. All depends on her awakening.'

'Poor, poor Flora,' said Meta, wiping away her tears.

'What have you done with the woman?'

'I sent her to Mrs. Larpent's. I knew she would receive her and keep her till she could write to her friends. Bellairs took her, but I could hardly speak to her—'

'She did it ignorantly,' said Dr. May.

'I could never be so merciful and forbearing as you,' said Meta.

'Ah! my dear, you will never have the same cause!'

They could say no more, for George awoke, and the argument of his exclusion had to be gone through again. He could not enter into it by any means; and when Dr. May would have made him understand that poor Flora could not acquit herself of neglect, and that even his affection was too painful for her in the present state; he broke into a vehement angry defence of her devotion to her child, treating Dr. May as if the accusation came from him; and when the Doctor and Meta had persuaded him out of this, he next imagined that his father-in-law feared that hè was going to reproach his wife, and there was no making him comprehend more than, that if she were not kept quiet, she might have a serious illness.

Even then, he insisted on going to look at her, and Dr. May could not prevent him from pressing his lips to her forehead. She half-opened her eyes, and murmured 'good-night,' and by this he was a little comforted; but he would hear of nothing but sitting up, and Meta would have done the same, but for an absolute decree of the Doctor.

It was a relief to Dr. May, that George's vigil soon became a sound repose on the sofa in the dressing-room; and he was left to read and muse uninterruptedly.

It was far past two o'clock before there was any movement; then Flora drew a long breath, stirred, and, as her father came and drew her hand into his, before she was well awake, she gave a long, wondering whisper—'Oh! papa! papa!' then sitting up, and passing her hand over her eyes, 'Is it all true?'

'It is true, my own poor dear,' said Dr. May, supporting her, as she rested against his arm, and hid her face on his shoulder, while her breath came short, and she shivered under the renewed perception, 'She is gone to wait for you.'

'Hush! Oh don't! papa!' said Flora, her voice shortened by anguish. 'O, think why—'

'Nay, Flora, do not, do not speak as if *that* should exclude peace, or hope!' said Dr. May, entreatingly. 'Besides, it was no wilful neglect—you had other duties—'

'You don't know me, papa!' said Flora, drawing her hands away from him, and tightly clenching them in one another, as thoughts far too terrible for words swept over her.

'If I do not, the most Merciful Father does,' said Dr. May. Flora sat for a minute or two, her hands locked together round her knees, her head bowed down, her lips compressed. Her father was so far satisfied, that the bodily dangers he had dreaded, were averted; but the agony of mind was far more terrible, especially in one who expressed so little, and in whom it seemed, as it were, pent up.

'Papa!' said Flora, presently, with a resolution of tone as if she would prevent resistance; 'I must see her!'

'You shall, my dear,' said the Doctor, at once; and she seemed grateful not to be opposed, speaking more gently, as she said, 'May it be now? While there is no daylight!'

'If you wish it,' said Dr. May.

The dawn, and a yellow waning moon, gave sufficient light for moving about, and Flora gained her feet; but she was weak and trembling, and needed the support of her father's arm, though hardly conscious of receiving it, as she mounted the same stairs, that she had so often lightly ascended in the like doubtful morning light; for never, after any party, had she omitted her visit to the nursery.

The door was locked, and she looked piteously at her father as her weak push met the resistance, and he was somewhat slow in turning the key with his left hand. The whitewashed, slightly furnished room, reflected the light, and the moonbeams showed the window-frame in pale and dim shades on the blinds, the dewy air breathed in coolly from the park, and there was a calm solemnity in the atmosphere—no light, no watcher present to tend the babe. Little Leonora needed such no more; she was with the Keeper, who shall neither slumber nor sleep.

So it thrilled across her grandfather, as he saw the little cradle drawn into the middle of the room, and, on the coverlet, some pure white rosebuds and lilies of the valley, gathered in the morning by Mary and Blanche, little guessing the use that Meta would make of them ere nightfall.

The mother sank on her knees, her hands clasped over her breast, and rocking herself to and fro uneasily, with a low, irrepressible moaning.

'Will you not see her face?' whispered Dr. May.

'I may not touch her,' was the answer, in the hollow voice, and, with the wild eye that had before alarmed him; but trusting to the soothing power of the mute face of the innocent, he drew back the covering.

The sight was such as he anticipated, sadly lovely, smiling and tranquil—all oppression and suffering fled away for ever.

It stilled the sounds of pain, and the restless motion; the compression of the hands became less tight, and he began to hope that the look was passing into her heart. He let her kneel on without interruption, only once he said, 'Of such is the kingdom of Heaven!'

She made no immediate answer, and he had had time to doubt whether he ought to let her continue in that exhausting attitude any longer, when she looked up and said, 'You will all be with her there.'

'She has flown on to point your aim more stedfastly,' said Dr. May.

Flora shuddered, but spoke calmly—'No, I shall not meet her.'

'My child!' he exclaimed, 'do you know what you are saying?'

'I know, I am not in the way,' said Flora, still in the same fearfully quiet, matter-of-fact, tone. 'I never have been'—and she bent over her child, as if taking her leave for eternity.

His tongue almost clave to the roof of his mouth, as he heard the words—words elicited by one of those hours of true reality that, like death, rend aside every wilful cloak of self-deceit, and self-approbation. He had no power to speak at first; when he recovered it, his reply was not what his heart had, at first, prompted.

'Flora! How has this dear child been saved?' he said. 'What has released her from the guilt she inherited through you, through me, through all? Is not the Fountain open?'

'She never wasted grace,' said Flora.

'My child! my Flora!' he exclaimed, losing the calmness he had gained by such an effort; 'You must not talk thus—it is wrong! Only your own morbid feeling can treat this—*this*—as a charge against you, and if it were, indeed'—he sank his voice 'that such consequences destroyed hope, oh Flora! where should I be?'

'No,' said Flora, 'this is not what I meant. It is that I have never set my heart right. I am not like you nor my sisters. I have seemed to myself, and to you, to be trying to do right, but it was all hollow, for the sake of praise and credit. I know it, now it is too late; and He has let me destroy my child here, lest I should have destroyed her Everlasting Life, like my own.'

The most terrible part of this sentence was to Dr. May, that Flora spoke as if she knew it all as a certainty, and without apparent emotion, with all the calmness of despair. What she had never guessed before had come clearly and fully upon her now, and without apparent novelty, or, perhaps, there had been misgivings in the midst of her complacent self-satisfaction. She did not even seem to perceive how dreadfully she was shocking her father, whose sole comfort was in believing her language the effect of exaggerated self-reproach. His profession had rendered him not new to the sight of despondency, and, dismayed as he was, he was able at once to speak to the point.

'If it were indeed so, her removal would be the greatest blessing.'

'Yes,' said her mother, and her assent was in the same tone of resigned despair, owning it best for her child to be spared a worldly education, and loving her truly enough to acquiesce.

'I meant the greatest blessing to you,' continued Dr. May 'if it be sent to open your eyes, and raise your thoughts upwards. Oh! Flora, are not afflictions tokens of infinite love?'

She could not accept the encouragement, and only formed, with her lips, the words, 'Mercy to her—wrath to me!'

The simplicity and hearty piety which, with all Dr. May's faults, had always been part of his character, and had borne him, in faith and trust, through all his trials, had never belonged to her. Where he had been sincere, erring only from impulsiveness, she had been double-minded and calculating; and, now that her delusion had been broken down, she had nothing to rest upon. Her whole religious life had been mechanical, deceiving herself more than even others, and all seemed now swept away, except the sense of hypocrisy, and of having cut herself off, for ever, from her innocent child. Her father saw that it was vain to argue with her, and only said, 'You will think otherwise by-and-by, my dear. Now, shall I say a prayer before we go down?'

As she made no reply, he repeated the Lord's Prayer, but she did not join; and then he added a broken, hesitating intercession for the mourners, which caused her to bury her face deeper in her hands, but her dull wretchedness altered not.

Rising, he said, authoritatively, 'Come, Flora, you must go to bed. See, it is morning.'

'You have sat up all night with me!' said Flora, with somewhat of her anxious, considerate self.

'So has George. He had just dropped asleep on the sofa when you awoke.'

'I thought he was in anger,' said she.

'Not with you, dearest.'

'No, I remember now, not where it was justly due. Papa,' she said, pausing, as to recal her recollection, 'what did I do? I must have done something very unkind to make him go away and leave me.'

'I insisted on his leaving you, my dear. You seemed oppressed, and his affectionate ways were doing you harm; so I was hard-hearted, and turned him out, sadly against his will.'

'Poor George!' said Flora, 'has he been left to bear it alone all this time? How much distressed he must have been. I must have vexed him grievously. You don't guess how fond he was of her. I must go to him at once.'

'That is right, my dear.'

'Don't praise me,' said she, as if she could not bear it. 'All that is left for me is to do what I can for him.'

Dr. May felt cheered. He was sure that hope must again rise out of unselfish love and duty.

Their return awoke George, who started, half-sitting up, wondering why he was spending the night in so unusual a manner, and why Flora looked so pale, in the morning light, with her loosened, drooping hair.

She went straight to him, and, kneeling by his side, said, 'George, forgive!' The same moment he had caught her to his bosom; but so impressed was his tardy mind, with the peril of talking to her, that he held her in his arms without a single word, till Dr. May had unclosed his lips—a sign would not suffice—he must have a sentence to assure him; and then it was such joy to have her restored, and his fondness and solicitude were so tender and eager in their clumsiness, that his father-in-law was touched to the heart.

Flora was quite herself again, in presence of mind and power of dealing with him; and Dr. May left them to each other, and went to his own room, for such rest as sorrow, sympathy, and the wakening city, would permit him.

When the house was astir for the morning kept by human creatures, and the Doctor had met Meta in the breakfast-room, and held with her a sad, affectionate conversation, George

came down with a fair report of his wife, and took her father to
see her.

That night had been like an illness to her, and, though perfectly
composed, she was feeble and crushed, keeping the room darkened,
and reluctant to move or speak. Indeed, she did not seem able
to give her attention to any one's voice, except her husband's.
When Dr. May, or Meta, spoke to her, she would miss what they
said, beg their pardon, and ask them to repeat it; and, sometimes,
even then, become bewildered. They tried reading to her, but
she did not seem to listen, and her half-closed eye had the expression of listless dejection, that her father knew betokened that,
even as last night, her heart refused to accept promises of comfort
as meant for her.

For George, however, her attention was always ready, and was
perpetually claimed. He was forlorn and at a loss without her,
every moment; and, in the sorrow which he too felt most acutely,
could not have a minute's peace unless soothed by her presence;
he was dependent on her to a degree which amazed and almost
provoked the Doctor, who could not bear to have her continually
harassed and disturbed, and yet was much affected by witnessing
so much tenderness, especially in Flora, always the cold utilitarian
member of his family.

In the middle of the day, she rose and dressed, because George
was unhappy at having to sit without her, though only in the
next room. She sat in the large arm-chair, turned away from
the blinded windows, never speaking nor moving, save when he
came to her, to make her look at his letters and notes, when
she would, with the greatest patience and sweetness, revise them,
suggest word or sentence, rouse herself to consider each petty
detail, and then sink back into her attitude of listless dejection.
To all besides, she appeared totally indifferent; gently courteous
to Meta and to her father, when they addressed her, but otherwise showing little consciousness whether they were in the room;
and yet, when something was passing about her father's staying
or returning, she rose from her seat, came up to him before he
was aware, and said, 'Papa! papa! you will not leave me!' in
such an imploring tone, that if he had ever thought of quitting
her, he could not have done so.

He longed to see her left to perfect tranquillity, but such could
not be in London. Though theirs was called a quiet house, the
rushing stream of traffic wearied his country ears, the door-bell
seemed ceaselessly ringing, and though Meta bore the brunt of
the notes and messages, great numbers necessarily came up to
Mr. Rivers, and of these Flora was not spared one. Dr. May

had his share, too, of messages and business, and friends and relations, the Rivers' kindred, always ready to take offence with their rich connections, and who would not be satisfied with inquiries at the door, but must see Meta, and *would* have George fetched down to them—old aunts, who wanted the whole story of the child's illness, and came imagining there was something to be hushed up; Lady Leonora extremely polite, but extremely disgusted at the encounter with them; George ready to be persuaded to take every one up to see his wife, and the prohibition to be made by Dr. May over and over again—it was a most tedious, wearing afternoon, and at last, when the visitors had gone, and George had hurried back to his wife, Dr. May threw himself into an arm-chair, and said, 'Oh! Meta, sorrow weighs more heavily in town than in the country!'

'Yes!' said Meta. 'If one only could go out and look at the flowers, and take poor Flora up a nosegay!'

'I don't think it would make much difference to her,' sighed the Doctor.

'Yes, I think it would,' said Meta; 'it did to me. The sights there speak of the better sights.'

'The power to look must come from within,' said Dr. May, thinking of his poor daughter.

'Aye,' said Meta, 'as Mr. Ernescliffe said, "heaven is as near—!" But the skirts of heaven are more easily traced in our mountain view, than here, where, if I looked out of window, I should only see that giddy string of carriages and people pursuing each other!'

'Well, we shall get her home as soon as she is able to move, and I hope it may soothe her. What a turmoil it is! There has not been one moment without noise in the twenty-two hours I have been here!'

'What would you say if you were in the City?'

'Ah! there's no talking of it, but if I had been a fashionable London physician, as my father-in-law wanted to make me, I should have been dead long ago!'

'No, I think you would have liked it very much.'

'Why?'

'Love's a flower that will not die,' repeated Meta, half smiling. 'You would have found so much good to do—'

'And so much misery to rend one's heart,' said Dr. May. 'But, after all, I suppose there is only a certain capacity of feeling.'

'It is within, not without, as you said,' returned Meta.

'Ha! there's another!' cried Dr. May, almost petulant at the sound of the bell again, breaking into the conversation that was a great refreshment.

'It was Sir Henry Walkinghame's ring,' said Meta. 'It is always his time of day.'

The Doctor did not like it the better.

Sir Henry sent up a message to ask whether he could see Mr. or Miss Rivers.

'I suppose we must,' said Meta, looking at the Doctor. 'Lady Walkinghame must be anxious about Flora.'

She blushed greatly, fancying that Dr. May was putting his own construction on the heightened colour which she could not control. Sir Henry came in, just what he ought to be, kindly anxious, but not overwhelming, and with a ready, pleased recognition of the Doctor, as an old acquaintance of his boyhood. He did not stay many minutes; but there was a perceptible difference between his real sympathy and friendly regard only afraid of obtruding, and the oppressive curiosity of their former visitors. Dr. May felt it due, both from kindness and candour, to say something in his praise when he was gone.

'That is a sensible, superior man,' he said. 'He will be an acquisition when he takes up his abode at Drydale.'

'Yes,' said Meta—a very simple yes—from which nothing could be gathered.

The funeral was fixed for Monday, the next day but one, at the church where Mr. Rivers had been buried. No one was invited to be present; Ethel wrote that, much as she wished it, she could not leave Margaret, and, as the whole party were to return home on the following day, they should soon see Flora.

Flora had laid aside all privileges of illness after the first day; she came down-stairs to breakfast and dinner, and though looking wretchedly ill, and speaking very low and feebly, she was as much as ever the mistress of her house. Her father could never draw her into conversation again, on the subject nearest his heart, and could only draw the sad conclusion that her state of mind was unchanged, from the dreary indifference with which she allowed every word of cheer to pass by unheeded, as if she could not bear to look beyond the grave. He had some hope in the funeral, which she was bent on attending, and more in the influence of Margaret, and the counsel of Richard, or of Mr. Wilmot.

The burial, however, failed to bring any peaceful comfort to the mourning mother. Meta's tears flowed freely, as much for her father as for her little niece; and George's sobs were deep and choking; but Flora, externally, only seemed absorbed in helping him to go through with it; she, herself, never lost her fixed, composed, hopeless look.

After her return, she went up to the nursery, and deliberately set apart and locked up every possession of her child's, then, coming down, startled Meta by laying her hand on her shoulder and saying, ' Meta, dear, Preston is in the housekeeper's room. Will you go and speak to her for a moment, to reassure her before I come?'

' Oh! Flora!'

' I sent for her,' said Flora, in answer. ' I thought it would be a good opportunity while George is out. Will you be kind enough to prepare her, my dear?'

Meta wondered how Flora had known whither to send, but she could not but obey. Poor Preston was an ordinary sort of woman, kind-hearted, and not without a conscience; but her error had arisen from the want of any high religious principle to teach her obedience, or sincerity. Her grief was extreme, and she had been so completely overcome by the forbearance and consideration shown to her, that she was even more broken-hearted by the thought of them, than by the terrible calamity she had occasioned.

Kind-hearted Mrs. Larpent had tried to console her, as well as to turn the misfortune to the best account, and Dr. May had once seen her, and striven gently to point out the true evil of the course she had pursued. She was now going to her home, and they augured better of her, that she had been as yet too utterly downcast to say one word of that first thought with a servant, her character.

Meta found her sobbing uncontrollably at the associations of her master's house, and dreadfully frightened at hearing that she was to see Mrs. Rivers; she began to entreat to the contrary with the vehemence of a person unused to any self-government; but, in the midst, the low calm tones were heard, and her mistress stood before her—her perfect stillness of demeanour, far more effective in repressing agitation, than had been Meta's coaxing attempts to soothe.

' You need not be afraid to see me, Preston,' said Flora, kindly. ' I am very sorry for you—you knew no better, and I should not have left so much to you.'

' Oh! ma'am—so kind—the dear, dear little darling—I shall never forgive myself.'

' I know you did love her,' continued Flora. ' I am sure you intended no harm, and it was my leaving her that made her fretful.'

Preston tried to thank.

' Only remember henceforth—' and the clear tone grew fainter than ever with internal anguish, though still steady, ' Remember strict obedience and truth henceforth; the want of them will have worse results by-and-by than even this. Now, Preston, I shall always wish you well. I ought not, I believe, to recommend you to the like place, without saying why you left me, but for any other I will give you a fair character. I will see what I can do for you, and if you are ever in any distress, I hope you will let me know. Have your wages been paid?'

There was a sound in the affirmative, but poor Preston could not speak. 'Good-bye, then,' and Flora took her hand and shook it. 'Mind you let me hear if you want help. Keep this.'

Meta was a little disappointed to see sovereigns instead of a book. Flora turned to go, and put her hand out to lean on her sister as for support; she stood still to gather strength before ascending the stairs, and a groan of intense misery was wrung from her.

'Dearest Flora, it has been too much!'

'No,' said Flora, gently.

'Poor thing, I am glad for her sake. But might she not have a book— a Bible?'

'You may give her one, if you like. I could not.'

Flora reached her own room, went in, and bolted the door.

CHAPTER XXI.

'O, where dwell ye, my ain sweet bairns?
I'm woe and weary grown!
O, Lady, we live where woe never is,
In a land to flesh unknown.'—ALLAN CUNNINGHAM.

IT had been with a gentle sorrow that Etheldred had expected to go and lay in her resting-place, the little niece, who had been kept from the evil of the world, in a manner of which she had little dreamt. Poor Flora! she must be ennobled, she thought, by having a child where hers is, when she is able to feel anything but the first grief; and Ethel's heart yearned to be trying, at least, to comfort her, and to be with her father, who had loved his grandchild so fondly.

It was not to be. Margaret had borne so many shocks with such calmness, that Ethel had no especial fears for her; but there are some persons who have less fortitude for others than for themselves, and she was one of these. Flora had been her own companion-sister, and the baby had been the sunbeam of her life, during the sad winter and spring.

In the middle of the night, Ethel knocked at Richard's door. Margaret had been seized with faintness, from which they could not bring her back; and, even when Richard had summoned Dr. Spencer, it was long ere his remedies took effect; but, at last, she revived enough to thank them, and say she was glad that papa was not there.

Dr. Spencer sent them all to bed, and the rest of the night was quiet; but Margaret could not deny, in the morning, that she felt terribly shattered, and she was depressed in spirits to a degree such as they had never seen in her before. Her whole heart was with Flora; she was unhappy at being at a distance from her, almost fretfully impatient for letters, and insisting vehemently on Ethel's going to London.

Ethel had never felt so helpless and desolate, as with Margaret thus changed and broken, and her father absent.

'My dear,' said Dr. Spencer, 'nothing can be better for both parties than that he should be away. If he were here, he ought to leave all attendance to me, and she would suffer from the sight of his distress.'

'I cannot think what he will do or feel!' sighed Ethel.

'Leave it to me. I will write to him, and we shall see her better before post time.'

'You will tell him exactly how it was, or I shall,' said Ethel, abruptly, not to say fiercely.

'Ho! you don't trust me?' said Dr. Spencer, smiling, so that she was ashamed of her speech. 'You shall speak for yourself, and I for myself; and I shall say that nothing would so much hurt her as to have others sacrificed to her.'

'That is true,' said Ethel; 'but she misses papa.'

'Of course she does; but, depend on it, she would not have him leave your sister, and she is under less restraint without him.'

'I never saw her like this!'

'The drop has made it overflow. She has repressed more than was good for her, and now that her guard is broken down, she gives way under the whole weight.'

'Poor Margaret! I am pertinacious; but, if she is not better by post time, papa will not bear to be away.'

'I'll tell you what I think of her by that time. Send up your brother Richard, if you wish to do her good. Richard would be a much better person to write than yourself. I perceive that he is the reasonable member of the family.'

'Did not you know that before?'

'All I knew of him, till last night, was, that no one could, by any possibility, call him Dick.'

Dr. Spencer was glad to have dismissed Ethel smiling; and she was the better able to bear with poor Margaret's condition of petulance. She had never before experienced the effects of bodily

ailments on the temper, and she was slow to understand the
change in one usually so patient and submissive. She was, by
turns, displeased with her sister and with her own abruptness;
but, though she knew it not, her bluntness had a bracing effect.
She thought she had been cross in declaring it was nonsense to
harp on her going to London; but it made Margaret feel that
she had been unreasonable, and keep silence.

Richard managed her much better, being gentle and firm, and
less ready to speak than Ethel, and he succeeded in composing
her into a sleep, which restored her balance, and so relieved Ethel,
that she not only allowed Dr. Spencer to say what he pleased,
but herself made light of the whole attack, little knowing how
perilous was any shock to that delicate frame.

Margaret's whole purpose was to wind herself up for the first
interview with Flora; and, though she had returned to her usual
state, she would not go down-stairs on the evening the party were
expected, believing it would be more grateful to her sister's feelings
to meet her without witnesses.

The travellers arrived and Dr. May hurried up to her. She
barely replied to his caresses and inquiries in her eagerness to
hear of Flora, and to convince him that he must not forbid the
meeting. Nor had he any mind so to do. 'Surely,' said he,
when he had seen the spiritualized look of her glistening blue
eyes, the flush on her transparent cheeks, and her hands clasped
over her breast, ' surely poor Flora must feel as though an angel
were waiting to comfort her.'

Flora came, but there was sore disappointment. Fond and
tender she was as ever; but, neither by word nor gesture, would
she admit the most remote allusion to her grief. She withdrew
her hand when Margaret's pressure became expressive; she
avoided her eye, and spoke incessantly of indifferent subjects.
All the time, her voice was low and hollow, her face had a settled
expression of wretchedness, and her glances wandered drearily
and restlessly anywhere but to Margaret's face; but her steadiness of manner was beyond her sister's power to break, and her
visit was shortened on account of her husband. Poor George
had quite given way at the sight of Gertrude, whom his little
girl had been thought to resemble; and, though Dr. May had
soothed him almost like a child, no one put any trust in his self-
control, and all sat round, fearing each word or look, till Flora
came down-stairs, and they departed.

Richard and Ethel each offered to go with them; they could
not bear to think of their spending that first evening in their
childless home, but Flora gently, but decidedly refused; and

Dr. May said that, much as he wished to be with them, he believed that Flora preferred having no one but Meta. 'I hope I have done Margaret no harm,' were Flora's last words to him, and they seemed to explain her guarded manner; but he found Margaret weeping as she had never wept for herself, and palpitation and faintness were the consequence.

Ethel looked on at Flora as a sad and perplexing mystery during the weeks that ensued. There were few opportunities of being alone together, and Flora shrank from such as there were—nay, she checked all expression of solicitude, and made her very kisses rapid and formal.

The sorrow that had fallen on the Grange seemed to have changed none of the usual habits there—visiting, riding, driving, dinners, and music, went on with little check. Flora was sure to be found the animated, attentive lady of the house, or else sharing her husband's pursuits, helping him with his business, or assisting him in seeking pleasure, spending whole afternoons at the coachmaker's, over a carriage that they were building, and, it was reported, playing écarté in the evening.

Had grief come to be forgotten and cast aside without effecting any mission? Yet Ethel could not believe that the presence of the awful messenger was unfelt, when she heard poor George's heavy sigh, or when she looked at Flora's countenance, and heard the peculiar low, subdued tone of her voice, which, when her words were most cheerful, always seemed to Ethel the resigned accent of despair.

Ethel could not talk her over with Margaret, for all seemed to make it a point that Margaret should believe the best. Dr. May turned from the subject with a sort of shuddering grief, and said, 'Don't talk of her, poor child—only pray for her!'

Ethel, though shocked by the unwonted manner of his answer, was somewhat consoled by perceiving that a double measure of tenderness had sprung up between her father and his poor daughter. If Flora had seemed, in her girlhood, to rate him almost cheaply, this was at an end now; she met him as if his embrace were peace, the gloom was lightened, the attention less strained, when he was beside her, and she could not part with him without pressing for a speedy meeting. Yet, she treated him with the same reserve; since that one ghastly revelation of the secrets of her heart, the veil had been closely drawn, and he could not guess whether it had been but a horrible thought, or were still an abiding impression. Ethel could gather no more than that her father was very unhappy about Flora, and that Richard understood why; for Richard had told her that he had written to

Flora, to try to persuade her to cease from this reserve, but that he had no reply.

Norman was not at home; he had undertaken the tutorship of two school-boys for the holidays; and his father owned, with a sigh, that he was doing wisely.

As to Meta, she was Ethel's chief consolation, by the redoubled assurances, directed to Ethel's unexpressed dread, lest Flora should be rejecting the chastening Hand. Meta had the most absolute certainty that Flora's apparent cheerfulness was all for George's sake, and that it was a most painful exertion. 'If Ethel could only see how she let herself sink together, as it were, and her whole countenance relax, as soon as he was out of sight,' Meta said, 'she could not doubt what misery these efforts were to her.'

'Why does she go on with them?' said Ethel.

'George,' said Meta. 'What would become of him without her? If he misses her for ten minutes, he roams about lost, and he cannot enjoy anything without her. I cannot think how he can help seeing what hard work it is, and how he can be contented with those dreadful sham smiles; but as long as she can give him pleasure, poor Flora will toil for him.'

'It is very selfish,' Ethel caught herself saying.

'No, no, it is not,' cried Meta. 'It is not that he will not see, but that he cannot see. Good honest fellow, he really thinks it does her good and pleases her. I was so sorry one evening, when I tried to take her place at that perpetual *écarté*, and told him it teased her; he went so wistfully to her, and asked whether it did, and she exerted herself into such painful enjoyment to persuade him to the contrary; and afterwards she said to me, "Let me alone, dearest—it is the only thing left me."'

'There is something in being husband and wife that one cannot understand,' slowly said Ethel, so much in her quaint way, that Meta laughed.

Had it not been for Norman's absence, Ethel would, in the warm sympathy and accustomed manner of Meta Rivers, have forgotten all about the hopes and fears that, in brighter days, had centred on that small personage; until one day, as she came home from Cocksmoor, she found 'Sir Henry Walkinghame's' card on the drawing-room table. 'I should like to bite you! Coming here are you?' was her amiable reflection.

Meta, in her riding-habit, peeped out of Margaret's room. 'O, Ethel, there you are! It is such a boon that you did not come home sooner, or we should have had to ride home with him! I heard him asking for the Miss Mays! And now I am in hopes that he will go home without falling in with Flora and George.'

' I did not know he was in these parts.'

' He came to Drydale last week ; but the place is forlorn, and George gave him a general invitation to the Grange.'

' Do *you* like him ?' said Ethel, while Margaret looked on, amazed at her audacity.

' I liked him very much in London,' said Meta ; ' he is pleasant enough to talk to, but somehow, he is not congruous here —if you understand me. And I think his coming oppresses Flora—she turned quite pale when he was announced, and her voice was lower than ever when she spoke to him.'

' Does he come often ?' said Ethel.

' I don't think he has anything else to do,' returned Meta, ' for our house cannot be as pleasant as it was ; but he is very kind to George, and for that we must be grateful. One thing I am afraid of, that he will persuade us off to the yachting after all.'

' Oh !' was the general exclamation.

' Yes,' said Meta. ' George seemed to like the plan, and I very much fear that he is taking a dislike to the dear old Grange. I heard him say, " anything to get away." '

' Poor George, I know he is restless,' said Margaret.

' At least,' said Ethel, ' you can't go till after your birthday, Miss Heiress.'

' No, Uncle Cosham is coming,' said Meta. ' Margaret, you must have your stone laid before we go !'

' Dr. Spencer promises it before Hector's holidays are over,' said Margaret, blushing, as she always did, with pleasure, when they talked of the Church.

Hector Ernescliffe had revived Margaret wonderfully. She was seldom down-stairs before the evening, and Ethel thought his habit of making her apartment his sitting-room, must be as inconvenient to her, as it was to herself ; but Hector could not be *de trop* for Margaret. She exerted herself to fulfil for him all the little sisterly offices that, with her brothers, had been transferred to Ethel and Mary ; she threw herself into all his schemes, tried to make him endure Captain Gordon, and she even read his favourite book of Wild Sports, though her feelings were constantly lacerated by the miseries of the slaughtered animals. Her couch was to him as a home, and he had awakened her bright soft liveliness, which had been only dimmed for a time.

The Church was her other great interest, and Dr. Spencer humoured her by showing her all his drawings, consulting her on every ornament, and making many a perspective elevation, merely that she might see the effect.

Richard and Tom made it their recreation to construct a model of the Church as a present for her, and Tom developed a genius for carving, which proved a beneficial interest to keep him from surliness. He had voluntarily propounded his intended profession to his father, who had been so much pleased by his choice, that he could not but be gratified; though now and then ambitious fancies, and discontent with Stoneborough, combined to bring on his ordinary moody fits, the more, because his habitual reserve prevented any one from knowing what was working in his mind.

Finally, the Rivers' party announced their intention of going to the Isle of Wight, as soon as Meta had come of age; and the council of Cocksmoor, meeting at tea at Dr. May's house, decided that the Foundation Stone of the Church should be laid on the day after her birthday, when there would be a gathering of the whole family, as Margaret wished. Dr. Spencer had worked incredibly hard to bring it forward, and Margaret's sweet smiles, and liquid eyes, expressed how personally thankful she felt.

' What a blessing this Church has been to that poor girl,' said Dr. Spencer, as he left the house with Mr. Wilmot. ' How it beguiles her out of her grief! I am glad she has the pleasure of the Foundation; I doubt if she will see the Consecration.'

' Indeed!' said Mr. Wilmot, shocked. ' Was that attack so serious ?'

' That recumbent position and want of exercise were certain to produce organic disease, and suspense and sorrow have hastened it. The death of Mrs. Rivers' poor child was the blow that called it into activity, and, if it last more than a year, I shall be surprised.'

' For such as she is, one cannot presume to wish, but her father—is he aware of this ?'

' He knows there is extensive damage; I think he does not open his eyes to the result, but he will bear it. Never was there a man to whom it came so naturally to live like the fowls of the air, or the lilies of the field, as it does to dear Dick May,' said Dr. Spencer, his voice faltering.

' There is a strength of faith and love in him, that carries him through all ' said Mr. Wilmot. ' His childlike nature seems to have the trustfulness that is, in itself, consolation. You said how Cocksmoor had been blessed to Margaret—I think it is the same with them all—not only Ethel and Richard, who have been immediately concerned; but that one object has been a centre and aim to elevate the whole family, and give force and unity to their efforts. Even the good Doctor, much as I always looked up to him—much good as he did me in my young days—I must confess that he was sometimes very provoking.'

'If you had tried to be his keeper at Cambridge, you might say so!' rejoined Dr. Spencer.

'He is so much less impetuous—more consistent—less desultory; I dare say you understand me,' said Mr. Wilmot. 'His good qualities do not entangle one another as they used to do.'

'Exactly so. He was far more than I looked for when I came home, though I might have guessed that such a disposition, backed by such principles and such—could not but shake off all the dross.'

'One thing was,' said Mr. Wilmot, smiling, 'that a man must take himself in hand, at some time in his life, and Dr. May only began to think himself responsible for himself, when he lost his wife, who was wise for both. She was an admirable person, but not easy to know well. I think you knew her at—'

'I say,' interrupted Dr. Spencer, 'it strikes me that we could not do better than get up our S.P.G. demonstration on the day of the stone—'

Hitherto the Stoneborough subscribers to the Society for the Propagation of the Gospel had been few and far between; but, under the new dynasty, there was a talk of forming an association, and having a meeting to bring the subject forward. Dr. Spencer's proposal, however, took the Vicar by surprise.

'Never could there be a better time,' he argued. 'You have naturally a gathering of Clergy—people ought to be liberal on such an occasion, and, as Cocksmoor is provided for, why not give the benefit to the missions, in their crying need.'

'True, but there is no time to send for any one to make a speech.'

'Husband your resources. What could you have better than young Harry and his islanders?'

'Harry would never make a speech.'

'Let him cram Norman. Young Lake tells me Norman made a great sensation at the Union at Oxford, and if his heart is in the work, he must not shrink from the face of his townsmen.'

'No doubt, he had rather they were savages,' said the Vicar. 'And yourself—you will tell them of the Indian Missions.'

'With all my heart,' said Dr. Spencer. 'When my Brahminhee Godson—the Deacon I told you of, comes to pay me his promised visit, what doings we shall have! Seriously, I have just had letters from him and from others, that speak of such need, that I could feel every moment wasted that is not spent on their behalf.'

Mr. Wilmot was drawn into Dr. Spencer's house, and heard the letters, till his heart burnt within him.

The meeting was at once decided upon, though Ethel could not see why people could not give without speechifying, and her two younger brothers declared it was humbug—Tom saying, he wished all blackamoors were out of creation, and Harry, that he could not stand palaver about his friend David. Dr. May threatened him with being displayed on the platform as a living instance of the effects of Missions, at which he took alarm, and so seriously declared that he should join the Bucephalus at once, that they pacified him by promising that he should do as he pleased.

The Archdeacon promised a Sermon, and the active Dr. Spencer worked the Nine Muses and all the rest of the town and neighbourhood into a state of great enthusiasm and expectation. He went to the Grange, as he said, to collect his artillery; primed Flora that she might prime the M.P.; made the willing Meta promise to entrap the uncle, who was noted for philanthropical speeches; and himself captured Sir Henry Walkinghame, who looked somewhat rueful at what he found incumbent on him as a country gentleman, though there might be some compensation in the eagerness of Miss Rivers.

Norman had hardly set foot in Stoneborough before he was told what was in store for him, and, to the general surprise, submitted as if it were a very simple matter. As Dr. Spencer told him, it was only a foretaste of the penalty which every Missionary has to pay for coming to England. Norman was altogether looking much better than when he had been last at home, and his spirits were more even. He had turned his whole soul to the career he had chosen, cast his disappointment behind him, or, more truly, made it his offering, and gathered strength and calmness, with which to set out on tasks of working for others, with thoughts too much absorbed on them, to give way to the propensity of making himself the primary object of study and contemplation. The praise of God, and love of man, were the best cures for tendencies like his, and he had found it out. His calm, though grave cheerfulness, came as a refreshment to those who had been uneasy about him, and mournfully watching poor Flora.

'Yes,' said Dr. Spencer, 'you have taken the best course for your own happiness.'

Norman coloured, as if he understood more than met the ear.

Mary and Blanche were very busy preparing presents for Meta Rivers, and every one was anxious to soften to her the thought of this first birthday without her father. Each of the family

contributed some pretty little trifle, choice in workmanship or
kind in device, and each was sealed and marked with the initials
of the giver, and packed up by Mary, to be committed to Flora's
charge. Blanche had, however, much trouble in extracting a
gift from Norman, and he only yielded at last, on finding that all
his brothers had sent something, so that his omission would be
marked. Then he dived into the recesses of his desk, and himself sealed up a little parcel, of which he would not allow his
sisters to inspect the contents.

Ethel had a shrewd guess. She remembered his having, in
the flush of joy at Margaret's engagement, rather prematurely
caused a seal to be cut with a Daisy, and 'Pearl of the meadow'
as the motto ; and his having said that he should keep it as a
wedding present. She could understand that he was willing to
part with it without remark.

Flora met Meta in her sitting-room, on the morning of the
day, which rose somewhat sadly upon the young girl, as she
thought of past affection and new responsibilities. If the fondness of a sister could have compensated for what she had lost,
Meta received it in no scanty measure from Flora, who begged
to call George, because he would be pleased to see the display
of gifts.

His own was the only costly one—almost all the rest were
homemade treasures of the greater price, because the skill and
fondness of the maker were evident in their construction ; and
Meta took home the kindness as it was meant, and felt the affection that would not let her feel herself lonely. She only wished
to go and thank them all at once.

'Do, then,' said Flora. 'If Lord Cosham will spare you, and
your business should be over in time, you could drive in, and try
to bring papa home with you.'

'O thank you, Flora. That is a kind treat, in case the morning
should be very awful !'

Margaret Agatha Rivers signed her documents, listened to explanations, and was complimented by her uncle on not thinking
it necessary to be senseless on money matters, like her cousin,
Agatha Langdale.

Still she looked a little oppressed, as she locked up the tokens
of her wealth, and the sunshine of her face did not beam out again
till she arrived at Stoneborough, and was dispensing her pretty
thanks to the few she found at home.

'Ethel out and Norman ? His seal is only too pretty—'
'They are all helping Dr. Spencer at Cocksmoor.'
'What a pity ! But it is so very kind of him to treat me as

a Daisy. In some ways I like his present for that the best of all,' said Meta.

'I will tell him so,' said Mary.

'Yes—no'—said Meta. 'I am not pretending to be anything half so nice.'

Mary and Blanche fell upon her for calling herself anything but the nicest flower in the world; and she contended that she was nothing better than a parrot tulip, stuck up in a parterre; and just as the discussion was becoming a game at romps, Dr. May came in, and the children shouted to him to say whether his hummingbird were a Daisy or a Tulip.

'That is as she comports herself,' he said, playfully.

'Which means that you don't think her quite done for,' said Meta.

'Not quite,' said the Doctor, with a droll intonation; 'but I have not seen what this morning may have done to her.'

'Come and see, then,' said Meta. 'Flora told me to bring you home—and it is my birthday, you know. Never mind waiting to tell Ethel. Margaret will let her know that I'll keep you out of mischief.'

As usual, Dr. May could not withstand her—and she carried him off in triumph in her pony carriage.

'Then you don't give me up yet?' was the first thing she said, as they were off the stones.

'What have you been doing to make me?' said he.

'Doing or not doing—one or the other,' she said. 'But indeed I wanted to have you to myself. I am in a great puzzle!'

'Sir Henry! I hope she won't consult me!' thought Dr. May, as he answered, 'Well, my dear.'

'I fear it is a lasting puzzle,' she said. 'What shall I do with all this money?'

'Keep it in the Bank, or buy railway shares?' said Dr. May, looking arch.

'Thank you. That's a question for my cousins in the City. I want you to answer me as no one else can do. I want to know what is my duty now that I have my means in my own hands?'

'There is need enough around—'

'I do not mean only giving a little here and there, but I want you to hear a few of my thoughts. Flora and George are kindness itself—but, you see, I have no duties. They are obliged to live a gay sort of life—it is their position; but I cannot make out whether it is mine. I don't see that I am like those girls who have to go out as a matter of obedience.'

Dr. May considered, but could only say, 'You are very young.'

'Too young to be independent,' sighed Meta. 'I must grow old enough to be trusted alone, and in the mean time—'

'Probably an answer will be found,' said the Doctor. 'You and your means will find their—their vocation.'

'Marriage,' said Meta, calmly speaking the word that he had avoided. 'I think not.'

'Why ?'—he began.

'I do not think good men like heiresses.'

He became strongly interested in a corn-field, and she resumed, 'Perhaps I should only do harm. It may be my duty to wait. All I wish to know is, whether it is ?'

'I see you are not like girls who know their duty, and are restless, because it is not the duty they like.'

'Oh! I like everything. It is my liking it so much that makes me afraid.'

'Even going to Ryde ?'

'Don't I like the sailing ? and seeing Harry too ? I don't feel as if that were waste, because I can sometimes spare poor Flora a little. We could not let her go alone.'

'You need never fear to be without a mission of comfort,' said Dr. May. Your " spirit full of glee" was given you for something. Your presence is far more to my poor Flora than you or she guess.'

'I never meant to leave her now,' said Meta, earnestly. 'I only wished to be clear whether I ought to seek for my work.'

'It will seek you when the time comes.'

'And meantime I must do what comes to hand, and take it as humiliation that it is not in the more obviously blessed tasks! A call might come, as Cocksmoor did to Ethel. But, oh! my money! Ought it to be laid up for myself ?'

'For your call, when it comes,' said Dr. May, smiling—then gravely, 'There are but too many calls for the interest. The principal is your trust, till the time comes.'

Meta smiled, and was pleased to think that her first-fruits would be offered to-morrow.

CHAPTER XXII.

'O DEAR !' sighed Etheldred, as she fastened her white muslin, 'I'm afraid it is my nature to hate my neighbour !'

'My dear Ethel, what is coming next ?' said Margaret.

'I like my neighbour at home, and whom I have to work for, very much,' said Ethel, 'but oh! my neighbour that I have to be civil to !'

'Poor old King! I am afraid your day will be spoilt with all your toils as lady of the house. I wish I could help you.'

'Let me have my grumble out, and you will!' said Ethel.

'Indeed I am sorry you have this bustle, and so many to entertain, when I know you would rather have the peaceful feelings belonging to the day undisturbed. I should like to shelter you up here.'

'It is very ungrateful of me,' said Ethel, 'when Dr. Spencer works so hard for us, not to be willing to grant anything to him.'

'And—but then I have none of the trouble of it—I can't help liking the notion of sending out the Church to the island whence the Church came home to us.'

'Yes—' said Ethel, 'if we could do it without holding forth!'

'Come, Ethel, it is much better than the bazaar—it is no field for vanity.'

'Certainly not,' said Ethel. 'What a mess every one will make! O if I could but stay away, like Harry! There will be Dr. Hoxton being sonorous and prosy, and Mr. Lake will stammer, and that will be nothing to the misery of our own people's work. George will flounder, and look at Flora, and she will sit with her eyes on the ground, and Dr. Spencer will come out of his proper self, and be complimentary to people who deserve it no more!— And Norman—I wish I could run away!'

'Richard says we do not guess how well Norman speaks.'

'Richard thinks Norman can do anything he can't do himself! It is all chance—he may do very well, if he gets into his "*funny state*," but he always suffers for that, and he will certainly put one into an agony at the outset. I wish Dr. Spencer would have let him alone! And then there will be that Sir Henry, whom I can't abide! Oh! I wish I were more charitable, like Miss Bracy and Mary, who will think all so beautiful.'

'So will you, when you come home,' said Margaret.

'If I could only be talking to Cherry, and Dame Hall! I think the school children enter into it very nicely, Margaret. Did I tell you how nicely Ellen Reid answered about the Hymn, "From Greenland's icy mountains." She did not seem to have made it a mere geographical lesson, like Fanny Grigg—'

Ethel's misanthropy was happily conducted off *via* the Cocksmoor children, and any lingering remains were dissipated by her amusement at Dr. Spencer's ecstasy on seeing Dr. May assume his red robe of office, to go to the Minster in state, with the Town Council. He walked round and round his friend, called him Nicholas Randall *redivivus*, quoted Dogberry, and affronted Gertrude, who had a dim idea that he was making game of papa!

Ethel was one of those to whom representation was such a penance, that a festival, necessitating hospitality to guests of her own rank, was burthen enough seriously to disturb the repose of thankfulness for the attainment of her object, and to render difficult the *recueillement* which she needed for the praise and prayer that she felt due from her, and which seemed to oppress her heart, by a sense of the inadequacy of her partial expression. It was well for her that the day began with the calm service in the Minster, where it was her own fault if cares haunted her, and she could confess the sin of her irritated sensations, and wishes to have all her own way, and then, as ever, be led aright into thanksgiving for the unlooked for crowning of her labours.

The Archdeacon's sermon amplified what Margaret had that morning expressed, so as to carry on her sense of appropriateness in the offerings of the day being bestowed on distant lands.

But the ordeal was yet to come, and though blaming herself, she was anything but comfortable, as the world repaired to the Townhall, the room where the same faces so often met for such diverse purposes—now an orrery displayed by a conceited lecturer, now a ball, now a magistrates' meeting, a concert or a poultry show, where rival Hamburg and Dorking uplifted their voices in the places of Mario and Grisi, all beneath the benignant portrait of Nicholas Randall, ruffed, robed, square-toed, his endowment of the scholarship in his hand, and a chequered pavement at his feet.

Who knows not an S. P. G. meeting ? the gaiety of the serious, and the first public spectacle to the young, who, like Blanche and Aubrey, gaze with admiration at the rows of bonnets, and with awe at the black coats on the platform, while the relations of the said black coats suffer, like Ethel, from nervous dread of the public speaking of their best friends.

Her expectations were realized by the Archdeacon's speech, which went round in a circle, as if he could not find his way out of it. Lord Cosham was fluent, but a great many words went to very small substance; and no wonder, thought Ethel, when all they had to propose and second was the obvious fact that Missions were very good things.

Dr. Hoxton pompously, Sir Henry Walkinghame creditably, assisted the ladies and gentlemen to resolve that the S. P. G. wanted help; Mr. Lake made a stammering, and Mr. Rivers, with his good-natured face, hearty manner, and good voice, came in well after him, with a straightforward speech, so brief, that Ethel gave Flora credit for the best she had yet heard.

Mr. Wilmot said something which the sharpest ears in the front row might, perhaps, have heard, and which resulted in Dr. Spencer standing up. Ethel hardly would have known who was speaking had her eyes been shut. His voice was so different, when raised and pitched, so as to show its power and sweetness; the fine polish of his manner was redoubled, and every sentence had the most graceful turn. It was like listening to a well-written book, so smooth and so fluent, and yet so earnest—his pictures of Indian life so beautiful, and his strong affection for the converts he described now and then making his eyes fill, and his voice falter, as if losing the thread of his studied composition—a true and dignified work of art, that made Dr. May whisper to Flora, ' You see what he can do. They would have given anything to have had him for a lecturer.'

With half a sigh, Ethel saw Norman rise, and step forward. He began with eyes fixed on the ground, and, in a low, modest tone, to speak of the islands that Harry had visited; but gradually the poetic nature, inherent in him, gained the mastery; and though his language was strikingly simple, in contrast with Dr. Spencer's ornate periods, and free from all trace of ' the lamp,' it rose in beauty and fervour at every sentence. The feelings that had decided his lot gave energy to his discourse, and repressed as they had been by reserve and diffidence, now flowed forth, and gave earnestness to natural gifts of eloquence of the highest order. After his quiet, unobtrusive beginning, there was the more wonder to find how he seemed to raise up the audience with him, in breathless attention, as to a strain of sweet music, carrying them without thought of the scene, or of the speaker, to the lovely isles, and the inhabitants of noble promise, but withering for lack of knowledge; and finally closing his speech, when they were wrought up to the highest pitch, by an appeal that touched them all home; ' for well did he know,' said he, ' that the universal brotherhood was drawn closest in circles nearer home, that beneath the shadow of their own old Minster, gladness and mourning floated alike for all; and that all those who had shared in the welcome to one, given back as it were from the grave, would own the same debt of gratitude to the hospitable islanders.'

He ceased. His father wiped his spectacles, and almost audibly murmured, ' Bless him !' Ethel, who had sat like one enchanted, forgetting who spoke, forgetting all save the islanders, half-turned, and met Richard's smiling eyes, and his whisper—' I told you so.'

The impress of a man of true genius and power had been made throughout the whole assembly; the Archdeacon put Norman out of countenance by the thanks of the meeting, for his admirable speech, and all the world, except the Oxford men, were in a state of as much surprise as pleasure.

'Splendid speaker, Norman May, if he would oftener put himself out,' Harvey Anderson commented. 'Pity he has so many of the good Doctor's prejudices!'

'Well, to be sure!' quoth Mrs. Ledwich. 'I knew Mr. Norman was very clever, but I declare I never thought of such as this! I will try my poor utmost for those interesting natives.'

'That youth has first-rate talents,' said Lord Cosham. 'Do you know what he is designed for? I should like to bring him forward.'

'Ah!' said Dr. Hoxton. 'The year I sent off May and Anderson was the proudest year of my life!'

'Upon my word!' declared Mrs. Elwood. 'That Dr. Spencer is as good as a book, but Mr. Norman—— I say, father, we will go without the new clock, but we'll send somewhat to they men that built up the Church, and has no Minister.'

'A good move that,' said Dr. Spencer. 'Worth at least £20. That boy has the temperament of an orator, if the morbid were but a grain less.'

'O Margaret!' exclaimed Blanche. 'Dr. Spencer made the finest speech you ever heard, only it was rather tiresome; and Norman made everybody cry—and Mary worse than all!'

'There is no speaking of it. One should live such things, not talk over them,' said Meta Rivers.

Margaret received the reports of the select few, who visited her up-stairs, where she was kept quiet, and only heard the hum of the swarm, whom Dr. May, in vehement hospitality, had brought home to luncheon, to Ethel's great dread, lest there should not be enough for them to eat.

Margaret pitied her sisters, but heard that all was going well; that Flora was taking care of the elders, and Harry and Mary were making the younger fry very merry at the table on the lawn. Dr. May had to start early to see a sick gardener at Drydale before coming on to Cocksmoor, and came up to give his daughter a few minutes.

'We get on famously,' he said. 'Ethel does well when she is in for it, like Norman. I had no notion what was in the lad. They are perfectly amazed with his speech. It seems hard to give such as he is up to those outlandish places—but there, his speech should have taught me better—one's best—and, now and then, he seems my best.'

'One comfort is,' said Margaret, smiling, 'you would miss Ethel more.'

Gallant old King! I am glad she has had her wish—Good-bye, my Margaret, we will think of you—I wish—'

'I am very happy,' was Margaret's gentle re-assurance. 'The dear little Daisy looks just as her godfather imagined her—' and happy was her face when her father quitted her.

Margaret's next visitor was Meta, who came to reclaim her bonnet, and, with a merry smile, to leave word that she was walking on to Cocksmoor. Margaret remonstrated on the heat.

'Let me alone,' said she, making her pretty wilful gesture. 'Ethel and Mary ought to have a lift, and I have had no walking to-day.'

'My dear, you don't know how far it is. You can't go alone.'

'I am lying in wait for Miss Bracy, or something innocent,' said Meta. 'In good time—here comes Tom.'

Tom entered, declaring that he had come to escape from the clack down-stairs.

'I'll promise not to clack, if you will be so kind as to take care of me to Cocksmoor,' said Meta.

'Do you intend to walk?'

'If you will let me be your companion.'

'I shall be most happy,' said Tom, colouring with gratification, such as he might not have felt, had he known that he was chosen for his innocence.

He took a passing glimpse at his neck-tie, screwed up the nap of his glossy hat to the perfection of its central point, armed himself with a knowing little stick, and hurried his fair companion out by the back-door, as much afraid of losing the glory of being her sole protector as she was of falling in with an escort of as much consequence, in other eyes, as was Mr. Thomas in his own.

She knew him less than any of the rest, and her first amusement was, keeping silence to punish him for complaining of clack; but he explained that he did not mean quiet, sensible conversation—he only referred to those foolish women's raptures over the gabble they had been hearing at the Town Hall.

She exclaimed, whereupon he began to criticise the speakers with a good deal of acuteness, exposing the weak points, but magnanimously owning that it was tolerable for the style of thing, and might go down at Stoneborough.

'I wonder you did not stay away, as Harry did.'

'I thought it would be marked,' observed the thread-paper Tom, as if he had been at least county member.

'You did quite right,' said Meta, really thinking so.

'I wished to hear Dr. Spencer, too,' said Tom. 'There is a

man who does know how to speak! He has seen something of the world, and knows what he is talking of.'

'But he did not come near Norman.'

'I hated listening to Norman,' said Tom. 'Why should he go and set his heart on those black savages?'

'They are not savages in New Zealand.'

'They are all niggers together,' said Tom, vehemently. 'I cannot think why Norman should care for them more than for his own brothers and sisters. All I know is, that if I were my father, I would never give my consent.'

'It is lucky you are not,' said Meta, smiling defiance, though a tear shone in her eye. 'Dr. May makes the sacrifice with a free heart and willing mind.'

'Everybody goes and sacrifices somebody else,' grumbled Tom. 'Who are the victims now?'

'All of us. What are we to do without Norman? He is worth all of us put together; and I—' Meta was drawn to the boy as she had never been before, as he broke off short, his face full of emotion, that made him remind her of his father.

'You might go out and follow in his steps,' said she, as the most consoling hope she could suggest.

'Not I. Don't you know what is to happen to me? Ah! Flora has not told you. I thought she would not think it grand enough. She talked about diplomacy—'

'But what?' asked Meta, anxiously.

'Only that I am to stick to the old shop,' said Tom. 'Don't tell any one; I would not have the fellows know it.'

'Do you mean your father's profession?'

'Ay!'

'Oh! Tom, you don't talk of that as if you despised it?'

'If it is good enough for him, it is good enough for me, I suppose,' said Tom. 'I hate everything when I think of my brothers' going over the world, while I, do what I will, I must be tied down to the slow place all the rest of my days.'

'If you were away, you would be longing after it.'

'Yes; but I can't get away.'

'Surely, if the notion is so unpleasant to you, Dr. May would never insist?'

'It is my free choice, and that's the worst of it.'

'I don't understand.'

'Don't you see? Norman told me it would be a great relief to him if I would turn my mind that way—and I can't go against Norman. I found he thought he must, if I did not; and, you know, he is fit for all sorts of things that— Besides, he has a squeamishness about him, that makes him turn white, if one does but cut one's finger, and how he would ever go through the hospitals—'

Meta suspected that Tom was inclined to launch into horrors. 'So you wanted to spare him,' she said.

'Aye! and papa was so pleased by my offering, that I can't say a word of the bore it is. If I were to back out, it would come upon Aubrey, and he is weakly, and so young, that he could not help my father for many years.'

Meta was much struck at the motives that actuated the self-sacrifice, veiled by the sullen manner which she almost began to respect. 'What is done for such reasons must make you happy,' she said, 'though there may be much that is disagreeable.'

'Not the study,' said Tom. 'The science is famous work. I like what I see of it in my father's books, and there's a splendid skeleton at the hospital, that I long to be at. If it were not for Stoneborough, it would be all very well; but if I should get on ever so well at the examinations, it all ends here! I must come back, and go racing about this miserable circuit, just like your gold pheasant rampaging in his cage, seeing the same stupid people all my days.'

'I think,' said Meta, in a low, heartfelt voice, 'it is a noble, beautiful thing to curb down your ambition for such causes. Tom, I like you for it.'

The glance of those beautiful eyes was worth having. Tom coloured a little, but assumed his usual gruffness.

'I can't bear sick people,' he said.

'It has always seemed to me,' said Meta, 'that few lives could come up to Dr. May's. Think of going about, always watched for with hope, often bringing gladness and relief; if nothing else, comfort and kindness, his whole business doing good.'

'One is paid for it,' said Tom.

'Nothing could ever repay Dr. May,' said Meta. 'Can any one feel the fee anything but a mere form? Besides, think of the numbers and numbers that he takes nothing from; and, oh! to how many he has brought the most real good, when they would have shut their doors against it in any other form? Oh! Tom, I think none of you guess how every one feels about your father. I recollect one poor woman saying, after he had attended her brother, "He could not save his body, but, surely, ma'am, I think he was the saving of his soul."'

'It is of no use to talk of my being like my father,' said Tom.

Meta thought perhaps not, but she was full of admiration of

his generosity, and said, 'You will make it the same work of love, and charity is the true glory.'

Any inroad on Tom's reserved and depressed nature was a benefit; and he was of an age to be susceptible of the sympathy of one so pretty and so engaging. He had never been so much gratified or encouraged, and, wishing to prolong the *tête-à-tête*, he chose to take the short cut through the fir-plantations, unfrequented on account of the perpendicular, spiked railings that divided it from the lane.

Meta was hummingbird enough to be undismayed. She put hand and foot wherever he desired, flattered him by letting him handily help her up, and bounded light as a feather down on the other side, congratulating herself on the change from the dusty lane to the whispering pine-woods, between which wound the dark path, bestrewn with brown slippery needle-leaves, and edged with the delicate feathering ling and tufts of soft grass.

Tom had miscalculated the chances of interruption. Meta was lingering to track the royal highway of some giant ants to their fir-leaf hillock, when they were hailed from behind, and her squire felt ferocious at the sight of Norman and Harry closing the perspective of fir-trunks.

'Hollo! Tom, what a guide you are!' exclaimed Norman. 'That fence which even Ethel and Mary avoid!'

'Mary climbs like a cow, and Ethel like a father-long-legs,' said Tom. 'Now, Meta flies like a bird.'

'And Tom helped me so cleverly,' said Meta. 'It was an excellent move, to get into the shade and this delicious pine-tree fragrance.'

'Halt!' said Norman—'this is too fast for Meta.'

'I cannot,' said Harry. 'I must get there in time to set Dr. Spencer's tackle to rights. He is tolerably knowing about knots, but there is a dodge beyond him. Come on, Tom.'

He drew on the reluctant Etonian, who looked repiningly back at the increasing distance between him and the other pair, till a turn in the path cut off his view.

'I am afraid you do not know what you have undertaken,' said Norman.

'I am a capital walker. And I know, or do not know, how often Ethel takes the same walk.'

'Ethel is no rule.'

'She ought to be,' said Meta. 'To be like her has always been my ambition.'

'Circumstances have formed Ethel.'

'Circumstances! What an ambiguous word! Either Providence pointing to duty, or the world drawing us from it.'

'Stepping-stones, or stumblingblocks.'

'And oh! the difficult question when to bend them, or to bend to them!'

'There must be always some guiding,' said Norman.

'I believe there is,' said Meta, 'but when trumpet-peals are ringing around, it is hard to know whether one is really "waiting beside the tent," or only dawdling.'

'It is great self-denial in the immoveable square not to join the charge,' said Norman.

'Yes, but they, being shot at, are not deceiving themselves.'

'I suppose self-deception on those points is very common.'

'Especially among young ladies,' said Meta. 'I hear so much of what girls would do, if they might, or could, that I long to see them like Ethel—do what they can. And then it strikes me that I am doing the same, living wilfully in indulgence, and putting my trust in my own misgivings and discontent.'

'I should have thought that discontent had as little to do with you, as with any living creature.'

'You don't know how I could growl!' said Meta, laughing. 'Though less from having anything to complain of, than from having nothing to complain of.'

'You mean,' he said, pausing, with a seriousness and hesitation that startled her. 'Do you mean that this is not the course of life that you would choose?'

A sort of bashfulness made her put her answer playfully,

' " All play and no work makes Jack a mere toy."

Toys have a kindly mission, and I may be good for nothing else; but I would have rather been a coffee-pot than a China shepherdess.'

The gaiety disconcerted him, and he seemed to try to be silent, or to reply in the same tone, but he could not help returning to the subject. 'Then you find no charm in the refinements to which you have been brought up?'

'Only too much,' said Meta.

He was silent, and fearing to have added to his fine lady impression, she resumed. 'I mean that I never *could* dislike anything, and kindness gives these things a soul; but, of course, I should be better satisfied if I lived harder, and had work to do.'

'Meta!' he exclaimed, 'you tempt me very much! Would you?—No, it is too unreasonable. Would you share—share the work that I have undertaken?'

He turned aside and leant against a tree, as if not daring to watch the effect of the agitated words that had broken from him.

She had little imagined whither his last sayings had been tending, and stood still, breathless with the surprise.

'Forgive me,' he said, hastily. 'It was very wrong. I never meant to have vexed you, by the betrayal of my vain affection.'

He seemed to be going, and this roused her. 'Stay, Norman,' exclaimed she. 'Why should it vex me? I should like it very much, indeed.'

He faced suddenly towards her; 'Meta, Meta! is it possible? Do you know what you are saying?'

'I think I do.'

'You must understand me,' said Norman, striving to speak calmly. 'You have been— Words will not express what you have been to me for years past, but I thought you too far beyond my hopes. I know I ought to be removed from you—I believe that those who are debarred from earthly happiness, are marked for especial tasks. I never intended you to know what actuated me, and now the work is undertaken, and—and I cannot turn back—' he added, quickly, as if fearing himself.

'No, indeed,' was her steady reply.

'Then I may believe it!' cried Norman. 'You do—you will —you deliberately choose to share it with me?'

'I will try not to be a weight on you,' answered the young girl, with a sweet mixture of resolution and humility. 'It would be the greatest possible privilege. I really do not think I am a fine lady in grain, and you will teach me not to be too unworthy.'

'I? O Meta, you know not what I am. Yet with you, with you to inspire, to strengthen, to cheer— Meta, Meta, life is so much changed before me, that I cannot understand it yet—after the long dreary hopelessness—'

'I can't think why—' Meta had half said, when feminine dignity checked the words, consciousness and confusion suddenly assailed her, dyed her cheeks crimson, and stifled her voice.

It was the same with Norman, and bashfulness making a sudden prey of both—on they went under its dominion, in a condition partaking equally of discomfort and felicity; dreading the sound of their own voices, afraid of each other's faces, feeling they were treating each other very strangely and ungratefully, yet without an idea what to say next, or the power of speaking first; and therefore pacing onwards, looking gravely straight along the path, as if to prevent the rabbits and foxgloves from guessing that anything had been passing between them.

Dr. May had made his call at Drydale, and was driving up a rough lane, between furzy banks, leading to Cocksmoor, when he was aware of a tall gentleman on one side of the road and a

little lady on the other, with the whole space of the cart-track
between them, advancing soberly towards him.

'Hollo! Why, Meta! Norman! what brings you here?
Where are you going?'

Norman perceived that he had turned to the left instead of to
the right, and was covered with shame.

'That is all your wits are good for. It is well I met you, or
you would have led poor Meta a pretty dance! You will know
better than to trust yourself to the mercies of a scholar another
time. Let me give you a lift.'

The courteous Doctor sprang out to hand Meta in, but something made him suddenly desire Adams to drive on, and then
turning round to the two young people, he said, 'Oh!'

'Yes,' said Norman, taking her hand, and drawing her
towards him.

'What, Meta, my pretty one, is it really so? Is he to be
happy after all? Are you to be a Daisy of my own?'

'If you will let me,' murmured Meta, clinging to her kind
old friend.

'No flower on earth could come so naturally to us,' said Dr.
May. 'And, dear child, at last I may venture to tell you that
you have a sanction that you will value more than mine. Yes,
my dear, on the last day of your dear father's life, when some
foreboding hung upon him, he spoke to me of your prospects,
and singled out this very Norman as such as he would prefer.'

Meta's tears prevented all, save the two little words, 'thank
you;' but she put out her hand to Norman, as she still rested on
the Doctor's arm, more as if he had been her mother than Norman's father. 'Did he?' from Norman, was equally inexpres-
sive of the almost incredulous gratitude and tenderness of his
feeling.

It would not bear talking over at that moment, and Dr. May
presently broke the silence in a playful tone. 'So, Meta, good
men don't like heiresses?'

'Quite true,' said Meta, 'it was very much against me.'

'Or it may be the other way,' said Norman.

'Eh? Good men don't like heiresses—here's a man who likes
an heiress—therefore here's a man that is not good? Ah, ha!
Meta, you can see that is false logic, though I've forgotten mine.
—And pray, Miss, what are we to say to your uncle?'

'He cannot help it,' said Meta, quickly.

'Ha!' said the Doctor, laughing, 'we remember our twenty-
one years, do we?'

'I did not mean—I hope I said nothing wrong,' said Meta,

in blushing distress. 'Only after what you said, I can care for nothing else.'

'If I could only thank him,' said Norman, fervently.

'I believe you know how to do that, my boy,' said Dr. May, looking tenderly at the fairy figure between them, and ending with a sigh, remembering, perhaps, the sense of protection with which he had felt another Margaret lean on his arm.

The clatter of horses' hoofs caused Meta to withdraw her hand, and Norman to retreat to his own side of the lane, as Sir Henry Walkinghame and his servant overtook them.

'We will be in good time for the proceedings,' called out the Doctor. 'Tell them we are coming.'

'I did not know you were walking,' said Sir Henry, to Meta.

'It is pleasant in the plantations,' Dr. May answered for her; 'but I am afraid we are late, and our punctual friends will be in despair. Will you kindly say we are at hand.'

Sir Henry rode on, finding that he was not to be allowed to walk his horse with them, and that Miss Rivers had never looked up.

'Poor Sir Henry!' said Dr. May.

'He has no right to be surprised,' said Meta, very low.

'And so you were marching right upon Drydale!' continued Dr. May, not able to help laughing. 'It was a happy dispensation that I met you.'

'Oh! I am so glad of it!' said Meta.

'Though to be sure you were disarming suspicion by so cautiously keeping the road between you. I should never have guessed what you had been at.'

There was a little pause, then Meta said rather tremulously, 'Please—I think it should be known at once.'

'Our idle deeds confessed without loss of time, Miss?'

Norman came across the path, saying, 'Meta is right—it should be known.'

'I don't think uncle Cosham would object, especially hearing it while he is here,' said Meta—'and if he knew what you told us.'

'He goes to-morrow, does he not?' said Dr. May.

A silence of perplexity ensued. Meta, brave as she was, hardly knew her uncle enough to volunteer, and Norman was privately devising a beginning by the way of George, when Dr. May said, 'Well, since it is not a case for putting Ethel in the forefront, I must e'en get it over for you, I suppose.'

'O thank you,' they cried, both at once, feeling that he was the proper person in every way, and Norman added, 'The sooner the better, if Meta—'

'O yes, yes, the sooner the better,' exclaimed Meta. 'And let me tell Flora—poor dear Flora—she is always so kind.'

A testimony that was welcome to Dr. May, who had once, at least, been under the impression that Flora courted Sir Henry's attentions to her sister-in-law.

Further consultation was hindered by Tom and Blanche bursting upon them from the common, both echoing Norman's former reproach of 'A pretty guide!' and while Blanche explained the sufferings of all the assembly at their tardiness, Tom, without knowing it, elucidated what had been a mystery to the Doctor, namely, how they ever met, by his indignation at Norman's having assumed the guidance for which he was so unfit.

'A shocking leader; Meta will never trust him again,' said Dr. May.

Still Blanche thought them not nearly sufficiently sensible of their enormities, and preached eagerly about their danger of losing standing-room, when they emerged on the moor, and beheld a crowd, above whose heads rose the apex of a triangle, formed by three poles, sustaining a rope and huge stone.

'Here comes Dr. Spencer,' she said. 'I hope he *will* scold you.'

Whatever Dr. Spencer might have suffered, he was far too polite to scold, and a glance between the two physicians ended in a merry twinkle of his bright eyes.

'This way,' he said, 'we are all ready.'

'But where's my little Daisy?' said Dr. May.

'You'll see her in a minute. She is as good as gold.'

He drew them on up the bank—people making way for them —till he had stationed them among the others of their own party, beside the deep trench that traced the foundation, around a space that seemed far too small.

Nearly at the same moment, began the soft, clear sound of chanting wafted upon the wind, then dying away—carried off by some eddying breeze, then clear, and coming nearer and nearer.

> 'I will not suffer mine eyes to sleep,
>   Nor mine eye-lids to slumber:
>   Neither the temples of my head to take any rest ;
>   Until I find out a place for the Temple of the Lord.
>   An habitation for the mighty God of Jacob.'

Few, who knew the history of Cocksmoor, could help glancing towards the slight girl, who stood, with bent head, her hand clasped over little Aubrey's; while, all that was not prayer and thanksgiving in her mind, was applying the words to him, whose head rested in the Pacific isle, while, in the place which he had chosen, was laid the foundation of the Temple that he had given unto the Lord.

There came forth the procession: the Minster choristers, Dr. Spencer as architect, and, in her white dress, little Gertrude, led between Harry and Hector, Margaret's special choice for the occasion, and followed by the Stoneborough clergy.

' Let thy Priests be clothed with righteousness.'

It came in well with the gentle, meek, stedfast face of the young Curate of Cocksmoor, as he moved on in his white robe, and the sunlight shone upon his fair hair and calm brow, thankful for the past, and hoping, more than fearing, for the future.

The prayers were said, and there was a pause, while Dr. Spencer and the foreman advanced to the machine and adjusted it. The two youths then led forward the little girl, her innocent face and large blue eyes wearing a look of childish obedient solemnity, only half understanding what she did, yet knowing it was something great.

It was very pretty to see her in the midst of the little gathering round the foundation, the sturdy workman smiling over his hod of mortar, Dr. Spencer's silver locks touching her flaxen curls as he held the shining trowel to her, and Harry's bright head and hardy face, as he knelt on one knee to guide the little soft hand, while Hector stood by, still and upright, his eyes fixed far away, as if his thoughts were roaming to the real founder.

The Victoria coins were placed—Gertrude scooped up the mass of mortar, and spread it about with increasing satisfaction, as it went so smoothly and easily, prolonging the operation, till Harry drew her back, while, slowly down creaked the ponderous corner-stone into the bed that she had prepared for it, and, with a good will, she gave three taps on it with her trowel.

Harry had taken her hand, when, at the sight of Dr. May, she broke from him, and, as if taking sudden fright at her own un-wonted part, ran, at full speed, straight up to her father, and clung to him, hiding her face as he raised her in his arms and kissed her.

Meanwhile the strain arose :—

> ' Thou heavenly, new Jerusalem,
> Vision of peace, in Prophet's dream ;
> With living stones, built up on high,
> And rising to the starry sky—'

The blessing of peace seemed to linger softly and gently in the fragrant summer breeze, and there was a pause ere the sounds of voices awoke again.

'Etheldred—' Mr. Wilmot stood beside her, ere going to unrobe in the school. 'Etheldred, you *must* once let me say, God bless you for this.'

As she knelt beside her sister's sofa, on her return home, Margaret pressed something into her hand. 'If you please, dearest,

GERTRUDE LAYING THE STONE.

give this to Dr. Spencer, and ask him to let it be set round the stem of the chalice,' she whispered.

Ethel recognised Alan Ernescliffe's pearl hoop, the betrothal ring, and looked at her sister without a word.

'I wish it,' said Margaret, gently. 'I shall like best to know it there.'

So Margaret joined in Alan's offering, and Ethel dared say no more, as she thought how the 'relic of a frail love lost,' was becoming the 'token of endless love begun.' There was more true union in this, than in clinging to the mere tangible emblem —for broken and weak is all affection that is not knit together above in the One Infinite Love.

CHAPTER XXIII.

'Of lowly fields you think no scorn,
Yet gayest gardens would adorn,
    And grace wherever set;
Home, seated in your lowly bower,
Or wedded, a transplanted flower,
    I bless you, Margaret.'—CHARLES LAMB.

GEORGE RIVERS had an antipathy to ladies' last words keeping the horses standing, and his wife and sister dutifully seated themselves in the carriage at once, without an attempt to linger.

Four of the young gentlemen were to walk across to Abbotstoke and dine at the Grange; and Tom, who, reasoning from analogy, had sent on his black tie and agate studs, was so dismally disconcerted on finding that Norman treated his own going as a matter of course, that Richard, whose chief use of his right of primogeniture was to set himself aside, discovered that he was wanted at home, and that Tom would be much better at the Grange, offering, at the same time, to send Norman's dressing things by Dr. Spencer.

'Which,' observed Thomas, 'he would never have recollected for himself.'

'Tom would have had to lend him the precious studs.'—'He would not have had them, who would wear imitation?' 'I say, Tom, what did you give for them?' 'Better ask what the Jew gave for them, that bought them at Windsor fair—not a bad imitation, either—pity they weren't Malachite; but, no doubt, the Jew thought green would be personal.' 'As if they had any business to talk, who didn't know a respectable stud when they saw it—Harry, especially, with his hat set on the back of his head, like a sailor on the stage—' (a leap to set it to-rights—a skirmish, knocking Tom nearly into the ditch). 'Fine experience of the stage—all came from Windsor fair.' 'Ay, Hector might talk, but didn't he pay a shilling to see the Irish giant. He wouldn't confess, but it was a famous take in—giant had potatoes in his shoes.' 'Not he; he was seven feet ten high.' 'Ay, when he stood upon a stool—Hector would swallow anything—even the lady of a million postage stamps had not stuck in his throat —he had made Margaret collect for her.' 'And had not Tom, himself, got a bottle of ointment to get the red out of his hair?' —(great fury). 'His hair wasn't red—didn't want to change the colour—not half so red as Hector's own.' 'What was it then? lively auburn?' But for fear of Norman's losing his bearings, Harry would fetch a carrot, to compare. 'Better colour than theirs would ever be.' 'Then, what was the ointment for? to produce whiskers?—that was the reason Tom oiled himself like a Loyalty islander—his hair was so shiny, that Harry recommended a topknot, like theirs, &c.'

Norman was, like the others, in such towering glee, and took so full a share of the witticisms, that were the more noisily applauded, the worse they were, that Harry suggested that 'old June had lost his way, and found his spirits in Drydale—he must have met with a private grog-shop in the plantations—would not Tom confess'—'not he; it was all in private. He thought it was laughing-gas, or the reaction of being fried all the morning, holding forth in that Town Hall. He had longed to make a speech himself—no end of the good it would have done the old stagers to come out with something to the purpose. What would old Hoxton have thought of it?

> 'They shall dive for alligators, catch the wild goats by the beard;
> Whistle to the cockatoos, and mock the hairy-faced baboon;
> Worship mighty Mumbo Jumbo in the mountains of the moon.
> I myself in far Timbuctoo, leopard's blood shall daily quaff;
> Ride a tiger hunting, mounted on a thorough-bred giraffe.'

'Not you, Tom,' cried Hector.

> 'You, the swell, the Eton fellow! You, to seek such horrid places.
> You to haunt with squalid negroes, blubber lips, and monkey faces.
> Fool, again the dream, the fancy; don't I know the words are mad,
> For you count the grey barbarian lower than the Brocas cad!'

'Nay, it is the consequence of misanthropy at the detection of the frauds of sophisticated society,' said Norman.

> 'The edge of life is rusted;
> The agate studs and whisker ointment left him very much disgusted.'

'Perhaps it was Miss Rivers forsaking him. Was not that rather spider-hearted, Tom?'

'Come, Harry, it is time to have done. We are getting into civilized society—here's Abbotstoke.'

'Poor Norman, he is very far gone! He takes that scarecrow for civilized society!'

'Much better clothed than the society you have been accustomed to, July.' 'What a prize his wardrobe would be to the Black Prince!' 'Don't insult your betters?' 'Which? The scarecrow, or the Black Prince?'

Norman tried to call his companions to order, for they were close upon the village, and he began to tax himself with unbecoming levity; the effect of spirits pitched rather low, which did not easily find their balance under unwonted exhilaration, but Harry's antics were less easily repressed than excited, and if Tom had not heard the Grange clock strike half-past six, and' had not been afraid of not having time to array himself, and watch over Harry's neck-cloth, they would hardly have arrived in reasonable time. Dr. May had gone home, and there was no one in the drawing-room; but, as Norman was following the boys up-stairs, Flora opened her sitting-room door, and attracted his attention by silently putting her cold fingers into his hand, and drawing him into the room.

'Dear Norman, this is pleasant,' she said, affectionately; but in a voice so sunken, that all gladness seemed to be dead within, and the effect was far more mournful than if she had not attempted to smile congratulation.

'I will give you till Dr. Spencer comes,' she said. 'Then Norman can dress, and you must be a good child, and come down to me.'

The playfulness ill-suited the wan, worn face that seemed to have caught a grey tint from her rich poplin, her full toilette making the contrast almost more painful; and, as she closed the door, her brother could only exclaim, 'Poor Flora!'

'She is so kind,' said the voice of the white figure that moved towards him. 'O, if we could comfort her!'

'I trust to her own kindness working comfort to her at last,' said Norman. 'But is she often thus?'

'Whenever she is not bearing up for George's sake,' said Meta. 'She never says anything when she is alone with me, only she does not struggle with her looks.'

'It must be very trying for you.'

'Nay, I feel grateful to her for even so far relaxing the restraint—If I could but do her any good.'

'You cannot help doing her good,' said Norman.

Meta sighed, and shook her head slightly, as she said, 'She is so gentle and considerate. I think *this* has been no fresh pain to her to-day, but I cannot tell. The whole day has been a strange intermixture.'

'The two strands of joy and grief have been very closely twisted,' said Norman. 'That rose is shedding its fragrant leaves in its glory, and there is much that should have chastened the overflowing gladness of to-day.'

'As I was thinking,' whispered Meta, venturing nearer to him, and looking into his face with the sweet reliance of union in thought. She meant him to proceed, but he paused, saying, 'You were thinking—'

'I had rather hear it from you.'

'Was it not that we were taught to-day what is enduring, and gives true permanence and blessedness to such—to what there was between Ernescliffe and Margaret?'

Her dewy eyes, and face of deep emotion, owned that he had interpreted her thought.

'Theirs would, indeed, be a disheartening example,' he said, 'if it did not show the strength and peace that distance, sickness, death, cannot destroy.'

'Yes. To see that Church making Margaret happy as she lies smiling on her couch, is a lesson of lessons.'

'That what is hallowed must be blest,' said Norman; 'whatever the sundry and manifold changes.'

Each was far too humble to deny aloud any inequality with the goodness of Alan and Margaret, knowing that it would be at once disputed, trusting to time to prevent the over-estimate, and each believing the other was the one to bring the blessing.

'But Meta,' said Norman, 'have you heard nothing of—of the elders?'

'O yes,' said Meta, smiling, 'have not you?'

'I have seen no one.'

'I have!' said Meta, merrily. 'Uncle Cosham is delighted. That speech of yours has captivated him. He calls me a wise little woman to have found out your first-rate abilities. There's for you, sir.'

'I don't understand it! Surely he must be aware of my intentions?'

'He said nothing about them; but, of course, Dr. May must have mentioned them.'

'I should have thought so, but I cannot suppose—'

'That he would be willing to let me go,' said Meta. 'But then you know he cannot help it,' added she, with a roguish look, at finding herself making one of her saucy independent speeches.

'I believe you are taking a would-be Missionary, instead of Norman May!' he answered, with a sort of teasing sweetness.

'All would-be Missionaries did not make dear papa so fond of them,' said Meta, very low ; ' and you would not be Norman May without such purposes.'

'The purpose was not inspired at first by the highest motive,' said Norman ; 'but it brought me peace, and, after the kind of dedication that I inwardly made of myself, in my time of trouble, it would take some weighty reason, amounting to a clear duty, or physical impossibility, to make me think I ought to turn back. I believe—' the tears rose to his eyes, and he brought out the words with difficulty—'that, if this greatest of all joys were likely to hinder me from my calling, I ought to seek strength to regard it as a temptation, and to forego it.'

' You ought, if it were so,' said Meta, nevertheless holding him tighter. ' I could not bear to keep back a soldier. If this were last year, and I had any tie or duty here, it would be very hard. But no one needs me, and if the health I have always had be continued to me, I don't think I shall be much in the way. There,' drawing back a little, and trying to laugh off her feeling —'Only tell me at once if you think me still too much of a fine lady.'

'I—you—a fine lady ! Did anything ever give you the impression that I did ?'

' I shall not get poor Harry into a scrape, shall I ? He told me that you said so, last spring, and I feared you judged me too truly.'

After a few exclamations of utter surprise, it flashed on Norman. 'I know—I know—Harry interpreted my words in his own blunt fashion !'

'Then you did say something like it ?'

'No, but—but—In short, Meta, these sailors' imaginations go to great lengths. Harry had guessed more than I knew myself, before he had sailed, and taxed me with it. It was a subject I could not bear then, and I answered that you were too far beyond my hopes.'

' Six years ago !' said Meta, slowly, blushing deeper and deeper. 'Some eyes saw it all that time, and you—and,' she added, laughing, though rather tearfully, ' I should never have known it, if Tom had not taken me through the plantations !'

'Not if I had not discovered that your preferences did not lie—'

Among boudoirs and balls ?' said Meta. ' Harry was right. You thought me a fine lady after all.'

The gay taunt was cut short by a tap at the door, and Flora looked in. ' Dr. Spencer has brought your things, Norman. I am sorry to disturb you—but come down, Meta—I ran away very uncivilly to fetch you. I hope it is not too cruel,' as she drew Meta's arm into her own, and added, 'I have not been able to speak to George.'

Meta suspected that, in the wish to spare her, Flora had abstained from seeking him.

The evening went off like any other evening—people ate and talked—thought Mrs. Rivers looking very ill, and Miss Rivers very pretty—Flora forced herself into being very friendly to Sir Henry, commiserating the disappointment to which she had led him ; and she hoped that he suspected the state of affairs, though Tom, no longer supplanted by his elder brother, pursued Meta into the sheltered nook, where Flora had favoured her seclusion, to apologize for having left her to the guidance of poor Norman, whose head was with the blackamoors. It was all Harry's fault.

'Nonsense, Tom,' said Harry ; 'don't you think Norman is better company than you, any day ?'

'Then why did you not walk him off instead of me ?' said Tom, turning round sharply.

'Out of consideration for Meta. She will tell you that she was very much obliged to me—' Harry checked himself, for Meta was colouring so painfully, that his own sunburnt face caught the glow. He pushed Tom's slight figure aside with a commanding move of his broad hand, and said, 'I beg your pardon, upon my word, though I don't know what for.'

'Nor I,' said Meta, rallying herself and smiling. 'You have no pardon to beg. You will know it all to-morrow.'

'Then I know it now,' said Harry, sheltering his face by leaning over the back of a chair, and taming the hearty gaiety of his voice. 'Well done, Meta—there's nothing like old June in all the world! You may take my word for it, and I knew you would have the sense to find it out.'

They were well out of sight, and Meta only answered by a good tight squeeze of his kind hand between both her own. Tom, suddenly recovering from his displeasure at being thrust aside, whisked round, dropped on a footstool before Meta, looked up in her face, and said, 'Hollo!' in such utter amazement that there was nothing for it but to laugh more uncontrollably than was convenient. 'Come along, Tom,' said Harry, pulling him up by force, 'she does not want any of your nonsense. We will not plague her now.'

'Thank you, Harry,' said Meta. 'I cannot talk rationally just yet. Don't think me unkind, Tom.'

Tom sat in a sort of trance all the rest of the evening.

Lord Cosham talked to Norman, who felt as if he were being

patronized on false pretences, drew into his shell, and displayed none of his 'first-rate abilities.'

Dr. Spencer discussed his architecture with the Archdeacon; but his black eyes roamed heedfully after the young gentleman and lady, in the opposite corners of the room; and, as he drove home afterwards, with the youths, he hummed scraps of Scottish songs, and indulged in silent smiles.

Those at home had been far more demonstrative. Dr. May had arrived, declaring himself the proudest Doctor in her Majesty's dominions, and Ethel needed nothing but his face to explain why, and tell her that dear old June's troubles were over, and their pretty little Meta was their own—a joy little looked for to attend their foundation stone.

The dreaded conference with Lord Cosham had proved highly gratifying. There might be something in the fact that he could not help it, which assisted in his ready acquiescence, but he was also a sensible right-minded man, who thought that the largeness of Meta's fortune was no reason that it should be doubled; considered that, in the matter of connection, the May family had the advantage, and saw in Norman a young man whom any one might have pleasure in bringing forward. Oxford had established confidence both in his character and talents, and his speech had been such as to impress an experienced man, like Lord Cosham, with an opinion of his powers, that prepared a welcome for him, such as no one could have dared to expect. His lordship thought his niece not only likely to be happier, but to occupy a more distinguished position with such a man as Norman May, than with most persons of ready-made rank and fortune.

The blushing and delighted Dr. May had thought himself bound to speak of his son's designs, but he allowed that the project had been formed under great distress of mind, and when he saw it treated by so good a man, as a mere form of disappointed love, he felt himself reprieved from the hardest sacrifice that he had ever been called on to make, loved little Meta the better for restoring his son, and once more gave a free course to the aspirations that Norman's brilliant boyhood had inspired. Richard took the same view, and the evening passed away in an argument—as if any one had been disputing with them—the father reasoning loud, the son enforcing it low, that it had become Norman's duty to stay at home to take care of Meta, whose father would have been horrified at his taking her to the Antipodes. They saw mighty tasks for her fortune to effect in England, they enhanced each other's anticipations of Norman's career, overthrew abuses before him, heaped distinctions upon him, and had made him Prime Minister, and settled his policy, before ten o'clock brought their schemes to a close.

Mary gazed and believed; Margaret lay still and gently assented; Ethel was silent at first, and only when the fabric became extremely airy and magnificent, put in her word with a vehement dash at the present abuses, which grieved her spirit above all; and, whether vulnerable or not, Norman was to dispose of, like so many giants before Mr. Great-heart.

She went up-stairs, unable to analyse her sentiments. To be spared the separation would be infinite relief—all this prosperity made her exult—the fair girl at the Grange was the delight of her heart, and yet there was a sense of falling off; she disliked herself for being either glad or sorry, and could have quarrelled with the lovers for perplexing her feelings so uncomfortably.

Though she sat up till the party returned, she was inclined to be supposed in bed, so as to put off the moment of meeting; but Margaret, who she hoped was asleep, said from her pillow, 'Ask dear Norman to let me give him one kiss.'

She ran down headlong, clutched Norman as he was taking off his great-coat, told him that Margaret wanted him, and dragged him up without letting him go, till she reached the first landing, where she stood still, saying, breathlessly, 'New Zealand.'

'If I wished to fail, she would keep me to it.'

'I beg your pardon,' said Ethel, claiming heartily his caress, 'I was wrong to doubt either of you. Now, I know how to feel! But Margaret must not wait.'

The happy youth, in the flush of love and joy, bent gently, almost tearfully, down in silence to the white form, half-seen in the twilight, whose hopes had fleeted away from earth, and who was calmly, softly gliding after them. Hardly a word was uttered, but of all the many heartfelt thoughts that had passed while the face was pressed into Margaret's pillow, and her sympathizing arms round the neck, surely none was ever deeper, than was his prayer and vow, that his affection should be like hers, unearthly, and therefore enduring.

The embrace was all. Margaret must not be agitated; and, indeed, the events of the day had been too much for her, and the ensuing morning brought the fluttering of her heart and prostration of strength, no longer a novelty and occasion of immediate terror, but the token of the waning power of life.

Till she was better, her father had no thoughts for aught else, but, as with many another invalid, the relief from present distress was as cheering as if it had been recovery, and ere night, her placid look of repose had returned, and she was devising pretty greetings for her newest Daisy.

Perhaps the sobering effect of these hours of anxiety was in Norman's favour, on entering into conversation with his father. Those visions, which had had their swing the night before, belonged to the earlier, more untamed period of Dr. May's life, and had melted away in the dim room, made sacred by lingering mementos of his wife, and in the sound of that panting breath and throbbing heart. His vehemence had been, after all, chiefly against his own misgivings; and when he heard of his son's resolution, and Meta's more than acquiescence, he was greatly touched, and recurred to his kind, sorrowful promise, that he would never be a stumbling-block in the path of his children. Still, he owned himself greatly allured by the career proposed by Lord Cosham, and thought Norman should consider the opportunities of doing good in, perhaps, a still more important and extensive field than that which he had chosen.

'Time was that I should have grasped at such a prospect,' said Norman; 'but I am not the man for it. I have too much ambition, and too little humility. You know, father, how often you have had to come to my rescue, when I was running after success as my prime object.'

'Vanity fair is a dangerous place, but you who have sound principles and pure motives—'

'How long would my motives be pure?' said Norman. 'Rivalry and party-spirit make me distrust my motives, and then my principles feel the shock. Other men are marked by station for such trials, and may be carried through them, but I am not.'

'Yet some of these men are far from your equals.'

'Not perhaps in speechifying,' said Norman, smiling; 'but in steadiness of aim, in patience, in callousness, in seeing one side of the question at once.'

'You judge rightly for your own peace, you will be the happier; I always doubted whether you had nerve to make your wits available.'

'It may be cowardice,' said Norman, 'but I think not. I could burn for the combat; and if I had no scruples, I could enjoy bearing down such as—'

Of course Dr. May burst in with a political name, and—'I wish you were at him!'

'Whether I could is another matter,' said Norman, laughing; 'but the fact is, that I stand pledged; and if I embraced what to *me* would be a worldly career, I should be running into temptation, and could not expect to be shielded from it.'

'Your old rule,' said Dr. May. 'Seek to be less rather than more. But there is another choice. Why not a parsonage at home?'

'Pleasant parishes are not in the same need,' said Norman.

'I wonder what poor old Rivers would say to you, if he knew what you want to do with his daughter! Brought up as she has been—to expose her to the roughness of a colonial life, such as I should hesitate about for your sisters.'

'It is her own ardent desire.'

'True; but are girlish enthusiasms to be trusted? Take care, Norman, take care of her—she is a bit of the choicest porcelain of human kind, and not to be rudely dealt with.'

'No, indeed; but she has the brave enterprising temper, to which I fully believe that actual work in a good cause is far preferable to what she calls idleness. I do not believe that we are likely to meet with more hardship than she would gladly encounter, and would almost—nay, quite enjoy.'

'You do not know what your aunt has had to go through.'

'A few years make a great difference in a colony. Still, it may be right for me to go out alone, and judge for her; but we shall know more if my aunt comes home.'

'Yes, I could trust a good deal to her. She has much of your mother's sense. Well, you must settle it as you can with Meta's people! I do not think they love the pretty creature better than I have done from the first minute we saw her—don't you remember it, Norman?'

'Remember it? Do I not? From the frosted cedar downwards! It was the first germ of spring in that dreary winter. What a Fairyland the Grange was to me!'

'You may nearly say the same of me,' confessed Dr. May, smiling; 'the sight of that happy little sunny spirit, full of sympathy and sweetness, always sent me brighter on my way. Wherever you may be, Norman, I am glad you have her, being one apt to need a pocket sunbeam.'

'I hope my tendencies are in no danger of depressing her!' said Norman, startled. 'If so—'

'No such thing—she will make a different man of you. You have been depressed by—that early shock, and the gap at our own fireside—all that we have shared together, Norman. To see you begin on a new score, with a bright home of your own, is the best in this world that I could wish for you, though I shall live over my own twenty-two years in thinking of you, and that sweet little fairy. But now go, Norman—she will be watching for you and news of Margaret. Give her all sorts of love from me.'

Norman fared better with the uncle than he had expected. Lord Cosham, as a philanthropist, could not, with any consistency, set his face against missions, even when the cost came so near home; and he knew that opposition made the like intentions assume a heroic aspect that maintained them in greater force. He therefore went over the subject in a calm dispassionate manner, which exacted full and grateful consideration from the young man.

The final compromise was, that nothing should be settled for a year, during which Norman would complete his course of study, and the matter might be more fully weighed. Mrs. Arnott would probably return, and bring experience and judgment, which would, or ought to, decide the question—though Meta had a secret fear that it might render it more complicated than ever. However, the engagement and the mission views had both been treated so much more favourably than could have been hoped, that they felt themselves bound to be patient and forbearing. As Meta said, 'If they showed themselves wilful children, they certainly did not deserve to be trusted anywhere.'

Lord Cosham made his niece listen to a kind exhortation not to press her influence towards a decision that might be repented, when too late to be repaired, without a degrading sense of failure —putting her in mind of the privations that would lose romance by their pettiness, and which money could not remedy; and very sensibly representing that the effect of these on temper and health was to be duly considered, as a serious impediment to usefulness.

'It would be worse for him alone,' said Meta.

'That is not certain,' said her uncle. 'A broken-down wife is a terrible drag.'

'I know it is so,' said Meta, firmly; 'but risks must be run, and he is willing to take the chance. I do not think it can be presumption, for, you know, I am strong; and Dr. May would say if he could not warrant me. I fancy household work would be more satisfactory, and less tiring, than doing a season thoroughly; and I mean to go through a course of Finchley manuals in preparation.'

'I hope you know what you are doing,' sighed her uncle. 'You see it all *couleur de rose.*'

'I think not. It is because it is not *couleur de rose* that I am so much bent upon it. I have had plenty of that all my life. I expect much that will be very disagreeable and not at all heroic; but if I can only make Norman think it fun, that will be one purpose answered. I do believe he will do his work better for having me, and, at least, I shall pay his passage.'

Her uncle shook his head, but did not try to say any more.

George had begun by loud exclamations against the project, in which he was vehemently abetted by Tom, who primed him with all sorts of outrageous abuse of the niggers and cannibals, who would make Norman's coats out of all shape, and devour little Meta at a mouthful—predictions which Meta accepted most merrily, talking of herself so resignedly, as bound upon a spit, and calling out to be roasted slower and faster, that she safely conducted off their opposition by way of a standing joke. As to Norman's coats, she threatened to make them herself, and silenced Tom for ever by supposing, in malicious simplicity, that he must be able to teach her the most unexceptionable cut.

Flora kept her opinions to herself. Only once, when urged to remonstrate, she said, 'I could not—I would not.'

She was gently and touchingly considerate towards the lovers, silently but unobtrusively obviating all that could jar on their feelings, and employing her exquisite tact in the kindest manner.

She released Meta from the expedition to Ryde, silencing scruples on the one hand, by a suggestion of 'poor Sir Henry,' and, on the other, by offering to exchange her for Mary. The first proposal made Mary take such a spring in her chair, with eyes so round, and cheeks so red, and such a shriek about Harry and the Bucephalus, that no one could have borne to say one word in opposition, even if it had not been the opinion of the Council that sea air would best repair Mary's strength.

Ethel had some private fears of a scene, since it was one of Miss Bracy's idiosyncrasies to be hurt whenever Mary was taken out of her hands; and she went to announce the design, in dread lest this shock should destroy the harmony that had prevailed for many months; nay, she almost believed, since the loss of the Alcestis had been known.

She was agreeably surprised. Miss Bracy thought Mary in need of the change, and discussed both her and Blanche in so pleasant and sensible a manner, that Ethel was quite relieved. She partook in Mary's anticipations of pleasure, forwarded her preparations, and was delighted with her promise of letters—promises that Mary bestowed so largely, in the fulness of her heart, that there were fears lest her whole time should be spent in writing.

Her soft heart indulged in a shower of tears when she wished them all good-bye; and Ethel and Blanche found the house was very empty without her; but that was only till Meta came in from a walk with Norman, and, under the plea of trying to supply Mary's place, did the work of five Maries, and a great deal besides.

Nothing could be happier than Meta's visit, brightening the house so that the Mays thought they had never known half her charms, helping whatever was going on, yet ready to play with Daisy, tell stories to Aubrey, hear Tom's confidences, talk to Margaret, read with Norman, and teach Richard singing for his school-children. The only vexation was, that every one could not always engross her entirely; and Dr. May used to threaten that they should never spare her to that long-legged fellow, Norman.

She had persuaded Bellairs to go and take care of Flora and Mary, instead of the French maid—a plan which greatly satisfied Margaret, who had never liked the looks of Coralie, and which Meta held to be a grand emancipation. She persuaded old nurse to teach her to be useful, and Margaret used to declare that she witnessed scenes as good as a play in her room, where the little dextrous scholar, apparently in jest, but really in sober earnest, wiled instruction from the old woman; and made her experiments, between smiles and blushes, and merrily glorying in results that promised that she would be a notable housewife. Whether it were novelty or not, she certainly had an aptitude and delight in domestic details, such as Ethel never could attain; and, as Dr. May said, the one performed by a little finger what the other laboured at with a great mind.

In the school-room, Meta was as highly appreciated. She found an hour for helping Blanche in her music, and for giving, what was still more useful, an interest and spirit to studies, where, it must be owned, poor good Mary had been a dead weight. She enlivened Miss Bracy so much, and so often contrived a walk or a talk with her, that the saucy Blanche told Hector that she thought Ethel would be quite second-fiddle with Miss Bracy.

No such thing. Miss Bracy's great delight was in having a listener for her enthusiasm about Miss Ethel. She had been lately having a correspondence with a former school-fellow, who was governess in a family less considerate than the Mays, and who poured out in her letters, feelings much like those with which Miss Bracy had begun.

Nothing could be more salutary than to find herself repeating all Ethel's pieces of advice; and, one day, when her friend had been more distressed than usual, she called Ethel herself, to consult on her answer, owning how much she was reminded of herself.

'Indeed,' she added, 'I am afraid it would only tease you to hear how much I am indebted to your decision and kindness—'

'Nay,' said Ethel, laughing her awkward laugh. 'You have often had to forget my savage ways.'

'Pray don't say that—'

'I think,' said Ethel, breaking in, 'the philosophy is this: I believe that it is a trying life. I know teaching takes a great deal out of one; and loneliness may cause tendencies to dwell on fancied slights in trifles, that might otherwise be hurried over. But I think the thing is, to pass them over, and make a conscience of turning one's mind to something fresh—'

'As you made me do, when you brought me amusing books, and taught me botany—'

'And still more, when you took to working for the Infant School. Yes, I think the way to be happy and useful is to get up many interests, so as to be fresh and vigorous, and think not at all of personalities. There's a truism!'

'Very true, though,' said Miss Bracy. 'Indeed, all your kindness and consideration would never have done me half the good they have, dear Miss Ethel, if you had not taught me that referring all to one's own feelings and self is the way to be unhappy.'

'Just so,' said Ethel. 'It is the surest way for any one to be miserable.'

'If I could only persuade poor dear Ellen to think that even if a slight were real, it ought to be borne forgivingly, and not brooded over. Ah! you are laughing; perhaps you have said the same of me.'

'You would forgive it now, I think,' said Ethel.

'I never thought I did not forgive. I did not see that brooding over vexations was not pardoning them. I have told her so now: and oh! if she could but have seen how true sorrows are borne here, she would be cured, like me, of making imaginary ones.'

'None could help being better for living with papa,' said Ethel.

Ethel made Miss Bracy happy by a kiss before she left her. It was a cheering belief that, whatever the future trials of her life might be, the gentle little lady would meet them with a healthier mind, more vigorous in overlooking troubles, and without punctilious sensitiveness on the look-out for affronts. 'Believing all things, bearing all things, hoping all things, enduring all things,' would be to her the true secret of serenity of spirits.

Ethel might not have been blameless or consistent in her dealings in this difficult intercourse, but her kind heart, upright intention, and force of character, had influence far beyond her own perception. Indeed, she knew not that she had personal influence at all, but went on in her own straight-forward humility.

CHAPTER XXIV.

'Enough of foresight sad, too much
    Of retrospect have I;
And well for me, that I, sometimes,
    Can put those feelings by.'

'There speaks the man we knew of yore,'
    Well pleased, I hear them say;
'Such was he, in his lighter moods,
    Before our heads were grey.

Buoyant he was in spirit, quick
    Of fancy, light of heart;
And care, and time, and change have left
    Untouch'd his better part.'—SOUTHEY.

ETHELDRED MAY and Meta Rivers were together in the drawing-room. The time-piece pointed towards ten o'clock, but the tea-things were on the table, prepared for a meal, the lamp shone with a sort of consciousness, and Ethel moved restlessly about, sometimes settling her tea equipage, sometimes putting away a stray book, or resorting by turns to her book, or to work a red and gold scroll on coarse canvas, on the other end of which Meta was employed.

'Nervous, Ethel?' said Meta, looking up with a merry provoking smile, knowing how much the word would displease.

'That is for you,' retorted Ethel, preferring to carry the war into the enemy's quarters. 'What, don't you know that prudent people say that your fate depends on her report?'

'At least,' said Meta, laughing, 'she is a living instance that every one is not eaten up, and we shall see if she fulfils Tom's prediction, of being tattooed, or of having a slice out of the fattest part of her cheek.'

'I know very well,' said Ethel, 'the worse she said it would be, the more you would go.'

'Not quite that,' said Meta, blushing, and looking down.

'Come! don't be deceitful!' said Ethel. 'You know very well that you are still more bent on it than you were last year.'

'To be sure I am!' said Meta, looking up with a sudden beamy flash of her dark eyes. 'Norman and I know each other so much better now,' she added, rather falteringly.

'Aye! I know you are ready to go through thick and thin, and that is why I give my consent and approbation. You are not to be stopped for nonsense.'

'Not for nonsense, certainly,' said Meta, 'but—' and her voice became tremulous—'if Dr. May deliberately said it would be wrong, and that I should be an encumbrance and perplexity, I am making up my mind to the chance.'

'But what would you do?' asked Ethel.

'I don't know. You should not ask such questions, Ethel.'

'Well! it won't happen, so it is no use to talk about it,' said Ethel. 'Fancy my having made you cry!'

'Very silly of me,' said Meta, brightening and laughing, but sighing. 'I am only afraid Mrs. Arnott may think me individually unfit for the kind of life, as if I could not do what other women can. Do I look so?'

'You look as if you were meant to be put under a glass case!' said Ethel, surveying the little elegant figure, whose great characteristic was a look of exquisite finish, not only in the features and colouring, the turn of the head, and the shape of the small rosy-tipped fingers, but in everything she wore, from the braids of black silk hair, to the little shoe on her foot, and even in the very lightness and gaiety of her movements.

'Oh! Ethel!' cried Meta, springing up in dismay, and looking at herself in the glass. 'What is the matter with me? Do tell me!'

'You'll never get rid of it,' said Ethel, 'unless you get yourself tattooed! Even separation from Bellairs hasn't answered. And, after all, I don't think it would be any satisfaction to Norman, or papa. I assure you, Meta, whatever you may think of it, it is not so much bother to be prettier than needful, as it is to be uglier than needful.'

'What is needful?' said Meta, much amused.

'I suppose to be like Mary, so that nobody should take notice of one, but that one's own people may have the satisfaction of saying, "she is pleasing," or "she is in good looks." I think Gertrude will come to that. That's one comfort.'

'That is your own case, Ethel. I have heard those very things said of you.'

'Of my hatchet face!' said Ethel, contemptuously. 'Some one must have been desperately bent on flattering the Member's family.'

'I could repeat more,' said Meta, 'if I were to go back to the Commemoration, and to the day you went home.'

Ethel crimsoned, and made a sign with her hand, exclaiming, 'Hark!'

'It went past.'

'It was the omnibus. She must be walking down!' Ethel breathed sort, and wandered aimlessly about—Meta put her arm round her waist.

'I did not think this would be so much to you,' she said.

'O Meta, it seems like dear mamma coming to see how we

have been going on. And then papa! I wish I had gone up to the station with him.'

'He has Richard.'

'Aye, but I am afraid Margaret is listening and will be restless, and have a palpitation, and I can't go and see, or I shall disturb her. O, I wish it were over.'

Meta stroked her, and soothed her, and assured her that all would do well, and presently they heard the click of the door. Ethel flew into the hall, where she stopped short, her heart beating high at the sound of overpoweringly familiar accents.

She was almost relieved by detecting otherwise little resemblance; the height was nearly the same, but there was not the plump softness of outline. Mrs. Arnott was small, thin, brisk and active, with a vivacious countenance, once evidently very fair and pretty, but aged and worn by toil, not trouble, for the furrows were the traces of smiles around her merry mouth, and beautiful blue eyes, that had a tendency to laugh and cry both at once. Dr. May, who had led her into the light, seemed to be looking her all over, while Richard was taking her wraps from her, and Ethel tried to encourage herself to go forward.

'Aye!' said the Doctor, kissing her. 'I *see* you Flora now. I have found you again.'

'I found you as soon as I heard your voice, Richard,' said she. 'And now for the bairnies.'

'Here is one, but there is but a poor show forthcoming to-night. Do you know her?'

There was an unspeakable joy in being pressed in aunt Flora's arms, like a returning beam from the sunshine of seven years ago.

'This must be Ethel! My dear, how you tower above me—you that I left in arms! And,' as she advanced into the drawing-room—'why, surely this is not Margaret.'

'A Margaret—not *the* Margaret. I wish I were,' said Meta, as Mrs. Arnott stood with an arm on her shoulder, in the midst of an embrace, Dr. May enjoying her perplexity and Meta's blushes. 'See, Flora, these black locks never belonged to Calton Hill daisies, yet a daisy of my own she is—Can't you guess?'

'Miss Rivers!' exclaimed Mrs. Arnott; and though she kissed her cordially, Meta suspected a little doubt and disappointment.

'Yes,' said Dr. May. 'We change Mary for this little woman, as Flora's lady-in-waiting, when she and her husband go out yachting and shooting.'

'Flora and her husband! There's a marvellous sound! Where are they?'

'They are staying at Eccleswood Castle,' said Ethel; 'and

Mary with them. They would have been at home to receive you, but your note yesterday took us all by surprise. Norman is away too, at a College meeting.'

'And Margaret—my Margaret! Does not she come down-stairs?'

'Ah! poor dear,' said Dr. May, 'she has not been in this room since that sultry day in July.'

'The eighteenth,' said Richard; the precision of the date marking but too well the consciousness that it was an epoch.

'We can keep her quieter up-stairs,' said Dr. May; 'but you must not see her to-night. She will enjoy you very much to-morrow; but excitement at night always does her harm, so we put her to bed, and told her to think about no one.'

Mrs. Arnott looked at him as if longing, but dreading, to ask further, and allowed her nephew and niece to seat her at the table, and attend to her wants, before she spoke again. 'Then the babies.'

'We don't keep babies, Gertrude would tell you,' said Dr. May. 'There are three great creatures, whom Ethel barbarously ordered off to bed. Ethel is master here, you must know, Flora —we all mind what she says.'

'O papa,' pleaded Ethel, distressed, 'you know it was because I thought numbers might be oppressive.'

'I never dispute,' said Dr. May. 'We bow to a beneficial despotism, and never rebel, do we, Meta?'

Seeing that Ethel took the imputation to heart, Meta rejoined. 'You are making Mrs. Arnott think her the strong-minded woman of the family, who winds up the clock and cuts the bread.'

'No; that she makes you do, when the boys are away.'

'Of course,' said Ethel, 'I can't be vituperated about hunches of bread. I have quite enough to bear on the score of tea.'

'Your tea is very good,' said Richard.

'See how they propitiate her,' maliciously observed the Doctor.

'Not at all; it is Richard standing up for his pupil,' said Ethel.

'It is all very well now, with people who know the capacities of mortal tea; but the boys expect it to last from seven o'clock to ten, through an unlimited number of cups, till I have announced that a teapot must be carved on my tombstone, with an epitaph, "Died of unreasonable requirements." '

Mrs. Arnott looked from one to the other, amused, observant, and perceiving that they were all under that form of shyness, which brings up family wit to hide embarrassment or emotion.

'Is Harry one of these unreasonable boys?' she asked. 'My dear Harry—I presume Ethel has not sent him to bed. Is there any hope of my seeing him?'

'Great hope,' said Dr. May. 'He has been in the Baltic fleet, a pretty little summer trip, from which we expect him to return any day. My old Lion! I am glad you had him for a little while, Flora.'

'Dear fellow! his only fault was being homesick, and making me catch the infection.'

'I am glad you did not put off your coming,' said Dr. May, gravely.

'You are in time for the Consecration,' said Richard.

'Ah! Cocksmoor! When will it take place?'

'On St. Andrew's day. It is St. Andrew's Church, and the Bishop fixed the day, otherwise it is a disappointment that Hector cannot be present.'

'Hector?'

'Hector Ernescliffe—poor Alan's brother, whom we don't well know from ourselves.'

'And you are curate, Ritchie?' said his aunt, 'if I may still call you so. You are not a bit altered from the mouse you used to be.'

'Church mouse to Cocksmoor,' said Dr. May, 'nearly as poor. We are to invest his patrimony in a parsonage, as soon as our architect in ordinary can find time for it. Spencer—you remember him?'

'I remember how you and he used to be inseparable! And he has settled down, at last, by your side?'

'The two old Doctors hope to bolster each other up till Mr. Tom comes down with modern science in full force. That boy will do great things—he has as clear a head as I ever knew.'

'And more—' said Ethel.

'Aye, as sound a heart. I must find you his tutor's letter, Flora. They have had a row in his tutor's house at Eton, and our boys made a gallant stand for the right, Tom especially, guarding the little fellows, in a way that does one good to hear of.'

'"I must express my strong sense of gratitude for his truth, uprightness, and moral courage,"' quoted Meta.

'Ah, ha! you have learnt it by heart! I know you copied it out for Norman, who has the best right to rejoice.'

'You have a set of children to be proud of, Richard!' exclaimed Mrs. Arnott.

'To be surprised at—to be thankful for,' said Dr. May, almost inarticulately.

To see her father so happy with Mrs. Arnott necessarily drew Ethel's heart towards her; and, when they had bidden him good night, the aunt instantly assumed a caressing confidence towards Ethel, particularly comfortable to one consciously backward and awkward, and making her feel as intimate as if the whole space of her rational life had not elapsed since their last meeting.

'Must you go, my dear?' said her aunt, detaining her over her fire. 'I can't tell how to spare you. I want to hear of your dear father. He looks aged and thin, Ethel, and yet that sweet expression is the same as ever. Is he very anxious about poor Margaret?'

'Not exactly anxious,' said Ethel, mournfully—'there is not much room for that.'

'My dear Ethel—you don't mean?—I thought—'

'I suppose we ought to have written more fully,' said Ethel, 'but it has been very gradual, and we never say it to ourselves. She is as bright, and happy, and comfortable as ever, in general, and, perhaps, may be so for a long time yet, but each attack weakens her.'

'What kind of attack?'

'Faintness—sinking. It is suspended action of the heart. The injury to the spine deranged the system, and then the long suspense, and the shock— It is not one thing more than another, but it must go on. Dr. Spencer will tell you. You won't ask papa too much about it?'

'No, indeed. And he bears it—'

'He bears everything. Strength comes up out of his great lovingness. But, oh! I sometimes long that he may never have any more sorrows.'

'My poor child!' said Mrs. Arnott, putting her arm round her niece's waist.

Ethel rested her head on her shoulder. 'Aunt Flora! aunt Flora! If any words could tell what Margaret has been ever since we were left. O, don't make me talk or think of ourselves without her. It is wrong to wish. And when you see her, that dear face of hers will make you happy in the present. Then,' added Ethel, not able to leave off with such a subject, 'you have our Norman to see.'

'Ah! Norman's project is too delightful to us; but I fear what it may be to your father.'

'He gives dear Norman, as his most precious gift, the flower and pride of us all.'

'But, Ethel, I am quite frightened at Miss Rivers's looks. Is it possible that—'

'Aunt Flora,' broke in Ethel, 'don't say a word against it. The choicest goods wear the best; and whatever woman can do, Meta Rivers can. Norman is a great tall fellow, as clever as possible, but perfectly *feckless*. If you had him there alone, he would be a bee without a queen—'

'Well, but—'

'Listen,' continued Ethel. 'Meta is a concentration of spirit and energy, delights in practical matters, is twice the housewife I am, and does all like an accomplishment. Between them, they will make a noble missionary—'

'But she looks—'

'Hush,' continued the niece. 'You will think me domineering; but please don't give any judgment without seeing; for they look to you as an arbitrator, and casual words will weigh.'

'Thank you, Ethel; perhaps you are right. When does he think of coming out?'

'When he is ordained—some time next year.'

'Does she live with you?'

'I suppose she lives with Flora; but we always manage to get her when Norman is at home.'

'You have told me nothing of Flora or Mary.'

'I have little *real* to tell. Good old Mary! I dare say Harry talked to you plentifully of her. She is a—a nice old darling,' said Ethel, fondly. 'We want her again very much, and did not quite bargain for the succession of smart visits that she has been paying.'

'With Flora?'

'Yes. Unluckily George Rivers has taken an aversion to the Grange, and I have not seen Flora this whole year.'

Ethel stopped short, and said that she must not keep Margaret expecting her. Perhaps her aunt guessed that she had touched the true chord of anxiety.

The morning brought a cheering account of Margaret; and Mrs. Arnott was to see her directly after breakfast. In the meantime, the firm limbs, blue eyes, and rosy face of Gertrude seemed a fair representation of the little bridesmaid, whom she remembered.

A very different niece did she find up-stairs, though the smiling, overflowing eyes, and the fond, eager look of recognition, as if asking to be taken to her bosom, had in them all the familiarity of old tenderness. 'Auntie! dear auntie! that you should have come back to me again!'

Mrs. Arnott fondly caressed her, but could not speak at first, for even her conversation with Ethel had not prepared her for so wasted and broken an appearance. Dr. May spoke briskly of Margaret's having behaved very well, and slept like a good child, told Margaret where he had to go that morning, and pointed out to Mrs. Arnott some relics of herself still remaining; but the nervous tremulousness of manner did not much comfort her, although Margaret answered cheerfully. Nothing was so effectual in composing the aunt, as Aubrey's coming headlong in to announce the gig, and to display to Margaret his last design for a Cathedral—drawing plans being just now his favourite sport.

'Architecture is all our rage at present,' said Margaret, as her father hurried away.

'I am so glad to have come in for the Consecration!' said Mrs. Arnott, following her niece's lead. 'Is that a model of the Church?'

'Oh! yes,' cried Margaret, lighting up. 'Richard made it for me.'

'May I show it to aunt Flora?' said Aubrey.

'Bring it here, if you can lift it,' said Margaret; and, aunt Flora helping, the great cumbersome thing was placed beside her, whilst she smiled and welcomed it like a child, and began an eager exhibition. 'Was it not a beautiful little pierced spire? —that was an extravagance of Dr. Spencer's own. Papa said he could not ask Captain Gordon to sanction it—the model did it no justice, but it was so very beautiful in the rich creamy stone rising up on the moor, and the blue sky looking through, and it caught the sunset lights so beautifully.' So animated was her description, that Mrs. Arnott could not help asking, 'Why, my dear, when have you seen it?'

'Never,' said Margaret, with her sweet smile. 'I have never seen Cocksmoor; but Dr. Spencer and Meta are always sketching it for me, and Ethel would not let an effect pass without telling me. I shall hear how it strikes you next.'

'I hope to see it by-and-by. What a comfortable deep porch! If we could build such churches in the Colonies, Margaret!'

'See what little Meta will do for you! Yes, we had the porch deep for a shelter—that is copied from the west-door of the Minster, and is it not a fine high-pitched roof? John Taylor, who is to be clerk, could not understand its being open; he said, when he saw the timbers, that a man and his family might live up among them. They are noble oak beams; we would not have any sham—here, Aubrey, take off the roof, and auntie will see the shape.'

'Like the ribs of a ship,' explained Aubrey, unconscious that the meaning was deeper than his sister could express, and he continued: 'Such fine oak beams! I rode with Dr. Spencer one day last year to choose them. It is a two-aisled Church, you see, that a third may be added.'

Ethel came up as Aubrey began to absorb the conversation. 'Lessons, Aubrey,' she said. 'So, Margaret, you are over your dear model?'

'Not forestalling you too much, I hope, Ethel, dear,' said Margaret; 'as you will show her the Church itself.'

'You have the best right,' said Ethel; 'but, come, Aubrey, we must not dawdle.'

'I will show you the stones I laid myself, aunt Flora,' said Aubrey, running off without much reluctance.

'Ethel has him in excellent order,' said Mrs. Arnott.

'That she has; she brings him on beautifully, and makes him enjoy it. She teaches him arithmetic in some wonderful scientific way that nobody can understand but Norman, and he not the details; but he says it is all coming right, and will make him a capital mathematical scholar, though he cannot add up pounds shillings and pence.'

'I expected to be struck with Ethel,' said Mrs. Arnott; 'and—'

'Well,' said Margaret, waiting.

'Yes, she does exceed my expectations. There is something curiously winning in that quaint, quick, decisive manner of hers. There is so much soul in the least thing she does, as if she could not be indifferent for a moment.'

'Exactly—exactly so,' said Margaret, delighted. 'It is really doing everything with all her might. Little, simple, everyday matters did not come naturally to her as to other people, and the having had to make them duties has taught her to do them with that earnest manner, as if there were a right and wrong to her in each little mechanical household office.'

'Harry described her to me thus,' said Mrs. Arnott, smiling: ' "As to Ethel, she is an odd fish; but Cocksmoor will make a woman of her after all." '

'Quite true!' cried Margaret. 'I should not have thought Harry had so much discernment in those days. Cocksmoor gave the stimulus, and made Ethel what she is. Look there—over the mantel-piece, are the designs for the painted glass, all gifts, except the East window. That one of St. Andrew introducing the lad with the loaves and fishes is Ethel's window. It is the produce of the hoard she began this time seven years, when she had but one sovereign in the world. She kept steadily on with it, spending nothing on herself that she could avoid, always intending it for the Church, and it was just enough to pay for this window.'

'Most suitable,' said Mrs. Arnott.

'Yes; Mr. Wilmot and I persuaded her into it; but I do not think she would have allowed it, if she had seen the application we made of it—the gift of her girlhood blessed and extended. Dear King Etheldred, it is the only time I ever cheated her.'

'This is a beautiful east window. And this little one—St. Margaret, I see.'

'Ah! papa would not be denied choosing that for his subject. We reproached him with legendary saints, and overwhelmed him with antiquarianism, to show that the Margaret of the dragon was not the Margaret of the daisy; but he would have it; and said we might thank him for not setting his heart on St Etheldreda.'

'This one?'

'That is mine,' said Margaret, very low; and her aunt abstained from remark, though unable to look, without tears, at the ship of the Apostles, the calming of the storm, and the scroll, with the verse—

'He bringeth them unto the haven where they would be.'

Beneath were the initials, 'A. H. E.,' and the date of the year, the only memorials of the founder.

Margaret next drew attention to St. Andrew with his Cross—Meta's gift. 'And, besides,' she said, 'George Rivers made us a beautiful present, which Meta hunted up. Old Mr. Rivers, knowing no better, once bought all the beautiful carved fittings of a Chapel in France, meaning to fit up a library with them; but, happily, he never did, and a happy notion came into Meta's head, so she found them out, and Dr. Spencer has adapted them, and set them all to rights; and they are most exquisite. You never saw such foliage.'

Thus Margaret proceeded with a description of everything in the Church, and all the little adventures of the building, as if she could not turn away from the subject; and her aunt listened and wondered, and, when called away, that Margaret might rest before nurse came to dress her, she expressed her wonder to Meta.

'Yes,' was the answer; 'it is her chief occupation and interest. I do not mean that she has not always her own dear full sympathy for every one's concerns, but Cocksmoor is *her* concern, almost more than even Ethel's. I think she could chronicle every stage in the building better than Dr. Spencer himself, and it is her daily delight to hear his histories of his progress. And not only with the Church but the people; she knows all about every family; Richard and Ethel tell her all their news; she talks over the school with the mistress every Sunday, and you cannot think what a feeling there is for her at Cocksmoor. A kind message from Miss May has an effect that the active workers cannot always produce.'

Mrs. Arnott saw that Meta was right when, in the afternoon, she walked, with her nieces, to see Cocksmoor. It was not a desolate sight, as in old times, for the fair edifice, rising on the slope, gave an air of protection to the cottages, which seemed now to have a centre of unity, instead of lying forlorn and scattered. Nor were they as wretched in themselves, for the impulse of civilization had caused windows to be mended and railings to be tidied, and Richard promoted, to the utmost, cottage gardening, so that, though there was an air of poverty, there was no longer an appearance of reckless destitution and hopeless neglect.

In the cottages, Mrs. Taylor had not entirely ceased to speak with a piteous voice, even though she told of the well-doing of her girls at service; but Granny Hall's merry content had in it something now of principle, and Sam had married a young Fordholm wife, who promised to be a pattern for Cocksmoor. Every one asked after Miss May, with a tenderness and affection that Mrs. Arnott well appreciated; and when they went into the large fresh school, where Richard was hearing a class, Cherry Elmwood looked quite cheered and enlivened by hearing that she had been able to enjoy seeing her aunt. Mrs. Arnott was set to enlighten the children about the little brown girls whom she was wont to teach, and came away with a more brilliant impression of their intelligence than she might have had, if she had not come to them fresh from the Antipodes.

She had to tell Margaret all her impressions on her return, and very pretty smiles repaid her commendations. She understood better the constant dwelling on the subject, as she perceived how little capable Margaret was of any employment. The book, the writing materials, and work-basket, were indeed placed by her side, but very seldom did the feeble fingers engage in any of the occupations once so familiar—now and then a pencilled note would be sent to Flora, or to Hector Ernescliffe, or a few stitches be set in her work, or a page or two turned of a book, but she was far more often perfectly still, living, assuredly in no ordinary sphere of human life, but never otherwise than cheerful, and open to the various tidings and interests which, as Ethel had formerly said, shifted before her like scenes in a magic lantern, and, perhaps with less of substance than in those earlier days, when her work among them was not yet done, and she was not, as it were, set aside from them. They were now little more than shadows reflected from the world whence she was passing.

Yet her home was not sad. When Dr. Spencer came in the evening, and old Edinburgh stories were discussed, Dr. May talked with spirit, and laughed with the merry note that Mrs.

Arnott so well remembered, and Meta Rivers chimed in with her gay, saucy repartees; nor, though Richard was always silent, and Ethel's brow seemed to bear a weight of thought, did it seem as if their spirits were depressed; while there was certainly no restraint on the glee of Blanche, Aubrey, and Gertrude, who were running into Margaret's room, and making as much noise there as they chose.

Mrs. Arnott was at home with the whole family from the first, and in every one's confidence; but what she enjoyed above all was, the sitting in Margaret's room in the morning, when there was no danger of interruption, the three children being all safe captives to their lessons, and Meta, in Richard's workshop, illuminating texts on zinc scrolls for the Church.

Margaret came out more in these interviews. It had been a kind of shyness that made her talk so exclusively of the Church at the first meeting; she had now felt her way, and knew again —and realized—the same kind aunt with whom she had parted in her childhood, and now far dearer, since she herself was better able to appreciate her, and with a certain resemblance to her mother, that was unspeakably precious and soothing to one deprived, as Margaret had been, at the commencement of her illness and anxiety.

She could hardly see her aunt come near her, without thanking her for having come home, and saying how every time she awoke, it was with the sense that something was comfortable, then remembering it was aunt Flora's being in the house. She seemed to have a feeling, as if telling everything to her aunt were like rendering up her account to her mother; and, at different times, she related the whole, looking back on the various decisions she had had to make or to influence, and reviewing her own judgments, though often with self-blame, not with acuteness of distress, but rather with a humble trust in the Infinite Mercy that would atone for all shortcomings and infirmities, truly sorrowed for.

On the whole, it was a peaceful and grateful retrospect; the brothers all doing so well in their several ways, and such a comfort to their father. Tom, concerning whom she had made the greatest mistake, might be looked upon as rescued by Norman. Aubrey, Margaret said, smiling, was Ethel's child, and had long been off her mind; Hector, to her quite a brother, would miss her almost more than her own brothers, but good honest fellow, he had a home here; and, whispered Margaret, smiling and glowing a little, 'Don't tell any one, for it is a secret of secrets. Hector told me one evening that, if he could be very steady, he hoped he might yet have Blanche at Maplewood. Poor little

White Mayflower, it won't be for want of liking on her part, and she so blushes and watches when Hector comes near, that I sometimes think he may have said something like it to her.'

Mrs. Arnott gave no opinion on the plan for Norman and Meta; but Margaret, however, took all for granted, and expressed warm hopes for their sakes, that they would go out with Mrs. Arnott; then, when the suggestion seemed to astonish her aunt, who thought they were waiting for his Ordination, she said, 'The fact is, that he would like to be ordained where he is to work; but I believe they do not like to say anything about the wedding, because of me. Now, of all persons, I must chiefly rejoice in what may help to teach in those islands. I cannot bear to be a hindrance. Whatever happens, Aunt Flora, will you take care that they know this?'

As to her father, Margaret was at rest. He had much more calmness than when he was more new to grief, and could bear far more patiently and hopefully than at first. He lived more on his affections above; and much as he loved those below, he did not rest in them as once, and could better afford to have them removed. 'Besides,' said Margaret, serenely, 'it has been good for him to have been gradually weaned from depending on me, so that it is Ethel who is really necessary to him.'

For herself, Margaret was perfectly content and happy. She knew the temptation of her character had been to be the ruler and manager of everything, and she saw it had been well for her to have been thus assigned the part of Mary, rather than of Martha. She remembered with thankful joy the engagement with Alan Ernescliffe, and though she still wore tokens of mourning for him, it was with a kind of pleasure in them. There had been so little promise of happiness from the first, that there was far more peace in thinking of him as sinking into rest in Harry's arms, than as returning to grieve over her decline; and that last gift of his, the Church, had afforded her continual delight, and, above all other earthly pursuits, smoothed away the languor and weariness of disease, as she slowly sank to join him. Now that her aunt had come to bring back a sunbeam of her childhood, Margaret declared that she had no more grief or care, except one, and that a very deep and sad one—namely, poor Flora.

Mrs. Arnott had at first been inclined to fear that her goddaughter was neglecting her own family, since she had not been at home this whole year, but the slightest betrayal of this suspicion roused Margaret to an eager defence. She had not a doubt that Flora would gladly have been with her, but she

believed that she was not acting by her own choice, or more
truly, that her husband was so devoted to her, that she felt the
more bound to follow his slightest wishes, however contrary to
her own.   The season had been spent in the same whirl that
had, last year, been almost beyond human power, even when
stimulated by enjoyment and success ; and now, when her spirits
were lowered, and her health weakened, Meta had watched and
trembled for her, though never able to obtain an avowal that it
was an overstrain ; and while treated most affectionately, never
admitted within her barrier of reserve.

'If I could see poor Flora comforted, or if even she would
only let me enter into her troubles,' Margaret said, sighing, 'I
should be content.'

The Consecration day came near, and the travellers began to
return.   Meta was in a state of restlessness, which in her was
very pretty, under the disguise of a great desire to be useful.
She fluttered about the house, visited Margaret, played with
Gertrude, set the drawing-room ornaments to rights—a task
which Ethel was very glad to depute to her, and made a great
many expeditions into the garden to put together autumn nosegays
for the vases—finally discovering that Ethel's potichomanie vases
on the staircase window must have some red and brown leaves.

She did not come back quite so soon with them, and Mrs.
Arnott, slyly looking out of window, reported, 'Ha! he is come
then ! At least, I see the little thing has found—'

'Something extremely unlike itself,' said Dr. May, laughing.

'Something I could easily set down as a student at Edinburgh,
thirty years ago.   That's the very smile! I remember dear Maggie
being more angry than I ever saw her before, because Mr. Fleet
said that you smiled to show your white teeth.'

'That is the best shadow of Maggie I ever saw,' said Dr. May.
'She has taught the lad to smile.   That is what I call a pretty
sight!'

'Come, Richard, it is a shame for old folks like us to stand
spying them !'

'They care very little for me,' said Dr. May, 'but I shall have
them in.   Cold winds blowing about that little head ! Ah ! here
they are.   Fine leaves you gather, Miss! Very red and brown.'

Meta rather liked, than otherwise, those pretty teasings of
Dr. May, but they always made Norman colour extremely, and
he parried them by announcing news.   'No, not the Bucephalus,
a marriage in high life, a relation.'

'Not poor Mary !' cried Ethel.

'Mary ! what could make you think of her ?'

'As a hen thinks of her ducklings when they go into waters beyond her ken,' said Ethel. 'Well, as long as it is not Mary, I don't care!'

'High life!' repeated Meta. 'O, it can be only Agatha Langdale.'

'There's only Lord Cosham further to guess,' said Ethel.

'Eh! why not young Ogilvie?' said Dr. May. 'I am right, I see. Well, who is the lady?'

'A Miss Dunbar—a nice girl that I met at Glenbracken. Her property fits in with theirs, and I believe his father has been wishing it for a long time.'

'It does not sound too romantic,' said Meta.

'He writes as if he had the sense of having been extremely dutiful,' said Norman.

'No doubt, thinking it needful in addressing a namesake, who *has* had an eye to the main chance,' said the Doctor. 'Don't throw stones, young people.'

'Well!' exclaimed Meta; 'he did not look as if he would go and do such a stupid thing as that!'

'Probably, it is anything but a stupid thing,' said Dr. May.

'You are using him very ill among you,' said Norman, eagerly. 'I believe her to be excellent in every way; he has known her from childhood; he writes as if he were perfectly contented, and saw every chance of happiness.'

'None the less for having followed his father's wishes—I am glad he did,' said Ethel, coming to her brother's side.

'I dare say you are right,' was Meta's answer; 'but I am disappointed in him. He always promised to come and stay with you, and made such friends at Oxford, and he never came.'

'I fancy there was a good deal to hinder him,' said Norman; and, as Mrs. Arnott proceeded to inquiries after the Ogilvies in general, the Master of Glenbracken was allowed to drop.

Meta, however, renewed the subject when walking to the Minster that evening with Norman.

'You may defend Mr. Ogilvie, Norman, but it is not what I should have expected from him. Why did he make promises, and then neglect his relations?'

'I believe that conscientiously he did not dare to come,' said Norman. 'I know that he was greatly struck with Ethel at the time of the Commemoration, and therefore I could never again press him to come here.'

'O Norman, you hard-hearted monster! What a bad conductor!'

'I did not wish to be a conductor,' said Norman. 'If you had seen Glenbracken and the old people, you would perceive that it would not have been suitable on our part to promote anything of the kind.'

'Would they have been so violent?'

'Not violent, but it would have been a severe struggle. They are good, kind people, but with strong prejudices; and, though I have no doubt they would have yielded to steady attachment on their son's part, and such conduct as Ethel's would have been, I could not lead in that direction.'

'Is that pride, Norman?'

'I hope not.'

'It is doing by others as you were doing by yourself,' half whispered Meta; 'but, after all, if he had no constancy, Ethel had an escape.'

'I was afraid that she had been rather touched, but I am glad to find myself mistaken.'

'If you thought so, how could you make such a public announcement?'

He laughed. 'I had made myself so nervous as to the effect, that, in desperation, I took her own way, and came out at once with it as unconsciously as I could.'

'Very naturally you acted unconsciousness! It was better than insulting her by seeming to condole. Not that I do, though, for she deserves more steadiness than he has shown! If a man could appreciate her at all, I should have thought that it would have been once and for ever.'

'Remember, he had barely known her a fortnight, and probably had no reason to believe that he had made any impression on her. He knew how such an attachment would grieve his parents, and, surely, he was acting dutifully, and with self-denial and consideration, in not putting himself in the way of being further attracted.'

'Umph! You make a good defence, Norman, but I cannot forgive him for marrying somebody else, who cannot be Ethel's equal.'

'She is a good little girl; he will form her, and be very happy; perhaps more so than with a great soul and strong nature, like Ethel's.'

'Only he is a canny Scot, and not a Dr. Spencer!'

'Too short acquaintance! besides, there were the parents. Moreover, what would become of home without Ethel?'

'The unanswerable argument to make one contented,' said Meta. 'And, certainly, to be wife to a Member of Parliament, is not so very delightful that one would covet it for her.'

'Any more than she does for herself.'

Norman was right in his view of his friend's motives, as well

as of Ethel's present feelings. If there had ever been any
disappointment about Norman Ogilvie, it had long since faded
away. She had never given away the depths of her heart, though
the upper surface had been stirred. All had long subsided, and
she could think freely of him as an agreeable cousin, in whose
brilliant public career she should always be interested, without
either a wish to partake it, or a sense of injury or neglect. She
had her vocation, in her father, Margaret, the children, home and
Cocksmoor; her mind and affections were occupied, and she
never thought of wishing herself elsewhere.

The new Church and the expected return of her sisters,
engrossed many more of her thoughts than did anything relating
to Glenbracken.

She could not bear to talk of Flora, though almost as uneasy
as was Margaret; and not able to lay aside misgivings, lest even her
good simple Mary might have had her head turned by gaiety.

Mr. and Mrs. Rivers arrived on the Saturday before the Tuesday
fixed for the Consecration, and stopped on their way, that they
might see Margaret, deposit Mary, and resume Meta.

It was a short visit, and all that Ethel could discover was, that
Flora was looking very ill, no longer able to conceal the worn and
fagged expression of her countenance, and evidently dreadfully
shocked by the sight of the havoc made by disease on Margaret's
frame. Yet she talked with composure of indifferent subjects—
the yacht, the visits, the Bucephalus, the Church, and the arrangements for St. Andrew's day. She owned herself overworked, and
in need of rest, and, as she was not well enough to venture on
being present at the Consecration, she undertook to spend the
day with Margaret, thus setting the others at liberty. This
settled, she took her leave, for the journey had fatigued her
greatly.

During the short visit, Mary had moved and spoken so quietly,
and looked so well-dressed, and young-lady-like, that, in spite of
her comfortable plump cheeks, Ethel felt quite afraid!

But the instant the carriage had driven off, there was a skipping,
a hugging, a screaming, ' O, it is so nice to be at home again!'—
and Ethel knew she had her own Mary. It was only a much
better looking and more mannerly Mary, in the full bloom of
seventeen, open and honest-faced, her profuse light hair prettily
disposed, her hands and arms more civilized, and her powers of
conversation and self-possession developed. Mary-like were her
caresses of Gertrude, Mary-like her inquiries for Cocksmoor,
Mary-like her insisting on bringing her boxes into Margaret's
room, her exulting exhibition of all the pretty things that Flora

and George had given to her, and the still more joyous bestowal of presents upon everybody.

Her tastes were not a whit altered, nor her simplicity diminished. If she was pleased by joining a large dinner-party, her satisfaction was in the amusement of seeing well-dressed people, and a grand table; her knowledge of the world only reached to pronouncing everything unlike home, 'so funny;' she had relished most freshly and innocently every pleasure that she could understand, she had learnt every variety of fancy work to teach Blanche and Miss Bracy, had been the delight of every school-room and nursery, had struck up numberless eternal friendships and correspondences with girls younger and shyer than herself, and her chief vexations seemed to have been first, that Flora insisted on her being called Miss May, secondly, that all her delights could not be shared by every one at home, and thirdly, that poor Flora could not bear to look at little children.

Grievous complaints were preferred by the dwellers in the attics the next morning, that Mary and Blanche had talked to an unmentionable hour of the night; but, on the whole, Blanche was rather doubtful whether Mary had made the most of her opportunities of observation.

CHAPTER XXV.

'Behold, with pearls they glittering stand,
Thy peaceful gates to all expand,
By grace and strength divinely shed,
Each mortal, thither may be led;
Who, kindled by Christ's love will dare
All earthly sufferings now to bear.

'By many a salutary stroke,
By many a weary blow, that broke
Or polished, with a workman's skill,
The stones that form that glorious pile;
They all are fitly framed to lie
In their appointed place on high.'
ANCIENT HYMN FOR THE DEDICATION OF A CHURCH.

THE thirtieth of November dawned with the grave brightness of an autumn day, as the sun slowly mounted from the golden east, drinking up the mists that rose tardily, leaving the grass thickly bedewed.

The bells of Stoneborough Minster were ringing gladsome 'peals, and the sunshine had newly touched the lime trees, whose last bright yellow leaves were gently floating down, as the carriage, from the Grange, drew up at Dr. May's door.

Norman opened it, to claim Meta at once for the walk; Mrs.

Arnott and Mary had gone on to assist Richard in his final arrangements, but even before Cocksmoor, with Ethel, was now the care of Margaret; and she had waited with her father to keep all bustle from her room, and to commit her into the charge of Flora and of nurse. Ethel seemed quite unwilling to go. There was that strange oppressed feeling on her as if the attainment of her wishes were joy too great to be real—as if she would fain hold off from it at the climax, and linger with the sister who had shared all with her, and to whom that Church was even more than to herself. She came back, and back again, with fresh injunctions, sometimes forgetting the very purpose of her return, as if it had been only an excuse for looking at Margaret's countenance, and drinking in her sympathy from her face; but she was to go in George's carriage, and he was not a man to allow of loitering. He became so impatient of Ethel's delays, that she perceived that he could bear them no longer, gave her final kiss, and whispered, 'In spirit with us!' then ran down and was seized on by George, who had already packed in the children and Miss Bracy, and was whirled away.

'Flora dear,' said Margaret, 'do you dislike having the window opened?'

Flora threw it up, protesting, in reply to her sister's scruples, that she liked the air. 'You always spoilt me,' said Margaret, fondly. 'Come and lie down by me. It is very nice to have you here,' she added, as Flora complied; and she took her hand and fondled it. 'It is like the old times to have you here taking care of me.'

'Very unlike them in some ways,' said Flora.

'It has been a great renewal of still older times,' said Margaret, 'to have aunt Flora here. I hope you will get to know her, Flora, it is so like having mamma here,' and she looked in her sister's face as she spoke.

Flora did not reply, but she lay quite still, as if there were a charm in the perfect rest of being alone with Margaret, making no effort, and being able to be silent. Time passed on, how long they knew not, but, suddenly, a thrill shot threw Margaret's frame; she raised her hand and lifted her head, with an eager 'Hark!'

Flora could hear nothing.

'The bells—his bells!' said Margaret, all one radiant look of listening, as Flora opened the window further, and the breeze wafted in the chime, softened by distance. The carnation tinted those thin white cheeks, eyes and smile beamed with joy, and uplifted finger and parted lips seemed marking every note of the cadence.

It ceased. 'Alan! Alan!' said she. 'It is enough! I am ready!'

The somewhat alarmed look on Flora's face recalled her, and, smiling, she held out her hand for the Consecration books, saying, 'Let us follow the service. It will be best for us both.'

Slowly, softly, and rather monotonously, Flora read on, till she had come more than half through the first Lesson. Her voice grew husky, and she sometimes paused as if she could not easily proceed. Margaret begged he' to stop, but she would not cease, and went on reading, though almost whispering, till she came to, 'If they return to Thee with all their heart and with all their soul in the land of their captivity, whither they have carried them captives, and pray toward their land, which Thou gavest unto their fathers, and toward the City which Thou hast chosen, and toward the House which I have built for Thy Name; then hear Thou from the Heavens, even from Thy dwelling-place—'

Flora could go no further; she strove, but one of her tearless sobs cut her short. She turned her face aside, and, as Margaret began to say something tender, she exclaimed, with low, hasty utterance, 'Margaret! Margaret! pray for me! for it is a hard captivity, and my heart is very, very sore. Oh! pray for me, that it may all be forgiven me—and that I may see my child again!'

'My Flora; my own poor, dear Flora! do I not pray? Oh! look up, look up. Think how He loves you. If I love you so much, how much more does not He? Come near me, Flora. Be patient, and I *know* peace will come!'

The words had burst from Flora uncontrollably. She was aware, the next instant, that she had given way to harmful agitation, and, resuming her quiescence, partly by her own will, partly from the soothing effect of Margaret's words and tone, she allowed herself to be drawn close to her sister, and hid her face in the pillow, while Margaret's hands were folded over her, and words of blessing and prayer were whispered with a fervency that made them broken.

Ethel, meanwhile, stood between Aubrey and Gertrude, hardly able to believe it was not a dream, as she beheld the procession enter the Aisle, and heard the Psalm that called on those doors to lift up their heads for Him who should enter. There was an almost bewildered feeling—could it indeed be true, as she followed the earlier part of the service, which set apart that building as a Temple for ever, separate from all common uses. She had imagined the scene so often that she could almost have supposed the present, one of her many imaginations; but, by-and-by, the strangeness passed off, and she was able to enter into, not merely to follow, the prayers, and to feel the deep thanksgiving that such had been the crown of her feeble efforts. Margaret was in her mind the whole time, woven, as it were, into every supplication and every note of praise; and when there came the intercession for those in sickness and suffering, flowing into the commemoration of those departed in faith and fear, Ethel's spirits sank for a moment at the conviction, that soon Margaret, like him, whom all must bear in mind on that day, might be included in that thanksgiving: yet, as the service proceeded, leaving more and more of earth behind, and the voices joined with Angel and Archangel, Ethel could lose the present grief, and only retain the certainty that, come what might, there was joy and union amid those who sung that Hymn of praise. Never had Ethel been so happy —not in the sense of the finished work—no, she had lost all that, but in being more carried out of herself than ever she had been before, the free spirit of praise so bearing up her heart that the cry of Glory came from her with such an exulting gladness, as might surely be reckoned as one of those foretastes of our Everlasting Life, not often vouchsafed even to the faithful, and usually sent to prepare strength for what may be in store.

The blessing brought the sense of peace, which hung on her even while the sounds of movement began, and the congregation were emerging. As she came out, greetings, sentences of admiration of the Church, and of inquiry for her absent sisters, were crowded upon her, as people moved towards the school, where a luncheon was provided for them, to pass away the interval until evening service. The half-dozen oldest Cocksmoorites were, meantime, to have a dinner in the former school-room, at the Elwood's house, and Ethel was anxious to see that all was right there, so, while the rest of her party were doing civil things, she gave her arm to Cherry, whose limping walk showed her to be very tired.

'Oh! Miss Ethel!' said Cherry; 'if Miss May could only have been here!'

'Her heart is,' said Ethel.

'Well, ma'am, I believe it is. You would not think, ma'am, how all the children take heed to anything about her. If I only begin to say "Miss May told me—" they are all like mice.'

'She has done more for the real good of Cocksmoor than any one else,' said Ethel.

More might have been said, but they perceived that they were being overtaken by the body of Clergy, who had been unrobing in the vestry. Ethel hastened to retreat within Mrs. Elwood's wicket gate, but she was arrested by Richard, and found herself being presented to the Bishop, and the Bishop shaking hands with her, and saying that he had much wished to be introduced to her.

Of course, that was because she was her father's daughter, and by way of something to say. She mentioned what was going on at the cottage, whereupon the Bishop wished to go in and see the old people; and, entering, they found the very comfortable-looking party just sitting down to roast-beef and goose. John Taylor, in a new black coat, on account of his clerkship, presiding at one end, and Mr. Elwood at the other, and Dame Hall finding conversation for the whole assembly; while Blanche, Aubrey, Gertrude, the little Larkinses, and the Abbotstoke Wilmots were ready to act as waiters with infinite delight. Not a whit daunted by the Bishop, who was much entertained by her merry manner, old Granny told him, 'she had never seen nothing like it since the Jubilee, when the Squire roasted an ox whole, and there wasn't none of it fit to eat; and when her poor father got his head broken. Well, to be sure, who would have thought what would come of Sam's bringing in the young gentleman and lady to see her the day her back was so bad!'

The Bishop said Grace, and left Granny to the goose, while he gave Ethel his arm, which she would have thought an unaccountable proceeding if she had not recollected that Richard might be considered as host, and that she was his eldest sister forthcoming.

No sooner, however, had they come beyond the wicket than she saw her father speaking to Will Adams, and there was that in the air of both which made it no surprise when Dr. May came up, saying, 'Ethel, I must carry you away;' and, in explanation to the Bishop, 'my poor girl at home is not so well.'

All was inquiry and sympathy. Ethel was frantic to be at home, and would have rushed off at once, if Richard had not held her fast, asking what good she would do by hurrying in, breathless and exhausted, so as to add to Flora's fright and distress, the anxiety which was most upon their minds, since she had never before witnessed one of the seizures, that were only too ordinary matters in the eyes of the home party. No one but Dr. May and Ethel should go. Richard undertook to tell the rest, and the gig making its appearance, Ethel felt that the peculiarly kind manner with which the Bishop pressed her hand, and gave them all good wishes, was like a continuation of his blessing to aid her, in her home scene of trial.

Perhaps, it was well for her that her part in the Consecration festivities should end here; at least so thought Mr. Wilmot, who, though very sorry for the cause, could not wish her to have been present at the luncheon. She had not thought of self hitherto, the Church was the gift of Alan and Margaret, the work of preparing the people belonged to all alike, and she did not guess that, in the sight of others, she was not the nobody that she believed herself. Her share in the work at Cocksmoor was pretty well known, and Dr. Hoxton could not allow a public occasion to pass without speeches, such as must either have been very painful, or very hurtful to her. The absence of herself and her father, however, permitted a more free utterance to the general feeling; and things were said, that did indeed make the rest of the family extremely hot and uncomfortable, but which gave them extreme pleasure. Norman was obliged to spare Richard the answer, and said exactly what he ought, and so beautifully, that Meta could not find it in her heart to echo the fervent wish, which he whispered as he sat down, that speechifying could be abolished by act of parliament.

Mrs. Arnott began to perceive that her nephew was something to be proud of, and to understand how much was sacrificed, while George Rivers expressed his opinion to her that Norman would be a crack speaker in the House, and he hoped she would say everything to hinder his going out, for it was a regular shame to waste him on the niggers.

Owing to George having constituted himself her squire, Mrs. Arnott had not arrived at an understanding of the state of affairs at home; but, as soon they rose up from luncheon, and she learnt the truth from Richard and Mary, nothing would hinder her from walking home at once to see whether she could be useful. Mary was easily persuaded to remain, for she was accustomed to Margaret's having these attacks, and had always been kept out of her room the while, so she had little uneasiness to prevent her from being very happy, in receiving in her own simple, good-humoured way, all the attentions that lapsed upon her in the place of her elder sisters.

'Cocksmoor really has a Church!' was note enough of joy for her, and no one could look at her round face without seeing perfect happiness. Moreover, when after evening service, the November mist turned into decided rain, she was as happy as a queen in her foresight, which had provided what seemed an unlimited supply of cloaks and umbrellas. She appeared to have an original genius for making the right people give a lift in their carriages to the distressed; and, regarding the Abbotstoke britska as her own, packed in Mrs. Anderson and Fanny, in addition to all their own little ones, Meta thrusting Miss Bracy into the demi-corner destined for herself at the last minute, and, remaining with Mary, the only ladies obliged to walk back to Stoneborough. So delighted were they 'at the fun,' that it might have been thought the most charming of adventures, and they laughed all the more at the lack of umbrellas. They went to Mrs. Elwood's, divested themselves of all possible finery, and tucked up the rest; Meta was rolled up from head to foot in a great old plaid shawl of Mrs. Elwood's, and Mary had a cloak of Richard's, the one took Norman's arm, the other Dr. Spencer's, and they trudged home through the darkness and the mud in the highest glee, quite sorry when the carriage met them half-way.

It was the last mirth that they enjoyed for many weeks. When they reached home, a sense of self-reproach for their glee thrilled over them, when they found a sort of hush pervading the drawing-room, and saw the faces of awe and consternation, worn by Blanche and George Rivers.

'It was a much worse attack than usual, and it did not go off,' was all that Blanche knew, but her father had desired to be told when Dr. Spencer came home, and she went up with the tidings.

This brought Flora down, looking dreadfully pale, and with her voice sunk away as it had been when she lost her child. Her husband started up, exclaiming at her aspect; she let him support her to the sofa, and gave the few particulars. Margaret had been as placid and comfortable as usual, till nurse came to dress her, but the first move had brought on the faintness and loss of breath. It did not yield to remedies, and she had neither looked nor spoken since, only moaned. Flora thought her father much alarmed; and then, after an interval, she began to entreat that they might stay there, sending Miss Bracy and the children to the Grange to make room.

Meantime, Dr. Spencer had come to the sick room, but he could only suggest remedies that were already in course of application to the insensible sufferer. Mrs. Arnott and Ethel were watching, and trying everything to relieve her, but with little effect, and Ethel presently stood by the fire with her father, as Dr. Spencer turned towards him, and he said, in a very low, but calm voice, 'It won't do—I believe it is the death-stroke.'

'Not immediate,' said Dr. Spencer.

'No,' said Dr. May; and he quietly spoke of what the disease had effected, and what yet remained for it to do, ere the silver bowl should be broken.

Dr. Spencer put in a word of agreement.

'Will there be no rally?' said Ethel, in the same tone.

'Probably not,' said Dr. May; 'the brain is generally reached at this stage. I have seen it coming for a long time. The thing was done seven years ago. There was a rally for a time when youth was strong; but suspense and sorrow accelerated what began from the injury to the spine.'

Dr. Spencer bowed his head, and looked at him anxiously, saying, 'I do not think there will be much acute suffering.'

'I fear it may be as trying,' said Dr. May, sighing; and then turning to Ethel, and throwing his arm round her, 'May God make it easy to her, and grant us " patient hearts." We will not grudge her to all that she loves best, my Ethel.'

Ethel clung to him, as if to derive strength from him. But the strength that was in them then, did not come from earth. Dr. Spencer wrung his hand, and stepped back to the bed to try another resource. Vain again, they only seemed to be tormenting her, and the silent helplessness prevailed again. Then Dr. May went down to Flora, told her the true state of the case, and urged on her to give up her plan of remaining. George joined with him, and she yielded submissively, but would not be refused going up once again and kissing her sister, standing beside her gazing at her, till her father came softly and drew her away. 'I shall be here to-morrow,' she said to Ethel, and went.

The morrow, however, brought no Flora. The agitation and distress of that day had broken her down completely, and she was so ill as to be unable to move. Her aunt went at once to see her, and finding that her presence at the Grange relieved some of Dr. May's anxieties, chiefly devoted herself to her. Flora was grateful and gentle, but as silent and impenetrable as ever, while day after day she lay on her couch, uncomplaining and undemonstrative, visited by her father, and watched over by her aunt and sister-in-law, who began to know each other much better, though Flora less than ever, in that deep fixed grief. She only roused herself to return her husband's affection, or to listen to the daily reports of Margaret. Poor George, he was very forlorn, though Meta did her best to wait on him, and he rode over twice a day to inquire at Stoneborough.

The Doctors were right, and the Consecration morning was her last of full consciousness. From the hour when she had heard the sound of Alan's bells, her ears were closed to earthly sounds. There was very little power of intercourse with her, as she lingered on the borders of the Land very far away, where skill and tenderness could not either reach body or spirit. Often the watchers could not tell whether she was conscious, or only incapacitated from expression, by the fearful weight on her breath, which caused a restlessness most piteous in the exhausted helpless frame, wasted till the softest touch was anguish. Now and then came precious gleams when a familiar voice, or some momentary alleviation would gain a smile, or thanks, and they thought her less restless when Richard read prayers beside her, but words were very rare, only now and then a name, and when in most distress, 'it will be soon over,' 'it will soon be over,' occurred so often, that they began to think it once her solace, and now repeated habitually without a meaning.

They could not follow her into the valley of the shadow of death, but could only watch the frail earthly prison-house being broken down, as if the doom of sin must be borne, though faith could trust that it was but her full share in the Cross. Calmly did those days pass. Ethel, Richard, and Mary divided between them the watching and the household cares, and their father bore up bravely in the fulness of his love and faith, resigning his daughter to the hands which were bearing her whither her joys had long since departed.

Hector Ernescliffe arrived when the holidays began; and his agony of sorrow, when she failed to recognise him, moved Dr. May to exert himself earnestly for his consolation; and, at the same time, Tom, in a gentle, almost humble manner, paid a sort of daughter-like attention to the smallest services for his father, as if already accepting him as his especial charge.

It was midnight, on the longest night of the year; Ethel was lying on her bed, and had fallen into a brief slumber, when her father's low, clear voice summoned her: 'Ethel, she is going!'

There was a change on the face, and the breath came in labouring gasps. Richard lifted her head, and her eyes once more opened; she smiled once more.

'Papa!' she said, 'dear papa!'

He threw himself on his knees beside her, but she looked beyond him, 'Mamma! Alan! oh! there they are! More! more!' and, as though the unspeakable dawned on her, she gasped for utterance, then looked, with a consoling smile, on her father. 'Over now!' she said—and the last struggle was ended. That which Richard laid down was no longer Margaret May.

Over now! The twenty-five years' life, the seven years' captivity on her couch, the anxious headship of the motherless household, the hopeless betrothal, the long suspense, the efforts for resignation, the widowed affections, the slow decay, the tardy, painful death agony—all was over; nothing left, save what they had rendered the undying spirit, and the impress her example had left on those around her

The long continuance of the last suffering had softened the actual parting; and it was with thankfulness for the cessation or her pain that they turned away, and bade each other good-night.

Ethel would not have believed that her first wakening, to the knowledge that Margaret was gone, could have been more fraught with relief than with misery. And, for her father, it seemed as if it were a home-like, comfortable thought to him, that her mother had one of her children with her. He called her the first link of his Daisy Chain drawn up out of sight; and, during the quiet days that ensued, he seemed as it were to be lifted above grief, dwelling upon hope. His calmness impressed the same on his children, as they moved about in the solemn stillness of the house; and when Harry, pale and shocked at the blow to him so sudden, came home, the grave silence soothed his violence of grief; and he sat beside his father or Mary, speaking in under-tones of what Margaret had loved to hear from him, of Alan Ernescliffe's last moments.

Mary gave way to a burst of weeping when she sought, in vain, for Daisies in the wintry garden; but Hector Ernescliffe went down to the Cloisters, and brought back the lingering blossoms to be placed on Margaret's bosom.

The dog Toby had followed him, unseen, to the Cloister; and he was entering the garden, when he was struck by seeing the animal bounding, in irrepressible ecstasy, round a lad, whose tarpaulin hat, blue bordered collar, and dark-blue dress, showed him to be a sailor, as well as the broad-shouldered, grizzled, elderly man, who stood beside him.

'I say, sir,' said the latter, as Hector's hand was on the door, 'do you belong to Dr. May?'

Hector unhesitatingly answered that he did.

'Then, may be, sir, you have heard of one Bill Jennings.'

Hector was all in one flush, almost choking, as he told that he was Mr. Ernescliffe's brother, and gave his hand to the sailor.

'What could he do for him?'

Jennings had heard from one of the crew of the Bucephalus that Mr. May had been met, on his return to Fortsmouth, by the news of his sister's death. The Mays had helped his boy; he had been with Mr. May in the island; he had laid Mr. Ernescliffe in his grave; and some notion had crossed the sailor that he must be at Miss Margaret's funeral—it might be they would let him lend a hand—and, in this expectation, he was spending his time on shore.

How he was welcomed need not be told, nor how the tears came forth from full hearts, as Dr. May granted his wish, and thanked him for doing what Margaret herself would indeed have chosen;

and, in his blue sailor garb, was Jennings added to the bearers, their own men, and two Cocksmoor labourers, who, early on Christmas Eve, carried her to the Minster. Last time she had been there, Alan Ernescliffe had supported her. Now, what was mortal of him lay beneath the palm tree, beneath the glowing summer sky, while the first snow flakes hung like pearls on her pall. But, as they laid her by her mother's side, who could doubt that they were together?

CHAPTER XXVI.

'At length I got unto the gladsome hill,
Where lay my hope;
Where lay my heart; and, climbing still,
When I had gained the brow and top,
A lake of brackish waters on the ground,
Was all I found.'—GEORGE HERBERT.

LATE in the evening of the same snowy 24th of December, a little daughter awoke to life at Abbotstoke Grange, and, not long after, Mrs. Arnott came to summon Dr. May from the anxious vigil in the sitting-room.

'Come and see if you can do anything to soothe her,' she said, with much alarm. 'The first sight of the baby has put her into such a state of agitation, that we do not know what to do with her.'

It was so, when he came to her bedside; that fixed stony look of despair was gone; the source of tears so long dried up, had opened again; and there she lay, weeping quietly indeed, but profusely, and with deep heaving sobs. To speak, or to leave her alone, seemed equally perilous, but he chose the first—he kissed and blessed her, and gave her joy. She looked up at him as if his blessing once more brought peace, and said, faintly, 'Now it is pardon—now I can die!'

'The cloud is gone! Thanks for that above all!' said Dr. May, fervently. 'Now, my dear, rest in thankful gladness—you are too weak to talk or think.'

'I am weak—I am tired of it all,' said Flora. 'I am glad to be going while I am so happy—there are Margaret—my own darling—rest—peace—'

'You are not going, dearest,' said her father; 'at least, I trust not, if you will not give way—here is a darling given to you, instead of the first, who needs you more.'

He would have taken the infant from the nurse and held her to her mother, but, recollecting how little Leonora had drawn her last breath in his arms, he feared the association, and signed to Mrs.

Arnott to show her the child; but she seemed as yet only able to feel that it was not Leonora, and the long sealed-up grief would have its way. The tears burst out again. 'Tell Ethel she will be the best mother to her. Name her Margaret—make her a Daisy of your own—don't call her after me,' she said, with such passionate caresses, that Mrs. Arnott was glad to take the babe away.

Dr. May's next expedient was to speak to her of her husband, who needed her more than all, and to call him in. There seemed to be something tranquillizing in his wistful manner of repeating, 'Don't cry, Flora;' and she was at last reduced, by her extreme exhaustion, to stillness; but there were still many fears for her.

Dr. May's prediction was accomplished—that she would suffer for having over-exerted herself. Her constitution had been severely tried by the grief and despondency that she had so long endured in silence, and the fresh sorrow for her favourite sister, coming at such a crisis. There was a weariness of life, and an unwillingness to resume her ordinary routine, that made her almost welcome her weakness and sinking; and now that the black terror had cleared away from the future, she seemed to long to follow Margaret at once, and to yearn after her lost child; while appeals to the affection that surrounded her, often seemed to oppress her, as if there were nothing but weariness and toil in store.

The state of her mind made her father very anxious, though it was but too well accounted for. Poor Flora had voluntarily assumed the trammels that galled her; worldly motives had prompted her marriage, and though she faithfully loved her husband, he was a heavy weight on her hands, and she had made it more onerous by thrusting him into a position for which he was not calculated, and inspiring him with a self-consequence that would not recede from it. The shock of her child's death had taken away the zest and energy which had rejoiced in her chosen way of life, and opened her eyes to see what Master she had been serving; and the perception of the hollowness of all that had been apparently good in her, had filled her with remorse and despair. Her sufferings had been the more bitter because she had not parted with her proud reserve. She had refused counsel, and denied her confidence to those who could have guided her repentance. Her natural good sense, and the sound principle in which she had been brought up, had taught her to distrust her gloomy feelings as possibly morbid; and she had prayed, keeping her hold of faith in the Infinite Mercy, though she could not feel her own part in it; and thus that faith was beginning at last to clear her path.

It was the harder to deal with her, because her hysterical agitation was so easily excited, that her father hardly dared to let a word be spoken to her; and she was allowed to see no one else except her aunt and the dear old nurse, whose tears for her child Margaret had been checked by the urgent requirements of another of her nurslings; and whom George Rivers would have paid with her weight in gold, for taking care of his new daughter, regarding her as the only woman in the world that could be trusted.

Those were heavy days with every one, though each brought some shade of improvement. They were harder to bear than the peaceful days which had immediately followed the loss of Margaret; and Ethel was especially unhappy and forlorn under the new anxiety, where she could be of no service; and with her precious occupation gone; her father absent, instead of resting upon her; and her room deserted. She was grieved with herself, because her feelings were unable to soar at the Christmas feast, as erst on St. Andrew's day; and she was bewildered and distressed by the fear that she had then been only uplifted by vanity and elation.

She told Richard so, and he said kindly, that he thought a good deal of what she complained of arose from bodily weariness.

This hurt her a little; but when he said, 'I think that the blessings of St. Andrew's day helped us through what was to follow;' she owned that it had indeed been so, and added, 'I am going to work again! Tell me what will be most useful to you at Cocksmoor.'

Sick at heart as she was, she bravely set herself to appropriate the hours now left vacant; and manfully walked with Richard and Harry to Church at Cocksmoor, on St. Stephen's day; but the Church brought back the sense of contrast. Next, she insisted on fulfilling their intention of coming home by Abbotstoke, to hear how Flora was, when the unfavourable account only added lead to the burthen that weighed her down. Though they were sent home in the carriage, she was so completely spent, that the effect of returning home to her room, without its dear inhabitant, was quite overwhelming, and she sat on her bed for half-an-hour, struggling with repinings. She came down-stairs without having gained the victory, and was so physically overcome with lassitude, that Richard insisted on her lying on the sofa, and leaving everything to him and Mary.

Richard seemed to make her his object in life, and was an unspeakable help and comforter to her, not only by taking every care for her for *her* sake, but by turning to her as his own friend and confidante, the best able to replace what they had lost. There were many plans to be put in operation for Cocksmoor, on which much consultation was needed, though every word reminded them sadly of Margaret's ever ready interest in those schemes. It was very unlike Ethel's vision of the first weeks of St. Andrew's Church; but it might be safer for her than that aught should tempt her to say, 'See what my perseverance has wrought!' Perhaps her Margaret had begun to admire her too much to be her safest confidante—at any rate, it was good still to sow in tears, rather than on earth to reap in confident joy.

Norman was as brotherly and kind as possible; but it was one of the dreary feelings of those days, that Ethel then first became aware of the difference that his engagement had made, and saw that he resorted elsewhere for sympathy. She was not jealous, and acquiesced submissively and resolutely; but they had been so much to each other, that it was a trial, especially at such a time as this when freshly deprived of Margaret.

Norman's own prospect was not cheerful. He had received a letter from New Zealand, begging him to hasten his coming out, as there was educational work much wanting him, and, according to his original wish, he could be ordained there in the autumnal Ember week.

He was in much perplexity, since, according to this request, he ought to sail with his aunt in the last week of February, and he knew not how to reconcile the conflicting claims.

Meta was not long in finding out the whole of his trouble, as they paced up and down the terrace together on a frosty afternoon.

'You will go!' was her first exclamation.

'I ought,' said Norman, 'I believe I ought; and if it had only been at any other time, it would have been easy. My aunt's company would have been such a comfort for you.'

'It cannot be helped,' said Meta.

'Considering the circumstances,' began Norman, with lingering looks at the little hummingbird on his arm, 'I believe I should be justified in waiting till such time as you could go with me. I could see what Mr. Wilmot thinks.'

'You don't think so yourself,' said Meta. 'Nobody else can give a judgment. In a thing like this, asking is, what you once called, seeking opinions as Balaam inquired.'

'Turning my words against me?' said Norman, smiling. 'Still, Meta, perhaps older heads would be fitter to judge what would be right for a little person not far off.'

'She can be the best judge of that herself,' said Meta. 'Norman,' and her dark eyes were steadfastly fixed, 'I always resolved that, with God's help, I would not be a stumbling-block in the way of your call to your work. I will not. Go out now —perhaps you will be freer for it without me, and I suppose I have a longer apprenticeship to serve to all sorts of things before I come to help you.'

'Oh! Meta, you are a rebuke to me!'

'What?—when I am going to stay by my own fireside?' said Meta, trying to laugh, but not very successfully. 'Seriously, I have much to do here. When poor Flora gets well, she must be spared all exertion for a long time to come; and I flatter myself that they want me at Stoneborough sometimes. If your father can bear to spare you, there is no doubt that you ought to go.'

'My father is as unselfish as you are, Meta—But I cannot speak to him until he is more easy about Flora. We always think the required sacrifice the hardest, but I must own that I could not grieve if he laid his commands on me to wait till the autumn.'

'Oh! that would make it a duty and all easy,' said Meta, smiling; 'but I don't think he will, and aunt Flora will be only too glad to carry you out without encumbrance.'

'Has not aunt Flora come to her senses about you?'

'I believe she would rather I belonged to any of her nephews but you. She is such a dear, sincere, kind-hearted person, and we are so comfortable together, that it will be quite like home to come out to her. I mean *there*, to convince her that I can be of something like use.'

Meta talked so as to brighten and invigorate Norman when they were together, but they both grew low-spirited when apart. The hummingbird had hardly ever been so downcast as at present —that is, whenever she was not engaged in waiting on her brother, or in cheering up Dr. May, or in any of the many gentle offices that she was ever fulfilling. She was greatly disappointed, and full of fears for Norman, and dread of the separation, but she would not give way; and only now and then, when off her guard, would the sadness reign on her face without an effort. Alone, she fought and prayed for resignation for herself, and protection and strength for him, and chid herself for the foolish feeling that he would be safer with her.

She told aunt Flora how it was one evening, as they sat over the fire together, speaking with a would-be-tone of congratulation.

'Indeed!' exclaimed Mrs. Arnott. 'But that is a great pity!'

Meta looked quite brightened by her saying so. 'I thought you would be glad,' she rejoined.

'Did you think me so hard-hearted?'

'I thought you believed he would be better without me.'

'My dear, we have not kept house and nursed together for a month for nothing,' said Mrs. Arnott, smiling.

'Thank you,' said Meta, trying to answer the smile. 'You have taken a load off me!'

'I don't like it at all,' said Mrs. Arnott. 'It is a very uncomfortable plan for every one—And yet, when I know how great is the want of him out there, I can say nothing against it without high treason. Well, my dear, I'll take all the care I can of Norman, and when you come—I shall be almost as glad as if we were coming home for good. Poor Flora, she is one person who will not regret the arrangement.'

'Poor Flora—you think her really better this evening?'

'Much better, indeed—if we could only raise her spirits, I think she would recover very well, but she is so sadly depressed. I must try to talk to Ethel—she may better understand her!'

'I have never understood Flora,' said Meta. 'She has been as kind to me as possible, and I very soon came to a certain point with her, but I never have known her thoroughly. I doubt whether any one did but dear Margaret.'

Flora was, however, much softened and less reserved than she had been. She found great repose in her aunt's attendance, retracing, as it did, her mother's presence, and she responded to her tenderness with increasing reliance and comfort; while, as her strength began to revive, and there was more disposition to talk, she became gradually drawn into greater confidence.

The seeing of Ethel was one of the difficult questions. Flora had begun to wish it very much, and yet the bare idea threw her into a nervous tremor, that caused it to be put off again and again. Her aunt found her one day almost faint with agitation —she had heard Ethel's voice in the next room, and had been winding up her expectations, and now was as much grieved as relieved, to find that she had been there seeing the baby, but was now gone.

'How does the dear Ethel look?' asked Flora, presently.

'She is looking better to-day; she has looked very worn and harassed, but I thought her brighter to-day. She walked over by Aubrey on his pony, and I think it did her good.'

'Dear old Ethel! Aunt, it is a thing that no one has told me yet. Can you tell me how she bore the news of Norman Ogilvie's engagement?'

'Do you mean—' and Mrs. Arnott stopped short in her interrogation.

'Yes,' said Flora, answering the pause.

'But I thought young Ogilvie a most unexceptionable person.'

'So he is,' said Flora. 'I was much annoyed at the time, but she was resolute.'

'In rejecting him?'

'In running away as soon as she found what was likely to happen;' and Flora, in a few words, told what had passed at Oxford.

'Then it was entirely out of devotion to your father.'

'Entirely,' said Flora. 'No one could look at her without seeing that she liked him. I had left her to be the only effective one at home, and she sacrificed herself.'

'I am glad that I have seen her,' said Mrs. Arnott. 'I should never have understood her by description. I always said that I must come home to set my correspondence going rightly.'

'Aunt Flora,' said her niece, 'do you remember my dear mother's unfinished letter to you?'

'To be sure I do, my dear.'

'Nothing ever was more true,' said Flora. 'I read it over some little time ago, when I set my papers in order, and understood it then. I never did before. I used to think it very good for the others.'

'It is what one generally does with good advice.'

'Do you recollect the comparison between Norman, Ethel, and me? It is so curious. Norman, who was ambitious and loved praise, but now dreads nothing so much; Ethel, who never cared for anything of the kind, but went straight on her own brave way; and, oh! aunt Flora—me—'

'Indeed, my dear, I should have thought you had her most full approbation.'

'Ah! don't you see the tone, as if she were not fully satisfied, as if she only could not see surface faults in me,' said Flora; 'and how she said she dreaded my love of praise, and of being liked. I wonder how it would have been if she had lived. I have looked back so often in the past year, and I think the hollowness began from that time. It might have been there before, but I am not so sure. You see, at that dreadful time, after the accident, I was the eldest who was able to be efficient, and much more useful than poor Ethel. I think the credit I gained made me think myself perfection, and I never did anything afterwards but seek my own honour.'

Mrs. Arnott began better to understand Flora's continued depression, but she thought her self-reproach exaggerated, and said something at once soothing and calculated to encourage her to undraw the curtain of reserve.

'You do not know,' continued Flora, 'how greedy I was of credit and affection. It made me jealous of Ethel herself, as long as we were in the same sphere; and when I felt that she was more to papa than I could be, I looked beyond home for praise.

I don't think the things I did were bad in themselves—brought up as I have been, they could hardly be so. I knew what merits praise and blame too well for that—but oh! the motive. I do believe I cared very much for Cocksmoor. I thought it would be a grand thing to bring about, but, you see, as it has turned out, all I thought I had done for it was in vain; and Ethel has been the real person and does not know it. I used to think Ethel so inferior to me. I left her all my work at home. If it had not been for that, she might have been happy with Norman Ogilvie—for never were two people better matched, and now she has done what I never thought to have left to another—watched over our own Margaret. Oh! how shall I ever bear to see her ?'

'My dear, I am sure nothing can be more affectionate than Ethel. She does not think these things.'

'She does,' said Flora. 'She always knew me better than I did myself. Her straightforward words should often have been rebukes to me. I shall see in every look and tone the opinion I have deserved. I have shrunk from her steadfast looks ever since I myself learnt what I was. I could not bear them now—and yet—oh! aunt! you must bring her. Ethel! my dear, dear old King—my darling's godmother—the last who was with Margaret !'

She had fallen into one of those fits of weeping when it was impossible to attempt anything but soothing her; but, though she was so much exhausted that Mrs. Arnott expected to be in great disgrace with Dr. May for having let her talk herself into this condition, she found that he was satisfied that she had so far relieved her mind, and declared that she would be better now.

The effect of the conversation was, that the next day, the last of the twelve Christmas days, when Ethel, whose yearning after her sister was almost equally divided between dread and eagerness—eagerness for her embrace, and dread of the chill of her reserve, came once again in hopes of an interview. Dr. May called her at once—'I shall take you in without any preparation,' he said, 'that she may not have time to be flurried. Only, be quiet and natural.'

Did he know what a mountain there was in her throat when he seemed to think it so easy to be natural ?

She found him leading her into a darkened room, and heard his cheerful tones saying, 'I have brought Ethel to you!'

'Ethel! oh!' said a low, weak voice, with a sound as of expecting a treat, and Ethel was within a curtain, where she began, in the dimness, to see something white moving, and her hands were clasped by two long thin ones. 'There!' said Dr. May, 'now, if you will be good, I will leave you alone. Nurse is by, to look after you, and you know she always separates naughty children.'

Either the recurrence to nursery language, or the mere sisterly touch after long separation, seemed to annihilate all the imaginary mutual dread, and, as Ethel bent lower and lower, and Flora's arms were round her, the only feeling was of being together again, and both at once made the childish gesture of affection, and murmured the old pet names of 'Flossy,' and 'King,' that belonged to almost forgotten days, when they were baby sisters, then kissed each other again.

'I can't see you,' said Ethel, drawing herself up a little. 'Why, Flora, you look like a little white shadow!'

'I have had such weak eyes,' said Flora, 'and this dim light is comfortable. I see your old sharp face quite plain.'

'But what can you do here?'

'Do? Oh! dear Ethel, I have not had much of *doing*. Papa says I have three years' rest to make up.'

'Poor Flora!' said Ethel, 'but I should have thought it tiresome, especially for you.'

'I have only now been able to think again,' said Flora; 'and you will say I am taking to quoting poetry. Do you remember some lines in that drama that Norman admired so much?'

'Philip von Artevelde?'

'Yes, I can't recollect them *now*, though they used to be always running in my head—something about time to mend and time to mourn.'

'These?' said Ethel—

> 'He that lacks time to mourn, lacks time to mend.
> Eternity mourns that.'

'I never had time before for either,' said Flora. 'You cannot think how I used to be haunted by those, when I was chased from one thing to another, all these long, long eighteen months. I am in no haste to take up work again.'

'Mending as well as mourning,' said Ethel, thoughtfully.

Flora sighed.

'And now you have that dear little Christmas gift to—' Ethel paused.

'She is not nearly so fine and healthy as her sister was,' said Flora, 'poor little dear. You know, Ethel, even now, I shall have very little time with her in that London life. Her papa

wants me so much, and I must leave her to—to the nurses.'
Flora's voice trembled again.

'Our own dear old nurse,' said Ethel.

'Oh! I wanted to thank you all for sparing her to us,' said
Flora. 'George wished it so much. But how does poor little
Daisy bear it?'

'Very magnanimously,' said Ethel, smiling. 'In fact, nurse
has had but little to do with Daisy of late, and would have been
very forlorn at home. It is better for Aubrey and for her, not
to return to be babies to comfort poor nurse. I have been breaking up the nursery, and taking Gertrude to live with me.'

'Have you gone back *there* again?'

'It would not have been better for waiting,' said Ethel; 'and
Gertrude was so proud to come to me. I could not have done it
without her, but papa must not have vacancy next to him.'

'It has been hard on you for me to engross him,' said Flora;
'but, oh, Ethel, I could not spare him. I don't think even you
can tell what papa is.'

'You have found it out,' said Ethel, in an odd, dry manner;
which, in sound, though not in feeling, was a contrast to the soft,
whispering, tearful murmurs of her sister.

'And my aunt!' continued Flora—'that I should have taken
up such a great piece of her short visit!'

'Ah! it is coming to an end very fast,' said Ethel, sighing;
'but you had the best right to her, and she and Meta have seen
so much of each other. She tells me she is quite satisfied about
Meta now.'

'I am sorry to see Meta looking out of spirits,' said Flora.
'I almost made her cry by saying something about Norman. Is
there anything going wrong?'

Ethel, as usual, blundered into the subject. 'Only about
Norman's going out.'

Flora asked further questions, and she was obliged to explain.
It roused Flora's energies at once.

'This will never do!' she said. 'They must marry, and go
with my aunt.'

Ethel was aghast. 'They would not hear of it now!'

'They must. It is the only reasonable thing. Why, Norman
would be miserable, and, as to Meta—Imagine his going out
and returning—a year's work, such an expense and loss of time,
besides the missing aunt Flora.'

'If it were not wrong—'

'The waste would be the wrong thing. Besides—' and she
told of Margaret's wishes.

'But, Flora, think—the last week in February—and you so ill!'

'I am not to marry them,' said Flora, smiling. 'If it could be in a fortnight, they could go and get their outfit afterwards, and come back to us when I am stronger. Let me see—there need be no fuss about settlements—Mr. Rivers's will arrange everything for her.'

'It would be a good thing to get rid of a fine wedding,' said Ethel; 'but they will never consent!'

'Yes they will, and be grateful.'

'Papa would be happier about Norman,' said Ethel; 'but I cannot fancy his liking it. And you—you can't spare Meta, for aunt Flora must go to the Arnott's in a week or two more.'

'Suppose papa was to let me have you,' said Flora. 'If he wants you, he must come after you.'

Ethel gasped at the thought that her occupation at home was gone, but she said—'If I am not too awkward for you, dear Flora. You will miss Meta terribly.'

'I can't keep the hummingbird caged, with her heart far away,' said Flora.

Dr. May came in to break up the conversation, and Ethel quickly guessed from his manner that Norman had been talking to him. Flora told him that she had been agreeing with Ethel that Meta had much better not miss this opportunity. He was far less startled than Ethel had expected; indeed, the proposal was rather a relief to his mind, and his chief objection was the fear that Flora would be fatigued by the extra bustle, but she promised not to trouble herself about it, otherwise than that if Norman could not persuade Meta, she would. The sisters parted, much more comfortable than before. Ethel felt as if she had found something like a dim reflection of Margaret, and Flora's fear of Ethel had fled away from the mere force of sisterhood.

As to Norman, he declared that he had not the audacity to make the proposal to Meta, though he was only too grateful—so his father carried it to the hummingbird; and, as soon as she found that it was not improper, nor would hurt any one's feelings, she gave ready consent—only begging that it might be as best suited every one, especially Flora; and ending by a whisper to her dear fatherly friend, owning that she was 'very glad—she meant she was very glad there would be nobody there.'

So Norman and Meta settled their plans as they walked home together from evening service, after listening to the prophecies of the blessings to be spread into the waste and desolate places,

which should yet become the heritage of the Chosen, and with
the evening star shining on them, like a faint reflex of the Star
of the East, Who came to be a Light to lighten the Gentiles.

CHAPTER XXVII.

' È una delle facoltà singolari ed incommunicabili della religione Cristiana questa·
di poter dare indirizzo e quiete a chiunque, in qualsivoglia congiuntura, a
qualsivoglia termine, ricorra ad essa. Se al passato v'è rimedio, essa lo pre-
scrive, lo somministra, presta lume e vigore per metterlo in opera a qualunque
costo ; se non v'è, essa dà il modo di fare realmente e in effeto, ciò che l' uom
dice in proverbio, della necessita virtù. Insegna a continuare con sapienza ciò
che è stato intrapreso per leggerezza, piega l'animo ad abbracciare con propen-
sione ciò che è stato imposto dalla prepotenza, e dà ad un elezione che fu
temeraria, ma che e irrevocabile, tutta la santità, tutto il consiglio, diciamolo
pur francamenta, tutte le gioje della vocazione.'—MANZONI.

THE wedding day was fixed for the 20th of January, since it
was less risk to Flora as an absolute invalid, than as convalescent
enough to take any share in the doings.

Meta managed her correspondence with her own relatives, and
obtained her uncle's kind approval, since he saw there could be
nothing else ; while her aunt treated her as an infatuated victim,
but wished, for her mother's sake, to meet her in London before
she sailed.

The worst stroke of all was to Bellairs, who had never chosen
to believe that her mistress could move without her, and though
mortally afraid in crossing to the Isle of Wight, and utterly
abhorring all ' natives,' went into hysterics on finding that her
young lady would take out no maid but a little hardworking
village girl ; and though transferred in the most flattering manner
to Mrs. Rivers's service, shed a tear for every stitch she set in
the trousseau, and assured her betrothed butler, that, if Miss
Rivers would only have heard reason, she would have followed
her to the world's end, rather than that her beautiful hair should
never look like anything again.

So the wedding-day came, and grass and trees wore a fitting suit
of crisp hoariness. Nothing could be quieter. Meta was arrayed
by the sobbing Bellairs in her simple bridal white, wrapped herself in a large shawl, took her brother's arm, and walked down
the frosty path with him and Mrs. Arnott, as if going merely to
the daily service.

The time had not been made known, and there was hardly an
addition to the ordinary congregation, except the May family and
Dr. Spencer ; but the Christmas evergreens still adorned aisle and
chancel, and over the Altar stood the motto that Meta herself

had woven of holly, on that Christmas eve of grief and anxiety, without knowing how it would speak to her.

'Fear not, for behold I bring unto you glad tidings of great joy, that shall be unto you and to all people.'

Fear not, for length of voyage, for distance from kindred, for hardship, privation, misunderstanding, disappointment. The glad tidings are to *all* people, even to the utmost parts of the earth. Ye have your portion in the great joy—ye have freely cast in your lot with those, whose feet are beautiful on the mountains, who bear the good tidings. Fear not, for He is with you, who will never forsake.

Thus Dr. May read the words with swelling heart, as he looked at his son's clear, grave, manful look, even as it had been when he made his Confirmation vow — his natural nervous excitability quelled by a spirit not his own, and chastened into strong purpose; and the bride, her young face the more lovely for the depth of enthusiasm restrained by awe and humility, as she stood without trembling or faltering, the strength of innocence expressed in the whole bearing of her slight figure in her white drapery. Around were the four sisterly bridesmaids, their black dresses showing that these were still the twilight days of mourning, and that none would forget her, whose prayers might still bless their labour of love.

When Margaret Agatha May, on her husband's arm, turned for a last look at the Altar of her own Church, 'Fear not,' in evergreen letters, was the greeting she bore away.

Ethel was left at the Grange for the ensuing fortnight—a time of unusual leisure both to her and to Flora, which they both prized highly, for it taught them to know each other as they had never done before. Flora's confidence to her Aunt had been a good thing for her, though so partial; it opened the way for further unreserve to one who knew the circumstances better, and, as to dread of Ethel, that could seldom prevail in her presence, partly from long habit, partly from her deficiency of manner, and still more from her true humility and affection. Gradually she arrived at the perception of the history of her sister's mind; understood what gloom had once overshadowed it; and how, since light had once shone upon her, she shrank not merely from the tasks that had become wearisome to her, but from the dread of losing among them her present peace.

'They are your duty,' argued Ethel. 'Duty brings peace.'

'They were not,' said Flora.

'They are now,' said Ethel.

'Dinners and parties, empty talk and vain show,' said Flora, languidly. 'Are you come to their defence, Ethel? If you could guess how sick one gets of them, and how much worse it is for them not to be hateful! And to think of bringing my poor little girl up to the like, if she is spared!'

'If they are not duties, I would not do them,' said Ethel.

'Ethel,' cried her sister, raising herself from her couch, eagerly, 'I will say it to you! What should you think of George resigning his seat, and living in peace here?'

'Would he?' said Ethel.

'If I wished it.'

'But what would he do with himself?' said Ethel, not in too complimentary a strain.

'Yachting, farming, Cochin-chinese—or something,' said Flora. 'Anything not so wearing as this!'

'That abominable candidate of Tomkins's would come in!' exclaimed Ethel. 'Oh! Flora, that would be horrid!'

'That might be guarded against,' said Flora. 'Perhaps Sir Henry—but, oh, let us leave politics in peace while we can. I thought we should do some great good, but it is all a maze of confusion. It is so hard to know principles from parties, and everything goes wrong! It is of no use to contend with it!'

'It is never vain to contend with evil,' said Ethel.

'We are not generalizing,' said Flora. 'There is evil nearer home than the state of parties, and I can't see that George's being. in Parliament—being what he is—is anything like the benefit to things in general—that it is temptation and plague to me, besides the risk of London life for the baby, now and hereafter.'

'I can't say that I think it is,' said Ethel. 'How nice it would be to have you here! I am so glad you are willing to give it up.'

'It would have been better to have given it up untasted—like Norman,' sighed Flora. 'I will talk to George.'

'But, Flora,' said Ethel, a little startled, 'you ought not to do such a thing without advice.'

'There will be worry enough before it is done!' sighed Flora. 'No fear of that!'

'Stop a minute,' said Ethel, as if poor Flora could have done anything but lie still on her sofa. 'I think you ought to consider well before you set it going.'

'Have not I longed for it day and night? It is an escape from peril for ourselves and our child.'

'I can't be sure!' said Ethel. 'It may be more wrong to make George desert the post which—'

'Which I thrust him into,' said Flora. 'My father told me as much.'

'I did not mean you to say that! But it is a puzzle. It seems as if it were right to give up such things; yet, when I recollect the difficulty of carrying an election right at Stoneborough, I think papa would be very sorry. I don't think his interest would bring in any sound man but his son-in-law; and George himself seems to like his parliamentary life better than anything else.'

'Yes,' said Flora, hesitatingly; for she knew it was true—he liked to think himself important, and it gave him something to think of, and regular occupation—not too active or onerous; but she could not tell Ethel what she herself felt; that all she could do for him could not prevent him from being held cheap by the men among whom she had placed him.

'Then,' said Ethel, as she heard her affirmative, 'I don't think it for his dignity, for you to put him into Parliament to please you, and then take him out to please you.'

'I'll take care of his dignity,' said Flora, shortly.

'I know you would do it well—'

'I am sick of doing things well!' said poor Flora. 'You little know how I dread reading up all I must read presently! I shall lose all I have scarcely gained. I cannot find peace any way, but by throwing down the load I gave my peace for.'

'Whether this is truth or fancy,' said Ethel, thoughtfully. 'If you would ask some one competent.'

'Don't you know there are some things one cannot ask?' said Flora. 'I don't know why I spoke to you! Ah! come in! Why, George, that is a finer egg than ever,' as he entered with a Shanghae egg in each hand, for her to mark with the date when it had been laid. Poultry was a new hobby, and Ethel had been hearing, in her *tête-à-tête* dinners with George, a great deal about the perfections of the hideous monsters that had obtained fabulous prices. They had been the best resource for conversation; but she watched, with something between vexation and softness, how Flora roused herself to give her full attention and interest to his prosing about his pets, really pleased as it seemed; and, at last, encouraging him actually to fetch his favourite cock to show her; when she went through the points of perfection of the ungainly mass of feathers, and did not at all allow Ethel to laugh at the unearthly sounds of disapproval which handling elicited.

'And this is our senator!' thought Ethel. 'I wonder whether Honorius's hen was a Shanghae! Poor Flora is right—it is poor work to make a silk purse out of a sow's ear! but, putting him into the place is one thing, taking him out another. I wish she would take advice; but I never knew her do that, except as a civil way of communicating her intentions. However, she is not quite what she was! Poor dear! Aunt Flora will never believe what a beautiful creature she used to be! It seems wrong to think of her going back to that horrid London; but I can't judge. For my part, I'd rather do work, than no work for George, and he is a good, kind-hearted fellow after all! I won't be a crab!'

So Ethel did her best, and said the cock had a bright eye—all she could say for him—and George instructed her to admire the awkward legs, and invited her to a poultry show, at Whitford, in two days' time—and they sent him away to continue his consultations with the poultry woman, which pullets should be preferred as candidates for a prize.

'Meta set him upon this,' said Flora. 'I hope you will go,' Ethel. You see he can be very happy here.'

'Still,' said Ethel, 'the more I think, the more sure I am that you ought to ask advice.'

'I have asked yours,' said Flora, as if it were a great effort. 'You don't know what to say—I shall do what I see to be the only way to rest.'

'I do know what to say,' said Ethel; 'and that is, do as the Prayer-book tells you, in any perplexity.'

'I am not perplexed,' said Flora.

'Don't say so. This is either the station to which God has called you, or it is not.'

'He never called me to it.'

'But you don't know whether you ought to leave it. If you ought not, you would be ten times more miserable. Go to Richard, Flora—he belongs to you as much as I—he has authority besides.'

'Richard!'

'He is the clearest of us all in practical matters,' said Ethel, preventing what she feared would be disparaging. 'I don't mean only that you should ask him about this parliament matter alone; but I am sure you would be happier and more settled, if you talked things over with him before—before you go to Church.'

'You don't know what you propose.'

'I do,' said Ethel, growing bolder. 'You have been going all this time by feeling. You have never cleared up, and got to the bottom of, your troubles.'

'I could not talk to any one.'

'Not to any one but a Clergyman. Now, to enter on such a

thing is most averse to your nature; and I do believe that, for that very reason, it would be what would do you most good. You say you have recovered sense of—Oh! Flora, I can't talk of what you have gone through; but if you have only a vague feeling that seems as if lying still would be the only way to keep it, I don't think it can be altogether sound, or the "quiet conscience" that is meant.'

'Oh! Ethel! Ethel! I have never told you what I have undergone, since I knew my former quietness of conscience was but sleep! I have gone on in agony, with the sense of hypocrisy and despair, because I was afraid, for George's sake, to do otherwise.'

Ethel felt herself utterly powerless to advise; and, after a kind sound of sympathy, sat shocked, pondering on what none could answer; whether this were, indeed, what poor Flora imagined, or whether it had been a holding-fast to the thread through the darkness. The proud reserve was the true evil, and Ethel prayed and trusted it might give way.

She went very amiably to Whitford with George, and gained great credit with him, for admiring the prettiest speckled Hamburgh present; indeed, George was becoming very fond of 'poor Ethel,' as he still called her, and sometimes predicted that she would turn out a fine figure of a woman after all.

Ethel heard, on her return, that Richard had been there; and three days after, when Flora was making arrangements for going to Church, a moment of confidence came over, and she said, 'I did it, Ethel! I have spoken to Richard.'

'I am so glad!'

'You were right. He is as clear as he is kind,' said Flora; 'he showed me that, for George's sake, I must bear with my present life, and do the best I can with it, unless some leading comes for an escape; and that the glare, and weariness, and being spoken well of, must be taken as punishment for having sought after these things.'

'I was afraid he would say so,' said Ethel. 'But you will find happiness again, Flora dear.'

'Scarcely—before I come to Margaret and to my child,' sighed Flora. 'I suppose it was Mercy that would not let me follow when I wished it. I must work till the time of rest comes!'

'And your own little Margaret will cheer you!' said Ethel, more hopefully, as she saw Flora bend over her baby, with a face that might one day be bright.

She trusted that patient continuance in well-doing, would one day win peace and joy, even in the dreary weird that poor Flora had chosen.

For her own part, Ethel found Flora's practical good sense and sympathy very useful, in her present need of the counsel she had always had from Margaret.

The visit to Flora lasted a fortnight, and Ethel was much benefited by the leisure for reading and the repose after the long nursing; though, before the end, her refreshed energies began to pine for Daisy and her hymns, for Aubrey and his Virgil, for Cherry and her scholars, and, above all, for her father; for, come as often as he would, it was not papa at home.

On the other hand, Mary was at a loss for Ethel every hour; Richard was putting off his affairs till Ethel should come home; Miss Bracy and Blanche longed for her to relieve the school-room from the children; Aubrey could not perform a lesson in comfort with any one else—never ended a sum without groaning for Ethel, and sometimes rode to Abbotstoke for the mere purpose of appealing to her; in short, no one could get on without her, and the Doctor least of all.

Dr. Spencer, and Mr. Wilmot, and all his sons and daughters, had done their best for him; but, in spite of his satisfaction at seeing the two sisters so happy together, he could not help missing Ethel every minute, as the very light of his home; and when, at last, Flora brought her back, she was received with uproarious joy by Aubrey and Daisy, while the rest of the household felt a revival and refreshment of spirits—the first drawing aside of the cloud that had hung over the winter. The pearl of their home might be missed every hour, but they could thankfully rest in the trust that she was a jewel stored up in safety and peace, to shine as a star for evermore.

A few weeks more, and there were other partings, sad indeed, yet cheery. Dr. May told Mrs. Arnott that, though he grieved that so much of sorrow had come to dim her visit, he could not but own that it was the very time when her coming could be most comforting; and this, as she truly said, was satisfaction enough for her, besides that she could not rejoice enough that her arrival had been in time to see their dear Margaret. She should carry away most precious recollections; and she further told Dr. Spencer that she was far more comfortable about her brother-in-law, than if she had only known him in his youthful character, which had seemed so little calculated to bear sorrow or care. She looked at him now only to wonder at, and reverence the change that had been gradually wrought by the affections placed above.

Norman and his wife went with her—the one grave but hopeful, the other trying to wile away the pain of parting, by her tearful mirth—making all sorts of odd promises and touching requests,

between jest and earnest, and clinging to the last to her dear father-
in-law, as if the separation from him were the hardest of all.

'Well, hummingbirds must be let fly?' said he, at last.
'Ah! ha! Meta, are they of no use?'

'Stay till you hear!' said Meta, archly—then turning back
once more. 'Oh! how I have thanked you, Ethel, for those first
hints you gave me how to make my life *real*. If I had only sat
still and wished, instead of trying what could be done as I was,
how unhappy I should have been!'

'Come, take your sprite away, Norman, if you don't want me
to keep her for good! God bless you, my dear children! Good-
bye! Who knows but when Doctor Tom sets up in my place,
Ethel and I may come out and pay you a visit?'

It had all been over for some weeks, and the home-party had
settled down again into what was likely to be their usual course,
excepting in the holidays, to which the Doctor looked forward
with redoubled interest, as Tom was fast becoming a very agreeable and sensible companion; for his moodiness had been charmed
away by Meta, and principle was teaching him true command of
temper. He seemed to take his father as a special charge, be-
queathed to him by Norman, and had already acquired that value
and importance at home which comes of the laying aside of all
self-importance.

It was a clear evening in March, full of promise of spring, and
Ethel was standing in the Church porch at Cocksmoor, after
making some visits in the parish, waiting for Richard, while the
bell was ringing for the Wednesday evening service, and the pearly
tints of a cloudless sunset were fading into the western sky.

Ethel began to wonder where Norman might be looking at the
sun dipping into the Western sea, and thence arose before her the
visions of her girlhood, when she had first dreamt of a Church on
Cocksmoor, and of Richard ministering before a willing congregation. So strange did the accomplishment seem, that she even
touched the stone to assure herself of the reality; and therewith
came intense thanksgiving that the work had been taken out of
her hands, to be the more fully blessed and accomplished—that
is, as far as the building went; as to the people, there was far
more labour in store, and the same Hand must be looked to for
the increase.

For herself, Ethel looked back and looked on. Norman Ogilvie's
marriage seemed to her to have fixed her lot in life, and what was
that lot? Home and Cocksmoor had been her choice, and they
were before her. Home! but her eyes had been opened to see
that earthly homes may not endure, nor fill the heart. Her dear

father might, indeed, claim her full-hearted devotion, but, to him, she was only one of many. Norman was no longer solely hers ; and she had begun to understand that the unmarried woman must not seek undivided return of affection, and must not set her love, with exclusive eagerness, on aught below, but must be ready to cease in turn to be first with any. Ethel was truly a mother to the younger ones ; but she faced the probability that they would find others to whom she would have the second place. To love each heartily, to do her utmost for each in turn, and to be grateful for their fondness was her call ; but never to count on their affection as her sole right and inalienable possession. She felt that this was the probable course, and that she might look to becoming comparatively solitary in the course of years—then tried to realize what her lonely life might be, but broke off smiling at herself, ' What is that to me ? What will it be when it is over ? My course and aim are straight on, and He will direct my paths. I don't know that I shall be alone, and I shall have the memory— the Communion with them, if not their presence. Some one there must be to be loved and helped, and the poor for certain. Only I must have my treasure above, and when I think what is there, and of—Oh ! that bliss of being perfectly able to praise— with no bad old self to mar the full joy of giving thanks, and blessing, and honour, and power ! Need I dread a few short years ? —and they have not begun yet—perhaps they won't—Oh! here is actually papa coming home this way ! how delightful ! Papa, are you coming to Church here ?'

' Aye ! Ethel. That weathercock of Spencer's is a magnet, I believe ! It draws me from all parts of the country to hear Richard in St. Andrew's Church.'

THE END